PLUM ISLAND

Novels by Nelson DeMille

By the Rivers of Babylon
Cathedral
The Talbot Odyssey
Word of Honor
The Charm School
The Gold Coast
The General's Daughter
Spencerville
Plum Island
The Lion's Game
Up Country
Night Fall
Wild Fire
The Gate House
The Lion
The Panther

With Thomas Block

Mayday

Nelson DeMille

Plum Island

GC

GRAND CENTRAL
PUBLISHING

NEW YORK   BOSTON

Author's Note: Concerning the United States Department of Agriculture Animal Disease Center at Plum Island, I took a small amount of literary license regarding the island and the work done there.

"Oklahoma" (by Richard Rodgers and Oscar Hammerstein II) Copyright © 1943 by WILLIAMSON MUSIC. Copyright Renewed. International Copyright Secured. Reprinted by Permission. All Rights Reserved.

"A Wonderful Guy" (by Richard Rodgers and Oscar Hammerstein II) Copyright © 1949 by Richard Rodgers and Oscar Hammerstein II. Copyright Renewed. WILLIAMSON MUSIC owner of publication and allied rights throughout the world. International Copyright Secured. Reprinted by Permission. All Rights Reserved.

Grand Central Publishing
Hachette Book Group
237 Park Avenue
New York, NY 10017
Visit our website at www.HachetteBookGroup.com

Grand Central Publishing is a division of Hachette Book Group, Inc.
The Grand Central Publishing name and logo is a trademark of Hachette Book Group, Inc.

The publisher is not responsible for websites (or their content) that are not owned by the publisher.

Printed in the United States of America

Originally published in hardcover by Hachette Book Group

First mass market edition: May 1998
First oversize mass market edition: August 2011
First special one-time offer edition: April 2013

10 9 8 7 6 5 4 3 2 1

To Larry Kirshbaum, friend, editor, and gambling partner.

ACKNOWLEDGMENTS

I am grateful to the following individuals for sharing their special knowledge with me. Any errors or omissions in the story are mine and mine alone. Also, I have taken a small measure of literary license here and there, but for the most part, I have tried to stay true to the information and advice provided to me by these men and women:

First and foremost, thanks to Detective Lieutenant John Kennedy of the Nassau County Police Department, the man who did almost as much work as I did on this novel. John Kennedy is a dedicated police officer, an honest lawyer, an expert sailor, a good husband to Carol, a good friend to me, and a tough literary critic. Many, many thanks for your time and expertise.

I would like to thank again Dan Starer of Research for Writers, NYC, for his diligent work.

I would also like to thank Bob and Linda Scalia of Southold for their help with local lore and customs.

My thanks to Martin Bowe and Laura Flanagan of the Garden City Public Library for their excellent research assistance.

Many thanks to Howard Polskin of CNN, and Janet Alshouse, Cindi Younker, and Mike DelGiudice of News 12 Long Island, for making available their video reporting on Plum Island.

Thanks again to Bob Whiting of Banfi Vintners for sharing with me his knowledge of and passion for wine.

My thanks to Dr. Alfonso Torres, Director of the Plum Island Animal Disease Center, for his time and patience, and my admiration for him and his staff for the important and selfless work they do.

Thanks and gratitude to my assistant, Dianne Francis, for hundreds of hours of arduous and dedicated work.

My sincere thanks to my agent and friend, Nick Ellison, and his staff, Christina Harcar and Faye Bender. An author couldn't have better representation or better colleagues.

Three may keep a secret, if two of them are dead.

—Benjamin Franklin,
Poor Richard's Almanac (1735)

PLUM ISLAND
LONG ISLAND
NEW YORK

CHAPTER ONE

Through my binoculars, I could see this nice forty-something-foot cabin cruiser anchored a few hundred yards offshore. There were two thirtyish couples aboard, having a merry old time, sunbathing, banging down brews and whatever. The women had on teensey-weensey little bottoms and no tops, and one of the guys was standing on the bow, and he slipped off his trunks and stood there a minute hanging hog, then jumped in the bay and swam around the boat. What a great country. I put down my binoculars and popped a Budweiser.

It was late summer, not meaning late August, but meaning September, before the autumnal equinox. Labor Day weekend had gone, and Indian summer was coming, whatever that is.

I, John Corey by name, convalescing cop by profession, was sitting on my uncle's back porch, deep in a wicker chair with shallow thoughts running through my mind. It occurred to me that the problem with doing nothing is not knowing when you're finished.

The porch is an old-fashioned wraparound, circling

three sides of an 1890s Victorian farmhouse, all shingle and gingerbread, turrets, gables, the whole nine yards. From where I sat, I could see south across a sloping green lawn to the Great Peconic Bay. The sun was low on the western horizon, which was where it belonged at 6:45 P.M. I'm a city boy, but I was really getting into the country stuff, the sky and all that, and I finally found the Big Dipper a few weeks ago.

I was wearing a plain white T-shirt and cutoff jeans that used to fit before I lost too much weight. My bare feet were propped on the rail, and between my left and right big toes was framed the aforementioned cabin cruiser.

About this time of day you can start to hear crickets, locusts, and who knows what, but I'm not a big fan of nature noises so I had a portable tape player beside me on the end table with *The Big Chill* cranking, and the Bud in my left hand, the binocs in my lap, and lying on the floor near my right hand was my off-duty piece, a Smith & Wesson .38 revolver with a two-inch barrel which fit nicely in my purse. Just kidding.

Somewhere in the two seconds of silence between "When a Man Loves a Woman" and "Dancing in the Street," I could hear or feel on the creaky old floor-boards that someone was walking around the porch. Since I live alone and was expecting no one, I took the .38 in my right hand and rested it on my lap. So you don't think I'm a paranoid citizen, I should mention that I was convalescing, not from the mumps, but from three bullet wounds, two 9mm and one .44 caliber Magnum, not that the size of the holes matters. As with real estate, what matters with bullet holes is location, location, location. Obviously these holes were in the right locations, because I was convalescing, not decomposing.

I looked to my right where the porch turned around the west side of the house. A man appeared around the corner, then stopped about fifteen feet from me, searching the long shadows cast by the setting sun. In fact, the man cast a long shadow himself which passed over me, so he didn't seem to see me. But with the sun at his back, it was also difficult for me to see his face or to guess his intentions. I said, "Help you?"

He turned his head toward me. "Oh...hey, John. Didn't see you there."

"Have a seat, Chief." I slipped my revolver into my waistband under my T-shirt, then lowered the volume on "Dancing in the Street."

Sylvester Maxwell, aka Max, who is the law in these here parts, sauntered toward me and plopped his butt on the rail, facing me. He was wearing a blue blazer, white button-down shirt, tan cotton slacks, boating shoes, and no socks. I couldn't tell if he was on or off duty. I said, "There're some soft drinks in that cooler."

"Thanks." He reached down and rescued a Budweiser from the ice. Max likes to call beer a soft drink.

He sipped awhile, contemplating a point in space about two feet from his nose. I directed my attention back toward the bay and listened to "Too Many Fish in the Sea"—The Marvelettes. It was Monday, so the weekenders were gone, thank God, and it was as I said after Labor Day when most of the summer rentals terminate, and you could feel the solitude returning again. Max is a local boy and he doesn't get right down to business, so you just wait it out. He finally asked me, "You own this place?"

"My uncle does. He wants me to buy it."

"Don't buy anything. My philosophy is, if it flies, floats, or fucks, rent it."

"Thank you."

"You going to be staying here awhile?"

"Until the wind stops whistling through my chest."

He smiled, but then got contemplative again. Max is a big man, about my age, which is to say mid-forties, wavy blond hair, ruddy skin, and blue eyes. Women seem to find him good-looking, which works for Chief Maxwell, who is single and hetero.

He said, "So, how're you feeling?"

"Not bad."

"Do you feel like some mental exercise?"

I didn't reply. I've known Max about ten years, but since I don't live around here, I only see him now and then. I should say at this point that I'm a New York City homicide detective, formerly working out of Manhattan North until I went down. That was on April twelfth. A homicide detective hadn't gone down in New York in about two decades so it made big news. The NYPD Public Information Office kept it going because it's contract time again, and with me being so personable, good-looking, and so forth, they milked it a little and the media cooperated, and round and round we go. Meanwhile, the two perps who plugged me are still out there. So, I spent a month in Columbia Presbyterian, then a few weeks in my Manhattan condo, then Uncle Harry suggested that his summer house was a fitting place for a hero. Why not? I arrived here in late May, right after Memorial Day.

Max said, "I think you knew Tom and Judy Gordon."

I looked at him. Our eyes met. I understood. I asked, "Both of them?"

He nodded. "Both." After a moment of respectful silence, he said, "I'd like you to take a look at the scene."

"Why?"

"Why not? As a favor to me. Before everyone else gets a piece of it. I'm short on homicide detectives."

In fact, the Southold Town Police Department has no homicide detectives, which usually works out okay because very few people get iced out here. When someone does, the Suffolk County police respond with a homicide detail to take over, and Max steps aside. Max does not like this.

A bit of locale here—this is the North Fork of Long Island, State of New York, the Township of Southold, founded, according to a plaque out on the highway, in sixteen-forty-something by some people from New Haven, Connecticut, who, for all anybody knows, were on the lam from the king. The South Fork of Long Island, which is on the other side of Peconic Bay, is the trendy Hamptons: writers, artists, actors, publishing types, and other assorted anals. Here, on the North Fork, the folks are farmers, fishermen, and such. And perhaps one murderer.

Anyway, Uncle Harry's house is specifically located in the hamlet of Mattituck, which is about a hundred road miles from West 102nd Street where two Hispanic-looking gentlemen had pumped fourteen or fifteen shots at yours truly, accomplishing three hits on a moving target at twenty to thirty feet. Not an impressive showing, but I'm not criticizing or complaining.

Anyway, the Township of Southold comprises most

of the North Fork, and contains eight hamlets and one village, named Greenport, and one police force of maybe forty sworn officers, and Sylvester Maxwell is the chief, so there it is.

Max said, "It doesn't hurt to look."

"Sure it does. What if I get subpoenaed to testify out here at some inconvenient time? I'm not getting paid for this."

"Actually, I called the town supervisor and got an okay to hire you, officially, as a consultant. A hundred bucks a day."

"Wow. Sounds like the kind of job I have to save up for."

Max allowed himself a smile. "Hey, it covers your gas and phone. You're not doing anything anyway."

"I'm trying to get the hole in my right lung to close."

"This won't be strenuous."

"How do you know?"

"It's your chance to be a good Southold citizen."

"I'm a New Yorker. I'm not supposed to be a good citizen."

"Hey, did you know the Gordons well? Were they friends?"

"Sort of."

"So? There's your motivation. Come on, John. Get up. Let's go. I'll owe you a favor. Fix a ticket."

In truth, I was bored, and the Gordons were good people. . . . I stood and put down my beer. "I'll take the job at a buck a week to make me official."

"Good. You won't regret it."

"Of course I will." I turned off "Jeremiah Was a Bullfrog" and asked Max, "Is there a lot of blood?"

"A little. Head wounds."

"You think I need my flip-flops?"

"Well...some brains and skull blew out the back...."

"Okay." I slipped into my flip-flops, and Max and I walked around the porch to the circular driveway in the front of the house. I got into his unmarked PD, a white Jeep Cherokee with a squawky police radio.

We drove down the long driveway, which was covered with about a hundred years' worth of raw oyster and clam shells because Uncle Harry and everyone before him threw shells on the driveway along with the ash and cinders from the coal furnace to keep the mud and dust down. Anyway, this used to be what's called a bay farm estate, and it's still bayfront, but most of the farm acreage has been sold. The landscape is a little overgrown, and the flora is mostly the kind of stuff they don't use much anymore, such as forsythia, pussy willow, and privet hedges. The house itself is painted cream with green trim and a green roof. It's all pretty charming, really, and maybe I will buy it if the cop docs say I'm through. I should practice coughing up blood.

On the subject of my disability, I have a good shot at a three-quarter, tax-free pension for life. This is the NYPD equivalent of going to Atlantic City, tripping over a tear in the rug at Trump's Castle, and hitting your head on a slot machine in full view of a liability lawyer. Jackpot!

"Did you hear me?"

"What?"

"I said, they were found at 5:45 P.M. by a neighbor—"

"Am I on retainer now?"

"Sure. They were both shot once in the head, and the neighbor found them lying on their patio deck—"

"Max, I'm going to see all this. Tell me about the neighbor."

"Right. His name is Edgar Murphy, an old gent. He heard the Gordons' boat come in about 5:30, and about fifteen minutes later he walks over and finds them murdered. Never heard a shot."

"Hearing aid?"

"No. I asked him. His wife's got okay hearing, too, according to Edgar. So maybe it was a silencer. Maybe they're deafer than they think."

"But they heard the boat. Edgar is sure about the time?"

"Pretty sure. He called us at 5:51 P.M., so that's close."

"Right." I looked at my watch. It was now 7:10 P.M. Max must have had the bright idea to come collect me very soon after he got on the scene. I assumed the Suffolk County homicide guys were there by now. They would have come in from a little town called Yaphank where the county police are headquartered and which is about an hour drive to where the Gordons lived.

Max was going on about this and that, and I tried to get my mind into gear, but it had been about five months since I had to think about things like this. I was tempted to snap, "Just the facts, Max!" but I let him drone on. Also, "Jeremiah Was a Bullfrog" kept playing in my head, and it's really annoying, as you know, when you can't get a tune out of your head. Especially that one.

I looked out the open side window. We were driving along the main east-west road, which is conveniently called Main Road, toward a place called Nassau Point where the Gordons live—or lived. The North Fork is sort of like Cape Cod, a windswept jut of land surrounded on three sides by water and covered with history.

The full-time population is a little thin, about twenty thousand folks, but there are a lot of summer and weekend types, and the new wineries have attracted day-trippers. Put up a winery and you get ten thousand wine-sipping yuppie slime from the nearest urban center. Never fails.

Anyway, we turned south onto Nassau Point, which is a two-mile-long, cleaver-shaped point of land that cuts into the Great Peconic Bay. From my dock to the Gordons' dock is about four miles.

Nassau Point has been a summer place since about the 1920s, and the homes range from simple bungalows to substantial establishments. Albert Einstein summered here, and it was from here in nineteen-thirty-whatever that he wrote his famous "Nassau Point Letter" to Roosevelt urging the president to get moving on the atomic bomb. The rest, as they say, is history.

Interestingly, Nassau Point is still home to a number of scientists; some work at Brookhaven National Laboratory, a secret nuclear something or other about thirty-five miles west of here, and some scientists work on Plum Island, a very top secret biological research site which is so scary it has to be housed on an island. Plum Island is about two miles off the tip of Orient Point, which is the last piece of land on the North Fork—next stop Europe.

Not incidental to all this, Tom and Judy Gordon

were biologists who worked on Plum Island, and you can bet that both Sylvester Maxwell and John Corey were thinking about that. I asked Max, "Did you call the Feds?"

He shook his head.

"Why not?"

"Murder is not a federal offense."

"You know what I'm talking about, Max."

Chief Maxwell didn't respond.

CHAPTER TWO

We approached the Gordon house nestled on a
small lane on the west shore of the point. The
house was a 1960s ranch type that had been made over
into a 1990s contemporary. The Gordons, from somewhere out in the Midwest, and uncertain about their
career paths, were leasing the house with an option to
buy, as they once mentioned to me. I think if I worked
with the stuff they worked with, I, too, wouldn't make
any long-range plans. Hell, I wouldn't even buy green
bananas.

I turned my attention to the scene outside the windows of the Jeep. On this pleasant, shady lane, little
knots of neighbors and kids on bicycles stood around
in the long purple shadows, talking, and looking at the
Gordon house. Three Southold police cars were parked
in front of the house, as were two unmarked cars. A
county forensic van blocked the driveway. It's a good
policy not to drive onto or park at a crime scene so as
not to destroy evidence, and I was encouraged to see
that Max's little rural police force was up to snuff so far.

Also on the street were two TV vans, one from

a local Long Island news station, the other an NBC News van.

I noticed, too, a bunch of reporter types chatting up the neighbors, whipping microphones in front of anyone who opened his mouth. It wasn't quite a media circus yet, but it would be when the rest of the news sharks got on to the Plum Island connection.

Yellow crime scene tape was wrapped from tree to tree, cordoning off the house and grounds. Max pulled up behind the forensic van and we got out. A few cameras flashed, then a bunch of big video lights went on, and we were being taped for the eleven o'clock news. I hoped the disability board wasn't watching, not to mention the perps who'd tried to ice *moi*, and who would now know where I was.

Standing in the driveway was a uniformed officer with a pad—the crime scene recorder—and Max gave him my name, title, and so forth, so I was officially logged in, now subject to subpoenas from the DA and potential defense attorneys. This was exactly what I didn't want, but I had been home when fate called.

We walked up the gravel driveway and passed through a moongate into the backyard, which was mostly cedar deck, multileveled as it cascaded from the house down to the bay and ended at the long dock where the Gordons' boat was tied. It was really a beautiful evening, and I wished Tom and Judy were alive to see it.

I observed the usual contingent of forensic lab people, plus three uniformed Southold town cops and a woman overdressed in a light tan suit jacket and matching skirt, white blouse, and sensible shoes. At first I thought she might be family, called in to ID the bodies and so forth, but then I saw she was holding a note-book and pen and looking official.

Lying on the nice silver-gray cedar deck, side by side on their backs, were Tom and Judy, their feet toward the house and their heads toward the bay, arms and legs askew as though they were making snow angels. A police photographer was taking pictures of the bodies, and the flash lit up the deck and did a weird thing to the corpses, making them look sort of ghoulish for a microsecond, à la *Night of the Living Dead*.

I stared at the bodies. Tom and Judy Gordon were in their mid-thirties, in very good shape, and even in death a uniquely handsome couple—so much so that they were sometimes mistaken for celebrities when they dined out in the more fashionable spots.

They both wore blue jeans, running shoes, and polo shirts. Tom's shirt was black with some marine supply logo on the front, and Judy's was a more chic hunter green with a little yellow sailboat on the left breast.

Max, I suspected, didn't see many murdered people in the course of a year, but he probably saw enough natural deaths, suicides, car wrecks, and such so that he wasn't going to go green. He looked grim, concerned, pensive, and professional, but kept glancing at the bod-ies as if he couldn't believe there were murdered people lying right there on the nice deck.

Yours truly, on the other hand, working as I do in a city that counts about 1,500 murders a year, am no stranger to death, as they say. I don't see all 1,500 corpses, but I see enough so that I'm no longer sur-prised, sickened, shocked, or saddened. Yet, when it's someone you knew and liked, it makes a difference.

I walked across the deck and stopped near Tom

Gordon. Tom had a bullet hole at the bridge of his nose. Judy had a hole in the side of her left temple.

Assuming there was only one shooter, then Tom, being a strapping guy, had probably gotten it first, a single shot to the head; then Judy, turning in disbelief toward her husband, had taken the second bullet in the side of her temple. The two bullets had probably gone through their skulls and dropped into the bay. Bad luck for ballistics.

I've never been to a homicide scene that didn't have a smell—unbelievably foul, if the victims had been dead awhile. If there was blood, I could always smell it, and if a body cavity had been penetrated, there was usually a peculiar smell of innards. This is something I'd like not to smell again; the last time I smelled blood, it was my own. Anyway, the fact that this was an outdoor killing helped.

I looked around and couldn't see any place close by where the shooter could hide. The sliding glass door of the house was open and maybe the shooter had been in there, but that was twenty feet from the bodies, and not many people can get a good head shot from that distance with a pistol. I was living proof of that. At twenty feet you go for a body shot first, then get in close and finish up with a head shot. So there were two possibilities: the shooter was using a rifle, not a pistol, or, the shooter was able to walk right up to them without causing them any alarm. Someone normal-looking, nonthreatening, maybe even someone they knew. The Gordons had gotten out of their boat, walked up the deck, they saw this person at some point and kept walking toward him or her. The person raised a pistol from no more than five feet away and drilled both of them.

I looked beyond the bodies and saw little colored pin flags stuck in the cedar planking here and there. "Red is for blood?"

Max nodded. "White is skull, gray is—"

"Got it." Glad I wore the flip-flops.

Max informed me, "The exit wounds are big, like the whole back of their skulls are gone. And, as you can see, the entry wounds are big. I'm guessing a .45 caliber. We haven't found the two bullets yet. They probably went into the bay."

I didn't reply.

Max motioned toward the sliding glass doors. He informed me, "The sliding door was forced and the house is ransacked. No big items missing—TV, computer, CD player, and all that stuff is there. But there may be jewelry and small stuff missing."

I contemplated this a moment. The Gordons, like most egghead types on a government salary, didn't own much jewelry, art, or anything like that. A druggie would grab the pricey electronics and such, and beat feet.

Max said, "Here's what I think—a burglar or burglars were doing their thing, he, she, or they see the Gordons approaching through the glass door; he, she, or they step out onto the deck, fire, and flee." He looked at me. "Right?"

"If you say so."

"I say so."

"Got it." Sounded better than Home of Top Secret Germ Warfare Scientists Ransacked and Scientists Found Murdered.

Max moved closer to me and said softly, "What do you think, John?"

"Was that a hundred an hour?"

"Come on, guy, don't jerk me around. We got maybe a world-class double murder on our hands."

I replied, "But you just said it could be a simple homeowner-comes-on-the-scene-and-gets-iced kind of thing."

"Yeah, but it turns out that the homeowners are... whatever they are." He looked at me and said, "Reconstruct."

"Okay. You understand that the perp did not fire from that sliding glass door. He was standing right in front of them. The door you found open was closed then so that the Gordons saw nothing unusual as they approached the house. The gunman was possibly sitting here in one of these chairs, and he may have arrived by boat since he wasn't going to park his car out front where the world could see it. Or maybe he was dropped off. In either case, the Gordons either knew him or were not unduly troubled by his presence on their back deck, and maybe it's a woman, nice and sweet-looking, and the Gordons walk toward her and she toward them. They may have exchanged a word or two, but very soon after, the murderer produced a pistol and blew them away."

Chief Maxwell nodded.

"If the perp was looking for anything inside, it wasn't jewelry or cash, it was papers. You know—bug stuff. He didn't kill the Gordons because they stumbled onto him; he killed them because he wanted them dead. He was *waiting* for them. You know all this."

He nodded.

I said, "Then again, Max, I've seen a lot of bungled and screwed-up burglaries where the homeowner got killed, and the burglar got nothing. When it's a druggie thing, nothing makes sense."

Chief Maxwell rubbed his chin as he contemplated a hop-head with a gun on one hand, a cool assassin on the other, and whatever might fall in between.

While he did that, I knelt beside the bodies, closest to Judy. Her eyes were open, really wide open, and she looked surprised. Tom's eyes were open, too, but he looked more peaceful than his wife. The flies had found the blood around the wounds, and I was tempted to shoo them away, but it didn't matter.

I examined the bodies more closely without touching anything that would get the forensic types all bent up. I looked at hair, nails, skin, clothing, shoes, and so on. When I was done, I patted Judy's cheek and stood.

Maxwell asked me, "How long did you know them?"

"Since about June."

"Have you been to this house before?"

"Yes. You get to ask me one more question."

"Well...I have to ask....Where were you about 5:30 P.M.?"

"With your girlfriend."

He smiled, but he was not amused.

I asked Max, "How well did *you* know them?"

He hesitated a moment, then replied, "Just socially. My girlfriend drags me to wine tastings and crap like that."

"Does she? And how did you know I knew them?"

"They mentioned they met a New York cop who was convalescing. I said I knew you."

"Small world," I said.

He didn't reply.

I looked around the backyard. To the east was the house, and to the south was a thick line of tall hedges, and beyond the hedges was the home of Edgar Murphy, the neighbor who found the bodies. To the north was an open marsh area that stretched a few hundred yards to the next house, which was barely visible. To the west, the deck dropped in three levels toward the bay where the dock ran out about a hundred feet to the deeper water. At the end of the dock was the Gordons' boat, a sleek white fiberglass speedboat—a Formula three-something, about thirty feet long. It was named the *Spirochete*, which as we know from Bio 101 is the nasty bug that causes syphilis. The Gordons had a sense of humor.

Max said, "Edgar Murphy stated that the Gordons sometimes used their own boat to commute to Plum Island. They took the government ferry when the weather was bad and in the winter."

I nodded. I knew that.

He continued, "I'm going to call Plum Island and see if I can find out what time they left. The sea is calm, the tide is coming in, and the wind is from the east, so they could make maximum time between Plum and here."

"I'm not a sailor."

"Well, I am. It could have taken them as little as one hour to get here from Plum, but usually it's an hour and a half, two at the outside. The Murphys heard the Gordon boat come in about 5:30, so now we see if we can find out the time they left Plum, then we know with a little more certainty that it *was* the Gordon boat that the Murphys heard at 5:30."

"Right." I looked around the deck. There was the

usual patio and deck furniture—table, chairs, outdoor bar, sun umbrellas, and such. Small bushes and plants grew through cutouts in the deck, but basically there was no place a person could conceal him- or herself and ambush two people out in the open.

"What are you thinking about?" Max asked.

"Well, I'm thinking about the great American deck. Big, maintenance-free wood, multileveled, landscaped, and all that. Not like my old-fashioned narrow porch that always needs painting. If I bought my uncle's house, I could build a deck down to the bay like this one. But then I wouldn't have as much lawn."

Max let a few seconds pass, then asked, "*That's* what you're thinking about?"

"Yeah. What are *you* thinking about?"

"I'm thinking about a double murder."

"Good. Tell me what else you've learned here."

"Okay. I felt the engines—" He jerked his thumb toward the boat. "They were still warm when I arrived, like the bodies."

I nodded. The sun was starting to dip into the bay, and it was getting noticeably darker and cooler, and I was getting chilly in my T-shirt and shorts, sans underwear.

September is a truly golden month up and down the Atlantic coast, from the Outer Banks to New-foundland. The days are mild, the nights pleasant for sleeping; it is summer without the heat and humidity, autumn without the cold rains. The summer birds haven't left yet, and the first migratory birds from up north are taking a break on their way south. I suppose if I left Manhattan and wound up here, I'd get into this nature thing, boating, fishing, and all that.

Max was saying, "And something else—the line is clove-hitched around the piling."

"Well, there's a major break in the case. What the hell's a line?"

"The *rope*. The boat's rope isn't tied to the cleats on the dock. The rope is just temporarily hitched to the pilings—the big poles that come out of the water. I deduce that they intended to go out in the boat again, soon."

"Good observation."

"Right. So, any ideas?"

"Nope."

"Any observations of your own?"

"I think you beat me to them, Chief."

"Theories, thoughts, hunches? Anything?"

"Nope."

Chief Maxwell seemed to want to say something else, like, "You're fired," but instead he said, "I've got to make a phone call." He went off into the house.

I glanced back at the bodies. The woman with the light tan suit was now outlining Judy in chalk. It's SOP in New York City that the investigating officer do the outline, and I guessed that it was the same out here. The idea is that the detective who is going to follow the case to its conclusion and who is going to work with the DA should know and work the entire case to the extent possible. I concluded, therefore, that the lady in tan was a homicide detective and that she was the officer assigned to investigate this case. I further concluded that I'd wind up dealing with her if I decided to help Max with this.

The scene of a homicide is one of the most interesting places in the world if you know what you're looking for and looking at. Consider people like Tom and Judy who look at little bugs under a microscope, and they can tell you the names of the bugs, what the bugs are up to at the moment, what the bugs are capable of doing to the person who's watching them, and so forth. But if I looked at the bugs, all I'd see is little squigglies. I don't have a trained eye or a trained mind for bugs.

Yet, when I look at a dead body and at the scene around the body, I see things that most people don't see. Max touched the engines and the bodies and noticed they were warm, he noticed how the boat was tied, and he registered a dozen other small details that the average citizen wouldn't notice. But Max isn't really a detective, and he was operating on about level two, whereas to solve a murder like this one, you needed to operate on a much higher plane. He knew that, which is why he called on me.

I happened to know the victims, and for the homicide detective on the case, this is a big plus. I knew, for instance, that the Gordons usually wore shorts, T-shirts, and docksiders in the boat on their way to Plum Island, and at work they slipped on their lab duds or their biohazard gear or whatever. Also, Tom didn't look like Tom in a black shirt, and Judy was more of a pastel person as I recall. My guess was that they were dressed for camouflage, and the running shoes were for speed. Then again, maybe I was making up clues. You have to be careful not to do that.

But then there was the red soil in the treads of their running shoes. Where did it come from? Not from the laboratory, probably not from the walkway to the Plum Island ferry dock, not their boat, and not the dock or deck here. It appeared they were somewhere else today, and they were dressed differently for the day, and for sure the day had ended differently. There was something else going on here, and I had no idea what it was, but it was definitely something else.

Yet, it was *still* possible that they just stumbled onto a burglary. I mean, this might have nothing to do with their jobs. The thing was, Max was nervous about that and sensitive to it, and it had infected me, too, pardon the pun. And before midnight, this place would be visited by the FBI, Defense Intelligence people, and the CIA. Unless Max could catch a hophead burglar before then.

"Excuse me."

I turned toward the voice. It was the lady in the tan suit. I said, "You're excused."

"Excuse me, are you supposed to be here?"

"I'm here with the band."

"Are you a police officer?"

Obviously my T-shirt and shorts didn't project an authority image. I replied, "I'm with Chief Maxwell."

"I could see that. Have you logged in?"

"Why don't you go check?" I turned and walked down to the next level of the deck, avoiding the little colored flags. I headed toward the dock. She followed.

"I'm Detective Penrose from Suffolk County homicide, and I'm in charge of this investigation."

"Congratulations."

"And unless you have official business here—"

"You'll have to speak to the chief." I got down to the dock and walked out to where the Gordons' boat was tied. It was very breezy out on the long dock and the sun had set. I didn't see any sailboats on the bay now, but a few powerboats went by with their running lights on. A three-quarter moon had risen in the southeast, and it sparkled across the water.

The tide was in and the thirty-foot boat was nearly at dock level. I jumped down onto the boat's deck.

"What are you doing? You can't do that."

She was very good-looking, of course; if she'd been ugly, I'd have been much nicer. She was dressed, as I indicated, rather severely, but the body beneath the tailored clothes was a symphony of curves, a melody of flesh looking to break free. In fact, she looked like she was smuggling balloons. The second thing I noticed was that she wasn't wearing a wedding ring. Filling out the rest of the form: age, early thirties; hair, medium length, coppery color; eyes, blue-green; skin, fair, not much sun for this time of year, light makeup; pouty lips; no visible marks or scars; no earrings; no nail polish; pissed-off expression on her face.

"Are you *listening* to me?"

She also had a nice voice despite the present tone. I suspected that because of the pretty face, great body, and soft voice, Detective Penrose had trouble being taken seriously, and thus she overcompensated with butchy attire. She probably owned a book titled *Dress to Bust Balls*.

"Are you listening to me?"

"I'm *listening* to you. Are you *listening* to me? I told you to talk to the chief."

"*I* am in charge here. In matters of homicide, the county police—"

"Okay, we'll go see the chief together. Just a minute."

I took a quick look around the boat, but it was dark now, and I couldn't see much. I tried to find a flashlight. I said to Detective Penrose, "You should post an officer here all night."

"Thank you for sharing your thoughts. Please come out of the boat."

"Do you have a flashlight on you?"

"Out of the boat. Now."

"Okay." I stepped onto the gunwale, and to my surprise she extended her hand, which I took. Her skin was cool. She pulled me up onto the dock and at the same time, quick as a cat, her right hand went under my T-shirt and snatched the revolver from my waistband. *Wow.*

She stepped back, my piece in her hand. "Stand where you are."

"Yes, ma'am."

"Who are you?"

"Detective John Corey, NYPD, homicide, ma'am."

"What are you doing here?"

"Same as you."

"No, I caught this case. Not you."

"Yes, ma'am."

"Do you have any official status here?"

"Yes, ma'am. I was hired as a consultant."

"*Consultant?* On a murder case? I've never heard of such a thing."

"Me neither."

"Who hired you?"

"The town."

"Idiotic."

"Right." She seemed undecided about what to do next, so to be helpful I suggested, "Do you want to strip-search me?"

I thought I saw a smile pass over her lips in the

moonlight. My heart was aching for her, or it might have been the hole in my lung acting up.

She asked me, "What did you say your name was?"

"John Corey."

She searched her memory. "Oh . . . you're the guy—"

"That's me. Lucky me."

She seemed to soften, then gave my .38 a twirl and handed it to me, butt first. She turned and walked away.

I followed her along the dock, up the three-leveled deck to the house where the outdoor lights lit up the area around the glass doors and moths circled around the globes.

Max was talking to one of the forensic people. Then he turned to me and Detective Penrose and asked us, "You two met yet?"

Detective Penrose responded, "Why is this man involved in this case?"

Chief Maxwell replied, "Because I want him to be involved."

"That's not your decision, Chief."

"And neither is it yours."

They kept bouncing the ball back and forth and my neck was getting tired, so I said, "She's right, Chief. I'm out of here. Get me a ride home." I turned and walked toward the moongate, then with a little practiced dramatics, I turned back to Maxwell and Penrose and said, "By the way, did anyone take the aluminum chest in the stern of the boat?"

Max asked, "What aluminum chest?"

"The Gordons had a big aluminum chest that they used to stow odds and ends, and sometimes they used it for an ice chest to hold beer and bait."

"Where is it?"

"That's what I'm asking *you*."

"I'll look for it."

"Good idea." I turned and walked through the gate and went out to the front lawn away from the parked police cars. The neighbors had been joined by the morbidly curious as word of the double homicide spread through the small community.

A few cameras popped in my direction, then video lights came on, illuminating me and the front of the house. Video cameras rolled, reporters called out to me. Just like old times. I coughed into my hand in case the disability board was watching, not to mention my ex-wife.

A uniformed cop from the backyard caught up to me, and we got into a marked Southold Township PD, and off we went. He said his name was Bob Johnson, and he asked me, "What do you think, Detective?"

"They were murdered."

"Yeah, no kidding." He hesitated, then inquired, "Hey, do you think it has to do with Plum Island or not?"

"Not."

"Tell you what—I've seen burglaries, and this wasn't burglary. It was supposed to look like a burglary, but it was a search—you know? They were looking for something."

"I didn't look inside."

"Germs." He glanced at me. "Germs. Biological warfare germs. That's what I think. Right?"

I made no reply.

Johnson continued, "That's what happened to the ice chest. I heard you say that."

Again, I made no reply.

"There were vials or something in the chest. Right? I mean, Jesus Christ, there could be enough stuff out there to wipe out Long Island...New York City."

Probably the planet, Bob, depending on which kind of bug it was and how much could be grown from the original stuff.

I leaned toward Officer Johnson and held his arm to get his attention. I said, "Do not breathe one fucking word of this to anyone. *Do you understand?*"

He nodded.

We drove in silence back to my place.

CHAPTER THREE

Everyone needs a hangout, at least guys do. When I'm in the city, I hang out at the National Arts Club and sip sherry with people of culture and refinement. My ex-wife had trouble believing that, too.

When I'm out here, I frequent a place called the Olde Towne Taverne, though I usually avoid places with that many silent "e's." I think the government should allocate one thousand silent "e's" to New England and Long Island, and when they're used up, no one can have any more. Anyway, the Olde Towne Taverne is in downtown (or downetowne) Mattituck, which is about a block long, and really charming. The OTT is okay, the motif is sort of early ship, despite the fact that it's a town tavern and a mile from the water. The wood is very dark and the floor is oak planking, and the thing that I love is the amber glass lanterns that cast this really mellow, mood-altering glow over the whole place.

So there I was in the OTT, and it was getting on to 10 P.M., and the Monday night crowd was watching The Game—Dallas vs. New York at the Meadowlands.

My mind was hopping between the game, the double murder, my food, and the waitress with the Nordic-Track ass.

I was more nattily dressed than earlier, having changed into evening attire of tan Levi's jeans, blue polo by Ralph, genuine Sperry Top-Siders, and Hanes all-cotton briefs. I looked like an ad for something.

I was sitting on a stool at one of those chest-high tables near the bar, and I had a good view of the TV, and I had my favorite meal in front of me—cheeseburger, french fries, stuffed potato skins, nachos, buffalo wings, and a Budweiser; a good balance of brown and yellow things.

Detective Penrose of the county police department sort of snuck up on me from behind, and the next thing I knew she was sitting on the stool facing me, a beer in her hand, and her head blocking the screen. She regarded my dinner, and I saw her eyebrows arch.

She turned her attention back to me and said, "Max thought I might find you here."

"Would you like some french fries?"

"No, thank you." She hesitated, then said, "I think we got off on the wrong foot back there."

"Nonsense. I don't mind having my own gun pulled on me."

"Look, I've been speaking to Max, and I've been thinking…if the town wants you as a consultant, that's okay with me, and if you wanted to pass on to me anything that you think is useful, feel free to call." She handed me her card, and I read, "Detective Elizabeth Penrose." Beneath that it said, "Homicide," then her office address, fax, telephone number, and so forth. On the left was the Suffolk County seal with the words

"Free and Independent" around a fearsome-looking bull. I commented, "Not a very good likeness of you."

She stared at me, her jaw sort of clenched and her nostrils flared as she took a long breath. She kept her cool, which is admirable. I can be annoying.

I leaned across the table until our noses were about a football apart. She smelled good, sort of soapy and healthy. I said, "Look, Elizabeth, cut the crap. You know that I knew the Gordons and that I've been to their house and I went out in their boat, and maybe I've met their friends and their coworkers, and maybe they opened up to me about their work a little because I'm a cop, and maybe I know more than you or Max put together, and maybe you're right about that. So, you realize you pissed me off, and Max is pissed at you, and you came here to apologize, and you give me permission to call you and tell you what I know. Wow! What a terrific opportunity for me. However, if I don't call you in a day or two, you'll have me down in your office for a formal interrogation. So let's not pretend I'm a consultant, your partner, your bud, or a willing informant. Just tell me where and when you want to take a statement from me." I sat back and turned my attention to the potato skins.

Detective Penrose stayed quiet awhile, then said, "Tomorrow, my office"—she tapped her card—"nine A.M. Don't be late." She stood, put her beer down, and left.

New York had the ball on their own thirty with third and six, and this idiot of a quarterback throws La Bomba fifty yards into the friggin' wind, and the ball hangs there like the Goodyear blimp, and the three pass receivers and three Dallas guys are all under it with their arms flapping, hopping around like they're praying for rain or something.

"Excuse me."

"Sit down."

She sat, but it was too late, and I missed the interception. The crowd at the stadium and in the OTT were going nuts, and the guys at the bar were yelling, "Pass interference!" though there were no yellow flags out there, and the Dallas guy ran it back to the fifty. I watched the replay in slow motion. No pass interference. Sometimes I wish I could replay parts of my life in slow motion like that. Like my marriage, which was a series of bad calls.

She said, "I'm going back to the scene now. Someone from the Department of Agriculture is going to meet me at about eleven. He's coming in from Manhattan. Would you like to be there?"

"Don't you have a partner you can annoy?"

"He's on vacation. Come on, Detective, let's start all over." She put her hand out.

I reminded her, "Last time I took your hand, I lost my gun and my manhood."

She smiled. "Come on, shake."

I shook hands with her. Her skin was warm. My heart was on fire. Or maybe the nachos were causing reflux. It's hard to tell after forty.

I held her hand a moment and looked at her perfect face. Our eyes met, and the same piggy thought passed through both our minds. She broke eye contact first. Someone has to or it gets geeky.

The cute waitress came over, and I ordered two beers. The waitress asked me, "Do you still want that bowl of chili?"

"More than ever."

She cleared some of the dishes and went to get beer and chili. I love this country.

Detective Penrose commented, "You must have a cast-iron stomach."

"Actually, my whole stomach was taken out after I was shot. My esophagus is attached to my intestine."

"Do you mean your mouth is connected directly to your asshole?"

I raised my eyebrows.

She said, "I'm sorry—that was crude. Shall we start yet again?"

"It wouldn't do any good. Turn around and watch the game."

She turned around, and we watched the game and had a beer. At halftime with a 7–7 tie, she looked at her watch and said, "I have to go meet this Department of Agriculture guy."

If you're wondering about this Department of Agriculture thing, Plum Island is officially a Department of Agriculture installation, and they do things with animal diseases, anthrax, and all that. But rumor has it that it goes beyond that. Way beyond. I said, "Don't keep the Department of Agriculture waiting."

"Do you want to come along?"

I contemplated this invitation. If I went along, I'd get deeper into this thing, whatever it was. On the pro side, I like solving murders, and I liked the Gordons. In the ten years I've been with homicide, I've put twenty-six murderers behind bars, and the last two guys are eligible to take advantage of the new death penalty law, which adds another whole dimension to homicide cases now. On the con side, this was something different, and

I was way off my turf. Also, a Department of Agriculture guy, like most government bureaucrats, wouldn't be caught dead working at night, so this guy was most probably CIA or FBI or Defense Intelligence or something like that. It didn't matter, and there'd be more of them later tonight or tomorrow. No, I didn't need this case at a buck a week, or a thousand bucks a day, or at any price.

"Detective? Hello?"

I looked at her. How do you say no to a perfect 10? I said, "I'll meet you there."

"All right. What do I owe you for the beers?"

"On me."

"Thanks. See you later." She walked toward the door and, with the game at halftime, the fifty or so guys in the OTT finally noticed that there was an incredible babe on the premises. There were a few whistles and invitations to stick around.

I watched a little of the halftime stuff. I wished they *had* taken my stomach out, because it was pumping acid into my ulcers now. The chili came, and I could hardly finish the bowl. I popped two Zantac, then a Maalox even though the gastro-doc said not to mix.

In truth, my health, once robust, had taken a decided dip since the April 12 incident. My eating, drinking, and sleeping habits were never good, and the divorce and the job had taken their toll. I was starting to feel forty-something, starting to feel my mortality. Sometimes in my sleep, I remember lying in the gutter in my own blood, lying on a storm drain and thinking, "I'm circling around the drain, I'm going down the drain."

On the upside, I was starting to notice things like

the waitress with the NordicTrack ass, and when Elizabeth Penrose walked into the bar, my little meat puppet sat up and stretched. Truly, I was on the road to recovery, and for sure I was in better shape than the Gordons.

I thought a moment about Tom and Judy. Tom was a Ph.D. who didn't mind killing his brain cells with beer and wine, and he cooked a good steak on the grill. He was a down-to-earth guy from Indiana or Illinois or someplace out there where they have this sort of twang. He was low-key about his work and joked about the danger, like last week when a hurricane was headed our way, he said, "If it hits Plum, you can call it Hurricane Anthrax, and we can kiss our asses goodbye." Ha. Ha. Ha.

Judy, like her husband, was a Ph.D., a Midwesterner, unpretentious, good-natured, spirited, funny, and beautiful. John Corey, like every guy who met her, was in love with her.

Judy and Tom seemed to have taken well to this maritime province in the two years since they'd been here, and they seemed to enjoy powerboating and had gotten involved with the Peconic Historical Society. In addition, they were enchanted by the wineries and had become connoisseurs of Long Island wine. In fact, they had befriended some of the local vintners, including Fredric Tobin, who threw lavish soirees at his chateau, one of which I attended as the Gordons' guest.

As a couple, the Gordons seemed happy, loving, caring, sharing, and all that 1990s stuff, and I really never noticed anything amiss between them. But that's not to say they were perfect people or a perfect couple.

I searched my memory for something like a fatal

flaw, the kind of thing that sometimes gets people murdered. Drugs? Not likely. Infidelity? Possible, but not probable. Money? They didn't have much to steal. So it came down to the job again.

I thought about that. It would appear on the face of things that the Gordons were selling superbugs and something went wrong, and they were terminated. Along the same lines, I recalled that Tom once confided to me that his biggest fear, aside from catching a disease, was that he and Judy would be kidnapped right off their boat one day, that an Iranian submarine or something would come up and snatch them away, and they'd never be seen or heard from again. This seemed a little far-fetched to me, but I remember thinking that the Gordons must have a lot of stuff in their heads that some people wanted. So maybe what happened was that the murder started out as a snatch job and went wrong. I thought about this. If the murders were related to the job, were the Gordons innocent victims, or were they traitors who sold death for gold? Were they killed by a foreign power or were they killed by someone closer to home?

I mulled this over as best I could in the OTT with the noise, the halftime crap, the beer in my brain, and the acid in my tummy. I had another beer and another Maalox. Gastro-doc never said *wh*y I wasn't supposed to mix.

I tried to think of the unthinkable, of handsome, happy Tom and beautiful, bouncy Judy selling plague to some nut cases, of water reservoirs filled with disease, or maybe aerial crop sprayers over New York or Washington, of millions of sick, dying, and dead....

I couldn't imagine the Gordons doing that. On

the other hand, everyone has a price. I used to wonder how they could afford to rent that house on the water and buy that expensive boat. Now maybe I knew how and also why they needed a high-speed boat and a house with a private dock. It all made sense, and yet my instincts were telling me not to believe the obvious.

I overtipped Ms. NordicTrack and returned to the scene of the crime.

CHAPTER FOUR

It was after eleven as I drove along the lane that led to the Gordons' house. The night was lit by a nice three-quarter moon, and a pleasant breeze brought the smell of the sea through the open windows of my new moss green Jeep Grand Cherokee Limited, a $40,000 indulgence that the nearly deceased John Corey thought he owed himself.

I stopped fifty yards from the house, put the vehicle into "park," and listened to a few more minutes of Giants-Dallas, then I shut off the engine. A voice said, "Your headlights are on."

"Shut up," I replied, "just shut up." I switched off the headlights.

There are many options in life, but one option you should never choose is the "Voice Warning and Advisory Option."

I opened the door. "Your key is in the ignition. Your emergency brake is not engaged." It was a female voice, and I swear to God it sounded like my ex-wife. "Thank you, dear." I took my keys, climbed down, and slammed the door.

The vehicles and crowds on the small street had thinned considerably, and I figured that the bodies had been removed, it being a fact of life that the arrival of the meat wagon usually satisfies most of the spectators and signals the end of Act One. Also, they all wanted to see themselves on the eleven o'clock news.

There was a new addition to the police presence since my earlier visit: a Suffolk County police mobile van was parked in front of the house near the forensic van. This new van was the command post that could accommodate investigators, radios, fax machines, cell phones, video equipment, and the other high-tech doodads that make up the arsenal in the never-ending battle against crime and all that.

I noticed a helicopter overhead, and I could see by the light of the moon that it was from one of the networks. Though I couldn't hear the reporter's voice, he or she was probably saying something like, "Tragedy struck this exclusive Long Island community earlier this evening." Then some stuff about Plum Island and so on.

I made my way through the last of the stragglers, avoiding anyone who looked like the working press. I stepped over the yellow tape, and this immediately attracted a Southold cop. I tinned the guy and got a half-assed salute.

The uniformed crime scene recorder approached me with a clipboard and time sheet, and again I gave him my name, my business, and so forth, as he requested. This is SOP and is done throughout the investigation of the crime, beginning with the first officer at the scene and continuing until the last officer leaves and the scene is returned to the owner of the property. In any case, they had me twice now and the hook was in deeper.

I asked the uniformed officer, "Do you have a guy from the Department of Agriculture logged in?"

He replied without even looking at the sheet, "No."

"But there is a man from the Department of Agriculture here. Correct?"

"You'll have to ask Chief Maxwell."

"I'm asking you why you haven't logged this guy in."

"You'll have to ask Chief Maxwell."

"I will." Actually, I already knew the answer. They don't call these guys spooks for nothing.

I walked around to the backyard and onto the deck. In the places where the Gordons had lain were now two chalk outlines, looking very ghostly in the moonlight. A big sheet of clear plastic covered the splatter behind them where their mortality had exited.

Regarding this, as I said, I was glad this was an open-air shooting, and there was no lingering smell of death. I hate it when I go back to the scene of an indoor murder and that smell is still there. Why is it that I can't get that smell out of my mind? Out of my nostrils? Out of the back of my throat? Why is that?

Two uniformed Southold guys sat at the round patio table drinking from steaming Styrofoam cups. I recognized one of them as Officer Johnson, whose kindness in driving me home I had repaid by getting a little rough with him. It's a tough world, you know, and I'm one of the people who make it that way. Officer Johnson gave me an unpleasant glance.

Down by the dock, I could make out the silhouette of another uniformed man, and I was glad someone had taken my advice to post a guard by the boat.

There was no one else around so I went into the house through the sliding screen door, which opened into a big living room and dining room combo. I'd been here before, of course, and recalled that Judy said most of the furnishings came with the rental, Scandinavian from Taiwan, as she described it.

A few forensic types were still messing around, and I asked one of them, a cute latent fingerprint lady, "Chief Maxwell?"

She jerked her thumb over her shoulder and said, "Kitchen. Don't touch anything on the way there."

"Yes, ma'am." I floated across the Berber carpet and alighted in the kitchen, where a conference seemed to be in progress. Present were Max, representing the sovereign Township of Southold, Elizabeth Penrose, representing the free and independent County of Suffolk, a gentleman in a dark suit who didn't need a sign that said FBI, and another gentleman, more casually dressed in denim jacket and jeans, a bloodred shirt, and hiking boots, a sort of parody of what a Department of Agriculture bureaucrat might look like if he ever left the office and had to visit a farm.

Everyone was standing, like they were giving the impression of literally thinking on their feet. There was a cardboard box filled with Styrofoam coffee cups, and everyone had a cup in his or her hand. It was interesting and significant, I thought, that this group wasn't assembled in the mobile command post, but was sort of out of sight in the kitchen.

Max, incidentally, had spiffed himself up for the Feds and/or the press by putting on a tie, a silly one decorated with nautical flags. Elizabeth was still wearing her tan suit, but had removed her jacket, revealing one holstered .38 and two holstered 36Ds.

A small black-and-white TV sat on the counter,

tuned to one of the networks, the volume low. The lead story was about a presidential visit to some strange place where everyone was short.

Max said to the two guys, "This is Detective John Corey, homicide," and let it go at that without mentioning that my jurisdiction began and ended about a hundred miles west of here. Max indicated the dark suit and said, "John, this is George Foster, FBI..." He looked at Mr. Bluejeans and said, "...and this is Ted Nash, Department of Agriculture."

We shook hands all around. I informed Penrose, "Giants scored in the first minute of the third quarter."

She didn't reply.

Max motioned toward the box of cups and asked, "Coffee?"

"No, thanks."

Ms. Penrose, who was closest to the TV, heard something on the news and raised the volume. We all focused on the screen.

A female reporter was standing in front of the Gordon house. We missed her lead-in and caught, "The victims of the double murder have been identified as scientists who worked at the top-secret government animal disease laboratory on Plum Island, a few miles from here."

An aerial shot now showed Plum Island from about two thousand feet. It was bright daylight, so it must have been stock footage. From the air, the island looked almost exactly like a pork chop, and I guess if you wanted to stretch an irony about swine fever.... Anyway, Plum is about three miles at its longest, and about a mile at its widest. The reporter, in voice-over, was saying, "This is Plum Island as it appeared last summer when this station did a report about persistent rumors that the island is home to biological warfare research."

Aside from the hackneyed phrases, the lady was right about the rumors. I recalled a cartoon I'd once seen in *The Wall Street Journal* where a school guidance counselor says to two parents, "Your son is vicious, mean-spirited, dishonest, and likes to spread rumors. I suggest a career in journalism." Right. And rumors could lead to panic. It occurred to me that this case had to be wrapped up quickly.

The reporter was now back in front of the Gordons' house, and she informed us, "No one is saying if the Gordons' murders were related to their work on Plum Island, but police are investigating."

Back to the studio.

Ms. Penrose turned off the volume and asked Mr. Foster, "Does the FBI want to be publicly connected with this case?"

"Not at this time." Mr. Foster added, "It makes people think there's a real problem."

Mr. Nash said, "The Department of Agriculture has no official interest in this case since there is *no* connection between the Gordons' work and their deaths. The department will issue no public statements, except an expression of sorrow over the murders of two well-liked and dedicated employees."

Amen. I mentioned to Mr. Nash, "By the way, you forgot to sign in."

He looked at me, a little surprised and a lot annoyed, and replied, "I'll...thank you for reminding me."

"Anytime. Every time."

After a minute of public relations chitchat, Max said

to Messrs. Foster and Nash, "Detective Corey knew the deceased."

Mr. FBI immediately got interested and asked me, "How did you know them?"

It's not a good idea to start answering questions—it gives people the idea that you're a cooperative fellow, which I'm not. I didn't reply.

Max answered for me, "Detective Corey knew the Gordons socially, only about three months. I've known John on and off about ten years."

Foster nodded. Clearly he had more questions and while he was hesitating about asking, Detective Penrose said, "Detective Corey is writing a full report on what he knew of the Gordons which I will share with all concerned agencies."

That was news to me.

Mr. Nash was leaning against a kitchen counter looking at me. We stared at each other, the two dominant males in the room, if you will, and we decided without a word that we didn't like each other, and that one of us had to go. I mean, the air was so thick with testosterone that the wallpaper was getting soggy.

I turned my attention to Max and Penrose and asked, "Have we determined that this is more than a homicide? Is that why the federal government is here?"

No one replied.

I continued, "Or are we just *assuming* that it is more? Did I miss a meeting or something?"

Mr. Ted Nash finally replied coolly, "We are being cautious, Detective. We have no concrete evidence that this homicide is connected to matters of...well, to be blunt, matters of national security."

I remarked, "I never realized the Department of

Agriculture was involved in national security. Do you have, like, undercover cows?"

Mr. Nash gave me a nice fuck-you smile and said, "We have wolves in sheep's clothing."

"Touché." Prick.

Mr. Foster butted in before it got nasty and said, "We're here as a precautionary measure, Detective. We'd be very remiss if we didn't check it out. We all hope it was just a murder with no Plum Island connection."

I regarded George Foster a moment. He was thirtyish, typical clean-cut, bright-eyed FBI type, wearing the FBI dark suit, white shirt, muted tie, black sturdy shoes, and halo.

I shifted my attention to Ted Nash wearing the aforementioned denims; he was closer to my age, tanned, curly salt-and-pepper hair, blue-gray eyes, impressive build, and all in all what the ladies would call a hunk, which is one of the reasons I didn't like him, I guess. I mean, how many hunks do you need in one room?

I might have been more pleasant to him except that he was throwing glances at Elizabeth Penrose, who was catching them and pitching them back. I don't mean they were leering and drooling; just real quick eye-to-eye flashes and neutral expressions, but you'd have to be blind not to figure out what was going through their dirty minds. Jeez, the whole friggin' planet was about to get anthrax and die or something, and these two are like dogs in heat, eye-fucking each other when we had important business at hand. Really disgusting.

Max interrupted my thoughts and said to me, "John, we have still not recovered the two bullets fired through their heads, but we can assume they went into the bay, and we'll be dredging and diving early tomorrow." He added, "There were no shell casings found."

I nodded. An automatic pistol would spit out shell casings whereas a revolver would not. If the weapon was an automatic, then the murderer was cool enough to bend down and gather the two shell casings.

So far, we had basically nothing. Two head shots, no bullets, no casings, no noise heard next door.

I regarded Mr. Nash again. He looked like a worried man, and I was happy to see that between thoughts of popping Ms. Penrose, he was thinking about saving the planet. In fact, everyone in the kitchen seemed to be thinking about things, probably germs, and they were probably wondering if they were going to wake up with red blotches or something.

Ted Nash reached into the cardboard box and asked Detective Penrose, "Another coffee, Beth?"

Beth? What the hell...?

She smiled. "No, thank you."

My stomach had settled down so I went to the refrigerator for a beer. The shelves were nearly empty and I asked, "Max, did you take things out of here?"

"The lab took everything that was not factory sealed."

"Do you want a beer?" No one answered, so I took a Coors Light, popped the top, and took a swig.

I noticed eight eyes on me, like they were waiting for something to happen. People get weird when they think they're in an infected environment. I had a crazy urge to clutch my throat, fall on the floor, and go into convulsions. But I wasn't with my buds in Manhattan North, chicks and dicks who would get a kick out of sick humor, so I passed on the opportunity to add some comic relief to the grimness. I said to Max, "Please continue."

He said, "We've searched the entire house and turned up nothing unusual or significant, except that half the drawers were intact, some closets didn't even look like they'd been searched, the books on the bookshelves weren't pulled out. A very amateur job of pretending it was a burglary."

I said, "It still could have been a junkie, strung out and not real focused." I added, "Or maybe the perp was interrupted, or the perp was looking for one thing and found it."

"Maybe," Max agreed.

Everyone looked pensive, which is good cover-up for clueless.

The striking thing about this double homicide, I thought, was still the outdoor shooting, the bang, bang, right on the deck without much preamble. There was nothing the killer needed or wanted from the Gordons, except that they be dead. So, yes, the killer either had what he wanted from inside the house, and/or the Gordons were carrying what the killer wanted, in plain view, i.e., the ice chest. It came back to the missing ice chest.

And the killer knew the Gordons and they knew him. I was convinced of that. *Hi Tom*, *Hi Judy*. *Bang*, *bang*. They fall, the ice chest falls...no, it's got vials of deadly virus in it. *Hi Tom*, *Hi Judy*. *Put that chest down*. *Bang*, *bang*. They fall. The bullets sail through their skulls into the bay.

Also, he *had* to have a silencer. No pro would pop off two big boomers outdoors. And it was probably an automatic, because revolvers don't adapt well to a silencer.

I asked Max, "Do the Murphys own a dog?"

"Nope."

"Okay.... Did you find any money, wallets, or anything on the victims?"

"Yes. They each had matching sports wallets; each had their Plum Island ID, driver's license, credit cards, and such. Tom had thirty-seven dollars in cash, Judy had fourteen." He added, "Each had a photo of the other."

It's little things, sometimes, that bring it all home, that make it personal. Then you have to remember Rule One: don't get emotionally involved—it doesn't matter, Corey, if it's a little kid who got greased, or a nice old lady, or pretty Judy who winked at you once, and Tom who wanted you to love the wines he loved and who cooked your steak just so. For the homicide dick, it does not matter who the victim is, it only matters who the killer is.

Max said, "I guess you figured out that we never found that ice chest. You're sure about the chest?"

I nodded.

Mr. Foster gave me his considered opinion. "We think the Gordons were carrying the chest, and the killer or killers wanted what was inside, and what was inside was you-know-what." He added, "I think the Gordons were selling the stuff and the deal went bad."

I looked around at the meeting of the kitchen cabinet. It's hard to read the faces of people whose job it is to read other people's faces. Still, I had the feeling that George Foster's statement represented the consensus.

So, if these people were right, that would presuppose

two things—one, the Gordons were really stupid, never considering that anyone who would want enough virus and bacteria to kill a zillion people might not hesitate to kill them, and two, it presupposed the Gordons were totally indifferent to the consequences of their selling death for gold. What I knew for sure about Tom and Judy was that they were neither stupid, nor heartless.

I would also assume that the killer was not stupid, and I wondered if he knew or could tell if what was in the chest was the real thing. How could he possibly know? *Hi Tom, Hi Judy. Got the virus? Good. Bang, bang.*

Yes? No? I tried different scenarios with and without the ice chest, with and without the person or persons whom the Gordons must have known, and so forth. Also, how did this person or these people get to the Gordons' house? Boat? Car? I asked Max, "Strange vehicles?"

Max replied, "There were no strange vehicles seen by anyone we've questioned. The Gordons' two cars are both in their garage." He added, "Forensics will take them to the lab tomorrow along with the boat."

Ms. Penrose spoke to me directly for the first time and said, "It's possible the killer or killers arrived by boat. That's my theory."

I said to her, "It's also possible, Elizabeth, that the killer or killers arrived in one of the Gordons' cars which the killer may have borrowed. I really think they *knew* each other."

She stared at me, then said a bit curtly, "I think it was a *boat*, Detective Corey."

"Maybe the killer walked here, or bicycled, or motorcycled." I continued, "Maybe he swam here, or was dropped off. Maybe he windsurfed in or paraglided. Maybe the killers are Edgar Murphy and his wife."

She stared hard at me, and I could tell she was pissed. I know that look. I was married.

Max interrupted our discussion and said, "And here's something interesting, John—according to the security people on Plum, the Gordons signed out at noon, got into their boat, and headed out."

You could hear the hum of the refrigerator in the silence.

Mr. Foster said to us, "One possibility that comes to mind is that the Gordons had secreted whatever it was they were selling somewhere in a cove or inlet on Plum, and they took their boat there and recovered the stuff. Or maybe they just walked out of the lab with that ice chest, put it aboard, and took off. In either case, they then met their customers out in the bay and transferred the chestful of vials at sea, so when they returned here, they didn't have the chest, but they had the money. They ran into their killer here, and after he shot them, he took the money back."

We all considered that scenario. Of course you have to wonder, if the transfer had taken place at sea, why wasn't the murder also done at sea? When homicide guys talk about the perfect murder, they talk about murder on the high seas—little or no forensic evidence, usually no noise, no witnesses, and most times no body. And if it's done right, it looks like an accident.

It stands to reason that pros who just copped a lethal bug are not going to draw attention to it by killing two Plum Island people on their back deck. Still, it was supposed to look like the Gordons surprised a burglar. But whoever staged *that* wasn't very convincing.

This whole thing looked amateurish, or maybe it was done by foreigners who didn't watch enough American cop shows on TV. Or, something else.

And what about those five and a half hours between the time the Gordons left Plum Island at noon, and the time Mr. Murphy said he heard the Gordons' boat at 5:30? Where were they?

Max said, "That's about all we have at the moment, John. We'll have the lab reports tomorrow, and there are people we have to speak to tomorrow. Can you suggest anyone we ought to see? Friends of the Gordons?"

"I don't know who the Gordons were friends with, and to the best of my knowledge, they had no enemies." I said to Mr. Nash, "Meanwhile, I want to speak to the people on Plum Island."

Mr. Nash replied, "It may be possible for you to speak to some people who work on Plum Island." He added, "But in the interest of national security, I must be present at all interviews."

I replied in my best New York obnoxious tone, "This is a murder investigation, remember? Don't pull that crap on me."

It got a little frosty in the kitchen. I mean, I work with FBI and Drug Enforcement types now and then, and they're okay people—they're cops. However, these spooks, like Nash, are real pains in the ass. The guy wasn't even saying if he was CIA, Defense Intelligence, Military Intelligence, or some other weird outfit. What I knew for sure was that he wasn't from the Department of Agriculture.

Max, feeling I suppose like the host at this gathering of egos, said, "I don't have any problem with Ted

Nash being present at any interviews or interrogations." He looked at Penrose.

My buddy Beth gave me a curt glance and said to Nash, the eye-fucker, "I have no problem with that either."

George Foster pointed out, "Any meeting, interview, interrogation, or working session at which Ted is present, the FBI will also be present."

I was really getting the crap kicked out of me, and I was wondering if Max was going to pull the plug on me.

The reasonable Mr. Foster went on, "My area of concern is domestic terrorism. Ted Nash is concerned with international espionage." He looked at me, Max, and Penrose, and said, "You are investigating a homicide under New York State law. If we all keep out of one another's way, we'll be fine. I won't play homicide detective if you won't play defenders of the free world. Fair? Logical? Workable? Absolutely."

I looked at Nash and asked him bluntly, "Who do you work for?"

"I'm not at liberty to say at this time." He added, "Not the Department of Agriculture."

"Fooled me," I said sarcastically. "You guys are sharp."

Penrose suggested, "Detective Corey, can we have a word outside?"

I ignored her and pressed on with Mr. Nash. I needed to get seven points on the board, and I knew how to do it. I said to Nash, "We'd like to go to Plum Island tonight."

He looked surprised. "Tonight? There aren't any ferries running—"

"I don't need a government ferry. We'll take Max's police boat."

"Out of the question," said Nash.

"Why?"

"The island is off-limits," he said.

"This is a murder investigation," I reminded him. "Didn't we just agree that Chief Maxwell, Detective Penrose, and I are investigating a murder?"

"Not on Plum Island you're not."

"We sure are." I love this stuff. I really do. I hoped Penrose was seeing what a putz this guy was.

Mr. Nash said, "There is no one on Plum now."

I replied, "There are security people on Plum now, and I want to speak to them. Now."

"In the morning and not on the island."

"Now, and on the island, or I'll get a judge out of bed and get a search warrant."

Mr. Nash stared at me and said, "It is unlikely that a local judge would issue a search warrant for U.S. government property. You would need to involve an assistant United States attorney and a federal judge. I assume you know that if you're a homicide detective, and what you may also know is that neither a U.S. attorney nor a federal judge will be enthusiastic about issuing such a warrant if it involves national security." He added, "So don't bluff and bluster."

"How about if I threaten?"

Finally, Max had had enough of Mr. Nash, whose sheep's clothing was slipping. Max said to Nash, "Plum Island may be federal land, but it's part of the Township of Southold, the County of Suffolk, and the State of New York. I want you to get us authorization to go to the island tomorrow, or we'll get a court order."

Mr. Nash now tried to sound pleasant. "There's really no need to go to the island, Chief."

Detective Penrose found herself on my side, of course, and said to her new friend, "We have to insist, Ted."

Ted? Wow, I really missed some stuff in the lousy hour I was late.

Ted and Beth looked at each other, tortured souls, torn between rivalry and ribaldry. Finally, Mr. Ted Nash, of the Bug Security Agency or whatever, said, "Well...I'll make a call about that."

"Tomorrow, A.M.," I said. "No later."

Mr. Foster didn't let the opportunity pass to tweak Mr. Nash and said, "I think we're all in agreement that we're going out there tomorrow morning, Ted."

Mr. Nash nodded. By now he'd stopped batting his eyelids at Beth Penrose and was concentrating his passions on me. He looked at me and said, "At some point, Detective Corey, if we determine that a federal crime has taken place, we probably won't need your services any longer."

I had reduced Teddy-boy to pettiness, and I knew when to leave well enough alone. I'd come back from a verbal drubbing, slain the slick Ted, and reclaimed the love of Lady Penrose. I'm terrific. I was really feeling better, feeling like my old unpleasant self again. Also, these characters needed a little fire under their asses. Rivalry is good. Competition is American. What if Dallas and New York were pals?

The other four characters were now making small talk, rummaging around the cardboard box and doing coffee stuff, trying to re-establish the amity and equilibrium that they'd established before Corey showed up. I got another beer from the fridge, then addressed Mr. Nash in a professional tone. I asked him, "What kind of bugs do they play around with on Plum? I mean, why would anyone, any foreign power, want bugs that cause hoof-and-mouth disease or Mad Cow Disease? Tell me, Mr. Nash, what I'm supposed to worry about so when I can't get to sleep tonight, I have a name for it."

Mr. Nash didn't reply for a good while, then cleared his throat and said, "I suppose you should know how high the stakes are here...." He looked at me, Max, and Penrose, then said, "Regardless of your security clearance, or lack of, you *are* sworn police officers, so—"

I said amiably, "Nothing you say will leave this room." Unless it suits me to blab it to someone else.

Nash and Foster looked at each other, and Foster nodded. Nash said to us, "You all know, or may have read, that the United States no longer engages in biological warfare research or development. We've signed a treaty to that effect."

"That's why I love this country, Mr. Nash. No bug bombs here."

"Right. However...there are certain diseases that make the transition between legitimate biological study and potential biological weapons. Anthrax is one such disease. As you know"—he looked at Max, Penrose, and me—"there have always been rumors that Plum Island is not only an animal disease research facility, but something else."

No one responded to that.

He continued, "In fact, it is not a biological warfare center. There is no such thing in the United States. However, I'd be less than truthful if I didn't say that biological warfare specialists sometimes visit the island to be briefed and to read reports on some of these experiments. In other words, there is a crossover between animal and human disease, between offensive biological warfare and defensive biological warfare."

Convenient crossovers, I thought.

Mr. Nash sipped his java, considered, then continued, "African swine fever, for instance, has been associated with HIV. We study African swine fever on Plum, and the news media makes up this junk about...whatever. Same with Rift Valley fever, the Hanta virus, and other retroviruses, and the filoviruses such as Ebola Zaire and Ebola Marburg...."

The kitchen was really quiet, like everyone knew this was the scariest topic in the universe. I mean, when it was nuclear weapons, people were either fatalistic or never believed it was going to happen. With biological warfare or biological terrorism, it was imaginable. And if the right plague got loose, it was lights out world, and not in a quick incandescent flash, but slowly, as it spread from the sick to the healthy, and the dead lay rotting where they fell, a Grade B movie coming to your neighborhood soon.

Mr. Nash continued in that sort of half-reluctant, half-hey-look-what-I-know-that-you-don't kind of voice. He said, "So...these diseases can and do infect animals, and therefore their legitimate study would fall under the jurisdiction of the Department of Agriculture.... The department is trying to find a cure for these diseases, to protect American livestock and by extension to protect the American public, because even though there is usually a species barrier in regard to animal diseases infecting humans, we're discovering that some of these diseases can jump species....With the recent Mad Cow Disease in Britain, for instance, there is some evidence that people were infected by this disease...."

Maybe my ex-wife was right about meat. I tried to picture a life of soybean cheeseburgers, chile no carne, and hot dogs made out of seaweed. I'd rather die. All of a sudden I felt love and warmth for the Department of Agriculture.

I realized, too, that what Mr. Nash was putting out was the official crap—stuff about animal diseases crossing species barriers and all that. In fact, if the rumors were correct, Plum Island was also a place where human infectious diseases were specifically and purposely studied as part of a biological warfare program that no longer officially existed. On the other hand, maybe it was rumor, and maybe, too, what they were doing on Plum Island was defensive and not offensive.

It struck me that there was a very thin line between all of this stuff. Bugs are bugs. They don't know cows from pigs from people. They don't know defensive research from offensive research. They don't know preventive vaccines from air-burst bombs. Hell, they don't even know if they're good or bad. And if I listened to Nash's crap long enough, I would start to believe that Plum Island was developing exciting new yogurt cultures.

Mr. Nash was staring into his Styrofoam coffee cup as if realizing that the coffee and the water could have already been infected with Mad Cow Disease. Mr. Nash continued, "The problem is, of course, that these bacteria and virus cultures can be...I mean, if someone got his hands on these micro-organisms, and has the knowledge to propagate more from the samples, then, well, you'd have a great deal of it reproducing, and if it got into the population somehow...then you may have a potential public health problem."

I asked, "You mean like an end-of-the-world plague with the dead piling up in the streets?"

"Yes, that kind of public health problem."

Silence.

"So," Mr. Nash said in a grave tone, "while we are all anxious to discover the identity of the murderer or murderers of Mr. and Mrs. Gordon, we're more anxious to discover if the Gordons took something off that island and transferred it to an unauthorized person or persons."

No one spoke for a time, then Beth asked, "Can you...can anyone on the island determine if anything is actually missing from the laboratories?"

Ted Nash looked at Beth Penrose the way a professor looks at a favorite student who has asked a brilliant question. Actually, it wasn't *that* good a question—but anything to get those panties off, right, Ted?

Mr. Cool replied to his new protégée, "As you probably suspect, Beth, it may not be possible to discover if anything is missing. The problem is, the micro-organisms can be propagated secretly in some part of the Plum Island laboratory or in other places on the island, then taken off the island, and no one would ever know. It's not like chemical or nuclear agents, where every gram is accounted for. Bacteria and virus like to reproduce."

Scary, if you think about it...microbugs are low-tech compared to nuclear fission or manufacturing nerve gas. This is home lab stuff, cheap to produce, and it replicates itself in—what did we use in bio lab? Beef bouillon? No more cheeseburgers for me.

Ms. Penrose, proud of her last question, asked Mr.-Know-It-All, "Can we assume the organisms studied on Plum Island are particularly deadly? What I mean is, do they genetically engineer these organisms to make them more lethal than they are in their natural state?"

Mr. Nash did not like that question and replied, "No." Then added, "Well, the laboratory at Plum Island does have genetic engineering capabilities, but what they do is take viruses and genetically alter them so they can't cause disease, but *can* stimulate the immune system to produce antibodies in the event the real virus ever infects the organism. This is sort of a vaccine, made not by weakening the infectious organism and injecting it, which can be dangerous, but by genetically changing the organism. To answer your question in short, any genetic engineering done on Plum Island is to weaken a virus or bacteria, not to increase its power to cause disease."

I said, "Of course not. But that's also possible with genetic engineering."

"Possible. But not on Plum Island."

It occurred to me that Nash was genetically altering information—taking the germ of the truth, if you will, and weakening it so we got a mild dose of the bad news. Clever fellow.

I was tired of the scientific crap, and I addressed my next question to Mr. Foster. "Are you people doing anything to keep this bottled? Airports, highways, and all that?"

Mr. Foster replied, "We've got *everyone* out there looking for...whatever. We have all area airports, seaports, and train stations being watched by our people, local police, and Customs people, and we have

the Coast Guard stopping and searchi...
we've even got the Drug Enforcement A...
their boats and planes. The problem is, the ...
tors would have had about a three-hour hea...
because quite frankly we weren't notified in a timely
fashion...." Mr. Foster looked at Chief Maxwell, who
had his arms crossed and was making a face.

A word here on Sylvester Maxwell. He's an honest
cop, not the brightest bulb in the room, but not stupid
either. He can be stubborn at times, though that seems
to be a North Fork trait and not peculiar to the chief.
Being in charge of a small rural police force that has to
work with the much larger county police force and on
occasion the state police, he's learned when to protect
his turf and when to retreat.

Another point: the geographical realities of a maritime jurisdiction in the era of drug running have put
Max in close proximity to the DEA and the Coast
Guard. The DEA always assumes the local gendarmes
may be in on the drug trade; the locals, like Max, are
positive the DEA is in on it. The Coast Guard and FBI
are considered clean, but they suspect the DEA and
the local police. The Customs Service is mostly clean,
but there have to be some bad guys who take bucks to
look the other way. In short, drugs are the worst thing
that has happened to American law enforcement since
Prohibition.

And this led me from thinking about Max to thinking about drugs, about the Gordons' thirty-foot Formula with big, powerful engines. Since the facts didn't
seem to fit the Gordons selling end-of-the-world
plague for money, maybe the facts *did* fit drug running.
Maybe I was onto something. Maybe I'd share this

with everyone as soon as I worked it out in my mind. Maybe I wouldn't.

Mr. Foster threw a few more zingers at Chief Maxwell for his tardiness in contacting the FBI, making sure he was on the record about that. Sort of like, "Oh, Max, if only you'd come to me sooner. Now, all is lost, and it's your fault."

Max pointed out to Foster, "I called county homicide within ten minutes of learning of the murder. It was out of my hands at that point. My ass is covered."

Ms. Penrose felt eight eyes on her ass and said, "I had no idea the victims were Plum Island people."

Max said, gently but firmly, "I reported that to the guy who answered the phone, Beth. Sergeant...something. Check the tape."

"I will," replied Detective Penrose. She added, "You may be right, Max, but let's not get into this now." She said to Foster, "Let's stick to solving the crime."

Mr. Foster replied, "Good advice." He looked around the room and offered, "Another possibility is that whoever took this stuff is not trying to take it out of the country. They could have a lab set up locally, an inconspicuous kind of operation that wouldn't attract attention, wouldn't require unusual materials or chemicals that could be traced. Worst-case scenario is that the organisms, whatever they are, are cultured, then introduced or delivered to the population in various ways. Some of these organisms are easy to deliver in the water supply, some can be airborne, some can be spread by people and animals. I'm no expert, but I phoned some people in Washington earlier, and I understand that the potential for infection and contagion is very high." He added, "A TV documentary once suggested that a coffee can full of anthrax, vaporized into the air by a single terrorist riding around Manhattan in a boat, would kill a minimum of two hundred thousand people."

The room got silent again.

Mr. Foster, enjoying the attention, it seemed, continued, "It could be worse. It's hard to gauge. Anthrax is bacterial. Viruses could be worse."

I asked, "Do I understand that we're not talking about the possible theft of a single type of virus or bacteria?"

George Foster replied, "If you're going to steal anthrax, you might as well steal Ebola, too, and anything else you can get. This would pose a multifaceted threat, the type of threat that would never be found in nature, and would be impossible to contain or control."

The mantel clock in the living room struck twelve chimes, and Mr. Ted Nash, with a sense for the dramatic and wanting to impress us with his education, undoubtedly Ivy League, quoted the Bard, thus: "'Ties now the very witching time of night, when churchyards yawn and hell itself breathes out contagion to this world."

On that cheery note, I said, "I'm going out for some air."

CHAPTER FIVE

I didn't go directly outside for air, but detoured to the west wing of the house where Tom and Judy had set up their office in what used to be a bedroom.

A comp-nerd sat at the PC where I had intended to sit. I introduced myself to the gent, who identified himself as Detective Mike Resnick, computer crime specialist with the county police department.

The printer was humming away and stacks of paper lay all over the desktop.

I asked Mike, "Did you find the killer yet?"

"Yeah, now I'm playing Jeopardy."

Mike was a real card. I asked him, "What do we have so far?"

"Oh...mostly...hold on, what's this? Nothing there...what do we...what...?"

"Have so far." I just love talking to butt holes at the computer. *"Have so far."*

"Oh...mostly letters...personal letters to friends and relatives, some business letters...some...what's this? Nothing...."

"Anything mentioning Plum Island?"

"No."

"Anything that looks interesting or suspicious?"

"No."

"Scientific papers—"

"No. I'll stop what I'm doing and let homicide know the minute I think I have something."

Mike sounded a little testy, like he'd been at this a few hours and it was past his bedtime. I asked him, "How about financial stuff? Investments, checkbook, household budget—?"

He glanced up from the monitor. "Yeah. That's the first thing I downloaded. They wrote their checks on the computer. There's the printout of all their checkbook activity for the past twenty-five months—since they opened the account." He pointed to a stack of paper near the printer.

I took the stack and said, "Do you mind if I look through this?"

"No, but don't go far with it. I have to attach all that to my report."

"I'll just take it into the living room where the light is better."

"Yeah . . ." He was playing with the computer again, which he found more interesting than me. I left.

Out in the living room, the latent fingerprint lady was still dusting and lifting prints. She glanced at me and asked, "Did you touch anything?"

"No, ma'am."

I walked over to the bookshelves on either side of the fireplace. To the left was fiction, mostly paperbacks, a nice mixture of trash and treasures. To the right was nonfiction, and I studied the titles, which ranged from technical biology stuff to standard health and fitness crap. There was also a whole shelf of locally published books about Long Island, flora, fauna, history, and so forth.

On the bottom shelf was a row of sailing books, navigational charts, and such. As I said, for land-locked Midwesterners, the Gordons had really gotten into boating. On the other hand, I'd been out with them a few times, and even I could tell they weren't great sailors. Also, they didn't fish, clam, crab, or even swim. They just liked to open up the throttles now and then. Which brought me back to the thought that this was a drug thing.

With that thought in mind, I put the computer printouts down and, using my handkerchief, took an oversized book of navigational charts from the shelf and propped it up on the mantelpiece. I flipped through the pages, my finger wrapped in the handkerchief. I was looking for radio frequencies, cellular phone numbers, or whatever else a drug runner might mark in his chart book.

Each page of the navigational charts showed an area of about four miles by four miles. The land that appeared on the charts was basically featureless except for landmarks that could be seen from the water. The seas, however, were marked with reefs, rocks, depths, lighthouses, sunken wrecks, buoys, and all sorts of aids and hazards to navigation.

I scanned page after page looking for "X's," I guess, rendezvous points, or grid coordinates, or names like Juan and Pedro or whatever, but the charts seemed clean except for a yellow highlighter line that connected the Gordons' dock with the Plum Island dock. This was the route they took to work, passing between the southern shore of the North Fork and Shelter Island, keeping to the deep and safe part of the channel. That wasn't much of a clue to anything.

I noticed that on Plum Island, printed in red, were the words, "Restricted Access—U.S. Government Property—Closed to the Public."

I was about to shut the large book when I saw something nearly hidden by my handkerchief—toward the bottom of the page, in the water south of Plum Island, was written in pencil, "44106818." Following this was a question mark, similar to the one that just popped out of my head like a little cartoon balloon—*44106818*? Make that two question marks and an exclamation point.

So, was this a standard eight-digit grid coordinate? A radio frequency? A disguised Dial-A-Joke? Drugs? Bugs? What?

There is a point in homicide investigations when you start to assemble more clues than you know what to do with. Clues are like ingredients in a recipe with no instructions—if you put them together in the right way, you have dinner. If you don't know what to do with them, you'll be in the kitchen a long time, confused and hungry.

Anyway, I held the chart book with my handkerchief and took it to the latent fingerprint lady. I asked her, "Could you do a real thorough job on this book for me?" I smiled nicely.

She gave me a tough look, then took the book in her latex-gloved hand and examined it. "This map paper's hard to do...but the cover is good glossy stock....I'll do what I can." She added, "Silver nitrate or ninhydrin. It's got to be done in the lab."

"Thank you, professionally competent woman."

She cracked a smile and asked, "Who has the most fingerprints? FBI, CIA, or EPA?"

"What's EPA? You mean Environmental Protection Agency?"

"No. Elizabeth Penrose's ass." She laughed. "That's going around headquarters. You haven't heard that one?"

"Don't think so."

She put out her hand. "I'm Sally Hines."

"I'm John Corey." I shook her gloved hand and remarked, "I love the feel of latex against my bare skin. How about you?"

"No comment." She paused, then asked, "Are you the NYPD guy working with county homicide on this thing?"

"Right."

"Forget that crack about Penrose."

"Sure will." I asked her, "What are we seeing here, Sally?"

"Well, the house was cleaned recently so we have nice fresh surfaces. I'm not studying the prints closely, but I'm seeing mostly the same two sets, probably the Mr. and Mrs. Only a few other sets now and then, and if you want my opinion, Detective, the killer was wearing gloves. This was no druggie leaving perfect fives on the liquor cabinet."

I nodded, then said, "Do the best job you can with that book."

"I only do perfect work. How about you?" She found a plastic bag in her kit and slipped the chart book inside. She said, "I need a set of elimination prints from you."

"Try Elizabeth Penrose's ass later."

She laughed and said, "Just put your hands on this glass coffee table for me."

I did as she asked, and inquired, "Did you take prints from the two guys with Chief Maxwell?"

"I was told that would be taken care of later."

"Yeah. Look, Sally, a lot of people, like the guys in the kitchen, are going to flash a lot of big-time ID at you. You report only to county homicide, preferably only to Penrose."

"I hear you." She looked around, then asked me, "Hey, what's with the germs?"

"This has nothing to do with germs. The victims happened to work on Plum Island, but that's only a coincidence."

"Yeah, right."

I retrieved the stack of computer printouts and walked toward the sliding glass door.

Sally called out, "I don't like how this crime scene is being handled."

I didn't reply.

I walked down to the bay where a nice bench faced the water. I threw the purloined papers on the bench and stared out at the bay.

It was breezy enough to keep the gnats and mosquitoes busy treading air and away from me. Little ripples rode the bay and rocked the Gordons' boat down at the dock. White clouds sailed past the big, bright moon, and the air smelled more of the land than the sea as the light wind shifted around and blew from the north.

Somewhere, somehow, through osmosis, I guess, I'd begun to understand the elemental forces of land and sea around me. I suppose if you add up all the

two-week summer vacations out here when I was a kid
and the autumn weekends, it's not too surprising that
something seeped into my urban brain.

There are times I want to get out of the city, and I
think about someplace like this. I guess I should come
out here in the winter and spend a few months in Uncle
Harry's big drafty house and see if I become an alco-
holic or a hermit. Hell, if people keep getting bumped
off around here, the Southold Town Board will make
me a full-time homicide consultant at a hundred bucks
a day and all the clams I can eat.

I was uncharacteristically ambivalent about returning to duty. I was ready to try something else, but I
wanted it to be my own decision, not the decision
of the docs; also, if the quackers said I was through,
I couldn't find the two hombres who plugged me.
That was serious unfinished business. I have no Italian blood, but my partner, Dominic Fanelli, is a Sicil-
ian, and he taught me the entire history and protocol of
revenge. He made me see *The Godfather* three times. I
think I get it. The two Hispanic gents had to stop living. Dominic was working on finding them. I was waiting for him to call one day when he did.

On the subject of my mortality, I was getting a little fatigued, and I sat on the bench. I wasn't quite the
superman I used to be before the shooting.

I leaned back and regarded the night awhile. On a
small patch of lawn to the left of the Gordons' dock
was a tall, white flagpole with a crossbar, called a yardarm, from which ran two ropes or lines called halyards.
Note how I have picked up some of the nautical lingo.
Anyway, the Gordons had found a whole collection of
flags and pennants in a locker in the garage, and they'd

sometimes hang signal pennants from the halyards for fun—such as the pennant for "Prepare to be boarded" or "The captain is ashore."

I had noticed earlier that at the top of the mast, the Gordons had run up the Jolly Roger, and I thought it ironic that the last flag they had flown was the skull and crossbones.

I noticed, too, that on each halyard was a signal pennant. I could barely make them out in the dark, but it didn't matter because I was clueless about nautical signals.

Beth Penrose sat down on the left end of the bench. She was wearing her jacket again, which was a disappointment, and her arms were crossed around her as if she were cold. Women are always cold. She didn't say anything, but kicked off her shoes, rubbed her feet in the grass, and wiggled her toes. They also wear uncomfortable shoes.

After a few minutes of companionable silence—or maybe frosty stillness—I chipped at the ice and said, "Maybe you're right. It could have been a boat."

"Are you armed?"

"No."

"Good. I'm going to blow your f-ing brains out."

"Now, Beth—"

"Detective Penrose to you, buster."

"Lighten up."

"Why were you so nasty to Ted Nash?"

"Which one is that?"

"You know f-ing well which one is that. What is your problem?"

"It's a guy thing."

"You made a fool out of yourself, everyone thinks

you're an arrogant idiot, and a totally useless incompetent. *And* you've lost my respect."

"Then I suppose sex is out of the question."

"*Sex*? I don't even want to breathe the same air you do."

"That hurts, Beth."

"Do *not* call me Beth."

"Ted Nash called you—"

"You know, Corey, I got this case because I slapped on the knee pads and begged the chief of homicide for it. This is my first real murder case. Before this, all I got was crap—hopheads blasting away at each other, mommas and poppas settling domestic disputes with cutlery, crap like that. And not much of it. There's a low homicide rate in this county."

"I'm sorry to hear that."

"Yeah. You do this all the time, so you're jaded, cynical, and smart-assed about it."

"Well, I wouldn't—"

"If you're here to make me look bad, fuck off." She stood.

I stood, too. "Hold on. I'm here to help."

"Then help."

"Okay. Listen up. First, some advice. Don't talk too much to Foster or your buddy Ted."

"I know that, and cut the 'buddy Ted' crap."

"Look...can I call you Beth?"

"No."

"Look, Detective Penrose, I know you think I'm attracted to you and you probably think I'm coming on to you...and you think this could be awkward...."

She turned her face away and looked out at the bay.

I continued, "...this is really hard to say, but...

well...you don't have to worry about that...about me...."

She turned back and looked at me.

I sort of covered my face with my right hand and rubbed my forehead. I continued as best I could. "You see...one of those bullets that hit me....God, how do I say this...? Well, it hit me in a funny place, okay? Now you know. So we can be sort of like...friends, partners...brother and sister...I guess I mean sister and sister...." I glanced at her and saw she was staring out to sea again.

Finally, she spoke. "I thought you said you were hit in the stomach."

"There, too."

"Max said you had a serious lung wound."

"That, too."

"Any brain damage?"

"Maybe."

"And now you want me to believe you've been neutered by yet another bullet."

"It's nothing a guy would lie about."

"If the furnace is out, why is there still fire in your eyes?"

"Just a memory, Beth—can I call you Beth? A good memory of a time when I could pole-vault over my car."

She put her hand up to her face, and I couldn't tell if she was crying or laughing.

I said, "Please don't tell anyone."

Finally, she got control of herself and replied, "I'll try to keep it out of the papers."

"Thanks." I let a few seconds pass, then asked her, "Do you live around here?"

"No, I live in western Suffolk."

"That's a long trip. Are you driving home, or staying around here?"

"We're all staying at the Soundview Inn out in Greenport."

"Who's 'we' all?"

"Me, George, Ted, some DEA guys, some other people who were here before . . . guys from the Department of Agriculture. We're all supposed to work day and night, round the clock, seven days a week. Looks good for the press and the public . . . in case the fudge hits the fan. You know, in case there's some concern about disease. . . ."

"You mean mass panic about a plague."

"Whatever."

"Hey, I have a nice place out here and you're welcome to stay there."

"Thanks anyway."

"It's an impressive Victorian mansion on the water."

"Doesn't matter."

"You'd be more comfortable. I told you, I'm safe. Hell, NYPD personnel says I'm allowed to use the ladies' room at headquarters."

"Cut it out."

"Seriously, Beth, I have a computer printout here— two years' worth of financial stuff. We can work on it tonight."

"Who authorized you to take that?"

"You did. Right?"

She hesitated, then nodded and said, "I want them back in my hands tomorrow morning."

"Okay. I'll pull an all-nighter with this. Help me out."

She seemed to mull that over, then said, "Give me your phone number and address."

I rummaged around my pockets for a pen and paper, but she already had her little notebook out and said, "Shoot."

I gave her the information, including directions.

She said, "I'll call first if I'm coming."

"Okay."

I sat back down on the bench, and she sat at the opposite end, the computer printouts between us. We stayed silent, sort of mentally regrouping, I guess.

Finally, Beth remarked, "I hope you're a whole lot smarter than you look or sound."

"Let me put it this way—the smartest thing Chief Maxwell has done in his career is to come calling on me for this case."

"And modest."

"There's no reason to be modest. I'm one of the best. In fact, CBS is developing a show called *The Corey Files*."

"You don't say?"

"I can get you a part."

"Thank you. If I can repay the favor, I'm sure you'll let me know."

"Seeing you in *The Corey Files* will be repayment enough."

"It sure will. Listen.... Can I call you John?"

"Please do."

"John, what's happening here? I mean with this case. You know something you're not sharing."

"What is your current status?"

"Excuse me?"

"Engaged, divorced, separated, involved?"

"Divorced. What do you know or suspect about this case that you haven't mentioned?"

"No boyfriend?"

"No boyfriend, no children, eleven admirers, five are married, three are control freaks, two possibilities, and one idiot."

"Am I being too personal?"

"Yes."

"If I had a male partner and I asked him these questions, it would be perfectly normal and okay."

"Well...we're not partners."

"You want it both ways. Typical."

"Look...well, tell me about yourself. Quickly."

"Okay. Divorced, no children, dozens of admirers, but no one special." I added, "And no venereal diseases."

"And no venereal parts."

"Right."

"Okay, John, what's with this case?"

I settled back on the bench and replied, "Well, Beth...what's happening with this case is that the obvious is leading to the improbable, and everyone is trying to make the improbable fit the obvious. But it don't work that way, partner."

She nodded, then said, "You're suggesting that this might have nothing to do with what we think it has to do with."

"I'm beginning to think there's something else going on here."

"Why do you think that?"

"Well...some evidence doesn't seem to fit."

"Maybe it will fit in a few days, when all the lab reports are in and everyone's been questioned. We haven't even spoken to the Plum Island people."

I stood and said, "Let's go down to the dock."

She slipped her shoes on, and we walked down toward the dock. I said, "A few hundred yards down the beach from here, Albert Einstein wrestled with the moral question of the atomic bomb and decided it was a go. The good guys had no choice because the bad guys had already decided it was a go without any wrestling with the moral questions." I added, "I knew the Gordons."

She thought a moment, then said, "You're saying you don't think the Gordons were capable—morally capable—of selling deadly micro-organisms."

"No, I don't. Like atomic scientists they respected the power of the genie in the bottle. I don't know exactly what they did on Plum Island, and we'll probably never know, but I think I knew them well enough to say they wouldn't sell the genie in the bottle."

She didn't reply.

I continued, "I remember Tom once told me that Judy was having a bad day because some calf that she'd become attached to had been purposely infected with something and was dying. These are not the kind of people who want to see children dying of plague. When you interview their Plum Island associates, you'll find this out for yourself."

"People sometimes have another side."

"I never saw a hint of anything in the Gordons' personalities to suggest that they'd traffic in deadly disease."

"Sometimes people rationalize their behavior. How about the Americans who gave atomic bomb secrets to the Russians? They were people who said they did it out of conviction—so one side wouldn't have all the power."

I glanced at her and saw she was looking at me as we walked. I was happy to discover that Beth Penrose was capable of some deeper thinking, and I knew she was relieved to discover that I wasn't the idiot she thought I might be.

I said, "Regarding the atomic scientists, that was a different time and a different secret. I mean, if nothing else, why would the Gordons sell bacteria and virus that could kill *them* and their families in Indiana or wherever, and wipe out everyone in between?"

Beth Penrose pondered that a moment, then replied, "Maybe they got paid ten million, and the money is in Switzerland, and they have a château on a mountain stocked with champagne and canned food, and they invited their friends and relatives to visit. I don't know, John. Why do people do crazy things? They rationalize, they talk themselves into it. They're angry at something or somebody. Ten million bucks. Twenty million. Two hundred bucks. Everyone has a price."

We walked out on the dock where a uniformed Southold policeman was sitting on a lawn chair. Detective Penrose said to him, "Take a break."

He stood and walked back toward the house.

The ripples lapped against the hull of the Gordons' boat, and the boat rocked against the rubber bumpers on the pilings. The tide was out, and I noticed that the boat was now tied to pulleys to allow the rope to play out. The boat had dropped about four or five feet below the dock. I noticed now that the writing on the hull said "Formula 303," which, according to Tom, meant it was thirty feet, three inches long.

I said to Beth, "On the Gordons' bookshelf, I found

a book of charts—nautical navigational maps—with an eight-digit number penciled on one of the pages. I asked Sally Hines to do a super print job on the book and report to you. You should take the book and keep it someplace safe. We should look at it together. There may be more marks on the book."

She stared at me for a few seconds, then asked, "Okay, what do you think this is about?"

"Well…if you ratchet down the moral dial about halfway, you go from selling plague for money to drugs for money."

"Drugs?"

"Yeah. Morally ambiguous in some minds, big money in everyone's mind. How does that sound to you? Drugs."

She stared at the high-powered boat and nodded. She said, "Maybe we got panicky with this Plum Island connection."

"Maybe we did."

"We should talk to Max and the others about this."

"We should not."

"Why not?"

"Because we're just speculating. Let them run with the plague theory. If that's the right theory, better keep it covered."

"Okay, but that's no reason not to confide in Max and the others."

"Trust me."

"No. Convince me."

"I'm not convinced myself. We have two strong possibilities here—bugs for money or drugs for money. Let's see if Max, Foster, and Nash come to any conclusions of their own, and if they share their thoughts with us."

"Okay...I'll play this one your way."

I motioned toward the boat. "What do you think that goes for?"

She shrugged. "I'm not sure...the Formula's a pricey item...you figure three thousand a running foot, so this one, new, would be about $100,000."

"And the rent on this house? About two thousand?"

"I guess about that, plus utilities." She added, "We'll find all this out."

"And what's with this commuting by boat? It's almost two hours one way from here, and a small fortune in fuel. Right?"

"Right."

"It takes maybe thirty minutes to drive from here to the government ferry on Orient Point. How long is the ferry ride? Maybe twenty minutes, compliments of Uncle Sam. Total about one hour door-to-door, as opposed to nearly two hours by speedboat. Yet, the Gordons took their own boat from here to Plum, and I know there were days when they couldn't take their boat back because the weather had turned bad during the day. They'd have to take the ferry back to Orient and hitch a ride home with someone. This never made sense to me, but I admit I never thought much about it. I should have. Now maybe it makes sense."

I jumped into the boat and landed hard on the deck. I put my arms up, and she jumped, grabbing my hands as she did. Somehow we wound up on the deck, me on my back, Beth Penrose on top of me. We stayed there about a second longer than we had to, then we got to our feet. We smiled awkwardly at one another, the way strangers of the opposite sex do when they find themselves accidentally bumping T&A and whatever.

She asked me, "Are you all right?"

"Yeah...." In truth, the wind had been knocked out of my bad lung, and I guessed she could see it.

I got my breath back and went to the rear, the stern, as they say, where the Formula 303 had a bench seat. I indicated the deck near the seat and informed her, "Here's where the chest always sat. It was a big one, about four feet long, three deep, and three high. Maybe thirty cubic feet on the inside, insulated aluminum. Sometimes, when I sat on the bench, I'd put my feet up on the chest and slug beers."

"And?"

"And, after work, on designated days, the Gordons leave Plum at the appointed hour and make a high-speed dash out to sea. There, out in the Atlantic, they rendezvous with a ship, maybe a South American freighter, maybe it's a seaplane, or whatever. They take on board about a hundred kilos of Colombian marching powder and dash back toward land. If they're spotted by the DEA or Coast Guard, they look like Mr. and Mrs. Clean out for a spin. Even if they're stopped, they flash the Plum Island ID and do a song and dance. In reality, they could probably outrun anything on the water. It would take an aircraft to chase this thing. More to the point, how many boats are stopped and searched? There are thousands of pleasure boats and commercial fishermen out there. Unless the Coast Guard or Customs or somebody has a serious tip, or someone is acting weird, they don't board and search. Right?"

"Usually. Customs has full authority to do that and sometimes they do." She added, "I'll see if there are any reports with DEA, Coast Guard, or Customs regarding the *Spirochete*."

"Good." I thought a moment, then said, "Okay, so after the Gordons cop the junk, they make land at some prearranged spot or rendezvous with a small boat, and transfer the ice chest to the local pharmaceutical distributors, who give them another chest in return with a bunch of bucks in it. The distributor then drives into Manhattan, and another duty-free import is completed. Happens every day. The question is, Did the Gordons participate, and if so, is that what got them killed? I hope so. Because the other thing scares me, and I'm not easily scared."

She mulled this over, looking around the speedboat. She said, "It *might* fit. But it might be wishful thinking."

I didn't reply.

She continued, "If we can determine it was drugs, we can rest easier. Until then, we have to go ahead with the idea that it's plague, because if it is and we're not on top of it, we could all be dead."

CHAPTER SIX

It was after two A.M., and I was getting cross-eyed reading the Gordons' computer printouts. I had a pot of coffee going in Uncle Harry's big old kitchen, and I was sitting at the round table by the bay window that faced east to catch the morning sun.

Uncle Harry and Aunt June had the good sense never to have the entire Corey clan as houseguests, but now and then they'd have me or my brother, Jim, or my sister, Lynne, stay in the guest room while the rest of the family was in some horrid 1950s tourist cabin.

I remember sitting at this table as a kid with my two cousins, Harry Jr. and Barbara, slopping up Cheerios or Wheaties, antsy to get out and play. Summer was magic. I don't think I had a care in the world.

Now, some decades later, same table, and I had a lot on my mind.

I turned my attention back to the checkbook register. The Gordons' salaries were deposited directly into their account, and their combined income, after being raped by the Feds and New York State, was about ninety thou. Not bad, but not that good for two Ph.D.'s doing brainy work with hazardous substances. Tom would have done better playing minor league baseball, and Judy could have worked in a titty bar in my old precinct and done as well. It's a strange country.

Anyway, it didn't take me long to see that the Gordons were overextended. It's not cheap to live on the East Coast, as they'd undoubtedly discovered. They had payments on two cars, the boat, the house rental, assorted insurances on same, utilities, five credit cards, big-time oil company bills, mostly for the powerboat, and regular living and breathing expenses. Also, there was a hefty $10,000 down payment on the Formula 303, the April before last.

Plus, the Gordons contributed to a number of worthy charities, making me feel guilty. They also belonged to a book and music club, hit the ATM frequently, sent checks to nieces and nephews, and were members of the Peconic Historical Society. They didn't appear to be in major trouble yet, but they were close to the edge. If they were making a nice side income from the drug trade, they were clever enough to stash the cash and get themselves in over their heads like all red-blooded fiscally fearless Americans. The question, then, was, Where was the loot?

I'm not an auditor, but I've done enough of these financial analyses to spot things that needed checking out. There was only one such thing in the last twenty-five months of the Gordons' checkbook printouts—a biggie, a check for $25,000 made out to a Margaret Wiley. The check had been certified for a fee of $10, and the funds to cover the check had been electronically transferred from the Gordons' money market account. In fact, it represented nearly all their savings.

The check was dated March 7 of this year, and there was no notation regarding the purpose of the check. Who, then, was Margaret Wiley? Why did the Gordons give her a certified check for twenty-five large? We would soon find out.

I sipped on my coffee and tapped my pencil on the table in time with the regulator clock on the far wall, and I thought about all of this.

I went to the kitchen cabinet beside the wall phone and found the local telephone directory among the cookbooks. I looked under "W" and located a Margaret Wiley who lived on Lighthouse Road in the hamlet of Southold. I actually knew where that was, it being the road that, as the name suggested, led to a lighthouse: Horton Point Lighthouse, to be exact.

I really wanted to call Margaret, but she might be annoyed at the two A.M. phone call. It could wait until dawn. But patience is not one of my virtues. In fact, to the best of my knowledge, I have no virtues. Also, I had the feeling that the FBI and CIA were not all asleep at this hour and that they were getting ahead of me on this case. Last, but not least, this was no ordinary murder; even as I hesitated to wake Margaret Wiley, a civilization-destroying plague could be spreading over the nation. I hate when that happens.

I called the number. The phone rang and an answering machine picked up. I hung up and dialed again. Finally, the lady of the house was awakened and she said, "Hello?"

"Margaret Wiley, please."

"Speaking. Who is this?" asked the groggy and elderly voice.

"This is Detective Corey, ma'am. Police." I let her

imagine the worst for a second or two. That usually wakes them up.

"*Police*? What's happened?"

"Mrs. Wiley, you've heard on the news about the murders on Nassau Point?"

"Oh...yes. How awful—"

"You knew the Gordons?"

She cleared the froggies from her throat and replied, "No...well, I met them once. I sold them a piece of land."

"In March?"

"Yes."

"For $25,000?"

"Yes...but what does that have to do with—"

"Where is the land, ma'am?"

"Oh...it's a nice piece of bluff overlooking the Sound."

"I see. They wanted to build a house?"

"No. They can't build there. I sold the development rights to the county."

"Meaning?"

"Meaning...it's a conservation plan. You sell the right to develop the land, but you still own the land. It has to stay undeveloped. Except for agriculture."

"I see. So the Gordons couldn't build a house on this bluff?"

"Lord, no. If the land could be developed, it would be worth over $100,000. I was paid by the county not to develop it. It's a restrictive covenant that runs with the land. It's a good plan."

"But you can sell the land?"

"Yes, and I did. For $25,000." She added, "The Gordons knew it couldn't be developed."

"Could they buy back the development rights from the county?"

"No. I sold the rights in perpetuity. That's the purpose of the plan."

"Okay...." I thought I understood now what the Gordons had done—they'd bought a nice piece of Sound-view land that, because it couldn't be built on, sold for less than market price. But they could plant on it, and I realized that Tom's fascination with local viniculture had led him to the ultimate hobby—Gordon Vineyards. Apparently, then, there was no connection between this purchase and their murders. I said, "I'm sorry I woke you, Mrs. Wiley. Thank you for your help."

"Not at all. I hope you find who did this."

"I'm sure we will." I hung up, turned from the phone, then went back and dialed again. She answered and I said, "I'm sorry, one more question. Is that land suitable for grapes?"

"Goodness, no. It's right on the Sound, much too exposed, and much too small. It's only a one-acre parcel that drops fifty feet to the beach. It's quite beautiful, but nothing much will grow there except scrub."

"I see...did they mention to you why they wanted it?"

"Yes...they said they wanted their own hill overlooking the water. A place to sit and watch the sea. They were a lovely couple. It's so awful."

"Yes, ma'am. Thank you." I hung up.

So. They wanted a place to sit and watch the sea. For twenty-five thousand bucks they could have paid the parking fee at Orient Beach State Park five thousand times and watched all the sea they wanted every day for the next eight years and still have money left over for hot dogs and beer. Did not compute.

I mulled a little. Mull, mull. Well, maybe it did compute. They were a romantic couple. *But twenty-five Gs?* That was almost all they had. And if they were transferred by the government, how would they unload an acre of land that had no use for building or agriculture? Who else would be crazy enough to pay $25,000 for encumbered property?

So. Maybe it had to do with maritime drug running. That would make sense. I'd have to take a look at that land. I wondered if anyone had yet found the deed to the property among the Gordons' papers. I wondered, too, if the Gordons had a safe deposit box and what was in it. It's tough when you have questions at two A.M., and you're flying high on caffeine and no one wants to talk to you.

I poured another cup of coffee. The windows above the sink were open, and I could hear the night things singing their September songs, the last of the locusts and tree frogs, an owl hooting nearby, and some night bird warbling in the foggy mist that rolled in from the Great Peconic Bay.

The autumn here is tempered by the big bodies of water that hold their summer heat until November. Terrific for grapes. Good boating until about Thanksgiving. There was the occasional hurricane in August, September, or October, and the odd nor'easter in the winter. But basically the climate was benign, the coves and inlets numerous, the fogs and mists frequent: an ideal place for smugglers, pirates, rum runners, and more recently, drug runners.

The wall phone rang, and for an irrational second

I thought it might be Margaret. Then I remembered that Max was supposed to call about the Plum Island outing. I picked up the receiver and said, "Pizza Hut."

After a confused second, Beth Penrose said, "Hello...."

"Hello."

"Did I wake you?"

"That's all right, I had to get up to answer the phone anyway."

"Very old joke. Max asked me to call. We're going to be on the eight A.M. ferry."

"Is there an earlier ferry?"

"Yes, but—"

"Why do we want the cover-up team to get to the island before us?"

She didn't reply to that but said, "We'll be accompanied by the island's security director, a Mr. Paul Stevens."

"Who's going on the earlier ferry?"

"I don't know....Look, John, if they're covering up, there's not much we can do about it. They've had some problems in the past, and they do cover-up real well. You're only going to see what they want you to see, hear what they want you to hear, and speak to who they want you to speak to. Don't get overly serious about this trip."

"Who's going?"

"Me, you, Max, George Foster, and Ted Nash." She asked, "Do you know where the ferry is?"

"I'll find it. What are you doing now?"

"I'm talking to you."

"Come on over. I'm looking at wallpaper samples. I need your opinion."

"It's late."

That almost sounded like yes, which surprised me. I pressed on. "You can sleep here, and we'll drive to the ferry together."

"That would look cute."

"Might as well get it over with."

"I'll think about it. Hey, did you find anything in the computer printouts?"

"Come over and I'll show you my hard drive."

"Cut it out."

"I'll pick you up."

"It's too late. I'm tired. I'm in my—I'm dressed for bed."

"Good. We can play hide the pickle."

I heard her take a long, patient breath, then say, "I would have thought there'd be a clue in their financial records. Maybe you're not looking hard enough. Or maybe you don't know what you're doing."

"Probably."

She said, "I thought we agreed to share information."

"Yes, with each other. Not the whole world."

"What...? Oh...I see."

We both knew that when you're working with the Feds, they'd slap a tap on your phone within five minutes of being introduced to you. They didn't even bother with a court order when they eavesdropped on friendlies. I was sorry I'd made the call to Margaret Wiley.

I asked Beth, "Where's Ted?"

"How do I know?"

"Keep your door bolted. He fits the description of a rapist-murderer I'm looking for."

"Give it a break, John." She hung up.

I yawned. While I was disappointed that Detective Penrose didn't want to come over, I was also a little relieved. I really think those nurses put saltpeter in a guy's Jell-O or something. Maybe I needed more red meat in my diet.

I turned off the coffeepot, flipped the light switch, and left the kitchen. I made my way in the dark through the big, lonely house, through the polished oak vestibule, up the winding, creaky staircase, and down the long hallway to the high-ceilinged room that I'd slept in as a boy.

As I undressed for bed, I reflected on this day, and tried to decide if I really wanted to make that eight A.M. ferry.

On the yes side, I liked Max, and he'd asked a favor of me. Two, I liked the Gordons and I wanted to do them a favor, to sort of pay them back for the good company and the wine and the steaks at a time when I was not feeling my best. Three, I didn't like Ted Nash and I had this childish desire to screw him big time. Four, I *did* like Beth Penrose and I had this grown-up desire to... whatever. And then there was me, and I was bored.... No, that wasn't it. I was trying to prove that I still had the stuff. So far, so good. And last, and certainly not least, the little problem of the plague, the black death, the red death, the multifaceted threat or whatever; the possibility that this would be the last autumn any of us on earth would see.

For all those reasons, I knew I should be on the eight A.M. ferry to Plum Island, not in bed with the covers pulled over me, like when I was a kid and there was something I didn't want to face....

I stood naked at the big window and watched the

fog climbing out of the bay, ghost white in the moonlight, creeping and crawling across the dark lawn toward the house. That used to scare the crap out of me. Still does. I felt goose bumps rising on my skin.

My right hand went unconsciously to my chest, and my fingers found the entry hole of bullet one, then I slid my hand down to my abdomen where the second, or maybe the third shot had ripped through my formerly tight muscles, drove through my intestines, chipped my pelvis, and blew out my rear end. The other shot passed through my left calf without much damage. The surgeon said I was lucky. And he was right. I'd flipped my partner, Dom Fanelli, to see who was going to go into the deli to buy coffee and donuts, and he lost. Cost him four bucks. My lucky day.

Somewhere out on the bay, a foghorn sounded, and I wondered who would be out in this weather at this hour.

I turned from the window and checked to see that my alarm clock was set, then made sure there was a round in the chamber of the .45 automatic I kept on the nightstand.

I tumbled into bed, and like Beth Penrose, and Sylvester Maxwell, and Ted Nash, and George Foster, and many others that night, I stared up at the ceiling and thought about murder, death, Plum Island, and plague. I saw in my mind's eye the image of the Jolly Roger flapping in the night sky, the death's head white and grinning.

It occurred to me that the only people resting in peace tonight were Tom and Judy Gordon.

CHAPTER SEVEN

I was up at six A.M., showered, and dressed in shorts, T-shirt, and Top-Siders: suitable attire for a quick change into biohazard gear or whatever they call it.

I did my Hamlet routine regarding my piece—to carry, or not to carry, that is the question. Finally, I decided to carry. You just never know what the day is going to bring. This might be a nice day to paint Ted Nash red.

By 6:45 A.M., I was traveling east on Main Road, through the heart of the wine country.

It occurred to me as I drove that it's not easy trying to pull a living out of the soil or the sea, as many of the locals did. But the vineyards had been surprisingly successful. In fact, to my left, as I passed through the hamlet of Peconic, was the most successful vineyard and winery, Tobin Vineyards, owned by Fredric Tobin, whom I'd met once briefly and who was a friend of the Gordons. I made a mental note to call on the gentleman and see if he could shed any light on the case at hand.

The sun was above the trees, off to my right front,

and my dashboard thermometer said 16 degrees centigrade, which meant nothing to me. Somehow I'd screwed up the computer, and I was on the metric system. Sixteen degrees sounded cold, but I knew it wasn't. Anyway, the sun was burning off the ground mist and sunlight filled my overpriced sports utility vehicle.

The road was gently curved, and the vineyards were more picturesque than the potato fields I remembered from thirty years ago. Now and then a fruit orchard or cornfield kept the vineyards from becoming monotonous. Big birds sailed and soared on the morning thermals, and little birds sang and chirped in the fields and trees. All was right with the world, except that Tom and Judy were in the county morgue this morning; and very possibly there was a sickness in the air, rising and falling with the thermals, carried on the ocean breeze, sweeping across the farms and vineyards, and carried in the blood of humans and animals. And yet, everything seemed normal this morning, including me.

I turned on the radio to an all-news channel from New York City and listened to the regular crap for a while, waiting for someone to say something about a mysterious outbreak of whatever. But it was too early for that. I tuned to the only local radio station and caught the seven A.M. news. The news guy was saying, "We spoke to Chief Maxwell by phone this morning, and here's what he told us."

A grumpy-sounding Max came out of my speakers, saying, "Regarding the deaths of Nassau Point residents Tom and Judy Gordon, we're calling this a double homicide, robbery, and burglary. This has nothing to do with the victims' work on Plum Island, and we want to put these speculations to rest. We urge all residents to be alert and aware of strangers and report anything suspicious to the town police. No need to be paranoid, but there's somebody out there with a gun who committed murder, robbery, and burglary. So you have to take some precautions. We're working with the county police on this, and we think we have some leads. That's all I have to say at this time. I'll talk to you later today, Don."

"Thanks, Chief," said Don.

That's what I like about this place—real down-to-earth and homey. I turned off the radio. What Chief Maxwell forgot to mention was that he was on his way to Plum Island, the place that had nothing to do with the double murders. He also forgot to mention the FBI and the CIA. I admire a man who knows how and when to gaslight the public. What if Max had said, "There's a fifty-fifty chance the Gordons sold plague viruses to terrorists who may be plotting the destruction of all life in North America"? That would cause a little dip in the Dow at the opening bell, not to mention a stampede for the airports and a sudden urge for a South American vacation.

Anyway, it was a nice morning, so far. I spotted a big pumpkin field to my right, and I recalled the autumn weekends out here as a kid, going nuts running through the pumpkin patches to find the absolutely biggest, roundest, orangest, and most perfect pumpkin. I remember having some disagreements with my kid brother, Jimmy, on the choice every year, but we settled it fairly with a fistfight that I always won since I was much bigger than he was. At least the kid had heart.

The hamlet after Peconic is Southold, which is

also the name of the whole township. It's about here where the vineyards end and the land narrows between the Sound and the bay, and everything looks a little more windswept and wild. The Long Island Rail Road tracks, which begin at Penn Station in Manhattan, paralleled the highway to my left for a while, then the road and the tracks crossed and diverged again.

There wasn't much traffic at this hour except for a few farm vehicles. It occurred to me that if any of my fellow travelers to Plum Island were on the road, I might see them at some point.

I drove into the village of Greenport, the main metropolis on the North Fork with a population, according to the sign, of 2,100. By comparison, Manhattan Island, where I worked, lived, and almost died, is smaller than the North Fork and has two million people piled on. The police force I work for has thirty thousand men and women, making it bigger than the entire population of Southold Township. Max, as I said, has about forty officers, if you include me and him. Greenport Village actually had its own police force once, about a half dozen guys, but they pissed off the populace somehow and were voted out of existence. I don't think that can happen in New York City, but it's not a bad idea.

Sometimes I think I should get Max to hire me— you know, big-time, big-city gunslinger rides into town, and the local sheriff pins a badge on him and says, "We need a man with your experience, training, and proven track record," or something like that. I mean, would I be a big fish in a small pond, or what? Would I have ladies stealing glances at me and dropping their handkerchiefs on the sidewalk, or what?

Back to reality. I was hungry. There are virtually no fast-food chains out here, which is part of the charm of the place, but also a pain in the ass. There are, however, a few convenience stores, and I stopped at one at the edge of Greenport and bought a coffee and a plastic-wrapped sandwich of mystery meat and cheese product. I swear you can eat the shrink wrap and Styrofoam, too, and not notice the difference. I grabbed a free weekly newspaper and had breakfast in the driver's seat. The newspaper, coincidentally, had an article on Plum Island. This is not uncommon as the locals seem very interested in this mist-shrouded island of mystery and all that. Over the years, I'd picked up most of my information about Plum from local sources. Now and then the island made the national news, but it was safe to guess that nine out of ten Americans never heard of the place. That might change real soon.

This article I was now reading had to do with Lyme disease, another obsession of the residents of eastern Long Island and nearby Connecticut. This disease, carried by deer ticks, had assumed plague-like proportions. I knew people who had Lyme; though rarely fatal, it could screw up a year or two of your life. Anyway, the locals were convinced that the disease came from Plum Island and was a bio-warfare experiment that had gotten loose by mistake or something. I would not be overstating if I said the locals would like Plum Island to sink into the sea. In fact, I had this image—like the scene in *Frankenstein*—of local farmers and fishermen, pitchforks and gaffing hooks in their hands, the women carrying torches, descending on the island and shouting, "To hell with your unnatural scientific experiments! God save us! Congressional investigation!" Or something like that. Anyway, I put the paper down and started the engine.

Properly fortified, I continued on, still keeping an eye out for my new colleagues.

The next hamlet was East Marion, though there doesn't seem to be a Marion around—I think it's in England, as with a lot of other "East" places on Long Island. Southold was once Southwold, after the place in England where a lot of the early settlers came from, but they lost the "w" in the Atlantic or someplace, or maybe they traded it for a bunch of "e's." Who knows? Aunt June, who was a member of the Peconic Historical Society, used to fill my little head with all this crap, and I guess some of it was interesting and some of it stuck, but maybe it stuck sideways.

The land narrowed to the width of a causeway, and there was water on both sides of the road—the Long Island Sound to my left and Orient Harbor to my right. The sky and water were filled with ducks, Canada geese, snowy white egrets, and gulls, which is why I never open the sunroof. I mean, these birds eat prunes or something, then come in like dive-bombers, and they *know* when you've got your sunroof open.

The land widened again, and I passed through the super-quaint, ye-olde hamlet of Orient, then ten minutes later finally approached Orient Point.

I passed the entrance to Orient Beach State Park and began to slow down.

Up ahead, on the right, I saw a flagpole from which flew the Stars and Stripes at half-mast. I assumed that the flag's position had to do with the Gordons, and therefore the flagpole was on federal property, no doubt the Plum Island ferry station. You can see how a great detective's mind works, even at seven-something A.M. with little sleep.

I pulled over to the side of the road in front of a marina and restaurant and stopped the car. I took my binoculars from the glove compartment and focused on a big, black and white sign near the flagpole, about thirty yards down the road. The sign said, "Plum Island Animal Disease Center." It didn't say "Welcome" and it also didn't say "Ferry," but the water was right there, and so I deduced this was indeed the ferry station. Civilians assume, detectives deduce. Also, to be truthful, I'd passed this place about a dozen times over the years on my way to the New London ferry, which was just beyond the Plum Island ferry. Although I'd never given it much thought, I suppose I was always curious about the mysterious Plum Island. I don't like mysteries, which is why I want to solve them. It bothers me that there are things I don't know.

Anyway, to the right of the sign and flagpole was a one-story brick building, apparently an administration and reception center. Behind and beyond the building was a large, blacktop parking lot that ran down to the water. The parking lot was surrounded by a high chain-link fence topped with razor wire.

Where the parking lot ended at the bay were several large warehouses and storage sheds attached to big wharfs. A few trucks were parked near the loading docks. I assumed—oops, deduced—that this was where they loaded the animals that were making the one-way trip to Plum.

The parking lot stretched along the bay for about a hundred yards and at the farthest end, through a light mist, I could see about thirty passenger vehicles parked near the ferry slips. There were no people visible.

I put down the binoculars and checked my dashboard digital clock, which read 07:29, and the temperature was now 17 degrees. I really had to get this car off the metric system. I mean, the friggin' computer was displaying weird French words, like "kilomètres" and "litres" and all kinds of French things. I was afraid to turn the seat warmer on.

I was a half hour early for the outbound ferry to Plum Island, but I was on time for the inbound from Plum, which is what I intended. As Uncle Harry used to say when he rousted me out of bed at dawn, "The early bird gets the worm, Johnny." And as I used to wisecrack to him, "The early worm gets *eaten*." What a character I was.

Out of the mist appeared a white and blue ferry boat that glided toward the ferry slip. I raised my binoculars again. On the bow of the boat was a government seal of some sort, probably Department of Agriculture, and the name of the boat—*The Plum Runner*, which showed a small sense of humor on someone's part.

I had to get closer, so I put the 4 x 4 into gear and drove toward the sign, flagpole, and brick building. To the right of the building, the chain-link gates were open, and I saw no guard around, so I drove into the parking lot and headed toward the warehouses. I parked near some delivery trucks and shipping containers, hoping my vehicle would be lost in the clutter. I was only about fifty yards from the two ferry slips now, and I watched through my binoculars as the ferry turned and backed into the closest of the slips. *The*

Plum Runner looked fairly new and sleek, about sixty feet with a top deck on which I saw chairs. The stern hit the bulkhead, and the captain shut down the engines as a mate jumped off and secured the lines to the pilings. I noticed there was no one on the dock.

As I watched through my binoculars, a group of men came out of the passenger cabin and onto the stern deck, where they disembarked from the open stern directly onto the parking lot. I counted ten men, all dressed in some sort of blue uniform, and either they were the Department of Agriculture band, sent out to greet me, or they were the night security guards who'd been relieved by the guards who'd taken the seven A.M. ferry to Plum. The ten guards all wore pistol belts, though I didn't see any holsters attached.

Next off the ferry was a big guy in a blue blazer and tie, chatting with the ten guards as if he knew them, and I guessed he could be Paul Stevens, the security chief.

Then came four guys in spiffy suits, and I had to think this was a little unusual. I mean, I doubt if these four dudes had spent the night on the island, so I had to figure they'd gone over on the seven A.M. ferry. But that would give them only a few minutes' turnaround time on the island. Therefore, they'd gone over earlier, either on a special ferry run or on another boat, or a helicopter.

And last but not least, waltzing off the boat, wearing casual attire, were Mr. George Foster and Mr. Ted Nash, which did not completely surprise me. Well, there you are—early to bed, early to rise, makes a man sneaky and full of lies. Those SOBs...I had expected they'd pull a fast one on me.

As I watched, Nash, Foster, and the four suits were in deep conversation, and the guy with the blue blazer stood respectfully to the side. I could tell by the body language that Ted Nash was The Man. The other four guys were probably up from D.C., and who knew who the hell sent them? This was all hard to figure, what with the FBI, CIA, Department of Agriculture, and no doubt the Army and Defense Department, and whoever else had their asses hanging out. As far as I was concerned, they were all the Feds and they, in turn, thought of me—if at all—as an annoying hemorrhoid.

Anyway, I put the binocs down and picked up the weekly newspaper and the empty coffee cup in case I had to play hide-the-face. So, here were all these bright boys pulling this early-bird crap on me, and they didn't even bother to look around to see if they were under surveillance. They had total disdain for lowly coppers, and that pissed me off.

The blue blazer guy spoke to the ten guards, dismissed them, and they went to their respective cars, got in, and drove off past me. Mr. Blue Blazer then went back onto the stern deck and disappeared into the ferry.

Then the four suits took their leave of Nash and Foster, got into a black Chevy Caprice, and came toward me. The Caprice slowed down opposite me, almost stopped, then went on, out the chain-link gates I'd entered.

At this point, I saw that Nash and Foster had noticed my vehicle, so I put it into gear and drove toward the ferry as if I'd just arrived. I parked away from the pier and sipped at the empty coffee cup and read about the return of the bluefish, ignoring Messrs. Nash and Foster, who stood near the ferry.

At about ten to eight, an old station wagon pulled up beside me, and Max got out wearing jeans, a windbreaker, and a fishing cap pulled down low on his forehead. I lowered my window and asked him, "Is that a disguise, or did you get dressed in the dark?"

He frowned. "Nash and Foster suggested I shouldn't be seen going to Plum."

"I heard you on the radio this morning."

"How'd I sound?"

"Totally unconvincing. Boats, planes, and cars have been leaving Long Island all morning. Total panic along the entire East Coast."

"Shove it."

"Right." I shut off the ignition and waited for my Jeep to tell me something, but I guess I hadn't screwed up this time. I took my keys out of the ignition, and a female voice said, "Votre fenetre est ouverte." Now why would a nice American car say that? Well, because when I tried to shut off the stupid voice thing, I somehow got it to speak French—these cars are exported to Quebec, which explained the metric thing, too. "Votre fenetre est ouverte."

"Mangez merde," I replied in my best graduate school French and got out of the car.

Max asked me, "You got somebody in there?"

"No."

"Somebody's talking—"

"Ignore it."

I was going to tell Max that I saw Nash and Foster get off the ferry from Plum, but since Max hadn't thought to get his butt here early, or ask me to do it, then he didn't deserve to know what I knew.

Cars started arriving and the experienced Plum

Island commuters hit the pier with split-second timing as the ferry horn blasted.

Ted Nash called out to Max and me, "Hey, all aboard!"

I looked around for Beth Penrose while making little misogynist remarks about women being late.

Max said, "There she is."

And there she was, walking away from a black Ford, probably her unmarked PD, that had been parked before even I arrived. Could it be that there were people in the world as bright as I? Not likely. I think I planted the idea in her head of arriving early.

Max and I walked across the misty parking lot toward the pier as the ferry horn sounded again. Detective Penrose joined Mr. Nash and Mr. Foster, and they were chatting near the ferry as we approached. Nash looked up and made an impatient gesture for us to hurry. I've killed people for less.

As Max and I got to the pier, Nash, without so much as a "good morning," looked at my shorts and said, "Aren't you a little cold, John?"

I mean, fuck you, Ted. He had that patronizing tone of voice that superiors adopt with inferiors, and this guy had to be set straight. I replied, apropos of his stupid rose-colored golf slacks, "Do those come with panty shields?"

George Foster laughed, and Ted Nash turned the color of his pants. Max pretended he didn't hear the exchange, and Beth rolled her eyes.

Mr. Foster said, belatedly, "Good morning. Ready to board?"

The five of us turned toward the ferry, and coming across the stern deck toward us was the gentleman with the blue blazer. He said, "Good morning. I'm Paul Stevens, security chief of Plum Island." He sounded like he had a computer-generated voice.

Mr. Red Pants said, "I'm Ted Nash with the Department of Agriculture."

What a load of crap. Not only had these three clowns just come from Plum Island together, but Nash was still putting out the agriculture manure.

Stevens had a clipboard in his hand—he looked like one of those whistle and clipboard types: short blond hair, icy blue eyes, Mr. Can-Do, ex-jock, fit and trim, ready to organize a sporting event or assign people to boxcars, whatever needed doing.

Beth, by the way, was wearing what she'd had on the day before, and I deduced she'd had no idea she'd be staying overnight out here when she caught the squeal, as we say, which may be appropriate in this case.... You know, animal disease center, swine fever, pork-chop-shaped island....

Mr. Stevens, glancing at his clipboard, said to Max, "And you're George Foster?"

"No, I'm Chief Maxwell."

"Right," said Mr. Stevens. "Welcome."

I said to Stevens, "I'm Beth Penrose."

He said to me, "No, you're John Corey."

"Right. Can I get aboard now?"

"No, sir. Not until we're all checked in." He looked at Beth and said, "Good morning, Detective Penrose," then at George Foster and said, "Good morning—Mr. Foster of the FBI. Correct?"

"Correct."

"Welcome aboard. Please follow me."

We boarded *The Plum Runner*, and within a minute,

we'd cast off and were on our way to Plum Island, or as the tabloids sometimes called it, Mystery Island, or somewhat less responsibly, Plague Island.

We followed Mr. Stevens into the big, comfortable, wood-paneled cabin where about thirty men and women sat on upholstered airplane-type seats, talking, reading, or nodding off. There seemed to be seating for maybe a hundred people, and I guessed that the next trip transported the majority of the people who worked on Plum.

We didn't sit with the passengers but followed Mr. Stevens down a set of stairs into a small room which seemed to serve as a chartroom or wardroom or whatever. In the center of the room was a round table and a carafe of coffee. Mr. Stevens offered seats and coffee, but no one wanted either. It was stuffy below deck, and the sound of the engine filled the room.

Stevens produced some papers from his clipboard, and he gave each of us a single printed sheet with a carbon copy attached. He said, "This is a waiver that you are required to sign before disembarking on Plum Island. I know you're all law officers, but rules are rules." He added, "Please read and sign."

I looked at the form, which was labeled "Visitor Affidavit." This was one of those rare government forms that were written in plain English. Basically, I was agreeing to stay with the group and hold hands, and to be accompanied at all times by a Plum Island employee. I also agreed to abide by all safety regulations, and I further agreed that I'd avoid hanging around with animals after I left the island, for at least seven days, and I promised I wouldn't associate with cattle, sheep, goats, swine, horses, and so on, and I wouldn't visit a farm, zoological garden, circus, or even a park, plus I had to stay away from sale barns, stockyards, animal laboratories, packing houses, zoos, menageries, and animal exhibits such as at fairs. Wow. That really limited my social life for the next seven days.

The last paragraph was interesting and read:

In the event of an emergency, the Center Director or Safety Officer may detain the visitor on Plum Island pending accomplishment of necessary biological safety precautionary measures. Personal clothing and other items may be temporarily held on Plum Island for decontamination and substitute clothing provided in order that the visitor may leave the Island after completion of a decontamination shower. The retained clothing items will be returned as soon as possible.

And to add to the enjoyment of my visit, I consented to any quarantine and detention necessary. I said to Stevens, "I guess this isn't the Connecticut ferry."

"No, sir, it isn't."

The efficient Mr. Stevens handed out a few government pens, and we laid the forms on the table and, still standing, we scratched, skipped, and clotted our names on them. Stevens collected the forms, then he gave us the carbon copies as souvenirs.

Stevens then handed out blue clip-on passes, which we dutifully affixed to our clothing. He asked us, "Are any of you armed?"

I replied, "I believe we all are, but you'd be well advised not to ask for our guns."

Stevens looked at me and replied, "That's exactly

what I'm going to ask for. Firearms are absolutely prohibited on the island." He added, "I have a lock box here where your pistols will be safe."

I said, "My pistol is safe where it is now."

Max added, "Plum Island is within the jurisdiction of Southold Township. *I* am the law on Plum Island."

Stevens considered a long moment, then said, "I suppose the prohibition doesn't apply to law officers."

Beth said, "You can be sure it doesn't."

Stevens, his little power play foiled, accepted defeat with good grace and smiled. It was, however, the kind of smile that, in the movies, the creepy villain gives before saying, "You have won this battle, sir, but I assure you, we will meet again." Click heels, turn, stomp off.

But Mr. Stevens was stuck with us for the time being, and he said, "Why don't we go on the top deck?"

We followed our host up the stairs, through the cabin, and outside to a staircase that led to a nice deck above the cabin. No one else was on the deck.

Mr. Stevens indicated a grouping of seats. The boat was making about fifteen miles an hour, which I think is about two hundred knots. Maybe a little less. It was a bit breezy up top, but quieter away from the engines. The mist was burning off and sunlight suddenly broke through.

I could see into the glass-enclosed bridge where the captain stood at the steering wheel, aka helm, talking to the mate. From the stern below flew an American flag, snapping in the wind.

I sat facing the bow, with Beth to my right, Max to my left, Stevens across from me, and Nash and Foster on either side of him. Stevens remarked, "The scientists who work in biocontainment always ride up here unless the weather is really foul. You know, they don't see the sun for eight to ten hours." He added, "I asked that we have some privacy this morning."

To my left, I saw the Orient Point Lighthouse, which is not one of the old-fashioned stone towers built on a headland, but a modern steel structure built on rocks. Its nickname is "The Coffeepot" because it's supposed to look like one, but I don't get it. You know, sailors mistake sea cows for mermaids, porpoises for sea serpents, clouds for ghost ships, and on and on. If you spend enough time at sea, you get a little batty, I think.

I looked at Stevens and our eyes met. The man really had one of those rare, never forgotten wax faces. I mean, nothing moved but the mouth, and the eyes bored right into you.

Paul Stevens addressed his guests and said, "Well, let me begin by saying that I knew Tom and Judy Gordon. They were well regarded by everyone on Plum—staff, scientists, animal handlers, lab people, maintenance people, security people—everyone. They treated all their fellow workers with courtesy and respect." His mouth made a sort of weird smile. "We'll sure miss them."

I had the sudden notion that this guy could be a government assassin. *Yeah.* What if it was the government who whacked Tom and Judy? Jeez, it just hit me that maybe the Gordons knew something or saw something, or were going to blow the whistle on something....As my partner, Dom Fanelli, would say, "Mama mia!" This was a whole new possibility. I looked at Stevens and tried to read something in those icy eyes, but he was a cool actor, as he'd shown on the gangplank.

Stevens was going on, "As soon as I heard about the deaths last night, I called my security sergeant on the island and tried to determine if anything was missing from the labs—not that I would suspect the Gordons of such a thing, but the way the murder was reported to me...well, we have standard operating procedures here."

I looked at Beth and our eyes met. I hadn't had a chance to say a word to her this morning, so I winked at her. She apparently couldn't trust her emotions so she turned away.

Stevens went on, "I had one of my security patrol boats take me to Plum very early this morning, and I did a preliminary investigation. As far as I can determine at this point in time, there is nothing missing from any of the stored micro-organisms or any stored samples of tissue, blood, or any other organic or biological material."

This statement was so patently self-serving and idiotic that no one even bothered to laugh. But Max did glance at me and shake his head. Messrs. Nash and Foster, however, were nodding as if they were buying Stevens' baloney. Thus encouraged, Mr. Stevens, aware that he was among fellow government-employed friends, continued to put out the line of official crap.

You can imagine how much bullshit I have to listen to in my professional life—suspects, witnesses, informants, and even my own team, like ADAs, brass, incompetent subordinates, low pols, and so forth. Bullshit and cowshit, the former being a gross and aggressive distortion of the truth, while the latter is a milder, more passive crock of crap. And that's the way it is with police work. Bullshit and cowshit. No one's going to tell you the truth. Especially if you're trying to send them to the electric chair, or whatever they're using these days.

I listened awhile as Mr. Paul Stevens explained why no one could get a single virus or bacterium off the island, not even a case of crotch itch, if we were to believe Pinocchio Stevens.

I gripped my right ear and twisted, which is how I tune out idiots. With Stevens' voice now far away, I looked out at the beautiful blue morning. The New London ferry was inbound and passed us off our left side, which I happen to know is called the port side. The one and a half miles of water between Orient Point and Plum Island is known as Plum Gut, another nautical term. There are a lot of nautical terms out here, and they give me a headache sometimes. I mean, what's wrong with regular English?

Anyway, I know that the Gut is a place where the currents get bad because the Long Island Sound and the open Atlantic sort of smack together in the Gut. I was with the Gordons once, in their speedboat, when we got into a situation right about here with the wind, the tide, and the currents slapping the boat around. I really don't need a day like that on the water, if you know what I mean.

But today was okay, and the Gut was calm and the boat was big. There was a little rocking, but I guess that can't be helped on the water, which is basically liquid and nowhere near as reliable as blacktop.

Well, it was a nice view from out here, and while Mr. Stevens was flapping his gums, I watched a big osprey circling. These things are weird, I mean totally crazy birds. I watched this guy circling, looking for breakfast, then he spotted it, and began this insane kamikaze dive into the water, shrieking like his balls were on fire, then he hit the water, disappeared, then shot up and out like he had a rocket up his ass. In his talons was a silver fish who'd been just paddling along down there, chomping minnows or something, and whoosh, he's airborne, about to slide down the gullet of this crazy bird. I mean, the silver fish maybe has a wife, kids, and whatever, and he goes out for a little breakfast and before he can bat an eye, he *is* breakfast. Survival of the fittest and all that. Awesome. Totally.

We were about a quarter mile from Plum Island when a strange but familiar noise caught our attention. Then we saw it—a big white helicopter with red Coast Guard markings passed us off our starboard side. The guy was going low and slow, and leaning out the door of the helicopter was a man, secured by straps or something. The man was wearing a uniform, a radio helmet, and was carrying a rifle.

Mr. Stevens commented, "That's the deer patrol." He explained, "As a purely precautionary measure, we look for deer that might swim to or from Plum Island."

No one spoke.

Mr. Stevens thought he should expand on that, and said, "Deer are incredibly strong swimmers, and they've been known to swim to Plum from Orient and even Gardiners Island, and Shelter Island, which is seven miles away. We discourage deer from taking up residence or even visiting Plum Island."

"Unless," I pointed out, "they sign the form."

Mr. Stevens smiled again. He liked me. He liked the Gordons, too, and look what happened to them.

Beth asked Mr. Stevens, "Why do you discourage deer from swimming to the island?"

"Well...we have what's called a 'Never Leave' policy. That is, whatever comes on the island may never leave unless it's decontaminated. That includes us when we leave later. Big items that can't be decontaminated, such as cars, trucks, lab equipment, construction debris, garbage, and so forth never leave the island."

Again, no one spoke.

Mr. Stevens, realizing he'd frightened the tourists, said, "I don't mean to suggest the island is contaminated."

"Fooled me," I admitted.

"Well, I should explain—there are five levels of bio-hazard on the island, or I should say, five zones. Level One or Zone One is the ambient air, all the places outside the biocontainment laboratories, which is safe. Zone Two is the shower area between the locker rooms and the laboratories and also some low-contagion workplaces. You'll see this later. Then Level Three is the biocontainment labs where they work with infectious diseases. Level Four is deeper into the building and includes the pens where diseased animals are held, and also where the incinerators and dissection rooms are." He looked at each of us to see if he had our attention, which he most certainly did, and continued, "Recently, we have added a Level Five capability, which is the highest biocontainment level. There are not many Level Five facilities in the world. We added this one because some of the organisms we were receiving from places such as Africa and the Amazon jungle were more virulent than suspected." He looked at each of us and said, sort of sotto voce, "In other words, we were getting blood and tissue samples infected with Ebola."

I said, "I think we can go back now."

Everyone smiled and tried to laugh. Ha, ha. Not funny.

Mr. Stevens continued, "The new laboratory is a state-of-the-art containment facility, but there was a time when we had the old post–World War Two facility, and that wasn't, unfortunately, as safe. So, at that time, we adopted the 'Never Leave' policy as a precaution against spreading infection to the mainland. The policy is still officially in effect, but it's somewhat relaxed. Still, we don't like things and people traveling too freely between the island and the mainland without being decontaminated. That, of course, includes deer."

Beth asked again, "But *why?*"

"*Why?* Because they might pick up something on the island."

"Like what?" I asked. "A bad attitude?"

Mr. Stevens smiled and replied, "Maybe a bad cold."

Beth asked, "Do you kill the deer?"

"Yes."

No one spoke for a long moment, then I asked, "How about birds?"

Mr. Stevens nodded and replied, "Birds could be a problem."

I asked my follow-up question, "And mosquitoes?"

"Oh, yes, mosquitoes could be a problem. But you must remember that all lab animals are kept indoors, and all experiments are done in negative air pressure biocontainment labs. Nothing can escape."

Max asked, "How do you know?"

Mr. Stevens replied, "Because you're still alive."

On that optimistic note, while Sylvester Maxwell contemplated being compared to a canary in a coal mine, Mr. Stevens said, "When we disembark, please stay with me at all times."

Hey, Paul, I wouldn't have it any other way.

CHAPTER EIGHT

A s we approached the island, *The Plum Runner* slowed. I stood, went to the port side, and leaned against the rail. To my left, the old stone Plum Island Lighthouse came into view, and I recognized it because it was a favorite subject of bad watercolor artists around here. To the right of the lighthouse, down by the shore, was a big billboard-sized sign that said, "CAUTION! CABLE CROSSING! NO TRAWLING! NO DREDGING!"

So, if terrorists were interested in knocking out power and communications to Plum Island, the authorities gave them a little hint. On the other hand, to be fair, I assumed Plum had its own emergency generators plus cell phones and radios.

Anyway, *The Plum Runner* slipped through this narrow channel and into a small cove which looked artificial, as though it had been called into being, not by God Almighty, but by the Army Corps of Engineers, who liked to put the finishing touches on Creation.

There weren't many buildings around the cove, just

a few tin warehouse-type structures, probably left over from the military days.

Beth came up beside me and said softly, "Before you got to the ferry, I saw—"

"I was there. I saw it. Thanks."

The ferry did a one-eighty and backed into the slip.

My colleagues were standing at the rail now, and Mr. Stevens said, "We'll wait until the employees disembark."

I asked him, "Is this an artificial harbor?"

He replied, "Yes, it is. The Army constructed it when they built the artillery batteries here before the Spanish-American War."

I suggested, "You may want to lose that cable crossing sign."

He replied, "We have no choice. We have to let boats know. Anyway, it's on the navigation charts."

"But it could say, 'Freshwater pipe.' You don't have to give the whole thing away."

"True." He glanced at me and was about to say something, but didn't. Maybe he wanted to offer me a job.

The last of the employees disembarked, and we went down the stairs and exited the ferry through the opening in the stern rail. And here we were on the mysterious Island of Plum. It was windy, sunny, and cool on the dock. Ducks waddled around the shoreline, and I was glad to see they didn't have fangs or flashing red eyes or anything.

As I said, the island is shaped like a pork chop— maybe a baby lamb chop—and the cove is at the fat end of the chop, as if someone took a little bite out of the meat, to continue the idiotic comparison.

There was only one boat tied up at the dock, a thirty-something-footer with a cabin, a searchlight, and an inboard motor. The name of this craft was *The Prune*. Someone had fun naming the ferry and this boat, and I didn't think it was Paul Stevens, whose idea of nautical humor was probably watching hospital ships being torpedoed by U-boats.

I noticed a wooden, weather-faded sign that said, "Plum Island Animal Disease Center." Beyond the sign was a flagpole, and I saw that the American flag was at half-staff here also.

The employees who'd just disembarked boarded a white bus that pulled away, and the ferry blasted its horn, but I didn't see anyone boarding for the trip back to Orient.

Mr. Stevens said, "Please stay here." He strode off, then stopped to speak to a man dressed in an orange jumpsuit.

There was a weird feel to this place—people in orange jumpsuits, blue uniforms, white buses, and all this "stay here" and "stay together" crap. I mean, here I was on a restricted island with this blond SS look-alike, an armed helicopter circling around, armed guards all over the place, and I'm feeling like I somehow stepped into a James Bond movie, except that this place is real. I said to Max, "When do we meet Dr. No?"

Max laughed, and even Beth and Messrs. Nash and Foster smiled.

Beth addressed Max. "Which reminds me, how is it that you never met Paul Stevens?"

Max replied, "Whenever there was a joint meeting of law enforcement agencies, we'd invite the Plum Island security director as a courtesy. None of them ever showed. I spoke to Stevens once on the phone, but never laid eyes on him until this morning."

Ted Nash said to me, "By the way, Detective Corey, I've discovered that you're not a Suffolk County detective."

"I never said I was."

"Oh, come on, fella. You and Chief Maxwell led me and George to believe you were."

Max said, "Detective Corey has been hired by the Town of Southold as a consultant in this case."

"Really?" asked Mr. Nash. He looked at me and said, "You are a New York City homicide detective, wounded in the line of duty on April twelfth. You're currently on convalescent leave."

"Who asked you?"

Mr. Foster, ever the peacemaker, interjected, "We don't care, John. We just want to establish credentials and jurisdictions."

Beth said to Messrs. Nash and Foster, "Okay, then, this is *my* jurisdiction and my case, and I have no problem with John Corey being here."

"Fine," said Mr. Foster.

Mr. Nash did not second that, leading me to believe he did have a problem, which was also fine.

Beth looked at Ted Nash and demanded, "Now that we know who John Corey works for, who do *you* work for?"

Nash paused, then said, "CIA."

"Thank you." She looked at George Foster and Ted Nash, and informed them, "If either of you ever visits the crime scene again without signing in, I will notify the DA. You will follow all procedures, just as the rest of us have to, understood?"

They nodded. Of course they didn't mean it.

Paul Stevens returned and said, "The director is not available just yet. I understand from Chief Maxwell that you'd like to see some of the island, so we can drive around now. Please follow—"

"Hold on," I said, pointing to *The Prune*. "Is that yours?"

"Yes. It's a patrol boat."

"It's not patrolling."

"We have another one out now."

"Is this where the Gordons docked their boat?"

"Yes. All right, please follow—"

"Do you have vehicle patrols around the island?" I asked.

He obviously didn't like being questioned, but he replied, "Yes, we have vehicle patrols around the island." He looked at me and asked impatiently, "Any more questions, Detective?"

"Yes. Is it usual for an employee to use his or her own boat to commute to work?"

He let a second or two go by, then replied, "When the 'Never Leave' policy was strictly enforced, it was prohibited. Now we've relaxed the rules a little, so we sometimes get an employee who takes his or her boat to work. Mostly in the summer."

"Did you authorize the Gordons to commute by boat?"

He replied, "The Gordons were senior staff and conscientious scientists. As long as they practiced good decontamination techniques and observed safety and security regulations and procedures, then I had no real problem with them commuting with their own boat."

"I see." I inquired, "Did it ever occur to you that

the Gordons could use their boat to smuggle deadly organisms out of here?"

He considered a second or two, then answered obliquely, "This is a workplace, not a jail. My main focus here is to keep unauthorized people out. We trust our people, but just to be sure, all our employees have gone through background checks by the FBI." Mr. Stevens looked at his watch and said, "We're on a tight schedule. Follow me."

We followed the tightly wound Mr. Stevens to a white mini-bus and boarded. The driver wore the same light blue uniform as the security guards, and in fact, I noticed he wore a holstered pistol.

I sat behind the driver and patted the seat beside me for Beth, but she must have missed my gesture because she sat in the double seat across the aisle from me. Max sat behind me, and Messrs. Nash and Foster sat in separate seats farther back.

Mr. Stevens remained standing and said, "Before we visit the main facility, we'll take a spin around the island so you can get a feel for the place and better appreciate the challenges of securing an island of this size with about ten miles of beach and no fences." He added, "There's never been a breach of security in the history of the island."

I asked Mr. Stevens, "What kind of sidearms am I seeing in the holsters of your guards?"

He replied, "The pistols are Army-issue Colt .45 automatics." He looked around the bus, then asked, "Did I say something interesting?"

Max informed him, "We think the murder weapon was a .45."

Beth said, "I'd like to do an inventory of your

weapons, and I'd like to run a ballistics test on each of them."

Paul Stevens didn't reply enthusiastically.

Beth asked, "How many .45 pistols do you have here?"

He said, "Twenty."

Max inquired, "Do you have one on you?"

Stevens patted his jacket and nodded.

Beth asked, "Do you always carry the same piece?"

"No." He added, "I draw one from the Armory every weekday." He looked at Beth and said, "It sounds like I'm being interrogated."

"No," Beth replied, "you're only being asked questions as a friendly witness. If you were being interrogated, you'd know it."

Mr. Nash, behind me, said, "Perhaps we should let Mr. Stevens get on with his agenda. We'll have time to question people later."

Beth said, "Proceed."

Mr. Stevens, still standing, said, "All right. Before we move on, I'll give you my little speech that I give to visiting scientists, dignitaries, and the press." He glanced at his stupid clipboard, then began in a rote tone, "Plum Island comprises 840 acres of mostly forest and some pastureland and a parade ground, which we'll see later. The island is mentioned in the ships' logs of early Dutch and English sailors. The Dutch named the island after the beach plum that grows along the shore—Pruym Eyland in old Dutch, if anyone is interested. The island belonged to the Montauk Indian tribe, and it was bought by a fellow named Samuel Wyllys in 1654 from Chief Wyandanch. Wyllys and other settlers after him used the island to pasture sheep and cattle, which is ironic considering what it is used for now."

I yawned.

"Anyway," Stevens continued, "there was no permanent settlement on this island. So, you might ask, how did the settlers pasture cattle on an island that was uninhabited? According to records, the Gut between Orient and Plum was so shallow in the sixteen and seventeen hundreds that cattle could cross at low tide. A hurricane around the late seventeen hundreds deepened the Gut and that ended the island's usefulness as pasture. However, from the beginning of the English presence, the island was visited by a succession of pirates and privateers who found the island's isolation very convenient."

I felt a sudden panic attack coming on. Here I was trapped in a small bus with this monotonal, monochromatic moron who was starting with Genesis, and we were only up to about 1700 or something with three centuries to go, and the friggin' bus wasn't even moving, and I couldn't leave unless I shot my way out. What did I do to deserve this? Aunt June was looking down on me from heaven and laughing her butt off. I could hear her, "Now, Johnny, if you can tell me what I said yesterday about the Montauk Indians, I'll buy you an ice cream cone." *No, no, no! STOP!*

Stevens went on, "During the Revolution, American patriots from Connecticut used the island to stage raids on the Tory strongholds in Southold. Then, George Washington, who'd visited the North Fork—"

I put my hands over my ears, but I could still hear a low hum.

Finally, I raised my hand and asked him, "Are you a member of the Peconic Historical Society?"

"No, but they helped me compile this history."

"Is there, like, a brochure or something that we can read later, and you can save this for a congressman?"

Beth Penrose said, "I find this fascinating."

Messrs. Nash and Foster made some seconding noises.

Max laughed and said, "You're outvoted, John."

Stevens smiled at me again. Why did I think he wanted to pull his .45 and empty his magazine in me? He said, "Bear with me, Detective. We have some time to kill anyway." He continued, but I noticed that he sped up his words. "So, on the eve of the Spanish-American War, the government purchased 130 acres of the island for coastal defenses, and Fort Terry was established. We'll see the abandoned Fort Terry later."

I glanced at Beth and saw she was staring intently at Paul Stevens, apparently absorbed in his narrative. As I stared at Beth Penrose staring at Paul Stevens, she turned toward me, and we made eye contact. She seemed embarrassed that I'd caught her looking at me, and she smiled quickly and turned back to Stevens. My heart skipped a beat. I was in love. Again.

Mr. Stevens was going on, "I should point out that there are over three hundred years of historical artifacts here on the island, and that if it weren't for the restricted access to this island, there would be a good number of archaeologists digging in what are mostly untouched sites. We're currently negotiating with the Peconic Historical Society to see if we can come to some arrangement about an experimental dig. In fact," he added, "the Gordons were members of the Peconic Historical Society, and they were the liaisons between the Department of Agriculture, the historical society, and some archaeologists at Stony Brook State University. The Gordons and I had identified some good sites that we felt wouldn't compromise or interfere with safety and security."

All of a sudden, I was interested. Sometimes a word or phrase or name comes up in an investigation, and then it comes up again, and it becomes something to think about. Such was the Peconic Historical Society. I mean, my aunt belonged to it, and you see flyers and bulletins around from this bunch, and they do cocktail parties, fund-raisers, lectures, and all that stuff, and that's pretty normal. Then the Gordons, who don't know Plymouth Rock from a scotch on the rocks, join up, and now Oberführer Stevens drops it into his spiel. Interesting.

Mr. Stevens prattled on, "In 1929, there was a devastating outbreak of foot-and-mouth disease in the United States, and the Department of Agriculture opened its first station on the island. This begins the modern history of the island in respect to its present mission. Any questions?"

I had a few questions about the Gordons snooping around the island away from where they were supposed to be working in the laboratory. These were clever people, I concluded. The speedboat, then the Peconic Historical Society, then the cover of the archaeological digs so they could recon the island. It was possible that none of this was related, and it was all coincidence. But I don't believe in coincidence. I don't believe that underpaid scientists from the Midwest often get involved in an expensive powerboating hobby and archaeology and local historical societies. These things are not consistent with the resources, the personalities, the temperaments, or the past interests of Tom and Judy Gordon. Unfortunately, the questions I had for Mr. Stevens couldn't be asked without giving away more than I was likely to get.

Mr. Stevens was going on about the Department of Agriculture, and I was able to safely tune out and do some noodling. I realized that before Stevens had mentioned the archaeological interest of the Gordons, he'd said something else that had pinged in my brain. I mean, think of a sonar wave moving through the water—the wave hits something and sends a ping back to the earphones. *Ping.* Something that Stevens said had pinged, but I was so bored senseless when he'd said it, I missed it and now I wanted to go back, but I couldn't remember what it was that caused the ping.

Stevens announced, "All right, we'll drive around the island a bit."

The driver woke up and threw the mini-bus into gear. The road, I noticed, was well paved, but there were no other vehicles to be seen, and no other people.

We drove around the area of the huge main building, and Mr. Stevens pointed out the water tower, the sewage decontamination plant, the power station, machine shops, and steam plants. The place seemed to be self-contained and self-sufficient, making me think again of a Bondian villain's lair where a madman plotted the destruction of the planet. All in all, this was some operation, and we hadn't even seen the inside of the main research building yet.

Now and then we passed a building that Mr. Stevens failed to identify, and if any of us asked him about the building, he'd say, "Paint Storage," or "Feed Storage," or something. And well they may have been, but the man didn't inspire credibility. In fact, I had the distinct feeling he enjoyed the secrecy crap and got his jollies by pulling our chains a little.

Nearly all the buildings, except for the new main research building, were former military structures, most made of red brick or reinforced concrete, and the vast majority of the buildings were deserted. All in all, this had once been a substantial military installation, one in a string of fortresses that guarded New York City against a hostile navy that never showed up.

We came to a grouping of concrete buildings with grass growing through the cement pavement. Stevens said, "The big building is called 257, after the old Army designation. It was the main laboratory some years ago. After we moved out, we decontaminated it with poison gas, then sealed it forever, just in case anything in there is still alive."

No one spoke for a few seconds, then Max asked, "Isn't this where there was a biocontainment leak once?"

"That was before my time," Stevens said. He looked at me and smiled his waxy smile. "If you'd like to take a look inside, Detective, I can get you the key."

I smiled back and asked, "Can I go alone?"

"That's the *only* way you can go into 257. No one will go in there with you."

Nash and Foster chuckled. Boy, I haven't had so much fun since I tripped on some slime and landed on a ten-day-old corpse. I said, "Hey, Paul, I'll go if you go."

"I don't particularly want to die," Stevens replied.

As the bus drew closer to Building 257, I saw that someone had painted in black on the concrete a huge skull and crossbones, and it struck me that this death's-head had actually two meanings—the Jolly Roger, the pirate flag that the Gordons had flown from their mast, and it was also the symbol for poison or contamination. I stared at the black skull and bones against the white wall, and when I turned away, the image was still in front of my eyes, and when I looked at Stevens, the death's-head was superimposed on his face, and the skull and Stevens were both grinning. I rubbed my eyes until the optical illusion faded. Jeez, if it hadn't been broad daylight with people around, this could get creepy.

Stevens continued, "In 1946, Congress authorized money to build a research facility. The law states that certain infectious diseases may not be studied on the mainland of the United States. This was necessary in the days when biocontainment wasn't very advanced. So, Plum Island, which was already wholly owned by the government and which happened to be shared by the Department of Agriculture and the Army, was a natural site for the study of exotic animal diseases."

I asked, "Are you saying that only animal diseases are studied here?"

"That's correct."

"Mr. Stevens, while we'd be upset if the Gordons stole foot-and-mouth virus, and the cattle herds of the United States, Canada, and Mexico were wiped out, that is not the reason we're all here. Are there diseases present in the Plum Island laboratory—crossover diseases—that can infect humans?"

He looked at me and replied, "You'll have to ask the director, Dr. Zollner, that question."

"I'm asking you."

Stevens thought a moment, then said, "I'll say

this—because of the coincidence of the Department of Agriculture sharing this island for a while with the Army, there was a lot of speculation and rumor that this was a biological warfare center. I guess you all know that."

Max spoke up and said, "There is plenty of evidence that the Army Chemical Corps was developing diseases here at the height of the Cold War to wipe out the entire animal population of the Soviet Union. And even I know that anthrax and other animal diseases can be used as biological weapons against a human population. You know that, too."

Paul Stevens cleared his throat, then explained, "I didn't mean to imply that there wasn't *any* biological warfare research done here. Certainly there was for a while in the early 1950s. But by 1954, the offensive biological warfare mission had changed to a defensive mission. That is to say, the Army was studying only ways to prevent our livestock industry from being purposely infected by the other side." He added, "I will not answer any more questions of that nature...but I will say that the Russians sent a biological warfare team here a few years ago, and they found nothing to cause them any anxiety."

I always thought that voluntary arms compliance inspections were sort of like a suspected murderer leading me on a guided tour of his house. *No, Detective, there's nothing in that closet of any interest. Now, let me show you my patio.*

The bus turned onto a narrow gravel road, and Mr. Stevens went on with his prescribed talk, concluding with, "So, since the mid-1950s, Plum Island is undoubtedly the world's foremost research facility for the study, cure, and prevention of animal diseases." He looked at me and said, "Now, that wasn't so bad, was it, Detective Corey?"

"I've survived worse."

"Good. Now we'll leave the history behind us and do some sightseeing. Right ahead of us is the old lighthouse, first commissioned by George Washington. This present one was built in the mid-1850s. The lighthouse isn't used any longer and is an historic landmark."

I looked out the window at the stone structure sitting in a field of grass. The lighthouse more resembled a two-story house with a tower rising out of its roof. I asked, "Do you use it for security purposes?"

He looked at me and said, "Always on the job, aren't you? Well, sometimes I have people stationed there with a telescope or a night-vision device when the weather is too nasty for helicopters or boats. The lighthouse is then our only means of 360-degree surveillance." He looked at me and asked, "Is there anything else you'd like to know about the lighthouse?"

"No, that's about it for now."

The bus turned onto another gravel lane. We were now heading east along the north shore of Plum Island, with the coastline to the left and gnarled trees to the right. I noticed that the beach was a pleasant stretch of sand and rocks, virtually virginal, and except for the bus and the road, you could imagine yourself as a Dutchman or Englishman in sixteen-whatever stepping onto this shore for the first time, walking along the beach, and trying to figure out how to screw the Indians out of the island. *Ping. Ping.*

There it was again. But what was it? Sometimes, if you don't force it, it just comes back by itself.

Stevens was prattling on about ecology and keeping the island as pristine and wild as possible, and while he was going on about that, the helicopter flew over, looking for deer to slaughter.

The road generally followed the coastline, and there wasn't much to see, but I was impressed with the loneliness of the place, the idea that not a solitary soul lived here and that you were unlikely to meet anyone on the beach or on the roads, which apparently went nowhere and had no purpose except for the one road that ran between the ferry and the main lab.

As if reading my mind, Mr. Stevens said, "These roads were all built by the Army to connect Fort Terry to the coastal batteries. The deer patrols use the roads, but otherwise, they're empty." He added, "Since we've consolidated the entire research facility into one building, most of the island is empty."

It occurred to me, of course, that the deer patrols and the security patrols were one and the same. The helicopters and boats may well have been looking for swimming deer, but they were also looking for terrorists and other bad actors. I had the disturbing feeling that this place could be breached. But that wasn't my concern, and it wasn't why I was here.

So far, the island had turned out to be less spooky than I'd expected. I didn't actually know *what* to expect, but like a lot of places whose sinister reputation precedes them, this place didn't seem too bad once you saw it.

When you see this island on maps and navigation charts, most of the time there aren't any features shown on the island—no roads, no mention of Fort Terry, nothing except the words, "Plum Island—Animal

Disease Research—U.S. Government—Restricted."
And the island is usually colored yellow—the color of
warning. Not real inviting, not even on a map. And
if you see it from the water, as I did several times with
the Gordons, it looks shrouded in mist, though I wonder how much of that is real and how much is in the
mind.

And if you go so far as to picture the place as you
might think it looks, you get this Poe-like image of the
ultimate dim Thule, a dark landscape of dead cattle
and sheep, bloating and rotting on the fields, vultures
feeding on the carrion, then dying themselves from
the infected flesh. That's what you think, if you think
about it. But so far, the place looked sunny and pleasant. The danger here, the real horror, was bottled up
in the biocontainment areas, in Zones Three and Four,
and the big-time Temple of Doom, Zone Five. Tiny
slides and test tubes and petri dishes crawling with the
most dangerous and exotic life forms that this planet
has evolved. If I were a scientist looking at this stuff,
I might wonder about God—not about His existence,
but His intent.

Anyway, that was about as much deep thought as I
was capable of without getting a headache.

Beth asked Paul Stevens, "How do boaters know
not to land here?"

"There's a warning on all maps and charts," Mr.
Stevens replied. "In addition, there are signs along all
of the beaches. Plus, the patrols can deal with anchored
or beached boats."

Beth asked, "What do you do with trespassers?"

Stevens replied, "We warn the boaters not to
come near or on the island again. Second offenders

are detained and turned over to Chief Maxwell." He looked at Max. "Right?"

"Right. We get one or two a year."

Paul Stevens tried a joke and said, "Only the deer get shot on sight."

Mr. Stevens got serious and explained, "It's not a dangerous breach of security or biocontainment if people stray onto the island. As I said, I don't mean to give the impression that the island is contaminated. This bus is not a biocontainment vehicle, for instance. But because of the proximity of the biocontainment areas, we would rather keep the island free of unauthorized people and all animals."

I couldn't help but point out, "From what I can see, Mr. Stevens, a boatload of even semi-competent terrorists could land on the island some night, knock off your handful of guards, and grab all kinds of scary things from the labs or blow the place sky-high, releasing deadly bugs into the environment. In fact, when the bay freezes over, they don't even need a boat—you're connected to the mainland."

Mr. Stevens replied, "I can only tell you that there's more security here than meets the eye."

"I hope so."

"Count on it." He looked at me and said, "Why don't you try it one night?"

I love a challenge and replied, "I'll bet you a hundred bucks I can get into your office, steal your high school equivalency diploma from the wall, and have it hanging in my office the next morning."

Mr. Stevens kept staring at me, his dead waxy face immobile. *Creepy.*

I said to him, "Let me ask you the question we're all

here to have answered—Could Tom and Judy Gordon have smuggled micro-organisms off this island? Tell us the truth."

Paul Stevens replied, "Theoretically, they could have."

No one in the bus spoke, but I noticed that the driver turned his head and did a double take.

Mr. Stevens asked, "But why would they?"

"Money," I replied.

"They really didn't seem the type," said Mr. Stevens. "They liked animals. Why would they want to wipe out the world's animals?"

"Maybe they wanted to wipe out the world's *people* so that the animals could have a happy life."

"Ridiculous," said Stevens. "The Gordons took nothing from here that would hurt any living thing. I'll bet my job on that."

"You already have. And your life."

I noticed that Ted Nash and George Foster were mostly quiet, and I knew they'd been briefed much earlier, and they were probably afraid they'd sound sort of like, "Been there, done that, got the T-shirt."

Mr. Stevens turned his attention back to the windshield and said, "We're approaching Fort Terry. We can get out here and look around."

The bus stopped, and we all got out.

CHAPTER NINE

It was a nice morning, and the sun was warmer here in the middle of the island. Paul Stevens led us around the fort.

Fort Terry had no walls, and actually resembled a deserted town. It was unexpectedly picturesque with a brick jailhouse, an old mess hall, a rambling, two-story brick barracks with a veranda, the commandant's house, a few other turn-of-the-century buildings, and a white clapboard chapel on a hill.

Mr. Stevens pointed to another brick building and said, "That's the only building still used—the firehouse."

Max commented, "This is a long distance to the lab."

"Yes," Stevens replied, "but the new laboratory is virtually fireproof and has its own internal fire-fighting system." He added, "These fire trucks are used mostly for brush fires and fires in buildings without biocontainment."

Max, who'd lived his whole life upwind or downwind from this island, said to Stevens, "But a fire or a hurricane could destroy the power generators that filter the biocontainment areas. Right?"

"Anything is possible." He added, "Some people live near nuclear reactors. This is the modern world—full of unimaginable horrors—chemical, biological, and nuclear nightmares waiting to clean the slate for the next evolving species."

I looked at Paul Stevens with new interest. It occurred to me that he was nuts.

In front of the barracks was a field of cut grass that swept down to the water some distance away. Flocks of Canada geese were strutting around the field, cackling and honking or whatever the hell they do when they're not crapping. Stevens explained, "That was the parade ground. We keep the grass cut so that aircraft can see the concrete letters that are embedded in the grass. The letters say, 'Plum Island—Restricted.' We don't want small planes landing here." He made a little joke. "The sign keeps airborne terrorists away."

We walked around a bit and Stevens said, "Before we built the main facility, a lot of the administration offices were housed here at Fort Terry. Now almost everything—labs, security, storage, administration, and animals—is under one roof, which is very good from the standpoint of security." He said to me, "So, even if the perimeter security were breached, the main building is virtually unbreachable."

"You're really tempting me," I said.

Mr. Stevens smiled again. I loved it when he smiled at me. He said, "For your information, I have a college degree from Michigan State, and it's hanging on the wall behind my desk, but you'll never see it."

I smiled back. God, I love pissing people off who annoy me. I liked Max, I liked George Foster, I loved Beth, but I didn't like Ted Nash or Paul Stevens. Liking three out of five people was really good for me—four out of six, if I counted myself. Anyway, I'm getting really intolerant of liars, fools, blowhards, and power freaks. I think I had more tolerance before I got shot. I have to ask Dom Fanelli.

The old parade ground ended abruptly in a steep drop to a rocky beach below, and we found ourselves standing at the edge overlooking the sea. It was a breathtaking view, but it highlighted the loneliness of this place, the otherworldly and end-of-the-world feeling associated with islands in general, and this island in particular. This must have been a very isolated duty station, an extremely boring outpost with little to do except watch the sea. Probably the artillerymen here would have welcomed the sight of an enemy armada.

Stevens said, "This beach is where the seals come every year in late autumn."

I asked, "Do you shoot them?"

"Of course not. As long as they stay on the beach."

As we walked back from the beach, Stevens drew our attention to a big boulder at the end of the parade ground. Sitting in a cleft of the boulder was a rusty cannonball. He said, "That's from about the time of the Revolution—British or American. It's one of the things the Gordons dug up."

"Where did they find it?"

"Right around here, I guess. They dug a lot around the seal beach and this parade ground."

"Did they?"

"They seemed to have a knack for knowing where to dig. They turned up enough musket balls to arm a regiment."

"You don't say?" Keep talking, Mr. Stevens.

"They used one of those metal detectors."

"Good idea."

"It's an interesting hobby."

"Indeed it is. My aunt was a big digger. I didn't know the Gordons were into digging. I never saw anything they uncovered."

"Well, they had to leave everything here."

"Because of contamination?"

"No, because it's federal land."

This was interesting, and Nash and Foster were starting to listen, which is not what I wanted, so I changed the subject by saying to Stevens, "I think the bus driver is trying to get your attention."

Stevens looked toward the bus, but the driver was just staring up at a flock of geese. Stevens glanced at his watch and said, "Well, let's see the rest of the island, then we have an appointment with Dr. Zollner."

We boarded the bus and off we went, heading east into the rising sun, out toward the spit of land that was the curved bone of the pork chop. The beach was magnificent, about two miles of unlittered, untrodden sand washed by the blue waters of the Long Island Sound. No one spoke in the presence of this majestic display of nature. Not even me.

Stevens, still standing, glanced at me now and then, and I smiled at him. He smiled back. It was not a really fun kind of smile.

Finally, at the narrow end of the island, the bus stopped, and Mr. Stevens said, "This is as far as we can go with the bus. Now we walk."

We all got out of the bus and found ourselves in the middle of an amazing old ruin. Wherever I looked,

I saw massive concrete fortifications overgrown with vines and brush—pillboxes, bunkers, gun emplacements, ammunition magazines, tunnels, brick and concrete roadways, and huge, three-foot-thick walls with rusty iron doors in them.

Stevens said, "One of these underground passages leads to a secret laboratory where captured Nazi scientists are still working to develop the ultimate, indestructible virus that will wipe out the world's population."

He let that sink in a second or two, then continued, "In another underground laboratory is the preserved remains of four aliens that were recovered from the UFO crash in Roswell, New Mexico."

Again, there was a silence. Finally, I said, "Can we see the Nazi scientists first?"

Everyone laughed—sort of.

Mr. Stevens smiled his winning smile and said, "These are two of the absurd myths associated with Plum Island." He added, "People report seeing strange-looking aircraft taking off and landing after midnight on the parade ground. They claim AIDS was originated here and also Lyme disease." He looked around and said, "I guess these old fortifications with all the underground passages and rooms can play on some fertile imaginations. You're welcome to look around. Go anywhere you please. If you find the aliens, let me know." He smiled again. He had a really weird smile, and I thought maybe *he* was an alien. Mr. Stevens said, "But, of course, we all have to stay together. I need everyone in my sight at all times."

This didn't quite square with, "Go anywhere you please," but it was close enough. So, John, Max, Beth,

Ted, and George reverted to adolescence and had some fun climbing around the ruins, up staircases, over parapets and all that, with Mr. Stevens always close by. At one point we walked along a long brick roadway that sloped down to a pair of steel doors. The doors were ajar, and we all went inside. It was dark, cool, damp, and probably crawling with things.

Stevens followed us and said, "This leads into a huge ammunition magazine." His voice echoed in the black void. "There was a narrow-gauge railroad on the island that carried the ammunition and gunpowder from the harbor to these underground storage areas. It's a very complex and sophisticated system. But, as you can see, it's entirely abandoned. There is nothing secret that goes on here." He said, "If I had a flashlight, we could go farther, and you'd see that no one lives, works, plays, or is interred in here."

"Then where are the Nazis and the aliens?" I inquired.

"I moved them to the lighthouse," replied Mr. Stevens.

I asked him, "But you can see our concern that the Gordons could have set up a clandestine lab in a place like this?"

Mr. Stevens replied, "As I said, I don't suspect the Gordons of anything. But because this possibility was raised, I'm having my men search this entire complex. Also, there are about ninety aboveground abandoned military buildings all over the island. We have a lot of searching to do."

I said, "Send your driver for a bunch of flashlights. I'd like to look around."

There was a silence in the darkness, then Stevens

said, "After you see Dr. Zollner, we can come back here and explore the underground rooms and passages if you wish."

We walked back into the sunlight and Stevens said, "Follow me."

We followed him and came onto a narrow road that led toward the eastern tip of Plum Island—the end of the curved bone. As we walked, Stevens said, "If you look around, you can see more gun emplacements. We once used these circular gun walls as animal pens, but now all animals are kept inside."

Beth remarked, "That sounds cruel."

Mr. Stevens replied, "It's safer."

Finally, we reached the easternmost tip of the island, a bluff rising maybe forty feet above a rock-strewn beach. Erosion had undermined a concrete bunker, and it lay in pieces down the face of the bluff and some of it had tumbled into the water.

It was a magnificent view, with the shoreline of Connecticut faintly visible to the left, and straight ahead a speck of land called Great Gull Island, about two miles away.

Stevens directed our attention to the south and said, "Do you see that rock pile there? That island was used for artillery and bombing practice. If you're a boater, you know to stay away from there because of all the unexploded shells and bombs in the area. Past that rock pile is the north shore of Gardiners Island, which, as Chief Maxwell knows, is the private property of the Gardiner clan and is off-limits to the public. Beyond Great Gull is Fishers Island, which, like Plum, was frequented by pirates in the 1600s. So, from north to south we have Pirates' Island, Plague Island, Perilous

Island, and Private Island." He smiled at his wit; appropriately it was a half smile.

Suddenly, we saw one of the patrol boats rounding the headland. The crew of three spotted us, and one of the men raised a pair of binoculars. Recognizing Paul Stevens, I suppose, the man waved, and Stevens waved back.

I looked down from the bluff at the beach below and noticed that the sand here had horizontal stripes of red, like a white layer cake with raspberry filling.

A voice called out behind us, and I saw the bus driver walking up the narrow road. Stevens said to us, "Stay here," and went to meet the driver. The driver handed Stevens a cell phone. This is the part where the guide disappears, and we see the bus driving off, leaving Bond alone with the girl, but then frogmen come out of the water with submachine guns and open fire, then the helicopter—

"Detective Corey?"

I looked at Beth. "Yes?"

"What do you think so far?"

I noticed that Max, Nash, and Foster were climbing over and around the gun emplacements, and, macho men that they were, they were discussing artillery ranges, calibers, and guy stuff.

I was alone with Beth. I said, "I think you're swell."

"What do you think about Paul Stevens?"

"Nuts."

"What do you think about what we've seen and heard so far?"

"Packaged tour. But now and then, I learn something." She nodded, then asked, "What's with this archaeological stuff? Did you know about that?"

"No." I added, "I knew about the Peconic Historical Society, but not about the archaeological digs here. For that matter, the Gordons never once mentioned that they bought an acre of useless land overlooking the Sound."

"What useless acre on the Sound?"

"I'll tell you later." I said, "There's like all these little pieces, you know, and they sort of point to drug running, but maybe they don't. There's something else going on here.... Did you ever hear a ping in your head?"

"Not lately. Do you?"

"Yeah, sounds like a sonar ping."

"Sounds like three-quarter disability."

"No, it's a sonar wave. The wave went out, it hit something, and it came back. Ping."

"Next time you hear it, raise your hand."

"Right. I'm supposed to be resting, and you've been upsetting me since I met you."

"Likewise." She changed the subject and said, "You know, the security here is not as good as I thought it would be, considering what's on this island. If this was a nuclear facility, you'd see a lot more security."

"Yeah. The barrier security sucks, but maybe the internal security in the lab is better. And maybe, as Stevens claims, there's more here than meets the eye. Basically, though, I get the feeling that Tom and Judy could have waltzed out of here with whatever they wanted. I just hope they didn't want anything."

"Well, I think we're going to find out later today or maybe tomorrow that they did steal something, and we're going to be told what it is."

"What do you mean?" I asked.

"I'll tell you later," she replied.

"Tell me over dinner tonight."

"I guess I have to get this over with."

"It really won't be that bad."

"I have a sixth sense for bad dates."

"I'm a good date. I've never pulled a gun on a date."

"Chivalry is not dead."

She turned and walked away. She stopped at the edge of the bluff and looked out over the water. The Sound was to the left and the Atlantic to the right and, as with the Gut on the other side of the island, the wind and currents mixed it up here. Gulls seemed to stand still in midair and whitecaps collided, causing the sea to churn. She looked good standing there in the wind, blue skies, white clouds, gulls, sea and sun, and all that. I pictured her naked in that same pose.

Mr. Stevens returned from his phone call and said, "We can get back on the bus now."

We all walked along the road that skimmed the bluff. In a few minutes, we were back in the area of the ruined artillery fortifications.

I noticed that one of the steep rises on which the fortifications were built had recently eroded, exposing strata of fresh earth. The topmost stratum was organic compost, which is what you'd expect, and beneath that was white sand, which was also normal. But the next stratum was a reddish streak of what looked like rust, then more sand, then another line of rust red, just like on the beach. I said to Stevens, "Hey, nature calls. I'll be right back."

"Don't get lost," said Mr. Stevens, not altogether joking.

I went around the base of the hill, picked up a piece

of deadwood, and began jabbing it into the vertical surface of the grassy slope. The black compost and grass fell away, and I could see the strata of white and red. I took a handful of the reddish brown soil and saw that it was actually clay mixed with sand and maybe some iron oxide. It looked very much like the stuff in and on Tom and Judy's running shoes. Interesting.

I put a handful of the soil in my pocket and turned around, only to see Stevens standing there watching me.

He said, "I think I mentioned the 'Never Leave' policy."

"I think you did."

"What did you put in your pocket?"

"My dick."

We stood staring at each other, then he finally said, "On this island, Detective Corey, I am the law. Not you, not Detective Penrose, not even Chief Maxwell, and not the two gentlemen with you." He fixed me with those icy eyes, then said, "May I see what you put in your pocket?"

"I can show it to you, but then I have to kill you." I smiled.

He thought a moment, running through his options, then came to the correct decision and said, "The bus is leaving."

I walked past him and he fell in behind me. I half expected a garrote around my neck, a blow to the head, a shiv in my spine—but Paul Stevens was smoother than that. He'd probably offer me a cup of coffee later, laced with anthrax.

We boarded the bus and off we went.

We'd all taken our former seats, and Stevens remained

standing. The bus headed west, back toward the area of the ferry dock and the main lab. A pickup truck with two men in blue uniforms carrying rifles passed us going the opposite way.

All in all, I'd learned more than I thought I would, seen more than I'd expected, and heard enough to make me curiouser and curiouser. I was convinced that the answer to why Tom and Judy Gordon had been killed was on this island. And, as I said, when I knew why, I would ultimately know who.

George Foster, who had been mostly silent up to now, asked Stevens, "You're quite sure the Gordons left in their own boat at noon yesterday?"

"Absolutely. According to the logbook, they had worked in the biocontainment section in the morning, signed out, showered, and gotten on a bus like this which took them to the ferry dock. They were seen by at least two of my men getting into their boat, the *Spirochete*, and heading out into Plum Gut."

Foster asked, "Did anyone in the helicopter or the patrol boat see them once they were out in the Gut?"

Stevens shook his head. "No. I asked."

Beth queried, "Is there anywhere along this shoreline where a boat can be hidden?"

"Absolutely not. There are no deep coves, no inlets, on Plum. It's a straight beach, except for the one man-made cove where the ferry comes in."

I asked, "If your patrol boat had seen the Gordons' boat anchored anywhere near the island, would your people have chased them off?"

"No. The Gordons, in fact, did sometimes anchor and fish or swim off the coast of Plum. They were well known to the patrols."

I didn't know the Gordons were such avid fishermen. I asked, "Were they ever seen by your people anchored near the beach after dark—late at night?"

Stevens thought a moment, then replied, "Only once that came to my attention." He added, "Two of my men in the patrol boat mentioned that the Gordons' boat was anchored close to the south beach one night in July, about midnight. My men noticed the boat was empty, and they shined their spotlights over the beach. The Gordons were on the beach...." He cleared his throat in a way that suggested what the Gordons were doing on the beach. Mr. Stevens said, "The patrol boat left them in peace."

I thought about this a moment. Tom and Judy struck me as the sort of couple who'd make love anywhere, so doing it on a deserted beach at night was not unusual. Doing it on Plum Island beach, however, raised both my eyebrows and a few questions. Oddly, I'd once had a sort of reverie about making love to Judy on a wave-washed beach. Maybe more than once. Every time I had this thought, I slapped myself in the face. Naughty, naughty, piggy, piggy.

The bus went past the ferry dock, then swung north, stopping in an oval-shaped driveway in front of the main research facility.

The curved front of the new two-story art deco–style building was made of some sort of pink and brown block. A big sign rising from the lawn said, "Department of Agriculture," and there was another flagpole with the flag at half-mast.

We all got out of the bus, and Paul Stevens said, "I hope you enjoyed your tour of Plum Island and that you got a good feel for our security arrangements."

I asked, "What security?"

Mr. Stevens looked hard at me and said, "Everyone who works here is well aware of the potential for disaster. We're all security-conscious, and we're all dedicated to the job and to the highest standards of safety that exist in this field. But you know what? Shit happens."

This profanity and flippancy from Mr. Ramrod Straight sort of surprised everyone. I said, "Right. But did it happen yesterday?"

"We'll know soon enough." He looked at his watch and said, "All right, we can go inside now. Follow me."

CHAPTER TEN

The semicircular lobby of the Plum Island research laboratory was two stories high with a mezzanine running around the central staircase. It was a light and airy space, pleasant and welcoming. The doomed animals probably came in the back.

On the left wall were the standard government chain-of-command photos—the president, the secretary of agriculture, and Dr. Karl Zollner; a rather short chain for a government agency, I thought, leading me to believe that Dr. Zollner was maybe a heartbeat or two away from the Oval Office.

Anyway, there was a reception counter, and we had to sign in and exchange our blue clip-on passes for white passes on a plastic chain that we hung around our necks. A good security procedure, I thought—the island was divided between this building and everything else. And within this building were the Zones. I should not underestimate Mr. Stevens.

An attractive young lady with a knee-length skirt had come down the staircase before I had a chance to check out her thighs, and she introduced herself as

Donna Alba, Dr. Zollner's assistant. She smiled and said, "Dr. Zollner will be with you shortly. Meanwhile, I'll show you around."

Paul Stevens said to us, "I'll take this opportunity to check in with my office and see if there are any further developments." He added, "Donna will take good care of you." He looked at me and said, "Please stay with Ms. Alba at all times."

"What if I have to go to the men's room?"

"You already did." He went up the stairs, stopping, I'm sure, at Dr. Zollner's to report on the five intruders.

I looked at Donna Alba. Mid-twenties, brunette, good face and body, blue skirt, white blouse, and running shoes. I suppose if you considered the daily boat commute and the possibility of having to travel somewhere on the island, then high heels weren't practical. In fact, I thought, if you liked a predictable commute and an average day at the office, Plum Island wasn't your kind of place.

In any case, Donna was attractive enough so that I recalled she'd been on the eight A.M. ferry with us this morning, and she was therefore not yet acquainted with Messrs. Nash and Foster and was therefore probably not on the inside of any cover-up.

Anyway, Donna asked that we all introduce ourselves, which we did, without using any upsetting job titles, such as "homicide detective," "FBI," or "CIA."

She shook hands all around and gave Nash a special smile. Women are such bad judges of character.

Donna began, "Welcome to the Plum Island Animal Disease Center research facility. I'm sure Paul briefed you and gave you a nice history of the island and a good tour."

Her face tried to remain smiley, but I could see it was forced. She said to us, "I'm very...it's terrible what happened. I really liked the Gordons. Everyone liked them." She glanced around, like people do in police states, and said, "I'm not supposed to discuss or comment on any of that. But I thought I should say how I felt."

Beth glanced at me, and seeing, I think, a possible weak spot in the Plum Island armor, said to Donna, "John and Max were good friends of Tom and Judy."

I looked into Donna Alba's eyes and said, "We appreciate all the help and cooperation we've gotten from the staff here." Which, so far, consisted of Mr. Stevens' giving us the fifty-cent tour of the ruins and wilderness, but it was important for Donna to believe that she could speak freely; not here and now, of course, but when we visited her home.

She said, "I'll show you around a bit. Follow me."

We did a little walk around the lobby, and Donna pointed out various things on the walls, including blown-up news articles and horror stories from around the world about Mad Cow Disease and something called rinderpest and swine fever, and other gruesome diseases. There were maps showing outbreaks of this and that, charts, graphs, and photos of cattle with blistered lips and stringy saliva running from their mouths, and pigs with horrible oozing sores. You wouldn't mistake this for the lobby of a steakhouse.

Donna now drew our attention to the doors in the rear of the lobby. The doors were painted that peculiar warning yellow, like the color of Plum Island on a map, and they stood out against the colors of the lobby, which were mostly shades of gray. On the left door was a sign that said, "Locker Room—Women," and on the right, "Locker Room—Men." Both doors said, "Authorized Personnel Only."

Donna said, "These doors lead to the biocontainment areas. This lobby along with the administrative offices is actually a separate building from the biocontainment building, though this appears to be one structure. But, in fact, what connects this area with biocontainment are those two locker rooms."

Max inquired, "Are there any other ways in or out of the biocontainment areas?"

Donna replied, "You can go in through the service entrance where the animals, the feed, supplies, and everything are brought in. But you can't leave that way. Everything and everybody that leaves has to go through the decontamination area, which includes the showers."

Mr. Foster inquired, "How are the products of dissection—wastes and all that—disposed of?"

"Through the incinerator or designated drains that lead to the water and waste decontamination plant," Donna replied. She added, "That's it—these two doors in, a service door in the rear, drains and incinerators, and on the roof, special air filters that can trap the smallest virus. This is a very tight building."

Each of us was thinking our own thoughts about the Gordons, about smuggling stuff out of the labs.

Donna continued, "The locker rooms are still Zone One, like this lobby. But when you move from the locker rooms, you go into Zone Two, and you have to be dressed in lab whites. Before you move out of Zone Two, Three, or Four, and back into Zone One, you have to shower. The shower is a Zone Two area."

"Is the shower co-ed?" I inquired.

She laughed. "Of course not." She added, "I understand that you all have been cleared to go into Zones Two, Three, and Four if you want to."

Ted Nash smiled his stupid smile and asked, "Will you be accompanying us?"

She shook her head. "I don't get paid for that."

Neither did I at a dollar a week. I asked Donna, "Why aren't we cleared for Zone Five?"

She looked at me, sort of surprised. "Five? Why would you want to go there?"

"I don't know. Because it's there."

She shook her head. "There are only ten or so people who are authorized to go into Five. You have to put on this kind of space suit—"

"Were the Gordons authorized to go into Five?"

She nodded.

"What goes on in Zone Five?"

"You should ask Dr. Zollner that question." She glanced at her watch and said, "Follow me."

"Stay together," I added.

We walked up the staircase, me trailing behind because my bad leg was getting draggy and also because I wanted to check out Donna's legs and butt. I know I'm a pig—I could conceivably contract swine fever.

So, we began a tour of the two wings that flanked the two-story lobby. Everything was painted the same dove gray or dark gray, which I guess has replaced the pukey green of older federal buildings. On the walls of the corridors were photos of past lab directors, scientists, and researchers.

I noticed that almost all the doors in the long corridors were closed and they were all numbered, but none of them had the name of a person or function on them, except the lavatories. Good security, I thought, and again I was impressed with Paul Stevens' paranoid mind.

We entered the research library where a few egghead types were browsing through the stacks or reading at tables. Donna said, "This is one of the finest libraries of its type in the world."

I couldn't imagine too many animal disease libraries in the universe, but I said to Donna, "Wow!"

Donna retrieved a handful of brochures, press releases, and other propaganda from a long table and handed them out to us. The tri-fold brochures had titles such as "Hog Cholera," "African Swine Fever," "African Horse Sickness," and something called "Lumpy Skin Disease," which, judging from the scary photos in the brochure, I think one of my old girlfriends had. I couldn't wait to get home and read this stuff, and in fact I said to Donna, "Can I have two more rinderpest brochures, please?"

"Two more...? Sure...." She retrieved them for me. She was really nice. She then got us each a copy of the monthly magazine called *Agricultural Research*, whose cover featured a hot story titled "Sex Pheromone to Foil Cranberry Fruitworm." I asked Donna, "Can I have a brown wrapper to cover this?"

"Uh...oh, you're kidding. Right?"

George Foster said to her, "Try not to take him too seriously."

Au contraire, Mr. Foster—you should take me very seriously. But if you confuse my doltish sense of humor with carelessness or inattention, so much the better.

So, we continued the fifty-cent tour, Part Two. We

saw the auditorium, then came to the second-floor cafeteria, a nice, clean modern room with big windows from which you could see the lighthouse, the Gut, and Orient Point. Donna offered us coffee, and we all sat at a round table in the nearly empty dining area.

We chatted a minute, then Donna said, "The researchers in biocontainment fax their lunch orders to the kitchen. It's not worth showering out—that's what we call it—showering out. Someone delivers all the orders into Zone Two, then whoever delivers has to shower out. The scientists are very dedicated, working in biocontainment eight or ten hours a day. I don't know how they do it."

I asked Donna, "Do they order hamburgers?"

"Excuse me?"

"The scientists. Do they order beef and ham and lamb and stuff like that from the kitchen?"

"I guess. . . . I date one of the researchers. He likes his steak."

"And he does dissections on diseased and putrid cows?"

"Yes. I guess you get used to it."

I nodded. The Gordons did dissections, too, and they loved their steaks. Weird. I mean, I just can't get used to stinking human corpses. Anyway, I guess it's different with animals. Different species and all that.

I knew this might be the only time I'd be able to get away from the herd so I glanced at Max and stood, announcing, "Men's room."

"Over there," Donna said, pointing to an opening in the wall. "Please don't leave the cafeteria."

I put my hand on Beth's shoulder and pressed down, indicating she should stay with the Feds. I said to her,

"Make sure Stevens doesn't come back and slip anthrax in my coffee."

I went to the passage where the two restrooms were located. Max joined me, and we stood in the dead-end corridor. Restrooms are much more likely to be bugged than corridors. I said, "They can say they fully cooperated, showed us the whole island, and the entire facility except for Zone Five. In fact, it would take a few days to cover this whole building, including the basement, and it would take a week to interrogate the staff."

Max nodded. He said, "We have to assume the people here are as anxious as we are to figure out what, if anything, is missing." He added, "Let's trust them on that."

I replied, "Even if they find out or already know what the Gordons stole, they're not going to tell us. They'll tell Foster and Nash."

"So what? We're investigating a murder."

"When I know what and why, I'm close to who," I said.

"In normal cases—with cases of national security and all that stuff, you're lucky if they tell you anything. There's nothing on this island for us. They control the island, the workplace of the victims. We control the murder scene, the home of the victims. Maybe we can horse-trade some information with Foster and Nash. But I don't think they care who killed the Gordons. They want to make sure the Gordons didn't kill the rest of the country. You know?"

"Yeah, Max, I know. But my cop instincts tell me—"

"Hey, what if we catch the killer, and we can't put him on trial because there aren't twelve people left alive in the state of New York to form a jury?"

"Cut the melodrama." I considered a moment, then said to him, "This may not have anything to do with bugs. Think drugs."

He nodded. "Thought about it. I like that one."

"Yeah. Really. What do you think of Stevens?"

Max looked over my shoulder, and I turned to see a blue-uniformed guard come into the passage. He said, "Gentlemen, can I help you find something?"

Max declined the offer, and we went back to the table. When they send someone to interrupt a private conversation, it means that they weren't able to eavesdrop.

After a few minutes of coffee and chitchat, Ms. Alba checked her watch again and announced, "We can see the rest of the wing now, then go to Dr. Zollner's office."

"You said that half an hour ago, Donna," I reminded her gently.

"He's very busy this morning," she replied. "The phone hasn't stopped ringing. Washington, newspeople from all over the *country*." She seemed amazed and incredulous. She said, "I don't believe what they're saying about the Gordons. Not for one minute. No way."

We all left the cafeteria and wandered around dull gray corridors awhile. Finally, while viewing the computer room, I'd had enough, and I said to Donna, "I'd like to see the laboratory where the Gordons worked."

"That's in biocontainment. You can probably see that later."

"Okay. How about Tom and Judy's office here in the admin area?"

She hesitated, then said, "You can ask Dr. Zollner. He didn't tell me to take you to the Gordons' office."

I didn't want to get rough with Donna, so I glanced at Max in a way cops understand—Max, you're now the bad cop.

Max said to Ms. Alba, "As the chief of police of Southold Township, of which this island is a part, I require you now to take us to the office of Tom and Judy Gordon, whose murders I am investigating."

Not bad, Max, despite the shaky syntax and grammar.

Poor Donna Alba looked like she was going to faint.

Beth said to her, "It's all right. Do what Chief Maxwell asks."

Now it was the turn of Messrs. Foster and Nash, and I already knew what they were going to say. George Foster turned out to be the designated dickhead. He said, "Because of the nature of the Gordons' work and the probability that their office contains papers or documents—"

"Relating to national security," I interjected helpfully, "and so forth, and blah, blah, blah."

Teddy Boy thought he should go on record and said, "The Gordons had a secret clearance, and therefore their papers are classified secret."

"Bullshit."

"Excuse me, Detective Corey—I'm speaking." He fixed me with a really nasty glare, then said, "However, in the interests of harmony and to avoid jurisdictional disputes, I will make a phone call, which I'm confident will get us access to the Gordons' office." He looked at me, Max, and Beth and asked, "All right?"

They nodded.

Of course the Gordons' office had already been completely searched and sanitized last night or early this morning. As Beth had said, we were only going to see what they wanted us to see. But I gave George and Ted credit for thinking to make a big stink over this, as though we were going to find some really interesting stuff in the Gordons' office.

Donna Alba seemed relieved and said to Nash, "I'll call Dr. Zollner." She picked up a telephone and hit the intercom button. Meanwhile, Ted Nash whipped out a flip phone and walked some distance away with his back to us and talked, or made believe he was talking, to the gods of National Security in the Great Capital of the Confused Empire.

Charade over, he returned to us mortals at the same time Donna finished with Dr. Zollner. Donna nodded that it was okay, and Nash also nodded.

Donna said, "Please follow me."

We followed her into the corridor and headed for the east wing of the building, past the open staircase we'd come up. We came to Room 265, and Donna opened the door with a master key.

The office had two desks, each with its own PC, a modem, shelves, and a long worktable covered with books and papers. There was no lab equipment or anything of that nature—just office stuff, including a fax machine.

We poked around the Gordons' desks awhile, opening drawers, looking at papers, but as I said, this office had been picked clean earlier. In any case, people who are involved in a conspiracy don't calendar it in or leave incriminating memos around.

Still, you never know what you might find. I rolled through their Rolodex cards, noting that they knew people from all over the world, mostly scientific types, it seemed. I looked under "Gordon" and saw a card for Tom's parents, and names of people who must have been his sister, his brother, and other family members. All in Indiana. I didn't know Judy's maiden name.

I looked for "Corey, John" and found my name, though I don't recall them ever calling me from work. I looked for "Maxwell, Sylvester" and found his office and home numbers. I looked for "Wiley, Margaret," but she wasn't there, and I wasn't surprised. Then I looked for "Murphy," the Gordons' next-door neighbors, and they were there, Edgar and Agnes, which made sense. I found "Tobin, Fredric" and I recalled the time I'd gone with the Gordons to the winery of Fredric Tobin for a wine tasting. I looked for and found the number of the Peconic Historical Society, and the home number of its president, one Emma Whitestone.

I looked under "D" for Drug Runner, Pedro, and "C" for Colombian Drug Cartel, but no luck. I tried "T" for Terrorists and "A" for Arab Terrorists, but I came up empty. I didn't see "Stevens" or "Zollner," but I imagined there must be a separate directory of every employee on the island, and I intended to get a copy of it.

Nash was playing with Tom's PC and Foster was playing with Judy's. This is probably the one thing they hadn't had time to fully check out this morning.

I noted that there were virtually no personal items in the office, not a photograph, not a piece of art, not even a desk item that wasn't government issue. I asked Donna about this, and she replied, "There's no rule against personal items in Zone One areas. But people tend not to bring much on the ferry to put in their office, except maybe cosmetics, medicines, and stuff like that. I don't know why. Actually, we can requisition almost anything we want, within reason. We're a little spoiled that way."

"My tax money at work."

She smiled. "We have to be kept happy on this crazy island."

I walked over to a big bulletin board where Beth and Max were reading the few scraps of paper pinned to the cork. Out of earshot of the Feds, I said, "This place has been picked clean already."

Max asked, "By who?"

Beth said, "John and I saw our two friends getting *off* the Plum Island ferry this morning. They've already been here, already met Stevens, already saw this office."

Max seemed surprised, then annoyed. He said, "Damn…that's against the law."

I said, "I'd let it go if I were you. But you can see why I'm not in the best of moods."

"I haven't noticed any difference, but now *I'm* pissed."

Donna, in her most accommodating voice, interrupted our discussion and said, "We're a little behind schedule now. Maybe you can come back here later."

Beth said to her, "What I would like you to do is to see that this room is padlocked. I am going to send people here from the county police force, and they will look around."

Nash said, "I assume what you mean by look around is that you're going to take items into custody."

"You can assume that."

Foster said, "I believe a federal law has been broken, and I intend to take whatever evidence I need from federal property, Beth. But I'll make all of it available to the Suffolk County police."

Beth said, "No, George, *I'll* take this whole office into custody and make it available to you."

Donna, sensing an argument, said quickly, "Let's go see the duty office. Then we'll see Dr. Zollner."

We went back into the corridor and followed her to a door marked "237." She punched in a code on a keypad and opened the door, revealing a large, windowless room. She said, "This is the duty office, the command, control, and communication center of all of Plum Island."

We all entered, and I looked around. Countertops ran along all the walls, and a young man sat with his back to us, talking on a telephone.

Donna said, "That's Kenneth Gibbs, Paul Stevens' assistant. Kenneth is duty officer today."

Kenneth Gibbs turned in his chair and waved at us.

I looked around the room. On the tables were three different types of radio transmitters and receivers, a computer terminal, a TV set, two fax machines, telephones, cell phones, a teletype, and a few other electronic gizmos. Two ceiling-mounted TV cameras scanned the room.

On the wall were all sorts of maps, radio frequencies, memos, a duty roster, and so forth. This was Paul Stevens' operation—command, control, and communication, known as CCC or C-Three. But I didn't see a door that could have led into Stevens' private office.

Donna said, "From here, we are in direct contact with Washington and with other research facilities all over the U.S., Canada, Mexico, and the world. We're also in contact with the Centers for Disease Control in Atlanta. In addition, we have a direct line to our fire department and to other key places on the island, plus the National Weather Service, and many other agencies and organizations who support Plum Island."

"Such as the military?" I asked.

"Yes. Especially the Coast Guard."

Gibbs put the phone down and joined us. We did the intro thing.

Gibbs was a tall guy of about thirty-something, blue eyes and short blond hair like his boss, neatly pressed trousers and shirt, with a blue tie. A blue blazer hung over one of the chairs. Gibbs, I was sure, was a product of the laboratory here, cloned from Stevens' pecker or something. Gibbs said, "I can answer any questions you may have about this office."

Beth said to Donna, "Would you mind leaving us with Mr. Gibbs for a few minutes?"

She looked at Gibbs, who nodded.

Donna went out into the corridor.

Max, being the only Plum Island neighbor in our group, had his own agenda and asked Gibbs, "What do you do if there's a major nor'easter or hurricane on the way?"

Gibbs replied, "During working hours, we evacuate."

"Everyone?"

"Some people have to stay behind to look after the store. I would stay behind, for instance. So would Mr. Stevens, a few other security people, some firemen, a maintenance man or two to be sure the generators and air filters keep working, and maybe one or two scientists to monitor the bugs. I guess Dr. Zollner would want to go down with his ship." He laughed.

Maybe it was just me, but I couldn't get into

the funny part of fatal diseases blowing all over the place.

Gibbs added, "During nonworking hours, when the island is nearly deserted, we would have to get key people *on* the island. Then, we would have to get our ferries and other watercraft to the submarine pens at New London where they'll be safe. The subs go out to the ocean and dive deep where *they're* safe." He added, "We know what we're doing here. We're prepared for emergencies."

Max said, "If there were ever a biocontainment leak, would you be kind enough to call me?"

"You'd be almost the first to know," Mr. Gibbs assured the chief.

Max replied, "I know that. But I'd like to know by telephone or radio—not by coughing up blood or something."

Gibbs seemed a little put off and said, "My SOP manual instructs me who to call and in what order. You are among the first."

"I've asked that a warning siren be installed here that can be heard on the mainland."

"If we call you, *you* can sound a siren for the civilian population if you want." Gibbs added, "I'm not anticipating any biocontainment leaks, so the point is moot."

"No, the point is this place scares the shit out of me, and I'm not feeling any better now that I see it."

"You have nothing to worry about."

I was glad to hear that. I asked Mr. Gibbs, "What if there were armed intruders on the island?"

Gibbs looked at me and asked, "You mean like terrorists?"

"Yeah, I mean like terrorists. Or worse, disgruntled postal workers."

He was not amused and replied, "Well, if our security people couldn't handle it, we would call the Coast Guard. Right from here." He jerked his thumb toward a radio.

"What if this room was knocked out first thing?"

"There's a second CCC in the building."

"In the basement?"

"Maybe. I thought you were investigating a murder?"

I love rent-a-cops giving me lip. I said, "That's correct. Where were you at 5:30 last night?"

"*Me?*"

"*You.*"

"Oh...let me think—"

"Where's your .45 automatic?"

"Uh...in the drawer over there."

"Has it been fired recently?"

"No...well, I sometimes take it to the pistol range—"

"When was the last time you saw the Gordons?"

"Let me think—"

"How well did you know the Gordons?"

"Not well."

"Did you ever have a drink with them?"

"No."

"Lunch? Dinner?"

"No. I said—"

"Did you ever have occasion to speak to them officially?"

"No...well..."

"Well?"

"A few times. About their boat. They liked to use the Plum Island beaches. The Gordons would come here by boat sometimes on Sundays and holidays, and they'd anchor their boat off one of the deserted beaches on the south side of the island, then swim to shore, trailing a rubber raft. On the raft they had their picnic stuff. We have no problem with that. In fact, we used to have a July Fourth picnic for all the employees and their families. It was the one time when we allowed non-workers on the island, but we had to stop that because of liability concerns. . . ."

I tried to picture such a holiday outing, sort of like beach blanket biocontainment.

Gibbs went on, "The Gordons never brought anyone with them, which would have been against the rules. But their boat presented a problem."

"What sort of problem?"

"Well, for one thing, during the day, it attracted other pleasure boaters who thought they could also come ashore and use the island. And after dark, it presented our patrol boats with a navigation hazard. So I spoke to them about both problems and we tried to work it out."

"How did you try to work it out?"

"The easiest solution would have been for them to come into the cove and take one of our vehicles to the remote end of the island. Mr. Stevens had no problem with that even though it bent the rules about official vehicle use and all that. It was better than what they were doing. But they didn't want to come into the cove or use a vehicle. They wanted to do it their way—take their speedboat to one of the beaches, rubber-raft, and swim. More fun, they said. More spontaneous and adventurous."

"Who runs this island? Stevens, Zollner, or the Gordons?"

"We have to pamper the scientists here or they get upset. The joke among the nonscientists is that if you annoy or argue with a scientist about anything, you wind up getting mysteriously sick with a three-day virus."

Everyone got a chuckle out of that.

Kenneth Gibbs went on, "Anyway, we got them to agree to leave their navigation lights on, and I made sure the Coast Guard helicopters and boats knew their boat. We also made them promise to anchor only where we had one of our big 'No Trespassing' signs on the beach. That usually keeps the fainthearted away."

"What were the Gordons doing on the island?"

Gibbs shrugged. "Picnicking, I guess. Hiking." He added, "They had the run of almost nine hundred deserted acres on holidays and after working hours."

"I understand they were amateur archaeologists."

"Oh, right. They ran around the ruins a lot. They were collecting things for a Plum Island museum."

"Museum?"

"Well, just a display. It was supposed to go in the lobby, I think. The stuff's stored in the basement."

"What kind of stuff?"

"Mostly musket balls and arrowheads. One cow bell...a brass button from a Continental Army uniform, some odds and ends from around the time of the Spanish-American War...a whiskey bottle...whatever. Mostly junk. It's all catalogued and stored in the basement. You can see it if you want."

Beth said, "Maybe later." She asked, "I understand that the Gordons were organizing an official dig. Do you know about that?"

"Yeah. We don't need a bunch of people from Stony Brook or the Peconic Historical Society rooting around the island. But they were trying to work it out with the USDA and the Department of the Interior." He added, "Interior has the final say about artifacts and all that."

I asked Mr. Gibbs, "Didn't it ever occur to you that the Gordons might be up to something? Like smuggling stuff out of the main building and hiding it out by a beach during a so-called archaeological dig, then recovering it later with their boat?"

Kenneth Gibbs did not reply.

I prompted, "Did it occur to you that the picnicking and archaeological crap was a cover for something?"

"I...guess in retrospect...hey, everybody's on my case, like I should have suspected something. Everybody forgets that those two were golden. They could do whatever the hell they wanted, short of pushing Zollner's face in a pile of cow crap. I don't need Monday-morning quarterbacking." He added, "I did my job."

Probably he did. And, by the way, I heard the ping again.

Beth was talking to Gibbs and she asked, "Did you or any of your people see the Gordons' boat after it left the cove yesterday at noon?"

"No. I asked."

"In other words, you can be certain that the boat was not anchored off this island yesterday afternoon?"

"No, I can't be certain of that."

Max inquired, "How often do your boats make the circuit of the island?"

Gibbs answered, "We usually use one of the two boats. Its route covers about eight or nine miles around the island, so at about ten to twelve knots, you're talking about a complete circle every forty to sixty minutes, unless they stop someone for something."

Beth said, "So if a boat were lying a half mile or so away from Plum Island and a person aboard was watching with binoculars, he or she would see your patrol boat—*The Prune*, right?"

"*The Prune* and *The Plum Pudding*."

"Right, he or she would see one of those patrol boats, and if that person or persons knew the routine, he, she, or they would know they had forty to sixty minutes to come toward shore, anchor, get to shore in a rubber raft, accomplish whatever, and get back to their boat without anyone seeing them."

Mr. Gibbs cleared his throat and said, "Possible, but you're forgetting the helicopter patrols and the vehicle patrols that skirt the beach. The helicopter and vehicles are completely random."

Beth nodded and observed, "We just did a tour of the island, and in the nearly two hours, I only saw the Coast Guard helicopter once, and a vehicle—a pickup truck—once, and your patrol boat once."

"As I say, it's random. Would you take a chance?"

"I might," Beth said. "Depends on the payoff."

Gibbs informed us, "There are also random Coast Guard boats that make passes now and then, and if you want me to be very candid, we have electronic devices that do most of the work."

I asked Gibbs, "Where are the monitors?" I motioned around the office.

"In the basement."

"What do you have? TV cameras? Motion sensors? Noise sensors?"

"I'm not at liberty to say."

"All right," Beth said. "Write out your name, address, and phone number. You'll be asked to come in for questioning."

Gibbs seemed annoyed, but also relieved he was off the hook for now. Also, I had the strong suspicion that Gibbs, Foster, and Nash had made one another's acquaintance earlier this morning.

I went over to look at the stuff on the wall near the radios. There was a big map of eastern Long Island, the Sound, and southern Connecticut. On the map were a series of concentric circles, with New London, Connecticut, at the center. It looked like one of those atomic bomb destruction maps that tell you how fried your ass is going to be relative to your distance from ground zero. I saw on this map that Plum Island was within the last circle, which I guess was either good or bad news, depending on what this map was about. The map didn't explain, so I asked Mr. Gibbs, "What is this?"

He looked to where I was pointing and said, "Oh, there's a nuclear reactor in New London. Those circles represent the various danger zones if there were an explosion or meltdown."

I considered the irony of a nuclear reactor in New London posing a danger to Plum Island, which itself posed a danger to everyone in New London, depending on the wind. I asked Kenneth Gibbs, "Do you think the nuke people have a map showing the danger to them of a biocontainment leak on Plum Island?"

Even straight Mr. Gibbs had to smile at that, though it was a weird smile. Gibbs and Stevens probably practiced that smile on each other. Gibbs said, "Actually, the people at the nuclear reactor do have a map such as you describe." He added, "I sometimes wonder what would happen if an earthquake caused a biocontainment leak *and* a nuclear leak at the same time. Would the radioactivity kill the germs?" He smiled again. Weird, weird. He mused philosophically, "The modern world is full of unimaginable horrors."

This seemed to be the Plum Island mantra. I suggested helpfully, "If I were you, I'd wait for a good southerly wind and release the anthrax. Get them before they get you."

"Yeah. Good idea."

I asked Mr. Gibbs, "Where is Mr. Stevens' office?"

"Room 250."

"Thanks."

The intercom buzzed and a male voice came out of the speaker saying, "Dr. Zollner will see his guests now."

We all thanked Mr. Gibbs for his time, and he thanked us for coming, which made us all liars. Beth reminded him that she'd be seeing him in her office.

We met Donna out in the corridor, and as we walked, I commented to her, "These doors don't have names or titles on them."

"Security," she replied tersely.

"Which is Paul Stevens' office?"

"Room 225," she replied.

Proving once again that the best security is a lie. She led us to the end of a corridor and opened door number 200.

CHAPTER ELEVEN

Donna said, "Please have a seat. Dr. Zollner's secretary, June, will be with us in a moment."

We all sat, and Donna stood there waiting for June.

After a minute or so, a middle-aged woman with a tight expression came out of a side door. Donna said, "June, these are Dr. Zollner's guests."

June barely acknowledged us and sat at her desk without a word.

Donna wished us a good day and departed. I noticed that we were never left alone for even a second. I'm a real fan of tight security, except when it's directed at me.

Anyway, I missed Donna already. She was really nice. There are a lot of nice women out there, but between my recent divorce and more recent hospitalization and convalescence, I hadn't really been in the game.

I regarded Beth Penrose. She looked at me, almost smiled, then turned away.

I next regarded George Foster. He always seemed the picture of composure. I assumed that behind those vacuous eyes was a fine brain. I hoped so.

Sylvester Maxwell was tapping his fingers impatiently on the arm of his chair. I think he was generally pleased that he'd hired me, but he might be wondering how he could control a dollar-a-week independent consultant who was generally pissing off everyone.

The waiting room was the same dove gray with dark gray trim and gray carpet as the rest of the structure. You could get sensory deprivation in this place.

Regarding Room 250, what I knew for sure about Room 250 is that neither Paul Stevens nor his diploma was in there. There were probably twenty rabid dogs in Room 250 waiting to eat my *cojones*. Regarding Room 225, I wasn't sure.... Nothing on this island was quite what it seemed, and no one was entirely truthful.

I said to the secretary, "My aunt was named June."

She looked up from her desk and stared at me.

I continued, "It's a pretty name. Reminds me of late spring and early summer, for some reason. Summer solstice, you know?"

June kept staring at me and her eyes narrowed. Scary.

I said to June, "Call Dr. Zollner on the intercom and tell him he has ten seconds to receive us, or we'll get an arrest warrant for obstruction of justice. Nine seconds."

She hit the intercom and said, "Dr. Zollner, please come here. Now."

"Five seconds."

The door to the right opened, and a big, beefy, bearded man in a white shirt and blue tie appeared. He said, "Yes? What is the problem?"

June pointed directly to me and said, "Him."

Beefy looked at me. "Yes?"

I stood. Everyone else stood. I recognized Dr. Zollner from the chain-of-command photos in the lobby, and I said, "We have come across the sea and have traveled many miles, Doctor, and overcome many obstacles to find you, and you repay us by jerking us off."

"Excuse me?"

June butted in, "Shall I call security, Doctor?"

"No, no." He looked at his guests and said, "Well, come in, come in."

We went in, went in.

Dr. Zollner's corner office was big, but the furniture, walls, and carpet were the same as all the others. There was an impressive array of framed things hanging on the wall behind his desk. On the other walls were crappy abstracts, real junk like you see in the best museums.

Still standing, we all introduced ourselves, using our titles and job descriptions this time. It appeared to me—and this had to be a guess again—that Zollner had already met Nash and Foster.

We all pressed the flesh, and Zollner smiled brightly. He said, "So, welcome. I trust Mr. Stevens and Ms. Alba have been helpful?"

He had a slight accent, German probably, if the name was any indication. As I said, he was big—fat, actually—and he had white hair and a white Van Dyke beard and thick glasses. In fact, he looked like Burl Ives, if you want the truth.

Dr. Zollner invited us to sit—"Sit, sit"—and we sat, sat. He began by saying, "I am still in shock over this tragedy. I couldn't sleep last night."

Beth inquired, "Who called you last night with the news, Doctor?"

"Mr. Stevens. He said he'd been called by the

police." Zollner continued, "The Gordons were brilliant scientists and very well respected among their colleagues." He added, "I hope you solve this case very quickly."

Beth replied, "So do we."

Zollner continued, "Also, let me apologize for keeping you waiting. I have been on the phone all morning."

Nash said, "I assume, Doctor, you've been advised not to give interviews."

Zollner nodded. "Yes, yes. Of course. No, I didn't give any information, but I read the prepared statement. The one that came from Washington."

Foster requested, "Can you read it to us?"

"Yes, of course, of course." He rummaged around his desk, found a sheet of paper, adjusted his specs, and read, "'The Secretary of Agriculture regrets the tragic deaths of Drs. Thomas and Judith Gordon, employees of the Department of Agriculture. We will not engage in speculation regarding the circumstances of these deaths. Questions regarding the investigation of the deaths should be directed to the local police, who can better answer those questions.'"

Dr. Zollner finished reading what amounted to nothing.

Max said to Zollner, "Please fax that to the Southold police so we can read it to the press after substituting the FBI for the local police."

Mr. Foster said, "The FBI is not involved in this case, Chief."

"Right. I forgot. Neither is the CIA." He looked at Beth. "How about the county police? You guys involved?"

Beth replied, "Involved and in charge." She said to Dr. Zollner, "Can you describe to us the duties of the Gordons?"

"Yes.... They were involved mostly with ... genetic research. Genetic alteration of viruses to make them unable to cause disease, but able to stimulate the body's immune system."

"A vaccine?" Beth asked.

"Yes, a new type of vaccine. Much safer than using a weakened virus."

"And in their work, they had access to all types of virus and bacteria?"

"Yes, of course. Mostly virus."

Beth went on, shifting to the more traditional homicide investigation questions regarding friends, enemies, debts, threats, relationships with co-workers, recalled conversations with the deceased, how the deceased appeared to act in the last week or so, and on and on. Good homicide stuff, but probably not totally relevant. Yet, it all had to be asked, and it would be asked again and again of almost everyone the Gordons knew, then asked again of those already interviewed to see if there were any inconsistencies in their statements. What we needed in this case, if you assumed the theft of deadly bugs, was a big break, the "Advance to Go" card, something to bypass the procedural crap before the world ended.

I looked at the abstracts on the walls and realized that these weren't paintings, but color photographs.... I had a feeling these were diseases—bacteria and stuff, infecting blood and cells and all that, photographed with a microscope. Weird. But actually, they weren't all that bad.

Zollner noticed my gaze and interrupted his reply to some question, saying, "Even disease-causing organisms can be beautiful."

"Absolutely," I agreed. "I have a suit with that pattern. The green and red squiggly ones there."

"Yes? That's a filovirus—Ebola, actually. Dyed, of course. Those little things could kill you in forty-eight hours. No cure."

"And they're here in this building?"

"Perhaps."

"Cops don't like that word, Doctor. Yes or no?"

"Yes. But safely stored—frozen and under lock and key." He added, "And we only play with simian Ebola here. Monkey Ebola, not human Ebola."

"And you've done an inventory of your bugs?"

"Yes. But to be honest, there is no way we could account for every specimen. And then you have the problem of someone propagating certain organisms in an unauthorized place. Yes, yes, I know what you're getting at. You believe the Gordons took some very exotic and deadly organisms, and perhaps sold them to...well, let's say a foreign power. But I assure you, they would not do that."

"Why not?"

"Because it's too terrible to contemplate."

"That's very reassuring," I said. "Hey, we can go home now."

Dr. Zollner looked at me, not used to my humor, I suppose. He really *did* look like Burl Ives, and I was going to ask him for a photo and autograph.

Finally, Dr. Zollner leaned across his desk toward me and said in his slight accent, "Detective Corey, if you had the key to the gates of hell, would you open them? If you did, you should be a very fast runner."

I contemplated this a moment, then replied, "If opening the gates of hell is so unthinkable, then why do you need a lock and key?"

He nodded and replied, "I suppose to protect us from madmen." He added, "Of course, the Gordons were not mad."

No one replied. We'd all been through this before, verbally and mentally, a dozen times since last night.

Finally, Dr. Zollner said, "I have another theory which I will share with you and which I believe will prove true within this day. Here is my theory—my belief. The Gordons, who were wonderful people, but somewhat carefree and terrible with money, stole one of the new vaccines they were working on. I believe they were further advanced on the research of a vaccine than they led us to believe. Unfortunately, this sometimes happens in science. They may have made separate notes and even separate sequencing gels—these are transparent plates where genetically engineered mutations, which are inserted into a disease-causing virus, show up as...something resembling a bar code," he explained.

No one said a word, and he continued, "So, consider that the Gordons could have discovered a wonderful new vaccine for a terrible disease-causing virus—animal, human, or both—and kept this discovery secret, and over the months assembled all their notes, genetic gels, and the vaccine itself in some hidden area of the laboratory, or in a deserted building on the island. Their purpose, of course, would be to sell this to perhaps a foreign pharmaceutical firm. Perhaps they intended to resign from here, take a job with a private firm, and pretend to make the discovery there. Then, they would get a very handsome bonus amounting to millions of dollars. And the royalties could be tens of millions of dollars, depending on the vaccine."

No one spoke. I glanced at Beth. She had actually predicted this when we were standing on the bluff.

Dr. Zollner continued, "This makes sense. No? People who work with life and death would rather sell life. If for no other reason than it's safer, and it's more profitable. Death is cheap. I could kill you with a whiff of anthrax. Life is more difficult to protect and preserve. So, if the death of the Gordons was in any way connected to their work here, then it was connected as I said. Why would you think of disease-causing virus and bacteria? Why do your minds work that way? As we say, if your only tool is a hammer, then every problem looks like a nail. Yes? Well, but I don't blame you. We always think the worst. And this is your job."

Again, no one spoke.

Dr. Zollner looked at each of us and continued. "If the Gordons did this, it was unethical and also illegal. And whoever was their agent—their middleman—was also unethical and greedy, and it would appear he was also murderous."

It appeared that the good Dr. Zollner had thought this through.

He went on. "This would not be the first time that government scientists or corporate scientists have conspired to steal their own discovery and become millionaires. It is very frustrating for geniuses to see others make millions from their work. And the stakes are very high. If this vaccine, for instance, could be used in a widespread disease, such as AIDS, then we are talking about hundreds of millions of dollars. Even billions for the discoverers."

We all glanced at one another. *Billions.*

"So, there you are. The Gordons wanted to be rich, but more, I think, they wanted to be famous. They wanted to be recognized, they wanted the vaccine named after them, like the Salk vaccine. That would not have happened here. What we do here is kept very quiet except within the scientific community. The Gordons were somewhat flamboyant for scientists. They were young, they wanted material things. They wanted the American Dream, and they were sure they had earned it. And, you know, they really had. They were brilliant, overworked, and underpaid. So they sought to remedy that. I only wonder what it was they discovered, and I worry that we will not recover it. I wonder, too, who killed them, though I'm sure I know why. So, what do you think? Yes? No?"

Ted Nash spoke first and said, "I think that's it, Doctor. I think you're right."

George Foster nodded. "We had the right idea, but the wrong bug. Vaccine. Of course."

Max, too, nodded and said, "Makes perfect sense. I'm relieved. Yeah."

Beth spoke. "I still have to find the murderer. But I think we can stop looking for terrorists and start looking for another type of person or persons."

I looked at Dr. Zollner awhile, and he looked back at me. His glasses were thick, but you could see the blue twinkling eyes. Maybe not Burl Ives. Maybe Colonel Sanders. That was it. How appropriate. The head of the world's largest animal disease research lab looks like Colonel Sanders.

He said to me, "Detective Corey? You have a contrary thought, perhaps?"

"Oh, no. I'm with the majority on this one. I knew the Gordons, and apparently you did too, Doctor. You're right on the mark." I looked at my colleagues and said, "I can't believe we never thought of that. Not death. Life. Not disease, but a cure."

"Vaccine," said Dr. Zollner. "A preventive. Not a cure. There's better money in vaccines. If it's a flu vaccine, for instance, then a hundred million doses are dispensed each year in America alone. The Gordons were doing brilliant work with viral vaccines."

"Right. Vaccine." I asked Dr. Zollner, "And you say they'd have had to plan this for some time?"

"Oh, yes. As soon as they realized they were onto something, they'd begin making false notes, false test results, and at the same time, keeping legitimate notes and so forth. It's the scientific equivalent of double bookkeeping."

"And no one would realize what was going on? There are no checks or controls?"

"Well, there are, of course. But the Gordons were each other's research partner, and they were very senior. Also, their area of expertise—viral genetic engineering—is somewhat exotic and not easily checked by others. And finally, if there's a will, and there's a genius IQ at work, then there's a way."

I nodded. "Incredible. And how did they smuggle this stuff out? I mean, how big is a Jell-O plate?"

"Gel plate."

"Right. How big?"

"Oh . . . perhaps a foot and a half wide, and two and a half feet long."

"How do you get that out of biocontainment?"

"I'm not sure."

"And their notes?"

"Fax. I'll show you later."

"And the actual vaccine?"

"That would be easier. Anal and vaginal."

"I don't want to sound crude, Doc, but I don't think they could get a thirty-inch gel plate up their ass without attracting a little attention."

Dr. Zollner cleared his throat and replied, "You don't actually need the gel plates if you could photocopy them or take a photo with one of those little spy cameras."

"Incredible." I thought of the fax machine in the Gordons' office.

"Yes. Well, let's go see if we can figure out what happened and how it happened." He stood. "If anyone does not want to go into biocontainment, you may sit in the lobby or in the cafeteria." He looked around, but no one said anything. He smiled, more Burl Ives than Colonel Sanders, I think. He said, "Well, everyone is brave then. Please, follow me."

We all stood and I said, "Stay together."

Dr. Zollner smiled at me and said, "When you are in biocontainment, my friend, you will naturally want to stay as close to me as possible."

It struck me that I should have gone to the Caribbean to convalesce.

CHAPTER TWELVE

We returned to the lobby and stood before the two yellow doors.

Dr. Zollner said to Beth, "Donna awaits you in the locker room. Please follow her instructions, and we will meet you at the rear door of the ladies' locker room." Zollner watched her go through the yellow door, then said to us, "Gentlemen, please follow me."

We followed the good doctor into the men's locker room, which turned out to be a hideous orange place, but otherwise typical of any locker room. An attendant handed us open locks without keys and freshly laundered lab whites. In a plastic bag were paper underwear, socks, and cotton slippers.

Zollner showed us to a row of empty lockers and said, "Please remove everything, including underwear and jewelry."

So, we all stripped down to our birthday suits, and I couldn't wait to tell Beth that Ted Nash carried a .38 with a three-inch barrel and that the barrel was longer than his dick.

George Foster said, apropos of my chest wound, "Close to the heart."

"I have no heart."

Zollner pulled on his oversized whites and now he looked more like Colonel Sanders.

I snapped my padlock on the locker hasp and adjusted my paper underwear.

Dr. Zollner looked us over and said, "So—we are all ready? Then please follow me."

"Hold on," Max said. "Don't we get face masks or respirators or something?"

"Not for Zone Two, Mr. Maxwell. Maybe for Zone Four, if you want to go that far. Come. Follow me."

We went to the rear of the locker room, and Zollner opened a red door marked with the weird-looking biohazard symbol and beneath the symbol the words "Zone Two." I could hear rushing air and Dr. Zollner explaining, "That's the negative air pressure you hear. It's up to a pound per square inch less in here than outside, so no pathogens can escape accidentally."

"I hate when that happens."

"Also, the particulate air filters on the roof clean all exhaust air from in here."

Max looked stubbornly skeptical, like a man who doesn't want any good news to interfere with his long-held belief that Plum Island was the biohazard equivalent of Three Mile Island and Chernobyl combined.

We went into a concrete block corridor, and Zollner looked around and asked, "Where is Ms. Penrose?"

I replied, "Doc, are you married?"

"Yes. Oh…of course, she may take longer to get changed."

"No 'mays' about it, feller."

Finally, from the door marked "Women," Lady Penrose appeared, dressed in loose-fitting whites and cotton slippers. She still looked sexy, more cupid-like in white, I thought.

She heard the rushing air sound, and Zollner explained the negative air pressure, gave us some instructions about being careful not to bump into carts or racks of vials, or bottles filled with lethal bugs or chemicals, and so forth.

Zollner said, "All right, please follow me, and I will show you what goes on here so you can tell your friends and colleagues that we are not making anthrax bombs." He laughed, then said in a serious tone, "Zone Five is off-limits because you need special vaccinations, and also training to put on the biohazard suits and respirators and all of that. Also, the basement is off-limits."

"Why," I asked, "is the basement off-limits?"

"Because that's where we hide the dead aliens and the Nazi scientists." He laughed again.

I love being the straight man for a fat Ph.D. with a Dr. Strangelove accent. Really. More to the point, I knew that Stevens had indeed spoken to Zollner. I would have liked to have been a tsetse fly on that wall.

Mr. Foster attempted humor and said, "I thought the aliens and the Nazis were in the underground bunkers."

"No, the dead aliens are in the lighthouse," Zollner said. "We moved the Nazis out of the bunkers when they complained about the vampires."

Everyone laughed—ha, ha, ha. Humor in biocontainment. I should write to *Reader's Digest*.

As we walked, Dr. Zany said, "It's safe in this zone—mostly we have genetic engineering labs, some offices, electron microscopes—low-risk, low-contagion work here."

We walked through concrete block corridors, and every once in a while Dr. Zollner would open a yellow steel door and say hello to someone inside an office or laboratory and inquire as to their work.

There were all sorts of weird windowless rooms, including a place that looked like a wine cellar except the bottles in the racks were filled with cultures of living cells, according to Zollner.

Zollner gave us a commentary as we walked through the battleship-gray corridors. "There are newly emerging viruses that affect animals or humans or both. We humans and the higher animal species have no immunological responses to many of these deadly diseases. Present antiviral drugs are not very effective, and so the key to avoiding a future worldwide catastrophe is antiviral *vaccines*, and the key to the new vaccines is genetic engineering."

Max asked, "*What* catastrophe?"

Dr. Zollner continued walking and talking very breezily, I thought, considering the subject. He said, "Well, regarding animal diseases, an outbreak of foot-and-mouth disease, for instance, could wipe out much of this nation's livestock and ruin the livelihoods of millions of people. The cost of other foods would probably quadruple. The foot-and-mouth virus is perhaps the most contagious and virulent in nature, which is why the biological warfare people have always been fascinated by it. A good day for the bio-warfare gentlemen is a day when their scientists can genetically engineer the FMD virus to infect humans. But worse, I think, some of these viruses mutate on their own and become dangerous to people."

No one had a comment or question on that. We peeked in on more labs, and Zollner would always say a few encouraging words to the pale eggheads in white who labored in surroundings that made me nervous just looking at them. He'd say things like, "What have we learned today? Have we discovered anything new?" And so on. It appeared that he was well liked, or at least tolerated by his scientists.

As we turned down yet another in a series of seemingly endless corridors, Zollner continued his lecture. "In 1983, for instance, a highly contagious and deadly influenza broke out in Lancaster, Pennsylvania. There were seventeen million dead. Chickens, I mean. Poultry. But you see what I'm getting at. The last big deadly human influenza epidemic in the world was in 1918. There were about twenty million dead worldwide, including five hundred thousand in the United States. Based on our present population, the equivalent number of dead now would be approximately one and a half million people. Could you imagine such a thing today? And the 1918 virus wasn't particularly virulent, and of course, travel was much slower then and less frequent. Today, the highways and skyways can spread an infectious virus around the world in days. The good news about the deadliest viruses, such as Ebola, is that they kill so fast, they barely have time to leave an African village before everyone in it is dead."

I asked, "Is there a one o'clock ferry?"

Dr. Zollner laughed. "You are feeling somewhat nervous, yes? Nothing to fear here. We are very cautious. Very respectful of the little bugs in this building."

"Sounds like the 'my dog doesn't bite' crap."

Dr. Zollner ignored me and continued on, "It is the

mission of the United States Department of Agriculture to prevent foreign animal pestilence from coming to these shores. We are the animal equivalent of the Centers for Disease Control in Atlanta. As you may imagine, we work closely with Atlanta because of these crossover diseases—animal to human, and vice versa. We have a huge quarantine complex in Newburgh, New York, where all animals coming into this country must stay in quarantine for a period of time. You know, it's like a Noah's Ark of animals arriving every day— foreign race horses, circus animals, zoo animals, breeding stock, exotic commercial animals such as ostriches and llamas, exotic pets such as Vietnamese potbellied pigs, and all sorts of birds from the jungle.... Two and a half million animals each year." He looked at us and said, "Newburgh has been called the Ellis Island for the animal kingdom. Plum Island is the Alcatraz. No animal that comes to us from Newburgh or from anywhere leaves here alive. I must tell you, all these animals being imported into this country for recreation and amusement have caused us here a lot of work and much anxiety. It's only a matter of time...." He added, "You can extrapolate from the animal kingdom to the human population."

I certainly could.

He stayed silent a moment, then said, "Plum Island's cannons once guarded the shores of this country, and now this facility does the same."

Rather poetic, I thought, for a scientist, then I recalled reading that line in one of the press releases that Donna handed me.

Zollner liked to talk, and my job is to listen, so, it was working out okay.

We walked into a room that Zollner said was an X-ray crystallography lab, and I wasn't about to argue with him.

A woman was bent over a microscope, and Zollner introduced her as Dr. Chen, a colleague and good friend of Tom and Judy. Dr. Chen was about thirty, and rather attractive, I thought, with a long shock of black hair, tied back with a sort of netting, suitable for close microscope work by day, I guess, and who knew what at night when the hair came down. Behave, Corey. This is a scientist, and she's a lot smarter than you are.

Dr. Chen greeted us, and she looked rather serious, I thought, but probably she was just upset and sad over the deaths of her friends.

Once again, Beth made sure that it was understood that I was a friend of the Gordons, and on that level, if no other, I was earning my buck a week. I mean, people don't like a bunch of coppers hammering them with questions, but if one of the cops is a mutual friend of the deceased, then you have a little edge. Anyway, we all agreed that the Gordons' deaths were a tragedy, and we spoke well of the dead.

The subject shifted to Dr. Chen's work. She explained, in lay terms so that I sort of understood her, "I am able to x-ray virus crystals so that I can map their molecular structure. Once we do that, we can then attempt to alter the virus to make it unable to cause disease, but if we inject this altered virus into an animal, the animal may produce antibodies that we hope will attack the natural, disease-causing version of the virus."

Beth asked, "And this is what the Gordons were working on?"

"Yes."

"What *specifically* were they working on? What virus?"

Dr. Chen glanced at Dr. Zollner. I'm not happy when witnesses do that. I mean, it's like the pitcher gets the signal from the coach to throw a curve or a slider or whatever. Dr. Zollner must have signaled for a fast ball because Dr. Chen said straightforwardly, "Ebola."

No one said anything, then Dr. Zollner said, "Simian Ebola, of course. Monkey Ebola." He added, "I would have told you sooner, but I thought you'd want it explained more fully by one of the Gordons' colleagues." He nodded to Dr. Chen.

Dr. Chen continued, "The Gordons were trying to genetically alter a simian Ebola virus so that it would not cause disease, but would produce an immune response in the animal. There are many strains of the Ebola virus, and we're not even sure which strains can cross the species barrier—"

"You mean," Max asked, "infect people?"

"Yes, infect humans. But this is an important first step toward a human Ebola vaccine."

Dr. Zollner said, "Most of our work here has traditionally been done with what you'd call farm animals— food- and leather-producing animals. However, over the years, certain government agencies have underwritten other types of research."

I asked, "Such as the military doing biological warfare research?"

Dr. Zollner didn't answer directly, but said, "This island is a unique environment, isolated, but close to major transportation and communication centers, and also close to the best universities in the nation, and close to a highly educated pool of scientists. In addition, this facility is technically advanced. So, aside from the military, we work with other agencies, here and abroad, whenever something very unusual or potentially... dangerous to humans comes along. Such as Ebola."

"In other words," I said, "you sort of rent rooms here?"

"It's a big facility," he replied.

"Did the Gordons work for the U.S. Department of Agriculture?" I asked.

"I'm not at liberty to say."

"Where did their paychecks come from?"

"All paychecks are from the USDA."

"But not every scientist who gets a USDA paycheck is a USDA employee. Correct?"

"I don't intend to get into a semantic duel with you, Mr. Corey." He looked at Dr. Chen. "Please continue."

She said, "There are so many separate tasks and steps to this sort of work that no one can see the whole picture except the project supervisor. That was Tom. Judy was the assistant project supervisor. In addition, they were both excellent researchers themselves. In retrospect, I can see what they were doing, which was to ask for tests on procedures that were something like a red herring, and sometimes they'd tell one of us on the project that they'd reached a dead end. They closely monitored the actual clinical tests on the monkeys, and the animal handlers were not well informed. Tom and Judy were the only ones who were privy to all the information."

She thought a moment, then said, "I don't believe they started out to deceive... I think when it hit them how close they were to a workable vaccine for simian

Ebola, they saw the possibilities of transferring the technology to a private laboratory where the next logical step was a human vaccine. Maybe they believed that this was the best thing in the interests of humanity. Maybe they thought they could develop this vaccine more quickly and effectively outside this place, which is—like most government agencies—prone to red tape and slowness."

Max said, "Let's stick to the theory of profit motive, Dr. Chen. The interests of humanity isn't cutting it for me."

She shrugged.

Beth motioned toward the microscope. "Can I take a look?"

Dr. Chen said, "Those are dead Ebola, of course. Live Ebola is only in Zone Five. But I can show you live Ebola viruses safely on videotape." She turned to a TV monitor and hit the VCR. The screen brightened to show four almost transparent crystals, tinted a sort of pink color, three-dimensional, reminding me of a prism. If they were alive, they were playing possum.

Dr. Chen said, "I'm mapping the molecular structure, as I said, so that the genetic engineers can cut and splice this or that piece, then the altered virus is propagated and injected into a monkey. The monkey has one of three responses—it contracts Ebola and dies, it doesn't contract Ebola but doesn't produce Ebola antibodies, or it doesn't contract Ebola and *does* produce Ebola antibodies. That is the response we're looking for. That means we have a vaccine. But not necessarily a safe or effective vaccine. The monkey may develop Ebola later, or more commonly, when we later inject the monkey with natural Ebola virus, the antibodies aren't effective in overcoming the disease. The immune response is too weak. Or the immune response does not protect against all strains. It's very frustrating work. Viruses are so simple, molecularly and genetically, but they are more challenging than bacteria in that they are easy to mutate, hard to understand, and hard to kill. In fact, the question is—are those crystals really alive as we understand life? Look at them. They look like ice chips."

Indeed, we were all staring at the crystals on the screen. They looked like something that dropped off a chandelier. It was hard to believe that those guys and their cousins and brothers had caused so much human misery and death, not to mention animal deaths. There was something scary about an organism that looked dead but came to life when it invaded living cells, and reproduced so fast it could kill a healthy two-hundred-pound man in forty-eight hours. What was God thinking?

Dr. Chen turned off the TV monitor.

Beth asked Dr. Chen about the Gordons' behavior yesterday morning, and Dr. Chen said that the Gordons seemed somewhat tense. Judy complained of a migraine, and they decided to go home. This did not surprise any of us.

I asked Dr. Chen directly, "Do you think they took anything out of here yesterday?"

She thought a moment, then replied, "I don't know. How can I say?"

Beth asked, "How difficult is it to smuggle something out of here? How would *you* do it?"

"Well...I could take any test tube here, or even in another lab, go into the ladies' room and insert the tube or vial in one of two orifices. No one would miss a single vial, especially if it hadn't been logged and identified. Then I go into the shower room, throw my lab clothes into a hamper, shower, and go to my locker. At this point I could remove the vial from wherever and put it in my handbag. I get dressed, leave through the lobby, get on the bus to the ferry, and go home. No one watches you shower. There are no cameras. You'll see when you leave here yourself."

I asked, "And larger items. Items too big to ... well, too big."

"Whatever will fit under your lab clothes can make it as far as the shower room. It is there where you have to be clever. For instance, if I took a sequencing gel into the shower room, I could hide it in my towel."

Beth said, "You could also hide it in the hamper with your lab clothes."

"No, you can never go back. The clothes are contaminated. In fact, after you use the towel, that must also go into a separate hamper. It is here that anyone who is looking would see if you were carrying anything. But if you shower out at an odd time, the chances are you will be alone."

I tried to picture this scene, of Judy or Tom smuggling God knew what out of this building yesterday afternoon when no one else was in the shower room. I asked Dr. Chen, "If it's assumed that everything in here has some degree of contamination, why would you want to put a vial of something in your whatever?"

She replied, "You practice some basic decon first, of course. You wash your hands with the special soap in the restrooms, you may use a condom to wrap a vial or test tube, or use sterile gloves or sheet latex for larger items. You have to be careful, but not paranoid."

Dr. Chen continued, "As for computer information, it can and is electronically transferred from biocontainment to the offices in the administration area. So it's not necessary to steal disks or tapes." She added, "As for handwritten and typewritten notes, graphs, charts, and so forth, it's standard procedure to fax all of that out of here and into your own office. There are fax machines all around, as you can see, and each office outside of biocontainment has an individual fax. That's the only way you can get notes out of here. Years ago, you had to use special paper, rinse it in a decontaminating fluid, leave it to dry, then retrieve it the next day. Now, with the fax, your notes are waiting for you when you return to the office."

Amazing, I thought. I'll bet the folks who invented the fax never thought of that. I can picture the TV commercial—"Laboratory notes covered with germs? Fax them to your office. *You* have to shower, but they don't." Or something like that.

Beth looked at Dr. Chen and asked her directly, "Do you think the Gordons took anything out of here that was dangerous to living things?"

"Oh, no. No, no. Whatever they took—if they took anything—wasn't pathogenic. Whatever it was, it was therapeutic, helpful, antidotal, however we want to term it. It was something good. I would bet my life on that."

Beth said, "We're all betting our lives on that."

We left Dr. Chen and the X-ray room and continued our tour.

As we walked, Dr. Zollner commented, "So, as I

said before, and as Dr. Chen seems to agree, if the Gordons stole anything, it was a genetically altered viral vaccine. Most probably a vaccine for Ebola since that was the main thrust of their work."

Everyone seemed to agree with that. My own thinking was that Dr. Chen had been a little too pat and perfect, and that she didn't know the Gordons as well as she or Zollner said she did.

Dr. Zollner gave a commentary as we strolled the labyrinthine corridors. He said, "Among the viral diseases we study are malignant catarrh, Congo Crimean hemorrhagic fever, and bluetongue. We also study a variety of pneumonias, rickettsial diseases, such as heartwater, a wide range of bacterial diseases, and also parasitic diseases."

"Doc, I got a C in biology and that's because I cheated. You lost me on the rickshaw disease. But let me ask you this—you have to produce a lot of this stuff in order to study it. Correct?"

"Yes, but I can assure you we don't have the capacity to produce enough of any organism in the quantities needed for warfare, if that's what you're getting at."

I said, "I'm getting at random acts of terrorism. Do you produce enough germs for that?"

He shrugged. "Perhaps."

"That word again, Doc."

"Well, yes, enough for a terrorist act."

"Is it true," I inquired, "that a coffee can full of anthrax, spritzed into the air around Manhattan Island, could kill two hundred thousand people?"

He thought a moment, then replied, "That could be. Who knows? It depends on the wind. Is it summertime? Is it lunchtime?"

"It's like tomorrow evening rush hour."

"All right...two hundred thousand. Three hundred thousand. A million. It doesn't matter because no one knows and no one has a coffee can full of anthrax. Of that, I can assure you. The inventory was quite specific on that."

"That's good. But not as specific on other things?"

"As I told you, if anything is missing, it is an antiviral vaccine. That is what the Gordons were working on. You'll see. Tomorrow you will all wake up alive. And the day after, and the day after that. But six or seven months from now, some pharmaceutical company, or some foreign government, will announce an Ebola vaccine, and the World Health Organization will purchase two hundred million doses to start with, and when you discover who is getting the richest from this vaccine, you will discover your murderer."

No one replied for a few seconds, then Max said, "You're hired, Doctor."

Everyone smiled and chuckled. In fact, we all wanted to believe, we *did* believe, and we were so relieved that we were walking on air, giddy over the good news, thrilled that we weren't going to wake up with terminal bluetongue or something, and in truth no one was focusing as closely on the case now as we had been earlier. Except me.

Anyway, Zollner continued showing us all sorts of rooms and talked about diagnoses and reagent production, monoclonal antibody research, genetic engineering, tick-borne viruses, vaccine production, and so forth. It was mind-boggling.

It takes an odd type to go into this sort of work, I thought, and the Gordons, whom I considered normal people, must have been considered by their peers as somewhat flamboyant by comparison—which was how Zollner described them. I mentioned this to Zollner and he replied, "Yes, my scientists here are rather introverted... like most scientists. Do you know the difference between an introverted biologist and an extroverted biologist?"

"No."

"An extroverted biologist looks at *your* shoes when he talks to you." Zollner laughed heartily at this one, and even I chuckled, though I don't like it when people upstage me. But it *was* his lab.

Anyway, we saw the various places where the Gordons' project had been worked on, and we also saw the Gordons' own lab.

Inside the Gordons' small lab, Dr. Zollner said, "As project directors, the Gordons mostly supervised, but they did some work here on their own."

Beth said, "No one else worked in this lab?"

"Well, there were assistants. But this laboratory was the private domain of the Doctors Gordon. You can be sure I spent an hour in here this morning looking for something that was not right, but they wouldn't leave anything incriminating around."

I nodded. In fact, there may have been incriminating evidence at any previous time, but if yesterday was to be the culmination of the Gordons' secret work and final theft, then they would have sanitized the place yesterday morning or the day before. But that supposed that I believed all of this stuff about an Ebola vaccine, and I wasn't sure I did.

Beth said to Dr. Zollner, "You are *not* supposed to enter the workplace of homicide victims and look around, remove things, or touch anything."

Zollner shrugged, as well he should under these circumstances. He said, "So, how was I supposed to know that? Do you know *my* job?"

Beth said, "I just want you to know—"

"For next time? All right, the next time two of my top scientists are murdered, I'll be sure not to go into their laboratory."

Beth Penrose was bright enough to let it go and said nothing.

Clearly, I thought, Ms. By-the-Book was not handling the unique circumstances of this case very well. But I gave her credit for trying to do it right. If she'd been one of the crew on the *Titanic*, she'd have made everyone sign for the life jackets.

We all looked around the lab, but there were no notebooks, no beakers labeled "Eureka," no cryptic messages on the blackboard, no corpses in the supply closet, and in fact, nothing at all that the average layperson could understand. If anything interesting or incriminating had been here, it was gone, compliments of the Gordons, or Zollner, or even Nash and Foster if they'd ventured this far on their earlier visit this morning.

So, I stood there and tried to commune with the spirits that possibly still occupied this room—*Judy, Tom...give me a clue, a sign.*

I closed my eyes and waited. Fanelli says the dead speak to him. They identify their murderers, but they always speak Polish or Spanish or sometimes Greek, so he can't understand them. I think he's pulling my leg. He's crazier than I am.

Unfortunately, the Gordons' lab was a bust, and we continued on.

We spoke to a dozen scientists who worked with or for the Gordons. It was obvious that (a) everyone loved Tom and Judy; (b) Tom and Judy were brilliant; (c) Tom and Judy wouldn't hurt a fly unless it advanced the cause of science in the service of man and beast; (d) the Gordons, while loved and respected, were different; (e) the Gordons, while scrupulously honest in their personal dealings, would probably screw the government and steal a vaccine worth its weight in gold, as someone phrased it. It occurred to me that everyone was reading from the same script.

We continued our walk and climbed a staircase to the second floor. My bad leg was dragging, and my bad lung was wheezing so loudly I thought everyone could hear it. I said to Max, "I thought this wasn't going to be strenuous."

He looked at me and forced a smile. He said to me softly, "I get claustrophobic sometimes."

"Me too." In truth, it wasn't claustrophobia that was troubling him. Like most men of courage and action, myself included, Max didn't like a danger he couldn't pull his gun on.

Dr. Zollner was going on about the training programs that were conducted here, the visiting scientists, graduate students, and veterinarians who came from all over the world to learn and teach here. He also spoke of the facility's foreign cooperative programs in places like Israel, Kenya, Mexico, Canada, and England. "In fact," he said, "the Gordons went to England about a year ago. Pirbright Laboratory, south of London. That's our sister lab there."

I asked Dr. Zollner, "Do you get visitors from the Army Chemical Corps?"

Dr. Zollner looked at me and commented, "Whatever I say, you see something to question. I'm glad you're listening."

"I'm listening for the answer to my question."

"The answer is it's none of your business, Mr. Corey."

"It is, Doctor. If we suspect that the Gordons stole organisms that can be used in biological warfare, and that's what got them murdered, then we have to know if such organisms exist here. In other words, are there biological warfare specialists here in this building? Do they work here? Experiment here?"

Dr. Zollner glanced at Messrs. Foster and Nash, and then said, "I would be less than truthful if I said no one from the Army Chemical Corps comes here. They are extremely interested in vaccines and antidotes for biological hazards. . . . The United States government does not study, promote, or produce agents of offensive biological warfare. But it would be national suicide not to study defensive measures. So, someday, when that bad fellow with the can of anthrax paddles his canoe around Manhattan Island, we can be ready to protect the population." Dr. Zollner added, "You have my assurances that the Gordons had no dealings with anyone from the military, did not work in that area, and in fact, had no access to anything so lethal—"

"Except Ebola."

"You *do* listen. My staff should pay as much attention. But why bother with an Ebola weapon? We have anthrax. Trying to improve on anthrax is like trying to improve on gunpowder. Anthrax is easy to propagate, easy to handle, it diffuses nicely into the air, kills slowly enough for the infected population to spread it around, and cripples as many victims as it kills, causing a collapse of the enemy's health care system. But, officially, we don't have anthrax bombs or artillery shells. The point is, if the Gordons were trying to develop a biological weapon to sell to a foreign power, they wouldn't bother with Ebola. They were too smart for that. So put that suspicion to rest."

"I feel much better. By the way, when did the Gordons go to England?"

"Let's see...May of last year. I recall that I envied them going to England in May." He asked me, "Why do you ask?"

"Doc, do scientists know why they're asking questions all the time?"

"Not all the time."

"I assume the government paid all expenses for the Gordons' trip to England."

"Of course. It was all business." He thought a moment, then said, "Actually, they took a week in London at their own expense. Yes, I remember that."

I nodded. What *I* didn't remember was any unusually large credit card bills in May or June of last year. I wondered where they'd spent the week. Not in a London hotel, unless they skipped out on the bill. I didn't recall any large cash withdrawals either. Something to think about.

The problem with asking really clever questions in front of Foster and Nash was that they heard the answers. And even if they didn't know where the questions were coming from, they were smart enough to know—contrary to what I indicated to Zollner—that most questions had a purpose.

We were walking down a very long corridor, and no

one was speaking, then Dr. Zollner said, "Do you hear that?" He stopped dead and put his hand to his ear. "Do you hear that?"

We all stood motionless, listening. Finally, Foster asked, "What?"

"Rumbling. It's a rumbling. It's..."

Nash knelt down and put the palms of his hands on the floor. "Earthquake?"

"No," Zollner said, "it's my stomach. I'm hungry." He laughed and slapped his fat. "Lighten up," he said in his German accent, which made it sound even more funny. Everyone was smiling except Nash, who stood stiffly and brushed his hands off.

Zollner went to a door painted bright red, on which was plastered six standard OSHA-type signs, as follows: Biohazard, Radioactive, Chemical Waste, High Voltage, Poison Hazard, and finally, Untreated Human Waste. He opened the door and announced, "Lunch Room."

Inside the plain white cement block room were a dozen empty tables, a sink, a refrigerator, microwave oven, bulletin boards covered with notices and messages, and a water cooler and coffee maker, but no vending machines, the fact being that no one wanted to come in here and service them. Sitting on a counter was a fax machine, a menu of the day's fare, and paper and pencil. Dr. Zollner said, "Lunch is on me." He wrote himself a big order which I saw included the soup du jour, which was beef. I didn't even want to think about where the beef came from.

For the first time since I left the hospital, I ordered Jell-O, and for the first time in my life, I skipped the meat dishes.

No one else seemed particularly hungry, and they all ordered salads.

Dr. Zollner faxed the order and said, "The lunch hour here doesn't start until one, but they will deliver quickly because I requested it."

Dr. Zollner suggested we wash our hands, which we all did at the sink with some weird brown liquid soap that smelled like iodine.

We all got coffee and sat. A few other people came in and got coffee and took things out of the refrigerator or faxed orders. I looked at my watch to see the time and saw my wrist.

Zollner said, "If you'd brought your watch in, I'd have to decontaminate it and quarantine it for ten days."

"My watch wouldn't survive a decontamination." I glanced at the clock on the wall. It was five minutes to one P.M.

We made small talk for a few minutes. The door opened and a man in lab whites entered, pushing a stainless steel cart which looked like any other lunch cart, except it was covered with a sheet of plastic wrap.

Dr. Zollner pulled off the wrap and disposed of it, then—perfect host—gave us each our orders and dismissed the man and the cart.

Max asked, "That guy has to shower now?"

"Oh, yes. The cart is first put in a decon room and retrieved later."

I asked, "Is it possible to use that cart to smuggle large items out of here?"

Dr. Zollner was arranging his large lunch in front of him with the expertise of a real trencherman. He looked up from his labor of love and said, "Now that you mention it, yes. That cart is the only thing that makes a regular journey between administration and biocontainment. But if you used it to smuggle, you'd have to have two other people in on it. The person who pushes it in and out, then the person who washes it and takes it back to the kitchen. You're very clever, Mr. Corey."

"I think like a criminal."

He laughed and dug into the beef soup. Yuck.

I regarded Dr. Zollner as I slurped my lime Jell-O. I liked the guy. He was funny, friendly, hospitable, and smart. He was lying through his teeth, of course, but other people had forced him to do that. Probably the two jokers across the table, for starters, and God knew who else in Washington had briefed Dr. Z on the phone all morning while we were rambling around the ruins and getting brochures on rinderpest and blue balls or whatever. Dr. Z in turn had briefed Dr. Chen, who was a little too perfect. I mean, of all the people we could have questioned, Zollner led us to Dr. Chen, whose work seemed to be only peripherally related to the Gordons' work. And she was introduced as a good friend of the Gordons, but wasn't; I'd never heard her name mentioned before today. And then there were the other scientists to whom we'd spoken briefly, before Zollner whisked us off—they, too, had been on the same page as Chen.

There was a lot of smoke and mirrors in this place, and I'm sure there always had been. I said to Zollner, "I don't believe this story about the Ebola vaccine. I *know* what you're hiding and what you're covering up."

Dr. Zollner stopped in mid-chew, which was a chore for him. He stared at me.

I said, "It's the Roswell aliens, isn't it, Doc? The

Gordons were about to blow the lid on the Roswell aliens."

The room was real quiet, and even some of the other scientists glanced at us. Finally, I smiled and said, "That's what this green Jell-O is—alien brains. I'm eating the evidence."

Everyone smiled and chuckled. Zollner laughed so hard he almost choked. Boy, I'm funny. Zollner and I could do a great routine; Corey and Zollner. That might be better than *The Corey Files*.

We all went back to our lunches and made chit-chat. I glanced at my companions. George Foster had looked a little panicky when I said I didn't believe the Ebola vaccine thing, but he was fine now, eating alfalfa sprouts. Ted Nash had looked less panicky and more murderous. I mean, whatever was going on here, this was not the time or place to yell bullshit or liar. Beth and I made eye contact, and as usual I couldn't tell if she was amused by me or if she was annoyed. The way to a woman's heart is through her funny bone. Women like men who make them laugh. I think.

I looked at Max, who seemed less phobic in this almost normal room. He seemed to enjoy his three-bean salad, which is not the thing that should be on a menu in an enclosed environment.

We picked at the chow, then the conversation got back to the possibly purloined vaccine. Dr. Z said, "Someone before mentioned that this vaccine would be worth its weight in gold, which made me recall something—a few of the vaccines that the Gordons were testing had a golden hue, and I recall the Gordons once referring to the vaccines as liquid gold. I thought that odd, perhaps, because we never speak in terms of money or profit here...."

"Of course not," I said. "You're a government agency. It's not your money, and you never have to show a profit."

Dr. Zollner smiled. "And the same in your business, sir."

"The very same. In any case, now we believe that the Gordons came to their senses, and, no longer satisfied with working in the interests of science for government wages, they discovered capitalism and went for the gold."

"Correct." He added, "You've spoken to their colleagues, you've seen what they did here, and now you can draw only one conclusion. Why are you still skeptical?"

"I'm not skeptical," I lied. Of course I was skeptical; I'm a New Yorker and a cop. But I didn't want to upset Dr. Zollner, Mr. Foster, or Mr. Nash, so I said, "I'm just trying to make sure the facts fit. The way I see it, either the Gordons' murders had *nothing* to do with their work here, and we're all following a false trail—or if their murders were related to their work, then most probably it had to do with the theft of a viral vaccine worth millions. Liquid gold. And it would appear that the Gordons were double-crossed, or maybe they tried to double-cross their partner, and were murdered—"
Ping.

Jeez. There it was again. What...? It was out there. I couldn't see it, but I could hear its echo, and I could sense its presence, but what *was* it?

"Mr. Corey?"

"Huh?"

Dr. Zollner's twinkling blue eyes were appraising me through his little wire frame glasses. He said, "Is there something on your mind?"

"No. Oh, yeah. If I had to remove my watch, why can you keep your glasses?"

"That's the one exception. There is an eyeglass bath on the way out. Does this lead you to yet another clever thought or theory?"

"Gel sequencing plates disguised as eyeglasses."

He shook his head. "Idiotic. I think the gel plates were smuggled out in the lunch cart."

"Right."

Dr. Z looked at the clock on the wall and said, "Shall we continue?"

We all stood and deposited our plastic and paper in a red trash can lined with a red plastic bag.

Out in the corridor, Dr. Zollner said, "We will now enter Zone Three. There is a higher risk of contagion in Zone Three, of course, so if anyone does not want to go, I will have someone escort you back to the shower room."

Everyone seemed eager to burrow farther into the bowels of hell. Well, that might be overstating the response. Presently, we moved through a red door that was marked "Zone Three." Here, Zollner explained, his researchers worked with live pathogens—parasites, viruses, bacteria, fungi, and other yuckies—and he showed us a lab where a woman sat on a stool at a sort of opening in the wall. She had a mask on and her hands were covered with latex gloves. In front of her face was a plastic shield, something like a sneeze shield at a salad bar, but she wasn't handling cole slaw. Zollner said, "There is an exhaust in the opening where the pathogens are, so the risk of anything floating into the room is small."

"Why," Max asked, "does she have a mask and we don't?"

"Good question," I agreed.

Zollner said, "She's much closer to the pathogen. If you want to get closer to take a look, I'll get you a mask."

"Pass," I said.

"Pass," everyone agreed.

Dr. Zollner moved closer to the woman and exchanged a few inaudible words with her. He turned, approached us, and said, "She's working on the virus that causes bluetongue disease." He thought a moment, then said, "Perhaps I got too close." He stuck out his tongue, which was actually bright blue, and looked down his nose. "God in heaven...or is it the blueberry pie I had for lunch?" He laughed. We laughed. In truth, the gallows humor was wearing thin, even for me, and I have a lot of tolerance for stupid jokes.

We all left the room.

This part of the building looked less populated than Zone Two, and the people I saw looked a bit less jolly.

Zollner said, "There isn't much to see here, but if I say that, then Mr. Corey will insist on seeing every nook and cranny of the place."

"Oh, Dr. Zollner," I said, "have I given you cause to say such things about me?"

"Yes."

"Well, then, let's see every nook and cranny of the place."

I heard some groans, but Dr. Z said, "Very well, follow me."

We spent the next half hour or so looking at nooks and crannies, and in truth, most of Zone Three looked the same—room after room of men and women peering through microscopes, making slides out of slime, slides from the blood and tissue of living and dead animals, and so on. Some of these people actually had their lunches with them and were eating while they played around with disgusting stuff.

We spoke to another dozen or so men and women who knew or worked with Tom and Judy, and while we were getting a more clear and more fully formed picture of their work, we didn't learn much new about their heads.

Still, I thought this was a useful exercise—I like to fix in my mind the milieu of the deceased, and later I usually think of something bright to follow up on. Sometimes, just casual chats with friends, family, and colleagues will turn up a word or two that can lead to the solution. Sometimes.

Zollner explained, "Most of these viruses and bacteria cannot cross the species barrier. You could drink a test-tube-ful of foot-and-mouth disease virus and not get much more than an upset stomach, though a cow would die from a quantity that would fit on the head of a pin."

"Why?"

"Why? Because the genetic makeup of a virus has to be able to ... well, mesh with a cell to infect it. Human cells do not mesh with FMD virus."

Beth said, "But there's some evidence that Mad Cow Disease has infected humans."

"Anything is possible. That's why we're careful." He added, "Bugs bite."

Actually, bugs suck.

We went into another brightly lit room, and Zollner said, "In here we work with parasites. The worst is the screwworm. We've found a clever way to control this disease. We have discovered that the male and female screwworms only mate once in their lives, so we sterilize millions of the males with gamma rays and drop them by plane over Central America. When the male mates with the female, no offspring result. Clever, yes?"

I had to ask, "But is the female screwworm fulfilled?"

"She must be," Zollner replied. "She never mates again."

Beth offered, "There's another way to look at that."

Zollner laughed. "Yes. There is a female point of view there."

The persiflage finished, we all took turns looking at screwworm larvae under a microscope. Disgusting.

And on we went, into laboratories, and into rooms where horrible microbes and parasites were grown and stored, and into all sorts of weird places whose purposes and functions I only dimly understood.

I kept in mind that my friends, Tom and Judy, walked these corridors and entered many of these rooms and labs every day. And yet, they seemed not to be depressed or anxious about any of it. At least not so I noticed.

Finally, Dr. Z said, "That's all of Zone Three. Now, once again I must ask you if you want to go farther. Zone Four is the most contaminated of all the zones, more so, actually, than Zone Five. In Five, you are always in a biohazard suit and respirator, and everything is decontaminated often. In fact, there is a separate shower for Zone Five. But Zone Four is where you will see the animal pens, the sick and dying animals, and also the incinerator and the necropsy rooms, if you wish. So, though we are clinically dealing here with animal diseases only, there may be other pathogens in the ambient environment." He added, "That means germs in the air."

Max asked, "Do we get face masks?"

"If you wish." He looked around and said, "All right. Follow me."

We approached yet another red door, this one marked "Zone Four," with the biohazard symbol. Some clown had stuck a particularly gruesome skull-and-crossbones decal on the door—the skull was cracked and a snake slithered out of the crack and threaded itself through one of the skull's eye sockets. Also, a spider was crawling out of the grinning mouth. In fact, Dr. Zollner said, "I believe Tom is responsible for that horrible thing. The Gordons added some levity to this place."

"Right." Until they died.

Our host opened the red door, and we found ourselves in a sort of anteroom. There was a metal cart in the small room on which was a box of latex gloves and a box of paper face masks. Dr. Z said, "For anyone who wishes."

This was sort of like saying parachutes or life vests are optional. I mean, either you need the damn things or you don't.

Zollner clarified his offer. "It's not mandatory. We're going to shower out after this anyway. I personally don't bother with gloves or masks. Too cumbersome. But you may feel better with them."

I had the distinct feeling he was daring us, as in, "I always take the shortcut through the cemetery, but if you'd rather walk the long way, that's okay with me. Wimp."

I said, "This place can't be any dirtier than my bathroom."

Dr. Zollner smiled. "Most probably a lot cleaner."

Apparently no one wanted to look like a pussy by practicing good prophylaxis, which is how little bugs get us in the end, so off we went, through the second red door, and found ourselves in the same kind of gray concrete corridor as in the rest of the biocontainment zones. The difference here was that the doors were wider, and each one had a big latching handle on it. Zollner explained, "These are airlock doors."

I noticed, too, that every door had a small window, and a clipboard hung from the wall beside each one.

Dr. Zollner took us to the closest door and said, "All these rooms are pens and all have viewing windows. What you see may upset you or make your lunch unsettled. So no one has to look." He examined the clipboard hanging on the concrete wall and said, "African equine fever...." He peeked through the viewing window and said, "This guy's not bad. Just a bit listless. Take a look."

We all took turns looking at the beautiful black horse in the enclosed, prison-like room. True enough, the horse looked okay, except now and then you could see him heave as if he were having trouble breathing.

Zollner explained, "All the animals in here have been challenged with a virus or bacteria."

"Challenged?" I asked. "Is that like infected?"

"Yes, we say challenged."

"Then what happens? They become less than well, then go into an involuntary nonbreathing mode?"

"Correct. They get sick and die. Sometimes, however, we sacrifice them. That means we kill them before the disease has run its full course." He added, "I think everyone who works here likes animals, which is why they are involved with this type of work. No one in this facility wants to see these creatures suffer, but if you ever saw millions of cattle infected with foot-and-mouth disease, you'd see why the sacrifice of a few dozen here is necessary." He put the chart back and said, "Come."

There was a great warren of these unhappy rooms, and we went from pen to pen where a variety of animals were in various stages of dying. At one pen, the cow saw us and walked unsteadily up to the door and looked at us looking at her. Dr. Zollner said, "This one is in bad shape. Advanced FMD—see how she walked? And look at those blisters on her mouth. She can't even eat at this stage because of the pain. The saliva looks like rope, it's so thick. This is a dreadful disease and an old enemy. There are accounts of this in ancient writings. As I said, this disease is highly contagious. An outbreak in France once spread to England on the wind across the Channel. It is one of the smallest viruses yet discovered, and it seems to be able to live dormant for long periods of time." He stayed silent a moment, then said, "Someday, something like this may mutate and begin infecting human hosts...."

By now, I think, we were all mentally and physically challenged, as Dr. Z might say. In other words, our minds were numb and our asses were dragging. Worse, though, our spirits were down, and if I had a soul, it would be troubled.

Finally I said to Dr. Zollner, "I don't know about anyone else, but I've seen enough."

Everyone seconded that.

I, however, had a last, stupid thought, and I said, "Can we see what the Gordons were working with? I mean, the simian Ebola?"

He shook his head. "That is Zone Five." He thought a minute, then said, "But I can show you a pig with African swine fever, which, like Ebola, is a hemorrhagic fever. Very similar."

He led the way to another corridor and stopped at a door numbered "1130." He examined the chart on the wall and said, "This one's in the final stages...the bleeding-out stage...he'll be gone by morning...if he goes before then, he'll be put in a cooler, then dissected first thing tomorrow, then incinerated. This is a very frightening disease that has nearly wiped out the swine population in parts of Africa. There is no known vaccine or treatment. As I say, it's a close cousin to Ebola...." He looked at me and motioned toward the viewing window. "Look."

I stepped up to the window and looked inside. The floor of the room was painted red, which surprised me at first, but then I understood. Near the center of the room was a huge pig, lying on the floor, almost motionless, and I could see blood around its mouth, snout, and even its ears. Despite the red floor, I noticed a glistening pool of blood near its hindquarters.

Behind me, Zollner was saying, "You see it bleeding out, yes? Hemorrhagic fever is terrible. The organs turn to mush.... You can see now why Ebola is so feared."

I noticed a big metal drain in the center of the floor, and the blood was running into the drain, and

I couldn't help it, but I was back in the gutter on West 102nd Street, and my life was draining into the damned sewer and I could see it, and I knew how the pig felt watching his own blood leaking out of him, and the rushing sound in the ears, and the pounding in the chest as the blood pressure dropped and the heart tried to compensate by beating faster and faster until you knew it was going to stop.

I heard Zollner's voice from far away. "Mr. Corey? Mr. Corey? You can step away now. Let the others take a look. Mr. Corey?"

CHAPTER THIRTEEN

e don't want any viruses or bacteria hitchhiking a ride back to the mainland," Dr. Zollner said, unnecessarily.

We stripped, put the lab whites and slippers in a hamper and the paper underwear in a trash can.

I was not totally focused, just sort of doing what everyone else was doing.

We all followed Dr. Z to the shower room—Max, Nash, Foster, and I—and we stood under the shower-heads washing our hair with a special shampoo, scrubbing our nails with a brush and disinfectant. We all gargled with some sort of horrid mouthwash, rinsed and spit. I kept soaping up and rinsing off until finally Zollner said, "That's enough. You'll catch pneumonia and die." He laughed.

I dried off with the provided towel, threw it in a hamper, then walked, naked, back to my locker, germ-free and squeaky clean, at least on the outside.

Other than the men I'd entered with, there was no one around. Even the attendant wasn't visible. I could see how a person could conceivably smuggle large items out of the lab and into the locker room. But I don't think that's what happened, so it didn't matter if it were possible or not.

Zollner had disappeared and come back with locker keys, which he distributed.

I opened my locker and began getting dressed. Some very thoughtful fellow, quite possibly Mr. Stevens, had been kind enough to launder my shorts and in doing so had inadvertently washed the red clay right out of my pocket. Oh, well. Good try, Corey.

I examined my .38 and it looked okay, but you never know when some joker is going to file the firing pin, clog the barrel, or take the powder out of your rounds. I made a mental note to check the piece and the ammo more closely at home.

Max, whose locker was beside mine, said softly, "That was an experience."

I nodded and asked, "Now do you feel better about living downwind from Plum Island?"

"Oh, yeah, I feel fucking terrific."

"I was impressed with the biocontainment," I said. "State-of-the art."

"Yeah. But I'm thinking about a hurricane or a terrorist attack."

"Mr. Stevens will protect Plum Island from a terrorist attack."

"Yeah. How about a hurricane?"

"Same drill as a nuclear attack—bend over, put your head between your legs, and kiss your ass goodbye."

"Right." He looked at me and asked, "Hey, are you okay?"

"Sure."

"You sort of got spacey back there."

"Tired. My lung is wheezing."

"I feel responsible about dragging you into this."

"I can't imagine why."

He smiled and said, "If you nail Ms. Tightass, you owe me one."

"I haven't the slightest idea what you're talking about." I slipped into my docksiders and stood. I said to Max, "You must be having an allergic reaction to the soap. Your face is all blotchy."

"*What?*" He put his hands to his cheeks and made for the closest mirror. He kept looking at himself, leaning closer over the washbasin. "What the hell are you talking about? My skin is fine."

"Must be the light in here."

"Cut the crap, Corey. This isn't a funny subject."

"Right." I went to the door of the locker room where Dr. Z was waiting. I said to him, "Despite my bad manners, I'm very impressed with your operation, and I thank you for your time."

"I enjoyed your company, Mr. Corey. I regret having met you under these sad circumstances."

George Foster joined us and said to Dr. Zollner, "I intend to make a favorable report regarding your biocontainment procedures."

"Thank you."

"But I think that perimeter security could be better, and I'll recommend that a study be conducted."

Zollner nodded.

Foster went on, "Fortunately, it would appear that the Gordons did not steal any dangerous substance, and if they stole anything, it was an experimental vaccine."

Dr. Zollner again nodded.

Foster concluded, "I would recommend a permanent detachment of Marines at Fort Terry."

I was anxious to get out of the orange locker room and into the sunlight, so I moved toward the door and everyone followed.

Out in the big, gleaming lobby, Dr. Z looked for Beth, still not getting it.

Anyway, we all walked to the reception counter where we exchanged our white plastic chain passes for the original blue clip-on ones. I said to Zollner, "Is there a gift shop where we can buy souvenirs and T-shirts?"

Zollner laughed. "No, but I'll suggest it to Washington. In the meantime, you should pray that you haven't picked up a souvenir of another kind."

"Thanks, Doc."

Dr. Zollner looked at his watch and said, "You can catch the 3:45 ferry if you wish, or you can come back to my office if you have anything further to discuss."

I'd wanted to go back to the artillery batteries and explore the underground passages, but I thought if I suggested that, I'd have a mutiny on my hands. Also, to be honest, I was not up to another trek around the island.

I said to Dr. Zollner, "We await the boss. We don't make major decisions without her."

Dr. Z nodded and smiled.

It appeared to me that Zollner didn't seem particularly worried about any of this—about people questioning his security or his biocontainment procedures, or even about the possibility that his two star scientists stole something good and valuable, or something bad and deadly. It occurred to me that Zollner was not worried because even if he'd somehow screwed up or if he could be held accountable for someone else's screwup, he was already off the hook—he'd already cut his deal with the government; he was cooperating in a cover-up in exchange for a free pass on this problem. There was also a possibility, however remote, that Dr. Z killed the Gordons or knew who killed them. As far as I was concerned, everyone who was close to the Gordons was a suspect.

Beth came out of the ladies' locker room and joined us at the reception counter. I noticed that she hadn't done a complete paint-by-numbers job, and her cheeks glowed with that freshly scrubbed look.

She exchanged passes, and Dr. Zollner related his offers and our options.

Beth looked at us and said, "I've seen enough, unless you want to do the underground bunkers or something else."

We all shook our heads.

She said to Dr. Zollner, "We reserve the right to revisit the island anytime until this case is closed."

"As far as I'm concerned, you're welcome anytime." He added, "But it's not my decision."

A horn sounded outside, and I looked through the glass doors. A white bus was out front, and a few employees were boarding.

Dr. Z said, "Forgive me if I don't accompany you to the ferry." He shook hands with all of us and bid us fond adieu, with not a hint of good riddance. A real gentleman.

We went out into the sunlight, and I breathed gallons of fresh air before boarding the bus. The driver was another security guy, and I guess he was our escort.

There were only six employees on the bus, and I didn't recognize any of them from our tour.

The bus made the five-minute trip to the dock and stopped.

We all got out and walked to the blue and white ferry, *The Plum Runner*. We went into the big cabin, the horn sounded, and we cast off.

The five of us remained standing, making small talk. One of the boat's crew, a weather-beaten gent, came around and collected our passes. He said, "So, did you like the island of Dr. Moreau?"

This literary reference took me aback coming from an old salt. We chatted with the guy for a minute and learned his name was Pete. He also told us that he felt pretty bad about the Gordons.

He excused himself and went up the stairs that led to the top deck and the bridge. I followed, and before he opened the door to the bridge, I said, "Got a minute?"

"Sure."

"Did you know the Gordons?"

"Sure did. We rode this boat together for two years on and off."

"I was told they used their own boat to commute."

"Sometimes. Nice new Formula 303. Twin Mercs. Fast as hell."

Time to be blunt. I asked, "Any chance they were running drugs with that thing?"

"*Drugs*? Hell, no. They couldn't find an island much less a drug ship."

"How do you know?"

"I talked boats with them once in a while. They couldn't navigate worth a damn. They didn't even have a navigation system on board. You know?"

"Right." Now that he mentioned it, I never saw a satellite nav device on board. But if you were a drug runner, you *needed* a satellite navigation device. I said to Pete, "Maybe they were pulling a fast one on you. Maybe they were the best navigators since Magellan."

"Who?"

"Why do you think they couldn't navigate?"

"I tried to get them into the Power Squadron course. You know? And they weren't interested."

Pete was a little dense. I tried again. "Maybe they were *making believe* they couldn't navigate. You know, so no one would think they were running drugs."

"Yeah?" He scratched his head. "Maybe. Don't think so. They didn't like the open water. If they were in their boat and they saw the ferry, they'd get on the leeward side and stay with us all the way. They never liked to lose sight of land. Does that sound like a drug runner to you?"

"I guess not. So, Pete, who killed them and why?"

He did a theatrical double take, then said, "Damned if I know."

"You *know* you thought about it, Pete. Who and why? What did you first think? What did people say?"

He hemmed and hawed, then replied, "Well, I guess I thought they stole something from the lab. You know? Like something to wipe out the world. And they were going to sell it to foreigners or something. You know? And the deal went bad, and they got knocked off."

"And you don't think that anymore?"

"Well, I heard something different."

"Like what?"

"Like what they stole was a vaccine worth millions." He looked at me. "Is that right?"

"That's it."

"They wanted to get rich quick and instead they got dead quick."

"The wages of sin is death."

"Yup." Pete excused himself and went into the wheelhouse.

It was interesting, I thought, that Pete, and probably everyone else, including yours truly, had the same initial reaction to the Gordons' deaths. Then, on second thought, I came up with drug running. Now we're doing vaccine. But sometimes your first reaction, your gut reaction, is the right one. In any event, what all three theories had in common was *money*.

I stood on the top deck and watched the green shore of Plum Island recede into the distance. The sun was still high in the west, and it felt good on my skin. I was enjoying the ride, the smell of the sea, even the movement of the boat. I had the disturbing thought that I was going native. Next I'd be shucking clams, whatever that means.

Beth Penrose came up on deck and watched the ship's wake awhile, then turned and leaned back against the rail, her face into the sun.

I said to her, "You predicted what Zollner was going to say."

She nodded. "It makes sense, and it fits the facts, and it resolves the problem we had with believing the Gordons were capable of stealing deadly organisms, and also the problem we had believing they were running drugs." She added, "The Gordons stole something good. Something profitable. Money. Money is the motivator. Saint-seducing gold, as Shakespeare said."

"I think I've had enough Shakespeare for this year." I mulled a moment and said, "I don't know why I never thought of that...I mean, we were so hung up on plague and stuff, we never thought of the antidotes— vaccines, antibiotics, and antivirals, and all of that. *That* is what the scientists are studying on Plum, and *that* is what the Gordons stole. Gee whiz, I'm getting dumb."

She smiled, then said, "Well, to tell you the truth, I started thinking about vaccines and all of that last night—then when Stevens mentioned foot-and-mouth vaccine, I knew where that was going."

"Right. Now everyone can rest easy. No panic, no hysteria, no national emergency. Jeez, I thought we'd all be dead by Halloween."

We looked at each other, and Beth said, "It's all a lie, of course."

"Yeah. But it's a really good lie. This lie takes the heat off Plum Island and off the Feds in general. Meanwhile, the FBI and CIA can work the case quietly without us and without media attention. You, Max, and I just got dealt out of the Plum Island part of this case."

"Right. Though we still have a double homicide to solve. On our own."

"That's right," I said to Beth, "and I think I'm going to miss Ted Nash."

She smiled, then looked at me with a serious expression and said, "I wouldn't cross a man like that."

"Screw him."

"So, you're a tough guy."

"Hey, I took ten slugs and finished my coffee before I walked to the hospital."

"It was three, you spent a month in the hospital, and you're still not completely recovered."

"You've been talking to Max. How sweet."

She didn't respond. She rarely took the bait, I noticed. I'd have to remember that.

She asked me, "What did you think of Stevens?"

"The right man for the right job."

She asked, "Does he lie?"

"Of course."

"How about Zollner?"

"I liked him."

"Does he lie?"

"Not naturally, the way Stevens does. He's been prompted though. Rehearsed."

She nodded, then asked, "Is he running scared?"

"No."

"Why not?"

"Nothing to be frightened about. It's all under control. Stevens and Zollner have made their deals with the government."

She nodded in understanding. "That was my impression. The cover-up was conceived, written, and directed late last night, early this morning. The lights burned all night in Washington and on Plum Island. This morning, we saw the play."

"You got it." I added, "I told you not to trust those two jokers."

She nodded again, then said, "I've never been in a situation where I couldn't trust the people I was working with."

"I have. It's a real challenge—watch your mouth, cover your ass, grow eyes in the back of your head, smell for rats, and listen for what's not said."

She glanced at me and asked, "Were you feeling okay back there?"

"I'm feeling fine."

"You should get some rest."

I ignored this and said to her, "Nash has a teeny weenie."

"Thank you for sharing that with me."

"Well, I wanted you to know because I saw that you were interested in him, and I didn't want you wasting your time with a guy who has a third pinky between his legs."

"That's very thoughtful of you. Why don't you mind your own business?"

"Okay."

The sea got a little choppier in the middle of the Gut, and I steadied myself against the rail. I looked at Beth, who had her eyes closed now, and with her head tilted back was catching a few UVs. I may have mentioned that she had one of those cupid-like faces, innocent and sensuous at the same time. Early thirties, as I said, and once married, as she said. I wondered if her ex was a cop or if he hated her being a cop, or what the problem was. People her age had some baggage; people my age have whole warehousesful of steamer trunks.

Her eyes still closed, Beth asked me, "What would you do if you were handed a disability retirement?"

"I don't know." I considered, then replied, "Max would hire me."

"I don't think you're supposed to do police work if you get a three-quarter. Do you?"

"I guess not. I don't know what I'd do. Manhattan is expensive. That's where I live. I think I'd have to move. Maybe out here."

"What would you do out here?"

"Grow wine."

"Grapes. You grow grapes and make wine."

"Right."

She opened her blue-green eyes and looked at me. Our eyes met, searched, penetrated, and all that. Then she closed her eyes again.

Neither of us spoke for a minute, then she opened her eyes and inquired, "Why don't we believe the Gordons stole a miracle vaccine in order to make a fortune?"

"Because that still leaves too many questions unanswered. First, what's with the power boat? You don't need a one-hundred-thousand-dollar boat to make a one-time score of golden vaccine. Right?"

"Maybe they knew they were going to steal the vaccine, so they knew they could afford the boat eventually, and they had some fun. When did they buy the boat?"

"April last year," I replied. "Right before the boating season. Ten thou down, and they're financing the rest."

"Okay, why else don't we believe the Plum Island version of events?"

"Well, why would the customers of this vaccine have to murder two people? Especially if the person or persons on the Gordons' deck couldn't be sure of what the Gordons were delivering in the ice chest."

She said, "As for the murders, we both know people are killed for small reasons. As for the goods in the chest...what if the Gordons had accomplices on Plum who loaded the vaccine on their boat? The person on Plum calls the person or persons who are waiting for the Gordons and says the goods are on the way. Think accomplice on Plum Island. Think Mr. Stevens. Or Dr.

Zollner. Or Dr. Chen. Or Kenneth Gibbs. Or anyone on the island."

"Okay...we'll put that in the clue bag."

"What else?" she asked.

"Well, I'm no geopolitical expert, but Ebola is pretty rare, and the chances of the World Health Organization or the affected African governments ordering this stuff in quantity seem a little remote. People are dying in Africa of all sorts of preventable diseases, like malaria and tuberculosis, and no one is buying two hundred million doses of anything for them."

"Right...but we don't understand the ins and outs of the trade in legitimate therapeutic drugs, whether they're stolen, black market, copied, or otherwise."

"Okay, but you agree that the Gordons stealing this vaccine sounds implausible?"

She replied, "No. It's *plausible*. I just feel it's a lie."

"Right. It's a plausible lie."

"A terrific lie."

"A terrific lie," I agreed. "It changes the case."

"It sure does. What else?"

"Well," I said, "there's the chart book. Not much there, but I'd like to know what 44106818 means."

"Okay. And how about the archaeology on Plum?" she asked.

"Right. That was a complete surprise to me and raises all sorts of questions," I said.

"Why did Paul Stevens give us that?"

"Because it's public knowledge, and we'd hear about it soon enough."

"Right. What's the meaning of the archaeological stuff?"

"I have no idea." I added, "But it has nothing to

do with the science of archaeology. It was a cover for something, a reason to go to remote parts of the island."

She said, "Or, it may be meaningless."

"It may be. And then we have the red clay that I saw in the Gordons' running shoes and which I saw on Plum. The route from the main lab, into the parking lot, onto the bus, then to the dock has no place where you could pick up soft red clay in your treads."

She nodded, then said, "I assume you took some of the clay when you went to tinkle?"

I smiled. "As a matter of fact, I did. But when I got dressed in the locker room, someone had been kind enough to launder my shorts."

She cracked, "I wish they'd done the same for me."

We both smiled.

She said, "I'll request soil samples. They can decontaminate them if they get hung up on the 'Never Leave' policy." She added, "You tend to take the direct approach, I see, such as filching the financial printouts, then stealing government soil, and who knows what else you've done. You should learn to follow protocols and procedures, Detective Corey. Especially since this is not your jurisdiction or your case. You're going to get into trouble, and I'm not going to stick my neck out for you."

"Sure you are. And by the way, I'm usually pretty good with the rules of evidence, suspects' rights, command structure, and all that crap when it's just regular homicides. This could have been—could still be—the plague-to-end-all-plagues. So I took a few shortcuts. Time is of the essence, the doctrine of hot pursuit, and all that. If I save the planet, I'm a hero."

"You'll play by the rules, and you'll follow procedures. Do not do anything to compromise an indictment or conviction in this case."

"Hey, we don't even have half a suspect and you're already in court."

"That's how I work a case."

I said, "I think I've done as much as I can here. I'm resigning my position as town homicide consultant."

"Stop sulking." She hesitated, then said, "I'd like you to stay. I may actually be able to learn something from you."

Clearly we liked each other, despite some run-ins and misunderstandings, some differences of opinion, dissimilar temperaments, differences of age and background, and probably blood type, and tastes in music, and God knew what else. Actually, if I thought about it, we had not one thing in common except the job, and we couldn't even agree on that. And yet, I was in love. Well, okay, lust. But significant lust. I was deeply committed to this lust.

We looked at each other again, and again we smiled. This was silly. I mean, really dopey. I felt like an idiot. She was so exquisitely beautiful...I liked her voice, her smile, her coppery hair in the sunlight, her movements, her hands...and she smelled soapy again, from the shower. I love that smell. I associate soap with sex. That's a long story.

Finally, she asked, "What useless land?"

"Huh...? Oh, right. The Gordons." I explained about the checkbook entry and my conversation with Margaret Wiley. I concluded, "I'm not a country boy, but I don't think people without bucks spend twenty-five Gs just to have their own trees to hug."

"It's odd," she agreed. "But land is an emotional thing." She added, "My father was one of the last farmers in western Suffolk County, surrounded by subdivisions of split-levels. He loved his land, but the countryside had changed—the woods and streams and the other farms were gone, so he sold. But he was not the same man afterward, even with a million dollars in the bank."

She stayed silent a moment, then said, "I suppose we should go speak to Margaret Wiley, take a look at that land, even though I don't think it's significant to this case."

"I think the fact that the Gordons never told me they owned a piece of land is significant. Same with the archaeological digs. Things that don't make sense need explaining."

"Thank you, Detective Corey."

I replied, "I don't mean to lecture, but I give a class at John Jay, and sometimes a line or two slips out like that."

She regarded me a moment, then said, "I never know if you're pulling my leg or not."

Actually, I wanted to pull her leg—both legs, but I let that thought go and said, "I really do teach at John Jay." This is John Jay College of Criminal Justice in Manhattan, one of the best such schools in the country, and I suppose she had a credibility problem with John Corey as professor.

She asked, "What do you teach?"

"Well, certainly not rules of evidence, suspects' rights, or any of that."

"Certainly not."

"I teach practical homicide investigation. Scene of

the crime, and that kind of thing. Friday nights. It's the ultimate murder mystery evening. You're welcome to sit in if I ever get back into it. Maybe January."

"I might do that."

"Come early. The class is always overflowing. I'm very entertaining."

"I'm sure of it."

And I was sure Ms. Beth Penrose was finally considering it. *It.*

The ferry was slowing as it approached the dock. I asked Beth, "Have you spoken to the Murphys yet?"

"No. Max did. They're on my list for today."

"Good. I'll join you."

"I thought you were quitting."

"Tomorrow."

She took her notebook out of her bag and began perusing the pages. She said, "I need from you the computer printouts that you borrowed."

"They're at my place."

"Okay. . . ." She scanned a page and continued, "I'll call fingerprints and forensic. Plus I've asked the DA for a subpoena for the Gordons' phone records for the last two years."

"Right. Also, get a list of licensed pistol holders in Southold Township."

She asked, "Do you think the murder weapon might be a locally registered weapon?"

"Maybe."

"Why do you think that?"

"Hunch. Meanwhile, keep dredging and diving for the bullets."

"We are, but that's a real long shot. Pardon the pun."

"I have a lot of tolerance for bad puns."

"Let me guess why."

"Right. Also, if you round up the hardware on Plum Island, make sure the county does the ballistics tests, not the FBI."

"I know."

She detailed a bunch of other odds and ends that needed doing, and I could see she had a neat and orderly mind. She was, also, intuitive and inquisitive. She only lacked experience, I thought, to make a really good detective. To make a great detective she had to learn to loosen up, to get people to talk freely and too much. She came on a little grim and strong, and most witnesses, not to mention colleagues, would get their defenses up. "Loosen up."

She looked up from her notebook. "Excuse me?"

"Loosen up."

She stayed quiet a moment, then said, "I'm a little anxious about this case."

"Everyone is. Loosen up."

"I'll try." She smiled. "I can do impersonations. I can do you. Want to see?"

"No."

She got all slouchy and wiggly, shoved one hand in her pocket, and scratched her chest with the other, then spoke in a bass voice with a New York City accent, "Hey, like, what the hell's goin' on with this case? Ya know? What's with this bozo, Nash? Huh? The guy don't know a cow pie from a pizza pie. Guy's got the IQ of a box of rocks. Ya know? The guy's—"

"Thank you," I said coolly.

She actually laughed, then said to me, "Loosen up."

"I do not speak with such a pronounced New York City accent."

"Well, it sounds like it out here."

I was a little annoyed, but a little amused, too. I guess.

Neither of us spoke for a few minutes, then I commented, "I'm thinking that this case doesn't have such a high profile anymore, and that's good."

She nodded.

I continued, "Fewer people to deal with—no Feds, no pols, no media, and for you, they won't be assigning more help than you need." I added, "When you solve this, you'll be a hero."

She looked at me a long second, then asked, "You think we'll solve it?"

"Of course."

"And if we don't?"

"No skin off my nose. You, on the other hand, will have a career problem."

"Thanks."

The ferry hit the rubber bumpers, and the crewmen threw down two lines.

Beth, sort of thinking out loud, said, "So...in addition to the possibility of bad bugs and bad drugs, now we have the possibility of good drugs, and don't forget that Max told the media it was a double homicide of two homeowners who came on the scene of an ordinary burglary. And you know what? It could still be that."

I looked at her and said, "Here's another one for you—and for you only. Consider that Tom and Judy Gordon knew something they weren't supposed to know or saw something on Plum Island that they weren't supposed to see. Consider that someone like Mr. Stevens or your friend Mr. Nash whacked them. Consider that."

She stayed silent a long time, then said, "Sounds like a bad movie-of-the-week." She added, "But I'll think about it."

Max called from the lower deck, "All ashore."

Beth moved toward the stairway, then asked me, "What's your cell phone number?"

I gave it to her, and she said, "We'll split up in the parking lot, and I'll call you in about twenty minutes."

We joined Max, Nash, and Foster on the stern deck, and we all walked off together with the six Plum Island employees. There were only three people on the dock for the return to Plum, and I was struck again by how isolated the island was.

In the parking field, Chief Sylvester Maxwell of the Southold PD said to everyone, "I'm satisfied that the most troubling part of this case has been cleared up. I have other duties, so I'm leaving Detective Penrose to work the homicide angle."

Mr. Ted Nash of the Central Intelligence Agency said, "I'm satisfied, too, and since there doesn't seem to be a national security breach or an international aspect to this situation, I'm going to recommend that my agency and I be relieved of this case."

Mr. George Foster of the Federal Bureau of Investigation said, "It appears that government property has been stolen, so the FBI will remain involved with the case. I'm heading back to Washington today to report. The local FBI office will take charge of this case, and someone will be contacting you, Chief." He looked at Beth. "Or you or your superior."

Detective Elizabeth Penrose of the Suffolk County PD replied, "Well, it looks like I'm it. I thank you all for your help."

We were ready to part, but Ted and I had to get in a few last friendly licks. He went first, and said to me, "I truly hope we meet again, Detective Corey."

"Oh, I'm sure we will, Ted. Next time try to impersonate a woman. That should be easier for you than an agriculture guy."

He stared at me and said, "By the way, I forgot to mention that I know your boss, Detective Lieutenant Wolfe."

"Small world. He's an asshole, too. But put in a good word for me, will you, pal?"

"I'll be sure to report that you send him your regards and that you're looking very fit to return to duty."

Foster interrupted as usual and said, "It's been an interesting and intense twenty-four hours. I think this task force can be proud of its accomplishments, and I have no doubt the local police will bring this case to a satisfactory conclusion."

I said, "In summation, long day, good job, good luck."

Everyone was shaking hands now, even me, though I didn't know if I was out of a job, or if I ever had a job to be out of. Anyway, brief goodbyes were said, and no one got smarmy or promised to write or meet again, and no one kissed and hugged or anything. Within a minute, Max, Beth, Nash, and Foster were in their own cars and were gone, and I was standing alone in the parking field with my finger up my nose. *Weird*. Last night everyone thought the Apocalypse had arrived, the Pale Horseman had begun his terrible ride. And now, no one gave a rat's ass about two dead vaccine thieves in the morgue. Right?

I began walking to my car. Who was in on the

cover-up? Obviously, Ted Nash and his people, and George Foster, since he'd also been on the earlier ferry with Nash and the four guys in suits who'd disappeared in the black Caprice. Probably Paul Stevens was in on it, too, and so was Dr. Zollner.

I was sure that certain agencies of the federal government had put together a cover, and it was good enough for the media, the nation, and the world. But it wasn't good enough for Detectives John Corey and Elizabeth Penrose. No sir, it was not. I wondered if Max was buying it. People generally want to believe good news, and Max was so paranoid about germs that he'd *really* love to believe Plum Island was spewing antibiotics and vaccine into the air. I should talk to Max later. Maybe.

The other question was this—if they were covering up, *what* were they covering up? It occurred to me that maybe they didn't know what they were covering up. They needed to change this case from high-profile horror to common thievery, and they had to do it quickly to get the heat off. Now they could start trying to figure out what the hell this was all about. Maybe Nash and Foster were as clueless as I was about why the Gordons were murdered.

Theory Two—they knew why and who murdered the Gordons, and maybe it was Nash and Foster themselves. I really had no idea who these clowns were.

With all this conspiracy stuff in mind, I remembered what Beth said regarding Nash... *I wouldn't cross a man like that.*

I stopped about twenty yards from my Jeep and looked around.

There were about a hundred Plum Island employee

vehicles in the ferry parking field now, but there weren't any people around, so I positioned myself behind a van and held out my keypad. Another feature that I got for my forty thousand bucks was a remote ignition. I pressed the ignition button in a sequence, two longs and one short, and waited for the explosion. There was no explosion. The vehicle started. I let it run for a minute, then walked toward it, and got inside.

I wondered if I was being a little overly cautious. I guess if my vehicle had exploded, the answer is no. Better safe than sorry, I say. Until I knew who the killer or killers were, paranoia was my middle name.

CHAPTER FOURTEEN

I drove west on Main Road, my engine humming, my radio tuned to easy listening, rural scenes sliding by, blue skies, gulls, the whole nine yards, the best that the third planet from the sun has to offer.

The car phone rang, and I answered, "Dial-a-stud. May I help you?"

"Meet me at the Murphy residence," said Detective Penrose.

"I don't think so," I replied.

"Why not?"

"I think I'm fired. If not, I quit."

"You were hired by the week. You have to finish out the week."

"Says who?"

"Murphy house." She hung up.

I hate bossy women. Nevertheless, I drove the twenty minutes to the Murphy house and spotted Detective Penrose parked out front, sitting in her unmarked black Ford LTD.

I parked my Jeep a few houses away, killed the engine, and got out. To the right of the Murphys' house, the crime scene was still taped off, and there was one Southold PD out front. The county mobile head-quarters van was still on the lawn.

Beth was on the cell phone as I approached, and she hung up and got out. She said, "I just finished a long verbal to my boss. Everyone seems happy with the Ebola vaccine angle."

I asked, "Did you indicate to your boss that you think it's a crock of crap?"

"No . . . let's leave that thought alone. Let's solve a double murder."

We went to the Murphys' front door and rang the bell. The house was a 1960s ranch, original condition, as they say, pretty ugly, but decently maintained.

A woman of about seventy answered the door, and we introduced ourselves. She stared at my shorts, probably remarking to herself about how freshly laun-dered they looked and smelled. She smiled at Beth and showed us inside. She disappeared toward the back of the house and called out, "Ed! Police again!"

She came back into the living room and indicated a love seat. I found myself cheek to cheek with Beth.

Mrs. Agnes Murphy asked us, "Would you like some Kool-Aid?"

I replied, "No, thank you, ma'am. I'm on duty."

Beth, too, declined.

Mrs. Murphy sat in a rocker facing us.

I looked around. The decorating style was what I call classical old fart: dark, musty, overstuffed furni-ture, six hundred ugly knickknacks, incredibly tacky souvenirs, photos of grandchildren, and so on. The walls were chalky green, like an after-dinner mint, and the carpet was . . . well, who cares?

Mrs. Murphy was dressed in a pink pants suit made of a synthetic material that would last three thousand years.

I asked Mrs. Murphy, "Did you like the Gordons?"

The question threw her, as it was supposed to. She got her thoughts together and replied, "We didn't know them very well, but they were mostly quiet."

"Why do you think they were murdered?"

"Well...how would I know?" We looked at one another awhile, then she said, "Maybe it had something to do with their work."

Edgar Murphy entered, wiping his hands on a rag. He had been in the garage, he explained, working on his power mower. He looked closer to eighty, and if I were Beth Penrose preparing a future trial in my mind, I wouldn't give odds that Edgar would make it to the stand.

He wore green overalls and work shoes and looked as pale as his wife. Anyway, I stood and shook hands with Mr. Murphy. I sat again, and Edgar sat in a recliner which he actually reclined so he was looking up at the ceiling. I tried to make eye contact with him, but it was hard to do given our relative positions. Now I remember why I don't visit my parents.

Edgar Murphy said, "I already spoke to Chief Maxwell."

Beth replied, "Yes, sir. I'm with homicide."

"Who's *he* with?"

I replied, "I'm with Chief Maxwell."

"No, you ain't. I know every cop on the force."

This was about to become a triple homicide. I looked up at the ceiling to about where his eyes were focused, and spoke, sort of like beaming up to a satellite and bouncing the signal down to the receiver. I said, "I'm a consultant. Look, Mr. Murphy—"

Mrs. Murphy interrupted, "Ed, can't you sit up? That's very rude to sit like that."

"The hell it is. It's my house. He can hear me okay. You can hear me okay, can't you?"

"Yes, sir."

Beth did some prelim, but related some of the details and times wrong, on purpose, and Mr. Murphy corrected her, demonstrating that he had good short-term memory. Mrs. Murphy also did some fine-tuning of the events of the prior day. They seemed like reliable witnesses, and I was ashamed of myself for showing impatience with the elderly—I felt awful about wanting to squash Edgar in his recliner.

Anyway, as Beth and I spoke to Edgar and Agnes, it was obvious that there was little new to be learned regarding the bare facts: the Murphys were both in their sunroom at 5:30 P.M., having finished dinner—the elderly eat dinner about 4 P.M. Anyway, they were watching TV when they heard the Gordons' boat—they recognized the big engines, and Mrs. Murphy editorialized, "My, they're loud engines. Why would people need such big, loud engines?"

To annoy their neighbors, Mrs. Murphy. I asked both of them, "Did you *see* the boat?"

"No," Mrs. Murphy replied. "We didn't bother to look."

"But you *could* see the boat from your sunroom?"

"We can see the water, yes. But we were watching TV."

"Better than watching the silly bay."

Beth said, "John."

Truly, I am a man of many prejudices, and I hate myself for all of them, but I'm a product of my age, my sex, my era, my culture. I smiled at Mrs. Murphy. "You have a beautiful house."

"Thank you."

Beth took over the questioning awhile. She asked Mr. and Mrs. Murphy, "And you're sure you didn't hear any noise that could be a gunshot?"

"Nope," Edgar Murphy replied. "My hearing's pretty good. Heard Agnes calling me, didn't I?"

Beth said, "Sometimes gunshots don't sound like what we think they sound like. You know, on TV, they sound one way, but in real life sometimes they sound like firecrackers or a sharp crack, or a car backfiring. Did you hear *any* sound after the engines stopped?"

"Nope."

My turn. I said, "Okay, you heard the engines stop. Were you still watching TV?"

"Yup. But we don't play it loud. We sit real close to it."

"Backs to the windows?"

"Yup."

"Okay, you watched TV for ten more minutes—what made you get up?"

"It was one of Agnes' shows. Some damn stupid talk show. Montel Williams."

"So you headed next door to chat with Tom Gordon."

"I needed to borrow an extension cord." Edgar explained that he went through a gap in the hedges, stepped onto the Gordons' wooden deck, and lo and behold, there were Tom and Judy, dead as doornails.

Beth asked, "How far were you from the bodies?"

"Not twenty feet."

"Are you sure?"

"Yup. I was at the edge of the deck, and they was like opposite their sliding glass door. Twenty feet."

"Okay. How did you know it was the Gordons?"

"Didn't, at first. I just sort of froze and stared, then it hit me."

"How did you know they were dead?"

"Didn't really know at first. But I could see the . . . well, what looked like a third eye on his forehead. You know? They didn't move an inch. And their eyes was open, but no breathing, no moaning. Nothing."

Beth nodded. "Then what did you do?"

"I got the hell out of there."

My turn. I asked Edgar, "How long do you think you actually stood there on the deck?"

"Oh, I don't know."

"Half an hour?"

"Hell, no. About fifteen seconds."

Probably closer to five, I suspected. I walked Edgar through these few seconds a couple of times, trying to make him remember if he heard or saw anything unusual at that moment, anything he'd forgotten to mention, but to no avail. I even asked if he recalled smelling gunpowder, but he was adamant; his first report to Chief Maxwell was all of it, and that was that. Mrs. Murphy agreed.

I wondered what would have happened if Edgar had gone through the hedges about ten minutes earlier. Probably he wouldn't have been sitting here now. I wondered if that had crossed his mind. I asked him, "How do you think the murderer got away if you didn't hear or see a car or boat?"

"Well, I thought about that."

"And?"

"Well, there's a lot of people around here that walk, bicycle, jog and all. You know? I don't think anybody would take notice of anybody doin' any of that."

"Right." But a jogger with an ice chest on his head might attract attention. There was a good chance the murderer was still somewhere in the area when Edgar came upon the bodies.

I left the time and scene of the murder and began another line of questions. I asked Mrs. Murphy, "Did the Gordons have much company?"

She replied, "A fair amount. They did a lot of cooking outside. Always had a few people over."

Beth asked Edgar, "Did they take the boat out late?"

"Sometimes. Hard to miss them engines. Sometimes they'd come in real late."

"How late is late?"

"Oh, like two, three in the morning." He added, "Night fishing, I guess."

One *can* fish from a Formula 303, as I'd done a few times with the Gordons, but a Formula 303 is *not* a fishing boat, as I'm sure Edgar knew. But Edgar was from the old school and believed that no one should speak badly of the dead—unless pressed.

We went round and round, asking about the Gordons' habits, about strange cars, and so forth. I'd never worked with Beth Penrose, of course, but we were on the same wavelength; we played a good duet.

After a few minutes, Mrs. Murphy opined, "They were a real good-looking couple."

I picked up the hint and asked, "Do you think he had a girlfriend?"

"Oh . . . I didn't mean—"

"Did she have a boyfriend?"

"Well . . ."

"When he wasn't home, she would have a gentleman caller. Correct?"

"Well, I'm not saying it was a boyfriend or anything."

"Tell us about it."

And she did, but it wasn't all that juicy. Once, back in June, when Tom was at work and Judy was home, a good-looking, well-dressed, and bearded gentleman came over in a white sports car of indeterminate make and left an hour later. Interesting, but not evidence of a torrid affair that could lead to a crime of passion. Then, a few weeks ago, on a Saturday when Tom was out in his boat, a man pulled into the driveway with a "green Jeep," went into the backyard where Mrs. Gordon was sunning in a teeny weenie bikini, took his shirt off, and sunned next to her for a while. Mrs. Murphy said, "I don't think that's right when the husband's not home. I mean, she was half naked, and this feller pulls off his shirt and lays down right next to her, and they're just chatting away, then he gets up and leaves before the husband comes back. Now what was that all about?"

I replied, "It was perfectly innocent. I stopped by to see Tom about something."

Mrs. Murphy looked at me, and I could feel Beth's eyes on me, too. I said to Mrs. Murphy, "I was a friend of the Gordons."

"Oh. . . ."

Mr. Murphy chuckled up at the ceiling. He informed me, "My wife's got a dirty mind."

"Me, too." I asked Mrs. Murphy, "Did you ever socialize with the Gordons?"

"We had them here to dinner once when they first moved in about two years ago. They had us over for a barbeque right after. Never got together since then."

I couldn't imagine why. I asked Mrs. Murphy, "Did you know any of their friends by name?"

"No. I expect they were mostly Plum Island people. They're a strange bunch of ducks, if you want my opinion."

And so on. They loved to talk. Mrs. Murphy rocked, Mr. Murphy played with the lever on the chair and kept changing inclines. During one of his flat-out positions, he asked me, "What'd they do? Steal a whole bunch of germs to wipe out the world?"

"No, they stole a vaccine that's worth a lot of money. They wanted to be rich."

"Yeah? They was only rentin' next door. You know that?"

"Yes."

"Payin' too damn much for the house."

"How do you know?"

"I know the owner. Young feller named Sanders. He's a builder. Bought the place from the Hoffmanns, who're friends of ours. Sanders paid too much, then fixed it up and rented it to the Gordons. They paid too much rent."

Beth said, "Let me be blunt, Mr. Murphy. Some people think the Gordons were running drugs. What do you think?"

He replied without hesitation, "Could be. They was out in the boat at odd hours. Wouldn't be surprised."

I asked, "Other than the bearded man in the sports

car and myself, did you ever see any suspicious types in the yard or out front?"

"Well...can't say as I have, to tell you the truth."

"Mrs. Murphy?"

"No, I don't think so. Most of the people seemed respectable. They drank too much wine...recycling bin was full of wine bottles...sometimes they got loud after they were drinking, but the music was soft—not this crazy stuff you hear."

"Did you have a key to their house?"

I saw Mrs. Murphy shoot a glance at Mr. Murphy, who was staring at the ceiling. There was a silence, then Mr. Murphy said, "Yeah, we had the key. We kept an eye on the house for them because we're usually around."

"And?"

"Well...maybe last week, we saw a locksmith truck there, and when the feller left, well, I just went over to try my key and it didn't work no more. I sort of expected Tom to give me a new key, but I never got one. He's got the key to my house. You know? So, I called Gil Sanders and asked him, you know, because the owner is supposed to have the key, but he didn't know nothing about that. It's none of my business, but if the Gordons wanted me to watch over the house, I guess I should have the key." He added, "Now I'm wondering if they was hiding something in there."

"We're going to make you an honorary deputy, Mr. Murphy. Hey, don't repeat anything that was said here to anyone except Chief Maxwell. If anyone comes around claiming to be FBI, or Suffolk County police, or New York State police, or anything like that, they might be lying. Call Chief Maxwell or Detective Penrose. Okay?"

"Okay."

Beth asked Mr. Murphy, "Do you own a boat?"

"Not anymore. Too much work and money."

"Did anyone ever visit the Gordons by boat?" Beth asked.

"Now and then I'd see a boat at their dock."

"Did you know who the boats belonged to?"

"Nope. But one time it was a boat like theirs. Speedboat. But it wasn't theirs. It had a different name."

"You were close enough to see that?" I asked him.

"I sometimes watch with binoculars."

"What was the name on the boat?"

"Can't remember. But it wasn't theirs."

"Did you see anyone on board?" Beth asked.

"Nope. Just happened to notice the boat. Never saw anyone get on or off."

"When was this?"

"Let's see...about June...early in the season."

"Were the Gordons home?"

"Don't know." He added, "I watched to see who left the house, but somehow they got by me and next thing I know, I hear the engine, and the boat is heading out."

"How is your distance vision?"

"Not real good, except with the binoculars."

"And yours, Mrs. Murphy?"

"Same."

Assuming there was more binocular watching of the Gordons' property than the Murphys cared to admit, I asked them, "If we showed you photos of people, could you tell me if you've ever seen them on the Gordons' property?"

"Maybe."

I nodded. Nosy neighbors can make good witnesses, but sometimes, like a cheap surveillance video camera, nosy neighbors witness too much that is irrelevant, blurry, boring, and muffled.

We put another half hour into the questioning, but the yield was diminishing by the minute. In fact, Mr. Murphy had accomplished the near impossible by falling asleep during a police interview. His snoring was starting to get on my nerves.

I stood and stretched.

Beth stood and gave Mrs. Murphy her card. "Thank you for your time. Call me if either of you think of anything else."

"I will."

"Remember," Beth said, "I am the investigating detective assigned to this case. This is my partner. Chief Maxwell is assisting us. You should not speak to anyone else about this case."

She nodded, but I didn't know if the Murphys could stand up to somebody like Ted Nash of the Central Intelligence Agency.

I asked Mrs. Murphy, "Do you mind if we walk around your property?"

"I guess not."

We bid Mrs. Murphy farewell, and I said, "I'm sorry if I bored Mr. Murphy."

"It's his nap time."

"I see that."

She walked us to the front door and said, "I'm scared."

"Don't be," Beth said. "There are police watching the neighborhood."

"We could get murdered in our beds."

Beth replied, "We think it was someone the Gordons knew. A grudge. Nothing for you to worry about."

"What if they come back?"

I was getting annoyed again. "Why would the murderer come back?" I asked a bit sharply.

"They always return to the scene of the crime."

"They *never* return to the scene of the crime."

"They do if they want to kill the witnesses."

"Did you or Mr. Murphy witness the murder?"

"No."

"Then you shouldn't worry about it," I said.

"The killer might *think* we witnessed it."

I glanced at Beth.

She said, "I'll have a patrol car keep an eye on things. If you feel nervous or hear anything, dial 911." She added, "Don't you worry."

Agnes Murphy nodded.

I opened the door and got out into the sunlight. I said to Beth, "She actually has a point."

"I know. I'll take care of it."

Beth and I went around the side yard where we found the gap in the hedges. From the hedges you could see the rear of the Gordons' house and the deck, and if you stepped through and looked to the left, you could see down to the water. Out in the bay was a blue and white boat, and Beth said, "That's the bay constable's boat. We have four scuba divers looking for two little bullets in the mud and seaweed. Fat chance."

The crime was not yet twenty-four hours old, and the scene was secured until at least the next morning, so we didn't enter the Gordon property, because to do so would have meant another sign-in, and I was trying to sign out and sign off. But we walked along the Murphy side of the hedges toward the bay. The hedges became stunted toward the saltwater and at a point some thirty feet from the water's edge, I could see over them. We kept walking to where the bay lapped against the Murphys' bulkhead. The Murphys had an old floating dock to the left, and to the right was the Gordons' fixed dock. The *Spirochete* was missing.

Beth said, "The Marine Bureau took the boat to their docking area. The lab will work on it there." She asked me, "What do you think about the Murphys?"

"I think they did it."

"Did what?"

"Murdered the Gordons. Not directly. But they intercepted Tom and Judy on the deck, spoke to them for thirty minutes about the supermarket sales in the Saturday paper, the Gordons drew their guns, and blew their own brains out."

"Possible," Beth conceded. "But what happened to the guns?"

"Edgar made toilet paper holders out of them."

She laughed. "You're terrible. You'll be old someday."

"No, I won't."

Neither one of us spoke for a few seconds. We stood watching the bay. Water, like fire, is mesmerizing. Finally, Beth asked, "Were you having an affair with Judy Gordon?"

"If I was, I'd have told you and told Max right up front."

"You would have told Max. Not me."

"All right—I was not having an affair with Judy Gordon."

"But you were attracted to her."

"Every guy was. She was beautiful." I remembered to add, "And very bright," like I really gave a rat's ass about that. Well, sometimes I do, but I sometimes forget to list brains as an attribute. I added, "When you have a young, sexually attractive couple, maybe we should consider a sex angle."

She nodded. "We'll think about it."

From where we stood, I could see the flagpole in the Gordons' yard. The Jolly Roger still flew from the mast, and the two signal pennants hung from the crossbeam, aka, the yardarm. I asked Beth, "Can you draw those pennants?"

"Sure." She took her notebook and pen and sketched the two pennants. "You think that's relevant? A signal?"

"Why not? They're signal pennants."

"I think they're just decorative. But we'll find out."

"Right." I said to Beth, "Let's return to the scene of the crime."

We crossed the property line and went down to the Gordons' dock. I said, "Okay, I'm Tom, you're Judy. We left Plum Island at noon, and now it's about 5:30. We're home. I kill the engines. You get off the boat first and tie the rope. I heft the chest up to the dock. Right?"

"Right."

"I climb onto the dock, we lift the chest by the handles and start walking."

We sort of simulated this, walking side by side. I said, "We look up at the house. If anyone were on any of the three deck levels, we could see them. Right?"

"Right," she agreed. "Let's say someone *is* there, but we know him, or her, or them, and we keep walking."

"Okay. But you'd think that person would come down to the dock to help. Common courtesy. Anyway, we're still walking."

We continued, side by side, up to the second level of the deck. Beth said, "At some point, we would notice if the sliding glass door or screen was open. If it were, we'd be concerned, and might stop or go back. The door shouldn't be open."

"Unless they were expecting someone to be waiting for them *in* the house."

"Right." She said, "But that would have to be someone with the new key."

We continued toward the house to the top level of the deck and stopped a few feet from the two chalk outlines, Beth opposite Judy's and me opposite Tom's. I said, "The Gordons have a few more feet to go, a minute or less to live. What do they see?"

Beth stared down at the chalk outlines, then looked at the house in front of us, at the glass doors, at the immediate area left and right. Finally, she said, "They're still heading toward the house, which is twenty feet away. There's no indication they were trying to run. They're still side by side, there's no concealment anywhere, except the house, and no one can get off two head shots from that distance. They had to know the killer, or they were not alarmed by the killer."

"Right. I'm thinking the killer could have been lying in a chaise lounge, faking sleep, which is why he or she didn't go down to greet the Gordons at the dock. The Gordons knew this person and maybe Tom called out, 'Hey, Joe, get up and help us with this chest of Ebola vaccine.' Or anthrax. Or money. So, the guy gets up, yawns, takes a few steps toward them from any of these chaises, gets within spitting range, pulls a pistol, and drills them through their heads. Right?"

She replied, "Possible." She walked around the chalk outlines and stood where the killer must have stood, not five feet away from the feet of the chalk outlines. I moved up to where Tom had been standing. Beth raised her right hand and held her right wrist with her left hand. She pointed her finger right at my face and said, "Bang."

I said, "They were not carrying the chest when they were shot. It would fly out of Tom's hand when he was shot. Tom and Judy put the chest down first."

"I'm not sure they were carrying any chest. That's your theory, not mine."

"Then where is the chest that was always in the boat?"

"Who knows? Anywhere. Look at those two outlines, John. They're lying so close together, I wonder if they could have been carrying a four-foot-long chest between them."

I looked back at the outlines. She had a point, but I said, "They could have put the chest down a few feet back, then walked toward their killer, who may have been lying on the chaise or standing here or had just walked out of this sliding door."

"Maybe. In any case, I think the Gordons were acquainted with their killer or killers."

"Agreed." I said to Beth, "I don't think it was chance that put the killer there and the Gordons there. It would have been easier for the killer to do the shooting inside the house rather than out here. But he *chose* this spot—he set up his shots right here."

"Why?"

"The only reason I can think of is that he had a registered pistol, and he didn't want the bullets subject to ballistics later, if he became a suspect."

She nodded and looked out toward the bay.

I continued, "Inside the house, the rounds would have lodged somewhere, and maybe he wouldn't have been able to recover them. So, he goes for two close-up head shots with a large-caliber pistol and with nothing between the exit wounds and the deep bay."

She nodded again. "Looks that way, doesn't it?" She added, "That changes the profile of the killer. He's not a hophead, or an assassin with an unregistered piece. It's someone with no access to an untraceable piece— it's a good citizen with a registered pistol. Is that what you're suggesting?"

I said, "It fits what I see here."

"That's why you want the names of locals with registered weapons."

"Right." I added, "Big-caliber, registered as opposed to an illegal or hot weapon, and probably an automatic pistol as opposed to a revolver because revolvers are nearly impossible to silence. Let's start with that theory."

Beth said, "How does a good citizen with a registered pistol get an illegal silencer?"

"Good question." I pondered the whole profile I'd come up with and said, "Like anything else in this case, there's always one inconsistency that screws up a good theory."

"Right." She added, "And then there are those twenty .45 caliber automatics on Plum Island."

"Indeed there are."

We talked it out awhile, trying to piece this thing

together, trying to make it 5:30 P.M. yesterday, instead of 5:30 P.M. today.

I could see a uniformed Southold policeman through the glass doors, but he didn't see us and moved away.

After about five minutes of noodling, I said to Beth Penrose, "When I was a kid, I used to come out here from Manhattan with my All-American-type family—Dad, Mom, brother Jim, and sister Lynne. We usually rented the same cottage near Uncle Harry's big Victorian, and we spent two weeks getting eaten by mosquitoes. We got poison ivy, we got fish hooks in our fingers, and then we got sunburned. We must have enjoyed it, because we looked forward to it every year, the Coreys on their annual S&M outing."

She smiled.

I continued, "One year, when I was about ten, I found a musket ball, and it blew my mind. I mean, some guy fired that thing a hundred or maybe two hundred years before. Then Harry's wife, my Aunt June—God rest her soul—took me to a place near the hamlet of Cutchogue that she said was once a Corchaug Indian village, and she showed me how to look for arrowheads and cooking pits and bone needles and all that. Incredible."

Beth said nothing, but she was looking at me as if this was very interesting.

I went on, "I remember that I couldn't sleep nights thinking about musket balls and arrowheads, settlers and Indians, British soldiers and Continental soldiers, and so forth. Before the two weeks of magic ended, I knew I wanted to be an archaeologist when I grew up. It didn't work out that way, but I think that was one reason I became a detective."

I explained to her about Uncle Harry's driveway and how they once used cinders and clam shells to keep down the dust and mud. I said, "So, a thousand years from now, an archaeologist is digging around, and he finds these cinders and shells, and he makes the assumption it was a long cooking pit. Actually, he's found a driveway, but he's going to make what he thinks is a cooking pit fit his theory. Follow?"

"Sure."

"Right. Okay, here's my speech to my class. Want to hear it?"

"Shoot."

"Okay, class—what you see at the scene of a homicide is frozen in time, it is no longer a moving, living dynamic. You can create several stories about this still life, but these are only theories. A detective, like an archaeologist, can assemble hard facts and solid scientific evidence, and still draw the wrong conclusions. Add to this, a few lies and red herrings and people who are trying to help but make mistakes. Plus people who tell you what you want to hear consistent with your theory, and people with hidden agendas, and the murderer himself, who may have planted false clues. Through all this mess of contradictions, inconsistencies, and lies is the truth." I said to Beth, "At this point, if my timing is right, the bell rings and I say, 'Ladies and gentlemen, it is your job to know the truth.' "

She said, "Bravo."

"Thank you."

"So, who killed the Gordons?" she asked.

"Beats the hell out of me," I replied.

CHAPTER FIFTEEN

We stood in the sun-dappled lane near Beth Penrose's black PD. It was approaching six o'clock. I said, "How about a cocktail?"

She replied, "Can you find Margaret Wiley's house?"

"Maybe. Is she serving cocktails?"

"We'll ask. Jump in." I got in. She started the big engine and off we went, north through Nassau Point, across the causeway, and onto the mainland of the North Fork.

"Which way?" she asked.

"Right, I think."

She took the turn with squealing tires. I said, "Slow down."

She slowed down.

It was pleasant with the windows down, the setting sun, the clean air, and all of that. We were away from the bay area now and were in farm and vineyard country. I said, "When I was a kid, there were two kinds of farms—potato farms owned mostly by Polish and German families who came here around the turn of the century, and the fruit and vegetable farms owned mostly by the original settlers. There are farms here that have been in the same family for three hundred and fifty years. Hard to comprehend."

She stayed silent awhile, then said, "My family owned the same farm for a hundred years."

"Really? And your father sold it?"

"Had to. By the time I was born, the farm sat in the middle of the suburbs." She added, "We were considered weird. I was laughed at in school. For being a farmer's daughter." She smiled and said, "But Dad had the last laugh. A million bucks for the acreage. Big money then."

"Big money now." I asked, "Have you inherited?"

"Not yet. But I'm squandering a trust fund."

I asked, "Will you marry me?"

"No, but I'll let you drive my BMW."

"Slow down and turn left there."

She turned, and we headed north again. She glanced at me and said, "I understood you were married."

"Divorced."

"Signed, sealed, and delivered?"

"I think so." In truth, I didn't remember getting my final discharge papers.

"I remember a story on TV...when you were hit...an attractive wife visiting the hospital with the mayor, the police commissioner...you remember that?"

"Not really. Heard about it." I said, "Right and a quick left."

We found ourselves on Lighthouse Road, and I said, "Go slow and we'll read numbers."

The small road, which led to Horton Point

Lighthouse about a mile farther on, had a scattering of small houses on both sides, surrounded by vineyards.

We came to a pleasant brick cottage whose mailbox said "Wiley." Beth stopped the car on the grass verge. "I guess this is it."

"Probably. The phone book was full of Wileys, by the way. Probably old originals."

We got out and went up a stone path to the front door. There was no bell and we knocked. We waited. There was a car parked under a big oak tree alongside the house, so we walked around to the side, then to the back.

A thin woman of about seventy wearing a flowered summer dress was puttering around in a vegetable garden. I called out, "Mrs. Wiley?"

She looked up from her garden, then came toward us. We met her on a patch of lawn between the house and the garden. I said, "I'm Detective John Corey. I phoned you last night. This is my partner, Detective Beth Penrose."

She stared at my shorts, and I thought maybe my fly was open or something.

Beth showed Mrs. Wiley her badge case, and the lady seemed satisfied with Beth, but still uncertain about me.

I smiled at Margaret Wiley. She had clear gray eyes, gray hair, and a sort of interesting face with translucent skin; a face that reminded me of an old painting—not any particular painting, or artist, or style, just an old painting.

She looked at me and said, "You called very late."

"I couldn't sleep. This double murder kept me awake, Mrs. Wiley. I apologize."

"I don't suppose I want an apology. What can I do for you?"

"Well," I said, "we were interested in the piece of land that you sold to the Gordons."

"I think I told you all I know."

"Yes, ma'am. You probably did. Just a few more questions."

"Sit over here." She led us to a grouping of green-painted Adirondack chairs beneath a weeping willow. We all sat.

The chairs, which had been popular when I was a kid, had made a big comeback, and you saw them all over now. These particular chairs in Mrs. Wiley's yard, I suspected, had never been away so that a comeback wasn't necessary. The house, the yard, the lady in the long cotton dress, the willow tree, the rusty swing set, and the old tire hanging by a rope from the oak tree—all of this had a 1940s or 1950s look, like an old photograph that had been color-tinted. Truly time moved more slowly here. There was a saying that in Manhattan the present was so strong, it obscured the past. But here, the past was so strong, it obscured the present.

I could smell the sea, the Long Island Sound, about a quarter mile away, and I thought I caught a whiff of the grapes that had fallen to the ground in the nearby vineyard. This was a unique environment of sea, farm, and vineyard, an unusual combination found only in a few places along the East Coast.

I said to Mrs. Wiley, "You have a beautiful place here."

"Thank you."

Margaret Wiley was my third old person of the day, and I determined to do better with her than I had with

Edgar and Agnes. In fact, Margaret Wiley wasn't going to take any crap from me; I could sense that. She was the no-nonsense, old-family, get-to-the-point, and mind-your-manners type. I'm a good interrogator because I can pick out personalities and types, and tailor my approach accordingly. This doesn't mean I'm simpatico, sensitive, or empathetic. I'm an overbearing, egocentric, and opinionated male chauvinist pig. That's my comfort zone. But I listen and I say what has to be said. It's part of the job.

I said to Mrs. Wiley, "Do you manage this place by yourself?"

"Mostly. I have a son and two daughters, all married and living in the area. Four grandchildren. My husband, Thad, died six years ago."

Beth said she was sorry.

That out of the way, Beth asked, "Do you own these vineyards?"

"I own some of this land. I lease it to the wine people. Regular farmer's lease for a season. Wine people need twenty years, they say. I don't know anything about grapevines." She looked at Beth. "Does that answer your question?"

"Yes, ma'am." Beth asked, "Why did you sell an acre to the Gordons?"

"What does that have to do with their murders?"

Beth replied, "We don't know until we find out more about the transaction."

"It was a simple land sale."

I said to Mrs. Wiley, "To be frank, ma'am, I find it odd that the Gordons spent so much money for land that couldn't be developed."

"I think I told you, Detective, they wanted a view of the Sound."

"Yes, ma'am. Did they mention any other use they might want to make of the land? For instance, fishing, boating, camping?"

"Camping. They mentioned pitching a tent. And fishing. They wanted to surf cast at night from their own beach. They also said something about wanting to buy a telescope. They wanted to study astronomy. They'd visited the Custer Institute. Have you been there?"

"No, ma'am."

"It's a small observatory in Southold. The Gordons had taken an interest in astronomy."

That was news to me. You'd think that people who looked at bugs through a microscope all day wouldn't want another lens in their eye at night. But you never know. I asked, "And boating?"

"You can't launch any boat from there, except maybe a canoe. The land is on a high bluff, and you couldn't get anything except a canoe up there, then down to the beach."

"But you could land a boat on the beach?"

"Maybe at high tide, but there are treacherous rocks along that stretch. You could probably anchor and swim or walk to the beach at low tide."

I nodded, then asked, "Did they mention any agricultural interest in the land?"

"No. It's not good for much. Didn't I tell you that?"

"I don't recall."

"Well, I did." She explained, "Whatever's growing on that bluff took a long time to get used to the wind and the salt air." She added, "You might try root vegetables on the landward side."

"Right." I tried another tack and inquired, "What was your impression of the Gordons?"

She looked at me, thought a moment, then replied, "A nice couple. Very pleasant."

"Happy?"

"They seemed happy."

"Were they excited about their purchase?"

"You could say so."

"Did they approach you about selling your land?"

"Yes. They made some inquiries first—I heard about that long before they came to me. When they asked me, I told them I wasn't interested."

"Why's that?"

"Well, I don't like to sell land."

"Why not?"

"Land should be held and passed on to the family." She added, "I've inherited some parcels through my mother's side. This piece of land that the Gordons were interested in was from my husband's side." She seemed to reflect a moment, then added, "Thad made me promise not to sell any of it. He wanted it to go to the children. But this was only an acre. I didn't really need the money, of course, but the Gordons seemed to have been heart-set on this bluff...." She glanced at me and Beth, and said, "I asked the children, and they thought that their father would approve."

It always amazed me that widows and children, who were entirely clueless about what to get the old boy for Christmas or Father's Day, knew exactly what the late great Pop would want after he popped off.

Mrs. Wiley continued, "The Gordons understood that the land couldn't be developed."

"You mentioned that." I asked pointedly, "And for

that reason, wouldn't you agree that twenty-five thousand dollars was above market price?"

She leaned forward in the deep Adirondack chair and informed me, "I also gave them an easement through my land to theirs." She added, "Let's see what the land goes for when the estate sells it."

"Mrs. Wiley, I'm not faulting you for making a good deal for yourself. I'm wondering why the Gordons wanted or needed that land so badly."

"I told you what they told me. That's all I know."

"The view must be breathtaking for twenty-five big ones."

"It is."

I said, "You mentioned that you lease your farmland."

"Yes. My children aren't interested in farming or in grape-growing for the wineries."

"Did that ever come up with the Gordons? I mean, about you leasing your farmland?"

"I suppose it did."

"And they never asked you if they could *lease* a part of the bluffs?"

She thought a moment, then said, "No, now that you mention it."

I glanced at Beth. Clearly this made no sense. Two government employees who could be transferred at any time rent a house on the south bay, then buy an acre on the north shore for twenty-five large to have another water view. I asked Mrs. Wiley, "If they'd offered to lease an acre or so of that bluff, would you have said yes?"

She nodded. "I might have preferred that."

"How much would you have asked by the year?"

"Oh...I don't know...the land has no use....I

suppose a thousand would be fair." She added, "A very nice view."

I said, "Would you be good enough to show us this land?"

"I can give you directions. Or you can look up the survey in the county clerk's office."

Beth said, "We would really appreciate it if you would come with us."

Mrs. Wiley looked at her watch, then at Beth. "All right." She stood. "I'll be right back."

She went inside through the rear screen door.

I said to Beth, "Tough old duck."

"You bring out the worst in people."

"I was being very nice this time."

"That's what you call nice?"

"Yes, I'm being *nice*."

"Scary."

I changed the subject and said, "The Gordons had to *own* the property."

She nodded.

"Why?"

"I don't know.... You tell me."

"Think about it."

"Okay...."

Mrs. Wiley came out of the back door, which she left unlocked. She was carrying her pocketbook and car keys. She walked toward her car, a basic gray Dodge about five years old. If Thad were alive, he'd approve.

Beth and I got in her car, and we followed Mrs. Wiley. We made a right on Middle Road, a four-lane road that ran east-west, parallel to the old colonial-era Main Road. Middle Road passed through the heart of the farmland and vineyards, with sweeping vistas in all directions. The sunshine on the windshield felt good, the air smelled of grapes, a copper-haired babe was driving, and if I wasn't investigating the murder of two friends, I'd be whistling.

On my left, about a mile away to the north, I could see where the flat tillable land suddenly rose up, like a wall, so steep it couldn't be farmed, and the slope was covered with trees and bush. This was, in fact, the bluff whose north slope fell into the sea, but from here, you couldn't see the water, and the sharp rise appeared to be a range of low hills.

Mrs. Wiley had a heavy foot, and we scooted past tractors and pickup trucks.

A sign told us we were in the hamlet of Peconic. There were a good number of vineyards on both sides of the road, all identified by wooden signs with gilded and lacquered logos, very upscale, promising expensive wines. I said to Beth, "Potato vodka. That's it. I need only twenty acres and a still. Corey and Krumpinski, fine potato vodka, natural and flavored. I'll get Martha Stewart to do cookbooks and suggested accompaniments to the vodka—clams, scallops, oysters. Very upscale. What do you think?"

"Who's Krumpinski?"

"I don't know. A guy. Polish vodka. Stanley Krumpinski. He's a marketing creation. He sits on his porch and says cryptic things about vodka. He's ninety-five years old. His twin brother, Stephen, was a wine drinker and died at thirty-five. Yes? No?"

"Let me think about it. Meanwhile, the overpriced acre seems more odd when you consider the Gordons could have had the same acre on a lease for a thousand dollars. Is this relevant to the murders or not?"

"Maybe. On the other hand, it could be nothing more than bad judgment on the Gordons' part, or even a land scam." I said, "The Gordons could have figured out a way to reverse the sale of the development rights. Therefore, they have a waterfront acre for twenty-five Gs that as a building plot is worth maybe a hundred. Neat profit."

She nodded. "I'll talk to the county clerk about comparative sale prices." She glanced at me as she drove and said, "You have formed another theory, obviously."

"Maybe. Not obviously."

She stayed silent awhile, then said, "They needed to *own* the land. Right? Why? Development? Right of way? Some big state park project in the works? Oil, gas, coal, diamonds, rubies...? What?"

"There are no minerals on Long Island, no precious metals, no gems. Just sand, clay, and rock. Even I know that."

"Right...but you're onto something."

"Not anything specific. I have this like...feeling... like I know what's relevant and what's not, sort of like one of those image association tests. You know? You see four pictures—a bird, a bee, a bear, and a toilet bowl. Which one doesn't belong?"

"The bear."

"The bear? Why the bear?"

"It doesn't fly."

"The toilet bowl doesn't fly either," I pointed out.

"Then the bear *and* the toilet bowl don't belong."

"You're not.... Anyway, I can sense what belongs in the sequence and what doesn't."

"Is this like the pings?"

"Sort of."

Mrs. Wiley's brake lights went on, and she swung off the highway onto a dirt farm road. Beth, not paying attention, almost missed the turn and two-wheeled it behind Margaret.

We headed north, toward the bluffs on the dirt road that ran between a potato field to the left and a vineyard to the right. We bumped along at about thirty miles an hour, dust flying up all over the place, and I could actually taste it on my tongue. I rolled up my window and told Beth to do the same.

She did and said, apropos of nothing, "We're approaching toidy-toid and toid."

"I do *not* speak with that kind of accent. I do *not* find that amusing."

"I hear ya."

Mrs. Wiley swung off onto a smaller rutted track that ran parallel to the bluff, which was only about fifty yards away now. After a few hundred yards, she stopped in the middle of the track, and Beth pulled up behind her.

Mrs. Wiley got out, and we followed suit. We were covered with dust and so was the car, inside and out.

We approached Mrs. Wiley, who was standing at the base of the bluff. She said, "Hasn't rained in two weeks. The grape growers like it that way this time of year. They say it makes the grape sweeter, less watery. Ready for harvest."

I was brushing dust off my T-shirt and eyebrows and really didn't give a damn.

Mrs. Wiley went on, "The potatoes don't need the rain either this time of year. But the vegetables and fruit trees could use a good soaking."

I really, *really* didn't care, but I didn't know how

to convey this without sounding rude. I said, "I guess some folks are praying for rain, and some are praying for sun. That's life."

She looked at me and said, "You're not from around here, are you?"

"No, ma'am. But my uncle has a place here. Harry Bonner. My mother's brother. Has a farm bay estate down in Mattituck. Or is it a bay farm estate? Anyway—"

"Oh, yes. His wife, June, passed away about the same time as my Thad."

"That would be about right." I wasn't totally blown away that Margaret Wiley knew Uncle Harry—I mean, the full-time population out here is, as I said, about twenty thousand, which is five thousand fewer people than work in the Empire State Building. I don't mean that all twenty-five thousand people who work in the Empire State Building know one another, but—anyway, Margaret and, I guess, the late Thad Wiley knew Harry and the late June Bonner. I had this bizarre thought that I'd get Margaret and crazy Harry together, they'd marry, she'd die, Harry would die, and leave me thousands of acres of North Fork real estate. I'd have to first bump off my cousins, of course. This sounded a little too Shakespearean. I had the strong feeling I'd been out here too long in the seventeenth century.

"John? Mrs. Wiley is speaking to you."

"Oh, sorry. I was badly wounded, and I have some residual consciousness lapses."

"You look awful," Mrs. Wiley informed me.

"Thank you."

"I was saying, how is your uncle?"

"Very fine. He's back in the city. Makes a lot of

money on Wall Street. But very lonely since Aunt June died."

"Give him my regards."

"I will."

"Your aunt was a fine woman." She said it with that inflection that means, "How'd she get such a dork of a nephew?"

Margaret continued, "June was a good amateur archaeologist and historian."

"Right. Peconic Historical Society. Are you a member?"

"Yes. That's how I met June. Your uncle was not interested, but he did finance a few digs. We excavated the foundation of a farmhouse that dated to 1681. You ought to see our museum if you haven't."

"In fact, I was going to see it today, but this other thing came up."

"We're only open weekends after Labor Day. But I have a key."

"I'll give you a call." I looked up at the bluff rising out of the flat earth. I asked Mrs. W, "Is this the Gordons' land?"

"Yes. You see that stake over there? That's the southwest corner. Down the trail here about a hundred yards is the southeast corner. The land starts here and rises to the top of the bluff, then down the other side, and ends at the high-water mark."

"Really? Doesn't sound too accurate."

"Accurate enough. It's custom and law. High-water mark. The beach belongs to everyone."

"That's why I love this country."

"Do you?"

"Absolutely."

She looked at me and said, "I'm a Daughter of the American Revolution."

"I thought you might be."

"My family, the Willises, have been here in this township since 1653."

"My goodness."

"They came to Massachusetts on the ship after the *Mayflower*, the *Fortune*. Then they came here to Long Island."

"Incredible. You just missed being a *Mayflower* descendant."

She replied, "I'm a *Fortune* descendant." She looked around, and I followed her gaze. South of us stretched the potato field to the right and the vineyard to the left. She said, "It's hard to imagine what life was like in the sixteen hundreds. Thousands of miles from England, woods where those fields are now, cleared by ax and ox, unknown climate, unknown soil, few domestic animals, an unreliable source of clothing, tools, seed, gunpowder, and musket balls, and hostile Indians all around."

"Sounds worse than Central Park after midnight in August."

Margaret Wiley ignored me and said, "It's very difficult for people like us—I mean my people—to part with even an acre of land."

"Right." But for twenty-five large, we can talk. I said, "I found a musket ball once."

She looked at me as if I were a half-wit. She directed her attention toward Beth and prattled on a bit, then said, "Well, you don't need me to show you up to the top. There's a path right there. It's not difficult going up, but be careful on the sea side. It drops steeply and there aren't many footholds." She added, "This bluff is actually the terminal moraine of the last ice age. The glacier ended right here."

In fact, the glacier stood before me now. I said, "Thank you for your time and patience, Mrs. Wiley."

She started to walk off, then looked at Beth and asked her, "Do you have any idea who could have done it?"

"No, ma'am."

"Did it relate to their work?"

"In a way. But nothing to do with germ warfare or anything dangerous."

Margaret Wiley didn't look convinced. She went back to her car, started it, and drove off in a cloud of dust. I called after her, "Eat my dust, Margaret. You old—"

"John!"

I brushed the dust off my clothes again. I said to Beth, "Do you know why Daughters of the American Revolution don't have group sex?"

"No, but I'm about to find out."

"You are. Daughters of the American Revolution don't have group sex because they don't want to have to write all those thank-you notes."

"Do these jokes come from an inexhaustible supply?"

"You know they do."

We both looked up at the bluff. I said, "Let's see that twenty-five-G view."

We found the small path, and I went first. The path led through some thick bushes, a lot of scrub oak, and a few bigger trees that looked like maples, but could have been banana trees, for all I knew.

Beth, dressed in a khaki poplin skirt and street shoes, wasn't having an easy time of it. I pulled her up over a few steep spots. She hiked her skirt up, or it rode up, and I was treated to a perfect pair of legs.

It was only about fifty feet to the top, the equivalent of a five-story walk-up, which I used to be able to do with enough energy left to kick down a door, wrestle a perp to the floor, slap the cuffs on, and drag him down to the street and into a PD. But that was then. This was now, and I felt shaky. Black spots danced before my eyes, and I had to stop and kneel down.

Beth asked, "Are you okay?"

"Yeah.... Just a minute...." I took a bunch of breaths and then continued on.

We reached the top of the bluff. The growth here was much more stunted because of the wind and salt air. We looked out over the Long Island Sound, and truly it was an incredible panorama. Although the south slope of the bluff was only fifty feet from the base to the crest, the north slope down to the beach was about a hundred feet. It was, as Mrs. Wiley warned, very steep, and when we peered down over the edge, we could see sea grasses, erosion gullies, mud slides, and rock falls that swept down to a nice long beach that stretched east and west for miles.

The Sound was calm, and we saw a few sailboats and powerboats. A huge cargo ship was heading west toward New York or one of the Connecticut ports. About ten miles away, we could make out the Connecticut coast.

The bluff ran west for a mile or so and disappeared at a point of land jutting into the Sound. To the east, the bluff ran with the beach for several miles and ended at Horton Point, which was identifiable because of the lighthouse.

Behind us, the way we had come up, were the flat farmlands, and from up here, we could see the quiltwork of potatoes, grapevines, orchards, and corn. Quaint clapboard houses and white, not red, barns dotted the green fields. I said, "What a view."

"Magnificent," Beth agreed. She asked, "Worth twenty-five thousand?"

"That is the question." I looked at her. "What do you think?"

"In theory, no. But up here, yes."

"Well put." I saw a boulder in the tall grass and sat on it, staring out to sea.

Beth stood to my side, also staring out to sea. We were both sweaty, dirty, dusty, out of breath, and tired. "Time for cocktails," I said. "Let's head back."

"Just a minute. Let's be Tom and Judy. Tell me what they wanted here, what they were seeking."

"Okay...." I stood on the boulder and looked around. The sun was setting, and way off to the east the sky was purple. To the west, it was pink and overhead it was blue. Gulls sailed, whitecaps raced across the Sound, birds sang in the trees, a breeze blew out of the northeast, and there was a smell of autumn as well as salt. I said to Beth, "We've spent the day on Plum Island. We were in biocontainment all day, wearing lab clothes, surrounded by viruses. We shower out, race to the *Spirochete* or to the ferry, cross the Gut, get into our car, and come here. This is wide open, clean, and invigorating. This is life....We brought a bottle of wine and a blanket. We drink the wine, we make love, we lie on the blanket, and watch the stars come out. Maybe we go down to the beach and swim or surf cast under the stars and moon. We are a million miles from the laboratory. We go home, ready for another day in biocontainment."

Beth stayed silent for a while, then, without replying, she moved to the edge of the bluff, then turned and walked to the only substantial tree on the crest, a ten-foot-tall, gnarled oak. She bent down, then straightened up, holding a coil of rope in her hand. "Look at this."

I joined her and looked at her find. The rope, made of green nylon about a half an inch thick, was knotted every three feet or so for handholds. One end was tied to the base of the tree. Beth said, "There's probably enough rope here to reach the beach."

I nodded. "That would certainly make the climb up and down easier."

"Yes." She knelt and looked down the slope. I did the same. We could see where the grass was worn from the climbs up and down the face of the bluff. It was, as I said, a steep slope, but not too difficult for anyone in decent shape, even without a rope.

I leaned farther over the edge and noticed that where the grass had eroded there were those reddish streaks of clay and iron in the soil. I noticed something else: about ten feet below, a sort of shelf or ledge appeared. Beth noticed it, too, and said, "I'm going to have a look."

She pulled at the rope, and satisfied that it was securely attached to the tree trunk, and the tree trunk was securely attached to the ground, she took the rope in both hands and walked backwards down the ten feet to the ledge, playing out the rope as she descended. She called up, "Come on down. This is interesting."

"Okay." I walked down the slope, holding the rope in one hand. I stood on the ledge beside Beth.

She said, "Look at that."

The ledge was about ten feet long and three feet deep at the widest. In the center of the ledge was a cave, but you could tell it was not natural. In fact, I could see shovel marks. Beth and I crouched down and peered into the opening. It was small, about three feet in diameter and only about four feet deep. There was nothing inside the excavation. I couldn't imagine what this was for, but I speculated, "You could stash a picnic lunch and a cooler of wine in there."

Beth added, "You could even put your legs in there and your body out on this ledge, and go to sleep."

"Or have sex."

"Why did I know you were going to say that?"

"Well, it's true." I stood. "They may have intended to make this bigger."

"For what?"

"I don't know." I turned toward the Sound and lowered myself into a sitting position, my feet dangling over the ledge. "This is nice. Have a seat."

"I'm getting cold."

"Here, you can have my T-shirt."

"No, it smells."

"You're no petunia yourself."

"I'm tired, I'm dirty, my pantyhose are ripped, and I have to go to the bathroom."

"This is romantic."

"It could be. But it's not now." She stood, grabbed the rope, and walked up to the crest. I waited until she got to the top, then followed.

Beth coiled the rope and put it back at the base

of the tree as she'd found it. She turned, and we found ourselves face-to-face, about a foot apart. It was one of those awkward moments, and we stood for exactly three seconds, then I put my hand out and brushed her hair, then her cheek. I moved in for the big smooch, confident we were about to lock lips, but she stepped back and uttered the magic word that all modern American men have been Pavloved to respond to. "No."

I immediately jumped back six feet, and I clasped my hands behind my back. My little woody dropped like a dead tree, and I exclaimed, "I mistook your friendly banter for a sexual come-on. Forgive me."

Actually, that's not exactly what happened. She did say "no," but I hesitated, a look of abject disappointment on my face, and she said, "Not now," which is good, then "maybe later," which was better, then "I like you," which was best.

I said, "Take your time," which I sincerely meant, as long as she didn't take more than seventy-two hours, which is sort of my limit. Actually, I've waited longer.

We didn't say anything else about that, but walked down the landward side of the bluff and got into the black PD.

She started the car, threw it into gear, then put it back into park, and leaned over and kissed me perfunctorily on the cheek, then into gear again and off we went, raising dust.

A mile later, we were on Middle Road. She had a good sense of direction and headed back to Nassau Point without my help.

She saw an open service station, and we both used the respective lavs to freshen up, as they say. I couldn't remember the last time I looked this dirty. I'm a pretty dapper guy on the job, a Manhattan dandy in tailor-made suits. I felt like a kid again, dirty Johnny rooting around the Indian burial sites.

In the service station office, I bought some really gross snacks—beef jerky, peanut butter crackers, and gummy bears. Out in the car, I offered some to Beth, who refused. I said, "If you chew this all together, it tastes like a Thai dish called Sandang Phon. I discovered that by accident."

"I hope so."

We drove a few minutes. The combo of beef jerky, peanut butter crackers, and gummy bears actually tasted awful, but I was starving, and I wanted that dust out of my throat. I asked Beth, "What do you think? I mean, about the bluff?"

She thought a moment, then replied, "I think I would have liked the Gordons."

"You would have."

"Are you sad?"

"Yeah...I mean, we weren't best buddies...I only knew them a few months, but they were good people, full of fun and life. They were too young to have ended their lives like that."

She nodded.

We drove across the causeway onto Nassau Point. It was getting dark.

She said, "My brain is telling me this piece of land is what it appears to be. A romantic retreat, a place to call their own. They were Midwesterners, they probably came from land, and they found themselves here as tenants in a place where land means a lot, like where they came from....Right?"

"Right."

"And yet...."

"Yes. And yet....And yet, they could have saved themselves about twenty Gs if they'd leased for five years." I added, "They had to *own* the land. Think about that."

"I'm thinking about it."

We wound up at the house where the Gordons had lived, and Beth pulled up behind my Jeep. She said, "It was a long day."

"Come back to my place. Follow me."

"No, I'm going home tonight."

"Why?"

"There's no reason to be here twenty-four hours a day any longer, and the county won't pay for the motel."

"Stop at my place first. I have to give you the computer printouts."

"They'll wait until tomorrow." She said, "I need to go to the office tomorrow morning. Why don't I meet you tomorrow about five o'clock?"

"My place."

"All right. Your place, five P.M. I'll have some information by then."

"Me, too."

"I'd rather you didn't proceed until you see me," she said.

"Okay."

"Get your status straight with Chief Maxwell."

"Will do."

"Get some rest," she said.

"You, too."

"Get out of my car." She smiled. "Go home. Really."

"I will. Really." I got out of her car. She made a U-turn, waved, and drove off.

I got into my Jeep, determined not to do anything that would make it speak French. Seat belt on, doors locked, emergency brake off. I started the engine and the car didn't utter a peep.

As I drove back to my bay farm estate, or farm bay estate, or whatever, I realized I hadn't remembered to use the remote to start the vehicle. Well, what difference did it make? The new car bombs all exploded after about five minutes anyway. Besides, no one was trying to kill me. Well, someone *had* tried to kill me, but that had to do with something else. Quite possibly, that was random, or if it were planned, the shooters considered that I was out of action, and whatever I'd done to piss them off was avenged without me having to be actually dead. That's the way the Mafia operated—if you survived, you were usually left alone. But these gentlemen who were blasting away at me looked decidedly Hispanic. And those hombres didn't always consider the job done until you were planted.

But that wasn't my concern at the moment. I was more concerned about what was going on around here, whatever it was. I mean, here I am in a very peaceful part of the planet, trying to get my mind and body to heal, and right beneath the surface we have all sorts of weird crap going down. I kept thinking about that pig bleeding from its ears and nose and mouth....I realized that people on that little island had discovered stuff that could exterminate almost every living thing on the planet.

The convenient thing about biological warfare has always been easy deniability, and its untraceable origins.

The entire culture of biological research and weapons development has always been permeated with lies, deception, and denial.

I pulled into the driveway of Uncle Harry's house. My tires crunched over the seashells. The house was dark, and when I shut off my headlights, the entire world fell into darkness. How do rural people live in the dark?

I tucked my T-shirt in so as to free the butt of my .38. I didn't even know if my piece had been tampered with—anyone who would tamper with a guy's shorts would certainly tamper with his revolver. I should have checked before.

Anyway, keys in my left hand, I opened the front door, my right hand ready to go for the gun. The gun should have been *in* my right hand, but men, even when completely alone, have to show balls. I mean, who's looking? I guess I'm looking. You have balls, Corey. You're a real man. The real man had a sudden urge to go tinkle, which I did in the bathroom off the kitchen.

Without turning on any lights, I checked the answering machine in the den and saw I had ten messages; quite a lot for a fellow who had none the whole preceding week.

Assuming that none of these messages would be particularly pleasant or rewarding, I poured a big, fat brandy from Uncle's crystal decanter into Uncle's crystal glass.

I sat in Uncle's recliner and sipped, vacillating between the message button, my bed, or another brandy. Another brandy won a few more times, and I postponed coming to grips with the electronic horror of the telephone answering machine until I had a little buzz on.

Finally, I hit the message button.

"You have ten messages," said the voice, agreeing with the message counter.

The first message came at seven A.M. and was from Uncle Harry, who'd seen me on TV the night before but didn't want to call so late, though he had no problem calling so early. Thankfully, I was already on my way to Plum Island at seven A.M.

There were four similar messages: one from my parents in Florida, who hadn't seen me on TV but had heard I was on TV; one from a lady named Cobi who I see now and then, and who may have wanted to be Cobi Corey for some reason; and then a call each from my siblings, Jim and Lynne, who are good about staying in touch. There would probably have been more calls about my brief TV appearance, but very few people had my number, and not everyone would recognize me since I had lost so much weight and looked terrible.

There was no call from my ex-wife, who despite no longer loving me, wants me to know that she likes me as a person, which is odd because I'm not that likable. Lovable, yes; likable, no.

Then there was my partner, Dom Fanelli, who called at nine A.M. and said, "Hey, you hump, I saw your mug on the morning news. What the hell are you doing out there? You got two Pedros looking for your ass, and you show up on TV, and now everyone knows you're out east. Why don't you put your poster in the Colombian post office? Jesus, John, I'm trying to find these guys before they find you again. Anyway, more good news— the boss is wondering what the hell you're doing at a crime scene. What's going on out there? Who iced those two? Hey, she was a looker. You need help? Give a call. Keep your pee-pee in the teepee. Ciao."

I smiled. Good old Dom. A guy I could count on. I still remember him standing over me as I lay bleeding in the street. He had a half-eaten donut in one hand and his piece in the other. He took another bite of the donut and said to me, "I'll get them, John. I swear to God, I'll get the bastards who killed you."

I remember informing him I wasn't dead, and he said he knew that, but I probably would be. He had tears in his eyes, which made me feel terrible, and he was trying to talk to me while chewing the donut, and I couldn't understand him, then the pounding started in my ears and I blacked out.

Anyway, the next call came at nine-thirty A.M. and was from the *New York Times*, and I wondered how they knew who I was and where I was staying. Then the voice said, "You can have the paper delivered to your door daily and Sunday as a new subscriber for only $3.60 weekly for thirteen weeks. Please call us at 1-800-631-2500, and we'll begin service immediately."

"I get it at the office. Next."

Max's voice came over the speaker and said, "John, for the record, you're no longer employed by the Southold Township PD. Thanks for your help. I owe you a buck, but I'd like to buy you a drink instead. Call me."

"Screw you, Max."

The next call was from Mr. Ted Nash, CIA superspook. He said, "I just want to remind you that a murderer or murderers are on the loose, and you may be a target. I thoroughly enjoyed working with you, and I know we'll meet again. Take care of yourself."

"Fuck you, Ted." I mean, if you're going to threaten me, at least have the balls to come out and say it, even if it is being recorded.

There was one more message on the machine, but I hit the stop button before it played, then I dialed the Soundview and asked for Ted Nash. The clerk, a young man, said there was no one there registered by that name. I asked, "How about George Foster?"

"No, sir."

"Beth Penrose?"

"She just checked out."

I described Nash and Foster to the clerk, and he said, "Yes, there are two gentlemen here that fit that description."

"They still there?"

"Yes."

"Tell the bigger guy, the one with the curly black hair, that Mr. Corey got his message and that he should heed his own warning. Got that?"

"Yes, sir."

"Also, tell him I said he should go fuck himself."

"Yes, sir."

I hung up and yawned. I felt like crap. I probably had gotten three hours sleep in the last forty-eight. I yawned again.

I hit the play button, and the final message came on. Beth's voice said, "Hi, I'm calling from the car. . . . I just wanted to say thanks for your help today. I don't know if I said that. . . . Anyway, I enjoyed meeting you, and if somehow we don't get together tomorrow—I may not get out that way—lots of office stuff and reports—well, I'll call either way. Thanks again."

The machine said, "End of messages."

I played the last one again. The call had come not ten minutes after I'd left her, and her voice sounded distinctly formal and distant. In fact, it was a brush-off. I had this totally paranoid thought that Beth and Nash had become lovers and were at that moment in his room having wild, passionate sex. Get a grip, Corey. Whom the gods wish to destroy, they first make horny.

I mean, what else could go wrong? I spend the day in biocontainment, and I'm probably infected with bubonic plague, I'm probably in trouble back on the job, Pedro and Juan know where I am, Max, my bud, fires me, then a CIA guy threatens my life for no reason...well, he may have had an imagined reason—and then my true love takes a powder, and I'm picturing her with her legs wrapped around bozo boy. Plus, Tom and Judy, who liked me, are dead. And it was only nine P.M.

The idea of a monastery suddenly popped into my head. Or better yet, a month in the Caribbean, following my big friend Peter Johnson from island to island.

Or, I could stay here and tough it. Revenge, vindication, victory, and glory. That's what John Corey was about. Furthermore, I had something no one else had—I had a half-assed idea of what this was about.

I sat in the dark, quiet den and for the first time all day, I was able to think without interruption. My mind had a whole bunch of things on hold, and now I started to put them together.

As I stared out the dark window, those little pings in my head were making white dots on the black screen, and the image was starting to take shape. I was far from seeing the complete picture let alone any of the details, but I could make a good guess about this thing's size, shape, and direction. I needed a few more points of light, a half dozen little pings, and then I would have the answer to why Tom and Judy Gordon were murdered.

CHAPTER SIXTEEN

Morning sunlight streamed into my second-floor bedroom windows, and I was happy to be alive; happy to discover that the bloody dead pig on the pillow beside me had been a bad dream. I listened for the sounds of birds just to be sure I wasn't the only living creature on earth. A gull squawked somewhere over the bay. Canada geese were honking on my lawn. A dog barked in the distance. So far, so good.

I arose, showered, shaved, and so forth, and made a cup of freeze-dried microwave coffee in the kitchen.

I had spent the night thinking, or, as we say in the biz, engaged in deductive reasoning. I had also made callbacks to Uncle Harry, parents, siblings, and Dom Fanelli, but not to the *New York Times* or to Max. I told everyone that the person on TV was not me, and that I had not seen the news show or shows in question; I said that I had spent the night watching *Monday Night Football* in the Olde Towne Taverne—which is what I should have done—and I had witnesses. Everyone bought it. I hoped my commanding officer, the aforementioned Detective Lieutenant Wolfe, would also buy it.

Also, I told Uncle H that Margaret Wiley had the hots for him, but he seemed uninterested. He informed me, "Dickie Johnson and I were born together, grew up together, had lots of women together, and got old together, but he died before me."

How depressing. Anyway, I called Dom Fanelli, but he was out, and I left a message with his wife, Mary, whom I used to get along with until I got married, but Mary and Ex didn't like each other at all. Neither my divorce nor my getting shot had made Mary and me buddies again. It's weird. I mean, with partners' wives. It's a bizarre relationship at best. Anyway, I said to Mary, "Tell Dom that wasn't me on TV. A lot of people made the same mistake."

"Okay."

"If I die, it's the CIA who did it. Tell him."

"Okay."

"There may be people on Plum Island who are also trying to kill me. Tell him that."

"Okay."

"Tell him to talk to Sylvester Maxwell, chief of police out here, if I die."

"Okay."

"How're the kids?"

"Okay."

"Gotta run. My lung is collapsing." I hung up.

Well, at least I was on record, and if my phone was tapped by the Feds, it's good for them to hear me tell people that I think the CIA is trying to kill me.

Of course, I didn't really think that. Ted Nash, personally, would like to kill me, but I doubted if the Agency would approve capping a guy just because he was a sarcastic prick. Point was, though, if this thing had to do with Plum Island in some significant way, then it wouldn't surprise me if a few more bodies did turn up.

Last night, while I made my phone calls, I checked out my piece and ammo with a flashlight and magnifying glass. Everything looked okay. Paranoia's kind of fun if it doesn't eat up too much time and doesn't get you off the track. I mean, if you're having a routine day, you can make believe someone's trying to kill you, or otherwise fuck you up, then you can play little games, like using the remote car ignition, imagining someone's tapped your phone, or tampered with your weapon. Some crazy people make up imaginary friends who tell them to kill people. Other crazy people make up imaginary enemies who are trying to kill *them*. The latter, I think, is a little less crazy and a lot more useful.

Anyway, I had spent the rest of the night going through the Gordons' financial records again. It was that or Jay Leno.

I had looked closely at May and June of the previous year to see how the Gordons had financed their one-week vacation in England after their business trip. I noticed now that the Visa card in June *was* slightly higher than usual and so was their Amex. A small bump in a usually smooth road. Also, their phone bill last June was about a hundred dollars higher than usual, indicating perhaps long-distance activity in May. Also, I had to assume they'd taken cash or traveler's checks with them, yet there were no unusual cash withdrawals. This was the first and only indication that there was outside cash available to the Gordons. People with illegal income often buy thousands of dollars in traveler's checks, go out of the country, and blow it out big time.

Or maybe the Gordons knew how to do England on twenty dollars a day.

Whatever the case might be, regarding the printouts, they basically had clean sheets, as we say. Whatever they were up to, they hid it well, or it didn't entail large expenses or large deposits. At least not in this account. The Gordons were very bright, I reminded myself. And they were scientists, and as such, they were careful, patient, and meticulous.

It was now eight A.M. Wednesday morning, and I was on my second cup of bad coffee, looking around the refrigerator for something to eat. Lettuce and mustard? No. Butter and carrots? That worked.

I stood at the kitchen window with my carrot and tub of butter, mulling, brooding, noodling, chewing, and so forth. I waited for the phone to ring, for Beth to confirm for five P.M., but the kitchen was quiet except for the clock.

I was dressed more spiffily this morning with tan cotton pants and striped oxford shirt. A blue blazer hung on the back of the kitchen chair. My .38 was on my ankle, and my shield—for what it was worth out here—was inside my jacket. And, optimist that I am, I also had a condom in my wallet. I was ready for battle or romance, or whatever the day would bring.

Carrot in hand, I walked down the sloping lawn to the bay. A light mist hung above the water. I walked out to the end of my uncle's dock, which needed major repair, and I watched where I stepped. I recalled the time the Gordons tied up to the dock—this would have been about mid-June, only a week or so after I'd met them for the first time, which had been in the bar of Claudio's Restaurant in Greenport.

On the occasion of their docking here at Uncle Harry's, I had been in my customary convalescing position on the back porch, drinking convalescent beer, checking out the bay with the binocs when I spotted them.

Back in Claudio's the week before, they had asked me to describe my house from the water and, sure enough, they'd found it.

I recalled that I had walked down to the dock to greet them, and they talked me into taking a spin with them. We tooled around the series of bays that lie between the North and South Forks of Long Island— Great Peconic Bay and Little Peconic, Noyack Bay and Southold Bay, then out into Gardiners Bay, and then to Orient Point. At one point, Tom opened the throttles on the speedboat, and I thought we were going to go airborne. I mean, that thing was nose up and breaking the sound barrier. Anyway, this was also the time when the Gordons showed me Plum Island. Tom had said, "That's where we work."

Judy had added, "Someday we'll see if we can get you a visitor's pass. It's really interesting."

And so it was.

That was the same day we got caught in the wind and currents in Plum Gut, and I thought I was going to puke my guts into the Gut and wondered if that was how the Gut got its name.

I recalled that we'd spent the whole day on the water and had come back here exhausted, sunburned, dehydrated, and hungry. Tom went for pizzas, and Judy and I slugged beers on the back porch and watched the sun go down.

I don't think I'm a particularly likable fellow, but

the Gordons went out of their way to befriend me, and
I never understood why. I didn't need or want the company, at first. But Tom was smart and funny, and Judy
was beautiful. And bright.

Sometimes things don't make sense while they're
happening, but after a period of time or after an incident or whatever, then the significance of what was
done or said is clear. Right?

The Gordons may have known they were in danger, or could be in danger. They'd already made the
acquaintance of Chief Maxwell, and they wanted some
person or persons to know they were tight with the
Chief. Next, they spent a good deal of time with yours
truly, and again, I think this may have been a way of
showing someone that Tom and Judy hung out with
the fuzz. Maybe Max or I would get a letter delivered if
anything happened to the Gordons, but I wasn't holding my breath.

Also, on the subject of things that made sense in
retrospect, on that particular night in June, before Tom
had returned with the pizza, Judy, who'd poured three
beers into an empty stomach, had asked me, regarding
Uncle's house, "What's a place like this worth?"

"I guess about four hundred thousand, maybe
more. Why?"

"Just wondering. Is your uncle selling it?"

"He offered it to me for below market, but I'd need
a two-hundred-year mortgage."

And there the discussion ended, but when people
ask you how much a house or a boat or car is worth,
then ask you if it's for sale, they're either nosy or in the
market. The Gordons weren't nosy. Now, of course, I
think that the Gordons expected to become rich very

quickly. But if the source of these newfound riches was an illegal transaction, the Gordons could hardly flash the money around and start buying four-hundred-thousand-dollar homes on the water. Therefore, the expected bucks were either legit, or would have the appearance of legit. Vaccine? Maybe.

And then something went wrong, and those bright brains got splattered across the cedar deck, like somebody dropped a five-pound package of ground beef near the barbeque grill.

I remembered later that night in June remarking to Tom that I thought we had been in some danger out in the Gut. Tom had switched from beer to wine and his mind was mellow. He had a philosophical streak for a techno-guy, and he'd said to me, "A boat in the harbor is a safe boat. But that's not what boats are for."

Indeed not, metaphorically speaking. It occurred to me that people who play with Ebola virus and other deadly substances must, by nature, be risk-takers. They had won for so long at the game of biohazard that they'd begun to think they were charmed. They decided to branch out into another dangerous game, but one that was more lucrative. They were, however, out of their element, like the scuba diver who goes mountain climbing, or vice versa; lots of guts and lung power, but not a clue about how it's done.

Well, back to Wednesday morning in September, about nine A.M. now. Tom and Judy Gordon, who stood right here on Uncle Harry's dock with me, are now dead, and the ball is in my court, to switch metaphors.

I turned and walked back toward the house, invigorated by the morning air and my carrot, motivated by my good memories of two nice people, my mind clear, the disappointments and worries of yesterday put in their proper perspective. I was rested and eager to do battle. To kick ass.

I had yet another seemingly unconnected dot that needed to be placed on the sonar screen: Mr. Fredric Tobin, vintner.

But first, thinking someone may have called whilst I was reflecting by the bay, I checked my answering machine, but there were no messages. "Bitch." Now, now, John.

More annoyed than hurt, I left the house. I was wearing Mr. Ralph Lauren's blazer, Mr. Tommy Hilfiger's oxford shirt, Mr. Eddie Bauer's pants, Mr. Perry Ellis' boxer shorts, Mr. Karl Lagerfeld's aftershave, and Messrs. Smith and Wesson's revolver.

I started the car with the remote and climbed in.

"Bonjour, Jeep."

I drove up to Main Road and turned east into the rising sun. Main Road is mostly rural, but becomes the main streets of many of the hamlets. Between the downtowns are barns and farmhouses, nurseries, lots of farm stands, a few good and simple restaurants, a bunch of antique stores, and some really charming New England–style clapboard churches.

One thing that has changed since I was a wee lad, however, is that Main Road now boasts about two dozen wineries. Regardless of where the vineyards are, most of the wineries have set up headquarters on Main Road to rope in the touristos. There are wine tours and free wine tastings, followed by a mandatory visit to the gift shop where the day-tripper feels obligated to buy the local grape nectar along with wine country calendars, cookbooks, corkscrews, coasters, and whatnot.

Most of these winery buildings are actually converted farmhouses and barns, but some are big new complexes that combine the actual wine-making facilities with the wine and gift shop, a restaurant, wine garden, and so forth. Main Road is not exactly the Rue de Soleil, and the North Fork is not the Côte du Rhône, but the overall ambience is pleasant, sort of a cross between Cape Cod and the Napa Valley.

The wines themselves aren't bad, I'm told. Some are quite good, I'm told. Some have won national and international competitions, I'm told. As for *moi*, I'll have a Bud.

In the hamlet called Peconic, I pulled into a big gravel parking field marked by a wooden sign that read "Fredric Tobin Vineyards." The sign was black lacquer, and the letters were carved into the wood and painted gold. Some weird streaks of various-colored paint crisscrossed the black lacquer, and I would have thought this was vandalism, except I'd seen the same streaks on the Tobin wine labels in the liquor stores and also on the wine labels while sitting on the back deck of Tom and Judy's house. Regarding the paint streaks on Mr. Tobin's sign, I concluded that this was art. It's getting harder to tell the difference between art and vandalism.

I exited my expensive sport utility vehicle and noticed a dozen others like my own. This was where they bred, perhaps. Or were these the vehicles-of-choice for urban and suburban cowboys whose definition of off-road meant a parking lot? But I digress.

I walked toward the Tobin complex. The smell of crushed and fermenting grapes was overwhelming, and a million bees flew around; about half of them liked my Lagerfeld.

How shall I describe the Tobin winery? Well, if a French château were built of American cedar shingle, it would look like this place. Clearly Mr. Tobin had spent a small fortune on his dream.

I'd been here before and knew the place. Even before I entered, I knew that the complex consisted of the visitors' reception area, to the left of which was the big gift and wine shop.

To the right was the actual wine-making wing, a sprawling two-story building filled with copper vats, crushers, and all that stuff. I once took a guided tour and listened to the blabber. Never in the course of human events has so much bullshit been concocted about something as small as a grape. I mean, a plum is bigger. Right? People make plum wine. Right? What's with this grape crap?

Anyway, rising above all of this is a broad central tower, sort of like a castle keep, about fifty feet high, from which flies a big flag. I don't mean Old Glory. I mean a black flag with the Tobin logo on it. Someone likes to see his name around.

All of this shingle is stained white, so from a distance it kind of looks like it could be one of those limestone châteaux you see in the travel brochures. Freddie put a big bucko into this thing, making me wonder exactly how much money there was in grape squeezing.

To continue the word picture of Château Tobin: farther to the left was a small restaurant that women and reviewers invariably described as cute. I called it prissy and stuffy. But no matter, it wasn't on my list of places to go if the Olde Towne Taverne was closed by the Board of Health.

The restaurant had a covered terrace where people who dressed with Eddie, Tommy, Ralph, Liz, Carole, and Perry could sit and bullshit about the wine, which, by the way, is really grape juice with alcohol.

Anyway, attached to and behind the cute restaurant is a bigger catering hall, a nice place to have a wedding, christening, or bar mitzvah, according to the brochure that was signed by Fredric Tobin, proprietor.

I'd been to the hall for one of Mr. Tobin's wine-tasting soirees, back in July. The occasion was to celebrate some new releases, by which I guess he meant wine that was ready to sell and guzzle. I had been a guest of the Gordons, as I may have mentioned, and there were about two hundred people present, the cream of North Fork society—bankers, lawyers, doctors, judges, politicians, a few attendees from Manhattan who had summer places here, successful merchants and realtors, and so forth. Mixed in with the local crème were a smattering of artists, sculptors, and writers who, for various and sundry reasons, didn't do the Hampton scene across the bay. Probably many of them weren't financially successful enough to afford the Hamptons, though, of course, they'd tell you they were more artistically honest than their Hampton colleagues. *Barf.* Also, Max had been invited, but couldn't attend. According to Tom and Judy, they were the only Plum Island people there. Tom said, "Hosts and hostesses avoid Plum Island people like the plague." We both got a good chuckle out of that. Gosh, I missed Tom. And Judy, too. She was bright.

I recalled that on this occasion of tasting the juice of the grape, Tom introduced me to our host, Fredric Tobin, a single gentleman who at first glance appeared to be a man who wore comfortable shoes, if you get my meaning. Mr. Tobin was dressed in a foppish purple suit, a white silk shirt, and a tie that sported vines and grape clusters. Gag me with a spoon.

Mr. Tobin was polite, but a bit cool toward *moi*, which always annoys me when I'm in La-Di-Da gatherings. I mean, a homicide detective sort of crosses social lines, and the average host or hostess enjoys a detective or two around to spin a yarn. Everyone loves murder. But Fredric sort of blew me off before I could tell him my theory about wine.

I had mentioned to Tom and Judy that Monsieur didn't even have the courtesy to make a pass at me. Tom and Judy informed me that Freddie (as no one dared call him to his face) was in fact an enthusiastic heterosexual. Some people, according to Judy, mistook Fredric's charm and refined manners as a sign that he was gay or bi. That has never happened to me.

I discovered from the Gordons that the suave and debonair Mr. Tobin had studied viniculture in France and held some grape juice degrees and all that.

Tom had pointed out to me a young lady who was Mr. Tobin's current live-in. She was an absolute knockout—about twenty-five, tall, blonde, blue eyes, and built like she came out of a Jell-O mold. Oh, Freddie, you lucky dog. How could I have misjudged you?

So, that was my sole encounter with the Lord of the Bees. I could see why Tom and Judy had sought this fellow out—for one thing, the Gordons loved wine and Tobin made some of the best. But beyond that, there was a whole social matrix to the wine biz, such as that party, and private dinner parties, and outdoor concerts at the vineyards, extravagant picnics on the beach, and so forth. The Gordons seemed to buy into this whole thing, which surprised me, and though they weren't fawning over Fredric Tobin or sucking up to him, they certainly had little in common with him socially, financially, professionally, or otherwise. Point is, I found it a little out of character for Tom and Judy to be involved with a guy like Fredric. Regarding that name, there's a case of getting rid of an "e" while everyone else around here was trying to tack "e's" onto things. To be succinct, Fredric the Grape seemed like a pompous ass, and I liked the idea of popping his balloons a little. Also, he had a beard, and perhaps a white sports car.

I was now in the gift shop, poking around, trying to find something nice for my lost love, something like a corkscrew whose handle said, "I got screwed on the North Fork." Lacking that, I found a nice hand-painted ceramic tile showing an osprey perching on a pole. This is a very strange-looking bird, but I liked the tile because it had no wine motif.

As the cashier wrapped it, I asked her, "Is Mr. Tobin in?" The attractive young lady glanced at me and replied, "I'm not sure."

"I thought I saw his car. White sports car. Right?"

"He may be around. That will be ten-ninety-seven with tax."

I paid ten-ninety-seven with tax and collected my change and package.

"Have you done the wine tour?" she asked me.

"No, but I saw beer made once." I took my shield case out of my jacket and held it up to her. "Police department, miss. What I'd like you to do is press whatever button on your phone there that will connect you with Mr. Tobin's office and have him come here chop, chop. Okay?"

She nodded and did as she was told. She said into the phone, "Marilyn, there's a policeman here who wants to see Mr. Tobin."

"Chop, chop."

"Without delay," she translated. "Okay...yes, I'll tell him." She hung up and said to me, "He'll be right down."

"Where's up?"

She pointed to a closed door in the far wall and said, "That leads to the tower suites—the business offices."

"Right. Thanks." I went to the door and opened it, finding myself in a large, round wood-paneled common area, sort of a lobby, that was the base of the tower. One door led to the fermenting vats, and one back to the reception area from which I'd entered. A glass-paneled door led outside to the rear of the winery. There was also a staircase leading up, and to the right of that, an elevator.

The elevator door opened, and Mr. Tobin strode out, barely giving me a glance in his haste to get to the gift shop. I noted that the expression on his face was one of concern. I said, "Mr. Tobin?"

He turned toward me. "Yes?"

"Detective Courtney." I sometimes mispronounce my own name.

"Oh....Yes, what can I do for you?"

"I just need some of your time, sir."

"What is this about?"

"I'm a homicide detective."

"Oh...the Gordons."

"Yes, sir." He apparently didn't remember my face,

which is the same one I had in July when I met him. True, my name had changed slightly, but anyway, I wasn't going to prompt him. Regarding my status, jurisdiction, and all that technical crap, I simply had not heard Max's message on my machine. I said to the proprietor, "I understand you were a friend of the victims."

"Well . . . we were social acquaintances."

"I see." Regarding Fredric Tobin, he was dressed, I'm chagrined to say, somewhat like I was dressed: a bunch of designer labels and docksiders. He had no grape tie, but sported a silly lilac-colored puff in the breast pocket of his blue blazer.

Mr. Tobin was a man of about fifty, perhaps younger, less than medium height, which might account for his Napoleon complex. He was of medium build, had a full head of short brown hair, though not all his own, and a neatly trimmed beard. His teeth, also not his own, were pearly white, and his skin was suntanned. All in all, he was a well-groomed fellow, well spoken, and he carried himself well. However, all the cosmetics and grooming couldn't change his beady, dark eyes which moved all over the place, like they were loose in their sockets.

Mr. Tobin wore a pine-scented aftershave lotion which I suspected did not attract bees.

He asked me, "Do I understand that you want to question me?"

"Just a few routine questions." There are no routine questions in a homicide investigation, by the way.

"I'm sorry, I don't . . . I mean, I have absolutely no knowledge of what could have happened to the Gordons."

"Well, they were murdered."

"I know. . . . I meant—"

"I just need some background."

"Perhaps I should call my attorney."

My eyebrows rose at that. I said, "That's your right." I added, "We can do this down at the station house with your attorney present. Or we can do this here in about ten minutes."

He seemed to mull this over. "I don't know. . . . I'm not used to this. . . ."

I spoke in my most engaging tone. "Look, Mr. Tobin, you're not a suspect. I'm just interviewing friends of the Gordons. You know—background."

"I see. Well . . . if you think I can help, I'll be happy to answer any questions you have."

"There you go." I wanted to get this guy away from a phone, so I said, "Hey, I've never walked through a vineyard. Can we do that?"

"Of course. Actually, I was about to do that when you arrived."

"This really works out for everyone."

I followed him out the glass-paneled door into the sunlight. Two small dump trucks were parked nearby, filled with grapes.

Mr. Tobin informed me, "We began harvesting two days ago."

"Monday."

"Yes."

"That's a big day for you."

"It's a fulfilling day."

"You were here all day, I guess."

"I was here early."

I nodded. "Good harvest?"

"Very good, so far, thank you."

We walked across the back lawn into the clos-est vineyard, between two rows of unpicked grapes. It really smelled good out here, and the bees hadn't located me yet, thank goodness.

Mr. Tobin indicated my little bag with his logo on it and inquired, "What did you buy?"

"A painted tile for my girlfriend."

"Which one?"

"Beth."

"I mean, which painted tile?"

"Oh. The osprey."

"They're making a comeback."

"Painted tiles?"

"No. Ospreys. Look, Detective—"

"They're weird. I read that they mate for life. I mean, they're probably not Catholic. Why do they mate for life?"

"Detective—"

"But then I read another version of that. The females *will* mate for life *if* the male comes back to the same nest. You know, the wildlife people put these big poles up with platforms on them, and they build their nests there. The ospreys. Not the wildlife people."

"Detective—"

"What it comes down to is that the female is not really monogamous. She's attached to the *nest*. She goes back to the same nest every year, and she'll screw for the first male who shows up. Sort of like Southampton ladies in their summer houses. You know? They never want to give up the Hampton house. I mean, okay, the guy may be dead, or he took a powder, and he'll never show up. But sometimes he's just late getting a train.

You know? Meanwhile, she's balling the pool guy. But anyway, back to ospreys—"

"Excuse me, Detective... what was—?"

"Just call me John."

He glanced at me, and I could see he was trying to place me, but wasn't quite getting it. In any case, after my little Columbo routine, Tobin had decided I was a simpleton, and he was a little more relaxed. He said to me, "I was shocked to hear the news." He added, "What a tragedy. They were so young and vibrant."

I didn't respond.

"Do you know anything about the funeral arrangements?"

"No, sir, I don't. I think the Gordons are still in the ME's office—the medical examiner. They're all, like, in pieces now, and then they get put back together later. Like a jigsaw puzzle except the ME saves the organs. I mean, how would anyone know the organs are missing?"

Mr. Tobin didn't comment.

We walked awhile in silence through the vineyards. Sometimes if you don't ask questions, the person you're interviewing gets fidgety and starts to babble to fill in the silence. After a minute or so, Mr. Tobin said, "They seemed like such nice people."

I nodded.

He let a few seconds pass, then added, "They couldn't have had an enemy in the world. But there are some strange goings-on at Plum Island. Actually, what happened sounds like a burglary. That's what I heard on the radio. Chief Maxwell said it was a burglary. But some of the media are trying to connect it to Plum Island. I should call Chief Maxwell. He and I are friends. Acquaintances. He knew the Gordons."

"Really? Everyone seems to know everyone else out here."

"It seems that way. It's the geography. We're bounded by water on three sides. It's almost like a small island. Eventually, everyone's paths cross. That's why this is so disturbing. It could have been one of us."

"You mean the killer or the victims?"

"Well, either," Mr. Tobin replied. "The killer could be one of us, and the victims could have been...Do you think the killer will strike again?"

"Oh, I hope not. I have enough to do."

We kept walking along this really long row of vines, but Mr. T had stopped running at the mouth, so I asked him, "How well did you know the Gordons?"

"We were social acquaintances. They were enamored with the glamour and romance of wine making."

"Really?"

"Are you interested in wine, Detective?"

"No, I'm a beer guy, myself. Sometimes I drink vodka. Hey, how does this sound?" I pitched him Krumpinski's real potato vodka, flavored and natural. "What do you think? A sister industry, right? There are potatoes all over the place here. This whole end of Long Island could be swimming in alcohol. Some people see grape jelly and mashed potatoes. We see wine and vodka. What do you think?"

"Interesting concept." He pulled a bunch of white grapes from the vine and squeezed one in his mouth. "Very nice. Firm, sweet, but not too sweet. Just enough sun and rain this year. This is going to be a vintage year."

"Terrific. When was the last time you saw the Gordons?"

"About a week ago. Here, try this." He put a few grapes in my hand.

I put one into my mouth, chewed, and spit out the skin. "Not bad."

"The skins have been sprayed. You should squeeze the pulp into your mouth. Here." He handed me half the bunch. We walked along like old buds, squeezing grape pulp into our mouths—but not each other's mouths. We weren't that close yet. Mr. Tobin went on about the weather, the vines, and all that. He said, "We have the same moderate annual rainfall as Bordeaux."

"You don't say?"

"But our reds are not as dense as Bordeaux-classed growths. Our texture is different."

"Of course."

"In Bordeaux, they let the skins macerate with the new wine for a long time after fermentation. Then they age the wine in the barrel for perhaps two or three years. That won't work for us. Our grapes and theirs are separated by an ocean. They are the same species, but they've developed their own character. Just like us."

"Good observation."

"We also have to handle the wine more gently when racking than they do in Bordeaux. I made some mistakes in the early years."

"We all do."

"Here, protecting the fruit is more important, for instance, than worrying about a tannic taste. We don't get the tannin they do in Bordeaux."

"That's why I'm proud to be an American."

"When making wine, one can't be too dogmatic or too theoretical. You have to discover what works."

"Same with my job."

"But we can learn from the old masters. In Bordeaux, I learned the importance of leaf spread."

"That's the place to learn it." This wasn't as bad as a history lesson, but it was a damned close second. Nonetheless, I let him babble. I stifled a yawn.

He said, "Leaf spread lets you capture sunlight at this northern latitude. They don't have that problem in southern France, or Italy or California. But here on the North Fork, as in Bordeaux, you have to strike a balance between leaf cover and sun on the grapes."

He went on. And on.

And yet, I found myself almost liking the guy, my first impression notwithstanding. I don't mean we were ever going to be big pals, but Fredric Tobin was a man of some charm, though a wee bit intense. You could tell he loved what he did; he seemed very much at home among the vines. I was beginning to understand why the Gordons might like him.

He said to me, "The North Fork is a microclimate. Different from the surrounding areas. Do you know that we get more sunlight than they do right across the bay in the Hamptons?"

"You're kidding. Do the rich people in the Hamptons know that?"

He continued, "More sunlight than right across the Sound in Connecticut?"

"You don't say? Why is that?"

"It has to do with the bodies of water and the prevailing winds around us. We have a maritime climate. Connecticut has a continental climate. It can be ten degrees colder over there in the winter. That would damage the vines."

"Goes without saying."

"Also, it never gets too hot here, which can also stress the vines. The bodies of water all around us have a moderating influence on the climate."

"Warmer, sunnier, ospreys coming back. That's great."

"And the soil is very special. This is very rich glacial soil, just the right nutrients, and it's drained by the sand stratum below."

"Boy, I'll tell you, when I was a kid, if anyone had said to me, 'Hey, John, this will all be vineyards someday,' you know, I'd have laughed in his face and kicked him in the balls."

"Does this interest you?"

"Very much." *Not a bit.*

We turned into another row where a mechanical harvester was beating the crap out of the vines, and the grape bunches were getting sucked into this contraption. Jeez. Who invents these things?

We got into another row where a couple of nubile young things in shorts and Tobin T-shirts were doing it by hand. Baskets of grapes sat in the row. The Lord of the Vines stopped and bantered with them. He was on his game today, and the nubes were responding well. He was probably old enough to be their father, but girls paid attention to money, pure and simple. I had to use all my charm and wit to get the little undies off, but I know rich guys who say less clever and charming things to young ladies—things like, "Let's fly Concorde to Paris this weekend." Works every time.

After a minute or so, we moved on from the little grape pluckers, and Mr. Tobin said to me, "I haven't heard the news this morning, but one of my employees told me that she heard on the radio that the Gordons had possibly stolen a new miracle vaccine and were going to sell it. Apparently they were double-crossed and murdered. Is that right?"

"That seems to be what happened."

"There's no danger of a ... a plague, or some kind of epidemic—"

"None at all."

"Good. There were a lot of worried people the other night."

"Worry no more. Where were you Monday night?"

"Me? Oh, I was at dinner with friends. In my own restaurant, right here, as a matter of fact."

"What time?"

"About eight. We hadn't even heard the news yet."

"Where were you earlier? Like about five, 5:30."

"I was home."

"Alone?"

"I have a housekeeper and a girlfriend."

"That's nice. Will they recall where you were at 5:30?"

"Of course. I was home." He added, "That was the day of the first pick. I arrived here about dawn. By four I was exhausted and went home to nap. Then I came back here for dinner. A little celebration to mark the harvest. You never know when the first pick will be, so it's always spontaneous. In a week or two, we'll have a big harvest dinner."

"What a life." I asked, "Who was at dinner?"

"My girlfriend, the estate manager, some friends...." He looked at me and said, "This sounds like an inter- rogation."

It should. It was. But I didn't want to get Mr. Tobin agitated and have him calling his lawyer, or Max. I said to him, "These are just standard questions, Mr. Tobin. I'm trying to get a picture of where everyone was Monday night, what everyone's relationship was to the deceased. That sort of thing. When we have a suspect, then some of the friends and co-workers of the Gordons may become witnesses. You see? We don't know until we know."

"I see."

I let him settle down awhile, and we did grape talk again. The guy was smooth, but like anyone else, he was a little jumpy around the fuzz. I asked him, "When and where did you see the Gordons last week?"

"Oh...let me think....Dinner at my house. I had a few people over."

"What was your attraction to the Gordons?"

"What do you mean?"

"Just what I said."

He replied, "I think I indicated it was the other way around, Detective."

"Then why would you invite them to your house?"

"Well...in truth, they told some fascinating tales about Plum Island. My guests always enjoyed that." He added, "The Gordons earned their dinner."

"Did they?" The Gordons rarely spoke about their job to me.

"Also," he said, "they were an exceptionally attractive couple." He asked me, "Did you...I mean, I suppose when you saw them...but she was a rare beauty."

"Indeed she was." I asked, "Were you popping her?"

"Excuse me?"

"Were you sexually involved with Mrs. Gordon?"

"Heavens, no."

"Did you give it a try?"

"Of course not."

"Did you at least *think* about it?"

He thought about if he thought about it, then said, "Sometimes. But I'm not a wife chaser. I have enough on my plate."

"Do you?" I guess champagne works when you own the vineyard, the château, the fermenting vats, and the bottling plant. I wonder if guys who own microbreweries get laid as much as vintners? Probably not. Go figure.

Anyway, I asked Mr. Tobin, "Have you ever been to the Gordons' house?"

"No. I don't even know where they lived."

"Then where did you send the social invitations?"

"Well...my public relations person does that. But now that I think about it, I recall that they live...lived in Nassau Point."

"Yes, sir. It was in all the news. Nassau Point residents found murdered."

"Yes. And I remember they mentioned they had a place on the water."

"Indeed they do. Did. They commuted to Plum Island often. They probably said that a few dozen times at dinner parties along with the Plum Island stories."

"Yes, they did."

I noticed that Mr. Tobin had little beads of sweat at the base of his hair weave. I had to keep in mind that the most innocent of people got the sweats when they were under the modified and civilized third degree. I mean, we used to talk about sweating information out of people in the old days—you know, the glaring lights, the nonstop interrogations, the third degree, whatever the hell that means. Today, we're very gentle, sometimes, but no matter how gentle you are, some people—innocent and guilty alike—just don't like being questioned.

It *was* getting a little warmer, and I took off my blue blazer and threw it over my shoulder. My S&W was on my ankle so Mr. T was not alarmed.

The bees had found me and I said, "Do these sting?"

"If you annoy them, they do."

"I'm not annoying them. I like bees."

"They're actually wasps. Yellow jackets. You must be wearing some cologne that they like."

"Lagerfeld."

"That's one of their favorites." He added, "Ignore them."

"Right. Were the Gordons invited to dinner Monday night?"

"No, I wouldn't have normally invited them to a small, spontaneous gathering....Monday's gathering was mostly close friends and people involved with the business."

"I see."

"Why do you ask that?"

"Oh, just for the irony of it. You know, if they'd been asked, maybe they'd have come home sooner, gotten dressed...you know, they might have missed their appointment with death."

He replied, "No one misses their appointment with death."

"Yeah, you know, I think you're right."

We were in a row of vines with purple grapes now.

I asked Mr. Tobin, "Why do purple grapes make red wine?"

"Why...? Well...I guess you could more properly call it purple wine."

"I would."

Mr. Tobin said, "This is actually called pinot noir. Noir means black."

"I took French. These grapes are called black, they look purple, and the wine is called red. You see why people are confused?"

"It's really not that complicated."

"Sure it is. Beer is easy. There's lager and pilsner. Right? Then you have ale and stout. Forget those and forget dark beer and bock. Basically you have lager and pilsner, light or regular. You go into a bar, and you can see what's on tap because the taps are labeled. You can ask, 'What do you have in bottles?' When they're through rattling it all off, you say, 'Bud.' End of story."

Mr. Tobin smiled. "That's very amusing. Actually, I enjoy a good, cold beer on a hot day." He leaned toward me conspiratorially and said, "Don't tell anyone."

"Your secret is safe with me. Hey, this goes on forever. How many acres do you have here?"

"Here I have two hundred acres. I have another two hundred scattered around."

"Wow. That's big. Do you lease land?"

"Some."

"Do you lease land from Margaret Wiley?"

He didn't reply immediately, and if I'd been facing him across a table, I could have seen his expression the moment I said, "Margaret Wiley." But the hesitation was interesting enough.

Finally, Mr. Tobin replied, "I believe we do. Yes, we do. About fifty acres. Why do you ask?"

"I know she leases land to the vintners. She's an old friend of my aunt and uncle. It's a small world. Small fork." I changed the subject and asked, "So, are you the biggest grape on the fork?"

"Tobin is the biggest vineyard on the North Fork, if that's what you mean."

"How'd you manage that?"

"Hard work, a good knowledge of viniculture, perseverance, and a superior product." He added, "And good luck. What frightens us here is hurricanes. Late August to early October. One year the harvest was very late. About mid-October. No fewer than six hurricanes came up from the Caribbean. But every one of them turned off in another direction. Bacchus was watching over us." He added, "That's the god of wine."

"And a hell of a composer."

"That's Bach."

"Right."

"By the way, we have concerts here and sometimes operas. I can put you on our mailing list, if you'd like."

We found ourselves heading back into the big shingled complex. I said, "That would be great. Wine, opera, good company. I'll send you my card. I'm out at the moment."

As we approached the winery, I looked around and said, "I don't see your house."

"I don't actually live here. I do have an apartment on the top of that tower, but my house is south of here."

"On the water?"

"Yes."

"Do you boat?"

"A little."

"Motor or sail?"

"Motor."

"And the Gordons were guests in your house?"

"Yes. A few times."

"They arrived by boat, I guess."

"I believe they did once or twice."

"And did you ever visit them in your boat?"

"No."

I was going to ask him if he owned a white Formula, but sometimes it's a good idea not to ask a question about something you can discover another way. Questions tend to tip people off, to spook them. Fredric Tobin, as I said, was not a murder suspect, but I had the impression he was hiding something.

Mr. Tobin showed me in through the entrance that we'd come out of. He said, "If I can be of any further help, please let me know."

"Okay...hey, I have a date tonight, and I'd like to get a bottle of wine."

"Try our Merlot. The '95 is incomparable. But a little pricey."

"Why don't you show me? I have a few more things to cover anyway."

He hesitated a moment, then led me into the gift shop, which was attached to a spacious wine-tasting room. It was a very handsome room with a thirty-foot-long oak tasting bar, a half dozen booths to one side, boxes and racks of wine all over the place, stained glass windows, a quarry tile floor, and so on. About a dozen wine lovers meandered around the room, commenting on the labels or slurping up freebies at the wine bar, making stupid talk with the young men and women who were pouring and trying to smile.

Mr. Tobin said hello to one of the pourers, Sara, by name, an attractive young lady in her mid-twenties. I assumed that Fredric picked the furniture himself, and he had a good eye for clean-cut pretties. The boss said, "Sara, pour Mr...."

"John."

"Pour John some of the '95 Merlot."

And she did, with a steady hand into a small glass.

I swirled the stuff around to show I was into this. I sniffed it and said, "Nice bouquet." I held it up to the light and said, "Good color. Purple."

"And nice fingers."

"Where?"

"The way it clings to the glass."

"Right." I sipped a little. I mean, it's okay. It's an acquired taste. It's actually not bad with a steak. I said, "Fruity and friendly."

Mr. Tobin nodded enthusiastically. "Yes. And forward."

"Very forward." *Forward?* I said, "This is a bit heavier and more robust than a Napa Merlot."

"Actually, it's a bit lighter."

"That's what I meant." I should have quit while I was ahead. "Good." I put the glass down.

Mr. Tobin said to Sara, "Pour the '95 Cabernet."

"That's all right."

"I want you to see the difference."

She poured. I sipped and said, "Good. Less forward."

We chitchatted a bit, and Mr. Tobin insisted I try a white.

He said, "This is my blend of Chardonnay and other

whites which I won't reveal. It has a beautiful color, and we call it Autumn Gold."

I sampled the wine. "Friendly, but not too forward."

He didn't reply.

I said, "Did you ever think of calling one of your wines the Grapes of Wrath?"

"I'll take that up with my marketing people."

I commented, "Nice labels."

Mr. Tobin informed me, "All my reds have labels with a piece of Pollock art, and my whites are de Kooning."

"Is that so?"

"You know—Jackson Pollock and Willem de Kooning. They both lived on Long Island and created some of their best works here."

"Oh, the painters. Right. Pollock is the splatter guy."

Mr. Tobin didn't reply, but glanced at his watch, clearly tired of my company. I looked around and spotted an empty booth, away from the wine pourers and customers. I said, "Let's sit over there a minute."

Mr. Tobin followed reluctantly and sat opposite me in the booth. I sipped at the Cabernet and said to him, "Just a few more routine questions. How long did you know the Gordons?"

"Oh...about a year and a half."

"Did they ever discuss their work with you?"

"No."

"You said they liked to tell Plum Island stories."

"Oh, yes. In a general way. They never gave away government secrets." He smiled.

"That's good. Did you know they were amateur archaeologists?"

"I...yes, I did."

"Did you know they belonged to the Peconic Historical Society?"

"Yes. In fact, that's how we met."

"Everyone seems to belong to the Peconic Historical Society."

"There are about five hundred members. That's not everyone."

"But everyone *I* come across seems to belong. Is this like a front for something else? Like a witches' coven or something?"

"Not as far as I know. That could be fun, though."

We both smiled. He seemed to mull something over; I can tell when a man is mulling, and I never interrupt a muller. Finally, he said, "As a matter of fact, the Peconic Historical Society is having a party Saturday night. I am hosting it on my back lawn. Last outdoor party of the season, weather permitting. Why don't you and a guest join us?"

I guess he had room for two more now that the Gordons couldn't make it. I replied, "Thanks. I'll try." Actually, I wouldn't miss it.

He said, "Chief Maxwell may be there. He has all the particulars."

"Great. Can I bring something? Wine?"

He smiled politely. "Just bring yourself."

"And a guest," I reminded him.

"Yes, and a guest."

I asked Mr. Tobin, "Did you ever hear anything... any gossip about the Gordons?"

"Such as?"

"Well, sexual, for instance."

"Not a word."

"Financial problems?"

"I wouldn't know."

And round and round we went for another ten minutes. Sometimes you catch a person in a lie, sometimes you don't. Any lie, no matter how small, is significant. I didn't exactly catch Mr. Tobin in any lies, but I was fairly certain he knew the Gordons more intimately than he was letting on. In and of itself, this was not significant. I asked Mr. Tobin, "Can you name any of the Gordons' friends?"

He thought a moment, then said, "Well, as I said, your colleague, Chief Maxwell, for one." He named a few other people whose names I didn't recognize. He said, "I really don't know their friends or professional associates well. As I said... well, let me put it bluntly— they were sort of hangers-on. But they were attractive, well spoken, and had interesting jobs. They were both Ph.D.'s. You can say we each got something out of the arrangement.... I like to surround myself with interesting and beautiful people. Yes, that's somewhat shallow, but you'd be surprised how shallow the interesting and beautiful people can be." He added, "I'm sorry about what happened to them, but I can't help you any further."

"You've been very helpful, Mr. Tobin. I really appreciate your time, and I appreciate your not making a big deal of this with an attorney."

He didn't reply.

I slid out of the booth, and he did the same. I said, "Will you walk me out to my car?"

"If you'd like."

I stopped at a counter on which was lots of literature about wine, including some brochures on and about Tobin Vineyards. I gathered a bunch of them and threw them in my little bag. I said, "I'm one of those brochure nuts. I have all these brochures from Plum Island—rinderpest, lumpy skin disease—anyway, I'm getting a real education on this case."

Again, he didn't reply.

I asked him to find me the Merlot '95, which he did. I said, apropos the label, "Jackson Pollock. I never would have guessed. Now I have something to talk about with my date tonight." I brought the wine to the cashier, and if I thought Mr. Tobin was going to charge it off to goodwill, I was wrong. I paid the full price, plus tax.

We walked out into the sunlight. I said, "By the way, I was, like yourself, an acquaintance of the Gordons."

He stopped walking and I, too, stopped. He looked at me.

I said, "John Corey."

"Oh...yes. I didn't catch the name...."

"Corey. John."

"Yes...I remember now. You're the policeman who was wounded."

"That's right. I'm feeling much better now."

"Aren't you a New York City detective?"

"Yes, sir. Hired by Chief Maxwell to help out."

"I see."

"So, the Gordons did mention me?"

"Yes."

"Did they say nice things about me?"

"I'm sure they did, but I don't recall precisely."

"We've actually met once. Back in July. You had a big wine-tasting thing in your big room there."

"Oh, yes...."

"You had on a purple suit and a tie with grapes and vines."

He looked at me. "Yes, I think we did meet."

"No doubt about it." I looked around the gravel lot and commented, "Everyone has a four-wheel drive these days. That's mine over there. It speaks French," I explained, as I started it with the remote. I asked Mr. Tobin, "Is that your white Porsche over there?"

"Yes, it is. How do you know that?"

"I just thought it might be. You're a Porsche kind of guy." I put my hand out, and we shook. I said, "I might see you at your party."

"I hope you find who did it."

"Oh, I'm sure I will. I always do. Ciao. Bonjour."

"Bonjour is hello."

"Right. Au revoir."

We parted, our footsteps crunching across the gravel in opposite directions. The bees followed me to my car, but I slipped inside quickly and drove off.

I thought about Mr. Fredric Tobin, proprietor, bon vivant, connoisseur of all things beautiful, local big wheel, acquaintance of the deceased.

My training told me he was clean as a whistle, and I shouldn't spend another minute thinking about him. Of all the theories I'd developed about why the Gordons were murdered and who may have done it, Mr. T did not fit one of them. Yet, my instinct told me to follow up on the gentleman.

CHAPTER SEVENTEEN

I headed west along Main Road, trying to read the vehicle owner's manual as I drove. I pushed a few buttons on the dashboard, and voilà, the LED displays all went from metric to one hundred percent American. This is the most fun you can have in the front seat of a car.

Feeling now technologically enriched, I accessed my telephone answering machine with my cell phone. "I'll tell ya, if those pilgrims could see us now, tooling around past their old farms and villages—"

The machine said, "You have three messages."

One must be from Beth. I listened, but the first was from Max, reiterating that I was no longer on the case and asking me to call him back, which I had no intention of doing. The second message was from Dom Fanelli. He said, "Yo, J.C. Got your message. If you need help out there, just holler. Meanwhile, I'm getting some leads about who used you for target practice, so I don't want to leave it up in the air unless you really need me there. Why do so many people want to kill my good bud? Hey, I spoke to Wolfe personally, and he's not buying that it wasn't you on TV. He says he has information that it was. He wants you to answer some questions. My advice is monitor your calls. That's it for now. Keep your bubble out of trouble."

"Thanks."

The last message was not from Beth, but was from none other than my commanding officer, Detective Lieutenant Andrew Wolfe. He didn't say much except, "I'd like you to call me back as soon as possible." Ominous.

I wondered if Nash and Wolfe really knew each other. The point was, however, that undoubtedly Nash had told Wolfe that, indeed, it had been John Corey on TV, and John Corey was working a homicide case when he was supposed to be on convalescent leave. All those statements were true, and I suppose Andrew Wolfe wanted an explanation from me. I know I could explain how I'd gotten involved with this case, but it would be difficult for me to explain to Detective Lieutenant Wolfe why he was an asshole.

All things considered, it would be best not to return that call. Maybe I should speak to my lawyer. No good deed goes unpunished. I mean, I'm just trying to be a good citizen, and the guy who talked me into this, my buddy Max, picks my brains, gets me into a pissing match with the Feds, then pulls my shield. Actually, he never gave me a shield. And Beth hasn't called.

I kept reminding myself I was a hero, though I'm not sure how getting shot is heroic. When I was a kid, only people who shot *at* bad guys were heroes. Now everyone who gets a disease, or who's held hostage, or who gets plugged is a hero. But if I could trade on the hero thing to get my ass out of hot water, I surely would.

Problem was, media-made heroes had only about ninety days shelf-life. I got shot in mid-April. Maybe I should call my lawyer.

I was in the hamlet of Cutchogue now, approaching downtown, which can get by you real quick if you're not paying attention. Cutchogue is ye olde quaint, neat, and prosperous, like most of these hamlets, partly because of the wine biz, I think. There were long banners strung across Main Street advertising a whole bunch of events, like the Annual East End Seaport Maritime Festival, and a concert at Horton Lighthouse featuring the Isotope Stompers. Don't ask.

Well, the summer was officially over, but the fall season had a lot going on for the residents and for the smaller number of tourists. I always suspected there was a big party held each November, open to locals only, and it was called, "The North Fork Residents Say Good Riddance to the Fucking Tourists Festival."

So there I was driving very slowly, looking for the Peconic Historical Society building that I remembered was somewhere around Main Road. To the south side of the road was the Cutchogue Village Green, which boasted the oldest house in New York State, circa 1649, according to the sign. This looked promising, and I drove down a small lane that bisected the green. There were a number of old clapboards and shingled buildings across the green which thankfully lacked pillories, stocks, dunking stools, or any other public displays of early American S&M.

Finally, a short distance from the village green, I saw a big white clapboard house, a mansion really, with tall white pillars in front. A wooden Chippendale-style sign on the lawn said, "Peconic Historical Society." Beneath that it said, "Museum," then, "Gift Shoppe." Two "p's" and an "e." I won a Scrabble game with that word once.

Hanging from two short chains was another sign giving the days and hours that the museum and gift shoppe were open. After Labor Day, the hours were confined to weekends and holidays.

There was a phone number on the sign, and I dialed it. There was a recorded message, a woman's voice that sounded like it was taped in 1640, which went on about hours and events and all of that.

Never one to be put off by other people's agendas, I got out, climbed the steps to the big porch, and knocked with ye olde brass knocker. I really gave it a good pounding, but no one seemed to be about, and there were no cars in the small lot to the side.

I got back into my vehicle and dialed my new friend, Margaret Wiley. She answered, and I said, "Good morning, Mrs. Wiley. This is Detective Corey."

"Yes."

"You mentioned yesterday about seeing the Peconic Historical Society museum, and I was thinking about that all day. Do you think it would be possible to go see it today and maybe speak to some of the officers—what was the president's name? Witherspoon?"

"Whitestone. Emma Whitestone."

"Right. Is that possible today?"

"I don't know...."

"Why don't I call Emma Whitestone—"

"I'll call her. She may consent to meet you at the museum."

"Great. I really appreciate—"

"Where can I reach you?"

"Tell you what. I'll call you back in ten or fifteen

minutes. I'm in my car, and I have to stop and get a gift for my mother. It's her birthday. Hey, I'll bet you have a gift shop in the museum."

"We do."

"Great. By the way, I spoke to my Uncle Harry and gave him your regards."

"Thank you."

"He said to say hello to you, and he'd like to call you when he gets out here." I didn't mention Uncle Harry's dead dick.

"That would be nice."

"Terrific. Okay, I'd really appreciate it if Mrs. White-stone or any of the other officers of the society could meet me this morning."

"I'll do what I can. I may have to come myself."

"Don't put yourself out. And thanks for your help yesterday."

"Don't mention it."

I almost didn't. "Fifteen minutes. Call around."

"Is your friend with you today?"

"My partner?"

"Yes, the young lady."

"She'll be along shortly."

"She's a delightful woman. I enjoyed speaking to her."

"We're going to get married."

"How unfortunate." She hung up.

Oh, well. I threw the vehicle into gear, and the female voice was back, telling me, "Release emergency brake," which I did. I messed around with the computer awhile, trying to delete this option, expecting the voice to say, "Why are you trying to kill me? Don't you like me? I'm only trying to help you."

What if the doors locked and the gas pedal went down to the floor? I threw the owner's manual in the glove compartment.

I turned south on the delightfully named Skunk Lane, then across the causeway to Nassau Point again.

I drove to the Gordons' street and noticed Max's white Jeep out front of the crime scene. I pulled into the Murphys' driveway, out of sight of the Gordons' house.

I went directly to the rear of the Murphys' house and saw them in the TV room, known also as the Florida room, a jalousied extension to the original building. The TV was going, and I rapped on the screen door.

Edgar Murphy stood, saw me, and opened the door. "Back again?"

"Yes, sir. I just need a minute of your time."

He motioned me inside. Mrs. Murphy stood and gave me a lukewarm hello. The TV stayed on. For a half second, I was at my parents' house in Florida—same room, same TV show, same people, really. Anyway, I said to them, "Describe the white sports car you saw next door in June."

They both gave it a go, but their descriptive powers were limited. Finally, I took a pen out of my pocket, picked up a newspaper, and asked them to draw an outline of the car, but they said they couldn't. I drew an outline of a Porsche for them. You're not supposed to lead a witness like this, but what the hell. They both nodded. Mr. Murphy said, "Yup, that's it. Big fat car. Like a turned-over washtub." Mrs. Murphy agreed.

I took the Tobin Vineyards brochure from my pocket and folded it so as to show only a small black-and-white photo of Fredric Tobin, proprietor. I didn't let them see the whole brochure because they would have told everybody that the police thought Fredric Tobin murdered the Gordons.

The Murphys studied the photo. Again, this is really leading the witness, showing only one photo without mixing it up with others, but I had no time or patience for procedure. I did not, however, say, "Is this the man you saw in the sports car?"

Mrs. Murphy, however, did say, "That's the man I saw in the sports car."

Mr. Murphy agreed. He asked me, "Is that a suspect?"

"No, sir. Okay, sorry to bother you again." I asked, "Did anyone try to question you about this case?"

"Nope."

"Remember, don't talk to anyone except Chief Maxwell, me, and Detective Penrose."

Mr. Murphy asked, "Where is she?"

"Detective Penrose? She's home with morning sickness."

"Pregnant?" asked Agnes.

"About a month," I replied. "Okay—"

"I didn't see a wedding ring," observed Agnes.

"You know how these young girls are." I shook my head sadly, then said, "Okay, thanks again." I exited quickly, got back into my Jeep, and drove off.

Apparently Mr. Fredric Tobin had been at the Gordons' on at least one occasion. Yet, he didn't seem to recall his June visit. But maybe it wasn't him. Maybe it was another brown-bearded man in a white Porsche.

Maybe I should find out why Mr. Tobin lied.

I tried my answering machine again, and there were

two new calls. The first was Max, who said, "John, this is Chief Maxwell. Maybe I didn't make myself clear about your status. You're no longer working for the township. Okay? I got a call from Fredric Tobin's attorneys, and they're not happy people. Understand? I don't know exactly what you and Mr. Tobin discussed, but I think that's the last official conversation you should have with him. Call me."

Interesting. All I'm trying to do is help, and I'm getting hometowned by the local old boys.

The next call was from my ex, whose name is Robin Paine, which fits her, and who also happens to be an attorney. She said, "Hello, John, this is Robin. I want to remind you that our one-year separation ends on October first, at which time we are legally divorced. You'll get a copy of the decree in the mail. There's nothing for you to sign or do. It's automatic." She put a light tone in her voice and said, "Well, you can't commit adultery after October first unless you remarry. But don't get married before you get your decree or it's bigamy. Saw you on the news. Sounds like a fascinating case. Be well."

Right. Robin, by the way, was a Manhattan assistant district attorney once, which is how I met her. We were on the same side. She switched sides and took a high-paying job with a big-name defense attorney who liked her style in court. He may have liked more than her style, but aside from that, our marriage became a conflict of interest. I mean, I'm trying to put scumbags in the slammer, and the woman I'm sleeping with is trying to keep them in business. The last straw was when she took the case of a high-level drug guy who, aside from his American problems, was wanted in

Colombia for icing a judge. I mean, Jeez, lady, I know somebody has to do it, and the money is terrific, but I was feeling matrimonially challenged. So I told her, "It's me or your job," to which she replied, "Maybe you should change *your* job" and she meant it—her firm needed a private investigator and she wanted me to take the job. I pictured doing PI work for her and her idiot boss. Maybe getting their coffee between cases. Right. Divorce, please.

Aside from these little career conflicts, we were actually in love once. Anyway, October first. Then she is officially ex, and I lose the opportunity to be an adulterer or a bigamist. Life just isn't fair sometimes.

Over the causeway and onto Main Road, heading back toward the hamlet of Cutchogue. I called Margaret Wiley.

She said, "I reached Emma at her florist shop, and she's on her way to the Peconic Historical Society house."

"That's very nice of her to give up her time."

"I told her it concerned the Gordon murders."

"Well, I'm not sure it does, Mrs. Wiley. I was just curious about—"

"You can discuss that with her. She's waiting for you."

"Thank you." I think she hung up before I did.

Anyway, I drove back to the Peconic Historical Society house and parked in the small lot beside a van marked "Whitestone Florist."

I went to the front door, and there was a yellow Post-it near the knocker that said, "Mr. Corey, please let yourself in."

So, I did.

The house, as I said, was large, circa about 1850s, typical of the home of a rich merchant or sea captain. The foyer was big, and to the left was a large sitting room, to the right was the dining room. The place was all antiques, of course, mostly junk if you want my opinion, but probably worth a bunch of buckos. I didn't see or hear anyone in the house, so I wandered about from room to room. It wasn't actually a museum in the sense of exhibits; it was just a decorated period house. I couldn't see anything sinister about the place, no paintings of burning churches on the walls, no black candles, no needlepoint pentagrams or black cats, and the kitchen had no bubbling witch's cauldron.

I wasn't sure why I was here, but something had drawn me here. On the other hand, I think I had geriatric overload, and the thought of talking to one more septuagenarian was more than I could handle. I should have opened the bottle of Tobin wine and chugged it before meeting Mrs. Whitestone.

Presently, I found the gift shop—Gift Shoppe—which had once been a summer kitchen, I think, and I went in. The lights were off, but sunlight came in through the windows.

The gifts ran the gamut from locally published books to local handicrafts, Indian crafts, needlepoint, dried herbs, pressed flowers, herbal teas, floral scents, candles (none black), watercolors, more painted tiles, seed packets, and so on. What do people do with all this crap?

I picked up a piece of weathered barn siding on which someone had painted an old sailing ship. As I studied the painting, I felt that someone was watching me.

I turned toward the entrance of the gift shop and a good-looking woman of about thirty-something was standing there, staring at me. I said, "I'm looking for Emma Whitestone."

"You must be John Corey."

"I must be. Do you know if she's in?"

"I'm Emma Whitestone."

The day was turning around. "Oh," I said. "I expected someone older."

"I expected someone younger."

"Oh...."

"Margaret said you were a young man. But you're closer to middle age, I think."

"Uh...."

She walked up to me and extended her hand. She said, "I'm president of the Peconic Historical Society. How can I help you?"

"Well...I don't know."

"Neither do I."

Okay, here's the deal: she was tall—only an inch or so shorter than I am—thin but shapely, shoulder-length brown hair that was washed but not ironed, light makeup, no nail polish, no jewelry, no earrings, no wedding or engagement ring. And she wasn't wearing much clothing either. She had on a knee-length, beige cotton summer dress with itty-bitty shoulder straps holding it up. Beneath this scanty number was little in the way of underwear. Certainly no bra, but I could see bikini panty lines. Also, she was barefoot. If I pictured Ms. Whitestone dressing this morning, she had slipped on the panties and the dress, put on a touch of lipstick, sort of combed her hair, and that was it. She could conceivably get out of that outfit in four seconds. Less with my help.

"Mr. Corey? Are you thinking about how I can help you?"

"Yes, I am. Just a second." She was not overly built, but was designed for speed and perhaps endurance. She had nice gray-green eyes and her face, aside from being pretty, was, at first glance, innocent. She reminded me of photos I'd seen of 1960s flower children, but maybe I thought that because she was a florist. On second look, there was a quiet sexuality in her features. Really.

I should mention, too, that she had a nice, even tan, giving her skin a café au lait color. This was one good-looking and sensual woman. Emma Whitestone.

"This has to do with the Gordons?"

"Yes." I put down the piece of barn siding and asked, "Did you know them?"

"Yes. We were friendly, but not friends." She added, "It was awful."

"Yes."

"Do you have any . . . leads?"

"No."

"I heard on the radio that they may have stolen a vaccine."

"Looks that way."

She thought a moment, then said to me, "You knew them."

"That's right. How do you know?"

"Your name came up a few times."

"Did it? In a nice way, I hope."

"Very nice." She added, "Judy had a little crush on you."

"Really?"

"Didn't you know?"

"Maybe." I wanted to change this subject, so I said, "Do you have, like, a list of members here?"

"Sure. The office is upstairs. I was doing some paperwork there when you arrived. Follow me."

I followed her. She had on a lavender scent. As we made our way through the mansion, I said, "Beautiful house."

She glanced back at me and said, "I'll give you a personal tour later."

"Terrific. Wish I had my camera."

We went up the wide, sweeping stairs, me still slightly behind her. Her panties really were skimpy. Also, she had nice feet, if you're into that.

On the second floor, she led me into a room that she described as the upstairs parlor. She invited me to sit in a wingback chair near the fireplace, which I did.

She said, "Can I offer you a cup of herbal tea?"

"I've had several cups already, thank you."

She sat in a wooden rocker opposite me and crossed her long, long legs. She asked, "What exactly do you need, Mr. Corey?"

"John. Please call me John."

"John. Please call me Emma."

"Well, Emma," I began, "I'd first like to ask you a few questions about the Peconic Historical Society. What's it all about?"

"It's about history. The North Fork has a number of local historical societies, most housed in historic buildings. This is the largest of all the societies and is named Peconic, an Indian name for this region. We have about five hundred members. Some are very prominent, some are simple farmers. We are dedicated to preserving, recording, and passing on our heritage."

"And discovering more about that heritage."

"Yes."

"Through archaeology."

"Yes. And research. We have some interesting archives here."

"Could I see them later?"

"You can see whatever you'd like later." She smiled.

Oh, my heart. I mean, was this a tease, or was this for real? I smiled at her. She smiled again.

Back to the job. I asked her, "Were the Gordons active members?"

"They were."

"When did they join?"

"About a year and a half ago. They'd moved here from Washington, D.C. They were from the Midwest, but they'd worked for the government in Washington. I suppose you know that."

"Did they ever discuss their work with you?"

"Not really."

"Have you ever been to their house?"

"Once."

"Did you socialize with them?"

"Now and then. The Peconic Historical Society is very social. That's one of the reasons they enjoyed us."

I asked, with some subtlety, "Did Tom have the hots for you?"

Instead of being insulted or shocked, she replied, "Probably."

"But you were not sexually involved with him?"

"No. He never asked."

I cleared my throat. "I see...."

"Look, Mr. Corey—John. You're wasting your time and my time with those kinds of questions. I don't know why or who murdered the Gordons, but it had nothing to do with me or with a sexual triangle involving me."

"I didn't say it did. I'm just exploring any sexual angles as part of the larger investigation."

"Well, I wasn't sleeping with him. I think he was faithful. She was faithful, too, as far as I know. It's hard to have an affair around here without everyone knowing about it."

"That may be your perception."

She regarded me a moment, then asked me, "Were you and Judy involved?"

"No, we weren't, Ms. Whitestone. This is not the afternoon soaps. This is a murder investigation, and I'll ask the questions."

"Don't be so touchy."

I took a deep breath and said, "I apologize."

"I want you to find the murderer. Ask your questions."

"Right. Okay...let me ask you this...what was your first thought when you heard they'd been murdered?"

"I don't know. I suppose I thought it had to do with their jobs."

"Okay. What do you think now?"

"I have no opinions."

"I find that hard to believe."

"Let's come back to that."

"Okay." I still wasn't sure where I wanted to go with this interview, or what I was specifically seeking. But I had this mental image in my mind, sort of a map, and on it was Plum Island, Nassau Point, the bluffs above Long Island Sound, Tobin Vineyards, and the Peconic Historical Society. If you connected these points with a line, you had a five-sided geometric shape with no meaning. But if you connected these points in a metaphysical way, maybe the shape made sense. I mean, what was the common element of these five points? Maybe there wasn't any; but somehow they seemed connected, they seemed to share something. What?

I thought about whatever it was that had pinged in my head on Plum Island. History. Archaeology. That was it. *What* was it?

I asked Ms. Whitestone, "Do you know any of the people who work on Plum Island?"

She thought a moment, then replied, "Not really. A few of my customers work there. Other than Tom and Judy, I don't know any of the scientists and none of them belong to the historical society." She added, "They're a close-knit group. Keep to themselves."

"Do you know anything about the proposed digs on Plum Island?"

"Only that Tom Gordon had promised the historical society a chance to root around on the island."

"You're not into archaeology?"

"Not really. I prefer archive work. I have a degree in archival science. Columbia University."

"Is that so? I teach at John Jay," which is actually about fifty blocks due south of Columbia. Finally, we had something in common.

"What do you teach?" she asked.

"Criminal science and ceramics."

She smiled. Her toes wiggled. She recrossed her legs. Beige. The panties were beige like the dress. I was at a point where I almost had to cross *my* legs lest Ms.

Whitestone notice that Lord Pudly was stirring from his nap. *Keep your pee-pee in the teepee.*

I said, "Archival science. Fascinating."

"It can be. I worked at Stony Brook for a while, then got a job out here in the Cutchogue Free Library. Founded in 1841, and they still pay the same salary. I was raised here, but it's hard to make a living out here unless you're in some sort of business. I own a florist shop."

"Yes, I saw the van."

"That's right. You're a detective." She asked, "So what are you doing out here?"

"Convalescing."

"Oh, right. Now I remember. You look fine."

So did she, but you're not supposed to hit on the witness, so I didn't mention it. She had a nice, soft, breathy voice which I found sexy.

I asked her, "Do you know Fredric Tobin?"

"Who doesn't?"

"He belongs to the Peconic Historical Society."

"He's our largest benefactor. He gives wine and money."

"Are you a wine connoisseur?"

"No. Are you?"

"Yes. I can tell the difference between a Merlot and a Budweiser. Blindfolded."

She smiled.

I said, "I'll bet a lot of people wish they'd gotten into wine years ago. I mean, as a business."

"I don't know. It's interesting, but not that lucrative."

"It is for Fredric Tobin," I pointed out.

"Fredric lives way above his means."

I sat up. "Why do you say that?"

"Because he does."

"Do you know him well? Personally?"

She asked me; "Do *you* know him personally?"

I really don't like to be interrogated, but I was on thin ice here. How are the mighty fallen. I replied, "I was at one of his wine-tasting things. Back in July. Were you there?"

"I was."

"I was with the Gordons."

"That's right. I think I saw you."

"I didn't see you. I would have remembered."

She smiled.

I asked again, "How well do you know him?"

"Actually, we were involved."

"In what?"

"I mean we were lovers, Mr. Corey."

This was disappointing to hear. Nevertheless, I stuck to business and asked, "When was this?"

"It began...oh, about two years ago, and it lasted— Is this relevant?"

"You can refuse to answer any question."

"I know that."

I asked her, "What happened to the relationship?"

"Nothing. Fredric just collects women. It lasted for about nine months. Not a record for either of us, but not bad. We did Bordeaux, the Loire, Paris. Weekends in Manhattan. It was all right. He's very generous."

I mulled this over. I had developed a tiny crush on Emma Whitestone, and I was a little annoyed that Fredric had beat me to the cookie jar. I said, "I'm going to ask you a personal question, and you don't have to answer. Okay?"

"Okay."

"Are you still...? What I mean is—"

"Fredric and I are still friends. He has a live-in now. Sondra Wells. A total phony, including the name."

"Right. You said he lives above his means."

"Yes. He owes the banks and private investors a small fortune. He spends too much. The sad thing is that he's very successful, and he could probably live very well on his profits if it weren't for Foxwoods."

"Foxwoods?"

"Yes, you know. The Indian gambling casino. In Connecticut."

"Oh, right. He gambles?"

"Does he ever. I went with him once. He lost about five thousand dollars in one weekend. Blackjack and roulette."

"My goodness. I hope he had a return ferry ticket."

She laughed.

Foxwoods. You took the Orient Point ferry with your car aboard to New London, or the Foxwoods high-speed ferry and bus to Foxwoods, blew it out, and came back to Orient on Sunday night. A nice diversion from the workaday world of the North Fork, and if you weren't compulsive, you had a nice time, you made a few hundred or you lost a few hundred, you had dinner, saw a show, slept in a nice room. A good date weekend. A lot of the locals, however, didn't like the proximity to sin. Some wives didn't like the boys going over with the grocery money. But, like anything else, it was a matter of degree.

So, Fredric Tobin, cool and dandy viniculturist, a man who seemed in control, was a gambler. But if you thought about it, was there a bigger gamble than the grape crop every year? The fact was, grapes were still experimental here, and so far, so good. No blight, no diseases, no frosts or heat spells. But one day, Hurricane Annabelle or Zeke was going to blow a billion grapes into the Long Island Sound, sort of like the biggest tub of Kool-Aid ever.

And then there were Tom and Judy, who gambled with little pathogenic bugs. Then they gambled with something else and lost. Fredric gambled with the crop and won, then gambled with cards and roulette and he, too, lost.

I said to Ms. Whitestone, "Do you know if the Gordons ever went with Mr. Tobin to Foxwoods?"

"I don't think so. But I wouldn't know. It's been about a year since Fredric and I parted."

"Right. But you're still friends. You still talk."

"I guess we're friends. He doesn't like it when his ex-lovers are angry with him. He wants to keep them all as friends. This is interesting at parties. He loves to be in a room with a dozen women that he's had sex with."

Who doesn't? I asked her, "And you don't think Mr. Tobin and Mrs. Gordon were involved?"

"I don't know for sure. I don't think so. He wasn't a wife chaser."

"How gallant."

"No, he was chicken. Husbands and boyfriends frightened him. He must have had a bad experience once." She sort of chuckled in her breathy way. She added, "In any case, he'd rather have Tom Gordon as a friend than Judy Gordon as a lover."

"Why is that?"

"I don't know. I never understood Fredric's attachment to Tom Gordon."

"I thought it was the other way around."

"That's what most people thought. It was Fredric who sought Tom out."

"Why?"

"I don't know. At first, I thought it was a way of getting to Judy, but then I came to learn that Fredric doesn't do wives. Then I figured it had to do with the Gordons' attractiveness and their jobs. Fredric is a collector of people. He fancies himself the leading social personage of the North Fork. Maybe he is. He's not the richest man, but the winery gives him some status. You understand?"

I nodded. Sometimes you dig for days and weeks and come up with nothing. Sometimes you hit gold. But sometimes it's fool's gold. I mean, this was fascinating, but was it relevant to the double homicide? Also, was this an exaggeration? A little revenge on Ms. Whitestone's part? This would not be the first ex-lover who sent me sniffing up the wrong tree in order to make life miserable for the party of the second part. So I asked her point-blank, "Do you think Fredric Tobin could have killed the Gordons?"

She looked at me as if I'd lost my mind, then said, "*Fredric?* He's not capable of violence of any sort."

"How do you know?"

She smiled and replied, "God knows, I gave him enough reason to take a swing at me." She added, "He just wasn't physical. He was in total control of his temper and his emotions. And why would he want to kill Tom and Judy Gordon?"

"I don't know. I don't even know why they *were* killed. Do you?"

She didn't reply for a second, then said, "Maybe drugs."

"Why do you think that?"

"Well...Fredric was concerned about them. They did coke."

"He told you that?"

"Yes."

Interesting. Especially since Fredric never mentioned it to me, and since there wasn't a grain of truth in it. I know what a cokehead looks and acts like, and the Gordons weren't cokeheads. So why would Tobin pin that on them? I asked her, "When did he tell you this?"

"Not long ago. A few months ago. He said they came to him and wanted to know if he wanted to score some good stuff. They dealt to support their habit."

"You believe that?"

She shrugged. "Could be."

"Okay...back to Mr. Tobin's relationship with the Gordons. You think he was the one who sought them out and cultivated the relationship."

"It seemed that way. I know in the nine months I was with him, he'd been on the phone with them a lot, and he rarely had a party without inviting them."

I thought about this. Certainly this didn't square with what Mr. Tobin had told me. I asked Ms. Whitestone, "What then was Mr. Tobin's attraction to the Gordons?"

"I don't know. Though I do know that he made it seem to everyone that it was the other way around. Funny thing is that the Gordons seemed to go along with it, as if they were honored to be in Fredric's company. Yet, when it was just the four of us a few times, you could see they considered themselves his equals. You understand?"

"Yes. But why were they playacting?"

Again, she shrugged. "Who knows?" She looked at me a moment, then said, "It was almost as if the Gordons were blackmailing Fredric. Like they had something on him. In public, he was the big cheese. In private, Tom and Judy were pretty familiar with him."

Blackmail. I let that percolate for a good half minute.

Emma Whitestone said, "I'm only guessing. Speculating. I'm not being vindictive or anything. I had a good time with Fredric, and I liked him, but I wasn't hurt when he broke it off."

"Okay." I looked at her, and we made eye contact. I asked her, "Have you spoken to Fredric since the murder?"

"Yes, yesterday morning. He called."

"What did he say?"

"Nothing more than anyone else was saying. Standard stuff."

We went into some detail about that phone conversation, and indeed, it seemed standard and pro forma.

I asked her, "Has he spoken to you today?"

"No."

"I visited him this morning."

"Did you? Why?"

"I don't know."

"You don't know why you're here, either."

"Right." I didn't want to explain that I was out of potential witnesses after Plum Island and the Murphys and that I was off the job and had to interview people that the county PD would not think to interview. I wasn't exactly scraping the bottom of the barrel, but I was sort of working the edge of the crowd. I asked her, "Do you know any of the Gordons' friends?"

"I didn't really travel in the same circles except for when we were with Fredric. And then it was his friends."

"Wasn't Chief Maxwell a friend of theirs?"

"I think so. I could never understand that relationship any more than I could understand the Gordons' relationship with Fredric."

"I seem to be having trouble finding friends of the Gordons."

"From what I can gather, all their friends are Plum Island people. That's not so unusual. I told you— they're a tight-knit group." She added, "You'd be better off looking there than around here."

"Probably."

She asked me, "What did you think of Fredric?"

"A delightful man. I enjoyed his company." Which was true. But now that I knew he'd popped Ms. Whitestone here, I was more convinced than ever that there was no sexual justice in the world. I added, "Beady eyes."

"Shifty, too."

"Right." I said to her, "Could I ask a favor of you?"

"You can ask."

"Would you not tell him of our conversation?"

"I won't go into details. But I'll tell him we spoke." She added, "I don't lie. But I can keep things to myself."

"That's all I ask."

In Manhattan, there are not that many of these interlocking relationships as there are here. I had to keep this in mind, and I had to deal with it, and I had to adjust my style accordingly. But I'm bright and I can do that. On that subject, I asked Emma Whitestone, "I assume you know Chief Maxwell."

"Who doesn't?"

"Did you ever date him?"

"No. But he's asked."

"You don't like cops?"

She laughed. She wiggled her toes again and crossed her legs again. My goodness.

We went round and round for the next fifteen minutes or so, and Emma Whitestone had a lot of gossip, a lot of insights into people, though not much of it seemed to relate to the case. The problem was that I still didn't know what I was doing here, but it was nice being here. I should say, though, that I was a gentleman. To hit on a female officer is okay because as a peer, she can tell you to take a hike. However, with civilians, especially ones who might wind up in front of the DA, you had to be careful. You didn't want to compromise yourself or the witness. Nevertheless, I was interested.

No, I'm not fickle. I was still pining for Beth. I asked Ms. Whitestone, "Can I use your phone?"

"Sure. Right in there."

I went into an adjoining room, which was like going from the nineteenth century into the twentieth. This was the office suite of the historical society, complete with modern office furniture, file cabinets, copy machine, and so forth. I used a phone on one of the desks and called my answering machine. There was one message. A male voice said, "Detective Corey, this is Detective Collins of the Suffolk County Police. Detective Penrose asked me to call you. She's in a lengthy conference. She says she can't meet you this afternoon, and she'll call you tonight or tomorrow." End of message. I hung up and looked around the office. Under one of the desks was a pair of leather thongs, most probably Ms. Whitestone's.

I went back to the library, but I didn't sit down.

Emma Whitestone looked at me and asked, "Anything wrong?"

"No. Where were we?"

"I don't know."

I looked at my watch, then asked her, "Can we finish this over lunch?"

"Sure." She stood. "First I'll give you a tour of our house."

And she did. Room by room. Most of the upstairs was used for offices, storage, exhibits, and archives, but there were two bedrooms decorated in ye olde. One, according to Emma, was mid–seventeen hundreds, and the other was contemporary with the house, mid–eighteen hundreds. She said, "The house was built by a sea merchant who made his fortune in South America."

"Cocaine?"

"No, silly. Semiprecious stones from Brazil. Captain Samuel Farnsworth."

I pushed down on the lumpy bed. "Do you nap here?"

She smiled. "Sometimes. It's a feather mattress."

"Osprey feathers?"

"Could be. They used to be all over."

"They're making a big comeback."

"Everything's making a big comeback. Damned deer devoured my rhododendrons." She led me out of the bedroom and said, "You wanted to see the archives."

"Yes."

She showed me into what had probably been a good-sized bedroom, and which was now filled with file cabinets, shelves, and a long oak table. She said,

"We have original books and documents going back as far as the mid–sixteen hundreds. Deeds, letters, wills, legal decisions, sermons, army orders, ships' manifests and logs. Some of it is fascinating."

"How did you get into this?"

"Well, I suppose it had something to do with growing up here. My own family goes back to the original settlers."

"You're not related to Margaret Wiley, I hope."

She smiled. "We have family connections. Didn't you enjoy Margaret?"

"No comment."

She went on, "Archive work must be a little like detective work. You know—mysteries, questions to be answered, things that need to be uncovered. Don't you think so?"

"I do, now that you mention it." I added, "To tell you the truth, when I was a kid, I wanted to be an archaeologist. I found a musket ball once. Somewhere out here. Can't remember where." I added, "Now that I'm old and infirm, maybe I should take up archive work."

"Oh, you're not that old. And you might enjoy it. I can teach you to read this stuff."

"Isn't it in English?"

"Yes, except that seventeenth- and eighteenth-century English can be difficult. The spelling is atrocious and the script is sometimes hard to decipher. Here, take a look at this." She offered a big looseleaf binder that was on the table. Inside were plastic sleeves and in the plastic were old parchments. She flipped to one of the pages and said, "Read that."

I bent over the book and looked at the faded script.

I read, "Dear Martha, Don't believe the rumors about me and Mrs. Farnsworth. I'm loyal and true. How about you? Your loving husband, George."

She laughed. "That's not what it says."

"That's what it looks like."

"Here, I'll read it." She pulled the binder toward her, and said, "This is a letter from a Phillip Shelley to the royal governor, Lord Bellomont, dated 3 August 1698." She read the letter, which to me had been indecipherable. The letter was full of "my lords" and "haths" and "your humble servant" stuff. The guy was complaining about some injustice regarding a land dispute. I mean, these people came across the ocean to a new continent and had the same gripes they had in Southwold with a "w."

I said to Ms. Whitestone, "Very impressive."

"There's nothing to it. You can learn it in a few months. I taught Fredric in two months, and he has no attention span."

"Really."

"The language isn't as difficult as the script and the spelling."

"Right." I asked her, "Can you give me a list of members?"

"Sure." We went into the office, and she gave me a paperbound membership directory, then slipped on her sandals.

I asked her, "How did you get this job?"

She shrugged. "I don't know.... It's a pain in the butt. This was another one of Fredric's stupid social-climbing ideas. I was the archivist here, which I didn't mind doing. Then he proposed me as president, and whatever Fredric wants, Fredric gets. Plus, I'm still the archivist. Flower girl and president and archivist of the Peconic Historical Society."

"Are you hungry?"

"Sure. Let me call the shop." She did, and I poked around the office a bit. I heard her say, softly, "I may not be back this afternoon."

No, Ms. Whitestone, you may not be if I have anything to say about it.

She hung up, and we went downstairs. She said, "We have small receptions and parties here. It's nice at Christmas."

"That reminds me—are you going to Mr. Tobin's soiree on Saturday?"

"Maybe. Are you?"

"I thought I would. In the line of duty."

She suggested, "Why don't you arrest him in front of everyone and take him away in handcuffs?"

"That sounds like fun, only I don't think he's done anything wrong."

"I'm sure he's done *something* wrong." She led me to the front door, and we went outside. It was getting warmer. She locked the door and took the Post-it note off. I said, "I'll drive."

I started my vehicle with the remote. She said, "That's a nice feature."

I said, "It's good to detonate car bombs from a distance."

She laughed. I was not joking.

We got into my sport utility vehicle, and I threw it into reverse, purposely leaving my door ajar. The female voice said, "The driver's side door is ajar."

Emma said, "That's a silly feature."

"I know. It sounds like my ex-wife. I'm trying to kill it. The voice, not my ex-wife."

Emma played with the computer buttons as she asked me, "How long have you been divorced?"

"Actually, it's not official until October first. In the meantime, I'm trying to avoid adultery and bigamy."

"That should be easy."

I wasn't sure how to take that. I pulled out of the parking area and said, "What do you like? You pick."

"Why don't we continue the mood and go to a historic inn? How about the General Wayne Inn? Do you know it?"

"I think so. Isn't that John Wayne's place?"

"No, silly. Mad Anthony Wayne. He slept there."

"Is that what made him mad? Lumpy mattress?"

"No...are you historically challenged?"

"Totally clueless."

"Mad Anthony Wayne was a Revolutionary War general. He was the leader of the Pennsylvania Volunteers."

"Right. Their big single was 'My Heart's on Fire and You're Sittin' on My Hose.' "

Emma Whitestone stayed silent awhile, wondering, I'm sure, if she'd made the right decision. Finally, she said, "It's on Great Hog Neck. I'll direct you."

"Okay." And off we went to a place called the General Wayne Inn, located in a place called Great Hog Neck. I mean, could I get into this scene? Did I miss Manhattan? Hard to say. If I had big bucks, I could do both. But I don't have big bucks. Which got me to thinking about Fredric Tobin, who, as it turns out, also doesn't have big bucks, and there I was envying him, figuring he was on top of the world—grapes, babes, bucks—turns out he's broke. Worse, he's in debt. For a man like Fredric Tobin, to lose it all would be the equivalent of losing his life. He might as well be dead. But he wasn't. Tom and Judy were dead. Connection? Maybe. This was getting interesting.

But time was running out for me. I could play cop for maybe forty-eight more hours before I was shut down by the Southold PD, the NYPD, and the Suffolk County PD.

Ms. Whitestone was giving me directions as I ruminated. Finally, she asked me, "Are they leveling with us about the vaccine?"

"I think so. Yes."

"This had nothing to do with germ warfare?"

"No."

"Or drugs?"

"Not that I can determine."

"Burglary?"

"It looks that way, but I think it has to do with a stolen vaccine." Who says I'm not a team player? I can put out the official bullshit as well as anyone else. I asked Ms. Whitestone, "You have another theory?"

"No, I don't. I just have this feeling that they were killed for some reason we don't yet understand."

Which is exactly what I thought. Bright woman.

I asked her, "Have you ever been married?"

"Yes. I married young, sophomore year in college. Lasted seven years." She added, "And I've been divorced seven years. Add it up."

"You're twenty-five."

"How did you get twenty-five?"

"Forty-two?"

She said, "Turn right here. Right is toward me."

"Thanks."

It was a pleasant drive, and we soon found ourselves

on Great Hog Neck—which is yet another peninsula that juts into the bay, lying somewhat east and north of Nassau Point, sometimes called Little Hog Neck.

I've noticed that around here there are three main sources of place names—Native Americans, English settlers, and realtors. The latter have maps with nice names that they make up to replace yucky names like Great Hog Neck.

We passed a small observatory called the Custer Institute, which Mrs. Wiley had mentioned, and I got a briefing on that and on the American Indian Museum across from the observatory.

I asked Emma, "Were the Gordons interested in astronomy?"

"Not that I knew about."

"You know they bought an acre of land from Mrs. Wiley."

"Yes." She hesitated, then said, "That was not a good deal."

"Why did they want that land?"

"I don't know. . . . It never made sense to me."

"Did Fredric know about the Gordons' buying that land?"

"Yes." She changed the subject to the immediate environs and said, "There's the original Whitestone house. Sixteen eighty-five."

"Still in the family?"

"No, but I'm going to buy it back." She added, "Fredric was supposed to help me out, but . . . That's when I realized he wasn't as well off as he appeared."

I didn't comment.

Like Nassau Point, Hog Neck was mostly cottages and some newer weekend homes, many of them gray-shingled to look like ye olde. There were some fields that Emma said had been common pastureland since colonial times, and there were woods here and there. I asked, "Are the Indians friendly?"

"There are no Indians."

"All gone?"

"All gone."

"Except the ones in Connecticut who opened the biggest casino complex between here and Las Vegas."

She said, "I have some Native American blood."

"Really?"

"Really. A lot of the old families do, but they're not advertising it. Some people come to me actually wanting to expunge relatives from the archives."

"Incredible." I knew there was a politically correct thing to say, but every time I try to do PC, I blow it. I mean, it changes, like weekly. I played it safe with, "Racist."

"Racial, though not necessarily racist. Anyway, I don't care who knows I have Indian blood. My maternal great-grandmother was a Corchaug."

"Well, you have nice color."

"Thanks."

We approached this big white clapboard building set on a few acres of treed land. I actually recalled seeing the place once or twice, when I was a kid. I have these childhood memories of places in my mind, still-life summer scenes, sort of like looking at slides through a viewfinder. I said to Ms. Whitestone, "I think I ate here with my family when I was a wee lad."

"Quite possible. It's two hundred years old. How old are you?"

I ignored this and asked, "How's the food?"

"Depends." She added, "It's a nice setting, and off the beaten path. No one will see us, and no one will gossip."

"Good thinking." I pulled into the gravel driveway, parked, and opened my door a crack with the engine still running. A tiny little bell chimed and the schematic of my vehicle showed a door ajar. I said, "Hey, you killed the voice."

"We don't want your ex-wife's voice annoying you."

We got out of the vehicle and walked toward the inn. She took my arm, which surprised me. She asked, "When do you get off duty?"

"Now."

CHAPTER EIGHTEEN

Lunch was pleasant enough. The place was nearly empty and had undergone a recent restoration, so if you let your imagination go, it was 1784 and Mad Anthony Wayne was stomping around ordering grog, whatever that is.

The food was basic American, nothing tricky, which appeals to my carnivorous tastes, and Ms. Emma Whitestone turned out to be a basic American girl, nothing tricky, which likewise appealed to my carnivorous tastes.

We didn't discuss the murders, or Lord Tobin, or anything unpleasant. She was really into history, and I was fascinated by what she was saying. Well, not really, but history coming from Emma Whitestone's breathy mouth was not too hard to take.

She went on about the Reverend Youngs, who led his flock here from Connecticut in 1640, and I wondered aloud if they took the New London ferry, which got me a cool look. She mentioned Captain Kidd and lesser-known pirates who sailed these waters three hundred years ago, then told me about the Hortons of lighthouse fame, one of which built this very inn. And then there was the Revolutionary War General, Francis Marion, the Swamp Fox, after whom, she said, East Marion was named, even though I argued there was probably a town called Marion in England. But she knew her stuff. She told me about the Underhills, the Tuthills, and a little about the Whitestones, who were actually Mayflower Pilgrims, and about people with first names like Abijah, Chauncey, Ichabod, and Barnabas, not to mention Joshua, Samuel, and Isaac, who weren't even Jewish. And so on.

Ping! Whereas Paul Stevens had bored me senseless with his computer-generated voice, Emma Whitestone had me bewitched with her sort of aspiring tones, not to mention her gray-green eyes. Anyway, the net result was the same—I'd heard something that caused a delayed reaction in my usually awake brain. *Ping!* I listened for her to say it again, whatever it was, and I tried to recall what it was and why I thought it was significant. But to no avail. This time, however, I knew it was on the tip of my brain, and I knew I'd have it out very soon. *Ping!*

I said to her, "I feel the presence of Mad Anthony Wayne here."

"Do you? Tell me about it."

"Well, he's sitting at that table by the window, and he's been sneaking glances at you. He's giving me dirty looks. He's mumbling to himself, 'What hath he got that I haveth not?' "

She smiled. "You're crazy."

"Haveth not got? Or goteth not?"

"I'll teach you eighteenth-century English if you stop being a jerk."

"I thank thee."

Well, before we knew it, it was three P.M. and the waiter was getting antsy. I hate to interrupt the flow and energy of a case to chase panties—*detectus interruptus*. It's a fact that the first seventy-two hours of a case are the most critical. But a fella has to answer certain biological calls, and my bells were ringing.

I said, "If you have time, we can take a spin in my boat."

"You have a boat?"

Actually, I didn't, so this might not have been a good line. But I had waterfront property and a dock, so I could say the boat sank. I said, "I'm staying at my uncle's place. A farm bay estate."

"Bay farm estate."

"Right. Let's go."

We left the General Wayne Inn and drove toward my place, which is about twenty minutes west of Hog Neck.

As we traveled west along Main Road, she informed me, "This used to be called King's Highway. They changed the name after the Revolution."

"Good idea."

"Funny thing is that my alma mater, Columbia University, was called Kings College, and they also changed it after the Revolution."

"I'll tell ya, if we have another revolution, there are a lot of names I'd like to change."

"Such as?"

"Well, first, East Seventy-second Street where my condo is. I'd like to call it Cherry Lane. Sounds nicer." I continued, "Then there's my ex-wife's cat, Snowball—I'd like to change his name to Dead Cat." I went on with a few more name changes, come the revolution.

She sort of interrupted by asking me, "Do you like it out here?"

"I think so. I mean, it's nice, but I'm not sure I fit."

She informed me, "There are a lot of eccentrics out here."

"I'm not eccentric. I'm nuts."

"There are a lot of those, too." She added, "This is no rural backwater. I know farmers with Ivy League degrees, I know astronomers from the Custer Institute, and there are the vintners who studied in France, and the scientists from Plum Island and Brookhaven labs, plus academics from Stony Brook University, artists, poets, writers, and—"

"Archivists."

"Yes. I get annoyed when people from the city think we're hicks."

"I certainly don't think that."

"I lived in Manhattan for nine years. I got tired of the city. I missed my home."

"I sensed a certain city sophistication about you, coupled with a country charm. You're in the right place."

"Thank you."

I think I passed one of the more important tests on my way to the sack.

We were driving through farm and wine country now, and she said, "The autumn is long and lazy here. The orchards are still heavy with fruit and many of the vegetables haven't been picked yet. It can be snowing in New England around Thanksgiving, and we're still harvesting here." She asked me, "Am I rambling on?"

"No, not at all. You're painting a beautiful word picture."

"Thank you."

I was now on the first landing of the staircase leading to the bedroom.

Basically, we both kept it light and airy, the way people do who are really sort of edgy because they know they might be headed for the sheets.

Anyway, we pulled up the long driveway to the big Victorian, and Emma said, "A big painted lady."

"Where?"

"The house. That's what we call the old Victorians."

"Oh. Right. By the way, my aunt used to belong to the Peconic Historical Society. June Bonner."

"Sounds familiar."

"She knew Margaret Wiley." I added, "Actually, my aunt was born here, which is why she talked Uncle Harry into this summer place."

"What was her maiden name?"

"I'm not sure—maybe Witherspoonhamptonshire."

"Are you making fun of my name?"

"No, ma'am."

"Find out your aunt's maiden name."

"Okay." I stopped in front of the painted lady.

She said, "If it's an old family, I can look it up. We have a lot of information on the old families."

"Yeah? Lots of skeletons in the closets?"

"Sometimes."

"Maybe Aunt June's family were horse thieves and whores."

"Could be. There are a lot of those in my family tree."

I chuckled.

She said, "Could be that her family and mine are related. You and I could be related by marriage."

"Could be." I was at the top of the stairs now, the

bedroom door was about ten feet away. Actually, I was still in the Jeep. I said, "Here we are," and got out.

She got out, too, and looked at the house. She said, "And this is her house?"

"Was. She's deceased. My Uncle Harry wants me to buy it."

"It's too big for one person."

"I can cut it in half." Okay, into the house, tour of the ground floor, check my answering machine in the den—no messages—into the kitchen for two beers and out onto the back porch and into two wicker chairs.

She said, "I love watching the water."

"This is a good place to do it. I've been sitting here for a few months."

"When do you have to go back to work?"

"I'm not sure. I'm scheduled to see the doc next Thursday."

"How did you get involved in this case?"

"Chief Maxwell."

She said, "I don't see your boat."

I looked out at the rickety dock. "Oh, it must have sunk."

"Sunk?"

"Oh, I remember. It's in for repairs."

"What do you have?"

"A . . . twenty-four-foot . . . Boston Whaler . . . ?"

"Do you sail?"

"You mean like a sailboat?"

"Yes. A sailboat."

"No. I'm into powerboats. Do you sail?"

"A little."

And so forth.

I'd taken off my jacket and docksiders and rolled up

my sleeves. She'd slipped off the thongs, and we both had our bare feet on the rail. Her little beige number had slipped north of the knees.

I got my binoculars, and we took turns looking out at the bay, the boats, the wetlands—which used to be called a swamp when I was a kid—the sky, and all that.

I was up to beer five, and she was going one for one with me. I like a woman who can pound down the suds. She was a little lit by now, but still had a clear head and voice.

She had the binoculars in one hand, and a Bud in the other. She said, "This is a major meeting point on the Atlantic Coastal Flyway, a sort of rest stop for migratory birds." She looked through the binoculars at the distant sky and continued, "I can see flights of Canada geese, long skeins of loons, and a ripply line of old-squaws. They'll all stay around until November, then continue on south. The osprey winds up in South America."

"That's good."

She rested the binoculars in her lap and stared out to sea. She said, "On stormy days, when the wind blows hard out of the northeast, the sky turns silvery gray and the birds act strange. There's a feeling of eerie isolation, an ominous beauty that has to be felt and heard as much as seen."

We stayed silent for a while, then I said, "Would you like to see the rest of the house?"

"Sure."

My first stop on the tour of the second floor was my bedroom, and we didn't get much farther.

It actually took three seconds for her to get out of her things. She had a really beautiful all-over tan, a firm body, everything exactly where it belonged, and exactly as I'd pictured it.

I was still unbuttoning my shirt by the time she was naked. She watched me getting undressed and stared at my ankle holster and revolver.

A lot of women aren't into armed men as I've learned, so I said, "I have to wear this by law," which was true in New York City but not necessarily out here.

She replied, "Fredric carries a gun."

Interesting.

Anyway, I was in the altogether now, and she came up to me and touched my chest. "Is that a burn?"

"No, a bullet hole." I turned around. "See? That's the exit wound."

"My God."

"Just a flesh wound. Here, look at this one." I showed her the entry wound in my lower abdomen, then turned again and showed her the exit on my rump. The grazing wound on my left calf was less interesting.

She said, "You could have been killed."

I shrugged. Aw shucks, ma'am.

Anyway, I was glad the cleaning lady had changed the sheets, glad I had condoms in the night table, and glad Willie Peter responded to Emma Whitestone. I turned the phone ringer off.

I knelt down at the side of my bed to say my prayers, and Emma got into the bed and wrapped her long, long legs around my neck.

Anyway, without going into details, we hit it off pretty well and fell asleep, wrapped in each other's arms. She felt good and didn't snore.

*   *   *

When I awoke, the sunlight was fading from the window, and Emma was sleeping on her side, sort of curled into a ball. I had a sense that I should be doing something more constructive than having afternoon sex. But what? I was being effectively sandbagged, and unless Max or Beth shared things with me like forensics, autopsies, and such, I had to proceed without any of the modern technical advantages of police science. I needed phone records, I needed the fingerprint reports, I needed more Plum Island stuff, and I needed access to the crime scene. But I didn't think I was going to get any of that.

So, I had to fall back on gumshoeing, phone calls, face time with people who might know something. I'd decided to stick this out no matter who didn't like the idea.

I looked at Emma in the fading light. A naturally beautiful woman. And bright.

She opened her eyes and smiled at me. She said, "I saw you looking at me."

"You're very nice to look at."

"Do you have a girlfriend out here?"

"No. But there's someone in Manhattan."

"I don't care about Manhattan."

I asked her, "How about you?"

"I'm between engagements."

"Good." I asked, "How about dinner?"

"Maybe later. I can make something."

"I have lettuce, mustard, butter, beer, and cookies."

She sat up, stretched, and yawned. "I need a swim." She rolled out of bed and slipped into her dress. "Let's take a swim."

"Okay." I got up and put on my shirt.

We went downstairs, out through the den, which led to the porch, across the lawn, and down to the bay.

She looked around. "Private here?"

"Pretty much."

She slipped off her dress and threw it on the foot of the dock. I did the same with my shirt. She picked her way across the stony beach, then dived in. I did the same.

The water was cool at first, and it took my breath away. We swam beyond the dock out into the dark bay. She was a good, strong swimmer. I felt my right shoulder stiffening, and my lung started to wheeze. I had thought I was getting stronger, but this exertion was too much for me. I swam back to the dock and grabbed on to the old wooden ladder.

Emma came up beside me and asked, "Are you all right?"

"I'm fine."

We treaded water near the dock. She said, "I love swimming naked."

"You don't have to worry about something biting your worm."

"Do you fish?"

"Now and then."

"You can get flounder right off this dock."

"I can get flounder in the supermarket."

"If you go out in your boat just a few hundred yards, you can get brown trout, porgy, and weakfish."

"Where can I get prime rib?"

"Beef is not good for you."

"You had a hamburger for lunch."

"I know. But it's not good for people." She added, "Neither is sex with strangers."

"I'm a high-risk kind of guy, Emma."

She said, "I guess I am, too. I don't even know you."

"That's why you like me."

She giggled.

In truth, most women considered cops safe. I mean, if a woman meets a cop in a bar, presumably he's not a homicidal maniac, he's probably got a clean bill of health, and he has a few bucks in his wallet. Women don't require much these days.

We bantered a little, we kissed and embraced, which is really nice, naked, half submerged, treading water. I like saltwater. It makes me feel clean and buoyant.

I put one hand on her incredible butt and the other on her breast as we kissed and treaded. This was as much fun as I'd had in a long time. She put one hand on my butt and the other on my periscope, which went immediately up.

I said, "Can we do it in the water?"

"It's possible. You have to be in good shape. You have to keep treading water and keep air in your lungs to stay buoyant, and at the same time...you know... do it."

"No problem. My flotation device is big enough to keep us both afloat."

She laughed. We actually consummated this aquatic feat, probably scaring a lot of fish in the process. My lung actually felt better.

Afterward, we both lay on our backs and floated. I commented, "Look, my rudder is out of the water."

She glanced over at me and said, "I thought that was a main mast."

Well, enough nautical naughties. I picked up my head a little and watched her floating out away from the shore with the ebbing tide. Truly, her breasts looked like twin volcanic islands in the moonlight.

She said, "Look up there, John. Shooting stars."

I looked in the southern sky and saw them.

"Make a wish," she said.

"Okay. I wish—"

"Don't tell or it won't come true."

"It already came true, Emma. Me and you." I mean, how's that for romantic? And I already had sex—twice. When the lust is gone, what's left is loathing or love. I think I was in love.

She didn't say anything for a few seconds, then said, "That's very nice."

"I meant it."

We continued to float. After a minute or two she said, "Look there, in the eastern sky. Can you see the constellation Andromeda?"

"Not without my glasses."

"Right there. Look." She attempted to connect a bunch of stars for me, but if there was somebody up there named Andromeda, I didn't see her. To be polite, I said, "Oh, yeah. Got it. She's wearing high heels."

Emma directed my gaze farther east and said, "There's Pegasus. You know, the winged horse of the Muses."

"I know. I had him to win in the fifth race at Belmont last Saturday. Came in fourth."

Emma had learned to ignore me and continued,

"Pegasus was born of the sea foam and the blood of the slain Medusa."

"It didn't say that on the scratch sheet."

"Do you want to get laid again?"

"Yes."

"Then stop being a wiseass."

"Consider it done." And I meant it.

So, what a night—a bright, nearly full moon overhead, a gentle shore breeze, the smell of sea and salt, stars twinkling in the deep purple sky, a beautiful woman, our bodies floating, rising and falling with the slow, rhythmic swells. It doesn't get much better than this. All things considered, this was a lot better than my somewhat unpleasant near-death experience.

Which got me thinking about Tom and Judy. I looked up at the sky and I sent out a nice thought to them, a sort of hello and goodbye, and a promise that I'd do everything I could to find their killer. And I asked them to please give me a hint.

I guess it was the feeling of total relaxation, the sexual release, or maybe looking up at the constellations, connecting the points of light—whatever it was, I had it now. The whole picture, the pings, the points, the lines, it all came together in a sort of rush, and my brain was racing so fast I couldn't keep up with my own thoughts. I yelled, "That's it!" and exhaled so much air that I sank.

I came to the surface sputtering, and Emma was there beside me, looking concerned. "Are you all right?"

"I'm terrific!"

"Are you—?"

"Captain Kidd's trees!"

"What about them?"

I grabbed her by the arms, and we treaded water. I said, "What did you tell me about Captain Kidd's trees?"

"I said there's a legend that Captain Kidd buried some of his treasure under one of the trees up by Mattituck Inlet. They're called Captain Kidd's Trees."

"We're talking about Captain Kidd the pirate, right?"

"Yes. William Kidd."

"Where are these trees?" I asked.

"Just due north of here. Where the inlet empties into the Sound. Why do you—?"

"What's with Captain Kidd? What does he have to do with this place?"

"Don't you know?"

"No. That's why I'm asking you."

"I thought everyone knew—"

"*I* don't know. Tell me."

"Well, his treasure is supposed to be buried somewhere around here."

"Where?"

"*Where?* If I knew, I'd be rich." She smiled. "And I wouldn't tell *you.*"

Jeez. This was mind-boggling. It all fit...but maybe I was totally wrong....No, damn it, it fit. It fit everything. All those disjointed pieces, which had looked like the Chaos Theory at work, now fell into place and became the Unified Theory, which explained everything. "Yeah...."

"Are you all right? You look pale or blue."

"I'm fine. I need a drink."

"Me, too. The wind is getting cold."

We swam back to shore, grabbed our clothes, and ran back naked across the lawn to the house. I got two thick bathrobes, then retrieved Uncle's decanter of brandy and two glasses. We sat on the porch, drinking, watching the lights across the bay. A sailboat glided over the water, its white sail ghostly in the moonlight, and thin wispy clouds raced across the starlit sky. What a night. What a night. I said to Tom and Judy, "I'm getting it. I'm getting close."

Emma glanced at me and held out her glass. I poured her more brandy and said, "Tell me about Captain Kidd."

"What would you like to know?" she asked.

"Everything."

"Why?"

"Why . . . ? I'm fascinated by pirates."

She regarded me for a moment, then asked, "Since when?"

"Since I was a kid."

"Does this have to do with the murders?"

I looked at Emma. Despite our recent intimacy, I barely knew her, and I wasn't sure I could trust her to keep this to herself. I realized, too, I'd been overly excited about Captain Kidd. Trying to be cool now, I asked, "How could Captain Kidd be related to the Gordons' murders?"

She shrugged. "I don't know. I'm asking you."

I said, "I'm off-duty now. I'm just curious about pirates and stuff."

"I'm off-duty, too. No history until tomorrow."

"Okay." I asked, "Will you stay the night?"

"Maybe. Let me think about it."

"Sure."

I put some Big Band dance music on my tape player, and we danced on the back porch in our bare feet and bathrobes and drank brandy and watched the bay and the stars.

It was one of those enchanted evenings, as they say, one of those magic nights that are often a prelude to something not so good.

CHAPTER NINETEEN

Ms. Emma Whitestone chose to spend the night.

She rose early, found the mouthwash, and gargled loud enough to wake me up. She showered, used my hair dryer, finger-combed her hair, found a lipstick and some eye stuff in her bag, which she applied in front of my dresser mirror while standing in the altogether.

As she pulled her panties on, she stepped into her sandals, then slipped her dress on over her head. Four seconds.

She was a sort of low-maintenance woman who didn't require a lot of life-support systems for an overnighter.

I'm not used to women being ready before me so I had to rush through my shower. I slipped on my tightest jeans along with a white tennis shirt and my docksiders. I left the .38 locked in my dresser.

At Ms. Whitestone's suggestion, we drove to the Cutchogue Diner, a real 1930s icon. The place was packed with farmers, deliverymen, local merchants, a few touristos, truck drivers, and maybe one other couple who were getting to know one another over breakfast and after sex.

We sat in a small booth, and I commented, "Won't people gossip if they see you in the same clothes you wore yesterday?"

"They stopped gossiping about me years ago."

"How about *my* reputation?"

"Your reputation, John, can only be enhanced by your being with me."

We were a bit tart this morning.

She ordered a huge breakfast of sausage, eggs, home fries, and toast, commenting that she hadn't had dinner last night.

I reminded her, "You drank your dinner. I offered to go for pizza."

"Pizza is not good for you."

"What you just ordered is not good for you."

"I'll skip lunch. How about dinner?"

"Sure. I was going to ask."

"Good. Pick me up at six at the florist."

"Okay." I looked around and spotted two uniformed Southold cops, but no Max in sight.

The food came, and we ate. I love other people's cooking.

Emma asked me, "Why were you so interested in Captain Kidd?"

"Who? Oh...the pirates. Well, it's fascinating. I mean, that he was right here on the North Fork. I sort of remember that now. From when I was a kid. No pun intended."

She looked at me and said, "You were all fired up last night."

After my initial outburst last night, which I'd

regretted, I had tried to play it cooler, as I said. But Ms. Whitestone was still curious about my curiosity. I said to her, "If I found that treasure, I'd share it with you."

"That's very sweet."

I said, as nonchalantly as possible, "I'd like to go back to the historical society house. How about this afternoon?"

"Why?"

"I need to buy my mother something in the gift shop."

"If you join the society, I'll give you a discount."

"Okay. Why don't I pick you up at, say, four?"

She shrugged. "Okay."

I regarded her across the table. Sunlight fell on her face. Sometimes, the morning after—and I really hate to say this—but sometimes, you wonder what the hell you were thinking the night before, or worse, you wonder if you have a grudge against your dick. But this morning, I had a good feeling. I liked Emma Whitestone. I liked the way she packed down two fried eggs, four sausages, a heap of home fries, buttered toast, juice, and tea with cream.

She glanced at the clock behind the counter, and I realized she didn't even wear a watch. This lady was something of a free spirit, and at the same time was president and archivist of the Peconic Historical Society. It was a nice contrast, I thought.

A lot of people smiled at her and said hello, and I could see she was well liked. That's always a good sign. If it sounds like I was falling in love for the second time that week, that might be true. However, I wondered about Emma Whitestone's judgment in men, specifically Fredric Tobin, and perhaps me as well. Possibly she was not judgmental regarding men, or people in general. Maybe she liked all men. Certainly Fredric and I couldn't have been more opposite. Her attraction to Fredric Tobin, I suppose, was probably the bulge in the hip pocket of his pants, whereas with me, it was certainly the bulge in the front of my pants.

In any case, we chatted awhile, and I was determined to stay away from the subject of pirates or Captain Kidd until the afternoon. Eventually, however, my curiosity got the better of me. A long shot popped into my head, and I borrowed a pencil from the waitress and wrote 44106818 on a napkin. I turned the napkin around and said, "If I played these lottery numbers, would I be a winner?"

She smiled between bites of toast. "Jackpot," she said. "Where'd you get those numbers?"

"Something I read. What do they mean?"

She looked around and lowered her voice. She said, "Well, when Captain Kidd was held in a Boston jail charged with piracy, he smuggled a note to his wife, Sarah, and on the bottom of the note were those numbers."

"And?"

"And everyone has been trying to figure it out for the last three hundred years."

"What do you think they mean?"

"The most obvious answer is that these numbers relate to his buried treasure."

"You don't think it was the number on his dry cleaning slip?"

"Are we being silly again?"

"Just kidding. Get it? Kidding?"

She rolled her eyes. In truth, it was a bit early for my

humor. She said, "I don't want to discuss this here. The last wave of Kidd-mania hit here in the 1940s, and I don't want to be accused of starting another mass treasure hunt."

"Okay."

She asked me, "Do you have any children?"

"Probably."

"Be serious." .

"No, I don't have any children. How about you?"

"No children. But I'd like to."

And so forth. After a while, I returned to the subject of numbers and in a whisper asked her, "Could those numbers be map coordinates?"

She clearly didn't want to discuss this, but replied, "That's the obvious thing. Eight-digit map coordinates. Minutes and seconds. Those coordinates are actually somewhere around Deer Isle, in Maine." She leaned across the table and continued, "Kidd's movements when he sailed back to the New York area in 1699 are pretty well documented, day by day, by reliable witnesses, so any visit to Deer Isle to bury treasure was unlikely." She added, "However, there's another legend surrounding Deer Isle. Supposedly, John Jacob Astor did find Kidd's or some other pirate's treasure on Deer Isle and that was the start of the Astor fortune." She sipped her tea and said, "There are dozens of books, plays, ballads, rumors, legends, and myths surrounding Captain William Kidd's buried treasure. Ninety-nine percent of them are just that—myth."

"Okay, but aren't those numbers that Kidd wrote to his wife solid evidence of *something*?"

"Yes, they mean *something*. Yet even if they are map coordinates, navigation in those days was too primitive to pinpoint a spot on the ground with any accuracy. Especially longitude. An eight-digit coordinate of minutes and seconds can be hundreds of yards off using the methods available in 1699. Even today, with a satellite navigation device, you can be off by ten or twenty feet. If you're digging for treasure, and you're off by even twenty feet, you could be digging a lot of holes. I think the theory of grid coordinates has been put aside in favor of other theories."

"Such as?"

She drew an exasperated breath, glanced around, and said, "Well, here—" She took the pencil and napkin and gave each number its corresponding letter in the alphabet and came up with DDAOFHAH. She said, "I think the last three letters are the key."

"H-A-H?"

"Right. Hah, hah, hah. Get it?"

"Hah, hah." I studied the letters, frontwards and backwards, then turned the paper upside down and said, "Was Kidd dyslexic?"

She laughed. "It's no use, John. Better brains than mine and yours have been trying to decipher that for three hundred years. For all anyone knows, it's a meaningless number. A joke. Hah, hah, hah."

"But why? . . . I mean, Kidd was in jail, charged with a hanging offense—"

"Well, okay, it's not meaningless, and it's not a joke. *But* it only made sense to Kidd and to his wife. She was able to visit him in jail a few times. They spoke. They were devoted to each other. He may have given her half a clue verbally, or another clue in a letter that's since been lost."

This was interesting. Like the kind of thing I do,

except this clue was three hundred years old. I asked her, "Any more theories?"

"Well, the prevailing theory is that these numbers represent paces, which is the traditional method of pirates recording the location of their buried treasure."

"Paces?"

"Yes."

"Paces from where?"

"That's what Mrs. William Kidd knew and you don't."

"Oh." I looked at the numbers. "That's a lot of paces."

"Again, you have to know the personal code. It could mean"—she looked at the napkin—"forty-four paces in a direction of ten degrees, and sixty-eight paces in a direction of eighteen degrees. Or vice versa. Or, read it backwards. Who knows? It doesn't matter if you don't know the starting point."

"Do you think the treasure is buried under one of those oak trees? Captain Kidd's Trees?"

"I don't know." She added, "Either the treasure has been found and the person who found it didn't advertise it to the world, or there was never any treasure, or it's still buried and will stay buried forever."

"What do you think?"

"I think I should go open my shop." She crumpled the napkin and stuffed it in my shirt pocket. I paid the bill and we left. The diner was five minutes from the Peconic Historical Society where Emma had left her van. I pulled into the lot, and she gave me a quick peck on the cheek, like we were more than just lovers.

She said, "See you at four. Whitestone Florist, Main

Road, Mattituck." She got out, hopped into her van, honked, waved, and pulled away.

I sat in my Jeep awhile, listening to the local news. I would have gotten on the road, but I didn't know where to go. In truth, I'd exhausted most of my leads, and I didn't have an office where I could go and shuffle papers. I wasn't going to get any calls from witnesses, forensics, and so forth. Very few people even knew where to send me an anonymous tip. In short, I felt like a private detective, though I wasn't even licensed to do that.

All things considered, however, I'd made some startling discoveries since meeting Emma Whitestone. If I had any doubts about why the Gordons had been murdered, that number, 44106818, which was in their chart book, should put the doubts to rest.

On the other hand, even if it were true that Tom and Judy Gordon were treasure hunters—and I had no doubt they were, based on all the evidence—it didn't necessarily follow that treasure hunting was what got them killed. What was the provable connection between their archaeological digs on Plum Island, and the bullets through their heads on their back deck?

I called my answering machine. Two messages—one from Max, asking where to mail my one-dollar check, and another call from my boss, Detective Lieutenant Wolfe, again strongly urging me to call his office and indicating that I was in deep doo-doo and sinking fast.

I put the car in gear and drove. Sometimes it's good to just drive.

On the radio, the news guy said, "An update on the double homicide of two Plum Island scientists in Nassau Point. The Southold Town police and the Suffolk

County police have issued a joint statement." The news guy—it sounded like Don from Tuesday morning— read the statement verbatim. Jeez, if we could get the network hotshots in the city to read our press releases without comment, we'd be in public relations heaven. The joint statement was a hot air balloon with no one in the gondola except two dead bodies. The statement stressed the theft of Ebola vaccine as a motive. A separate statement from the FBI said that they didn't know if the perpetrators were foreign or domestic, but they were pursuing some good leads. The World Health Organization expressed concern over the theft of this "vital and important vaccine" that was desperately needed in many Third World countries. And so forth.

The thing that really pissed me off was that the official version of what happened had the effect of branding Tom and Judy as cynical, heartless thieves: first they stole their employer's time and resources, then when they secretly developed a vaccine, they stole the formula and presumably some samples, and intended to sell it for a huge profit. Meanwhile, people in Africa were dying by the thousands of this horrible disease.

I could picture Nash, Foster, the four suit guys I'd seen coming off the ferry, and a bunch of White House and Pentagon spin-control types burning up the phone lines between Plum Island and D.C. As soon as everyone learned that the Gordons were involved with genetically altered vaccines, then the perfect cover story presented itself to these geniuses. To be fair, they wanted to avoid panic about plague, but I'd bet my potential three-quarter lifetime disability pension that not one person in Washington considered the Gordons' reputations or their families when they concocted the story branding them as thieves.

The irony, if there was an irony here, was that Foster, Nash, and the government were undoubtedly still convinced that the Gordons stole one or more biological warfare diseases. The Washington insiders, from the president on down through the chain of command, were still sleeping with biocontainment suits over their jammies. Good. Screw them.

I stopped at a deli in Cutchogue and bought a container of coffee and a bunch of newspapers—the *New York Times*, the *Post*, the *Daily News*, and Long Island's *Newsday*. In all four papers, the Gordon story had been relegated to a few inches on the inside pages. Even *Newsday* didn't give the local murder much attention. I'm sure a lot of people in Washington were happy that the story was fading. And so was I. It gave me as much of a free hand as it gave them.

And while Foster, Nash, and Company were looking for foreign agents and terrorists, I'd followed my hunch and gone with my feelings about Tom and Judy Gordon. I was happy and not too surprised to discover that what I'd thought all along was true—this was not about biological warfare, or about narcotics, or anything illegal. Well, not too illegal.

Anyway, I still didn't know who murdered them. Equally important, I knew they were not criminals, and I intended to give them their reputations back.

I finished the coffee, threw the newspapers in the back seat, and got on the road. I drove up to the Soundview, a 1950s waterfront motel. I went into the office and inquired after Messrs. Foster and Nash. The young man behind the desk said the gentlemen I was describing had both checked out already.

I drove around—I hesitate to say aimlessly, but if you don't know where you're going or why, you're either a government employee or you're aimless.

Anyway, I decided to drive to Orient Point. It was another nice day, a bit cooler and breezier, but pleasant.

I drove to the Plum Island ferry station. I wanted to check out the cars in the lot, see if there was any unusual activity, and maybe see if I ran into anyone interesting. When I pulled into the facility and approached the gate, a Plum Island security guard stepped into my path and held up his hand. Softie that I am, I didn't run him over. He came around to my window and asked me, "Can I help you, sir?"

I held up my shield case and said, "I'm working with the FBI on the Gordon case."

He studied the shield and ID closely, and I watched his face. Clearly, I was on this man's short list of saboteurs, spies, and perverts, and he wasn't very cool about it. He stared at me a moment, cleared his throat, and said, "Sir, if you'll pull over here, I'll get you a pass."

"Okay." I pulled to the side. I hadn't expected a security guy at the gate, though I should have. The guy went into the brick building, and I continued on into the parking lot. I have a problem with authority.

The first thing I noticed was that there were two military humvees parked at the ferry slip. I could see two uniformed men in each humvee, and as I got closer, I was able to identify them and the humvees as Marine Corps. I hadn't seen a single military vehicle on Plum Island Tuesday morning, but the world had changed since then.

I also spotted a big black Caprice that could have been the one I'd seen Tuesday with the four suit guys in it. I noted the license plate number.

Then, riding around through the hundred or so parked cars, I saw a white Ford Taurus with rental plates, and I was pretty certain this could be the car that Nash and Foster drove. Big doings at Plum Island today.

Neither ferry was in the slip or on the horizon, and except for the Marines waiting to drive their humvees onto an arriving ferry, there was no one around.

Except, when I looked in my sideview mirror, I saw four—count 'em, four—blue uniformed security guards running toward me, waving and hollering. Obviously I'd misunderstood the gate guard. Oh, dear.

I drove my vehicle toward the four guards. I could hear them now yelling, "Stop! Stop!" Fortunately, they weren't going for their guns.

I wanted the report to Messrs. Foster and Nash to be entertaining, so I drove in circles around the four guards, waving back at them, and yelling to them, "Stop! Stop!" I did a couple of figure eights, then, before anyone closed the steel gate or got crazy with the guns, I drove toward the exit. I cut hard left onto Main Road and hit the gas, heading back west. No one fired. That's why I love this country.

Within two minutes, I was on the narrow strip of land that connects Orient to East Marion. The Sound was to my right, the bay to my left, and lots of birds were in between. Atlantic Coastal Flyway. You learn something new every day.

Suddenly, this big white gull came in at me from twelve o'clock high. It was a beautifully timed and executed flight, a long steep dive, followed by a slight flare-out which resulted in a more shallow dive, then a pull-out and climb; then with perfect timing, he let loose his payload, which splattered purple and green across my windshield. It was that kind of day.

I hit the windshield wipers, but the washer reservoir was empty, and I had this stuff smeared across my field of vision. Yuck, yuck. I pulled over. "Damn." Ever resourceful, I got my expensive bottle of Tobin Merlot out of the backseat, and got my trusty Swiss Army knife with the corkscrew from the glove compartment. I opened the wine and poured some of the Merlot over the windshield as the wipers swept back and forth. I drank a little of the wine. Not bad. I poured more on the windshield, then drank some more. A guy in a passing car honked and gave me a wave. Fortunately, the bombload was made up of pretty much what the wine was made of and the windshield was reasonably clean, except for a purple film. I finished the bottle and threw it in the backseat.

On my way again. I thought about Emma Whitestone. I'm the kind of guy who *always* sends flowers the next day. However, sending flowers to a florist might be redundant. For all I knew, my FTD order would go through her. She'd make up the bouquet and hand it to herself. Enough silliness, as Emma would say. I needed a gift for her. A bottle of Tobin wine was also not appropriate. I mean, what with them being ex-lovers and all. And, she had access to all the local handicrafts and gift shop junk she'd ever need. Jeez, this one had me stumped. I hate to buy jewelry or clothes for women, but maybe that's what I had to do.

Back on Main Road, I stopped at a service station

and got gas. I also filled my windshield washer reservoir, washed my windshield, and invested in a local map.

I took the opportunity to scope out the road to see if anyone was parked nearby, watching me. It didn't appear that I was being followed, and I'm good at spotting a tail, the incident on West 102nd Street notwithstanding.

I didn't think I was in any danger, yet I considered going home for my piece, then decided against it.

Armed now with nothing more than a map and my superior intellect, I headed north, up to the bluffs. With some difficulty, I finally found the right dirt road that led to the right bluff. I parked, got out, and climbed to the top of the bluff.

This time, I poked around through the underbrush and the sawgrass. I found the rock I'd sat on and noted that it was big enough to be used as a point of reference if you were going to bury something.

I went to the edge of the bluff. It was obvious that a good deal of erosion must have taken place over the last three hundred years so that something buried on the north side—the Sound side—of the bluff might well have been exposed by wind and water, and maybe tumbled down onto the beach. I was putting this together now.

I came down from the bluff and got in my Jeep. Using my new map, I made my way to the west side of Mattituck Inlet. And there it was—no, not Captain Kidd's Trees, but a sign that said "Captain Kidd Estates." Apparently some subdivider had a marketing dream. I drove into Captain Kidd Estates, a small collection of 1960s ranches and Cape Cods. A kid—no pun intended—was riding by on his bicycle, and I stopped and asked him, "Do you know where Captain Kidd's Trees are?"

The boy, about twelve, didn't reply.

I said, "There's supposed to be a place near the inlet where there are a bunch of trees called Captain Kidd's Trees."

He looked at me, looked at my four-wheel drive, and I guess I struck him as an Indiana Jones type, because he asked me, "You gonna look for the treasure?"

"Oh...no, I just want to take a picture of the trees."

"He buried his treasure chest under one of those trees."

It seemed like everyone but me was hip to this. That's what happens when you don't pay attention. I said to the lad, "Where are the trees?"

"My friends and me dug a big hole once, before the cops chased us away. The trees are in a park, so you can't dig there."

"I just want to take a few pictures."

"If you wanna dig, I'll watch for the cops."

"Okay. Lead on."

I followed the boy on his bike to a winding lane that led downhill to the Sound and ended at a beach park where a few young mothers sat with toddlers in strollers. To the right was the Mattituck Inlet and a marina farther up the inlet. I pulled off to the side and got out. I didn't see any large oaks, only a field of brush and scrub trees across the lane. The field was bordered by the beach on the north and by the inlet on the east. Across the field, to the west, I could see a bluff descending to the water. On the south from where I'd come was a rise of land which were the Captain Kidd Estates.

The boy asked me, "Where's your shovel?"

"I'm just taking pictures."

"Where's your camera?"

"What's your name?"

"Billy. What's yours?"

"Johnny. Is this the right place?"

"Sure."

"Where are Captain Kidd's Trees?"

"There. In the park."

He pointed to the big field. It was apparently an undeveloped piece of parkland, part of the beach park, more a nature preserve than what my Manhattan mind thought of as a park. Still, I saw no towering oaks. I said to him, "I don't see the trees."

"There." He pointed out to me all the scrub oak, wild cherry, and other assorted trees, none taller than twenty feet high. He said, "See that big one there? That's where me and Jerry dug. We're gonna go back some night."

"Good idea. Let's take a look."

Billy dropped his bike in the grass, and my new partner and I walked onto the field. The grass was high, but the bushes were widely spaced and the walking was easy. Obviously, Billy hadn't paid attention in earth science class or he'd have known that these few trees weren't three and four hundred years old. In fact, I really hadn't expected to see hundred-foot-high oaks with skulls and crossbones carved in them.

Billy said, "Do you have a shovel in your car?"

"No, I'm just scoping it out for now. Tomorrow we're coming back with bulldozers."

"Yeah? If you find the treasure, you have to share."

In my best pirate accent, I said, "If I find the treasure, me lad, I'll cut the throats of all who ask for their share."

Billy grabbed his throat with two hands and made gurgling sounds.

I kept walking, kicking at the sandy soil, until finally I found what I was looking for—a huge tree stump half rotted, covered with soil and vegetation. I said to Billy, "Did you ever see any more stumps like this?"

"Oh, yeah. They're like all over."

I looked around, picturing primeval oaks that once stood here in colonial times on this flat piece of land beside this big inlet in the Sound. This was a natural haven for ships and men, and I could picture a three-master coming into the Sound and anchoring offshore. A few men take a dinghy into the inlet and land about where my vehicle was parked on the lane. They moor the dinghy to a tree and wade ashore. They're carrying something—a chest—just as Tom and Judy carried a chest ashore. The seamen—William Kidd and a few others—enter the oak forest, pick a tree, dig a hole, bury the treasure, then somehow mark the tree and leave, intending to return someday. Of course, they never do. That's why there are so many legends of buried treasure.

Billy said, "That's the tree where me and Jerry dug. Want to see?"

"Sure."

We walked over to a gnarled windblown wild cherry, about fifteen feet high. Billy pointed to the base of the tree where a shallow hole was half filled with sand. He said, "There."

"Why not the other side of the tree? Why not a few feet away from the tree?"

"I don't know...we guessed. Hey, do you have a map? A treasure map?"

"I do. But if I show it to you, I have to make you walk the plank."

"Aaahhh!" He did a passable imitation of going off the end of eternity's diving board.

I started back toward the car, Buddy Billy at my side. I asked him, "How come you're not in school today?"

"Today is Rosh Hashanah."

"You Jewish?"

"No, but my friend Danny is."

"Where's Danny?"

"He went to school."

This kid had lawyer potential.

We got back to my vehicle, and I found a fiver in my wallet. "Okay, Billy, thanks for your help."

He took the bill and said, "Hey, thanks! You need more help?"

"No, I have to go back and report to the White House."

"The White House?"

I picked up his bicycle and gave it to him. I got in my Jeep and started it up. I said to him, "That tree where you were digging isn't old enough to have been there in Captain Kidd's day."

"Yeah?"

"Captain Kidd was three hundred years ago."

"Wow."

"You know all those old rotten stumps in the

ground? Those were big trees when Captain Kidd came ashore here. Try digging around one of those."

"Hey, thanks!"

"If you find the treasure, I'll be back for my share."

"Okay. But my friend Jerry might try to cut your throat. I wouldn't, 'cause you told us where the treasure is."

"Jerry might cut *your* throat."

"Aaaaarrrghh!"

And off I went.

Next stop, a gift for Emma. On my way, I put more of the mental puzzle together.

Indeed, there may have been more than one treasure buried, but the one the Gordons were looking for, and may well have found, was buried on Plum Island. I was reasonably certain of that.

And Plum Island was government land, and anything taken from the ground there belonged to the government, specifically, the Department of the Interior.

So, the simple solution to cheating Caesar out of the treasure on Caesar's land is to move the treasure to your own land. If you rent, however, you have a problem. So, voilà, the one acre of waterfront purchased from Margaret Wiley.

Some questions remained, however. One question was, how did the Gordons know there was possibly a hoard of treasure buried on Plum Island? Answer: they found out through their interest and membership in the Peconic Historical Society. Or, someone else had figured out long ago that there was treasure on Plum Island and that person or persons had no access to Plum Island, so he, she, or they befriended the Gordons, who, as senior staff, had almost unlimited access to the island. Eventually, this person or persons confided this knowledge to the Gordons, and a plot was hatched, a deal was made, signed in blood by the light of a flickering candle or something.

Tom and Judy were good citizens, but they weren't saints. I thought of what Beth had said—"saint-seducing gold"—and realized now how appropriate that was.

The Gordons obviously intended to rebury the treasure on their land, then discover it and announce it to the world, and pay their honest taxes to Uncle and New York State. Maybe their partner had other ideas. That was it. The partner wasn't satisfied with his or her fifty percent of the loot on which presumably some heavy taxes had to be paid.

This got me to wondering how much the treasure could be worth. Obviously enough to commit double murder.

A theory, as I teach in my class, has to fit all the facts. If it doesn't, you have to examine the facts. If the facts are correct, and the theory doesn't work, then you have to alter the theory.

In this case, most of the early facts pointed to the wrong theory. That aside, I finally had what the physicists would call a unified theory—the Plum Island so-called archaeological digs, the high-priced powerboat, the expensive rental house on the water, the *Spirochete* anchored off Plum Island, the membership in the Peconic Historical Society, and the one acre of apparently useless land on the Sound, and maybe the trip to England. Add to this the Gordons' whimsical flying of the Jolly Roger, the missing ice chest, and the eight-digit number on their sea chart, and you had a pretty solid unified theory that tied all these seemingly unconnected things together.

Or—and this was the big or—I had lost too much blood from my brain, and I was totally wrong, completely off base, mentally unfit for detective duty, and lucky to be allowed to walk a beat in Staten Island.

That, too, was possible. I mean, look at Foster and Nash, two reasonably smart guys with all the resources in the world behind them, and *they* were totally off base, chasing the wrong leads. They had good minds, yet they were confined by their narrow worldview: international intrigue, biological warfare, international terrorism, and all that. They probably never even *heard* of Captain Kidd. Good.

Anyway, my unified theory notwithstanding, there were still things I didn't know and things I didn't understand. One thing I didn't know was who murdered Tom and Judy Gordon. Sometimes you catch the murderer even before you have all the facts or before you understand what you do have—in those cases, the murderer will sometimes be nice and explain to you what you missed, what you misunderstood, what his motives were, and so forth. When I get a confession, I want more than an admission of guilt—I want a lesson in the criminal mind. This is good for next time around, and there's always a next time around.

In this case, I had what I thought was the motive, but not the murderer. All I knew about the murderer was that he or she was very clever. I couldn't imagine the Gordons plotting a crime with an idiot.

One of the points in my mental map of this case was Tobin Vineyards. Even now, after I'd gotten hip to the Kidd thing and come up with my unified theory,

I couldn't figure out how the relationship between Fredric Tobin and the Gordons fit into the whole picture.

Well, maybe I could....I headed toward Tobin Vineyards.

CHAPTER TWENTY

The white Porsche which belonged to the proprietor was in the parking field. I parked, got out of my Jeep, and made my way to the winery.

The ground floor of the central tower connected various wings, and I entered the tower through the visitors' reception area. The staircase and elevator each had signs reading "Employees Only." In fact, the elevator that Mr. Tobin had gotten off when I first met him had a key entry, so I took the stairs, which I prefer in any case. The staircase was actually a steel and concrete fire exit built within the cedar-shingled tower, and at each floor was a steel door, and there was a sign on each door: "Second Floor, Accounting, Personnel, Billing"; "Third Floor, Sales, Marketing, Shipping"; and so forth.

On the fourth floor the sign said "Executive Offices." I continued up to the fifth floor where there was another steel door, this one unmarked. I pulled on the handle, but it was locked. I noticed a surveillance camera and an intercom.

I went back down to the fourth floor where the

executive offices door opened into a reception area. There was a circular reception counter in the center, but no one was at the counter. From the reception area, four open doors led to offices that I could see were sort of pie-shaped, an obvious function of the circular floor plan. Each office had a nice big window in the tower. A fifth door was closed.

I couldn't see anyone at any of the desks in the open offices, and as it was now 1:30, I assumed everyone was at lunch.

I stepped into the reception area and looked around. The furniture looked like real leather, purple, of course, and on the walls were reproductions of de Kooning and Pollock—or the staff's children and grandchildren had been allowed to hang their dribbles. A video surveillance camera was trained on me, and I waved.

The closed door opened and an efficient-looking woman of about thirty appeared. She asked me, "May I help you?"

"Please tell Mr. Tobin that Mr. Corey is here to see him."

"Do you have an appointment, sir?"

"I have a standing appointment."

"Mr. Tobin is about to go to lunch. In fact, he's running late."

"Then I'll drive him. Please tell him I'm here." I hate to flash the tin in a guy's office unless I'm there to help him or to put the cuffs on him. It's the in-between stuff where the guy sometimes gets pissed off if you scare the staff with the tin and bully your way in. I said to the young lady, "Tell him it's important."

She turned back to the closed door, knocked, went

in, and shut it behind her. I waited a full minute, which is really patient for me, then I went in. Mr. Tobin and the young lady were both standing at his desk in conversation. He was rubbing his short-cropped beard, looking somewhat Mephistophelian. He was wearing a burgundy blazer, black slacks, and a pink oxford shirt. He turned to me, but did not return my big friendly grin.

I said, "I'm sorry to barge in this way, Mr. Tobin, but I'm kind of pressed for time, and I knew you wouldn't mind."

He dismissed the young lady and remained standing. The man was a real gentleman, and he didn't even show any anger. He said, "This is an unexpected pleasure."

I love that expression. I replied, "For me, too. I mean, I didn't think I was going to see you until your party, then all of a sudden, your name pops up."

"How did it pop up?"

When I popped your ex-girlfriend. Actually, I had a more polite reply and said, "I was just talking to somebody about the case, you know, about Tom and Judy and their love of wine and how they were so pleased to know you. Anyway, this person happened to mention that she also knew you and knew Tom and Judy. So, that's how your name came up."

He wouldn't go for the bait and replied, "And that's why you're here?"

"Well, no." I didn't elaborate. I let it sit. He was still standing, the window at his back. I walked around his desk and looked out the window. "What a view."

"The best view on the North Fork, unless you live in a lighthouse."

"Right." Mr. Tobin's view was to the north, across his acres of vineyards. A few farms and orchards within the vineyards created a sort of patchwork effect which was very nice. In the far distance, the land rose up into the glacial bluffs, and from this height, I could actually see over them to the Sound. I said, "Do you have binoculars?"

He hesitated, then went to a credenza and fetched me a pair of binoculars.

"Thanks." I focused on the Sound and commented, "I can see the Connecticut coastline."

"Yes."

I craned to the left and focused on the bluff I thought might be Tom and Judy's. I said to Mr. Tobin, "I just learned that the Gordons bought an acre of bluff out there. Did you know that?"

"No."

That's not what Emma told me, Fredric. I said, "They could have used some of your business sense. They paid twenty-five Gs for a parcel that couldn't be developed."

"They should have known if the development rights had been sold to the county."

I put down the binoculars and said, "I didn't say anything about the development rights being sold to the county. I said they couldn't develop their parcel. That could be because of zoning, no well water, no electric service, or whatever. Why did you think the development rights had been sold on their land?"

He replied, "Actually, I may have heard that."

"Oh. Then you did know they bought a piece of land."

"I think someone mentioned it to me. I didn't know

where the land was. Only that it came without development rights."

"Right." I turned back to the window and trained Tobin's binoculars on the bluffs again. To the west, the high ground dropped off where the Mattituck Inlet came through, and I could see the area known as Captain Kidd's Trees and Captain Kidd Estates. To the far right, the east, I could see clearly as far as Greenport and could also make out Orient Point and Plum Island. I said, "This is better than the observation deck in the Empire State Building. Not as high, but—"

"How can I help you, Mr. Corey?"

I ignored his question and said, "You know, you're on top of the world. I mean, look at all of this. Four hundred acres of prime real estate, a house on the water, a restaurant, a Porsche, and who knows what else. And you sit here in this five-story tower—what's on the fifth floor, by the way?"

"My apartment."

"Wow. Wow. I mean, do the ladies like that or what?"

He didn't respond to that and said, "I spoke to my attorney after I saw you yesterday."

"Did you?"

"And he advised me not to speak to the police without counsel present."

"That's your right. I told you that."

"Further inquiries by my attorney turn up the fact that you are no longer employed by Chief Maxwell as a consultant in this case, and that, in fact, you were not employed by the township when you spoke to me."

"Well, now, that's a debatable point."

"Debatable or not, you have no official status here any longer."

"Right. And since I'm not the police any longer, you can speak to me. That works."

Fredric Tobin ignored this and said, "My attorney promised to cooperate with the town police, until he discovered that Chief Maxwell doesn't need or want his or my cooperation. Chief Maxwell is annoyed that you came and questioned me. You have embarrassed me and him." Mr. Tobin added, "I am a generous contributor to key politicians here, and I've been very generous with time and money to renovate historic homes, put up historical markers, contribute to the hospital and other worthy charities, including the Police Benevolent Association. Do I make myself clear?"

"Oh, absolutely. About ten sentences ago. I just came here to see if I could take you to lunch."

"I have a lunch date, thank you."

"Okay, maybe some other time."

He glanced at his watch and announced, "I really have to go."

"Sure. I'll go downstairs with you."

He took a deep breath and nodded.

We left his office and went into the reception area. He said to his receptionist, "Mr. Corey and I have concluded our business, and it will not be necessary for him to return again."

Wow, talk about polite. This guy could slip you the greased weenie, and you wouldn't even feel it for a few days.

Mr. T put his key in the elevator lock, and it arrived in short order. We got in, and on the way down, to break the awkward silence, I said, "You know that

Merlot I bought? Well, it came in handy. This is really stupid, maybe funny, but I don't think you'll find it funny—I had to use the stuff to clean birdshit off my windshield."

"What?"

The elevator door opened, and we walked out into the common area. I said, "A big gull dive-bombed my windshield." I explained. He glanced at his watch again. I concluded, "The half I drank was very good. Not too forward."

He said, "That's a terrible waste of vintage wine."

"I knew you'd say that."

He went through the door that connected to the visitors' reception area. I walked with him.

Out in the parking field, I said, "By the way, the lady who made you pop into my head—remember?"

"Yes."

"She said she was a friend of yours. But a lot of people claim to be your friend, like the Gordons, but they're just acquaintances who want to bask in your reflected light."

He didn't reply. It's hard to bait a man who's playing Lord of the Manor. Mr. Tobin was not going to lose his cool.

I said, "Anyway, she said she was your friend. Do you know Emma Whitestone?"

He may have broken his stride a bit, then continued on and stopped at his car. He said, "Yes, we dated about a year ago."

"And you stayed friends?"

"Why not?"

"All my exes want to murder me."

"I can't imagine why."

I chuckled at that one. I mean, it was odd that I still kinda liked this guy, even though I suspected that he'd murdered my friends. Don't get me wrong—if he really did it, I'd do my best to see him get the hot squat, or whatever this state decides to use when they dispatch the first condemned murderer. For now, if he was polite, I'd be polite.

The other thing that was so bizarre is that since the last time we'd spoken, we had developed something in common. I mean, we had both gone where few men had gone before...well, maybe more than a few. I wanted to kind of slap him on the back and say, "Hey, Freddie, was it as good for you as it was for me?" or something like that. But gentlemen don't kiss and tell.

Fredric Tobin was saying, "Mr. Corey, I sense that you think I know more than I'm telling you about the Gordons. I assure you I don't. However, if the county or town police wish to take a statement from me, I'll be happy to oblige. Meanwhile, you're welcome here as a customer, and you're welcome to my home as an invited guest. You are not welcome to my office, and you're not welcome to question me any further."

"Sounds reasonable."

"Good day."

"Have a good lunch."

He got into his Porsche and off he went.

I looked back at the Tobin tower flying the black Tobin flag. If Mr. Tobin had any physical evidence to hide, it might be at his waterfront home or perhaps in his apartment on the top floor of that tower. Obviously, a consent search was out of the question, and no judge was going to issue a search warrant, so it looked like I'd have to issue a midnight search warrant to myself.

Back in my Jeep and on the road again. I called my answering machine and retrieved two messages. The first was from an unidentified Snippybitch from the NYPD Absence Control Unit telling me my physical was moved up to next Tuesday and asking me to acknowledge the message. Whenever the bosses can't get ahold of you, they ask personnel or payroll section or health services division to call you about something that you have to reply to. I hate sneakiness.

The next message was from my former partner, Beth Penrose. She said, "Hi, John. Sorry I didn't get back to you sooner, but it's been crazy here. Anyway, I know you're not officially involved with the case, but I have a few things I'd like to discuss with you. Why don't I come out tomorrow afternoon? Call me or I'll call you, and we'll come up with a time and place. Take care."

So. The tone was friendly, but not as friendly as when we'd last spoken in person. Not to mention the kiss on the cheek. I suppose it's not a good idea to be too gushy on an answering machine. More to the point, whatever heat had developed during that intense two days would naturally cool off when she returned to her turf and her own world. It happens.

Now she wanted to discuss a few things with me, which meant she wanted to know what, if anything, I'd discovered. To Beth Penrose, I had become just another witness. Well, maybe I was being cynical. Though maybe I had to move Beth Penrose out of my mind in order to fit Emma Whitestone in. I was never good at balancing multiple relationships. It's worse than carrying a dozen homicide cases at the same time, and a lot more dangerous.

Anyway, I needed a gift for Emma, and I spotted an antique shop on Main Road. Perfect. I pulled over and got out. The wonderful thing about America is that there are more antiques in circulation than were originally made.

I rummaged around inside the musty place and the proprietress, a nice little old lady, asked me if she could help.

"I need a gift for a young lady."

"A wife? Daughter?"

Someone I don't know well but had sex with. "A friend."

"Ah." She showed me a few things, but I'm totally clueless about antiques. Then I had a brilliant idea and asked her, "Are you a member of the Peconic Historical Society?"

"No, but I belong to the Southold Historical Society."

Good lord, there were certainly enough of these things around. I asked, "Would you know Emma Whitestone?"

"I surely do. A very fine young lady."

"Exactly. I'm looking for something for her."

"How nice. What is the occasion?"

Standard postcoital token of affection and thanks. "She's helped me do some research in the archives."

"Oh, she's very good at that. What were you looking for?"

"Well . . . this is silly, but ever since I was a kid, I was fascinated by pirates."

She sort of chuckled. Maybe cackled. She said, "The famous Captain Kidd was a visitor to our shores."

"Was he?"

"There were many pirates who came through here before the Revolution. They plundered the French and Spanish in the Caribbean, then came north to spend their ill-gotten gains, or to refit their ships. Some settled in these parts." She smiled and said, "With all that gold and jewels, they quickly became leading citizens." She added, "Many an original fortune around here was founded on pirate's plunder."

I sort of liked the old-fashioned way the woman spoke. I commented, "Many a modern-day fortune has corporate piracy behind it."

"Well, I wouldn't know about that, but I do know that these drug runners today are much like the old pirates." She added, "When I was a girl, we had the rum runners. We're law-abiding people here, but we're on the sea routes."

"Not to mention the Atlantic Coastal Flyway."

"That's for birds."

"Right."

After another minute of chat, I introduced myself as John, and she introduced herself as Mrs. Simmons. I asked her, "Does the Southold Historical Society have any information on pirates?"

"We do. Though not much. There are some original documents and letters in the archives. And even a reward poster in our little museum."

"Would you happen to have an authentic pirate treasure map I could photocopy?"

She smiled.

I asked her, "Do you know Fredric Tobin?"

"Well, doesn't everyone? Rich as Croesus."

Who? I asked, "Does he belong to the Southold Historical Society? Mr. Tobin, not Croesus."

"No, but Mr. Tobin's a generous contributor."

"Does he visit your archives?"

"I understand he did. Though not in the last year or so."

I nodded. I had to keep reminding myself that this wasn't Manhattan, that this was a community of about twenty thousand people and that while it wasn't literally true that everyone knew everyone else, it was true that everyone knew someone who knew someone else. For a detective, this was like walking knee-deep in pay dirt.

Anyway, at least one of my searches was over, and I asked Mrs. Simmons, "Could you recommend something for Ms. Whitestone?"

"What is your price range?"

"Nothing is too good for Ms. Whitestone. Fifty dollars."

"Oh...well..."

"A hundred."

She smiled and produced a porcelain chamber pot with a big jug handle, decorated with painted roses. She said, "Emma collects these."

"Chamber pots?"

"Yes. She uses them as planters. She has quite a collection."

"Are you sure?"

"Of course. I've been holding this for her to see. It's late Victorian. Made in England."

"Okay...I'll take it."

"It's actually a bit over a hundred dollars."

"How big a bit?"

"It's two hundred."

"Has it ever been used?"

"I imagine so."

"Do you take Visa?"

"Of course."

"Can you wrap it?"

"I'll put it in a nice gift bag."

"Can you put a bow on the handle?"

"If you'd like."

Transaction complete, I left the antique store with the glorified bedpan in a nice pink and green gift bag.

Okay, off I went to the Cutchogue Free Library, founded in 1841 and still paying the same wages. The library was at the edge of the village green, a big clapboard building with a steeple that looked as if it had once been a church.

I parked and went inside. There was a tough-looking old bird at the front desk who peered at me over a pair of half specs. I smiled and breezed past her.

There was a big banner hung at the entrance to the stacks which read: *"Find Buried Treasure—Read Books."* Excellent advice.

I found the card catalogue, which, thank God, wasn't computerized, and within ten minutes I was sitting in a reading alcove with a reference book in front of me, titled *The Book of Buried Treasure*.

I read about a John Shelby of Thackham, England, who in 1672 was thrown from his horse into a thicket where he found an iron pot containing more than five hundred gold coins. According to the treasure trove laws of England, all hidden or lost property belonged to the Crown. However, Shelby refused to give the gold to the king's officers, and he was arrested, tried for treason, and beheaded. This was probably a favorite story of the IRS.

I read about the treasure trove laws of the United

States government and of the various states. Basically, all the laws say, "Finders keepers, losers weepers."

There was, however, something called the Act for the Preservation of American Antiquities, and it was pretty clear that anything found on federal land came under the jurisdiction of the secretary of either Agriculture, Defense, or the Interior, depending on the land in question. Furthermore, you needed a permit to dig on federal land and whatever you found belonged to Uncle Sam. What a great deal that was.

If, however, you found money, valuables, or any sort of treasure on your own land, it was pretty much yours, as long as you could prove that the original owner was dead, and/or the heirs were unknown, and that the property wasn't stolen. And even if it was stolen, you could claim it if the rightful owners were known to be dead or unknowable, or enemies of the country at the time the money, goods, or treasure was obtained. The example given was pirate treasure, plunder, bounty, and all that good stuff. So far, so good.

And to make a nice situation even nicer, the IRS, in some unbelievable lapse of greed, required that you pay tax only on the portion you sold or otherwise turned into cash each year, as long as you weren't a *professional* treasure hunter. So, if you were a biologist, for instance, and you owned a piece of land, and you found buried treasure on it by accident, or as a result of your archaeological hobby, and it was worth, say, ten or twenty million, then you didn't pay a dime in taxes until you sold some of it. What a sweet deal. It almost made me want to go into treasure hunting as a hobby. On second thought, that's what I was doing.

The book also said that if the treasure has historical

value or is associated with popular culture—and here, lo and behold, the book gave the specific example of Captain Kidd's lost treasure—then the value of the treasure would be greatly enhanced, and so forth.

I read for a while longer, learning about the treasure trove laws and reading some interesting examples and case histories. One particular case caught my eye—in the 1950s, a man was going through some old papers in the Admiralty Section of the Public Records Office in London. He found a faded letter written in 1750 by a famous pirate named Charles Wilson, addressed to Wilson's brother. The letter had originally been found on a pirate ship that was captured by the British navy. The letter read, "My brother, there are three creeks lying one hundred paces or more north of the second inlet above Chincoteague Island, Virginia, which is the southward end of the peninsula. At the head of the third creek to the northward is a bluff facing the Atlantic Ocean with three cedar trees growing on it, each about one and a half yards apart. Between the trees I have buried ten ironbound chests, bars of silver, gold, diamonds, and jewels to the sum of 200,000 pounds sterling. Go to the woody knoll secretly and remove the treasure."

Obviously, Charles Wilson's brother never got the letter since it was captured by the British navy. So, who found the treasure? The British navy? Or maybe it was the man who found the letter in the Public Records Office two hundred years later. The author of *The Book of Buried Treasure* didn't finish the story.

Point was, there is a place called the Admiralty Section of the Public Records Office in London, and God knew what you could find there if you had time, patience, a magnifying glass, a knowledge of old English, and a little greed, optimism, and sense of adventure. I was sure that now I understood the Gordons' lost week in London last year.

I had to assume the Gordons had read what I was reading now and knew the treasure trove laws. Beyond that, common sense would tell them that anything they found on Plum Island belonged to the government—no fifty-fifty split or anything—and that anything they claimed to have found on their rented property belonged to the owner, not the tenants. You didn't need a law degree to figure out any of that.

It had probably crossed Tom's and Judy's minds that an easy solution to the problems of ownership was to simply keep their mouths shut if they found anything on Plum Island. But maybe somewhere along the line, they realized that their best course of action—the most profitable in the long run—was simply to change the location of the discovery, announce the find, bask in the publicity, pay taxes only on what they sold each year, and go down in history as the handsome young Ph.D.'s who found Captain Kidd's lost treasure and became filthy rich. This was what any bright and logical person would do. It was what I would have done.

But there were a few problems. The first was that they had to get anything they found on Plum Island off Plum Island. The second problem was to rebury the treasure in such a way that its rediscovery not only seemed plausible, but would withstand scientific scrutiny. The answer to that was the eroded bluffs.

It all made sense to me. It made sense to them, too, but somewhere along the line, Tom and Judy did or said something that got them killed.

Fredric Tobin had lied to me about a few facts, and about his relationship with the Gordons, which seemed to be open to different interpretations. Plus, Tobin was either broke or on his way. To a homicide detective, this was like a flashing red light and an alarm bell.

Not only had Tobin befriended the Gordons, but he'd seduced—or at least charmed—Emma Whitestone, historian and archivist. It all seemed to fit. It was probably Tobin who'd somehow tumbled onto the possibility that there was buried treasure on Plum Island. And it was probably Tobin who paid for the Gordons' week in England to research this and maybe try to pinpoint the location.

Fredric Tobin was my prime suspect, but I wasn't discounting Paul Stevens or anyone else on Plum Island. For all I knew, this was a larger conspiracy than I first thought, and it could involve Stevens, Zollner, and others on the island, plus Tobin, plus...well, Emma Whitestone.

CHAPTER TWENTY-ONE

I found Whitestone Florist easily enough; I'd passed it dozens of times in the last three months.

I parked close by, checked my hair in the visor mirror, got out, and strode into the store.

It was a very nice place, full of...well, flowers. It smelled good. A young fellow behind the counter asked, "Can I help you?"

"I have an appointment with Emma Whitestone."

"Are you John?"

"None other."

"She had to do some errands—hold on." He called into the back, "Janet. John is here for Emma."

From the back came Janet, a woman of about forty-plus, and also a younger woman of about twenty-five whom Janet introduced as Ann. Janet said to me, "Emma asked if you could meet her at the historical society house."

"No problem."

Janet continued, "Emma said she had no way to get in touch with you."

"Well, no problem. I can find the house easy enough."

Ann said, "She may be a little late. She had some deliveries and errands."

"Not to worry. I'll wait there for her. I'll wait all night if I have to." Did I need three people to brief me? Obviously, I was on display.

The young man handed me a business card and said, "Call here if there's any problem."

"I surely will. Thank you all for your help." I got to the door, turned, and said, "Emma has a really nice place here."

They all smiled.

I left. I easily got a passing grade on that.

Back in my Jeep and on the way to Cutchogue Green. I really didn't like myself for even *thinking* that Emma Whitestone was in cahoots with Tobin and who knew who else. I mean, she had the entire staff of Whitestone Florist there to check out her new friend.

On the other hand, when you wind up in the sack with a woman you just met, you have to wonder if it's your charm or her agenda. Still, it was I who sought her out, not vice versa. Where did I get her name? Margaret Wiley? No, I'd found it earlier in the Gordons' Rolodex on Plum Island. All of these people seemed to be interconnected. Maybe Margaret was in on it. Maybe the entire adult population of the North Fork was in on it and I was the only outsider. I mean, it was like one of those creepy horror flicks where the whole village is witches and warlocks, and this clueless tourist shows up and before long, he's dinner.

I drove into the small parking lot of the historical

society mansion. There was no florist van there, but there was a ten-year-old Ford in the lot.

I left the chamber pot on the rear seat, thinking this might not be an appropriate time to present it. Perhaps after dinner.

Anyway, I went to the front door, and there was another Post-it note that said simply, "Enter."

So I did. Inside the big foyer, I called out, "Emma!" No answer. I walked through the various rooms of the large house and called out again, "Emma!" No answer. It seemed inconceivable that she'd unlock the door and leave the house with all these antiques around.

I went to the foot of the stairs and called out again, but no answer. It occurred to me that she could be on the potty, and I shouldn't be calling out to her. If she had waited, she could have used her gift.

Anyway, I began climbing the stairs, which were creaky. I'm not saying I would have liked to have had my gun, but I would have liked to have had my gun.

So, I got to the top of the stairs and listened. No sound except the sound a creaky old house makes. I decided to go into the upstairs parlor, which was half-way down the long hallway.

I tried to walk without making the damned floorboards creak, but every step made them squeak and moan.

I got to the door that led to the parlor. It was closed, and I swung it open. The damned hinges absolutely squealed. Jeez.

I stepped inside, and from behind the half-open door, there was a scream. I turned quickly, and Emma lunged at me with a sword and stuck it in my gut. She yelled, "Take that, you blackhearted pirate."

My heart raced and my bladder almost let loose. I smiled. "Funny."

"Scared you, didn't I?"

She had on a blue tricornered hat and in her hand was a soft plastic cutlass.

"Kind of surprised me."

"You looked more than surprised."

I got myself settled down and noticed she was wearing tan slacks today, a blue blouse, and sandals.

She said, "I got this sword and hat in the gift shop. There's a whole section of kids' junk." She went over to the armchair near the fireplace and held up a black pirate hat with a white skull and crossbones on it, a plastic saber, an eye patch, and something that looked like a parchment. She gave me the hat and patch, which she insisted I put on as she stuck the sword in my belt. She showed me the yellowed parchment on which was a map that said, "Pyrate Mappe." There was the usual island with the palm tree, a compass, a fat face blowing a westerly wind, a dotted sea route, and a three-master plus a sea serpent—the whole nine yards, including the big black X that marked the chest of gold.

Emma said, "This is one of our biggest sellers for children of all ages." She added, "People are fascinated by pirate treasure."

"Are they?"

"Aren't you?"

"It's interesting." I asked her, "Was Fredric interested in pirate treasure?"

"Maybe."

I asked, "Didn't you tell me you taught him to read old English script?"

"Yes, but I don't know specifically what he was

interested in reading." We looked at each other awhile, then she asked me, "What's going on, John?"

"I'm not sure."

"Why are you asking me about Fredric?"

"I'm jealous."

She didn't respond to that, but asked me, "Why did you want to meet me here?"

"Well...can I rely on you to keep this to yourself?"

"Keep what to myself?"

"Pirates."

"What about them?"

It's a balancing act between telling a witness *what* you want and *why* you want it. I changed the subject and said, "I met your employees. Janet, Ann, and..."

"Warren."

"Right. I passed the test."

She smiled and took my hand. "Come look at yourself in the mirror."

She led me into the hall, then into the eighteenth-century bedroom. I looked at myself in a wall mirror with the pirate hat, eye patch, and sword. "I look stupid."

"You really do."

"Thanks."

She said, "I'll bet you never did it on a feather bed."

"No, I never did."

"You have to keep the hat and patch on."

"Is this my fantasy or yours?"

She laughed, then before I knew it, she was getting out of her clothes, which she left on the floor. She kept the cocked hat on, and holding it with one hand, she tumbled into bed, onto the quilt comforter, which was probably an expensive antique that had never had sex before.

I played along with the game, leaving the hat and patch on as I undressed.

As I said, she was tall with long legs, and the beds in those days were short, so her head and hat were at the headboard and her feet were touching the footboard. It looked kind of funny and I laughed.

"What are you laughing at?"

"You. You're bigger than the bed."

"Let's see how big you are."

Anyway, if you've never done it on a feather mattress, you're not missing much. I can see why no one in those old portraits on the walls is smiling.

CHAPTER TWENTY-TWO

Later, in the archive room, sans costumes, we both sat at the oak table. Emma had a mug of herb tea that smelled like rubbing liniment.

She had gathered some material—original documents encased in plastic, some old books, and some reproductions of historical letters and documents. She was perusing her papers as she sipped her tea. I was in a typical male postcoital mood, thinking I should be sleeping or leaving. But I could do neither; I had work to do.

Emma asked me, "What exactly are you interested in?"

"I'm interested in pirate treasure. Is there any around here?"

"Sure. Almost anywhere you dig, you'll find silver and gold coins, diamonds and pearls. The farmers say it makes plowing difficult."

"I can imagine. But seriously." I hate it when people are smart-asses.

She said, "There are a number of pirate legends and

truths associated with this area. Would you like to hear the most famous? The story of Captain Kidd?"

"Yes, I would. I mean, not from year one, but as Captain Kidd relates to this place and to buried treasure."

"Okay...first of all, Captain William Kidd was a Scotsman, but he lived in Manhattan with his wife, Sarah, and their two children. In fact, he lived on Wall Street."

"Still full of pirates."

"Kidd was not really a pirate. He was, in fact, a privateer, hired by Lord Bellomont, who was then governor of Massachusetts, New York, and New Hampshire." She took a sip of tea. "So, with a royal commission, Captain William Kidd set sail in 1696 from New York harbor to search for pirates and seize their plunder. Bellomont put up a lot of his own money to buy and outfit Kidd's ship, the *Adventure Galley*. There were also rich and powerful backers of this enterprise in England, including four English lords and King William himself."

"I see trouble coming. Never go into a joint venture with the government."

"Amen."

I listened as she related this tale by heart. I wondered if Tobin knew this story, and if so, did he know it before or after he met Emma Whitestone? And why would anybody seriously think a three-hundred-year-old treasure could still be buried and/or found? Kidd's treasure, as I'd discovered by talking to Billy at Mattituck Inlet, was a dream, a child's story. Of course, the treasure may have existed, but there was so much myth and legend surrounding it, as Emma had said in the

Cutchogue Diner, and so many false maps and clues, that it had become meaningless over the last three centuries. Then I remembered the guy who found Charles Wilson's letter in the Public Records Office...so maybe Tobin and the Gordons had tumbled onto some real hard evidence.

Emma went on, "So after a lot of bad luck in the Caribbean, Kidd sailed to the Indian Ocean to search for pirates. There, he plundered two ships owned by the Great Mogul of India. On board were fabulous riches, worth in those days about two hundred thousand pounds. Today, that could be twenty million dollars."

"Not a bad day's work."

"No. Unfortunately, however, Kidd had made a mistake. The Mogul was allied with the king, and he complained to the British government. Kidd defended his actions by saying the Mogul's ships were sailing under French passes, and England and France were at war at the time. So even if the Mogul's ships weren't pirate ships, they were technically enemy ships. Unfortunately for Kidd, the British government had a good relationship with the Mogul through the British East India Company, which did big business with the Mogul. So Kidd was in trouble, and the only thing that was going to get him out of trouble was the two hundred thousand pounds' worth of loot."

"Money talks."

"Always has."

Apropos of money, Fredric Tobin popped into my head again. While I wasn't exactly jealous of Emma's past relationship with him, I thought it would be nice if I could get Freddie fried in the electric chair. Now, now, John.

Emma continued. "So, William Kidd sailed back to the New World. He stopped in the Caribbean, where he learned he was a wanted man himself, charged with piracy. Thinking ahead, he left about a third of his booty in the West Indies in the care of a person he could trust. Many of his crew wanted no part of this problem, so they took their share of the loot and stayed in the Caribbean. Kidd then bought a smaller ship, a sloop called the *San Antonio*, and sailed back to New York—to answer the charges. On the way, more of his crew wanted to be put ashore with their share, which they were, in Delaware and New Jersey. But Kidd still had a fantastic amount of treasure on board, worth today perhaps ten or fifteen million dollars."

I asked, "How do you know that he had that much treasure on board?"

"Well, no one knows for sure. These are guesses based partly on the Mogul's complaint to the British government, which may have been inflated."

"Moguls lie."

"I suppose. You know, aside from what the treasure is worth ounce for ounce, consider that some of the jewelry must be museum quality. Consider, too, that if you took a simple gold coin of that era, worth maybe a thousand dollars, and put the coin in a presentation case with a certificate authenticating that it was part of Captain Kidd's treasure, you could probably get double or triple for it."

"I see you took marketing at Columbia."

She smiled, then looked at me a long time. She said, "This is about the Gordon murders, isn't it?"

Our eyes met. I said, "Please continue."

She stayed silent a moment, then went on. "All

right...we know from documents and public records that Kidd then sailed into Long Island Sound from the eastern end, and that he landed at Oyster Bay, where he made contact with a James Emmot, who was a lawyer famous for defending pirates."

"Hey, my ex-wife works for that firm. They're still in the same business."

She ignored this and continued. "At some point, Kidd contacted his wife in Manhattan, who joined him on board the *San Antonio*. We know that at this time all the treasure was still on board."

"You mean the lawyer didn't get it yet?"

"Actually, Emmot *was* paid a generous sum by Kidd to defend him against the piracy charge."

I watched Emma Whitestone as she spoke. In the lamplight of the archive room, with papers piled in front of her, she looked and almost sounded schoolmarmish. She reminded me of some of the female instructors I know at John Jay—self-assured, knowledgeable, cool, and competent in the classroom, which somehow made them seem sexy and sensual to me. Maybe I have this schoolteacher hang-up from the sixth grade, specifically Miss Myerson, who I still have naughty dreams about.

Anyway, Emma continued, "Mr. Emmot went to Boston on Kidd's behalf and met with Lord Bellomont. Emmot delivered a letter that Kidd had written to Bellomont, and also gave Bellomont the two French passes that were on the Great Mogul's two ships, proving that the Mogul was double-dealing with the English and French, and therefore the ships were fair game for Kidd."

I asked, "How did Kidd know that when he attacked the ships?"

"Good question. It never came out in his trial."

"And you're saying that Kidd's lawyer turned over these passes, this important defense evidence, to Bellomont?"

"Yes, and Bellomont, for political reasons, wanted Kidd hanged."

"Fire that lawyer. You should always give photocopies and keep the originals."

She smiled. "Yes. The originals were never produced at Kidd's trial in London, and without those French passes, Kidd was convicted and executed." She added, "The passes were found in the British Museum in 1910."

"A little late for the defense."

"For sure. William Kidd was basically framed."

"Tough break. But what happened to the treasure aboard the *San Antonio*?"

"That's the question. I'll tell you what happened after Emmot went to Lord Bellomont in Boston, and since you're a detective, you tell me what happened to the treasure."

"Okay. I'm on the spot."

She went on, "Emmot, not a very good attorney apparently, got the impression from Lord Bellomont that Kidd would be treated fairly if he turned himself in at Boston. In fact, Bellomont wrote a letter to Kidd which he gave Emmot to deliver. The letter says, among other things…" She read from a reproduction in front of her, "'I have advised with his Majesty's council, and they are of the opinion that if you be so clear as you have said, that you may safely come hither and be equipped and fitted out to go and fetch your other ship, and I make no manner of doubt but to obtain the King's pardon for you.'"

"Sounds like royal poopy to me," I said.

Emma nodded and continued from Lord Bellomont's letter to Kidd, " 'I assure you on my word and on my honor I will perform nicely what I have now promised, tho' this I declare beforehand that whatever treasure of goods you bring hither, I will not meddle with the least bit of them, but they shall be left with such trusty persons as the council will advise until I receive orders from England how they shall be disposed of.' "

Emma looked up at me and asked, "Would that get you to come hither to Boston to answer a hanging charge?"

"Not me. I'm a New Yorker. I can smell a rat a mile away."

"So could William Kidd. He was a New Yorker *and* a Scotsman. But what was he going to do now? He was a man of some substance in Manhattan, he had his wife and two children on board the sloop, and he felt he was innocent. More importantly, he had the money—a third of it down in the Caribbean and the rest on board the *San Antonio*. He intended to use this treasure to bargain for his life."

I nodded. It was interesting, I thought, how little some things had changed in three hundred years. Here's a situation where the government hires this guy to do its dirty work, he does part of the job but by mistake he creates a political problem for the government, so they try to get not only their money back, but also his fair share, then they frame him, and finally hang him. But somewhere along the line, most of the bucks slipped through their hands.

Emma continued, "Meanwhile, Kidd kept his ship

moving, sailing back and forth through the Sound, from Oyster Bay to Gardiners Island and as far as Block Island. It was during this time that the ship apparently got a little lighter."

"He was dumping the loot."

"That's what seems to have happened, and that's how all the legends about buried treasure got started." She said, "Here's a man with about ten or fifteen million dollars' worth of gold and jewels on board, and he knows he can be captured at sea at any time. He's got a small ship with only four cannon. It's fast, but no match for a warship. So, what would you do?"

"I think I'd make a run for it."

"He's got almost no crew left, and he's short on provisions. His wife and children are on board."

"But he's got the money. Take the money and run."

"Well, that's not what he did. He decided to turn himself in. But he's not stupid, so he decides to hide the loot—remember, this is the share that Bellomont, the four lords, and the king are to get for their investment. This treasure now becomes Kidd's life insurance."

I nodded. "So he buried the loot."

"Correct. In 1699, there was very little population outside of Manhattan and Boston, so Kidd had thousands of places he could land and safely bury treasure."

"Like Captain Kidd's Trees."

"Yes. And farther east, there are Captain Kidd's Ledges, which are probably a section of the bluffs since there are no actual ledges or cliffs on Long Island."

I sat up. "You mean, there's a part of the bluffs called Captain Kidd's Ledges? Where?"

"Someplace between Mattituck Inlet and Orient

Point. No one really knows for certain. It's just part of the whole myth."

"But some of it is true. Right?"

"Yes, that's what makes it interesting."

I nodded. One of those myths—Captain Kidd's Ledges—was what prompted the Gordons to buy Mrs. Wiley's acre on the bluffs. How clever.

Emma added, "There's no doubt that Kidd dumped treasure in several spots, either here on the North Fork, or on Block Island, or Fishers Island. That's where most accounts put the buried treasure."

"Any other locations?"

"One more that we know is true. Gardiners Island."

"Gardiners?"

"Yes. This is documented history. In June of 1699, while sailing around trying to make a deal with Lord Bellomont, Kidd anchored off Gardiners Island to get provisions. The island was then called the Isle of Wight on maps, but it was, and still is, owned by the Gardiner family."

"You mean, the people who own the island now are Gardiners, and this is the same family who owned the island in 1699?"

"Yes. The island has been in the same family line since it was given to them by King Charles the first in 1639. In 1699, John Gardiner, the Third Lord of the Manor, lived there with his family." She added, "The Captain Kidd story is very much a part of the Gardiner family history. In fact, on Gardiners Island is Kidd Valley and a stone monument that marks the spot where John Gardiner buried some of Kidd's treasure for him. The whole island is private, but the present lord of the manor will sometimes give you a tour." She hesitated, then said, "Fredric and I were guests of the gentleman."

I didn't comment on that, but said, "So there really *was* buried treasure."

"Yes. William Kidd showed up in the *San Antonio,* and John Gardiner went out in a small boat to see who was anchored off his island. It was by all accounts a friendly meeting, and the two exchanged gifts. There was at least one more meeting between the two, and on that occasion, Kidd gave John Gardiner quite a bit of loot and told Gardiner to bury it for him."

I said, "I hope Kidd got a receipt."

"Better yet, Kidd's last words to John Gardiner were, 'If I call for it and it is gone, I will take your head or your son's.'"

"Better than a signed receipt."

Emma sipped her tea, then looked at me and said, "Kidd, of course, never returned. Having received another nice letter from Bellomont, he was ready to go to Boston and face the charges. He landed there on July first. He was allowed to remain free for a week to see who he associated with, then he was arrested on Bellomont's orders and put into chains. His ship and his Boston lodgings were searched, turning up bags of gold, silver, and some jewelry and diamonds. It was a lot of treasure, but not as much as Kidd was supposed to have, and not nearly enough to cover the cost of the expedition."

I asked, "What happened to the treasure on Gardiners Island?"

"Well, somehow—and the stories here differ—it came to the attention of Bellomont, who sent John Gardiner a nice letter by special messenger...." She pulled a reproduction toward her and read, "'Mr. Gardiner, I have secured Captain Kidd in the gaol of this town and some of his men. He has been examined by myself and the Council and has confessed among other things that he left with you a parcel of gold made up in a box and some other parcels besides, all of which I require you in his Majesty's name immediately to fetch hither to me that I may secure them for his Majesty's use, and I shall recompense your pains in coming hither. Signed, Bellomont.'"

Emma handed me the letter, and I glanced at it. I could actually make out some of it. Incredible, I thought, that stuff like this survived three centuries. It occurred to me that maybe some other three-hundred-year-old document regarding the location of more of Kidd's treasure had led to the murder of two twentieth-century scientists.

I said to Emma, "I hope John Gardiner sent a letter back to Bellomont saying, 'What Kidd? What gold?'"

She smiled. "No, John, Gardiner wasn't about to cross the governor and the king. He duly carried the treasure to Boston himself."

"I'll bet you he kept some of it."

Emma pushed a piece of paper toward me and said, "That is a photostat of the original inventory of the treasure delivered by John Gardiner to Lord Bellomont. The original is in the Public Records Office in London."

I looked at the photostat of the original, which was ripped in places and totally indecipherable to me. I pushed it back to Emma. "Can you actually read that?"

"I can." She held the photostat up to the lamp and read, "'Received the 17th July of Mr. John

Gardiner—one bag dust gold, one bag coined gold and silver, one parcel dust gold, one bag three silver rings and sundry precious stones, one bag of unpolished stones, one parcel of crystal and bazer stone, two carnelian rings, two small agates, two amethysts all in the same bag, one bag silver buttons, one bag broken silver, two bags gold bars, and two bags silver bars. The whole of the gold abovementioned is eleven hundred and eleven ounces, Troy weight. The silver is two thousand, three hundred fifty-three ounces, the jewels and precious stones' weight are seventeen ounces....' "

Emma looked up from the inventory and said, "This is a good-sized treasure, but if you believe the Mogul's claim to the British government, then there was twenty times more gold and jewels still missing than had so far been recovered on Gardiners Island or seized on the *San Antonio* and in Kidd's Boston lodgings." She smiled at me and asked, "Okay, Detective, where is the rest of the loot, booty, and plunder?"

I smiled in return. "Okay...a third is still in the Caribbean."

"Yes. That treasure, which is well documented, disappeared and has spawned a hundred Caribbean legends to match the hundred legends here."

"Okay...also, the crew got their share before they all jumped ship."

"Yes, but the whole of the crew's share would not have been more than ten percent of the total treasure. That's the deal."

"Plus medical and dental benefits."

"Where's the rest of the treasure?"

"Well, we can assume John Gardiner skimmed a little."

"We might assume that."

"The lawyer, Emmot, got his, for sure."

She nodded.

"How much is left?"

She shrugged. "Who knows? Estimates range anywhere between five and ten million of today's dollars unaccounted for. But, as I said, the treasure, if found in situ, rotted chest and all, would be worth double or triple its intrinsic value if it were auctioned at Sotheby's." She added, "The treasure map alone, if it existed and if it was in Kidd's handwriting, would be worth hundreds of thousands of dollars at auction."

"How much do you get for the maps in the gift shop?"

"Four dollars."

"They're not authentic?"

She smiled and finished her tea.

I said, "We're assuming that Kidd buried treasure in one or more other locations as insurance, as a bargaining point to buy his freedom and keep himself from the gallows."

"That's always been the assumption. If he buried some treasure at Gardiners Island, then he probably buried some elsewhere for the same reason." She added, "Captain Kidd's Trees and Captain Kidd's Ledges."

I said to her, "I went to see Captain Kidd's Trees."

"Did you?"

"I think I found the place, but they're all cut down."

"Yes, there were still a few big oaks standing around the turn of the century. They're all gone now." She added, "People used to dig around the stumps."

I said, "You can still see some of the stumps."

Emma informed me, "In colonial times, digging for pirate treasure became such a national obsession that Ben Franklin wrote newspaper pieces against it. As late as the 1930s, people were still digging around here." She added, "The craze has almost entirely disappeared, but it's part of the local culture here, which is why I didn't want anyone in the Cutchogue Diner to hear us talking about buried treasure. Half the damned town would have been dug up by now." She grinned.

"Amazing." I asked Emma, "So Kidd's buried treasure was supposed to be his life insurance. Why didn't it save him from the gallows?"

"Because of a variety of misunderstandings, bad luck, vindictiveness. For one thing, no one in Boston or London believed Kidd could recover the loot in the Caribbean, and they were probably right. That was long gone. Also, you had the mogul's complaint and the political problem. Then Kidd himself was playing it cute. He was holding out for a full pardon from the king in exchange for turning over the plunder. But the king and the others may have felt that to protect the British East India Company they had to return the plunder to the Mogul so they had no interest in pardoning Kidd in exchange for the location of the loot. They would rather *hang* Kidd, which they did."

"Did Kidd say anything about the hidden treasure at his trial?"

"Nothing. There are transcripts of the trial, and you can see that Kidd realized he was going to be hanged no matter what he did or said. I think he accepted this and decided as a last act of spite to take any secrets he had to the grave with him."

"Or, he told his wife."

"That's a strong possibility. She had some money of her own, but she seemed to live quite well after her husband's death."

"They all do."

"No sexist remarks, please. Tell me what happened to the treasure."

I replied, "I don't have enough information. The clues are old. Yet, I would make the assumption that there was still some treasure buried somewhere."

"Do you think Kidd told his wife where all of it was?"

I reflected on this a moment, then replied, "Kidd knew that his wife could also be arrested, and she might be made to talk. So...I think at first he didn't tell her, but by the time he was in the slammer in Boston and was about to be shipped out to London, he probably gave her a few clues. Like that eight-digit number."

Emma nodded. "It's always been assumed that Sarah Kidd managed to recover *some* of the treasure. But I don't think Kidd would have told her where *all* of it was because if she *were* arrested and made to talk, then any slim chance that Kidd had of trading buried treasure for his life would have been lost." She added, "I really think he took the location of some buried treasure to the grave with him."

I said, "Did they torture Kidd?"

"No," she replied, "and people have always wondered why they didn't. In those days, they tortured people for much less reason." She added, "A lot of the Kidd story never made sense."

"If I'd been around, I'd have made sense of it all."

"If you had been around then, they'd have hanged you as a troublemaker."

"Be nice, Emma."

I processed all this information and played with it awhile. I again thought about Charles Wilson's detailed letter to his brother, and I asked Emma, "Do you think Kidd could recall from memory all the locations of where he'd buried his treasure? Is that possible?"

"Probably not." She added, "Bellomont did look for evidence of hidden treasure and recovered some papers from Kidd's Boston lodgings and from the *San Antonio,* but there were no maps or locations of buried treasure among the papers—or if there were, Bellomont kept it to himself. I should mention that Bellomont died before Kidd was hanged in London, so if Bellomont had any of Kidd's treasure maps, they may have disappeared on Bellomont's death." She said to me, "So, you see, John, there are lots of little clues and hints and inconsistencies. People who have an interest in this have been playing historical detective for centuries." She smiled at me and asked, "So, do you have it figured out?"

"Not yet. I need a few more minutes."

"Take as long as you need. Meanwhile, I need a drink. Let's go."

"Hold on. I get to ask a few more questions."

"Okay. Shoot."

"Okay...I'm Captain Kidd, and I've been sailing around Long Island Sound for...how long?"

"A few weeks."

"Right. I've been to Oyster Bay where I got into contact with a lawyer, and my wife and children have come aboard from Manhattan. I've been to Gardiners Island....I asked Mr. Gardiner to bury some treasure for me. Do I know where he buried it?"

"No, which is why a map wasn't needed. Kidd simply told Gardiner to make sure the treasure was available when he returned, or he'd cut off a Gardiner head."

I nodded. "That's better than a map. Kidd didn't even have to dig the hole."

"That's right."

"Do you think Kidd did the same thing at other locations?"

"Who knows? The more common method was to go ashore with a few men and bury the treasure secretly, then make a map of the location."

"Then you have witnesses to where the treasure is buried."

She replied, "The traditional pirate method of insuring secrecy is to kill the person who dug the hole and throw him in. Then the captain and his trusted mate fill the hole. It was believed that the ghost of the murdered seaman haunted the treasure. In fact, skeletons have been found buried with treasure chests."

"Presumptive evidence of homicide," I said.

She continued, "As I mentioned, Kidd's crew at this point may have been reduced to six or seven. If he trusted at least one to watch the ship and the crew and his family, he could easily row to any bay or inlet and bury a chest of treasure himself. It's not a major engineering project to dig a hole in the sand. The old movies usually show a big party going ashore, but depending on the size of the chest, you only need one or two people."

I nodded, "A lot of our perception of history is influenced by inaccurate movies."

"That's probably right," Emma said. "But one thing

in the movies is pretty accurate—all treasure hunting starts with the discovery of a long-lost map. We sell them for four bucks downstairs, but they've sold for tens of thousands of dollars to gullible people over the centuries."

I mulled this over, thinking that it may have been one of these maps—a real one—that had somehow come into the possession of Tom and Judy, and/or Fredric Tobin. I said to Emma, "You mentioned that Gardiners Island was once called the Isle of Wight."

"Yes."

"Are there other islands around here that once had other names?"

"Sure. All the islands initially had Indian names, obviously. Then some acquired Dutch or English names." She added, "And even those changed over the years. There was a real problem with geographic place names in the New World. Some English sea captains had only Dutch maps, some had maps showing the wrong name for an island or river, for instance, and the spelling was atrocious, and some maps simply had blanks and some had purposely misleading information."

I nodded and said, "Let's take, for instance, Robins Island or, say, Plum Island. What were they called in Kidd's day?"

"I'm not sure about Robins Island, but Plum Island was the same, except spelled P-L-U-M-B-E. This came from the earlier Dutch name for Plum Island, which was spelled P-R-U-Y-M E-Y-L-A-N-D." She added, "There could have been an even earlier name, and someone like William Kidd, who hadn't been to sea for years before he accepted this commission from Bellomont, may have had or purchased navigation charts that were decades old. That was not uncommon." She went on, "A pirate's treasure map, which would be drawn from a chart, could start with some inaccuracies. And you have to remember there are not many authentic treasure maps in existence today, so it's hard to draw any conclusions about the general accuracy of buried-treasure maps. It depended on the pirate himself. Some were really stupid."

I smiled.

She continued, "If the pirate chose not to draw a map, then the chances are much smaller of finding a treasure based on his written instructions. For instance, suppose you found a parchment that said, 'On Pruym Eyland, I buried my treasure—from Eagle Rock go thirty paces to the twin oaks, thence, forty paces due south' and so on. If you couldn't figure out where Pruym Eyland was, you had a major problem. If research said Pruym Eyland was once the name for Plum Island, then you have to find the rock that everyone at that time knew was Eagle Rock. And forget the oaks. You see?"

"I do."

After a bit, Emma said to me, "Archivists are sort of like detectives, too. Can I make a guess?"

"Sure."

She thought a moment, then said, "Okay...the Gordons got onto some information about Captain Kidd's treasure, or maybe some other pirate's treasure, and then someone else found out about it, and that's why the Gordons were murdered." She looked at me. "Am I right?"

I said, "Something like that. I'm working on the details."

"Did the Gordons actually retrieve the treasure?"

"I'm not sure."

She didn't press me.

I asked, "How would the Gordons have stumbled onto that information? I mean, I don't see any files here marked 'Pirate Treasure Maps.' Right?"

"Right. The only pirate treasure maps here are in the gift shop. There are, however, a lot of documents here and in the other museums and historical societies that are still unread, or if read, their significance is not understood. You understand?"

"I do."

She continued, "You know, John, people who haunt archives like the Public Records Office in London, or the British Museum, find new things that other people either missed or didn't understand. So, yes, there may be information here or in other collections or in private homes."

"Private homes?"

"Yes, at least once a year we get something donated that was turned up in an old house. Like a will or an old deed. My guess—and this is only a guess—is that someone like the Gordons, who were not professional archivists or historians, simply stumbled onto something that was so obvious that even they could understand what it was."

"Like a map?"

"Yes, like a map that clearly shows a recognizable piece of geography, and gives landmarks, directions, paces, compass headings, and the whole works. If they had something like that, they could pretty much go right to the spot and dig." She reflected a moment, then said, "The Gordons did a lot of archaeological digging on Plum Island...maybe they were really looking for treasure."

"No maybes about it."

She looked at me a long time, then said, "From what I hear, they had holes dug all over the island. That doesn't sound like they knew what or where—"

"The archaeological digs were cover. It gave them the ability to walk around remote parts of the island with shovels. Also, I wouldn't be surprised if a lot of the archival work wasn't also a cover."

"Why?"

"They wouldn't be allowed to keep anything they found on Plum Island. It's government land. So they had to create a legend of their own. The legend of how Tom and Judy Gordon saw something in the archives— here or in London—that mentioned Captain Kidd's Trees, or Captain Kidd's Ledges, and, they would later claim, this got them to thinking about hunting for the treasure." I added, "In reality, they already knew the treasure was on Plum Island."

"Incredible."

"Yes, but you have to work the problem backwards. Start with an authentic map or written directions that pinpoint a treasure on Plum Island. Let's say you had this information in your possession. What would you, Emma Whitestone, do?"

She didn't think about it long before she said, "I'd simply turn the information over to the government. This is an important historical document, and the treasure, if any, is historically important. If it's located on Plum Island, then it should be found on Plum Island. To do otherwise is not only dishonest, it's also a historical hoax."

"History is full of lies, deceit, and hoaxes. That's how the treasure got there to begin with. Why not just pull off another hoax? Finders keepers. Right?"

"No. If the treasure is on anyone else's land—even the government's—then they own it. If I discovered its whereabouts, I would accept a reward."

I smiled.

She looked at me. "What would *you* do?"

"Well...in the spirit of Captain Kidd, I'd try to cut a deal. I wouldn't just turn the location over to the person whose land is represented on the map. It would be fair to trade the secret for a share. Even Uncle Sam will make a deal."

She thought about that and said, "I suppose." She added, "Only that's not what the Gordons did."

"No. The Gordons had a partner or partners who I believe was more larcenous than they were. And probably murderous, too. Really, we don't know *what* the Gordons were up to, or what they intended, because they wound up dead. We can assume they began with hard information about the location of a treasure on Plum Island, and everything we see them do after that is simply a deliberate and clever ruse—the Peconic Historical Society, the archaeological digs, the archive work, even the week in the Public Records Office in London—it's all in preparation for the transportation and reburial of the treasure from Uncle Sam land to Gordon land."

Emma nodded. "And that's why the Gordons bought that land from Mrs. Wiley—a place to rebury the treasure...Captain Kidd's Ledges."

"That's right. Does it make sense to you or am I crazy?"

"You're crazy, yet it makes sense."

I ignored this and continued, "If there's ten or twenty million bucks at stake, you do it right. You take your time, you cover your tracks before anyone even knows you're making tracks, you anticipate problems with historians, archaeologists, and the government. You're going to be not only rich, you're going to be famous, and you're going to be in the spotlight for better or worse. You're young, handsome, bright, and in the money. And you don't want any problems."

She stayed silent awhile, then said, "But something went wrong."

"It must have—they're dead."

Neither of us spoke for a while. I now had a lot of answers, and I still had a lot more questions. Some of them might never be answered, since Tom and Judy Gordon, like William Kidd, had taken some secrets to the grave with them.

Emma finally asked me, "Who do you think killed them?"

"Probably their partner or partners."

"I know . . . but *who*?"

"I don't know yet. Do you have any suspects in mind?"

She shook her head, but I think she had a suspect in mind.

I'd confided a lot of information to Emma Whitestone, who I really didn't know. But I have a good sense of who to trust. On the chance that I'd misjudged, that she was part of the plot, then it didn't matter because she knew all of this anyway. And if she went and told Fredric Tobin or someone else that I'd figured it out, so much the better. Fredric Tobin lived very high in the tower, and it would take a lot of smoke to reach him up there. And if someone else were involved that I didn't know about, then the smoke might reach him or her, too. There comes a time in an investigation where you just let it rip. Especially when time is running out.

I pondered my next question, then decided to go for broke. I said to her, "I understand that some people from the Peconic Historical Society were on Plum Island to do a survey of possible digs."

She nodded.

"Was Fredric Tobin one of those people?"

She actually hesitated, which I guess was out of an old habit of loyalty. Finally, she said, "Yes. He was on the island once."

"With the Gordons as guides?"

"Yes." She looked at me and asked, "Do you think... I mean...?"

I said to her, "I can speculate about motive and method, but I never speculate out loud about suspects." I added, "It's important that you keep all of this to yourself."

She nodded.

I looked at Emma. She seemed to be what she appeared to be—an honest, intelligent, and pleasantly crazy woman. I liked her. I took her hand, and we played hand squeezies.

I said, "Thank you for your time and knowledge."

"It was fun."

I nodded. My mind went back to William Kidd. I said, "So they hanged him?"

"They did. They kept him in chains in England for more than a year before he was tried at Old Bailey. He was allowed no legal counsel, no witnesses, and no evidence. He was found guilty and hanged at Execution Dock on the Thames. His body was covered with tar and hung in chains as a warning to passing seamen. Crows ate the rotting flesh for months."

I stood. "Let's get that drink."

CHAPTER TWENTY-THREE

I needed a major pasta fix so I suggested dinner at Claudio's and Emma agreed.

Claudio's is in Greenport, which as I said has a population of about two thousand, which is fewer than the number of people in my condo building.

We traveled east along Main Road. It was about seven P.M. when we entered the village, and it was getting dark.

The village itself is not as quaint or ye olde as the hamlets; it was, and still is, a working port and a commercial fishing town. There has been some gentrification in recent years, boutiques, trendy restaurants, and all that, but Claudio's remains pretty much the same as it was when I was a kid. At a time where there were very few places to dine on the North Fork, there was Claudio's, sitting on the bay at the end of Main Street, near the wharf, just as it had been since the last century.

I parked, and we walked out on the long wharf. A big, old three-master was permanently moored at the wharf, and there was a clam bar nearby, people strolling, and a few motor vessels tied up whose passengers were probably in Claudio's. It was another nice evening, and I commented on the fair weather.

Emma said, "There's a tropical depression forming in the Caribbean."

"Would Prozac help?"

"A baby hurricane."

"Oh, right." Like a baby lion. Hurricanes were nice to watch in your condo in Manhattan. They weren't nice out on this spit of land less than fifty feet above sea level. I remembered an August hurricane out here when I was a kid. It started as fun, then got scary.

So, we strolled, we talked. There's an excitement in the early stages of a relationship—like the first three days—after that, you sometimes realize you don't like each other. It's usually something the other person says, like, "I hope you're a cat lover."

But with Emma Whitestone, so far, so good. She seemed to enjoy my company, too. In fact, she said, "I enjoy being with you."

"Why is that?"

"Well, you're not like most of the men I date—all they want to do is hear about me, talk about me, discuss art, politics, and philosophy, and get my opinion on everything. You're different. You just want sex."

I laughed.

She took my arm, and we walked to the end of the wharf and watched the boats.

She said, "I was thinking...if Tom and Judy had lived, and they announced that they'd found this fabulous treasure—a pirate's treasure, Kidd's treasure—then the newspeople would have been all over the place, like they were when the Gordons were murdered.

They were all over Southold asking questions of people on the street, filming Main Street, and all that."

"That's what they do."

"So, it's ironic that they were here to report the murders of the Gordons instead of their fortune."

I nodded. "Interesting observation."

"I wonder if the newspeople would have come to the Peconic Historical Society for the treasure story."

"Probably."

She said, "You know, as I was saying before, there used to be treasure-hunting frenzies. As recently as the 1930s—the Depression—and right into the late 1950s, Kidd-mania would sweep over this area, usually started by some stupid rumor, or some minor find of coins on the beach. People would come from all over and start digging up the beaches, bluffs, the woods...that hasn't happened in a while....Maybe times have changed." She asked me, "Did you play pirate when you were a kid?"

"I was thinking about that....I remember now hearing about pirates out here when I was a kid. But not too much...." I added, "My aunt was a little more sophisticated. She was into Indians before Indians were in."

"My family was into the early settlers and the Revolution. I do remember talk of pirates....I have an older brother, and I remember him playing pirates once or twice with his friends. I guess it was a boy thing. Like cops and robbers, cowboys and Indians."

"I guess. Now they play narc and dealer." I added, "But there was this kid—no pun intended—up in Captain Kidd Estates." I told Emma the story of Billy the treasure hunter.

She commented, "It comes in circles. Maybe pirates are in again." She asked me, "Did you ever read Robert Louis Stevenson's *Treasure Island*?"

"Sure did. And Poe's 'The Gold Bug.' Remember that dumb clue with a sketch of a goat—baby goat—a kid. Get it?"

"Got it. Did you ever read Washington Irving's *Wolfert Webber*?"

"Never heard of that one."

"A terrific pirate story," she informed me. She smiled and asked me, "Did you ever see any of those old swashbuckler movies from the 1930s and 1940s?"

"Loved 'em."

She said, "You know, the English language has few words more intriguing and romantic than words like pirate, buried treasure, galleon...what else?"

"Swashbuckler. I like that one."

"How about the Spanish Main?"

"Right. Whatever that is."

And so, standing on the wharf near this big, old three-master, with the sun setting, we played this silly word game, coming up with words and phrases like buccaneers, doubloons, cutlasses, eye patches, peg legs, parrots, walking the plank, desert islands, booty, plunder, pillage, the Jolly Roger, treasure maps, treasure chests, X marks the spot, and—scraping the bottom of the rum barrel—phrases like, "Shiver me timbers" and "Ahoy, me hardies." We both laughed, and I said, "I like you."

"Of course you do."

We walked back along the wharf toward Claudio's, actually holding hands, which I hadn't done in a long time.

Claudio's was busy for a weeknight, and we sat at the bar and had a drink while a table was readied.

As I said, this is an old place, built in 1830, and claims to be the oldest restaurant in America that has been run continuously by the same family—the Claudios, since 1870. My family had trouble sharing the kitchen and bathroom every morning; I couldn't imagine doing it for a hundred and thirty years.

Anyway, according to what a bartender told me, the building was once an inn when Greenport was a whaling port, and the bar where Emma and I sat was transported here by barge from Manhattan in eighteen-eighty-something.

The bar and the shelves behind it are all mahogany, etched glass, and Italian marble, and it's vaguely foreign and exotic with none of the ye olde colonial look that's more common in this area. In here, I can imagine I'm back in Manhattan, especially when I smell the Italian food from the restaurant side. Sometimes I miss Manhattan and places like Little Italy, where the Feast of San Gennaro was right now in progress, for instance. If I was back in New York City, Dom Fanelli and I would be down on Mulberry Street this very night, stuffing our faces at each outdoor food stand and ending the evening in some coffeehouse. Clearly, I had some decisions to make about my future.

Emma asked for a white wine and the bartender said to her, "We have six different local whites by the glass. Any preference?"

"Yes...Pindar," she replied.

That's my girl. Loyal and true. Won't drink her ex-lover's wine in front of the new beau. I'll tell you, the older you get, the more baggage you have to carry, and the less you're able to lift it.

I ordered a Budweiser, and we clinked glasses. I said, "Thanks again for everything."

"What historical lesson did you most enjoy?"

"The history of the feather bed."

"Me, too."

And so forth.

On the walls were lots of memorabilia, black-and-white photos of the Claudio ancestors, old photos of past sailing races, old Greenport scenes, and so on. I like old restaurants—they're sort of living museums where you can get a beer.

It was also in Claudio's, back in June, where I'd first met the Gordons, which is one of the reasons I'd wanted to come here, aside from my stomach demanding red sauce. Sometimes it's good to physically return to a particular scene when you want to recall something that happened there.

I found myself remembering my parents, my brother and sister, sitting at these tables, discussing the day's activities and planning the next day. I hadn't thought about that in years.

Anyway, I left my childhood memories, which are better recalled on a shrink's couch, and I put my mind back into June of this year.

I'd come here, to the bar, because it was one of the few places I knew. I recall still feeling a little shaky, but there's nothing like a bar and a beer to buck a boy up.

I ordered my usual cocktail, a Bud, and immediately noticed this very attractive woman a few stools down. It was pre–tourist season, early weeknight, raining, and there weren't many people at the bar. I made eye contact with her. She sort of smiled, and I moved in. "Hi," I said.

"Hello," she said.

"My name is John Corey."

"Judy Gordon."

"Are you alone?"

"Yes, except for my husband, who's in the men's room."

"Oh...." I now noticed the wedding ring. Why can't I remember to look for the wedding ring? Well, but even if she's married, and she's alone—but I digress. I said, "I'll go get him for you."

She smiled and said, "Don't run off."

I was in love, but I gallantly said, "See you around." I was about to move back to my original bar stool when Tom showed up, and Judy introduced me.

I excused myself, but Tom said, "Have another beer."

I'd noticed they both had these sort of out-there accents, and I figured they were early tourists or something. They had none of the New York abruptness I was used to. Like the joke goes, the guy from the Midwest goes up to a New Yorker on the street and says, "Excuse me, sir, can you tell me how to get to the Empire State Building, or should I just go fuck myself?"

Anyway, I didn't want to have a drink with them, feeling awkward, I guess, that I'd tried to pick up his wife and all that, but for some reason that I'll never completely understand, I decided to have one drink with them.

Well, I can be taciturn, but these were such open people that before long, I'd told them about my recent misfortune, and they both remembered seeing the story on TV. I was a celebrity to them.

They mentioned they worked on Plum Island, which

I found interesting, and that they'd come directly here from work by boat, which I also found interesting. Tom had invited me to see the boat, but I put it off, not being that interested in boats.

It came out that I had a house on the water, and that's when Tom asked me where it was and to describe it from the water so he could visit. I did, and to my surprise, he and Judy had actually shown up a week later.

Anyway, we all got along very well in Claudio's, and an hour later, we were having dinner together. That had been about three months ago, not a very long time, but I felt I knew them well. I was finding out, however, that there were things about them I didn't know.

Emma said, "Hello? John?"

"Sorry. I was thinking about the first time I met the Gordons. Right here at this bar."

"Really?" She asked me, "Are you very upset about...?"

"I didn't realize how much I enjoyed their company." I added, "I'm taking this a little more personally than I thought I would."

She nodded. We chatted about this and that. It occurred to me that if she were in cahoots with the killer, or was in any way part of the plot, she'd try to pump me a little. But she seemed to want to avoid the whole subject, which was fine with me.

Our table was ready, and we went to this sort of enclosed patio that looked out toward the bay. It was getting noticeably colder, and I was sorry to see summer coming to an end. I had tasted my own mortality— literally tasted it when my blood came running out of my mouth—and I suppose the shorter days and the chilly wind reminded me of the fact that my summer was over, that little Johnny, who'd been so bug-eyed over the musket ball, had finally grown up as he lay in the gutter of West 102nd Street, with three musket ball holes in him.

America is a country of second and third chances, a place of multiple resuscitations, so that, given enough retakes, only a total idiot can't eventually get it right.

Emma said, "You seem distracted."

"I'm trying to decide if I want to start with the fried calamari or the scungilli."

"Fried is not good for you."

"Do you miss the city?" I asked her.

"Now and then. I miss the anonymity. Here, everyone knows who you're sleeping with."

"I suppose so, if you parade all your boyfriends in front of your employees."

She asked me, "Do *you* miss the city?"

"I don't know....I won't know till I get back." I excused myself, saying, "I have to go to the potty." I went to my car and got the potty, which I brought back in the gift bag.

I put the bag down in front of her, and she asked, "Is that for me?"

"Yes."

"Oh, John, you didn't have to...Should I open it now?"

"Please."

She reached inside the bag and pulled out the pot, which was swathed in pink tissue paper. "What is...?"

I had this sudden panic attack. What if the old bird in the antique store was wrong? What if she'd confused Emma Whitestone with someone else? "Wait," I said, "maybe you shouldn't open it—"

Other diners were looking now, curious, nosy, smiling.

Emma unfolded the tissue paper, revealing the white chamber pot with pink roses. She held it up by its jug handle.

A gasp arose from the crowd. Or at least it sounded that way. Someone laughed.

Emma said, "Oh, John! It's beautiful. How did you know?"

"I'm a detective." *Aw, shucks.*

She admired the chamber pot, turning it, looking at the potter's mark and all that.

The waiter came by and said, "There are rest rooms in the rear if you'd prefer."

Well, anyway, we all got a nice chuckle, and Emma said she'd plant miniature roses in it, and I said that would definitely keep people from sitting on it, and so forth. We ran out of potty humor and ordered dinner.

We had a pleasant meal, talking and watching the harbor. She asked me if I'd like her to spend the night again, which I did. She opened her purse and pulled out a toothbrush and a pair of panties. She said, "I'm prepared."

The stand-up comic waiter happened by at that moment, and said, "Can I get you more coffee, or are you in a real hurry to get home?"

On the drive back to my digs in Mattituck, I had this strange feeling again that none of this was going to end well, not this case, not this thing with Emma, not the thing with Beth, whatever that was, and not my career. It felt to me like the eerie silence and clear skies of an approaching hurricane before it hits.

CHAPTER TWENTY-FOUR

The next morning while I was dressing, the doorbell rang, and I assumed that Emma, who was downstairs, would answer it.

I finished dressing—tan slacks, striped oxford shirt, blue blazer, and docksiders, sans socks: standard outfit of the maritime provinces. In Manhattan, people who didn't wear socks often carried tin cups; here it was très chic.

I came downstairs about ten minutes later and found Emma Whitestone at the kitchen table having coffee with Beth Penrose. *Uh-oh.*

It was one of those moments that called for savoir faire, and I said to Beth, "Good morning, Detective Penrose."

Beth replied, "Good morning."

I said to Emma, "This is my partner, Beth Penrose. I guess you've met."

Emma replied, "I guess so. We're having coffee."

I said to Beth pointedly, "I thought I'd see you later."

Beth replied, "I had a change of plans. I left a message on your machine last night."

"I didn't check it."

Emma stood. "I have to get to work."

"Oh . . . I'll drive you," I said.

Beth stood also and said to me, "I have to go, too. I just stopped by to pick up those financial printouts. If you have them, I can take them now."

Emma said to both of us, "Sit. You must have work to do." She moved toward the door. "I'll call Warren for a ride. He lives close by. I'll be in the den." She didn't make eye contact with me on her way out of the kitchen.

I said to Beth, "She's the president of the Peconic Historical Society."

"Really? A bit young for the job."

I poured myself a cup of coffee.

Beth said, "I thought I would brief you, as a courtesy."

"You don't owe me any courtesies."

"Well, you were very helpful."

"Thank you."

We both remained standing, me drinking my coffee, Beth cleaning up her coffee mug, spoon, and napkin, as if she were ready to leave. I noticed a briefcase beside her chair. I said, "Sit."

"I should go."

"Let's have one cup of coffee together."

"Okay." She poured herself another cup of coffee and sat opposite me. She said, "You look very dapper this morning."

"I'm trying to change my image. No one was taking me seriously." She was wearing another tailored suit, this one navy blue with a white blouse. She looked yummy this morning, fresh and bright-eyed. I said, "You look very good yourself."

"Thank you. I dress well."

"Right." A little severe, but that's my opinion. I couldn't tell what she thought about my houseguest, if in fact she thought anything at all. Aside from a small emotional rush that I'd felt for Beth, I reminded myself that she'd cut me loose professionally. Now she was back.

I wasn't sure if I should tell her that I'd made some significant progress in her absence; that, indeed, I believed I'd found the motive for the double murders, and that Fredric Tobin needed to be checked out. But why should I stick my neck out? I might be wrong. In fact, having slept on it, I was less certain that Fredric Tobin was the actual murderer of Tom and Judy Gordon. He might very well know more than he was saying, but it seemed more likely that someone else pulled the trigger—someone like Paul Stevens.

I decided to see what she had that I might need, and what she wanted that I might have. This was going to be a sparring match. Round One—I said, "Max terminated my career with the Township of Southold."

"I know."

"So, I don't think I should be privy to any police information."

"Do you mean that? Or are you sulking?"

"A little of both."

She played with her coffee spoon awhile, then said, "I really respect your opinions and your insights."

"Thank you."

She looked around the kitchen. "This is some house."

"A big painted lady."

"Your uncle owns it?"

"Yes. He's Wall Street. There's lots of money on the Street. I'm mentioned in his will. He's a heavy smoker."

"Well, it's nice that you were able to have a place to convalesce."

"I should have gone to the Caribbean."

She smiled. "You wouldn't have had this much fun." She asked, "How are you feeling, by the way?"

"Oh, fine. I'm good until I try to exert myself."

"Don't exert yourself."

"I won't."

"So, what have you been up to the last few days? Have you followed up on anything?"

"A little. But, as I said, I had the plug pulled on me by Max, and my boss saw me on TV the night of the homicide. Also, I think your friend, Mr. Nash, put in a bad word for me with my superiors. Very petty."

"You gave him a *very* hard time, John. I'll bet he's a little annoyed at you."

"Could be. He probably wants to terminate my life cycle."

"Well, I don't know about that."

I do. I said, "More importantly, I probably have some explaining to do with the big bosses at Police Plaza."

"That's too bad. Let me know if I can help."

"Thank you. It'll work out. It's bad PR to screw around with a shot cop."

"What do you want from the job? In or out?"

"In."

"Are you sure?"

"Yes. I want to go back. I'm ready."

"Good. You look ready."

"Thank you." I asked her, "So, who killed Tom and Judy Gordon?"

She forced a smile. "I thought you'd tell me by now."

"You don't get much for a dollar a week. Or was it a dollar a month?"

She played with her spoon awhile, then looked at me and said, "When I first met you, I didn't like you. You know why?"

"Let me think…arrogant, smart-ass, too good-looking."

To my surprise, she nodded. "That's about it. Now I realize there's more to you."

"No, there isn't."

"Sure there is."

"Maybe I'm trying to get in touch with my inner child."

"Oh, you do that just fine. You should try to get in touch with your suppressed adult side."

"That's no way to speak to a wounded hero."

She continued, "On the whole, I think you're loyal to your friends and dedicated to your job."

"Thank you. Let's get to the case. You want me to brief you about what I've done."

She nodded. "Assuming you've done anything." She said, with a touch of sarcasm, "You appear to have been busy with other things."

"Job related. She's president of the—"

Emma popped her head into the kitchen. "Okay, I think I heard a horn outside. Nice meeting you, Beth. Talk to you later, John." She left, and I heard the front door open and close.

Beth said, "She's nice." She added, "Travels light."

I didn't comment.

Beth said, "Do you have those financial printouts for me?"

"Yes." I stood. "In the den. I'll be right back."

I went into the center hallway, but instead of going into the den, I went out the front door.

Emma was sitting in a wicker chair, waiting for her ride. Beth's PD, the black Ford, was in the circle. Emma said, "I thought I heard a horn. I'll just wait here."

I said, "I'm sorry I can't drive you to work."

"No problem. Warren lives right near here. He's on the way."

"Good. Can I see you later?"

"Friday night I go out with the girls."

"What do the girls do?"

"Same as the boys do."

"Where do the girls go?"

"Usually, the Hamptons. We're all looking for rich husbands and lovers."

"At the same time?"

"Whatever comes first. We do deals."

"Okay. I'll stop by the shop later." I asked, "Where's your potty?"

"In the bedroom."

"I'll bring it with me later."

A car pulled into the long driveway, and Emma stood. She said, "Your partner seemed surprised to see me."

"Well, I suppose she was expecting me to answer the door."

"She seemed more than surprised. She was a little . . . put off. Subdued. Unhappy."

I shrugged.

"You said you weren't seeing anyone else out here."

"I'm not. I just met her for the first time Monday."

"You met me Wednesday."

"Right, but—"

"Look, John, I don't care, but—"

"She's just—"

"Warren's here. I have to go." She started down the steps, then came back up, kissed me on the cheek, and hurried off to the car.

I waved to Warren.

Oh, well. I went back inside and walked to the den. I hit the play button on my answering machine. The first message at seven P.M. last night was from Beth, who said, "I have a ten A.M. appointment with Max tomorrow. I'd like to stop by on the way—about 8:30 or so. If this is a problem, call me tonight." She gave me her home number, then said, "Or call me in the morning, or call my car." She gave me her car phone number, then said, "I'll bring donuts if you make coffee."

Very friendly tone in her voice. She really should have called me from the car phone this morning. But okay. My experience over the years has always been that if you miss a message, something interesting usually happens.

The next message was from Dom Fanelli at eight P.M. He said, "Hey, are you home? Pick up if you're there. Well, okay.... Listen, I got a visit today from two gents from the Anti-Terrorist Task Force. An FBI guy named Whittaker Whitebread, or something like that, real buttoned-down dandy, and his cop counterpart, a guy we met a few times, a paisano. You know who I mean. Anyway, they wanted to know if I'd heard from you. They want to see you Tuesday when you come in for your doc meet, and I have to deliver you to them. I think the FBI doesn't believe its own press release about the Ebola vaccine. I think I smell a cover-up. Hey, are we all going to get the black clap and watch our dicks fall off? By the way, we're going down to San Gennaro tomorrow night. Get your ass in here and meet us. The bar at Taormina's, six P.M. Kenny, Tom, Frank, and me. Maybe some babes. We're gonna mange, mange, mange. Bellissimo. Molto bene. Come meet us if your pepperoni is lonely. Ciao."

Interesting. I mean about the Anti-Terrorist Task Force. That surely didn't sound as though they were concerned about a miracle cure for Ebola getting into the black market. Obviously, Washington was still in a state of panic. I should tell them not to worry—it's pirate treasure, guys. You know, Captain Kidd, doubloons, pieces of eight, whatever the hell that is. But let them look for terrorists. Who knows, they might find one. It's a good training exercise.

The Feast of San Gennaro. My mouth was watering for fried calamari and calzone. Jeez, I felt like an exile here sometimes. Sometimes I got into it—nature, quiet, no traffic, ospreys....

I could conceivably be at Taormina's at six tonight, though I didn't want to fly that close to the flame. I needed some more time, and I had until Tuesday before they got their hands on me—first the docs, then Wolfe, then the ATTF guys. I wondered if Whittaker Whitebread and George Foster were in communication. Or were they the same guy?

Anyway, I retrieved the pile of financial printouts.

Also on the desk was the bag from Tobin Vineyards that held the painted tile with the osprey. I picked it up, then thought, "no," then thought, "yes," then "no" again, then "maybe later." I put it down and went back into the kitchen.

CHAPTER TWENTY-FIVE

Beth Penrose had her papers from the briefcase spread out on the table, and I now noticed a plateful of donuts. I gave her the stack of printouts, which she put to the side. I said, "Sorry I took so long. I had to play my phone messages. I got your message."

She replied, "I should have called from the car phone."

"That's all right. You had a standing invitation." I indicated the paper on the table and asked, "So, what do you have there?"

"Some notes. Reports. Do you want to hear this?"

"Sure." I poured us both coffee and sat.

Beth said, "Did you discover anything else in these printouts?"

"Just some increases in their phone, Visa, and Amex after their England trip."

She asked me, "Do you think the trip to England was anything other than business and vacation?"

"Could be."

"Do you think they met a foreign agent?"

"I don't think we'll ever know what they did in

England." I was fairly certain, of course, they'd spent the week wading through three-hundred-year-old papers, making sure they signed in and out of the Public Records Office, and/or the British Museum, thereby establishing their bona fides as treasure seekers. However, I wasn't prepared to share that thought yet.

Beth made a short note in her book. Maybe some archivist would be interested in a late-twentieth-century homicide detective's notebook. I used to keep a notebook, but I can't read my own handwriting so it's sort of useless.

Beth said, "Okay, let me begin at the beginning. First, we still have not recovered the two bullets from the bay. It's an almost hopeless task, and they've given up on it."

"Good decision."

"All right, next. Fingerprints. Almost every print in the house is the Gordons'. We tracked down the cleaning lady, who had cleaned that very morning. We also found her prints."

"How about prints on that book of charts?"

"Only the Gordons' and yours." She added, "I examined every page of that book with a magnifying glass and an ultraviolet lamp, looking for marks, pinholes, secret writing—whatever. Nothing."

"I really thought that might yield something."

"No such luck." She glanced at her notes and said, "The autopsy shows what you'd expect. Death in both cases came as a result of massive brain trauma caused by an apparent gunshot wound to the decedents' respective heads, the bullets both entering from the frontal lobes, and so forth....Burned powder or propellant found, indicating close range, so we can probably discount a rifle from a distance. The ME won't commit, but he's saying the murder weapon was probably fired from five to ten feet away and that the caliber of the bullets was in the larger range—maybe a forty-four or forty-five."

I nodded. "That's what we figured."

"Right. The rest of the autopsy..." She glanced at the report. "...Toxicology—no drugs, legal or illegal, found. Stomach contents, almost none, maybe an early and light breakfast. No marks on either body, no infections, no discernible disease...." She went on for a minute or so, then looked up from the report and said, "The deceased female was about a month pregnant."

I nodded. What a nice way to celebrate sudden fame and wealth.

Neither of us spoke for a minute or so. There's something about an autopsy protocol that sort of ruins your mood. One of the more disagreeable tasks that a homicide detective has to perform is to be present at the autopsy. This has to do with the chain-of-evidence requirement and makes sense legally, but I don't like seeing bodies cut open, organs removed and weighed, and all that. I knew that Beth had been present when the Gordons were autopsied, and I wondered if I could have handled seeing people I knew having their guts and brains plucked out.

Beth shuffled some papers and said, "The red earth found in their running shoes is mostly clay, iron, and sand. There's so much of it around here, it's not even worth trying to match it to a specific site."

I nodded and asked, "Did their hands show any signs that they'd been doing something manual?"

"Actually, yes. Tom had a blister on the heel of

his right hand. Both of them had been handling soil, which was embedded in their hands and under their nails, despite attempts to wash with saltwater. Their clothes, too, showed smudges of the same soil."

I nodded again.

Beth asked me, "What do you think they were doing?"

"Digging."

"For what?"

"Buried treasure."

She took this as another example of my smart-ass attitude and ignored me, which I knew she'd do. She went through some other points in the forensic report, but I didn't hear anything significant.

Beth continued, "The search of their house, top to bottom, didn't turn up too much of interest. They didn't save much on the computer, except financial and tax records."

I asked her, "What's the difference between a woman and a computer?"

"Tell me."

"A computer will accept a three-and-a-half-inch floppy."

She closed her eyes for a second, rubbed her temples, took a deep breath, then continued, "They had a file cabinet, and there is some correspondence, legal stuff, personal, and so forth. We're reading and analyzing it all. This may be interesting, but so far, nothing."

"Whatever was relevant or incriminating was probably stolen."

She nodded and continued, "The Gordons owned expensive clothing, even the casual clothes, no pornography, no sexual aids, a wine cellar with seventeen

bottles, four photo albums—you're in a few pictures—
no audiotapes, a Rolodex which we're comparing to
the one in their office, nothing unusual in the medicine
cabinet, nothing in any of the pockets of their summer clothes or their stored winter clothes, no keys that
don't belong, and one that seemed to be missing—the
Murphys' key, if you believe what Mr. Murphy said
about giving the house key to the Gordons...." She
turned a page and kept reading. This is the kind of stuff
that gets my undivided attention, though so far, there
was nothing out of the ordinary.

She went on, "We found the deed to the Wiley land,
by the way. All in order. Also, we can't find any evidence of a safe deposit box. Or other bank accounts.
We found two life insurance policies in the amount of
$250,000, one on each of them naming the other as
beneficiary with secondary beneficiaries of parents and
siblings. Same with their government life insurance.
There is also a will, very simple, again naming each
other, parents and siblings and so forth."

I nodded. "Good detail work."

"Right. Okay...nothing interesting on the walls...
family photos, reproduction art, diplomas."

"How about an attorney?"

"On the wall?"

"No, Beth—an attorney...who is their attorney?"

She smiled at me and said, "You don't like it when
people are smart-ass with you, do you? But you—"

"Please continue. Attorney."

She shrugged and said, "Yes, we found the name of
an attorney in Bloomington, Indiana, so we'll contact
him." She added, "I spoke to both sets of parents on
the phone....This is the part of the job I don't like."

"Me neither."

"I talked them out of coming here. I explained that as soon as the medical examiner finished, we'd send the remains to whatever funeral home they wanted. I'll let Max tell them we may need to keep a lot of personal stuff until we, hopefully, wrap it up, go to trial, and all that." She added, "It's all so rough, you know, when you have a murder...death is bad enough. Murder is... well, hard on everyone."

"I know."

She pulled another sheet of paper toward her and said, "I made inquiries about the *Spirochete* with the DEA, Coast Guard, and even Customs. Interesting that they all knew this boat—they pay attention to these Formulas. Anyway, as far as everyone was concerned, the Gordons were clean. The *Spirochete* was never spotted in the open Atlantic as far as anyone recalls, and there was never any suspicion that the boat was engaged in smuggling, drug running, or any other illegal activity."

I nodded. "Okay." Not quite true, but not worth mentioning right now.

Beth continued, "For your information, the Formula 303 SR–1 has a draft of thirty-three inches, which will get it into reasonably shallow water. It carries eighty-eight gallons of fuel and has twin 454-cubic-inch MerCruiser engines putting out 350 horsepower. It can reach speeds of seventy-five miles per hour. Cost, new, is about ninety-five thousand dollars, but this was a used one and the Gordons bought it for seventy-five thousand." She looked up from the report and said, "This is a top-of-the-line craft, much more than the Gordons could afford to buy and maintain, and more than they needed to commute—sort of like buying a Ferrari for a station car."

I said, "You've been busy."

"Yes, I have. What did you think I was doing?"

I ignored the question and said, "I think we can rule out drug running and all that. As for the Gordons buying a performance boat, it may be that they didn't need the performance on a daily basis, but they wanted the capability, just in case."

"In case of what?"

"In case they were chased."

"Who would chase them? And why?"

"I don't know." I took a cinnamon donut and bit into it. "Good. Did you make this?"

"Yes. I also made the crème-filled donuts, the eclairs, and the jelly donuts."

"I'm impressed, but the bag says Nicole's Bakery."

"You're some detective."

"Yes, ma'am. What else do you have?"

She moved some papers around and said, "I got the DA to subpoena the Gordons' phone records for the last two years."

I sat up. "Yes?"

"Well, as you'd expect, a lot of calls back home— parents, friends, relatives, and so forth—Indiana for Tom, Illinois for Judy. Lots of calls to Plum Island, service people, restaurants, and on and on. A few calls to the Peconic Historical Society, calls to Margaret Wiley, two to the Maxwell residence, one to Paul Stevens at his Connecticut home, and ten calls to you over the last twelve weeks."

"That would be about right."

"It *is* right. Also, about two or three calls a month

to Tobin Vintners in Peconic as well as Fredric Tobin in Southold and Fredric Tobin in Peconic."

I said, "The gentleman has a house on the water in Southold and keeps an apartment at the winery, which is in Peconic."

She looked at me. "How do you know all that?"

"Because Emma—the president of the Peconic Historical Society, who just left—is a close friend of Mr. Tobin. Also, I was invited to a party at His Lordship's waterfront home tomorrow night. I think you should be there."

"Why?"

"It's a good opportunity to chat with some locals. Max will probably be there."

She nodded. "Okay."

"You should get the details from Max. I don't actually have a formal invite."

"Okay."

"Phone calls."

She looked down at her sheets of computer printouts and said, "In May of last year, there were four phone calls from London, England, charged to their phone credit card . . . one each to Indiana and Illinois, one to the general number on Plum Island, and a forty-two-minute call to Fredric Tobin in Southold."

"Interesting."

"What's with Mr. Fredric Tobin?"

"I'm not sure."

"Tell me the part you're sure of."

"I think you were giving a report, and I don't want to interrupt."

"No, it's your turn, John."

"I'm not playing that game, Beth. You finish, just as

if you're briefing a roomful of bosses. Then I'll tell you what I've discovered."

She thought a moment, clearly not wanting to be bamboozled by John Corey. She asked me, "*Do* you have anything?"

"I do. I truly do. Proceed."

"Okay...where was I?"

"Phone records."

"Yes. There are twenty-five months' worth here, which is about a thousand calls, and I'm having them computer-analyzed. I did turn up an interesting fact— when the Gordons got here in August two years ago, they first rented a house in Orient, near the ferry, then moved to the Nassau Point house only four months later."

I asked, "Was the Orient house on the water?"

"No."

"There's the answer. Within four months of coming here, they decided they needed a house on the water and a dock and a boat. Why?"

"That," said Beth, "is what we're trying to figure out."

"Right." I'd already figured it out. It had to do with the Gordons somehow discovering that something on Plum Island needed to be found and dug up. So, way back in the autumn of two years ago, the first part of the plot—getting a house on the water, then a boat— was already in place. I said to Beth, "Proceed."

"All right...Plum Island. They're being cute there, and I had to get rough with them."

"Good for you."

"I had the entire contents of the Gordons' office transported by ferry to Orient Point, then loaded on a police truck, and transported to the Suffolk County lab."

"The taxpayers of the county will be happy to hear that."

"Also, I had their office fingerprinted and vacuumed and had a padlock put on it."

"My goodness. You're thorough."

"This is a double homicide, John. How do you handle a double homicide in the city?"

"We call the Department of Sanitation. Please proceed."

She took a deep breath. She said, "Okay...I also obtained the directory of everyone who works on Plum Island, and we have five detectives assigned to do interviews."

I nodded. "Good. I want to interview Donna Alba myself."

"I'm sure you do. If you find her, let us know."

"Gone?"

"Vacation." Beth added, "That's what I mean about them being cute."

"Right. They're still covering up. They can't help it. It's in their bureaucratic bones." I said, "Where are your buddies, Nash and Foster?"

"They're not my buddies, and I don't know. Around, but not visible. They left the Soundview."

"I know. Okay, next."

"I got a court order to take into evidence all the government weapons on Plum Island, including the .45 automatics, a few revolvers, and a dozen M-16s, and two World War Two carbines."

"My goodness. Were they going to invade us?"

She shrugged. "It's a lot of Army stuff, left over,

I guess. Anyway, they howled about giving up the armory. I'm having each weapon test-fired by ballistics, and we'll have a report on each one in case we ever find a slug."

"Good thinking." I asked, "When will you re-arm Plum Island?"

"Probably Monday or Tuesday."

I said, "I saw some Marine Corps activity at the ferry. I guess after you disarmed poor Mr. Stevens' security force, they felt they needed protection."

"Not my problem."

I said, "By the way, I'm sure they didn't give you the whole arsenal."

"If they didn't, I'll get an arrest warrant for Stevens."

No judge was going to issue that warrant, but it didn't matter so I said, "Please proceed."

"Okay, more Plum Island. I paid a surprise call on Dr. Chen, who lives in Stony Brook. I got the distinct impression she had been coached before we met her in the lab, because she could not extemporize when I spoke to her in her house." Beth added, "I got Dr. Chen to say that yes, maybe, perhaps, possibly, the Gordons stole a dangerous virus or bacterium."

I nodded. This was very good police work, topnotch procedural. Some of it was relevant, some of it was not. As far as I knew, there were only three people who would use the words "pirate treasure" in regard to this case—me, Emma, and the murderer.

Beth said, "I re-interviewed Kenneth Gibbs, also at his house. He lives in Yaphank, not far from my office. He's a bit of a snot, but aside from that, I don't think he knows any more than he's told us." She added, "Paul Stevens is another story...."

"Indeed he is. Did you speak to him?"

"I tried to...he's been giving me the slip." She added, "I think he knows something, John. As security chief of Plum Island, there's not too much that gets past that guy."

"Probably not."

She looked at me and asked, "Do you think he's a suspect?"

"He makes me suspicious, so he's a suspect."

She thought a moment, then said, "This is not very scientific, but he looks like a killer."

"He sure does. I have a whole class called 'People Who Look and Act Like Killers.'"

She didn't know if I was pulling her leg or not, which, actually, I wasn't. She said, "Anyway, I'm trying to run a background check on him, but the people who would have the most information—the FBI—are dragging their feet."

"Actually, they've already done what you're asking them to do, but they're not going to share any of it with you."

She nodded and said unexpectedly, "Fucked-up case."

"That's what I've been telling you." I asked her, "Where does Stevens live?"

"Connecticut. New London. There's a government ferry from New London to Plum."

"Give me his address and phone number."

She found it in her notes and started to write it out, but I said, "I have a photographic memory. Just tell me."

She looked at me, again with an expression of slight disbelief. Why doesn't anyone take me seriously? In any case, she told me Paul Stevens' address and phone number, which I tucked away in a crevice of my brain. I stood and said, "Let's take a walk."

CHAPTER TWENTY-SIX

We went out back and walked down to the water. She said, "This is very nice."

"I'm beginning to appreciate it." I picked up a flat stone and skimmed it across the water. It made three skims before it sank.

Beth found a nice skimmer, cocked her arm, and let loose, throwing her whole body into the motion. The stone did four hits before it sank.

I said, "Hey, nice arm."

"I pitch. Homicide softball team." She took another stone and threw it at the piling at the end of the pier. It missed the piling by inches and she tried again.

I watched her chucking stones at the piling. What had turned me on, still turned me on. It was her looks, for sure—but also her aloofness. I love it when they're aloof. I think. Anyway, I was fairly sure that finding Emma in the house had embarrassed her and annoyed her. More important, she was surprised at how she felt, and maybe what she felt was competition. I said, "I missed your company. Absence makes the heart grow fonder."

She glanced at me between throws and said, "Then

you're absolutely going to love me, because this will probably be the last time you'll ever see me."

"Don't forget the party tomorrow."

She ignored that and said, "If I suspected one person out of all the people we spoke to, it would be Paul Stevens."

"Why?"

She aimed a stone at the piling again and this time hit it. She said to me, "I called him at Plum Island yesterday, and they said he was out. I pressed and they said he was home sick. I called his home, but no one answered." She added, "Another disappearing Plum Islander."

We walked along the stony shore.

I, too, was not satisfied with Mr. Stevens' last performance. He *was* a possible murder suspect. As I said, I could very well be wrong about Fredric Tobin, or it could be that Tobin was in cahoots with Stevens, or it could be neither. I had thought that when I had the motive, I'd have the murderer. But the motive had turned out to be money, and when the motive is money, the suspects are everybody and anybody.

We walked east along the shore, past my neighbors' houses. The tide was coming in and the water lapped over the stones. Beth had her hands tucked in the side pockets of her jacket, and she walked with her head down as if in deep thought. Every now and then, she'd kick at a stone or seashell. She saw a small starfish stranded on the beach, bent down, picked it up, and threw it back into the bay.

We walked in silence for a while longer, then she said, "Regarding Dr. Zollner, we had a pleasant chat on the phone."

"Why don't you call him in?"

"I would, but he's in Washington. He was summoned to give a statement to the FBI, the Department of Agriculture, and others. Then, he's on a traveling schedule—South America, England, a lot of other places that need his expertise." She said, "They're keeping him out of my reach."

"Get a subpoena."

She didn't reply.

I asked, "Are you getting interference from Washington?"

She replied, "Not me, personally. But people I work for are.... You know how it is when your calls are not returned, things you ask for take too long, meetings you want are put off."

"I worked a case like that once." I advised her, "Politicians and bureaucrats will run you around until they figure out if you can help them or hurt them."

She asked me, "What are they really afraid of, and what are they covering up?"

"Politicians are afraid of anything they don't understand, and they don't understand anything. Just keep working the case."

She nodded.

I said, "You've done a very good job."

"Thanks." We turned around and began walking back to my house.

Beth, I reflected, seemed to enjoy the paperwork, the details, the little building blocks that made up the case. There were detectives who believed that you could solve a case by working with the known elements of forensics, ballistics, and so forth. Sometimes, that was true. In this case, however, the answers started coming out of left field, and you had to be there to catch them.

Beth said, "The lab has done a complete job on the Gordons' two vehicles and their boat. All fingerprints were theirs, except mine, yours, and Max's on the boat. Also, on the deck of the boat, they found something strange."

"Yes?"

"Two things. First, soil, which we know about. But also they found small, very small, slivers of wood that were decayed, rotted. Not driftwood. There was no salt in the wood. This was buried wood, still showing some soil." She looked at me. "Any ideas?"

"Let me think about it."

"Okay."

Beth continued, "I contacted the county sheriff, a fellow named Will Parker, regarding pistol permits he's issued in Southold Township."

"Good."

"I also checked with the county pistol license section, and I have a computer printout that shows that there are 1,224 pistol permits issued by the sheriff and by the county to residents of Southold Township."

"So, out of the twenty-some thousand residents of this township, we have about twelve hundred registered pistol license holders. That's a big number, a lot of people to call on, but not an impossible task."

"Well," Beth informed me, "the irony is that when the subject was plague, no task was impossible. But we're no longer pledging the whole police budget to solve this case."

"The Gordons are important to *me*. Their murder is important to me."

"I know that. And to me. I'm just explaining reality."

"Why don't I call your boss so I can explain reality to *him*?"

"Let it go, John. I'll take care of it."

"All right." In truth, while the county PD was turning down the flame on this one, the Feds were secretly working very hard looking for the wrong type of perp. But that wasn't my problem. I asked, "Is Mr. Tobin on the pistol license list?"

"Actually, yes. I scanned the list and pulled a few names I knew. Tobin was one."

"Who else?"

"Well, Max." She added, "He has an off-duty .45."

"There's your perp," I said, half jokingly. I asked her, "What does Tobin pack?"

She glanced at me and said, "Two pieces—a 9mm Browning and a Colt .45 automatic."

"My goodness. Is he afraid of grape rustlers?"

"I suppose he carries cash or something. You don't need a lot of reasons to get a pistol permit in this township if you're tight with the sheriff and the chief."

"Interesting." Concealed weapons were closely regulated in New York State, but there were places where it was a wee bit easier to get a permit. Anyway, having two pistols didn't make F. Tobin a killer, but it was suggestive of certain personality types. Freddie, I thought, fit into the mild-mannered type who, as Emma suggested, was not physically or verbally violent, but who would put a bullet through your head if he felt in the least bit threatened by you.

As we approached my piece of the shoreline, Beth stopped and turned toward the water. She stood there, looking at the bay—a classical pose, I thought, like some oil painting titled, *Woman Gazes at the Sea*. I wondered if Beth Penrose was a spontaneous skinny-dipper, and decided she was definitely not the type.

Beth asked me, "Why does Fredric Tobin interest you?"

"I told you . . . well, it turns out he was closer to the Gordons than even I realized."

"So what?"

"I don't know. Please continue."

She glanced at me again, then turned from the bay and continued walking. She said, "Okay. Next, we searched the wetlands to the north of the Gordons' house, and found a place where a boat may have been dragged into the bulrushes."

"Really? Good work."

"Thank you." She said, "It's quite possible someone came that way in a shallow draft craft. High tide Monday was at 7:02 P.M., so at about 5:30, it was near high, and there was almost two feet of water in the wetlands beside the Gordon house. You could pole a shallow-draft boat in through the reeds, and no one would see you on the boat."

"Very good. Why didn't I think of that?"

"Because you're spending time thinking of wiseass remarks."

"I actually don't think about them."

She continued, "I'm not saying for certain that a boat was in those reeds, though it appears there was. There are recently broken bulrushes." She added, "The muck shows no signs of compression, but we've had eight tides since the murder, and that may have erased any marks in the mud."

I nodded. "Boy, this is not like a Manhattan homicide. I mean, bulrushes, wetlands, muck, tides, big deep bays with bullets at the bottom. This is like Sergeant Preston of the Yukon."

"You see what I mean? You're a total wiseass."

"Sorry—"

"Okay, I spoke to Max on the phone, and he's very annoyed at you for putting Fredric Tobin through the wringer."

"Fuck Max."

She said, "I have smoothed things over for you with Max."

"Thank you so much."

She asked me, "Did you learn anything from Fredric Tobin?"

"Did I ever. Leaf spread. Maceration of the skins with the juice in the barrels. What else . . . ?"

"Should I interview him?"

I thought a moment, then replied, "Yes, you should."

"Are you going to give me any clues about why I should interview him?"

"I will. But not right now. You should, however, forget drugs, bugs, vaccines, and anything to do with the Gordons' work."

She stayed silent for a really long time as we walked. Finally, she asked, "Are you certain?"

"I kid you not." Get it?

"Then *what* is the motive? Tell me."

"I think I'm getting your goat a little." Get it?

She looked at me, sort of funny, then asked, "Romance? Sex? Jealousy?"

"Nope."

"The Wiley land?"

"That's part of it."

She seemed deep in thought.

We were back at my uncle's property now, and we stopped near the dock. We sort of faced one another, both of us with our hands in our jacket pockets. I was trying to figure out how I felt about this woman in light of Emma, and Beth was trying to figure out who killed the Gordons. It occurred to me that maybe after the case was solved, then we'd all have to resolve how we felt, and who we felt it for.

Beth said, "Pick a rock and give it your best shot."

"Is this a contest?"

"Of course."

"What's the prize?"

"Don't worry about it. You're not going to win."

"Well, aren't we a little overconfident?" I found a really great skimmer—round, flat on the bottom, and concave on the top—a perfect airfoil. I wound up like it was the final pitch of a three-and-two count and let loose. The rock hit, skipped, hit, skipped, hit, skipped, hit, skipped, and sank. Wow. "Four," I said, just in case she wasn't counting.

She'd already found her skimmer—round, a little bigger than mine, and concave on both sides. That's another theory. She took off her jacket and handed it to me. She hefted the stone in her hand like she was considering braining me with it, then, probably psyched up at the mental image of my head bobbing out there on the water, she let loose.

The stone hit and skipped four times and would have sunk, but it caught a small ripple wave and went airborne one more time before disappearing.

Beth wiped her hands and took her jacket from me.

"Very good," I said.

"You lose," she said. She put her jacket back on and said, "Tell me what you know."

"You're such a great detective, I'll just give you the clues, and you can figure it out. Okay, listen up—the rented house on the water with the speedboat, the acre of Wiley land, the Peconic Historical Society, the history of Plum Island and surrounding islands, the lost week in England...what else...the numbers 44106818...what else?"

"Paul Stevens?"

"Possibly."

"Fredric Tobin?"

"Possibly."

"How does he fit? Suspect? Witness?"

"Well, Mr. Tobin and his winery may be dead broke. Or so I heard. So he may be a desperate man. And desperate men do desperate things."

Beth replied, "I'll check out his financials. Meanwhile, thanks for the great clues."

I replied, "It's all there, kid. Look for a common denominator, a thread that runs through those clues."

She didn't like this game and said, "I have to go. I'll tell Max you solved the case, and he should give you a call." She started back across the lawn toward the house. I followed.

Back in the kitchen, she began gathering her papers.

"By the way," I asked, "what do those two signal flags mean?"

She continued packing her briefcase and said, "The flags are the letters B and V. In the phonetic alphabet, they are Bravo Victor." She looked at me.

I asked, "How about the other meaning? The word meaning?"

"The Bravo flag also means dangerous cargo. The Victor flag means require assistance."

"So, the two flags could mean dangerous cargo, require assistance."

She replied, "Yes, which would make sense if the Gordons were carrying dangerous micro-organisms. Or even illegal drugs. This could have been a signal to their partner. But you say this has nothing to do with bugs or drugs."

"That's what I say."

She informed me, "According to a guy in my office who's a sailor, a lot of people on land run up pennants as nothing more than a decoration or a joke. You couldn't do that on the water, but on the land, no one takes it seriously."

"True enough. That's what the Gordons often did." But this time...dangerous cargo, need assistance....I said, "Go with the assumption it was a signal to someone." I added, "It's a terrific signal. No telephone record, no cell phone, just an old-fashioned flag signal. Probably prearranged. The Gordons are saying, 'We got the goods on board, come help us unload this stuff.'"

"*What* stuff?"

"Ah. *That* is the question."

She looked at me and said, "If you have information or evidence that you're holding back—and I suppose you do—then you may have a legal problem, Detective."

"Now, now. No threats."

"John, I'm investigating a *double murder*. They were your friends, and this is not a game—"

"Hold on. I don't need a lecture. I was sitting on

my back porch minding my own business when Max comes calling with his hat in his hand. By the same time the next evening, I'm standing in an empty parking lot at the ferry after a day in biocontainment with my thumb up my nose. And now—"

"You hold on. I've treated you very well—"

"Oh, come on. You took a two-day walk on me—"

"I was *working*. What were *you* doing?"

And so on. After about two minutes of this, I said, "Truce. This is not productive."

She got herself under control and said, "I'm sorry."

"You should be." I added, "I'm also sorry."

And so we made up, without kissing.

She said, "I'm not pressing you for what you know, but you did indicate that after I told you about what I knew, you'd do the same."

"I will. But not this morning."

"Why not?"

"Speak to Max first. It would be much better if you just briefed him from *your* notes and not from my theories."

She thought about that and nodded, "Okay. When can I hear your theories?"

"I just need a little more time. Meanwhile, think about those clues I gave you and see if you come up with what I came up with."

She didn't reply.

I added, "What I will promise you is that if I get it all together, I'll hand it to you on a silver platter."

"That's very generous of you. What would you like in return?"

"Nothing. You need the career boost. I'm at the top of my career."

"You're actually in trouble and solving this case won't get you out of it—it'll get you further into it."

"Whatever."

She looked at her watch and said, "I have to meet Max."

"I'll walk you to your car."

We walked outside, and she got into her car. She said, "I'll see you tomorrow night at the Tobin party, if not sooner."

"Right. You can be Max's date." I smiled. "Thanks for stopping by."

She drove around the circle, but instead of heading down the driveway, she came tearing around again to the front door, jammed on her brakes, and said, almost breathlessly, "John! You said the Gordons were digging for buried treasure. Like an important archaeological find—on Plum Island—government land—they had to steal it from Plum Island and bury it on their own land—the Wiley property. Right?"

I smiled and gave her a thumbs-up, then turned and went inside.

The phone was ringing, and I answered it. It was Beth. She asked, "What did they dig up?"

"The phone is not secure."

"John, when can I meet you? Where?"

She sounded excited, as well she should.

I said, "I'll get in touch with you."

"Promise."

"Sure. Meanwhile, you'd be well advised to keep that to yourself."

"I understand."

"Bye—"

"John."

"Yes?"

"Thanks."

I hung up. "You're welcome."

I went out the back kitchen door and walked out to the end of the dock. I've found that this is a good place to think.

A morning mist hung over the water, and I saw a small skiff making its way through the gray vapor. A cabin cruiser was going to cross its path, and the man in the skiff picked something up, then I heard a loud horn, a foghorn, and I recalled seeing these aerosol cans that emitted a foghorn sound, a sort of poor man's version of an electric foghorn or a brass bell. It was a common enough sound on the water, so much so that you'd never notice it, probably not even if you heard it on a clear sunny day because I recalled the big boats also used it to signal for a tender to pick up the crew after they moored in the deep water. And if you heard it close by, you might not hear the sound of two gunshots in quick succession. A poor man's silencer. Very clever, actually.

It was, indeed, all coming together now, even the tiny details. I was satisfied that I had the motive for murder—Captain Kidd's treasure. But I couldn't quite connect Tobin, Stevens, or anybody else to the murders. In fact, in my more paranoid moments, I thought that Max and Emma could also be in on it.

Given the milieu out here, it really could be a wide-ranging conspiracy. But who actually pulled the trigger? I tried to picture Max, Emma, Tobin, and Stevens, and maybe even Zollner, all on the back deck of the Gordons' house. . . . Or maybe someone else, someone I hadn't even met or thought about. You have to be very careful and damned sure before you start calling someone a murderer.

What I also needed to do—not because I gave a damn about it, but everyone else would—was to find the treasure. Little Johnny goes treasure hunting. But he must outwit some evil pirates and get the treasure and turn it over to the government. Now there's a depressing thought.

I wondered if a few million in gold and jewels would make me happy. Saint-seducing gold. Before I got too deep into that one, I thought about all the people who'd died because of that gold—presumably the men whose ship it was on when Kidd attacked them, then some of Kidd's own men, then Kidd himself when they hanged him at the execution dock, then who knew how many men and women died or were ruined over the last three centuries looking for Captain Kidd's fabled treasure. Then, finally, Tom and Judy Gordon. I had an uneasy premonition that the chain of death wasn't going to stop there.

CHAPTER TWENTY-SEVEN

At about noon, I stopped by Whitestone Florist and delivered the chamber pot. I hadn't had breakfast so I asked Emma to lunch, but she said she was busy. Fridays in flowerland were busy days—parties, dinners, and so forth. Plus, there were three funerals, which by their nature are unscheduled events. And, she had a standing order from Tobin Vineyards for flowers every weekend for their restaurant and lobby. And, of course, there was Fredric's big soiree the next evening. I said, "Does he pay his bills?"

"No. That's why I get it up front with him. Cash or credit card. No checks. And I cut off his house charge."

She said it in a way that suggested she'd like to cut off more than that. I asked, "Can I bring you a sandwich?"

"No, thanks. I really have to get back to work."

"See you tomorrow."

I left and took a walk on Main Street. Somehow the nature of our short relationship had changed. She was definitely a little cool. Women have a way of frosting you, and if you try to thaw them, they just turn the temperature lower. It's a game that takes two to play, and the deck is already stacked, so I always choose not to play.

I bought a sandwich and a beer in a deli, got in my Jeep, and drove to Tom and Judy's acre on the bluff. I sat on the rock and had my lunch. Captain Kidd's Ledge. Incredible. And I had no doubt that the numbers 44106818, which were known history, would be made to fit the eroded spot on the face of this bluff where the treasure was going to be found—forty-four paces or forty-four degrees, ten paces or ten degrees, or whatever. You could play with numbers and their meaning and work backwards toward a spot of your own choosing. "Nice going, you two. I wish the hell you'd confided in me. You wouldn't be dead."

A bird chirped somewhere, as if in reply.

I stood on the rock and with my binocs, I looked south, scanning the farms and vineyards until I spotted the Tower of Tobin the Terrible, rising above the flat glacial plain, the tallest thing out there: Lord Freddie's penis substitute. I said aloud, "You little shit."

I decided I wanted to get away—away from my telephone, my house, Beth, Max, Emma, the FBI, the CIA, my bosses, and even my buds in the city. As I looked across the Sound at Connecticut, I had the idea to go to Foxwoods Resort Casino.

I went down the bluff, got into my Jeep, and drove to the Orient ferry. It was a calm crossing, a nice day on the Sound, and in one hour and twenty minutes, my Jeep and I were in New London, Connecticut.

I drove to Foxwoods, this sprawling gambling casino and hotel in the middle of nowhere—actually on the land of the Mashantucket Pequot tribe—a sort of Fuck-You-White-Man-We're-Getting-Even kind of place. I checked in, bought some toiletries, went to my room, unpacked my toothbrush, then went down to the cavernous casino to meet my fate.

I was very lucky with blackjack, broke even on the slots, lost a little at craps, and got taken a wee bit at the roulette wheel. By eight P.M., I was down only about two thousand dollars. What fun I was having.

I tried to put myself in Freddie Tobin's light shoes—babe on my arm, down about ten Gs a weekend, winery pumping out the juice, but not quick enough. Everything that is my world is about to come crashing down. Still, I'm holding on and even becoming more reckless with my gambling and spending because I'm about to hit the jackpot. Not this jackpot at Foxwoods; the jackpot that has been buried for three hundred years, and I know where it is, and it's tantalizingly close—I can probably see where it's buried as I go past Plum Island on my boat. But I can't grasp this treasure without the help of Tom and Judy Gordon, whom I've taken into my confidence and recruited to be my partners. And I, Fredric Tobin, have picked well. Of all the Plum Island scientists, staff, and workers I've ever met, Tom and Judy are the ones I want to recruit—they're young, they're bright, they're stable, they have a little flair, and most of all, they've shown a taste for the good life.

I assumed that Tobin recruited the Gordons not long after they'd come here, as evidenced by the fact that within four months the Gordons had moved from their inland house near the ferry to their present house on the water. That had been Tobin's suggestion, and so had the boat.

Obviously, Fredric Tobin had been actively on the

prowl for his Plum Island connection and had probably rejected a number of candidates. For all I knew, he'd once had another Plum Island partner, and something had gone wrong, and that person or persons were now dead. I'd have to check and see if any Plum Island employees had met an untimely death two or three years ago.

I realized that I was displaying an unacceptable prejudice toward Fredric Tobin, that I really wanted *him* to be the murderer. Not Emma, not Max, not Zollner, not even Stevens. Fredric Tobin—Fry Freddie.

Try as I might to cast others in the role of murderer, it came back to Tobin in my mind. Beth, without actually saying so, suspected Paul Stevens, and all other things being equal, it was more likely him than Tobin. My thoughts about Tobin were too involved with my feelings for Emma. I just couldn't get the image out of my mind of those two screwing. I mean, I haven't felt that way in a decade or so.

I didn't want to railroad Freddie, but I decided to proceed on the assumption that he did it, and I'd see if I could make a case against him.

Regarding Paul Stevens, he might well be in on this, but if Tobin had recruited Stevens, why did he need the Gordons? And if Stevens was not *in on* the plan, was he *onto* the plan? Was he like a vulture waiting to swoop in and take his share after the long, hard work of the hunt had been done by others? Or was it Stevens acting alone without Tobin or anyone else? I could certainly make a case against Stevens, who had knowledge of Plum Island, the opportunity, the guns, the daily proximity to the victims, and above all, the personality to hatch a conspiracy and kill his partners. Maybe if I was lucky, I'd get Stevens *and* Tobin a hot squat.

And then there was the possibility of someone else....

I thought about all that had come before Tom and Judy Gordon wound up with their brains blown out. I could see Tom and Judy and Fredric living too high, spending too much, alternatingly confident and frantic about the success of their venture.

They were meticulous in laying the groundwork for the so-called discovery of the treasure. Interestingly, they decided not to locate it on Tobin's waterfront estate. They decided to go with a local legend, Captain Kidd's Ledges. Of course, they would tell the world afterward that their research led them to that particular spot, and they'd confess that they hoodwinked poor Margaret Wiley, who will kick herself for selling the land, and she'd be convinced that Thad was punishing her. The Gordons would have presented Mrs. Wiley with a jewel as a consolation prize.

Often, in a murder investigation, I look for the simplest explanation, and the simplest explanation was simple indeed: it was greed. Freddie had never learned to share and even if he wanted to share, I wondered if the treasure was big enough to cover his debts and save his vineyard. His share would certainly be no more than fifty percent, and the government's share, state and federal, would be about the same. Even if the treasure were worth ten million dollars, Freddie would be lucky to see two and a half million. Not nearly enough for a spendthrift like Lord Tobin. And if there was another partner—a live one, such as Paul Stevens— then certainly the Gordons had to go.

But I still had unanswered questions—assuming the Gordons had uncovered the treasure on Plum Island, did they have it all with them on the day they'd met their end in their own backyard? Was the treasure in that ice chest? And where was the original treasure chest, which had to be reburied and found in a way that might satisfy a nosy archaeologist or Treasury agent?

While I was mulling this over, I wasn't paying attention to the roulette wheel. Roulette is good for people with things on their minds because it's such a mindless game; like the slots, it's pure luck. But with the slots you can time your rate of loss and pass the night in a catatonic, slack-jawed state in front of the one-armed bandits and not lose much more than the grocery money. With roulette, however, at the ten-dollar table, with a fast croupier and fast bettors, you could get hurt fast.

I got up from the table, took another cash advance on my credit card, and went to find a friendly poker game. Ah, the things I do for my job.

I did okay at the poker table, and by midnight, I was back to minus two thousand and change. Plus, I was starving. I got a beer and a sandwich from one of the cocktail ladies and played poker until one A.M., still down two large.

I retired to one of the bars and switched to scotch. I watched a rerun of the news on TV, which failed to mention the Gordon murders at all.

I reran the entire case in my mind—from the time Max stepped on my porch to here and now. And while I was at it, I thought about my love life, my job, and all that, which brought me to confront the question of where I was going.

So, there it was, about two in the morning, I was two thousand dollars poorer, I was alone but not lonely, I was slightly lit, I was supposed to be three-quarters physically disabled, and maybe a hundred percent mentally disabled, and I could have easily felt sorry for myself. Instead, I went back to the roulette wheel. I was unlucky at love, so I had to be lucky at gambling.

At three A.M., another thousand dollars down, I went to bed.

I woke up on Saturday morning with that weird where-am-I? feeling. Sometimes the woman next to me can help out, but there was no woman next to me. Presently, my head cleared and I remembered where I was, and I remembered getting scalped by the Mashantucket Pequots—or, perhaps I should say I was financially challenged by my Native American brothers.

I showered, dressed, packed my toothbrush, and had breakfast in the casino.

Outside, it was another beautiful late summer, almost autumn day. Maybe this was Indian summer. I got in my Jeep and headed south toward New London.

On the northern outskirts of the town, I stopped at a service station and asked directions. Within fifteen minutes, I was on Ridgefield Road, a sort of exurban street of neat New England clapboards set on good-sized pieces of land. The area was semirural; it was difficult for me to figure out if you needed buckos to live here or not. The houses were medium-sized and the cars were medium-priced, so I figured it was a medium neighborhood.

I stopped at number seventeen, a typical white clapboard Cape Cod set about a hundred feet back from the road. The nearest neighbors were some distance away. I got out of my Jeep and walked up the front path and rang the doorbell.

As I waited, I looked around. There was no car in the driveway. Also, there was no sign of kids' stuff around so I concluded that Mr. Stevens was either unmarried, or married no children, or married with grown children, or he'd eaten his children. How's that for deductive reasoning?

I noticed, too, that the place was too neat. I mean, it looked like someone with a sick, fascist, orderly mind lived here.

No one answered my call, so I went to the attached garage and peeked through the side window. No car. I went around to the rear yard, whose lawn stretched about fifty yards to a woods. There was a nice slate patio, grill, lawn furniture, and so forth.

I went to the back door and peeked through the windows into a neat and clean country kitchen.

I seriously contemplated a quick B&E job, giving the place a toss and maybe stealing his diploma for fun, but as I gave the house the once-over, I noticed that all the windows had alarm tape on them. Also, under the eaves to my right was a TV surveillance camera doing a one-eighty-degree sweep. This guy was a piece of work.

I went back out front, got into my Jeep, and dialed Stevens' phone. A voice mail came on, giving me several options having to do with his home fax and home e-mail, his beeper number, his post office box mailing address, his office phone, office fax, office e-mail, and finally a chance to leave a voice message after two beeps. I haven't had that many options since I stood in front of a condom vending machine. I pushed three on my phone pad, got Stevens' beeper number, dialed it, punched in my mobile number, and hung up. A minute later, my phone rang and I answered, "New London Water Authority."

"Yes, this is Paul Stevens. You beeped me."

"Yes, sir. Water main break in front of your house on Ridgefield Road. We'd like to put a pump in your basement to make sure it doesn't flood."

"Okay...I'm in my car now....I can be there in twenty minutes."

"That'll be fine." I hung up and waited.

About five minutes later—not twenty—a gray Ford Escort pulled into the driveway, and out of it came Paul Stevens, wearing black slacks and a tan windbreaker.

I got out of my Jeep, and we met on his front lawn. He greeted me warmly by saying, "What the hell are you doing here?"

"Just out for a drive and thought I'd stop by."

"Get the hell off my property."

My goodness. I hadn't expected such a nasty greeting. I said, "I really don't like to be spoken to that way."

"You shit—you busted my balls for half the fucking morning—"

"Hey, fella—"

"Fuck you, Corey. Get the fuck out of here."

Indeed, this was a different Mr. Stevens than the one on Plum Island, who had been at least civil, if not friendly. Of course, he'd had to be civil then. Now, the tiger was in his own den and his keepers weren't around. I said, "Now, hold on, Paul—"

"Are you deaf? I said, get the hell out of here. And, by the way, you stupid shit, there's well water here. Now get out."

"Okay. But I have to get my partner." I motioned toward the house. "Beth Penrose. She's behind the house."

"You get in your fucking car. I'll get her." He turned and began walking away, then called back over his shoulder, "I should have you both arrested for trespassing. You're lucky I didn't get out of my car shooting."

I turned and walked back toward my Jeep. I looked over my shoulder in time to see him turn the corner of his garage.

I sprinted across the lawn, across the driveway, and caught up to him as he rounded the far end of the house and turned toward his backyard. He heard me, spun around, and reached into the pit for his gun, but much too late. I caught him on the chin with my fist, and he made one of those *umph* sounds and did a little backspring with his arms and legs askew. It was almost comical.

I knelt beside poor Paul and patted him down, finding his little Saturday afternoon special—a 6.5mm Beretta—tucked in the inside pocket of his windbreaker. I took the magazine out and emptied it, putting the rounds in my pocket. I cleared the chamber, replaced the magazine, and returned his piece.

I looked through his wallet—some cash, credit cards, driver's license, medical card, a Plum Island ID card, and a Connecticut pistol permit that listed the Beretta, a .45 Colt, and a .357 Magnum. There were no photos, no phone numbers, no business cards, no keys, no condoms, no lottery tickets, and nothing of any special interest, except the fact that he owned two big-caliber guns that we might not have turned up if

I hadn't cold-cocked him and rummaged through his wallet.

Anyway, I put the wallet back, stood, and waited patiently for him to bounce up and apologize for his behavior. But he just lay there, his stupid head rolling from side to side, and dopey sounds coming out of his mouth. There was no blood on him, but a red spot was starting to form where I'd hit him. Later, it would be blue, then an interesting purple.

Anyway, I went over to a coiled garden hose, turned on the faucet, and spritzed Mr. Stevens. That seemed to help and presently he staggered to his feet, sputtering, wobbling, and all that.

I said to him, "Did you find my partner?"

He seemed sort of confused, reminding me of myself this morning when I woke up with a size ten hangover. I could sympathize. Really.

I said, "Well water. Jeez, I never thought of that. Hey, Paul, who killed Tom and Judy?"

"Fuck you."

I squirted him again and he covered his face.

I dropped the hose and moved closer to him. "Who killed my friends?"

He was drying his face with a corner of his windbreaker, then he seemed to remember something and his right hand went into his jacket and came out with the peashooter. He said, "You bastard! Hands on your head."

"Okay." I put my hands on my head and that seemed to make him feel a little better.

He was rubbing his jaw now and you could tell it hurt. He seemed to be realizing in stages that he'd been tricked, cold-cocked, and doused with the hose. He looked like he was getting angry, working himself up. He said to me, "Take off your jacket."

I took it off, revealing my off-duty .38 in the shoulder holster.

"Drop the jacket, and slowly unstrap the holster and let it fall."

I did as he said.

He asked, "You carrying anywhere else?"

"No, sir."

"Pull up your pants legs."

I pulled up my pants legs, showing him I had no ankle holster.

He said, "Turn around and pull up your shirt."

I turned, pulled up my shirt, showing him I had no holster in the small of my back.

"Turn around."

I turned and faced him.

"Hands on your head."

I put my hands on my head.

"Step away from your gun."

I stepped forward.

"Kneel."

I knelt.

He said, "You shit—you bastard. Who the hell do you think you are coming here like this and violating my privacy and my civil rights?" He was really, really pissed and used a lot of profanity.

It is almost axiomatic in this business that guilty people proclaim their innocence and innocent people get totally pissed off and make all sorts of legal threats. Alas, Mr. Stevens seemed to be falling into the innocent category. I let him vent awhile.

Finally, I got a word in edgewise and asked him,

"Well, do you at least have any idea of who could have done it?"

"If I did, I wouldn't tell you, you wiseass son of a bitch."

"Any ideas why they were killed?"

"Hey, don't you question me, you shit. You shut your fucking mouth."

"Does that mean I can't count on your cooperation?"

"Shut up!" He thought a moment, then said, "I should shoot you for trespassing, you stupid bastard. You're going to pay for hitting me. I should make you strip and dump you in the woods." He was getting worked up again and also creative about ways of getting revenge and all that.

I was sort of getting cramped in the kneeling position, so I stood.

Stevens screamed, "Kneel! Kneel!"

I walked over to him, and he pointed the Beretta right at my dingdong and pulled the trigger. I winced even though the gun was empty.

He realized he'd done something very bad, trying to shoot my balls off with an empty gun. He kept staring at the Beretta.

I used a left hook this time, not wanting to reinjure his right jaw. I hoped he'd appreciate that when he woke up.

Anyway, he toppled back onto the grass.

I knew he'd feel really terrible when he woke up, really stupid and embarrassed and all, and I felt sort of bad for him. Well, maybe not. In any case, he wasn't going to volunteer any information after the second KO, and I didn't think I could cajole or trick him into talking. Torturing him was really out of the question, though he was tempting me.

Anyway, I gathered my gun and holster and my jacket and then, fun guy that I am, I tied Mr. Stevens' shoelaces together.

I walked back to my Jeep, got in, and drove off, hoping I'd get some distance between me and there before Stevens woke up and called the cops.

As I drove, I thought about Paul Stevens. The fact was that he was borderline crazy. But was he a murderer? He didn't seem to be, yet there was something about him...he *knew* something. I was convinced of that. And whatever he knew, he was keeping it to himself and that meant he was either protecting someone, or blackmailing someone, or maybe he was trying to figure out how to turn a buck on this thing. In any case, he was now a hostile witness, to say the least.

So, instead of taking the New London ferry back to Long Island—which could put me at one of the points of an all-points bulletin and subject to a hassle by the Connecticut fuzz—I drove west through some scenic back roads, singing along to some dopey show tune station—Ooowk—lahoma! where the wind comes sweeping down the plains, and all that.

Meanwhile, my right hand was aching and my left hand was stiffening up. In fact, my right knuckles were a little swollen. Jeez. "Gettin' old." I flexed both hands. Oow!

My cell phone rang. I didn't answer it. I crossed into New York State where I had a better shot at jukin' and jivin' the fuzz if they were on my case.

I passed the Throgs Neck Bridge exit where most people would cross to Long Island, and I continued on and crossed at the Whitestone Bridge, which may have been appropriate. "The Emma Whitestone Bridge." I sang, "I'm in love. I'm in love, I'm in love with a wonderful girl!" I love soppy show tunes.

Over the bridge, I headed east on the parkway, back toward the North Fork of Long Island. It was a very roundabout way because I had to avoid the ferry, but I couldn't judge what Paul Stevens was going to do about being decked twice in his own backyard. Not to mention falling on his face when he tried to take a step with his tied shoelaces.

My guess, though, was that he had not called the cops. And if he did not want to report a trespassing and assault, then that was very suggestive. Paul conceded this round, knowing there'd be another. My problem was, he'd pick the next time and place and sort of surprise me with it. Oh, well. If you play hardball, to switch sports metaphors, you have to expect a beanball now and then.

By seven P.M., I was back on the North Fork, having driven some three hundred miles. I didn't want to go home, so I stopped at the Olde Towne Taverne and had a beer or two. I said to the bartender, a guy named Aidan, whom I knew, "Did you ever meet Fredric Tobin?"

He replied, "I bartended a party he had once at his house. But I didn't exchange five words with him."

"What's the story on him?"

Aidan shrugged. "I don't know. . . . I hear all kinds of things."

"Such as?"

"Well, some people say he's gay, some say he's a ladies' man. Some people say he's broke and owes everybody.

Some people say he's cheap, others say he's easy with a buck. You know? You get a guy like that, comes here, starts a whole business from scratch, and you're going to get mixed reviews. He's stepped on some toes, but he's been good to some people, too, I guess. He's tight with the pols and the cops. You know?"

"I do." I asked Aidan, "Where does he live?"

"Oh, he's got a place down in Southold by Founders Landing. You know where that is?"

"No."

Aidan gave me directions and said, "Can't miss it. Big, big."

"Right. Hey, somebody told me that there's pirate treasure buried around here."

Aidan laughed. "Yeah. My old man said there used to be holes dug all over the place when he was a kid. If anybody found anything, they're not talking."

"Right. Why share with Uncle Sam?"

"No kidding."

"Have you heard anything new about the double murder at Nassau Point?"

He said, "Nope. I think, personally, those people stole something dangerous, and the government and the cops are making up a lot of crap about some vaccine. I mean, what are they gonna say? The world's coming to an end? No. They say, 'Don't worry—it can't hurt you.' Bullshit."

"Right." I think the CIA, the FBI, and the government in general should always try out their bullshit on bartenders, barbers, and taxi drivers before they try to sell it to the country. I mean, I usually bounce things off bartenders or my barber when I need a reality check, and it works.

Aidan said, "Hey, what's the difference between Mad Cow Disease and PMS?"

"What?"

"There *is* no difference." He slapped his rag on the bar and laughed. "Get it?"

"Yup." I left the OTT, saddled up, and drove to a place called Founders Landing.

CHAPTER TWENTY-EIGHT

It was getting dark when I got to Founders Landing, but I could see a waterfront park at the end of the road. I also saw a stone monument that said, "Founders Landing—1640." I deduced that this was where the group from Connecticut first landed. If they had stopped at Foxwoods first, they would probably have arrived here in their skivvies.

To the east of the park was a big, big house, bigger than Uncle Harry's and more colonial than Victorian. The house was surrounded by a nice wrought iron fence, and I could see cars parked in front of it and some cars up on the side lawn. I could also hear music coming from the rear of the property.

I parked on the street and walked down to the open wrought iron gate. I wasn't sure of the attire, but I spotted a couple in front of me, and the guy was dressed pretty much as I was—blue blazer, no tie, no socks.

I found my way to the back lawn, which was wide and deep, sloping down to the bay. There were striped tents, colored party lights strung from tree to tree, blazing tonga torches, hurricane candles on the umbrellaed tables, flowers by Whitestone, a six-piece combo playing Big Band stuff, a few bars, and a long buffet table; the very height of East Coast seaside chic, the very best that the old civilization had to offer— and the weather was cooperating. Truly F. Tobin was blessed.

I noticed, too, a big blue and white banner strung between towering oak trees. The banner read, "Peconic Historical Society Annual Party."

A pretty young woman wearing a period costume came up to me and said, "Good evening."

"So far."

"Come and choose a hat."

"Excuse me?"

"You have to wear a hat to get a drink."

"Then I want six hats."

She giggled, took my arm, and led me to a long table on which were about two dozen idiotic hats— tricornered hats of various colors, some with feathers, some with plumes, some with gold braid like navy hats of the period, and some black hats with the white skull and crossbones. I said, "I'll take the pirate hat."

She picked one off the table and put it on my head. "You look dangerous."

"If you only knew."

Out of a big cardboard box she fetched a plastic cut-lass, such as the one Emma had attacked me with, and she slid it into my belt. "There you are," she said.

I left the young lady so she could greet a group who had just arrived, and I walked farther onto the sweep-ing lawn, hatted and armed. The band was playing "Moonlight Serenade."

I looked around and saw that there weren't too many people yet, about fifty, all hatted up, and I suspected the big crowd would arrive after sundown in about half an hour. I didn't see Max, Beth, Emma, or anyone I knew for that matter. I did, however, locate the closest bar and asked for a beer.

The bartender, dressed in a pirate costume, said, "Sorry, sir, only wine and soft drinks."

"*What*? That's outrageous. I need a beer. I have my hat."

"Yes, sir, but there's no beer. May I suggest a sparkling white? It has bubbles, and you can pretend."

"May I suggest you find me a beer by the time I get back here?"

I wandered around, beerless, and checked out the acreage. I could see the park from here, the place where the first settlers landed, sort of the local Plymouth Rock, I guess, but virtually unknown outside of this area. I mean, who knew that the *Fortune* followed the *Mayflower*? Who cares about second and third place? This is America.

I watched Mr. Tobin's guests spread out over his broad lawn, standing, walking, sitting at the white round tables, everyone wearing a hat with a feather, glass in hand, chatting. They were a sedate group, or so they appeared at this early hour—no rum and sex on the beach or skinny-dipping or naked volleyball or anything like that. Just social intercourse.

I saw that Mr. Tobin had a long dock, at the end of which was a good-sized boathouse. Also, several boats were tied up at the long dock, and I assumed they belonged to guests. If this party had been held a week earlier, the *Spirochete* would have been here.

Anyway, curious sort that I am, I walked the length of the dock toward the boathouse. Right before the opening of the boathouse was a big cabin cruiser, about thirty-five feet long. It was named the *Autumn Gold*, and I assumed it was Mr. Tobin's boat, named after his new wine, or named after Mr. Tobin's as-yet-to-be-discovered treasure. In any case, Mr. T liked his toys.

I entered the boathouse. It was dark, but there was enough light coming from both ends to see two boats, one on either side of the dock. The boat to the right was a small, flat-bottomed Whaler of the type you could take into shallow water or wetlands. The other on the left side of the dock was a speedboat, in fact, a Formula 303, the exact same model as the Gordons'. For a half second, I had the spooky feeling that the Gordons had returned from the dead to crash the party and scare the crap out of Freddie. But it wasn't the *Spirochete*—this 303 was named *Sondra*, presumably after Fredric's current squeeze. I suppose it was easier to change the name of a boat than to get a tattoo off your arm.

Anyway, neither the cabin cruiser nor the speedboat interested me, but the flat-bottomed Whaler did. I lowered myself into the small boat. It had an outboard motor, and it also had oarlocks. There were two oars lying on the dock. More interesting, there was a pole, about six feet long, of the type used to move a boat through bulrushes and reeds where neither oars nor motor could be used. Also, the Whaler's deck was a little muddy. In the stern was a plastic crate filled with odds and ends and among them was a compressed-air foghorn.

"Are you looking for something?"

I turned to see Mr. Fredric Tobin standing on the

dock, wineglass in hand, wearing a rather elaborate purple tricornered hat with a flowing plume. He was stroking his short beard as he stared at me. Mephistophelian, indeed.

I said, "I was admiring your boat."

"*That* boat? Most people notice the speedboat or the Chris-Craft," he said, indicating the cabin cruiser docked just outside the boathouse.

I said, "I thought that was the *Autumn Gold*."

"The *make* of the boat is a Chris-Craft."

He was speaking to me with a tiny tone of irritation in his tiny voice which I did not like. I said, "Well, this little guy here is more in my price range." I smiled disarmingly. I do that before I fuck somebody big-time. I said, "When I saw the Formula 303, I thought the Gordons had returned from the dead."

He did not like that at all.

I added, "But then I saw it wasn't the *Spirochete*— it's called the *Sondra*, which is appropriate. You know— fast, sleek, and hot." I love pissing off assholes.

Mr. Tobin said coolly, "The party is on the lawn, Mr. Corey."

"I noticed." I climbed up to the dock and said, "This is some place you have here."

"Thank you."

In addition to the fruity hat, Mr. T was wearing white ducks, a blue double-breasted blazer, and an outrageous scarlet ascot. My goodness. I said, "I like your hat."

He said, "Let me introduce you to some of my guests."

"That would be terrific."

And off we went, out of the boathouse and along

the dock. I asked him, "How far is the Gordon dock from here?"

"I have no idea."

"Take a guess."

"Maybe eight miles. Why?"

"More like ten," I said. "You have to go around Great Hog Neck. I checked my car map. About ten."

"What is your point?"

"No point. Just making seaside conversation."

We were back on the lawn now, and Mr. Tobin reminded me, "You will not question any of my guests about the Gordon murders. I've spoken to Chief Maxwell, and he has agreed to that, and he further reiterated that you have no official standing here."

"You have my word that I won't bother any of your guests with police questions about the Gordon murders."

"Or anything to do with the Gordons at all."

"I promise. But I need a beer."

Mr. Tobin looked around, saw a young lady with a tray of wine, and said to her, "Please go into the house and get this gentleman a beer. Pour it into a wineglass."

"Yes, sir." And off she went. Boy, it must be nice to be rich and to tell people, "I want this, and I want that."

Mr. Tobin said to me, "You're not a hat person." He excused himself and left me standing alone. I was afraid to move lest the serving girl with the beer not find me.

It was deep dusk now, and the colored party lights twinkled, the torches blazed, the candles glowed. A nice gentle land breeze blew the bugs out to sea. The band was playing "Stardust." The trumpet player was terrific. Life is good. I was glad I wasn't dead.

I watched Fredric work the party, person by person, couple by couple, group by group, laughing, joking, adjusting their hats, and putting plastic swords in the belts of ladies who had belts. Unlike the most famous Long Island party-giver, Jay Gatsby, Fredric Tobin did not watch his party from afar. Quite the opposite, he was right in there, mixing it up, being the most perfect host ever.

The man had some cool, I'll give him that. He was near broke, if I could believe Emma Whitestone, and he was a double murderer, if I could believe my instincts, not to mention what I'd just seen in the boathouse. And he must have known that I knew both his secrets, yet he was not ruffled. He was more concerned that I not fuck up his party than that I might fuck up his life. A very cool customer, indeed.

The serving girl returned with the wineglass of beer on a tray. I took the beer and commented, "I don't like wine."

She smiled. "Me neither. There's more beer in the refrigerator." She winked and moved off.

Sometimes I think I'm blessed with sex appeal, charisma, and animal magnetism. Other times, I think I must have bad breath and body odor. Tonight, I felt I was on, hot as a three-dollar pistol; I tilted my hat rakishly, adjusted my sword, and began working the party.

It was mostly a young and early-middle-age crowd, not too many of the grandes dames and DAR types. I didn't see Margaret Wiley, for instance. It was mostly couples—the world is mostly couples—but there were a few strays who looked able to make conversation if neither of my one and only true loves showed up.

I noticed a woman in a white, sort of silky dress,

wearing the required chapeau from which fell long blonde hair. I recognized her as Lord Freddie's little thing, who the Gordons had pointed out to me at the wine tasting. She was crossing the lawn, alone, so I set course and intercepted. "Good evening," I said.

She smiled. "Good evening."

"I'm John Corey."

The name obviously meant nothing to her, and she kept smiling. She said, "I'm Sondra Wells. A friend of Fredric Tobin."

"Yes, I know. We met in July at the vineyard. A wine tasting. I was with the Gordons."

Her smile dropped, and she said, "Oh, that was terrible."

"It certainly was."

"A tragedy."

"Yes. You were close to the Gordons?"

"Well...Freddie was. I liked them...but I don't know if they liked me."

"I'm sure they did. They always spoke highly of you." Actually, they never spoke of her at all.

She smiled again.

She spoke well and carried herself well as if she'd gone to school to learn how to do those things; it was all too practiced, and I could imagine Tobin sending her off someplace where she had to walk with a book on her head and recite Elizabeth Barrett Browning while sucking on a pencil.

I personally couldn't see why anyone would trade Emma Whitestone for Sondra Wells. Then again, beauty is in the eye of the beholder and all that. I said to Ms. Wells, "Do you like boating?"

"No, I don't. Fredric seems to enjoy it."

"I have a place on the water west of here. I love to boat."

"How nice."

"In fact, I'm sure I saw Mr. Tobin...let's see, last Monday, about cocktail time, I guess, in his little Whaler. I thought I saw you with him."

She thought a moment, then said, "Oh...Monday...I was in Manhattan all day. Fredric had a car and driver take me and the housekeeper to the city, and I spent the day shopping."

I saw her little brain working and a frown passed over her lips. She asked me, "You saw Fredric in the Whaler with a...another person?"

"Perhaps it wasn't him, or if it was, he may have been alone, or perhaps with a man...."

She frowned again.

I love to stir up the shit. Beyond that, I had now placed Ms. Wells and the housekeeper in Manhattan at the time of the murders. How convenient. I asked her, "Do you share Fredric's interests in local history and archaeology?"

She replied, "No, I don't. And I'm glad he's given it up. Of all the hobbies a man can have, why that one?"

"It might have had something to do with the Peconic Historical Society's archivist."

She gave me a very cool look, indeed, and would surely have walked away, except that Fredric himself popped up and said to Ms. Wells, "May I steal you a moment? The Fishers want to say hello." Fredric looked at me and said, "You'll excuse us?"

"I guess, unless the Fishers want to say hello to me, too."

Fredric gave me an unpleasant smile, Ms. Wells gave

me a frown, and off they went, leaving their boorish guest to contemplate his gauche behavior.

About 8:30 I saw Max and Beth. Max also had on a pirate hat, and Beth had a sort of silly bonnet on her head. She was wearing white slacks and a blue and white striped boat top. She looked different. I walked over to them at the long buffet. Max was stuffing his face with a plate of pigs in the blanket, my very favorite. We exchanged greetings, and I stole one of his hot dogs.

Beth said, "Nice evening. Thank you for suggesting I come."

"You never know what you can learn by listening."

Max said to me, "Beth briefed me on the Suffolk PD's progress so far. She did a lot of work in the last four days."

I glanced at Beth to see if she'd said anything to Max about her visit to my house. Beth shook her head slightly.

Max said to me, "Thanks again for your help."

"No problem. Don't hesitate to call again."

Max said to me, "You never returned any of my phone calls."

"No, and I never will."

"I don't think you have any reason to be angry."

"No? Try reversing the situation, Max." I added, "I should have kicked you off my porch."

Max replied, "Well... I apologize if I caused you any inconvenience."

"Yeah. Thanks."

Beth interjected and said to Max, "John is in some trouble with his bosses because he helped you."

Max said again, "Sorry. I'll make a few calls, if you tell me who to call."

"No offense, Max, but they don't want to hear from a rural police chief."

Actually, I wasn't that angry with Max and even if I had been, it's hard to stay angry with Max. Basically, he's a good egg, and his only real fault is that he *always* looks out for Number One. Sometimes I make believe I'm angry so the other person thinks they owe me something. Like a small piece of information. I asked Max, "By the way, have there been any other deaths among Plum Island workers that have come to your attention? Say, two or three years ago?"

He thought a moment, then said, "There was a drowning accident, two years ago this summer. A guy...Dr. somebody...a veterinarian...I think."

"How'd he drown?"

"I'm trying to think...he was in his boat...right, he was night fishing or something, and when he didn't come home, his wife called us. We got the Coast Guard out, and they found his boat empty about one in the morning. The next day, he washed up from the bay there...." He cocked his head toward Shelter Island.

"Any evidence of foul play?"

"Well, there was a bump on his head, and an autopsy was done, but it appeared he'd slipped in the boat, hit his head on the gunnel, and gone overboard." Max added, "It happens." He looked at me. "Why do you ask that?"

I replied, "I promised Mr. Tobin, and so did you, Max, that we wouldn't discuss any of this at his party." I added, "I need a beer." I walked off, leaving Max with a weenie in his hand.

Beth caught up to me and said, "That was rude."

"He deserved it."

"Remember, I have to work with him."

"Then work with him." I saw my favorite server, and she saw me. She had a glass of beer on her tray and handed it to me. Beth took a glass of wine.

Beth said, "I want you to tell me about the archaeological digs, about Fredric Tobin, about everything you've found out, and all your conclusions. In return, I'll get you an official status, and you'll have all the resources of the county PD behind you. What do you say?"

"I say, keep your official status, I'm in enough trouble, and I'll tell you all I know tomorrow. Then I'm outta here."

"John, stop playing hard to get."

I didn't reply.

"Do you want me to make an official call to your boss? What's his name?"

"Chief Inspector Asshole. Don't worry about that." The band was playing "As Time Goes By," and I asked her, "Want to dance?"

"No. Can we talk?"

"Sure."

"Do you think the drowning of that other Plum Island employee is related to this case?"

"Maybe. We might never know. But I see a pattern."

"What pattern?"

"You look good in that hat."

"I want to talk about the case, John."

"Not here, and not now."

"Where and when?"

"Tomorrow."

"Tonight. You said tonight. I'll go back to your place."

"Well...I don't know if I can do that...."

"Look, John, I'm not offering to have sex with you. I just need to talk to you. Let's go to a bar or something."

"Well...I don't think we should leave together...."

"Oh...right. You're in love."

"No...well...maybe I am...in any case, this can wait until tomorrow. If I'm right about this, then our man is right over there, and he's hosting a party. If I were you, I'd keep him under loose surveillance tomorrow. Just don't spook him. Okay?"

"Okay, but—"

"We'll meet tomorrow, and I'll give you the whole thing, then I'm through with it. Monday I'm heading back to Manhattan. I have medical and professional appointments all day Tuesday. Okay? Tomorrow. Promise."

"Okay." She touched glasses with me, and we drank.

We chatted awhile, and while we were doing that, I saw Emma in the distance. She was speaking with a group of people among whom was Fredric Tobin, exlover and suspected murderer. I don't know why it annoyed me to see them chatting. I mean, get sophisticated, John. When my wife took long business trips with her Randy Dan boss, did I get bent up? Not too much.

Beth followed my gaze and said, "She seems very nice."

I didn't reply.

Beth went on, "I happened to mention her to Max."

I definitely didn't respond to that.

Beth said, "She used to be Fredric Tobin's...girlfriend. I guess you know that. I only mention it in case you don't. I mean, you should be careful of pillow talk if Tobin is a suspect. Or is that why you've befriended her? To find out more about Tobin? John? Are you listening to me?"

I looked at her and said, "You know, Beth, I sometimes wish one of those bullets really had neutered me. Then I'd be completely free of the control of women."

She observed, "Next time you're having sex, you won't be thinking like that." She turned and walked off.

I looked around, realizing again that Tom and Judy would have been here tonight. I wondered if the treasure was supposed to be discovered on the bluff this week. Would they have announced it to the press by now? Or would they have announced it here tonight?

In any case, the Gordons were in cold storage tonight, the treasure was hidden somewhere, and their probable killer was about fifty feet from me, talking to a woman I'd become very fond of. In fact, I noticed that Tobin and Emma were alone now, talking tête-à-tête.

I'd had enough of this and made my way around the side of the house, discarding my hat and sword on the way. About halfway across the front lawn, I heard my name called, but I kept walking.

"JOHN!"

I turned.

Emma hurried across the lawn. "Where are you going?"

"Someplace where I can get a beer."

"I'll go with you."

"No, I don't need the company."

She informed me, "You need lots of company, my

friend. That's your problem. You've been alone too long."

"Do you write a lovelorn column for the local weekly?"

"I will not let you bait me, and I will not let you leave alone. Where are you going?"

"Ye Olde Towne Taverne."

"My favorite dive. Have you had their nacho platter?" She took my arm and off we went.

I got in her old car and within twenty minutes, we were ensconced in a booth at the Olde Towne Taverne, beers in hand, nachos and chicken wings on the way. The Saturday night regulars didn't look as if they were on their way to, or back from, Freddie's fabulous fete.

Emma said, "I called you last night."

"I thought you went out with the girls."

"I called you when I got back. About midnight."

"No luck with the hunt?"

"No." She said, "I guess you were sleeping."

"Actually, I went to Foxwoods. You can lose your drawers there."

"Tell me about it."

We talked awhile, and I said to her, "I'm assuming you didn't say anything to Fredric about what we've been discussing."

She hesitated a half second too long, then replied, "I didn't... but I did tell him... I said that you and I were dating." She smiled. "Are we dating?"

"Archivists are always dating—July 4, 1776, December 7, 1941—"

"Be serious."

"Okay, I seriously wish you hadn't mentioned me at all."

She shrugged. "I'm happy, and I want everyone to know it. He wished me luck."

"What a gentleman."

She smiled. "Are you jealous?"

"Not at all." *I'm going to see him fry.* "I think you should not discuss us with him and certainly not discuss pirate treasure."

"Okay."

And so we had a pleasant dinner and then went to her place, a little cottage in a residential section of Cutchogue. She showed me her chamber pot collection, ten of them, all used as planters and placed in a big bay window. My gift was now filled with soil and held miniature roses.

She disappeared for a moment and returned with a wrapped gift for me. She said, "I got it at the historical society gift shop. I didn't lift it, but I took forty percent off for myself."

"You didn't have to—"

"Just open it."

And I did. It was a book titled *The Story of Pirate Treasure.*

She said, "Open to the flyleaf."

I opened it and read, "To John, my favorite buccaneer, Love, Emma." I smiled and said, "Thank you. This is what I've always wanted."

"Well, not always. But I thought you might want to look it over."

"I will."

Anyway, the cottage was cute, it was clean, there was no cat, she had scotch and beer, the mattress was firm, she liked the Beatles and the Bee Gees, and she had two pillows for me. What more could I ask? Well, whipped cream. She had that, too.

*   *   *

The next morning, Sunday, we went out for breakfast at the Cutchogue Diner, then without asking me, she drove to church, a nice clapboard Methodist church. She explained, "I'm not a fanatic about it, but it gives me a lift sometimes. It's not bad for business either."

So I attended church, ready to dive under the pew if the ceiling caved in.

After church, we retrieved my car in front of Mr. Tobin's mansion, and Emma followed me back to my mansion.

While Emma made tea for herself, I called Beth at her office. She wasn't in so I left a message with a guy who said he was working the Gordon case. I said to him, "Tell her I'll be out all day. I'll try to speak to her tonight. If not, she should come to my place tomorrow morning for coffee."

"Okay."

I called Beth's house and got her answering machine. I left the same message.

Feeling that I'd done what I could to keep my promise, I went into the kitchen and said, "Let's take a Sunday drive."

"Sounds good to me."

She drove her car home and I followed, then we went to Orient Point in my Jeep and took the New London ferry. We spent the day in Connecticut and Rhode Island, visiting the mansions in Newport, having dinner in Mystic, then taking the ferry back.

We stood on the deck of the ferry and watched the water and the stars.

The ferry passed through Plum Island Gut, and I could see the Orient Point Lighthouse on the right. To the left, the old stone Plum Island Lighthouse was dark and forbidding against the night sky.

The Gut was choppy, and Emma remarked, "That storm's tracking this way. The seas get rough long before the weather moves in." She added, "Also, the barometer drops. Can you feel it?"

"Feel what?"

"The falling air pressure."

"Uh...." I stuck my tongue out. "Not yet."

"I can feel it. I'm very weather sensitive."

"Is that good or bad?"

"I think it's a good thing."

"So do I."

"Are you sure you can't feel it? Don't your wounds ache a little?"

I focused on my wounds and sure enough, they did ache a little. I said to Emma, "Thanks for bringing it to my attention."

"It's good to get in touch with your body, to understand the relationships between the elements and your body and mind."

"Absolutely."

"For instance, I get a little crazy during a full moon."

"Crazier," I pointed out.

"Yes, crazier. How about you?"

"I get very horny."

"Really? During a full moon?"

"Full moon, half-moon, quarter-moon."

She laughed.

I glanced at Plum Island as we passed by. I could see a few channel lights and, on the horizon, a glow from where the main lab would be behind the trees. Otherwise, the island was as dark as it had been three hundred years ago, and if I squinted I could imagine William Kidd's sloop, the *San Antonio*, reconnoitering the island one July night in 1699. I could see a boat being lowered off the side with Kidd and maybe one or two others aboard, and I could see someone in the boat rowing toward the shore....

Emma interrupted my thoughts and asked me, "What are you thinking?"

"Just enjoying the night."

"You were staring at Plum Island."

"Yes.... I was thinking about...the Gordons."

"You were thinking about Captain Kidd."

"You must be a witch."

"I'm a good Methodist and a bitch. But only once a month."

I smiled. "And you're weather sensitive."

"That's right." She asked me, "Are you going to tell me any more about this...this murder?"

"No, I'm not."

"All right. I understand. If you need anything from me, just ask. I'll do whatever I can to help."

"Thanks."

The ferry approached the slip, and she asked me, "Do you want to stay at my place tonight?"

"Well...I do, but...I should go home."

"I can stay at your place."

"Well...to tell you the truth, I was supposed to talk or to meet with Detective Penrose today, and I should see if I can still do that."

"All right."

And we left the matter there.

I dropped her off at her home. I said to her, "I'll see you tomorrow after work."

"Good. There's a nice restaurant on the water that I'd like to take you to."

"Looking forward to it." We kissed on her doorstep, and I got into my Jeep and drove home.

There were seven messages for me. I was in no mood for them and went to bed without playing them. They'd be there in the morning.

As I drifted off, I tried to figure out what to do about Fredric Tobin. There's sometimes this situation when you have your man, yet you don't have your man. There is a critical moment when you have to decide if you should keep stalking him, confront him, smoke him out, or pretend to lose interest in him.

I should have also been thinking that when you corner an animal or a man, he can become dangerous—that the game is played by both hunter and hunted, and that the hunted had a lot more to lose.

But I forgot to consider Tobin as a thinking, cunning animal because he struck me as such a fop, the same way I'd struck him as a simpleton. We both knew better, but we'd both been lulled a little bit by each other's act. In any event, I blame myself for what happened.

CHAPTER TWENTY-NINE

It was raining Monday morning when I woke up, the first rain we'd had in weeks, and the farmers were happy even if the vintners were not. I knew at least one vintner who had bigger problems than a heavy rain.

As I dressed, I listened to the radio and heard that a hurricane named Jasper was off the coast of Virginia, causing unsettled weather conditions as far north as New York's Long Island. I was glad I was driving back to Manhattan today.

I hadn't been to my Seventy-second Street condo in over a month, and I hadn't accessed my answering machine messages either, partly because I didn't want to, but mostly, I guess, because I forgot my access code.

Anyway, at about nine A.M., I went downstairs dressed in designer jeans and polo shirt and made coffee. I was sort of waiting for Beth to call or come by.

The local weekly was on the kitchen counter, unread from Friday, and I was not too surprised to see last Monday's murder on the front page. I took the paper out on the back porch with a mug of coffee and read the local hotshot reporter's version of the double

murder story. The guy was imprecise enough, opinionated enough, and was a bad enough stylist to write for
Newsday or the *Times.*

I noticed an article about Tobin Vineyards in which
Mr. Fredric Tobin was quoted as saying, "We will begin
the harvest any day now, and this promises to be a vintage year, perhaps the best in the last ten years, barring
a heavy rain."

Well, Freddie, it's raining. I wondered if condemned
men are allowed to request wine with their last meal.

Anyway, I threw the local weekly aside and
picked up Emma's gift, *The Story of Pirate Treasure.* I
flipped through it, looked at the pictures, saw a map of
Long Island, which I studied for a minute or so, then
found the chapters on Captain Kidd and read at random a deposition of Robert Livingston, Esq., one of
Kidd's original financial backers. The deposition read
in part,

> *That hearing Capt. Kidd was come into these parts
> to apply himself unto his Excellency, the Earl of
> Bellomont, the said Narrator came directly from
> Albany ye nearest way through the woods to meet
> the said Kidd here and wait upon his Lordship.
> And at his arrival at Boston, Capt. Kidd informed
> him there was on board his Sloop then in Port, forty
> bales of Goods, and some Sugar, and also said he
> had about eighty pound weight in Plate. And fur-
> ther the said Kidd said he had Forty pound weight
> in Gold which he hid and secured in some place in
> the Sound betwixt this and New York, not naming
> any particular place, which nobody would find but
> himself.*

I did a little math in my head and figured that forty pounds of gold would be worth about three hundred thousand dollars, on the hoof, so to speak, not counting whatever historical value or numismatic value it would have, which could easily quadruple the value according to what Emma had said.

I spent the next hour reading and the more I read, the more I was convinced that nearly every narrator in this episode, from Lord Bellomont to the lowest seaman, was a liar. No two stories were alike, and the value and amount of the gold, silver, and jewels were all over the lot. The only thing everyone agreed on is that treasure had been put ashore in various spots around the Long Island Sound. Not once was Plum Island mentioned, but what better place to hide something? As I'd learned on my trip to Plum, the island had no harbor then, so it was unlikely to be visited by random ships looking for food or water. It was owned by white settlers, and therefore off-limits to Indians, but was apparently uninhabited by anyone. And if Kidd dropped off a valuable treasure with John Gardiner, a man he didn't know, why wouldn't he sail the five or six miles across the bay to Plum Island and bury more treasure there? It made sense to me. I wondered, though, how Fredric Tobin had figured it out. He would be happy to tell us at his press conference when he announced his discovery. He'd probably say, "Hard work, a good knowledge of viniculture, perseverance, and a superior product. And good luck."

Anyway, I dawdled on the back porch for a long time, reading, watching the weather, working the case in my mind, waiting for Beth, who I thought should have arrived by now.

Finally, I went inside through the French doors that led to the den and played the seven messages on my answering machine.

Number one was from Uncle Harry saying he had a friend who wanted to rent the house, so would I mind buying it or leaving. Two, Detective Lieutenant Wolfe, who said simply, "You're pissing me off." Three, Emma's old unplayed message, a little before midnight on Friday just saying hello; four, Max on Saturday morning with the particulars on the Tobin party and saying he had a nice chat with Beth and would I call him. Five, Dom Fanelli, who said, "Hey, paisano, you missed a good time. What a night. The wine was flowing, we picked up four Swedish tourists in Taormina's, two of them airline stewardesses, one model, one actress. Anyway, I called our friend, Jack Rosen at the *Daily News*, and he's going to do a story on your return to New York after convalescing in the country. Wounded hero comes home. Beautiful. Give him a call Monday A.M. and the story will run Tuesday, so the humps at Police Plaza can read it before they bust your cojones. Am I good, or what? Call me Monday, and we'll have a drink P.M., and I'll tell you about the Swedes. Ciao."

I smiled. Four Swedes, my ass. Number six was Beth on Sunday morning asking where I'd disappeared to Saturday night, and when could we meet. And number seven was Beth on Sunday afternoon, acknowledging my message to her office and saying she'd be at my house on Monday morning.

So, when the doorbell rang a little before noon, I wasn't too surprised to see Beth there. I said, "Come in."

She left her umbrella on the porch and came in. She

was wearing another tailored suit, this one sort of a rust color.

I thought I should say I was alone, so I said, "I'm alone."

She said, "I know."

We looked at each other for some very long seconds. I knew what she was going to say, but I didn't want to hear it. She said it anyway. "Emma Whitestone was found in her house by one of her employees this morning, dead, apparently murdered."

I said nothing. What could I say? I just stood there.

Beth took my arm and led me into the living room to the couch. "Sit down," she said. I sat.

She sat beside me and took my hand. She said, "I don't know how you feel...I mean, I know you must have been fond of her...."

I nodded. For the second time in my life, I wasn't the one giving the bad news. I was the one hearing about the murder of someone I cared about. It was mind-numbing. I couldn't quite grasp it because it didn't seem real. I said to Beth, "I was with her until about ten last night."

Beth said, "We have no time of death yet. She was found in her bed...apparently killed by blows to the head with a fireplace poker that was found on the floor...there was no sign of forced entry...the back door was unlocked."

I nodded. He would have had a key which he never returned, and she never thought to change the lock. He knew there was a poker handy.

Beth continued, "There was the appearance of a burglary...pocketbook emptied, cash gone, jewelry box emptied. That sort of thing."

I took a deep breath, and said nothing.

Beth then told me, "Also, the Murphys are both dead. Apparently also murdered."

"My God."

Beth said, "A Southold PD was patrolling their street about once an hour and was keeping an eye on the Murphy house, but...he didn't see anything." She added, "When a new shift came on at eight A.M., the officer noticed that the newspaper was on the lawn and it was still there at nine. He knew that the Murphys rose early and took the paper in, so—" She asked me, "Do you want to hear this?"

"Go on."

"Okay...so he phoned them, then knocked on the front door, then went around back and saw that the rear door in the Florida room was unlocked. He went inside and found them in their bed. Both had died of apparent head injuries caused by a crowbar that he found on the floor with blood on it." She added, "The house was ransacked. Also, with the police presence on the street, it's assumed that the house was approached from the bay side."

I nodded.

Beth said, "You can imagine the Southold PD is in a state of uproar, and the whole North Fork will soon be. If they get one murder a year, that's a lot."

I thought of Max, who liked things quiet and peaceful.

Beth continued, "The county PD is sending a task force because now the thinking is that this is a psychotic who burglarizes houses and murders the occupants." She added, "I think that whoever killed the Gordons could have taken the Murphys' key from the

Gordon house, and that's why there was no forced entry and why the back door was unlocked." She added, "That would indicate some premeditation."

I nodded. Tobin knew he might have to get rid of the Murphys at some point and thought ahead far enough to take the key. When Beth mentioned that the Murphys' key was not found in the Gordon house, that should have alerted us. Another example of underestimating the killer. I said, "We should have predicted..."

She nodded. "I know." She continued, "As for Emma Whitestone...well, either she left her door unlocked or, again, someone had the key...someone she knew."

I looked at Beth and saw that we both knew who she was talking about. In fact, she said, "I had that surveillance put on Fredric Tobin Sunday morning, as you suggested, and it ran all day, but some higher-ups called it off from midnight to eight...for budgetary reasons...so, basically no one was watching Tobin after midnight."

I didn't respond.

She said, "I had trouble getting them to agree to *any* surveillance of Tobin. He's just not a suspect." She said pointedly, "I didn't have anything on him to warrant around-the-clock surveillance."

I was paying attention, but my mind kept returning to images of Emma, at my house, swimming in the bay, at the historical society party, in her bedroom where she was found murdered...what if I'd spent the night there? How would anyone know that she was alone...? It occurred to me that Tobin would have killed me, too, if he'd found me there, sleeping beside her.

Beth said, "By the way, I met Fredric Tobin at his

party, and he was very charming. But he's a little *too* slick...I mean, there's another side to that man... There's something not so nice right behind that smile."

I thought of Fredric Tobin and pictured him talking to Emma on the lawn at his party. As he spoke to her, he must have known he was going to murder her. I wondered, though, if he decided to kill her to keep her from talking to me anymore, or if he just wanted to say, "Fuck you, Corey. Fuck you for being a wiseass, fuck you for figuring out I killed the Gordons, fuck you for fucking my ex-girlfriend, and just plain fuck you."

Beth said, "I feel a little responsible for the Murphys."

I forced myself to think about the Murphys. They were decent people, helpful citizens, and unfortunately for them, witnesses to too much that had taken place next door over the last two years. I said, "I brought a photo of Fredric Tobin to the Murphys on Wednesday, and they ID'ed him as the guy with the white sports car....Tobin owns a white Porsche...." I explained my short visit to Edgar and Agnes Murphy.

Beth nodded. "I see."

I said, "The murderer is Fredric Tobin."

She didn't reply.

I said, "He killed Tom and Judy Gordon, Edgar and Agnes Murphy, maybe that Plum Island veterinarian, and Emma Whitestone. And maybe others." I added, "I'm taking this very personally."

I stood and said, "I need some air." I went out back and stood on the porch. The rain was heavier now, gray rain falling from a gray sky into a gray sea. The wind was coming off the bay from the south.

Emma. Emma.

I was still in the shock and denial stage, working up to the anger stage. The more I thought about Tobin bashing her head in with an iron poker, the more I wanted to bash his head in with an iron poker.

Like a lot of cops who have a personal and close-up encounter with crime, I wanted to use my power and knowledge to take care of it myself. But a cop can't be a vigilante, and a vigilante can't be a cop. On the other hand, there were times when you had to put the badge away and keep the gun....

CHAPTER THIRTY

Beth left me alone for a while, during which time I was able to get myself together. Finally, she came out on the back porch and gave me a mug of coffee laced with what smelled like brandy.

We both stood silently watching the bay. After a few minutes, she asked me, "What is this all about, John?"

I knew that I owed her some information. "Gold," I replied.

"Gold?"

"Yes. Buried treasure, maybe a pirate's treasure, maybe the treasure of Captain Kidd himself."

"Captain Kidd?"

"Yes."

"And it was on Plum Island?"

"Yes... as far as I can guess, Tobin somehow got onto this, and realizing he could never get access to one of the most inaccessible places in the country, he began looking for a partner who had unlimited access to the island."

She thought about that, then finally said, "Of course... it all makes sense now... the historical society, the digging, the house on the water, the speedboat...we were all so hung up on plague and then drugs...."

"Right. But when you completely discount those possibilities, as I did because I knew the Gordons weren't capable of that, then you have to rethink the whole thing."

She nodded and observed, "As Dr. Zollner said, When the only tool you have is a hammer, every problem looks like a nail."

I nodded.

"Tell me all of it. Go ahead."

I knew she was trying to get my mind off Emma's murder, and she was right that I had to work the case and do something positive. I said, "Okay...when I was on Plum Island, these archaeological digs struck me as totally out of character for Tom and Judy, and they knew I'd think that so they never mentioned it to me. I believe they were thinking ahead to a day—after they supposedly discovered treasure on their own land—when certain people might remember their digging on Plum Island and make a connection. So, the fewer people who knew, the better."

Beth remarked, "It wouldn't be the first time something valuable was moved and suddenly discovered in a more convenient place."

"That was the crux of the entire plan. The X on the pirate map had to be moved from Uncle Sam's land to Tom and Judy's land."

She thought a moment and asked me, "Do you think the Gordons knew exactly where the treasure was buried on Plum Island? Or were they trying to find it? I don't remember seeing too many fresh digs on the island."

"I think Tobin's information was reliable and believable, but maybe not very accurate. I learned a few things about pirate maps from Emma...and from this book here...." I pointed to the book on the end table. "And, as I learned, these treasures were meant only to be buried temporarily, so some of the landmarks on a map or some instructions turn out to be long-vanished trees, rocks that have been quarried or fallen into the sea...that sort of thing."

Beth asked me, "How is it that you decided to interview Emma?"

"I just wanted to check out the Peconic Historical Society. I was going to give it about an hour, and I really didn't care who I spoke to...then, I met her and in the course of conversation, it turns out she was once Tobin's girlfriend."

Beth contemplated all of this for a while as she stared out at the bay, then said, "So, next you interviewed Fredric Tobin."

"No, I interviewed him before I interviewed Emma."

"Then what led you to interview him? What possible connection would you think he had with the murders?"

"None, at first. I was doing junior detective work, talking to friends, not suspects. I'd met Tobin at his vineyard, back in July, with the Gordons." I explained about that and added, "I didn't care for him then, and I wondered why the Gordons did. After I spent a few hours with him on Wednesday, I decided he was an okay guy, personally, but he wasn't giving me the right answers to simple questions. You understand?"

She nodded.

"Then, after I spoke to Emma, I started to triangulate some relationships."

Again, she nodded, stared out at the rain, and seemed to be thinking. Finally she said, "I spent the same two days with forensics, the ME, Plum Island, and all that. Meanwhile, you're following a completely different scent."

"The very faintest of scents, but I didn't have much else to do."

"Are you still annoyed at the way you were treated?"

"I was. Maybe that's what motivated me. Doesn't matter. Point is, I'm giving this to you. I want Fredric Tobin arrested, convicted, and fried."

She looked at me and said, "That may not happen, and you know it. Unless we get some real solid evidence, this guy is not going to be convicted of anything. I don't even think the DA would try to indict him."

I knew that. I also knew that when the problem *was* a nail, all you needed was a hammer. I had a hammer.

Beth asked, "Well? Do you have anything more in the way of evidence?"

"Actually, I found a small flat-bottomed boat in Tobin's boathouse with a pole—the kind of thing you can use to move through wetlands. Also, an aerosol foghorn." I related my encounter with Tobin in the boathouse.

She nodded, then said to me, "Sit down." I sat in my wicker chair, and she sat in the rocker. She said, "Talk to me."

I spent the next hour briefing her, telling her everything I'd done since we parted Tuesday night, up to and including the fact that Tobin's girlfriend, Sondra

Wells, and the housekeeper had been away on the afternoon of the Gordon murders, yet Tobin had led me to believe they had been home.

Beth listened, staring out at the rain and the sea. The wind was getting heavier and actually howled once in a while.

When I finished, Beth said, "So, the Gordons' purchase of the Wiley property was not to double-cross Tobin."

"No. Tobin *told* the Gordons to buy the land, based on this legend of Captain Kidd's Ledges. There is also a place called Captain Kidd's Trees, but that's a public park now. Regarding the ledge or the bluff, this spot is not as well pinpointed in history books as the trees are, so Tobin knew that any bluff in the area would do. But he didn't want it to get around that *he* was buying useless land up on the bluffs—that would lead to all sorts of gossip and speculation. So he had the Gordons buy the land with their own money, which was limited, but they got lucky with that piece of Wiley land—or maybe Tobin knew about it. The plan then was to wait awhile before burying the treasure, then discovering it."

"Incredible."

"Yes. And because it's almost impossible to fake the age of a vertical shaft, they intended to tuck the treasure chest into the side of that bluff—on that ledge that we found—and then say it was exposed by erosion. Then, when they hacked it loose from the sand and clay, using picks and shovels, the site is basically destroyed, and the chest itself is in splinters, so the recovery of the chest makes it impossible for anyone to study the site."

She said again, "Incredible."

"These were three very bright people, Beth, and they had no intention of screwing up. They were going to snatch ten or twenty million dollars worth of treasure right from under Uncle Sam's nose, and the first that Uncle was going to hear about it was when it made the news. Enter the IRS, which they were prepared for." I explained about the treasure trove laws, income tax, and all that.

She thought a moment, then asked me, "But how was Tobin to get in on the money after the Gordons announced their find?"

"First of all, these three established that they'd been friends for almost two years. The Gordons had developed this interest in wine, which I don't think was real, but it was a good way to get Fredric Tobin and the Gordons seen together in public as friends." I explained what I'd discovered from Emma about the nature of the relationship. I said, "However, that didn't agree with what Tobin had told me about the relationship. So I had another interesting inconsistency."

She nodded. "Being friends is no reason to share millions of dollars in found treasure."

"No. So they concocted a whole story to go along with the discovery. Here's what I think.... First, they pretended they had developed a mutual interest in local history, and eventually that interest led to some information on pirate treasure. At this point, according to what they were going to put out to the press, they entered into a friendly agreement to search for and share whatever they found."

Beth nodded again. I could see she was mostly convinced of my reconstruction of what had taken place before the murders. I added, "The Gordons and Tobin would say they all pored through old archives in the various historical societies here, which is true, and they did the same in England, and so forth. They became convinced that the treasure was on the land owned by Margaret Wiley, and while they had some regrets about having suckered her out of that parcel, all's fair in treasure hunting, and so forth. They'd give Margaret a nice jewel or something. They'd also point out that they took a twenty-five-thousand-dollar risk because they couldn't be positive the treasure was there."

I sat back in my chair and listened to the wind and rain. I felt about as bad as I'd ever felt in my life, and I was surprised at how much I missed Emma Whitestone, who'd come into my life so quickly and unexpectedly, then moved into another life, somewhere among the constellations perhaps.

I took another deep breath, then continued, "I assume the Gordons and Tobin had some sort of phony documentation to back up their claim to have discovered this location in some archive. I don't know what they had in mind regarding this—a counterfeit parchment, or a photostat of what was supposed to be an original that was lost, or they could simply say, 'None of your business how we found this. We're still researching for more treasure.' The government doesn't care how they found it, only *where* they found it, and how much it's all worth." I looked at her. "Does this make sense to you?"

She thought about that and said, "It makes sense the way you laid it out . . . but I still think that someone would make the Plum Island connection."

"That's possible. But having a suspicion of where the treasure was found and proving it are very different."

"Yes, but it's a weak link in an otherwise good plan."

"Yes, it is. So let me give you another theory, one that fits what actually happened—Tobin had no intention of sharing anything with the Gordons. He led the Gordons to believe all of what I just said, he put them up to buying the land, and the three of them constructed this whole story about how they found the treasure and why they were going to share. In reality, Tobin, too, was afraid of the Plum Island connection. The Gordons were the solution to his problem of how to locate the treasure and move it from Plum Island. Then the Gordons became a liability, a weak link, an obvious clue to where the treasure had actually come from."

Beth stayed silent, rocking in the chair, and she nodded her head and said, "Three may keep a secret, if two of them are dead."

"Exactly."

I continued, "The Gordons were bright, but also a little naive, and they'd never come across anyone as evil and deceitful as Fredric Tobin. They never smelled a rat because they'd gone through this whole scenario, bought the land, and so forth. In reality, Tobin knew from the beginning that he was going to kill them. Most likely, he intended to either bury the treasure on his own property near Founders Landing, which is also an old historical site, and discover the treasure there—or he was going to fence the treasure, here or overseas, thereby keeping not only the Gordons' share, but Uncle Sam's share."

"Yes. I think that's a strong possibility, now that we see he's capable of cold-blooded murder."

"In any case, he's your man."

Beth sat with her chin in her hand, her feet hooked over the front rung of the rocker. She finally asked me, "How did you meet the Gordons? I mean, how is it that people with such an agenda took the time to... Are you following me?"

I tried to smile and replied, "You underestimate my charm. But it's a good question." I considered the question, not for the first time, and replied, "Maybe they really did just like me. Maybe, though, they did smell a rat, and they wanted a rat catcher close by. They also made the acquaintance of Max, so you should ask him how that came about."

She nodded, then asked me, "So, how *did* you meet them? I should have asked you that on Monday at the crime scene."

"You should have." I replied, "I met them at the bar in Claudio's. You know it?"

"Everyone does."

"I tried to pick up Judy at the bar."

"There's an auspicious start to a friendship."

"Right. Anyway, I thought the meeting was serendipitous, and maybe it was. On the other hand, the Gordons already knew Max, and Max knew me, and it may have been mentioned that the shot cop on TV was a friend of Max's and was convalescing in Mattituck. I had—and still only have—two hangouts, the Olde Towne Taverne and Claudio's. So, it's possible... but maybe not...it's hard to say. Almost doesn't matter, except as a point of interest." I added, "Sometimes things just happen by fate."

"They do. But in our job, we have to look for motives and agendas. Whatever is left over is fate." She looked at me and asked, "How do you feel, John?"

"Okay."

"I mean really."

"A little down. The weather doesn't help."

"Are you hurting?"

I didn't reply.

She informed me, "I spent some time talking to your partner on the phone."

"Dom? He never told me that. He would have told me."

"Well, he didn't."

"What did you speak to him about?"

"About you."

"*What* about me?"

"Your friends are worried about you."

"They damn well better be worried about *themselves* if they're talking about me behind my back."

"Why don't you cut the tough-guy stuff?"

"Change the subject."

"Fine." She stood and went to the railing and watched the bay, which was starting to swell and form whitecaps. She said, "Hurricane coming. May miss us." She turned to me and asked, "So, where is the treasure?"

"That's a very good question." I stood also and looked out at the rolling water. There wasn't a boat in sight, of course, and debris was starting to blow across the lawn. Whenever the wind dropped for a few seconds, I could hear the water slapping against the stony shore.

Beth asked me, "And where is our hard evidence?"

Still staring at the weather, I replied, "The answer to both of those questions may be in Mr. Tobin's home, office, or apartment."

She thought a moment, then said, "I'll present the

facts as I know them to an ADA and request that the DA's office apply for a search warrant."

"Good idea. If you can get a search warrant without probable cause, you're a lot smarter than I am." I added, "A judge would be a little skittish about issuing a search warrant on the homes and business of a prominent citizen with no previous problems with the law. You know that." I studied her face as she thought this over. I said, "That's what's so great about America. You don't have the police and the government crawling up your butt without due process. And if you're rich, you get even more due process than the average Joe."

She didn't reply to that, but asked me, "What do you think we ... I should do next?"

"Whatever you want. I'm off the case." The swells were turning into breaking waves now, unusual for this part of the bay. I recalled what Emma said about watching the water as a storm approached.

Beth said to me, "I know I can ... well, I *think* I can nail this guy if he did it."

"That's good."

"You're sure it was him?"

"I'm sure."

"And Paul Stevens?"

I replied, "He's still the joker in the deck. He may be Tobin's accomplice to murder, or Tobin's blackmailer, or a jackal waiting to pounce on the treasure, or he may be nothing more than a guy who always looks suspicious and guilty of *something*."

"We should talk to him."

"I did."

She raised her eyebrows. "When?"

I explained my unannounced visit to Mr. Stevens'

Connecticut home, leaving out the part where I decked him. I concluded, "At the very least, he's guilty of lying to us and conspiring with Nash and Foster."

She mulled that over and added, "Or he may be more deeply involved." She said, "Well ... maybe we can catch a forensic break at the two new murder scenes. That would be a clincher."

"Right. Meanwhile, Tobin will know what's going on around him, and he's got half the local politicians in his pocket, and probably has friends in the Southold PD."

"We'll keep Max out of this."

"Do what you have to do. Just don't spook Tobin because if he gets onto you, whatever evidence exists that's under his control is going to disappear."

"Like the treasure?"

"Right. Or the murder weapon. Actually, if I'd killed two people with my registered pistol and all of a sudden the cops were in my office, I'd ditch that thing in mid-Atlantic and claim it was lost or stolen." I added, "You should announce that you found one of the slugs. That will spook him if he still has the pistol. Then keep a tail on him and see if he tries to ditch the gun if he hasn't already."

She nodded and looked at me. She said, "I'd like you to work this case with me. Will you do that?"

I took her arm and led her inside to the kitchen. I took the phone off the hook and said, "Call his office, and see if he's there."

She dialed information, got the number of Tobin Vintners, and dialed. She said, "Mr. Tobin, please." She waited and looked at me. She asked, "What should I say to him?"

"Just thank him for a wonderful party."

Beth spoke into the phone. "Yes, this is Detective Penrose of the Suffolk County Police Department. I'd like to speak to Mr. Tobin."

She listened, then said, "Just tell him I called to thank him for a wonderful evening." She listened again, then asked, "Is there any way to reach him?" She glanced at me, then said into the phone, "Okay. Yes, that's a good idea." She hung up and said to me, "He's not in, not expected, and she doesn't know where to reach him. Also, they're about to close the winery because of the weather."

"Okay. Call his house."

She took her notebook out of her bag, found Tobin's unlisted number, and dialed. She said to me, "Am I calling his home to thank him for a wonderful evening?"

"You lost your grandmother's gold locket on his lawn."

"Right." She said into the phone, "Is Mr. Tobin in?" She listened, then asked, "Is Ms. Wells in then?" She listened again, then said, "Thank you. I'll call again...no, no message...no, don't be frightened. You should go to a designated emergency shelter.... Well, then call the police or fire department, and they'll come and get you. Okay? Do that now." Beth hung up. "The housekeeper. Eastern European lady. Doesn't like hurricanes."

"I'm not too keen on them either. Where is Mr. Tobin?"

"He's absent without explanation. Ms. Wells has gone to Manhattan until the storm blows over." Beth looked at me. "Where is he?"

"I don't know. But we know where he's not."

She said, "By the way, you should get out of this house. All waterfront residents have been advised to evacuate."

"Weather people are professional alarmists."

And with that, the lights flickered.

Beth said, "Sometimes they're right."

"I have to head back to Manhattan sometime today anyway. I have appointments tomorrow morning with those who will decide my fate."

"Then you'd better leave now. This is not going to get any better."

While I contemplated my options, the wind took a chair off my porch and the lights flickered again. I remembered I was supposed to call Jack Rosen at the *Daily News*, but I'd already missed the deadline for his column. Anyway, I didn't think the wounded hero cop was going to make it home today or tomorrow. I said to Beth, "Let's take a ride."

"Where?"

"To find Fredric Tobin—so we can thank him for a wonderful evening."

CHAPTER THIRTY-ONE

The rain was heavy and the wind sounded like a freight train.

I found two yellow ponchos in the coat closet and retrieved my .38, which I wore in my shoulder holster. The next thing to do was to get out of the driveway, which was covered with limbs and debris. I started the Jeep, threw it into gear, and ran over the fallen branches. I said to Beth, "Fourteen-inch clearance, four-wheel drive."

"Does it float?"

"We may find out."

I drove through the narrow lanes of my waterfront section of Mattituck, over more fallen limbs and past sailing trash can lids, then I found the road blocked by a toppled tree. I said, "I haven't been out in the country during a hurricane since I was a kid."

Beth informed me, "This isn't the hurricane, John."

I drove up on someone's lawn, around the huge fallen tree, and observed, "Looks like a hurricane to me."

"It has to reach wind speeds of sixty-five knots to be a hurricane. Now it's a tropical storm."

She turned on the radio to an all-news channel and, as expected, the top story was Jasper. The news guy said, "... tracking north-northeast, with wind speeds of up to sixty knots, which is about seventy miles an hour for you landlubbers. Its forward speed is about fifteen miles an hour, and if it continues on its present course, it will make landfall somewhere on the south shore of Long Island at about eight P.M. tonight. There are small craft warnings posted for the ocean and the Sound. Travelers are advised to stay at home and—" I shut off the radio. "Alarmist."

Beth said, "My house is pretty far inland, if you want to stop by later. From there, it's less than two hours by car or train to Manhattan, and you could leave after the worst of the storm has passed."

"Thank you."

We drove in silence awhile, then finally reached Main Road, which was clear of debris but flooded. There wasn't much traffic and almost all the businesses along the way were closed and some were boarded up. I saw an empty farm stand that had collapsed, and a utility pole that had fallen over, taking the telephone and electric wires with it. I said, "I don't think this is good for the vines."

"This is not good for anything."

Within twenty minutes, I pulled into the gravel parking lot of Tobin Vineyards. There were no cars in the lot, and a sign said, "Closed."

I looked up at the tower and saw there were no lights in any of the windows, though the sky was almost black.

On both sides of the parking lot were vineyards, and the staked vines were taking a beating. If the storm got any worse, the crop would probably be wiped out. I remembered Tobin's little lesson about the moderating influence of the maritime climate—which was true enough until you were in the path of a hurricane.

"Jasper."

"That's what it's called." She looked around at the parking lot and the winery and said, "I don't think he's here. I don't see any cars, and the place is dark. Let's try his house."

"Let's pop into the office first."

"John, the place is closed."

"Closed is a relative term."

"No, it isn't."

I drove toward the winery, then swung off to the right, out of the parking lot and onto a grassy area between the winery and the vineyard. I turned into the back of the big building where a few trucks sat parked among stacked empty wine barrels.

"What are you doing?" Beth asked.

I drove up to the back door at the base of the tower. "See if it's open."

She looked at me and started to say something.

"Just see if it's open. Do what I say."

She got out of the Jeep and ran to the door, pulling at the handle. She looked at me and shook her head, then started back toward the Jeep. I hit the gas and plowed the Jeep into the door, which flew open. I shut off the engine and jumped out. I grabbed Beth's arm and ran through the open door into the tower.

"Are you crazy?"

"There's a nice view at the top." The elevator, as I'd noticed, had a keyed entry, so I started up the stairs. Beth grabbed my arm and said, "Stop! This is called burglary, not to mention any civil rights violations—"

"This is a public building."

"It's closed!"

"I found the door broken in."

"John—"

"Go back to the Jeep. I'll take care of this."

We looked at one another, and she gave me that look that said, "I know you're angry, but don't do this."

I turned away from her and went up the stairs alone. On each landing, I tried the door to the offices, but they were all locked.

On the third-floor landing, I heard footsteps behind me and drew my .38. I waited at the back of the landing and saw Beth turn the corner. She looked up at me.

I said to her, "This is my felony. I don't need an accomplice."

She replied, "The door was broken in. We're investigating."

"That's what I said."

We continued up the stairs together.

On the fourth floor, the executive offices, the door was also locked. This didn't mean there was no one there—these fire exit doors could be locked on this side, but would have to open out from the other side. I banged on the steel door and kept banging.

Beth said, "John, I don't think anyone's in—"

"I hope not."

I ran up to the fifth floor and she followed. Again, I tried the knob, but it was locked.

Beth asked, "Is this his apartment?"

"Yes." In a glass case on the wall was the mandatory

steel-cut fire ax and a fire extinguisher. I took the extinguisher from the wall, smashed the glass, and extracted the ax. The noise of the breaking glass echoed up and down the stairs.

Beth almost screamed, "*What* are you doing?"

I pushed her back and swung the ax at the doorknob, which came right off, but the locking mechanism held. A few more swings opened the steel around the mechanism, and a final blow caused the door to swing inward.

I took a few deep breaths. My lung felt funny, as though I might have reopened something that had taken a long time to close.

"John, listen to me—"

"Quiet. Listen for footsteps." I pulled my piece from under my poncho, and she did the same. We stood motionless, and I peered into the doorway I'd just opened. Blocking my view into Tobin's apartment was a Japanese silk screen which hid the steel door from Mr. Tobin's delicate eyes. The apartment was dark and quiet.

I still had the ax in my left hand, and I pitched it through the door at the silk screen, which toppled over, revealing a large living room and dining room combination.

Beth whispered, "We can't go in there."

"We *have* to go in there. Someone smashed the door open. There're burglars somewhere."

The noise we'd made so far was loud enough to attract anyone who was around, but I didn't hear anything. I had to assume that the rear door was alarmed, but the storm had probably set off dozens of alarms all over the North Fork to various central station monitors.

In any case, we could handle the cops if they showed up—in fact, we *were* the cops.

I moved into the living room, my piece held in both hands, swinging in an arc from left to midpoint. Beth did the same from right to midpoint. She said, "John, this is not a good idea. Just calm down. I know you're upset, and I don't blame you, but you can't do this. We're going to back out of here and—"

"Quiet." I called out, "Mr. Tobin! Are you home, sir? You have visitors."

There was no reply. I went farther into the living room, which was lit only by the dark sky outside the big arched windows and by light filtering in from two big skylights in the twelve-foot-high ceiling. Beth slowly followed.

It was quite a place, as you can imagine—the living room was a semicircle with the round wall on the north. The other half of the tower, the south half, was divided into an open kitchen, which I could see into, and a bedroom that occupied the southwest quarter of the circle. The bedroom door was open, and I peered inside. I was satisfied that we were alone, or if Tobin was here, he was hiding under the bed or in a closet, scared witless.

I looked around the living room. In the gray light, I could see that the decor was sort of light-and-airy modern, to match the mood of a tower suite. The walls were decorated with watercolors that depicted local scenes which I recognized—Plum Island Lighthouse, Horton Point Lighthouse, some seascapes, a few ye olde shingled houses, and even the General Wayne Inn. I said, "Nice digs."

"Very nice."

"A fella could get lucky with the ladies up here."

No response from Ms. Penrose.

I moved to one of the windows facing north and watched the storm raging outside. I could see that some of the vines were down, and I imagined that the grapes that had not yet been picked were past ready now and would be taken by the wind.

Beth, sticking to my script, said, "There are no burglars here. We should leave and report that we found evidence of a break-in here."

"Good idea. I'll just make sure the perp fled." I gave her my keys. "Go sit in the Jeep. I'll be right down."

She hesitated, then said, "I'm going to move the Jeep to the parking lot. I'll wait fifteen minutes. No longer."

"Okay." I turned away from her and went into the bedroom.

This was a little more plush and soft, the room where God's gift to women carried the champagne bottles. In fact, there was a champagne stand and bucket near the bed. I'd be lying if I said I couldn't picture Emma in the bed with Mr. Wino. But that didn't matter anymore. She was dead, and he soon would be.

To the left was a big bathroom, multihead shower, Jacuzzi, bidet, the whole works. Yes, life had been good to Fredric Tobin, until he started spending more than he was making. It occurred to me that this storm would have wiped him out without a transfusion of gold.

There was a desk in the bedroom, and I pulled it apart, but I didn't find anything incriminating or useful.

I spent the next ten or so minutes tearing the place apart. Back in the living room, I found a locked closet and broke open the door with the fire ax, but the big walk-in closet seemed to contain only a sterling silver dinner service, some linens and crystal, a glass-doored wine refrigerator, a cigar humidor, and other necessities of the good life, including a large collection of video porn.

I ripped the closet apart, including the wine refrigerator, and again found nothing.

I walked around the living room with the fire ax in my hand, searching for whatever, and also working off a little frustration by smashing things with the ax.

There was a wall unit, or entertainment center, as they're called, with a TV, VCR, CD player, and all that, plus a few shelves of books. I took this apart, too, shaking out the books and tossing them aside.

Then something caught my eye. In a gold frame, about the size of a book, was an old parchment. I picked it up and turned it into the dim light from the window. It was a faded ink-sketched map with some writing on the bottom. I took it into the kitchen and laid it down on the counter near one of those plug-in emergency lights that give off a weak glow. I opened the frame and pulled out the parchment, which had ragged edges. I could see what it was now—a section of shoreline and a small inlet. The writing was really difficult, and I wished Emma was here to help.

At first, I thought the map might be of a piece of the Plum Island shore, but there were no inlets on Plum Island, only the harbor, which looked much different than what I could see on this map.

I then considered that this sketch might be of Mattituck Inlet, where Captain Kidd's Trees were, but there seemed to be little or no resemblance to the inlet I'd seen on my road atlas and in person. There was a third possibility, which was the bluffs or ledges, though again, I could see no similarity between that shoreline, which was very straight, and the one on this map, which was curved and showed an inlet.

Finally, I decided it had no meaning other than an old parchment that Tobin had decided to frame as a decoration. Right? Wrong. I kept staring at it, trying now to make out the faint words—then I saw two words I could read; they said, Founders Landing.

Now that I was oriented, I could see that this was in fact a map of about a quarter mile of coastline that took in Founders Landing, an unnamed inlet, and what today was the property of Fredric Tobin.

The writing on the bottom was obviously directions, and I could see numbers and made out the word "Oak."

I heard a noise in the living room and drew my piece.

Beth said, "John?"

"In here."

Beth came into the kitchen. I said, "I thought you were leaving."

"The Southold police arrived on a phone call from a watchman. I told them it was under control."

"Thanks."

She looked out at the living room and said, "This place is wrecked."

"Hurricane John."

"Feel better?"

"No."

"What do you have there?"

"A treasure map. It was in plain view, in this gold frame."

She looked at it. "Plum Island?"

"No. The Plum Island map or whatever led them to the treasure is long destroyed. This is a map of Founders Landing and what is now Tobin's property."

She said, "And?"

"Well, I'm sure it's a forgery. In my archival studies, I learned that you can buy authentic blank parchment from any time period in the last few centuries. Then, there are people in the city who will mix a little lamp carbon and oil or whatever, and write anything you ask them to write."

She nodded. "So, Tobin had this map made showing that there was treasure buried on his property."

"Yes. If you look hard, you can see that the writing seems to give directions. And if you look real hard... see that X?"

She held the parchment up and said, "I see it." She put it down and said, "He never intended to have the Gordons bury the treasure on the bluff."

"No. He intended to get the treasure from them, kill them, and bury it on his property."

"So, is the treasure now buried on Tobin's property?"

"Let's go find out."

"Another burglary?"

"Worse. If I find him home, I'm going to break his legs with this ax, then threaten to really hurt him if he doesn't talk." I added, "I can drop you off somewhere."

"I'll come along. You need taking care of, and I have to look for Grandma's locket on the lawn."

I put the parchment in my shirt under the poncho and grabbed the fire ax. On my way to the staircase, I flung a table lamp through one of the tall, arched windows. A gust of wind blew in through the shattered glass, whipping some magazines off the coffee table. "Sixty-five knots yet?"

"Getting there."

CHAPTER THIRTY-TWO

The ride from Tobin Vineyards to Founders Landing, usually about twenty minutes, took an hour because of the storm. The roads were strewn with branches and the rain was so hard on the windshield, I had to crawl along with my headlights on, though it was only five P.M. Every once in a while, a gust of wind blew the Jeep off-course.

Beth turned on the radio, and the weather guy said the storm had not been upgraded to a hurricane, but it was close. Jasper was still tracking north at fifteen miles per hour, and the edge of the storm was about sixty miles from the Long Island coast. The storm was picking up lots of moisture and strength over the open Atlantic. I commented, "These guys try to scare everyone."

"My father said the hurricane of September 1938 totally destroyed large areas of Long Island."

"My father told me about that one. Old people tend to exaggerate."

She changed the subject and said, "If Tobin is home, I'm going to handle it."

"Fine."

"I mean it. You'll play this my way, John. We're not going to do anything to compromise this case."

"We already did. And don't worry about perfecting a case."

She didn't respond. I tried to call my answering machine, but the phone kept ringing. I said, "The power's out in my house."

"Probably out all over by now."

"This is awesome. I think I like hurricanes."

"Tropical storm."

"Right. Those, too."

It occurred to me that I wasn't going to get back to Manhattan tonight, and therefore I wasn't going to make my mandatory meeting, and thus, I was in deep doo-doo on the job. I realized I didn't care.

I thought again of Emma, and it occurred to me that had she lived, my life would have gotten happier. For all my waffling about town or country living, I'd actually pictured myself here with Emma Whitestone, fishing, swimming, collecting chamber pots, or whatever people did out here. It occurred to me, too, that all my North Fork connections were now ended—Aunt June was dead, Uncle Harry was selling his place, Max and I would never repair whatever relationship we'd once had, the Gordons were dead, and now Emma was gone, too. Add to this, things didn't look too good in Manhattan either. I glanced at Beth Penrose.

She sensed my glance and looked back at me. Our eyes met and she said, "The sky is very beautiful after a storm passes."

I nodded. "Thanks."

The area around Founders Landing had a lot of

old-growth trees, and unfortunately, big pieces of them were on the road and lawns. It took another fifteen minutes of weaving around to get to the Tobin property.

The wrought iron gates were shut, and Beth said, "I'll get out and see if they're locked," but in the interest of time, I drove through them.

Beth said, "Why don't you see if you can get your adrenaline level down?"

"I'm trying."

As we moved up the long drive, I could see that the lawn where we'd had our party not so long ago was now covered with broken limbs, garbage cans, lawn furniture, and all sorts of debris.

The bay at the end of the lawn was wild, big waves breaking past the stone beach and onto the grass itself. Tobin's dock was holding up all right, but the boathouse had a lot of missing shingles. I said, "That's funny."

"What?"

"The Chris-Craft is missing."

Beth said, "Well, it must be in dry dock somewhere. No one would go out on the water on a night like this."

"Right."

I didn't see any cars in the driveway and the house was completely dark. I drove to the two-car garage, which was a separate building to the side and rear of the house. I veered right and drove the Jeep into the garage door, which crashed down in sections. I peered out the windshield and saw the white Porsche in front of me with a section of the garage door on top of it and a Ford Bronco on the other side of the garage. I said to Beth, "Two cars here—maybe the bastard's home."

"Let me handle him."

"Of course." I whipped the Jeep around and drove toward the rear of the house, across the back lawn to the patio where I stopped among some wind-scattered lawn furniture.

I got out, carrying the fire ax, and Beth rang the doorbell. We stood under the door canopy, but no one answered, so I opened the door with the ax. Beth said, "John, for God's sake, calm down."

We entered the kitchen. The electricity was off, and it was dark and quiet. I said to Beth, "Cover this door."

I went into the center hall and called up the stairs, "Mr. Tobin!" No one answered. "Are you home, Fredric? Hey, buddy!" *I'm going to chop your fucking head off.*

I heard a creak on the floor overhead, and I dropped the ax, drew my .38, and charged up the stairs, taking them four at a time. I swung around the newel post and headed for the area where I'd heard the creak. I shouted, "Hands up! Police! Police!"

I heard a noise in one of the bedrooms, and I charged in just in time to see the closet door close. I pulled it open, and a woman screamed. And screamed again. She was about fifty, probably the housekeeper. I said, "Where is Mr. Tobin?"

She covered her face with her hands.

"Where is Mr. Tobin?"

Beth was in the bedroom now, and she brushed past me and took the woman's arm. She said, "Everything is okay. We're the police." She led the woman out of the closet and sat her on the bed.

After a minute of nice talk, we learned that the

woman's name was Eva, that her English was not good, and that Mr. Tobin was not home.

Beth said to her, "His cars are in the garage."

"He come home, then he go."

"Go where?" Beth asked.

"He take the boat."

"The *boat*?"

"Yes."

"When? How long ago?"

"Not long," Eva replied.

"Are you sure?" Beth asked.

"Yes. I watch him." She pointed to the window. "The boat goes out there."

"He was alone?"

"Yes."

I said to Eva, "Stand here at the window."

She stood up and went to the window.

I said, "The boat—which way did the boat go? Which way?" I motioned with my hands.

She pointed to the left. "Go that way."

I looked at the bay. The Chris-Craft, the *Autumn Gold*, had headed east from the boathouse, but I couldn't see anything on the water except waves.

Beth asked me, "Why did he take the boat out?"

I replied, "Maybe to ditch the murder weapon."

"I think he could have picked a better day." She turned to Eva and asked, "*When* did he leave? Ten minutes? Twenty?"

"Maybe ten. Maybe more."

"*Where* was he going?"

She shrugged. "He say he be back tonight. Tell me to stay here. To not be afraid. But I am afraid."

"It's just a tropical storm," I informed her.

Beth took Eva by the hand and led her out of the bedroom, then down the stairs into the kitchen. I followed. Beth said to her, "You must stay on the ground floor. Stay away from the windows. Okay?"

Eva nodded.

Beth said, "Find candles, matches, and a flashlight. If you are afraid, go to the basement. Okay?"

Eva nodded again and went to one of the cupboards to get candles.

Beth thought a moment, then asked me, "Where is he *going* in this weather?"

I said, "He should be at the winery doing what he can to protect his property. But he's not going to the winery by boat." I said to Eva, "Did you see him walk to the boat? You understand?"

"Yes. I see him go to boat."

"Was he carrying anything?" I did a little pantomime. "In his hands?"

"Yes."

"What?"

She decided to clam up.

Beth said, "What did he carry?"

"Gun."

"Gun?"

"Yes. Big gun. Long gun."

"Rifle?" Beth pantomimed aiming a rifle.

"Yes, rifle." She held up two fingers and said, "Two."

Beth and I looked at each other.

Eva said, "And to dig." It was her turn to pantomime, and she made a digging motion. "To dig."

"Shovel?"

"Yes. Shovel. In garage."

I thought a moment and said to Eva, "And box? To carry? Bag? Box?"

She shrugged.

Beth said to me, "What do you think?"

I said, "Well, what I don't think is that Fredric Tobin went fishing with two rifles and a shovel." I said to Eva, "Keys. Where are keys?"

She led us to the wall phone, beside which was a key board. Tobin, compulsive neat-freak that he was, had tagged all the keys. I saw that the keys for the Chris-Craft were missing, but the Formula key was still there.

While I was contemplating my next rash move, Eva said, "Downstairs. Down to cellar."

We both looked at her. She was pointing to a door at the far end of the kitchen. She said, "He go downstairs. Something downstairs."

Beth and I looked at each other.

Clearly, Mr. Tobin was not Employer of the Year, and Eva was happy for the opportunity to rat him out—though I could see fear in her eyes, and I knew it was more than the hurricane that frightened her. I had no doubt Tobin would have murdered her if it weren't for the inconvenience of having a dead body on the property.

I walked to the door and turned the knob, but it was locked. I retrieved the fire ax and took up a batting stance.

Beth said, "Wait! We need probable cause to do that."

I said to Eva, "Do we have your consent to search?"

"Please?"

"Thank you." I swung the steel-cut ax at the door knob and smashed it right through the wood. I opened the door, revealing a narrow, dark staircase leading down to the basement. I said to Beth, "You're free to leave anytime."

Ms. Do-Right seemed to have an epiphany, an understanding that we were both in so deep, we might as well break any laws we may have missed. She got a flashlight from Eva and handed it to me. "You first, hero. I'll cover."

"Right." I went first, carrying the flashlight in one hand and the fire ax in the other. Beth drew her 9mm and followed.

It was a very old cellar with less than a seven-foot clearance. The foundation was stone and so was the floor. At first glance, it seemed that there wasn't much down there—it was too damp for storage and too grim and spooky for even a laundry room. Basically, it seemed to have only a furnace and hot water tank. I couldn't imagine what Eva was trying to tip us off to.

Then the flashlight beam rested on a long brick wall at the far end of the cellar, and we moved toward it.

The brick and mortar wall was of newer construction than the ancient stone foundation. The wall was basically a partition that bisected the cellar from front to rear and all the way up to the old oak beams.

In the dead center of the wall was a very nice carved oak door. My flashlight picked out a brass sign on the door that read, "His Lordship's Private Wine Cellar."

Since His Lordship was lacking a sense of humor, I assumed the sign was a gift from an admirer, or perhaps even Emma.

Beth whispered, "Should we go in?"

I replied, "Only if the door is unlocked. Rules of search and seizure." I handed her the flashlight and tried the big brass handle, but the door was locked and I noticed a brass keyhole above the handle. I said, "It's not locked, it's just stuck." I swung the ax at the keyhole and the oak door split, but held. I gave it a few more whacks and eventually it swung open.

Beth had switched off the flashlight as soon as the door swung in, and we were standing on either side of the door now with our backs to the brick wall, pistols drawn.

I called out, "Police! Come out with your hands up!"

No reply.

I pitched my ax in through the door and it landed with a metallic clank. But no one fired at it.

I said to Beth, "You go first. I've already been shot this year."

"Thanks." She got into a crouch and said, "I'm going right." She moved quickly through the door and I followed. I broke left, and we stayed motionless in a crouch with our pistols up and out.

I couldn't see a thing, but I felt that the room was cooler and maybe drier than the rest of the basement. I called out, "Police! Hands up!"

We waited another half minute, then Beth snapped on the flashlight. The beam traveled across the room illuminating a row of wine racks. She moved the light around the room. There was a table in the center of the room on which were two candelabra and some candlesticks. There were packs of matches on the table, and I lit about ten candles, which cast a flickering glow around the wine cellar and which danced off the bottles.

There were wooden racks all over the place as you'd expect in a wine cellar. There were also wooden crates and cardboard wine boxes, opened and unopened, piled here and there. There were six barrels of wine in cradles, each one tapped. I could see refrigeration coils on the walls protected by Plexiglas. The ceiling looked like cedar and the rough stone floor had been covered with smooth slates set in concrete. I remarked to Beth, "I keep my two bottles of wine in a kitchen cupboard."

Beth took the flashlight from me and examined some of the dust-covered bottles in one of the racks. She said, "These are vintage French wines."

I replied, "He probably keeps his own stuff in the garage."

She shone the light on the foundation wall where a few dozen cardboard boxes were stacked. She said, "There's some of his stuff there. And the barrels have his wine labels on them."

"Right."

We poked around awhile, noting a cabinet that held glasses, corkscrews, napkins, and such. We found thermometers hung here and there, all reading about 60 degrees Fahrenheit.

Finally, I said, "What was Eva trying to tell us?"

Beth shrugged.

I looked at Beth in the candlelight. She looked back at me. She said, "Maybe we should look at those crates and boxes."

"Maybe we should."

So, we started moving wooden crates and cardboard boxes. We ripped open a few of them, but there was only wine inside. Beth asked, "What are we looking for?"

"I don't know. Not wine."

In a corner where the two foundation walls met

was a stack of Tobin Vineyards wine boxes, all labeled "Autumn Gold." I went over to them and started pitching them off into an aisle between two wine racks. The sound of breaking glass filled the room as did the smell of wine.

Beth said, "You don't have to ruin good wine. Take it easy. Hand the boxes to me."

I ignored her and said, "Move out of the way."

I pitched the last layer of boxes away, and there, in the corner, between the wine boxes was something that wasn't wine. In fact, it was an aluminum ice chest. I stared at it in the candlelight.

Beth came up beside me, the flashlight in her hand shining on the chest. She said, "Is that what you were talking about? The aluminum chest from the Gordons' boat?"

"It certainly looks like it. But it's a common enough chest, and unless it has their fingerprints on it, which I'm sure it doesn't, then we'll never know for sure." I added, "My guess is that this is it—the chest everyone was convinced held dry ice and anthrax."

"It still may." She added, "I'm not completely buying the pirate treasure thing."

I said, "Well, I hope the fingerprint people can lift some prints off that brushed aluminum." I turned toward the door and started to leave.

"Wait. Aren't you going to . . . I mean . . ."

"Open it? Are you crazy? And tamper with evidence? We don't even belong here. We don't have a search—"

"Cut it out!"

"Cut what—?"

"Open the damned chest—no, I'll open it. Hold

this." She handed me the flashlight and crouched in front of the chest that lay between two wine boxes. "Give me a handkerchief or something."

I handed her my handkerchief, and with it in her hand, she opened the latch, then lifted the hinged lid.

I kept the beam of the flashlight pointed at the chest. I guess we expected to see gold and jewels, but before the lid was fully open, what we saw staring back at us was a human skull. Beth let out a startled sound, jumped back, and the lid fell shut. She stood a few feet from the chest and caught her breath. She pointed to the chest, but couldn't speak for a second, then said, "Did you see that?"

"Yeah. The guy's dead."

"Why...? What...?"

I crouched beside the chest and said, "Handkerchief." She handed it to me, and I opened the lid. The flashlight moved around the interior of the big aluminum chest, and I saw that the skull sat amongst some bones. The skull itself had a copper coin in each eye socket, thick with verdigris.

Beth crouched beside me and had her hand on my shoulder for balance or reassurance. She'd gotten herself under control and said, "It's part of a human skeleton. A child."

"No, a small adult. People were smaller then. Did you ever see a seventeenth-century bed? I slept in one once."

"My God....Why is there a skeleton...? What is that other stuff...?"

I reached into the chest and extracted something unpleasant to the touch. I held it up to the flashlight.

"Rotted wood." I could see now that beneath the bones were a few pieces of rotted wood, and on closer examination, I found brass fittings covered with verdigris, and some iron nails which were mostly rust, and a piece of rotted cloth.

The bones were not bleached white, they were reddish brown, and I could see that soil and clay still clung to them, indicating they hadn't been buried in a coffin, but had lain in the earth for a long time.

I poked around the stuff in the ice chest and found a rusted iron padlock and four gold coins, which I gave to Beth.

I stood and wiped my hand on the handkerchief. "Captain Kidd's treasure."

She looked at the four gold coins in her hand. *"This?"*

"That's part of it. What I see here is part of a wooden chest, pieces from the lid that was forced open, I would guess. The chest was wrapped in that rotting oilcloth or canvas to keep it waterproof for a year or so, but not for three hundred years."

She pointed to the skull and said, "Who's *that*?"

"I guess that's the guardian of the treasure. Sometimes a condemned man or a native or a slave or some unlucky guy was murdered and thrown in on top of the chest. They believed in those days that a murdered man's ghost was restless and would drive away anyone who dug up his grave."

"How do you know that?"

"I read it in a book." I added, "And for those who weren't superstitious, and who may have seen people burying something or saw fresh earth, if they dug, the first thing they saw was a corpse, and they might think it was only a grave. Clever, yes?"

"I guess. It would keep *me* from digging any further."

We both stood there in the wine cellar awhile, deep in our own thoughts. The contents of the aluminum chest didn't smell all that good, so I bent over and closed the lid. I said to Beth, "I suppose this was all going to be displayed at some place and time, along with the gold and jewels."

She stared at the four gold coins in her hand and again asked, "But *where* is the treasure?"

"If bones could speak, I'm sure he'd tell us."

"Why does he have coins in his eyes?"

"Something to do with some superstition or another."

She glanced at me and said, "Well, you were right. I congratulate you on a remarkable piece of detective work."

"Thank you," I said. "Let's get some fresh air."

CHAPTER THIRTY-THREE

We went back upstairs, and I saw that Eva was no longer in the kitchen. Beth said to me, "I may have enough here to get a search warrant."

"No, you don't. What we found here is not connected in any way to any of the murders except through circumstantial evidence. And then only if you believe my line of reasoning." I reminded her, "Three potential witnesses are dead."

Beth said, "Okay... but I have human remains here. That's a start."

"That's true. It's worth a phone call." I added, "Don't mention that the bones could be about three hundred years old."

Beth picked up the wall phone. "Dead," she said.

I gave her my car keys and said, "Try my cell phone."

She went out the back door and jumped in the Jeep. I saw her dial and speak to someone.

I walked around the ground floor of the house. It was decorated in what appeared to be real antiques, but could have been good reproductions. The style and period seemed mostly English country stuff, maybe mid-eighteen hundreds. The point was, Fredric Tobin knew how to spend it. He'd constructed an entire world of leisure, good taste, and sophistication more suitable to the Hamptons than to the North Fork, which prided itself on simple American tastes and virtues. Undoubtedly Tobin would rather have been in Bordeaux, or at least living in the Hamptons next door to Martha Stewart, swapping recipes with her for stuffed hummingbird tongues; but for the time being, like most people, he had to live near where he worked, where the wine made his bread. In the living room, there was a beautiful carved wood curio cabinet with curved and beveled glass filled with what looked like priceless objects. I pushed the cabinet over, and it made a loud crash followed by little tinkling sounds. I love that sound. My ancestors must have been Vandals or Visigoths or something.

There was a small den off the living room, and I poked around His Lordship's desk, but he kept very little there. There were a few framed photos, one of Sondra Wells, another of his true love—himself, standing on the fly bridge of his cabin cruiser.

I found his address book and looked up Gordon. Tom and Judy were listed, but they'd been crossed off. I looked up Whitestone and saw that Emma, too, had a line through her name. Considering he'd murdered her only this morning, and the news was not even out yet, this showed a very sick and orderly mind. The sort of mind that sometimes worked against the person who possessed it.

There was a fireplace in the room, and above the mantel were rifle pegs for two weapons, but neither weapon was there. Eva was proving to be a reliable witness.

I went back to the kitchen and looked out the rear window. The bay was angry, as the old salts would say, but not totally pissed off yet. Still, I couldn't imagine what would send Fredric Tobin out on a day like this. Actually, I could imagine what. I had to play with it in my mind a little.

Beth came back in the house, her poncho wet from the short run between the Jeep and the door. She gave me my keys and said, "There is a forensic team at the Murphy house, and another at...the other scene." She added, "I am no longer heading the Gordon investigation."

"Tough break." I added, "But don't worry about it. You've already solved the case."

"You solved it."

"*You* have to make it stick. I don't envy you that job. Tobin can bring you down, Beth, if you're not careful with how you proceed."

"I know...." She glanced at her watch and said, "It's 6:40. There are forensic and homicide people on the way here, but it'll take them a while to get through this storm. They'll be working on a search warrant before they enter. We should be outside when they get here."

"How do you explain that you were already inside the premises?"

"Eva let us in. She was frightened—felt she was in danger. I'll finesse that." She added, "You don't have to worry about it. I'll say I went down to the basement to check the electric."

I smiled. "You're getting good at covering your ass. You must be hanging out with street cops."

"You owe me some cover on this, John. You broke every rule in the book."

"I barely got through page one."

"And that's as far as you're getting."

"Beth, this guy killed three people I was fond of and an innocent elderly couple. The last three people wouldn't have died if I'd moved faster and thought harder."

She put her hand on my shoulder. "Do *not* blame yourself. The police were responsible for the Murphys' safety....As for Emma...well, I know I wouldn't have guessed that she was in danger—"

"I don't want to discuss it."

"I understand. Look, you don't need to speak to the county cops when they get here. Take off, and I'll handle it."

"Good idea." I tossed her my car keys and said, "See you later."

"Where are you going without your keys?"

"For a boat ride." I took the Formula key from the keyboard.

"Are you crazy?"

"The jury's out on that. See you later." I headed toward the back door.

Beth held my arm. "No, John. You'll get killed out there. We'll catch up with Fredric Tobin later."

"I want him, now, with fresh blood on his hands."

"No." She was really squeezing my arm now. "John, you don't even know where he went."

"There's only one place he would go on a night like this in a boat."

"Where is that?"

"You know where—Plum Island."

"But why?"

"I think the treasure is still there."

"How do you know that?"

"Just a guess. Ciao." Before she could get in my way again, I left.

I headed across the lawn toward the boat. The wind was really howling, and a huge branch fell not far from me. There was almost no daylight left, which was fine because I didn't want to see what the water looked like.

I made my way along the dock, holding on to the pilings, then sprinting to the next one so as not to get blown off into the water. Finally, I reached the boathouse, which was creaking and groaning. In the dim light, I saw that the Formula 303 was still there, but I noticed that the Whaler was gone, and I wondered if it had broken loose and been washed away, or if Tobin was towing it behind the Chris-Craft, either as a lifeboat or as a way to get onto the beach at Plum Island.

I stared at the Formula rising and falling on the swells and thumping against the rubber bumpers on the floating dock. I hesitated a moment, trying to get into a rational frame of mind, telling myself that it wasn't necessary for me to take a boat into a storm. Tobin was finished, one way or another. Well...maybe not. Maybe I had to finish him before he got himself lawyered up and alibied and outraged at my violations of his civil rights. Dead men can't sue.

I kept staring at the Formula, and in the dim light, I thought I saw Tom and Judy on board, smiling and motioning for me to join them. Then, an image of Emma flashed in my mind, and I saw her again, swimming in the bay smiling at me. And then I saw Tobin's face at his party as he was speaking to her, knowing he was going to kill her. . . .

Beyond the legal necessities, I realized that the only way I could bring closure to this case for me personally was to capture Fredric Tobin myself, and having captured him, to . . . well, I'd think about that later.

The next thing I knew, I was jumping from the dock into the speedboat.

I caught my balance on the pitching deck and made my way to the right-hand seat, the captain's seat.

I experienced my first problem, which was finding the ignition. I finally found it near the throttle. I tried to recall what I'd seen the Gordons do and remembered that they'd once handed me a printed plastic card titled "Suddenly in Command," and told me to read it. I had read it and decided I didn't want to be suddenly in command. But now I was. I wished I still had the card.

Anyway, I remembered to put both gear selectors in neutral, put the key in the ignition, move it to on . . . then . . . what . . . ? Nothing was happening. I saw two buttons marked "start" and pushed the right one. The starboard engine turned over and fired. Then I pressed the second button and the port engine started. I felt them running a little rough, and I pushed both throttles slightly forward and gave them more gas. I remembered I had to let the engines warm a few minutes. I didn't want to stall out in that sea. While they were warming, I found a knife in the open glove compartment in the dashboard and cut the spring line, then both mooring lines, and the Formula immediately rolled with a wave and smashed into the side of the boathouse about five feet from the dock.

I shifted into forward gear and gripped the dual throttles. The bow was pointed to the bay, so all I had to do was push forward on the throttles, and I would be out into the storm.

Just as I was about to do this, I heard something behind me and looked over my shoulder. It was Beth, calling my name over the noise of the wind, water, and motors.

"JOHN!"

"What?"

"Wait! I'm coming!"

"Then come on!" I shifted the boat into reverse, grabbed the wheel, and managed to back the boat closer to the dock. "Jump!"

She jumped and landed on the rolling deck behind me, then fell.

"Are you okay?"

She stood, then a swell pitched the boat, and she fell again, then stood again. "I'm okay!" She made her way to the left-hand seat and said, "Let's go."

"Are you sure?"

"Go!"

I pushed the throttles forward, and we cleared the boathouse into the driving rain. A second later, I saw a huge wave coming at us from the right, and it was going to hit us broadside. I cut the wheel right and got the bow into the wave. The boat rode up, hung on to the crest as if it were in midair, then the wave broke behind me, leaving the boat literally in midair. The boat came down, bow first, digging into the swelling sea. Then the bow rose and the stern hit the water. The propellers caught, and we were off, but in the wrong direction. In the trough between waves, I swung the boat around 180 degrees and headed east. As we passed the boathouse, I heard a sharp crack and the entire structure leaned to the right, then collapsed onto the boiling sea. "Jeez!"

Beth called out over the noise of the storm, "Do you know what you're doing?"

"Sure. I took a course once called Suddenly in Command."

"About boats?"

"I think so." I looked at her, and she looked back at me. I said, "Thanks for coming."

She said, "Drive."

The Formula was at half throttle, which is how I think you're supposed to keep control in a storm. I mean, we seemed to be above the water about half the time, flying over the troughs, then slicing right into the oncoming waves where the propellers would whine, then bite into the water and shoot us forward like a surfboard into the oncoming sea again. The one thing I knew I had to do was to keep the bow into the oncoming waves and keep from being broadsided by a big one. The boat would probably not sink, but it could capsize. I'd seen capsized boats in the bay after lesser storms than this.

Beth called out, "Do you know how to navigate?"

"Sure. Red right return."

"What does that mean?"

"You keep the red marker on your right when returning to harbor."

"We're not returning to the harbor. We're leaving."

"Oh...then look for green markers."

"I don't see *any* markers," she informed me.

"Neither do I." I added, "I'll just stay to the right of the double white line. Can't go wrong doing that."

She didn't reply.

I tried to get my head into a nautical frame of mine. Boating is not my number one hobby, but I'd been a guest on a lot of boats over the years, and I figured I'd sucked up some facts since I was a kid. And in June, July, and August, I'd been out with the Gordons about a dozen times, and Tom was a nonstop chatterer, and he liked to share his nautical enthusiasm and knowledge with me. I don't recall paying a lot of attention (being more interested in Judy in her bikini), but I was positive there was a little pigeonhole in my cerebral cortex labeled "Boats." I just had to locate it. In fact, I was sure I knew more about boats than I realized. I hoped so.

We were now well into the Peconic Bay, and the boat was slamming very hard into the water—jarring, teeth-rattling thumps, one after the other, like a car driving over railroad ties, and I could feel my stomach getting out of sync with the vertical movement of the boat; when the boat was down, my stomach was still up, and when the boat was tossed into the air, my stomach dropped down. Or so it seemed. I couldn't see a thing through the windshield, so I stood and looked over the windshield, my butt braced against the seat behind me, my right hand on the steering wheel, my left on a handgrip on the dashboard. I'd swallowed enough saltwater to raise my blood pressure fifty points. Also, the salt was starting to burn my eyes. I glanced at Beth and saw she was wiping her eyes, too.

To my right, I saw a huge sailboat lying on its side in the water, its keel barely visible and its mast and sail swamped. "Good God...."

Beth said, "Do they need help?"

"I don't see anyone."

I got closer to the sailboat, but there was no sign of anyone clinging to the masts or rigging. I found the horn button on the dashboard and gave a few blasts, but I still didn't see any signs of life. I said to Beth, "They may have taken a life raft to shore."

Beth didn't reply.

We pressed on. I remembered that I was the guy who didn't even like the gentle rolling of the ferryboat, and here I was in a thirty-foot open speedboat plowing through a near hurricane.

I could feel the impacts in my feet, like someone was slapping the soles of my shoes with a club, and the shock traveled up my legs to my knees and hips, which were starting to ache now. In other words, it sucked.

I was getting nauseous from the salt, the motion, the constant slamming into the waves, and also from my inability to see or separate the horizon from the water. Add to this my precarious post-trauma physical condition....I recalled Max assuring me this wouldn't be strenuous. If he were here now, I'd tie him to the bow.

Through the rain, I could see the shoreline to my left about two hundred yards, and up ahead to my right I could see the dim outline of Shelter Island. I knew we would be a little safer once I got into the protected passage on the leeward side of the island, which I guess is why it's called Shelter Island. I said to Beth, "I can put you ashore on Shelter Island."

"You can steer the damned boat and stop worrying about frail little Beth."

"Yes, ma'am."

She added, in a nicer tone of voice, "I've been on rough water before, John. I know when to panic."

"Good. Tell me when."

"Close," she said. "Meanwhile, I'm going below to get some life vests and see if I can find something more comfortable to wear."

"Good idea." I added, "Wash the salt out of your eyes and also look for a chart."

She disappeared down the companionway between the two seats. The Formula 303 has a good-sized cabin for a speedboat and also has a head, which might come in handy real soon. Basically, it's a comfortable, seaworthy craft, and I always felt safe when Tom or Judy was at the helm. Also, Tom and Judy, like John Corey, didn't like rough weather, and at the first sign of a whitecap, we'd be heading back. Yet here I was, confronting one of my A-List fears, looking it right in the eye, so to speak, and it was spitting at me. And crazy as it sounds, I almost enjoyed the ride—the feel of the throttles as I adjusted power, the vibrations of the engines, the helm in my hand. Suddenly in command. I'd been sitting on the back porch too long.

I stood, one hand on the wheel, one on the top of the windshield to keep my balance. I peered into the driving rain, scanning the heaving sea for a boat, a Chris-Craft to be exact, but I could barely make out the horizon or the shore, let alone another boat.

Beth came up the stairs and handed me a life vest. "Put this on." She shouted, "I'll hold the wheel." Still standing, she took the wheel as I put on the life vest. I saw that she had a pair of binoculars hung around her neck. She also had a pair of jeans under her yellow slicker and was wearing a pair of boating shoes as well as an orange life vest. I asked, "Are you wearing Fredric's clothes?"

"I hope not. I think these belong to Sondra Wells. A little tight." She added, "I laid a chart out on the table if you want to take a look."

I asked her, "Can you read a chart?"

"A little. How about you?"

"No problem. Blue is water, brown is land. I'll look at it later."

Beth said, "I looked for a radio down there, but I didn't see one."

"I can sing. Do you like 'Oklahoma'?"

"John . . . please don't be an idiot. I mean, the ship-to-shore radio. To send distress calls."

"Oh . . . that. Well, there's no radio here either."

She said, "There's a mobile phone recharger down below, but no phone."

"Right. People tend to use mobile phones in small boats. Me, I prefer a two-way radio. In any case, what you're saying is that we're out of touch."

"That's right. We can't even send an SOS."

"Well, neither could the people on the *Mayflower*. Don't worry about it."

She ignored me and said, "I found a signal pistol." She tapped the big pocket of her slicker.

I didn't think anyone could see a signal flare tonight, but I said, "Good. We may need it later."

I took the helm again, and Beth sat on the stairs in the companionway beside me. We took a break from shouting above the storm and sat in silence awhile. We were both soaked, our stomachs were churning, and we were scared. Yet some of the terror of riding through the storm had passed, I think, as we realized that every wave was not going to sink us.

After about ten minutes, Beth stood and moved

close to me so she could be heard. She asked, "Do you really think he's going to Plum Island?"

"I do."

"Why?"

"To recover the treasure."

She said, "There won't be any of Stevens' patrol boats or any Coast Guard helicopters around in this storm."

"Not a one. And the roads will be impassable, so the truck patrols can't get around."

"True...." She asked, "Why didn't Tobin wait until he had all the treasure before he killed the Gordons?"

"I'm not sure. Maybe the Gordons surprised him while he was searching their house. I'm sure that all the treasure was supposed to be recovered, but something went wrong."

"So he has to recover the treasure himself. Does he know where it is?"

I replied, "He must, or he wouldn't be heading there. I found out from Emma that Tobin was on the island once with the survey group from the Peconic Historical Society. At that time, he would have made sure that Tom or Judy showed him the actual site of the treasure, which, of course, was supposed to be one of Tom's archaeological holes." I added, "Tobin was not a trusting man, and I have no doubt that the Gordons didn't particularly like him or trust him either. They were using one another."

She said, "There's always a falling-out among thieves."

I wanted to say that Tom and Judy were not thieves, yet they were. And when they crossed that line from honest citizens to conspirators, their fate was basically sealed. I'm no moralist, but in my job, I see this every day.

Our throats were raw from shouting and from the salt, and we lapsed back into silence.

I was approaching the passage between the south coastline of the North Fork and Shelter Island, but the sea seemed to be worse at the mouth of the strait. A huge wave came up out of nowhere and hung for a second over the right side of the boat. Beth saw it and screamed. The wave broke right over the boat, and it felt as if we'd run into a waterfall.

I found myself on the deck, then a torrent of water washed me down the stairs, and I landed on the lower deck on top of Beth. We both scrambled to our feet and I clawed my way up the stairs. The boat was out of control, and the wheel was spinning all over the place. I grabbed the wheel and held it steady as I got myself into the seat, just in time to turn the bow into another monster wave. This one took us up on its rising slope, and I had the weird experience of being about ten feet in the air with both shorelines appearing lower than I was.

The wave crested and left us in midair for a second before we dropped into the next trough. I fought the wheel and got us headed east again trying to make it into the strait, which had to be better than this.

I looked to my left for Beth, but didn't see her on the companionway stairs. I called out, "Beth!"

She shouted from the cabin, "I'm here! Coming!"

She came up the stairs on her hands and knees, and I saw that her forehead was bleeding. I asked, "Are you all right?"

"Yes…just got knocked around a little. My butt is sore." She tried to laugh, but it almost sounded like a sob. She said, "This is crazy."

"Go below. Make yourself a martini—stirred, not shaken."

She said, "Your idiotic sense of humor seems to fit the situation." She added, "The cabin is starting to take on water, and I hear the bilge pumps going. Can you come up with a joke for that?"

"Well...let's see...that's not the bilge pump you hear, it's Sondra Wells' electric vibrator underwater. How's that?"

"I may jump." She asked me, "Can the pumps keep up with the water we're taking on?"

"I guess. Depends on how many waves break on board." In fact, I'd noticed the response to the helm was sluggish, the result of the weight of the water now in the bilge and cabin.

Neither of us spoke for the next ten minutes. Between gusts of wind-driven rain, I could see about fifty yards ahead for a few seconds, but I didn't see Tobin's cabin cruiser, or any boat for that matter, except two small craft, capsized and tossed like driftwood by the storm.

I noticed a new phenomenon, or perhaps I should say a new horror—it was something that the Gordons called a following sea, which I had experienced with them in the Gut that day. What was happening was that the sea behind the boat was overtaking it, smashing into the Formula's stern and whipping the boat almost out of control in a violent side-to-side motion, called yawing. So now, along with rolling and pitching, I had to contend with yawing. About the only two things that were going right were that we were still heading east and we were still afloat, though I don't know why.

I tilted my head back so that the rain could wash

some of the salt from my face and my eyes. And since I was looking up at the sky anyway, I said to myself, *I went to church Sunday morning, God. Did you see me there? The Methodist place in Cutchogue. Left side, middle pew. Emma? Tell Him. Hey, Tom, Judy, Murphys— I'm doing this for you guys. You can thank me in person in about thirty or forty years.*

"John?"

"What?"

"What are you looking at up there?"

"Nothing. Getting some freshwater."

"I'll get you some water from below."

"Not yet. Just stay here awhile." I added, "I'll give you the wheel later, and I'll take a break."

"Good idea." She stayed silent a minute, then asked me, "Are you . . . worried?"

"No. I'm scared."

"Me, too."

"Panic time?"

"Not yet."

I scanned the dashboard and noticed the fuel gauge for the first time. It read about an eighth full, which meant about ten gallons left, which, considering the rate of fuel burn of these huge MerCruisers at half throttle fighting a storm, meant we didn't have much time or distance left. I wondered if we could make it to Plum Island. Running out of gas in a car is not the end of the world. Running out of gas in an airplane *is* the end of the world. Running out of gas in a boat during a storm is *probably* the end of the world. I reminded myself to keep an eye on the gas gauge. I said to Beth, "Is it a hurricane yet?"

"I don't know, John, and I don't give a damn."

"I'm with you."

She said, "I had the impression you were not fond of the sea."

"I like the sea just fine. I just don't like to be *on* it or *in* it."

"There are a few marinas and coves along here on Shelter Island. Do you want to put in?"

"Do you?"

"Yes, but no."

"I'm with you," I said.

Finally, we got into the passage between the North Fork and Shelter Island. The mouth of the strait was about half a mile wide, and Shelter Island to the south had enough elevation and mass to block at least some of the wind. There was less howling and splashing, so we could talk easier, and the seas were just a bit calmer.

Beth stood and steadied herself by holding on to the grab handle mounted on the dashboard above the companionway. She asked me, "What do you think happened that day? The day of the murders?"

I replied, "We know the Gordons left the harbor at Plum Island about noon. They went far enough offshore so that the Plum Island patrol boat couldn't identify them. The Gordons waited and watched with binoculars and saw the patrol boat pass. They then opened the throttles and raced toward the beach. They had forty to sixty minutes before the boat came around again. We established this fact on Plum Island. Correct?"

"Yes, but I thought we were talking about terrorists, or unauthorized persons. Are you telling me you were thinking about the Gordons even then?"

"Sort of. I didn't know why, or what they were up

to, but I wanted to see *how* they could pull something off. A theft. Whatever."

She nodded. "Go on."

"Okay, they make a high-speed dash and get close to the shore. If a patrol vehicle or a helicopter spots their boat anchored, it's not a major problem because by now everyone knows who they are and recognizes their distinctive boat. Yet according to Stevens, no one did see their boat that day. Correct?"

"So far."

"Okay, it's a nice, calm summer day. The Gordons take their rubber raft onto the beach and drag it into the bush. On the raft is the aluminum chest."

"And shovels."

"No, they've already uncovered this treasure and hidden it where they could get at it easily. But first, they had to do a lot of groundwork, like archival and archaeological work, buying the Wiley land, and so forth."

Beth thought a moment, then asked, "Do you think the Gordons were holding out on Tobin?"

"I don't think so. The Gordons would be satisfied with half the treasure, minus half of that to the government. Their needs weren't anywhere near what Tobin's were. And also, the Gordons wanted the publicity and the acclaim of being the finders of Captain Kidd's treasure." I added, "Tobin's needs, however, were different and his agenda was different. He had no scruples about killing his partners, taking the whole treasure, fencing most of it, and then discovering a small portion of it on his own land and holding an auction at Sotheby's, complete with media and the IRS guy in the back."

Beth reached under her slicker and retrieved the four gold coins. She held them out toward me, and

I took one and examined it while I steered the boat. The coin was about the size of an American quarter, but it was heavy—the weight of gold always surprised me. The gold was amazingly bright, and I could see a guy's profile on it and some writing that looked Spanish. "This could be what's called a doubloon." I handed it back to her.

She said, "Keep it for luck."

"*Luck*? I don't need the kind of luck this brought to anyone."

Beth nodded, looked awhile at the three coins in her hand, then threw them over the side. I did the same.

This was an idiotic gesture, of course, but it made us feel better. I could understand the universal sailors' superstition about throwing something valuable—or someone—over the side to appease the sea and make it stop doing whatever the hell it was doing that was scaring the crap out of everybody.

So we felt better after we threw the gold overboard, and sure enough the wind dropped a little as we made our way along the Shelter Island coast, and the waves had diminished in height and frequency as if the gift to the sea had worked.

The land masses around me looked black, totally devoid of color like piles of coal, while the sea and sky were an eerie gray luminescence. Normally at this hour, you could see lights along the coast, evidence of human habitation, but apparently the power was out all over and the coasts had slipped back a century or two.

All in all, the weather was still a horror show, and it would become deadly again once we cleared Shelter Island and got out into Gardiners Bay.

I knew I was supposed to turn on my running

lights, but there was only one other boat out here, and I didn't want to be seen by that boat. I was certain he wasn't running with his lights either.

Beth said, "So the Gordons didn't have time to go back for a second load before the Plum Island patrol boat came around again."

"Right," I answered, "a rubber raft can hold only so much, and they didn't want to leave the bones and so forth unguarded on the Formula while they went back for a second trip."

Beth nodded and said, "So they decided to get rid of what they'd already recovered and come back for the main treasure some other time."

"Right. Probably that very night, if the temporary clove hitch was an indication." I added, "They had to pass Tobin's house on Founders Landing on the way back to their house. I have no doubt they pulled into his boathouse, maybe intending to leave the bones, the rotted sea chest, and the four coins—as a sort of souvenir of the find—at his house. When they saw that the Whaler was gone, they figured Tobin was gone, so they continued on to their house."

"Where they surprised Tobin."

"Right. He'd already ransacked their house to simulate a burglary, as well as to see if the Gordons were holding out on any treasure."

"Also, he'd want to see if there was any incriminating evidence in their house linking them to him."

"Exactly. So the Gordons pull into their dock, and maybe it's at this point that they raise the flags signaling Dangerous Cargo, Need Assistance." I added, "I'm sure they'd raised the Jolly Roger in the morning, signaling to Tobin that this was, indeed, the day as agreed. Calm seas, no rain, and a lot of confidence and good vibes, or whatever."

"And when the Gordons pulled into their dock, Tobin's Whaler was in the wetlands nearby."

"Yes." I thought a minute and said, "We'll probably never know what happened next—what was said, what Tobin thought was in the chest, what the Gordons thought Tobin was up to. At some point, all three of them knew that their partnership had ended. Tobin knew he'd never have another opportunity to murder his partners. So...he raised his gun, pressed on the handle of the air horn, and squeezed on the trigger of his pistol. The first round hits Tom in the forehead at close range, Judy screams and turns toward her husband and the second round hits her in the side of the head.... Tobin stops squeezing the air horn. He opens the aluminum chest and sees that there isn't much gold or jewels in it. He figures the rest of the loot is on board the *Spirochete*, and he goes down to the boat and searches it. Nothing there. He realizes he's killed the geese that were supposed to deliver the golden eggs. But all is not lost. He knows or believes that he can complete the job himself. Right?"

Beth nodded, thought a moment, then said, "Or, Tobin has another accomplice on the island."

I said, "Indeed." I added, "Then killing the Gordons is no big deal."

We continued east through the passage, which is about four miles long and half a mile wide at its narrowest. It was definitely dark now—no lights, no moon, and no stars, only an ink-black sea and a smoke-black sky. I could barely see the channel markers, and if it weren't for them, I'd have been totally lost and disoriented, and would have wound up on the rocks or shoals.

To our left, I saw a few lights onshore, and·realized we were passing Greenport where there was obviously some emergency generator lighting. I said to Beth, "Greenport."

She nodded.

We both had the same thought, which was to make for this safe harbor. I pictured us in some bar at a traditional hurricane party—candlelight and warm beer.

Somewhere to our right, though I couldn't see it, was Dering Harbor on Shelter Island, and I knew there was a yacht club there where I could put in. Greenport and Dering Harbor were the last of the big easily navigable ports before the open sea. I looked at Beth and reminded her, "As soon as we clear Shelter Island, it's going to get rough."

She replied, "It's rough *now*." She shrugged, then said, "Let's give it a shot. We can always turn back."

I thought it was time to tell her about the fuel, and I said, "We're low on gas and at some point out in Gardiners Bay, we will reach that legendary point of no return."

She glanced at the gas gauges and said, "Don't worry about that. We'll capsize long before then."

"That sounds like some idiotic thing I'd say."

She smiled at me, which was unexpected. Then she went below and came back with a lifesaver, meaning a bottle of beer. I said, "Bless you." The boat was banging around so badly, I couldn't put the neck of the bottle to my lips without knocking my teeth out, so I poured the beer into my upturned and open mouth, getting about half of it on my face.

Beth had a plastic-coated chart, which she spread out on the dashboard and said, "Coming up on our left over there is Cleeves Point, and to the right over there is Hays Beach Point on Shelter Island. When we pass those points, we're in this sort of funnel between Montauk Point and Orient Point where the Atlantic weather blows right in."

"Is that good or bad?"

"This is not funny."

I took another swig of the beer, an expensive imported brand, which is what I'd expect from Fredric Tobin. I said, "I sort of like the idea of stealing his boat and drinking his beer."

Beth replied, "Which has been the most fun— wrecking his apartment or sinking his boat?"

"The boat is not sinking."

"You ought to go look below."

"I don't have to—I can feel it in the helm." I added, "Good ballast."

"You're a real sailor all of a sudden."

"I'm a quick learner."

"Right. Go take a break, John. I'll take the helm."

"Okay." I took the chart, gave the wheel to Beth, and went below.

The small cabin was awash in about three inches of water, which meant we were taking in more water than the bilge pumps could handle. As I indicated, I didn't mind a little water to add weight and ballast to make up for the lighter fuel tanks. It was too bad the engine wouldn't burn water.

I went into the head and retched about a pint of salt-water into the toilet. I washed the salt off my face and hands, and came back into the cabin. I sat on one of the bench beds, studied the chart, and sipped my beer. My arms and shoulders ached, my legs and hips ached, and my chest was heaving, though my stomach felt better. I stared at the chart for a minute or two, went to the bar refrigerator, and found another beer, which I carried topside along with the chart.

Beth was doing fine in the storm, which, as I said, wasn't too bad here on the leeward side of Shelter Island. The seas were high, but they were predictable, and the wind at sea level wasn't so bad as long as the island sheltered us.

I looked out at the horizon and was able to see the black outline of the two points of land that marked the end of the safe passage. I said to Beth, "I'll take the wheel. You take the chart."

"Okay." She tapped the chart and said, "There's some tricky navigating coming up. You have to stay to the right of Long Beach Bar Lighthouse."

"All right," I replied. We exchanged places. As she sidestepped past me, she glanced toward the stern and let out a scream.

I thought it must be a monster wave that caused that reaction and I looked quickly back over my shoulder as I took the wheel.

I couldn't believe what I was seeing. A huge cabin cruiser—a Chris-Craft to be exact, the *Autumn Gold* to be specific—was no more than twenty feet off our tail on a collision course and gaining fast.

CHAPTER THIRTY-FOUR

Beth seemed mesmerized by the specter of the huge boat looming over us.

It kind of surprised me, too. I mean, I hadn't heard it over the roar of the storm and the sound of our own engines. Also, visibility was limited and the Chris-Craft wasn't showing any running lights.

In any event, Fredric Tobin had outflanked us and all I could think of was the bow of the *Autumn Gold* cleaving through the stern of the *Sondra*; a Freudian image if ever there was one.

Anyway, it looked as if we were going to be sunk.

Realizing we'd seen him, Mr. Tobin turned on his electric hailing horn and shouted, "Fuck you!"

I mean, really.

I pushed forward on the throttles and the distance between us and him widened. He knew he couldn't overtake a Formula 303, even in these seas. He greeted us again with, "Fuck you both! You're dead! You're dead!"

Freddie's voice was kind of screechy, but maybe that was a result of the electric distortion.

Beth had drawn her 9mm Glock at some point, and she was crouched behind her chair, trying to steady her aim on the back of the seat. I thought she should be firing, but she wasn't.

I glanced back at the Chris-Craft and noticed now that Tobin wasn't on the exposed fly bridge, but was in the deckhouse cabin where I knew there was a complete second set of controls. I noticed, too, that the hinged windshield on the helm side of the cabin was raised. More interesting than that, the skipper, Captain Freddie, was leaning out the open window, holding a rifle in his right hand, and I assume steadying the helm with his left. His right shoulder was braced against the window frame and the rifle was now pointed at us.

Well, here we were in two wildly moving boats in the dark with no lights, the wind and waves and all that, and I guessed that's why Tobin hadn't opened fire yet. I yelled to Beth, "Pop off a couple."

She called back, "I'm not supposed to fire until he fires."

"Shoot the fucking gun!"

She did. In fact, she popped off all fifteen rounds, and I saw the windshield beside Tobin shatter. I also noticed that F. Tobin was no longer leaning out the window with his rifle. I called to Beth, "Good job!"

She slammed another fifteen-round magazine into the pistol and covered the cabin cruiser.

I kept glancing over my shoulder as I tried to control the Formula in the steadily worsening sea. All of a sudden, Tobin popped up at the open window, and I saw his rifle flash. "Down!" I yelled. The rifle flashed three more times, and I heard a round thud into the dashboard, then my windshield shattered.

Beth was returning the fire, slower, steadier than before.

I knew we couldn't match the accuracy of his rifle so I gave the engines full throttle and we took off, crashing through the tops of the waves and away from the Chris-Craft. At about sixty feet, neither of us was visible to the other. I heard his hailing horn crackle, then his tinny, tiny voice came across the stormy seas. "Fuck you! You'll drown! You'll never survive this storm! Fuck you!"

This didn't sound like the suave and debonair gentleman I'd come to know and dislike. This was a man who had lost it.

"You're dead! You're both fucking dead!"

I was really annoyed at being taunted by a man who had just murdered my lover. I said to Beth, "That bastard dies."

"Don't let him get to you, John. He's finished and he knows it. He's desperate."

He's desperate? We weren't in great shape either.

Anyway, Beth stayed in her firing stance, facing the stern, trying to steady her pistol on the back of the seat. She said to me, "John, come around in a wide circle, and we'll get behind him."

"Beth, I'm not John Paul Jones and this is not a naval engagement."

"I don't want him behind us!"

"Don't worry about it. Just keep an eye out." I glanced at the fuel gauge and saw the needle between one eighth and E. I said, "We don't have the fuel for maneuvers."

She asked me, "Do you think he's still going to Plum Island?"

"That's where the gold is."

"But he knows we're onto him."

"Which is why he's going to keep on trying to kill us." I added, "Or at least witness that we capsized and drowned."

She didn't reply for a while, then asked me, "How did we get ahead of him?"

"I guess we were going faster than him. Law of physics."

"Do you have a plan?"

"Nope. Do you?"

"Is it time to head for a safe harbor?"

"Maybe. But we can't go back. I don't want to run into Freddie's rifle again."

Beth found the plastic-coated chart on the deck and unfolded it on the dashboard. She pointed and said, "That must be Long Beach Bar Lighthouse over there."

I looked off to our right front and saw a faint blinking light.

She continued, "If we head to the left of the lighthouse, we may be able to see some channel markers that will lead us to East Marion or Orient. We can dock someplace, and call the Coast Guard or the security people on Plum Island and alert them to the situation."

I glanced at the chart, which was lit by the faint glow of a reading light on the dashboard. I said, "There's no way I can navigate this boat in this storm through these narrow channels. The only place I can get into is Greenport or maybe Dering, and Freddie's between us and those harbors."

She thought a moment, then said, "In other words, we're not chasing him anymore. He's chasing us—out into the open water."

"Well...you could say we're leading him into a trap."

"What trap?"

"I knew you'd ask that. Trust me."

"Why?"

"Why not?" I cut back on the throttles and the Formula settled down a little. I said to Beth, "Actually, I like it this way. Now I know for sure where he is and where he's going." I added, "I'd rather deal with him on land. We'll meet him on Plum Island."

Beth folded her chart. "Right." She glanced back over her shoulder and said, "He's got us outgunned and outboated."

"Correct." I set a course that would take us to the right of the lighthouse out into Gardiners Bay, which in turn would put us on a course to Plum Island. I asked her, "How many rounds do you have left?"

She replied, "I have nine left in this magazine and a full magazine of fifteen in my pocket."

"Good enough." I glanced at her and said, "Nice shooting back there."

"Not really."

"You upset his aim. You may also have hit him."

She didn't reply.

I said to her, "I heard that last round go past my ear before it went through the windshield. Jeez! Just like old times back in the city." I asked her, as an afterthought, "You okay?"

"Well..."

I looked quickly toward her. "What's the matter?"

"Not sure..."

"*Beth*? What's the matter?" I could see her left hand moving over her rain slicker and she winced. She brought her hand out and it was covered in blood. She said, "Damn...."

I was literally speechless.

She said, "Funny....I didn't realize I was hit... then I felt this warm...It's okay though...just a graze."

"Are you...are you sure...?"

"Yeah....I can feel where it passed through...."

"Let's see. Come here."

She moved closer to where I stood at the wheel, turned toward the stern and loosened her life vest, then raised her slicker and shirt. Her rib cage, between her breast and her hip, was covered with blood. I reached out and said, "Steady." I felt for the wound and was relieved to discover that it was indeed a graze running along the lower rib. The gash was deep, but had not exposed the bone.

Beth let out a gasp as my fingers probed into the wound. I took my hand away and said, "It's okay."

"That's what I told you."

"I just get a kick out of sticking my fingers into gunshot wounds. Hurt yet?"

"It didn't. Now it does."

"Go below and find the first-aid kit."

She went below.

I scanned the horizon. Even in the darkness, I could see the two points of land on either side that marked the end of the relatively calm strait.

Within a minute, we were out into Gardiners Bay. Within two minutes, the sea looked like someone switched the dial to spin and rinse. The wind howled, the waves crashed, the boat was nearly out of control, and I was weighing my options.

Beth scrambled up from the cabin and held on to the handgrip on the dashboard.

I called out over the sound of the wind and the waves, "Are you okay?"

She nodded, then yelled, "John! We have to turn back!"

I knew she was right. The Formula was not made for this and neither was I. Then I recalled Tom Gordon's words to me on my porch that night which seemed so long ago. *A boat in the harbor is a safe boat. But that's not what boats are for.*

In truth, I was no longer frightened by the sea or by the possibility of my death, for that matter. I was running on pure adrenaline and hate. I glanced at Beth and our eyes met. She seemed to understand, but she didn't want to share my psychotic episode. She said, "John...if we die, he gets away with it. We have to get into some harbor or inlet somewhere."

"I can't....I mean, we'd run aground and sink. We have to ride it out."

She didn't reply.

I said, "We can put in at Plum Island. I can get into that cove. It's well marked and lit. They have their own generator."

She opened the chart again and stared at it as if trying to find an answer to our dilemma. In fact, as I'd already concluded, the only possible harbors, Greenport and Dering, lay behind us, and between us and those harbors was Tobin.

She said, "Now that we're out in the open sea, we should be able to circle around and get past him and back to Greenport."

I shook my head. "Beth, we have to stay in the

marked channel. If we lose sight of these channel markers, we're finished. We're on a narrow highway and there's a guy with a rifle behind us and the only way to go is straight."

She looked at me and I could tell she didn't completely believe me, which was understandable because I wasn't completely telling the truth. The truth was, I wanted to kill Fredric Tobin. When I thought he'd killed Tom and Judy, I would have been satisfied seeing the great State of New York kill him. Now, after he murdered Emma, I had to kill him myself. Calling the Coast Guard or Plum Island security was not going to even the score. In fact, regarding score, I wondered where Paul Stevens was this night.

Beth broke into my thoughts and said, "Five innocent people are dead, John, and that's five too many. I won't let you throw away my life or yours. We're heading back. Now."

I looked at her and said, "Are you going to pull your gun on me?"

"If you make me."

I kept staring at her and said, "Beth, I can handle this weather. I *know* I can handle it. We're going to be okay. Trust me."

She stared back at me a long time, then said, "Tobin murdered Emma Whitestone right under your nose and that was an attack on your manhood, an insult to your macho image and your ego. That's what's driving you on. Right?"

No use lying, so I said, "That's part of it."

"What's the other part?"

"Well . . . I was falling in love with her."

Beth nodded. She seemed contemplative, then said,

"Okay...if you're going to get us killed anyway, then you may as well know the whole truth."

"*What* whole truth?"

She replied, "Whoever killed Emma Whitestone... and I guess it was Tobin...also first raped her."

I didn't reply. I should say I wasn't completely shocked either. There is a primitive side to all men, including fops like Fredric Tobin, and this dark side, when it takes over, plays itself out in a predictable and very scary way. I could say I've seen it all—rape, torture, kidnapping, maiming, murder, and everything else in the penal code. But this was the first time that a bad guy was sending a personal message to me. And I wasn't handling it with my usual cool. *He raped her*. And while he was doing it to her, he was—or thought he was—doing it to me.

Neither of us spoke for a while, and in fact, the noise of the engines and the wind and sea made any talk difficult, which was okay with me.

Beth sat in the left seat and held the arms tightly as the boat pitched, rolled, yawed, and did everything else but spin and dive.

I remained standing at the wheel, braced against the seat. The wind blew through the shattered glass in front of me, and the rain sliced in from all angles. The fuel was low, I was cold, wet, exhausted, and very troubled by that image of Tobin doing that to Emma. Beth seemed strangely silent, almost catatonic, staring straight ahead at each onrushing wave.

Finally, she seemed to come alive, and looked back over her shoulder. Without a word, she got out of the chair and went to the rear of the boat. I glanced at her and saw her take up a kneeling position in the stern as she drew her 9mm. I looked out at the sea behind us, but saw only the walls of waves trailing the boat. Then, as the Formula rode up on a big wave, I could see the fly bridge of the Chris-Craft behind us again, not more than sixty feet away and closing fast. I made a decision and cut the throttles back, leaving only enough power to control the boat. Beth heard the engines rev down and glanced back at me, then nodded in understanding. She turned back toward the Chris-Craft and steadied her aim. We had to meet the beast.

Tobin had not noticed the sudden difference in relative speed and before he knew it, the Chris-Craft was less than twenty feet from the Formula, and he hadn't gotten his rifle into position. Before he did, Beth began a steady volley of fire at the dark figure at the window of the cabin. I watched all of this, dividing my time between keeping the bow of the Formula into the waves, and looking back to be sure Beth was okay.

Tobin seemed to disappear from the cabin, and I wondered if he'd been hit. But then, all of a sudden, the Chris-Craft spotlight, mounted on the bow, went on, illuminating the Formula and also revealing Beth kneeling in the stern. "Damn it." Beth was slipping her last magazine into the Glock, and Tobin was now back at the windshield, aiming the rifle with both hands and letting the wheel go.

I drew my .38, spun around, and jammed my back against the wheel to hold it as I tried to steady my aim. Tobin's rifle was pointing right at Beth from less than fifteen feet away.

For a half second, it seemed as if everything was frozen—both boats, Beth, Tobin, me, and the sea itself. I fired. The barrel of Tobin's rifle, which was clearly lined up on Beth, all of a sudden swung toward me and I saw the muzzle flash at about the same time that the Chris-Craft, with no hand on the helm, lurched to port, and Tobin's shot went wide. The Chris-Craft was now at right angles to the stern of the Formula, and I could see Tobin in the side window of the cabin. In fact, he saw me and we made eye contact. I fired three more rounds into the cabin and his side window shattered. When I looked again, he was gone.

I noticed now that trailing behind the Chris-Craft was the small Whaler that had been in the boathouse. I had no doubt now that Tobin intended to use the Whaler to land on Plum Island.

The Chris-Craft bobbed around aimlessly, and I could tell there was no one at the helm. Just as I was wondering if I'd hit him, his bow came around very deliberately, and the spotlight again illuminated us. Beth fired at the light, and on the third shot, it exploded in a shower of sparks and glass.

Tobin was not to be foiled, and he gunned the Chris-Craft's engines. His bow was closing on the stern of the Formula. He would have rammed us except that Beth had pulled the flare pistol from her pocket and fired it right into the windshield of the cabin cruiser's bridge. There was a blinding white explosion of phosphorus and the Chris-Craft veered off as Tobin, I imagined, let go of the helm real fast and dived for cover. In fact, maybe he was burned, blinded, or dead.

Beth was yelling, "Go! Go!"

I had already opened the throttles and the Formula was picking up speed.

I could see flames licking around the bridge of the Chris-Craft. Beth and I looked at one another, both wondering if maybe we'd gotten lucky. But as we watched Tobin's boat behind us, the flames seemed to subside. At a distance of about forty feet, we again heard the hailing horn crackle and again the little bastard had something to say.

"Corey! I'm coming for you! And for you, too, Ms. Bitch! I'll kill you both! I'll kill you!"

I said to Beth, "I think he means it."

"How dare he call me bitch."

"Well . . . of course he's just taunting you. He doesn't know you, so how can he know that you're a bitch? I mean, *if* you're a bitch."

"I know what you mean."

"Right."

"Haul ass, John. He's getting close again."

"Right." I gave it more throttle, but the extra speed made the Formula unstable. In fact, I hit an oncoming wave so hard the bow pitched up at too steep an angle, and I thought we were going to back-flip. I could hear Beth scream, and I thought she'd been pitched overboard, but when the boat came down, she rolled across the deck and dropped halfway down the companionway stairs before she came to a stop. She lay on the stairs, and I called out, "Are you okay?"

She got up on all fours and crawled up the companionway. "I'm all right. . . ."

I cut back on the throttles and said, "Go below and take a break."

She shook her head and positioned herself between her seat and the dashboard. She said, "You watch for waves and channel markers. I'll watch for Tobin."

"Okay." I had the thought that maybe Beth was right, and I should try to circle around and come up behind him, rather than him coming up behind us again. Maybe if he was sitting in his nice dry cabin, he wouldn't see us and we could board him. But if he saw us, we'd be looking down the muzzle of that rifle again.

The only advantage we had was our speed, but as we saw, we couldn't take full advantage of it in this weather.

I said to Beth, "Nice going. Good thinking."

She didn't reply.

"Do you have any more signal flares?"

"Five more."

"Good."

"Not really. I lost the flare gun."

"Do you want to go back and try to find it?"

"I'm tired of your jokes."

"Me, too. But it's all we've got."

So, we continued on in silence, through the storm, which was getting worse if that were possible.

Finally, she said, "I thought I was dead."

I replied, "We can't let him get that close again."

She looked at me and said, "He passed me up to get you."

"That's the story of my life. Whenever somebody has only one shot, I'm the one they pick."

She almost smiled, then disappeared below. Less than a minute later, she came back and handed me another beer. She said, "Every time you do good, you get a beer."

"I don't have many tricks left. How many more beers do you have?"

"Two."

"That should work out."

I contemplated my options and realized I'd run out

of most of them. There were only two possible harbors left now—the ferry slip at Orient Point and the cove at Plum Island. Orient Point was probably coming up to the left by now and Plum Island was two miles farther. I looked at the gas gauge. The needle was in the red but not yet touching E.

The sea was so bad now I couldn't even see the channel markers for long periods at a time. I knew that Tobin, sitting high in his cabin bridge, had a better view of the markers and of us. As I thought about that, it suddenly struck me that he must have radar—ship-hazard radar, which was how he'd found us. And he must also have a depth-finder, which made navigation much easier for him even if he lost sight of the channel markers. In short, the *Sondra* was no match for the *Autumn Gold*. "Damn it."

Every once in a while with increasing frequency, a wave broke over the bow or sides, and I could feel the Formula getting heavier. In fact, I was sure we were riding lower in the water. The extra weight was slowing us up and burning more gas. I realized that Tobin could overtake us at the speed we were going. I realized, too, that we were losing the battle against the sea as well as the naval engagement.

I glanced at Beth, and she sensed me looking at her and our eyes met. She said, "In case we capsize or sink, I want to tell you now that I actually like you."

I smiled and replied, "I know that." I looked at her and said, "I'm sorry. I never should have—"

"Drive and shut up."

I turned my attention back to the wheel. The Formula was moving so slowly now that the following sea was coming over the stern. In a short time, we would be swamped, or the engine compartment would be flooded, and/or Tobin would be on top of us and we weren't going to outrun him this time.

Beth kept looking for Tobin and, of course, she saw the sea washing over the stern and couldn't help but realize the boat was lower and slower. She said, "John, we're going to swamp."

I looked again at the gas gauge. The only chance we had at this point was to gun the engines and see what happened. I put my hand on the throttles and pushed them all the way forward.

The Formula moved out, slowly at first, then gathered some speed. We were taking on less water from the stern, but the boat was slamming hard and heavy into the oncoming waves. So hard, in fact, it was like hitting a brick wall every five seconds. I thought the craft was going to break up, but the fiberglass hull held.

Beth was holding on in her seat, rising and falling with each encounter with a wave.

Leaving it at full throttle was working, as far as keeping control and keeping from getting swamped, but it wasn't doing much for fuel economy. Yet, I had no choice. In the great realm of trade-offs, I had traded off the certainty of sinking now against the certainty of running out of gas shortly. Big deal.

But my experience with fuel gauges—ever since I had my first car—was that they show either more fuel than you have left, or less fuel than you have left. I didn't know how this gauge lied, but I would soon find out.

Beth said, "How's the gas?"

"Fine."

She tried to put a light tone in her voice and said, "Do you want to stop for gas and ask directions?"

"Nope. Real men don't ask directions, and we have enough gas to get to Plum Island."

She smiled.

I said to her, "Go below awhile."

"What if we capsize?"

"We're too heavy now to capsize. We'll sink. But you'll have plenty of warning. Take a break."

"Okay." She went below. I took the chart out of the open glove compartment and divided my attention between it and the sea. Off to the left in the far distance, I caught a glimpse of a flashing strobe light, and I knew that had to be Orient Point Lighthouse. I glanced at the chart. If I turned due north now, I would probably be able to find the Orient Point ferry slips. But there were so many rocks and shoals between the ferry and the lighthouse that it would take a miracle to get past them. The other possibility was to go on another two miles or so and try for the cove at Plum Island. But that meant going into Plum Gut, which was treacherous enough in normal tides and winds. In a storm—or hurricane—it would be . . . well, challenging, to say the least.

Beth came up the companionway, lurching from side to side and pitching forward, then back. I caught her outstretched hand and hauled her up. She presented me with an unwrapped chocolate bar. I said, "Thanks."

She said, "The water's ankle deep below. Bilge pumps are still working."

"Good. The boat's feeling a little lighter."

"Terrific. Take a break below. I'll drive."

"I'm okay. How's your little scratch?"

"It's okay. How's your little brain?"

"I left it onshore." As I ate my chocolate bar, I explained our options.

She understood our chances clearly and said, "So, we can smash up on the rocks at Orient Point or drown in the Gut?"

"Right." I tapped the fuel gauge and said, "We're well past the point where we can turn back to Greenport."

"I think we missed our opportunity there."

"I guess so...." I asked her, "So? Orient or Plum?"

She looked at the chart awhile and said, "There are too many navigation hazards between here and Orient." She looked out to the left and added, "I don't even see any channel markers leading to Orient. I wouldn't be surprised if some of them haven't broken loose and floated away."

I nodded. "Yeah...."

Beth said, "And forget the Gut. Nothing less than an ocean liner could get through there in this storm." She added, "If we had more fuel, we could ride this out until the eye passes over." She looked up from the chart and said, "We have no options."

Which may have been true. Tom and Judy once told me that the instinct to sail toward land in a storm was often the wrong thing to do. The coast was treacherous; it was where the breaking waves could pulverize or capsize your boat or drive you into the rocks. It was actually safer to ride out the storm in the open sea as long as you had fuel or sail left. But we didn't even have that option because we had a guy with a rifle and radar on our ass. We had no choice but to press on and see what God and nature had in store for us. I said, "We'll hold course and speed."

She nodded. "Okay. That's about all we can do.... What—?"

I looked at her and saw she was staring toward the stern. I looked back, but saw nothing.

She said, "I saw him...I think I saw him." Beth jumped up on the chair and managed to keep her balance for a second before she was pitched off and onto the deck. She scrambled to her feet and shouted, "He's right behind us!"

"Damn it!" I knew now that the son of a bitch definitely had radar. I was glad I hadn't tried to get around him. I said to Beth, "It's not that our luck is so bad, it's that he has radar. He's had a fix on us from the start."

She nodded and said, "No place to run, no place to hide."

"No place to hide for sure, but let's try to run."

I opened the throttles all the way, and we picked up more speed.

Neither of us spoke as the Formula cut heavily through the waves. I estimated we were making about twenty knots, which was about one-third of what this boat could do in a calm sea and without a bilge- and cabinful of seawater. I guessed that the Chris-Craft could do at least twenty knots in this weather, which was why he was able to catch up to us. In fact, Beth said, "John, he's gaining on us."

I looked back and saw the vague outline of Tobin's boat as it crested a huge wave about forty feet behind us. In about five minutes or less, he'd be able to place fairly accurate rifle fire on us, while my .38 and Beth's 9mm pistol were really useless except for the occasional lucky shot. Beth asked me, "How many rounds do you have left?"

"Let's see...the cylinder holds five...I shot four... so, how many bullets does the copper have left in—"

"This is *not* a fucking joke!"

"I'm trying to lighten the moment."

I heard some four-letter words coming from Ms. Penrose's prim mouth, then she asked me, "Can you get any more speed out of this fucking thing?"

"Maybe. Get something heavy down below and smash that windshield."

She dove down below and came up with a fire extinguisher, which she used to smash the glass out of her windshield. Then she threw the extinguisher overboard.

I said, "At this speed, we're not taking on as much water, and the pumps will lighten the weight a little more every minute, and we'll pick up a little more speed." I added, "Plus we're burning all that heavy fuel."

"I don't need a lesson in physics."

She was angry and that was much better than the quiet resignation I'd seen taking hold earlier. It's good to be pissed off when man and nature conspire to do you in.

Beth made a few more trips below and came back each time with something to toss overboard, including, unfortunately, the beer from the refrigerator. She managed to get a portable TV set up the stairs and over the side. She also threw some clothes and shoes overboard, and it occurred to me that if we lost Freddie, he might see the flotsam and jetsam and conclude that we'd gone under.

We were picking up a little more speed, but the Chris-Craft was gaining on us and there was no escaping the fact that he was going to begin laying down rifle fire very soon. I asked Beth, "How many rounds do you have left?"

"Nine."

"You only had three magazines?"

"*Only?* You're running around with a damned five-shot peashooter and not a single extra bullet on you, and you have the nerve—" She suddenly crouched behind the seat and pulled her pistol. She said, "I saw a muzzle flash."

I glanced back and sure enough, there was Fearless Fucking Freddie in his shooting post. The muzzle flashed again. Shooting at one another from storm-tossed boats is easy; hitting anything is difficult, so I wasn't overly concerned yet, but there would be a moment when both boats were hanging on a crest and Tobin had the advantage of the higher perch and the long barrel.

Beth was wisely holding her fire.

I saw the Orient Point Lighthouse directly to my left and much closer than before. I realized I'd been blown north even as I'd kept an easterly heading. I realized, too, there was only one thing left to do, and I did it. I cut the wheel hard left, and the boat headed toward the Gut.

Beth called out, "What are you doing?"

"We're running for the Gut."

"John, we'll drown there!"

"It's either that or Tobin picks us off with his rifle or he rams and sinks us and laughs as he watches us drown." I added, "If we go down in the Gut, maybe he'll go down with us."

She didn't reply.

The storm was coming in from the south, and as soon as I got my bow heading north, the boat picked up some speed. Within a minute, I could see the outline of Plum Island to my right front. To my left front was the Orient Lighthouse. I aimed at a point between the light and the coast of Plum Island, right into Plum Gut.

At first, Tobin followed, but as the waves got worse and as the wind blowing between both bodies of land got supersonic, we lost sight of him, and I guessed that he'd given up the chase. I was pretty sure I knew what he was going to do next and where he was headed. I hoped I'd be alive in fifteen minutes to see if I was right.

We were into the Gut now, smack in the middle of it, between Orient Point to the west and Plum Island to the east, Gardiners Bay to the south, and Long Island Sound to the north. I recalled that Stevens said that a hurricane a few hundred years before had deepened the seafloor here, and I could believe it. I mean, it was like a washing machine with all kinds of stuff being turned up from the seabed—sand, seaweed, wood, junk, and debris of every type. There was no pretense of me controlling the boat any longer. The Formula was nothing more than another piece of flotsam and jetsam now, going with the flow. The boat actually broached, which in plain English means it spun around a few times, and we found ourselves pointing south, east, and west at various times, but the storm kept driving us north into the Sound, which is where I wanted to be.

The idea of trying to get into Plum Island cove was almost laughable now that I saw what a horrendous place this was.

Beth managed to make her way toward me, and she wedged herself into my chair behind me. She wrapped her legs and arms around me as I held on to the wheel for dear life. It was nearly impossible to talk, but she buried her face in my neck, and I could hear her say, "I'm scared."

Scared? I was terrorized out of my fucking mind. This was easily the worst experience of my life, if you don't count my walk down the aisle to the altar.

The Formula was being tossed around so badly now that I was totally disoriented. There were times when I realized we were literally airborne, and I knew that the boat—which had shown good stability in the water—could actually flip upside down in midair. I think it was only the bilgewater that kept us hull-side down during our launches into the stratosphere.

I'd had the presence of mind to cut the throttles to idle as soon as I saw that the propellers were spending more time in the air than the water. Fuel management is a long-term strategy, and I was in a short-term situation—but, hey, you never know.

Beth was clinging tighter, and if it weren't for our imminent deaths by drowning, I might have found this pleasant. As it was, I hoped the physical contact gave her some comfort. I know it did for me. She spoke again into my ear and said, "If we go in the water, hold me tight."

I nodded. I thought again of how Tobin had already killed five good people and was about to be the cause of two more dying. I couldn't believe that this little turd had actually caused all this death and misery. The only explanation I had for it was that short people with beady eyes and big appetites were ruthless and dangerous. They really had a bone to pick with the world. You know? Well, maybe there was more to it.

Anyway, we were blown through the Gut like a spitball through a straw. Ironically, I think it was the very ferocity of the storm that got us through okay, and we were probably on an incoming tide. I mean, the whole thrust of the sea, wind, and tide was north, which sort of canceled out the usual treacherous swirling of the wind and the tides in the Gut. Sort of like the difference between being caught in a flushing toilet bowl or being in the waste pipe, to stretch an analogy.

We were in the Long Island Sound now, and the seas and wind were a little better. I revved up the engines and headed the boat east.

Beth was still behind me, holding on, but not as tight.

Off to our right front was the dark shape of the old Plum Island Lighthouse. I knew if we could get behind that headland, we would be a little more protected from the wind and seas, just as we had been when we had Shelter Island between us and the storm. Plum Island was not as elevated as Shelter Island, and it was a lot more exposed to the open Atlantic, but it should offer some protection.

Beth said, "Are we alive?"

"Sure." I added, "You were very brave. Very calm."

"I was paralyzed with fear."

"Whatever." I took one hand off the wheel and squeezed her right hand, which was clamped on to my tummy.

So, we got on the leeward side of Plum Island, and we passed the lighthouse on our right. I could see now into the lantern of the lighthouse, and what I saw was a green dot, sort of following us. I drew Beth's attention to it, and she said, "Night-seeing device. We're being watched by some of Mr. Stevens' men."

"Indeed," I agreed. "That's about all the security they have left on a night like this."

The wind was partly blocked by Plum Island, and the sea was just a bit calmer. We could hear the waves crashing up on the beach about a hundred yards away.

Through the driving rain, I could see a glow of lights behind the trees, and I realized this was the security lighting of the main laboratory building. This meant the generators were still working and this in turn meant that the air filters and scrubbers were still doing their job. It would have been really unfair if we'd survived the storm, landed on Plum Island, and died of anthrax. Really.

Beth let go of me and squeezed out of her nook between my seat and my butt. She stood beside me, holding the grip on the dashboard. She asked me, "What do you think happened to Tobin?"

"I think he continued on around the south end of the island. I think he thinks we're dead."

"Probably," Beth replied. "I thought so, too."

"Right. Unless he has radio contact with someone on Plum Island who knows from the guy in the lighthouse that we made it."

She thought a moment and asked, "Do you think he has an accomplice on Plum Island?"

"I don't know. But we're about to find out."

"Okay...so where is Tobin going now?"

"There's only one place he can go and that's right here, on this side of the Island."

She nodded. "In other words, he's coming around

from the other direction, and we'll meet him coming at us."

"Well, I'll try to avoid that. But he's definitely got to get on the leeward side if he's going to anchor and get onto the beach with that Whaler."

She thought a moment, then asked, "Are we going to land on the island?"

"I hope so."

"How?"

"I'll try to run up on the beach."

She took the chart out again and said, "There are rocks and shoals along most of this beach."

"Well, pick a place where there aren't any rocks or shoals."

"I'll try."

We moved east for another ten minutes. I looked at the fuel gauge and saw it read Empty. I knew I should make my run to the beach now because if I ran out of fuel, we'd be at the mercy of the weather, and we would either blow out to sea or wash up onto the rocks. But I wanted to at least catch sight of Tobin's boat before I beached.

Beth said, "John, we're about out of gas. You'd better head in."

"In a minute."

"We don't have a minute. It's about a hundred yards to the beach. Turn now."

"See if you can spot the Chris-Craft in front of us."

The binoculars were still on the strap around her neck, and she raised them and peered out over the bow. She said, "No, I don't see any boat. Turn into the beach."

"Another minute."

"No. Now. We did all of this your way. Now we do it my way."

"Okay...." But before I began my turn into the beach, the wind suddenly dropped and I could see this incredible wall of towering clouds rising above us. More incredibly, I saw the night sky overhead, circled by these swirling walls of clouds, as if we were at the bottom of a well. Then I saw stars, which I never thought I'd see again.

Beth said, "The eye is passing over us."

The wind was much calmer though the waves weren't. The starlight filtered into this sort of round hole, and we could see the beach and the sea.

Beth said, "Go for it, John. You won't get another chance like this."

And she was right. I could see the breaking waves so I could time them, and I could also see any rocks protruding out of the water as well as shoaling waves, which indicated shoals and sandbars.

"Go!"

"One minute. I really want to see where that bastard made land. I don't want to lose him on the island."

"John, you're out of gas!"

"Plenty of gas. Look for the Chris-Craft."

Beth seemed resigned to my idiocy, and she raised the binoculars and scanned the horizon. After what seemed like a half hour, but was probably a minute or two, she pointed and called out, "There!" She handed me the binoculars.

I looked into the rainy darkness and sure enough, silhouetted against the dark horizon, was a shape that could have been the fly bridge of the Chris-Craft—or could have been a pile of rocks.

As we got a little closer, I saw that it was definitely the Chris-Craft, and it was relatively motionless, indicating that Tobin had at least two anchors out, bow and stern. I handed Beth the binoculars. "Okay. We're going in. Hold on. Look for rocks and stuff."

Beth knelt on her seat and leaned forward, her hands gripped on the top of the glassless windshield frame. Whenever she moved, I could tell by the expression on her face that she was in some pain from her wound.

I turned the Formula ninety degrees to starboard and pointed the bow at the distant beach. Waves began breaking over the stern, and I gave the engines more gas. I needed about one more minute of fuel.

The beach got closer and more distinct. The waves smashing onto the sand were monstrous and getting louder as we got closer. Beth called out, "Sandbar right ahead!"

I knew I couldn't turn in time so I gave it full throttle, and we ripped across the sandbar.

The beach was less than fifty yards away now, and I thought we actually had a chance. Then the Formula hit something a lot harder than a sandbar, and I heard the unmistakable sound of splitting fiberglass and a half second later, the boat lifted out of the water, then came down with a thud.

I glanced at Beth and saw she was still hanging on.

The boat was very sluggish now, and I could picture water pouring in through the smashed hull. The engines seemed to be laboring even at full throttle. The incoming waves were pushing us toward the beach, but now the undertow was pulling us back between waves. If we were making any forward headway at all, it was very slow. Meanwhile, the boat was filling with water, and in fact I could see the water sloshing on the bottom step of the companionway.

Beth called out, "We're not moving! Let's swim for it!"

"No! Stay with the boat. Wait for the perfect wave."

And we waited, watching the shoreline get closer, then receding for about six wave cycles. I looked behind me and watched the swells forming. Finally, I saw a huge wave forming behind us, and I threw the nearly swamped Formula into neutral. The boat pitched backwards a little and caught the wave just below its mounting crest. I called out, "Get down and hold on!"

Beth dropped down and clung to the base of her chair.

The wave propelled us like a surfboard on its hanging crest with such force that the eight-thousand-pound Formula, filled with thousands more pounds of water, acted like a reed basket caught in a raging river. I had anticipated an amphibian-type landing, but this was going to be an airborne drop.

As we hurtled toward the beach, I had the presence of mind to switch off the engines so that if we actually survived the landing, the Formula wouldn't explode, assuming there was any fuel left. I was also concerned about the twin props chopping our heads off. "Hold on!" I yelled.

"No shit!" she replied.

We came down bow first onto the wave-washed beach. The Formula rolled to the side, and we both jumped clear of the boat, just as another wave came crashing in. I found a rock outcropping and wrapped my arm around it as my free hand found Beth's wrist. The wave broke and receded, and we stood and ran like hell for the higher ground, Beth holding her side where she'd been hit.

We came to the face of an eroded bluff and began scrambling up it, the wet sand, clay, and iron oxide falling away in great chunks. Beth said, "Welcome to Plum Island."

"Thank you." Somehow, we got to the top of the bluff and collapsed on the high ground. We lay in the grass for a full minute. Then I sat up and looked down at the beach. The Formula was capsized, and I could see that its white hull was split open. The boat rolled again as the backwash took it out to sea, and then it righted itself for a minute, then capsized again and another wave took it toward the beach. I said to Beth, "I wouldn't want to be in that boat."

She replied, "No, and I also don't want to be on this island."

"Out of the fire," I said, "and into the frying pan."

"You bug me," she replied.

"There's an idea for a T-shirt," I suggested. "I got bugged on Plum Island. Get it?"

"Would you mind shutting up for about five minutes?"

"Not at all."

In fact, I welcomed the relative silence after hours of wind, rain, and ship's engines. I could actually hear my heart thumping, the blood pounding in my ears, and my lung wheezing. I could also hear a little voice in my head saying, "Beware of little men with big rifles."

CHAPTER THIRTY-FIVE

We sat in the grass, sort of collecting ourselves and catching our breaths. I was wet, tired, cold, and banged up, plus my punctured lung ached. I'd lost my boating shoes, and I noticed that Beth, too, was barefoot. On the positive side, we were alive, and I still had my .38 in my shoulder holster. I drew the revolver and made sure the one remaining round was next in line to fire. Beth was patting her pockets and she announced, "Okay...got mine."

We still had on our slickers and life vests, but I noticed that Beth had lost the binoculars around her neck.

We watched the sea and the eerie swirling of the towering clouds around the eye of the storm. It was still raining, but it wasn't a hard, driving rain. When you're drenched to the bones, a little rain is no big deal. My concern was hypothermia if we sat still too long.

I looked at Beth and asked, "How's that cut on your forehead?"

"It's okay." She added, "I soaked it in saltwater."

"Good. How about your bullet wound?"

"It's just terrific, John."

"And all your other cuts and bruises?"

"Every one of them is feeling great."

I thought I detected a touch of sarcasm in her voice. I stood and felt very wobbly.

Beth asked me, "Are *you* okay?"

"I'm fine." I reached down, and she took my hand and pulled herself to her feet. "Well," I said, mixing clichés, "we're out of the frying pan, but not out of the woods."

She said to me in a serious tone, "I think Tom and Judy Gordon would be proud of your seamanship."

I didn't reply. There was another unspoken sentence hanging there, and it was something like, "Emma would be pleased and flattered to see what you've done for her."

Beth said, "I think we should head back in the direction of the Gut and find the main lab."

I didn't reply.

She continued, "We can't miss the lights. We'll get the Plum Island security force to help us. I'll put in a telephone call or radio call to my office."

Again, I didn't reply.

She looked at me. "John?"

I said, "I did not come this far to run to Paul Stevens for help."

"John, we're not in great shape, and we have about five bullets between us and no shoes. Time to call the cops."

"You can go to the main building if you want. I'm going to find Tobin." I turned and began walking east along the bluff, toward where we'd seen Tobin's boat anchored about a half mile farther down the beach.

She didn't call after me, but a minute later, she

was walking beside me. We continued on in silence. We kept our life vests on, partly for warmth, partly, I guess, because you just never know when you're going to wind up back in the drink.

The trees came right up to the eroded bluff and the underbrush was thick. Without shoes, we stepped gingerly and were not making good time.

The wind was calm in the eye of the storm, and the air was very still. I could actually hear birds chirping. I knew that the air pressure was extremely low here in the eye, and though I'm not usually barometer sensitive, I did feel sort of…edgy, I guess, maybe a bit cranky, too. In fact, maybe pissed off and murderous was what I felt.

Beth spoke to me in a sort of hushed tone and asked, "Do you have a plan?"

"Of course."

"What's the plan, John?"

"The plan is to stay loose."

"Great plan."

"Right." There was some moonlight coming through the smoky clouds, and we could see about ten feet in front of us. Despite that, walking along the edge of the bluff was a little treacherous because of the erosion, so we cut inland and found the gravel road that Paul Stevens' tour bus had taken to the east end of the island. The narrow road was clogged with uprooted trees and fallen limbs, so we didn't have to worry about a motor patrol surprising us.

We rested on a fallen tree trunk. I could see our breaths fogging in the damp air. I took off my life vest and slicker, then my shoulder holster and polo shirt. I managed to rip the polo shirt in half, and I wrapped both pieces around Beth's feet. I said, "I'm taking off my undershorts. Don't peek."

"I won't peek. Mind if I stare?"

I got my tight, wet jeans off, then my shorts, which I ripped in two.

Beth said, "Boxers? I took you for a Jockey guy."

Ms. Penrose seemed in a playful mood for some reason. Post-trauma survivor euphoria, I guess. I tied the pieces of cloth around my feet.

Beth said, "I'd donate my panties, but they were so wet when I changed on the boat, I didn't bother to put them back on. Do you want my shirt?"

"No, thanks. This is okay." I pulled my jeans back on, then the shoulder holster against my bare skin, then the slicker, then the life vest. I was so cold now, I was starting to shiver.

We checked Beth's bullet wound, which was seeping some blood but otherwise seemed all right.

We continued on along the dirt road. The sky was darkening again, and I knew the eye was traveling north and we'd soon be in the back end of the storm, which would be as violent as the leading edge had been. I whispered to Beth, "This is about where Tobin anchored. Careful and quiet from here on."

She nodded, and we both moved north, off the trail and through the woods back down to the edge of the bluff. And sure enough, about fifty yards off-shore was the Chris-Craft, and I could see it straining in the swells against two anchor lines that Tobin had set fore and aft. In the dim light, we could see the Whaler on the beach below, so we knew Tobin had come ashore. In fact, there was a line from the Whaler that ran up the bluff and was tied to a tree right near where we were crouched.

We remained motionless, listening and peering into the darkness. I was fairly certain Tobin had struck off for the interior of the island, and I whispered to Beth, "He's off to find the treasure."

She nodded and said, "We can't track him. So we'll wait here for him to return." She added, "Then I'll arrest him."

"Miss Goody-Two-Shoes."

"What the hell does that mean?"

"It means, Ms. Penrose, that one does not *arrest* a person who has tried to kill you three times."

"You are not going to kill him in cold blood."

"Wanna bet?"

"John, I risked my life to help you on that boat. Now you owe me one." She added, "I'm still assigned to this case, I'm a cop, and we'll do it my way."

I didn't see any reason to argue what was already decided in my mind.

Beth suggested we untie the line and let the waves take the Whaler out, thereby cutting off Tobin's line of retreat. I pointed out that if Tobin approached from the beach below, he'd see that the Whaler was gone and he'd be spooked. I said to Beth, "Wait here and cover me."

I grabbed the line and lowered myself the fifteen feet down to the Whaler onto the rocky beach. In the stern, I found the plastic crate that I'd seen when the Whaler was in Tobin's boathouse. There was an assortment of odds and ends in the crate, though I noticed the air horn was gone. Fredric Tobin had probably figured out that I'd figured him out and he was ditching little pieces of the puzzle. No matter—he wasn't going to face a twelve-person jury.

Anyway, I found a pair of pliers, and I pulled out

the shear pin that held the propeller to the drive shaft. I found some spare pins in the crate and pocketed them. I also found a small fish scaling and fleshing knife in the crate, which I took. I looked for a flashlight, but there wasn't one on board the small boat.

I pulled myself up the bluff using the line, my underwear-wrapped feet digging into the sandy bluff. At the top, Beth reached out and helped me up.

I said, "I took the shear pin out of the prop."

She nodded. "Good. Did you save it in case we need it later?"

"Yes. I swallowed it. How stupid do I look?"

"You don't *look* stupid. You do stupid things."

"That's part of my strategy." I gave her the pins, and kept the knife.

Beth, to my surprise, said, "Look, I'm sorry for some of my nasty remarks. I'm a little tired and tense."

"Don't worry about it."

"I'm cold. Can we ... huddle?"

"Cuddle?"

"*Huddle.* You're supposed to huddle to conserve body heat."

"Right. I read that someplace. Okay...."

So, a little awkwardly, we huddled, or cuddled, with me sitting at the base of a big toppled tree trunk, and Beth sitting across my lap, her arms wrapped around me, and her face buried in my chest. It *was* a little warmer that way, though in truth it wasn't sensual or anything, given the circumstances. It was just human contact, as well as teamwork and survival. We'd been through a lot together, and we were close to the end now, and we both sensed, I think, that something had changed between us since Emma's death.

Anyway, this was also very Robinson Crusoe, or Treasure Island, or whatever, and I guess I was sort of enjoying it as boys of all ages enjoy matching themselves against man and nature. I had the distinct impression, though, that Beth Penrose was not sharing my boyish enthusiasm. Women tend to be a little more practical and less likely to have fun splashing in the mud. Also, I think, the hunt and the kill don't appeal much to females. And that's what this was really all about—hunt and kill.

So, we huddled there awhile, listening to the wind and the rain, and I watched the Chris-Craft roll and pitch in the waves, straining at the anchor lines, and I kept an eye on the beach below, and we listened for footsteps in the woods.

Finally, after about ten minutes, we unhuddled and I stood and worked the stiffness out of my joints, noticing another, unexpected stiffness in the old crankshaft.

I said to Beth, "I feel warmer."

She sat at the base of the fallen tree, her arms wrapped around her drawn-up knees. She didn't reply.

I said, "I'm trying to put myself in Tobin's shoes."

"At least he *has* shoes."

"Right. Let's say he's making his way inland toward where the treasure is hidden. Right?"

"Why inland? Why not along the beach?"

"The treasure may have been originally found near the beach, maybe on one of these bluffs—maybe these are Captain Kidd's Ledges—but the Gordons would most likely move the loot out of the shaft or hole where they'd uncovered it, because the hole could easily collapse and they'd have to dig again. Right?"

"Probably."

"I think the Gordons hid the treasure somewhere in or around Fort Terry or maybe that maze of artillery fortifications that we saw when we were here."

"Possible."

"So, assuming Tobin knows where it is, he now has to pack it out, through the woods and back here. It may take two or three trips depending on how heavy the loot is. Right?"

"Could be."

"So, if I were him, I'd go get the loot, bring it back here, then get it down to the Whaler. I wouldn't try to get the Whaler back to the Chris-Craft in this weather, or try to transfer the treasure in those waves. Right?"

"Right."

"So, he's going to wait in the Whaler until the storm blows out, but he'd want to get moving before dawn, before the helicopter and boat patrols get out and about. Right?"

"Right again. So?"

"So, we have to try to follow his trail and jump him as he's recovering the loot. Right?"

"Right—no, not right. I don't follow that line of reasoning."

"It's complicated, but logical."

"It's actually bullshit, John. Logic says we stay here. Tobin will be back here no matter what, and we'll be waiting for him."

"*You* can wait for him. I'm going to track down the son of a bitch."

"No, you're not. He's better armed than you are, and I'm not giving you my piece."

We looked at each other, and I said, "I'm going to

find him. I want you to stay here, and if he shows up while I'm gone—"

"Then he's probably killed you. Stay here, John. There's safety in numbers." She added, "Get rational."

I ignored this and knelt beside her. I took her hand and said, "Go down to the Whaler. That way, you can see him if he comes along the beach or if he goes down the rope. Take cover down there among the rocks. When he's so close to you that you can see him clearly in the dark, put the first round in his midsection, then move in fast and close and put a bullet in his head. Okay?"

She didn't reply for a few seconds, then she nodded. She smiled and said, "Then I say, 'Freeze, police!'"

"Right. You're learning."

She drew her 9mm Glock and held it out to me. She said, "I only need one shot if he comes back here. Take this. It has four rounds left. Give me yours."

I smiled and said, "The metric system confuses me. I'll stick with my real American .38 caliber six-shooter."

"Five-shooter."

"Right. I have to remember that."

"Can I talk you out of this?"

"No."

Well, a quick kiss might have been appropriate, but neither of us was in the mood, I guess. I did squeeze her hand and she squeezed back, and I stood, turned, and walked through the trees, away from the windy bluff and away from Beth.

Within five minutes, I came to the gravel road again. Okay, I am Fredric Tobin now. I might have a compass, but whether or not I do, I'm smart enough to know I should put a blaze mark of some kind on one of these trees to show me where I am on this road relative to my landing spot on the beach.

I looked around and sure enough, I found a white length of cord tied between two trees about ten feet apart. I took this to be Tobin's compass heading, and though I had no compass, and no Empire State Building to guide me, it appeared that Tobin had gone almost due south. I struck out through the trees, trying to maintain that heading.

In truth, if I hadn't gotten lucky and hadn't found anything to indicate where Tobin had gone, I might have turned back and rejoined Beth. But I had this feeling—amounting to almost an assurance—that something was pulling and pushing me toward Fredric Tobin and Captain Kidd's treasure. I had a clear vision of me, Tobin, and the treasure all together, and in the shadows around us were the dead—Tom and Judy, the Murphys, Emma, and Kidd himself.

The land rose and I soon found myself at the edge of a clearing. On the other side of the clearing, I could make out two small buildings silhouetted against the dark horizon. I realized I was at the edge of the abandoned Fort Terry.

I searched around for a marker and found a length of rope hanging from a tree. This was Tobin's exit point from the woods, and it would be his entry point when he returned. Apparently, the inertial navigation system in my head was working fairly well. If I was a migrating bird heading south, I'd be right on track to Florida.

It was no surprise that Tobin was heading to Fort Terry. Virtually all the roads and paths on Plum Island converged there, and there were hundreds of good hiding places among the abandoned buildings and nearby artillery bunkers.

I knew if I waited right there, I'd be able to ambush him when he returned. But I was in more of a hunter-stalker mood than a patient ambusher mood.

I waited a few minutes, trying to determine if anyone with a rifle was waiting for me on the far side of the clearing. From a hundred war movies, I knew I wasn't supposed to cross a clearing—I was supposed to go around. If I did that, though, I'd either miss Tobin, or get myself lost. I had to go the route he'd gone. The rain was getting heavier and the wind was picking up. I was miserable. I put my head back, opened my mouth, and got some fresh water on my face and down my throat. I felt better.

I entered the clearing and continued in a southerly direction across the open land. The cloth around my feet was in tatters and my feet were sore and bleeding. I kept reminding myself that I was tougher than twinkle-toes Tobin, and that all I needed was one bullet and a knife.

I approached the end of the field and saw that a thin treeline separated the field from the large expanse of Fort Terry. I had no way of knowing where he'd headed, and there'd be no further markings because the buildings were now his landmarks. All I could do was press on.

I zigzagged from one building to another, looking for some sign of Tobin. After about ten minutes, I found myself near the old headquarters building. I realized that I'd lost him, that he could have gone anywhere from here—south to the seal beach, or west toward the main building, or east out onto the pork chop bone. Or, he could be waiting somewhere for me to get closer. Or, I could have somehow missed him, as I'd done on the water, and he was behind me. Not good.

I decided to check out the rest of the buildings in the fort, and I began moving in a running crouch toward the chapel. All of a sudden, I heard a gunshot ring out, and I dived to the ground. I stayed motionless as another shot rang out. They were oddly muffled shots, not followed by a sharp crack, or by anything whistling over my head. I realized the shots weren't meant for me.

I sprinted to the side of the clapboard chapel and looked toward the direction where I thought the shots had come from. I could see the fire station about fifty yards away, and it occurred to me that the shots were fired inside, which was why they were muffled.

I started to move toward the firehouse, but hit the ground again as one of the big overhead doors began to open. It seemed as if it was going up in short lurches, as if someone were opening it with a pulley rope, and I figured the electric power was out here. In fact, in the upstairs windows, I saw a flickering light—candle or kerosene.

Anyway, before I had to decide what to do next, a big ambulance without any lights showing came out of the garage bay and turned onto the road, heading east toward the narrow bone of land where the ruined artillery batteries were.

The ambulance had a high chassis and ran easily over the deadfall on the road. Soon, it disappeared in the dark.

I ran as quickly as I could barefoot toward the

firehouse, drew my revolver, and dashed in through the open garage door. I could make out three fire trucks in the garage.

I had been in the rain so long that the lack of rain felt sort of strange for about ten seconds, but I got used to it real fast.

As my eyes adjusted to the darkness, I saw a fire pole toward the rear of the garage, and the flickering light from the bunkroom upstairs filtered down through the hole in the ceiling. To the left of the pole, I saw a wide staircase. I went to the staircase and climbed the creaky steps, my pistol out front. I knew there was no danger to me, and I knew what I was going to find.

At the top of the stairs was the bunkroom, lit by kerosene lamps. By the light of the lamps, I saw two men in their bunks, and I didn't have to get closer to see they were dead. That brought the known number of people murdered by Tobin to seven. We definitely didn't need a silly old trial to settle these scores.

Boots and socks sat at the side of each bed. I sat on a bench and pulled on a pair of heavy socks and a pair of vulcanized rubber boots that fit well enough. There were lockers against the wall, and on another wall there were raincoats and sweatshirts hanging on hooks. But I had on about as much of a dead man's clothing as I wanted. Not that I'm superstitious.

There was a small, galley-type kitchen at the rear of the firehouse bunkroom and on the counter was a box of chocolate donuts. I took one and ate it.

I went down the stairs and out to the road that ran east-west in front of the firehouse. I headed east, up the rising paved road in the trail of the ambulance. Broken limbs and branches lay in the road where the ambulance had run over them.

I walked for about a half mile, and even in the dark, I recalled this road from Stevens' tour. The rain was driving hard now, and the wind was starting to rip branches from the trees again. Every now and then, I'd hear a crack that sounded like a rifle shot and it made my heart skip a beat, but the sound came from limbs snapping off and falling through the trees.

The paved road was running with a torrent of water that was coming from the higher ground on both sides of the road. The drainage ditches along the road were full and overflowing as I tried to fight my way uphill against the current and through the mudslides and fallen limbs. This was definitely worse than slush in front of my condo. Nature is awesome. Sometimes, nature sucks.

Anyway, I wasn't paying enough attention to my front because when I looked up, the ambulance sat right in front of me, no more than fifteen feet away. I stopped dead, drew my pistol, and dropped to one knee. Through the rain, I could see that a huge tree had toppled over and blocked the road in front of the ambulance.

The ambulance took up most of the narrow road and I edged around it to the left, knee-deep in the torrent of water from the drainage ditch. I got to the driver's side door and peeked inside, but there was no one in the cab.

I wanted to disable the vehicle, but the cab doors were locked, and the engine hood was latched from the inside. *Damn*. I crawled under the high chassis and drew my knife. I don't know much about auto mechanics, and Jack the Ripper didn't know much about anatomy. I slashed a few hoses that turned out to be water and hydraulic, then for good measure, I cut a few electrical wires. Reasonably certain I'd committed enginecide, I crawled out from under, and continued on, up the road.

I was in the midst of the artillery fortifications now, massive concrete, stone, and brick ruins, covered with vines and brush, looking very much like the Mayan ruins I'd once seen in the rain forest outside of Cancún. In fact, that had been on my honeymoon. This was no honeymoon. Neither was my honeymoon.

I stuck to the main road though I could see smaller lanes and concrete ramps and steps to my right and left. Obviously Tobin could have taken any one of these passages into the artillery fortifications. I realized that I'd probably lost him. I stopped walking and crouched beside a concrete wall that abutted the road. I was about to turn back, when I thought I heard something in the distance. I kept listening, trying to still my heavy breathing, and I heard it again. It was a sharp, whiny noise, and I finally recognized it as a siren. It was very far away and barely audible over the wind and rain. It came from the west, a long, shrill sound, followed by a short blast, then a long sound again. It was obviously a warning siren, an electric horn, and it was probably coming from the main building.

When I was a kid, I'd come to recognize an air raid siren, and this wasn't it. Neither was it a fire signal or an ambulance or police car siren, or a radiation leak signal, which I'd heard once in a police training film. So, partly by process of elimination and partly because I'm not really stupid, I knew—though I'd never heard this signal before—that I was listening to a warning siren for a biohazard leak. "Jesus..."

The electricity from the mainland was down and the backup generator near the main building must have died; the negative air flow pumps had stopped and the electronic air filters were breached. "Mary..."

Somewhere, a big, battery-powered siren was putting out the bad news, and everyone who was pulling hurricane duty on the island now had to suit up in biohazard gear and wait it out. I didn't have any biohazard gear. Hell, I didn't even have underwear. "...and Joseph. Amen."

I didn't panic because I knew exactly what to do. This was just like in school when we went into the basement as the air raid sirens wailed and the Russian missiles were supposed to be streaking toward Fiorello H. La Guardia High.

Well, maybe it wasn't as bad as all that. The wind was blowing hard from the south to the north...or was it? Actually, the storm was *tracking* north, but the *wind* was blowing in a counterclockwise direction, so that conceivably whatever the wind picked up at the main laboratory on the west end of the island could wind up here on the eastern edge of the island. "Damn it."

I crouched there in the rain and thought about all this—all these murders, all this chasing around through the storm and narrowly escaping death and all that—and after all this mortal foolishness and silly vanity, greed, and deceit, then the Grim Reaper steps in and clears the board. *Poof.* Just like that.

I knew in my heart that if the generators conked out, then the entire lab was leaking everything it had inside into the outside air. "I knew it! I knew this would happen!" But why today? Why did this happen on the second day of my whole life that I was on this idiotic island?

Anyway, what I decided to do was run as fast as I could back to the beach, get Beth, get in the Whaler, get on the Chris-Craft, and haul ass away from Plum Island, hoping for the best. At least we'd have a chance, and the Grim Reaper could take care of Tobin for me.

Another thought passed through my mind, but it wasn't a nice thought—what if Beth, recognizing the warning siren for what it was, took the Whaler to the Chris-Craft and left? I mulled that over a moment, then decided that a woman who would jump aboard a small boat in a storm with me wouldn't abandon me now. Yet...there was something about plague that was more terrifying than a storm-tossed sea.

As I hurried down the sloping road toward the ambulance, I came to some realizations and conclusions: one, I'd come too far to run away now; two, I didn't want to discover what Beth had decided; three, I had to find and kill Fredric Tobin; four, I was a dead man anyway. Suddenly ashamed at my loss of nerve, I turned back toward the fortifications to meet my fate. The siren continued to wail.

As I approached the crest of the road, my eye caught a flash of light—a beam, actually, that brushed past the horizon to my right for a second, then disappeared.

I explored the area around the side of the road and found a narrow brick lane that led through the vegetation. I could see that someone had been through there recently. I made my way through the tangle of brush and fallen branches, and finally came out into a sort of sunken courtyard, surrounded by concrete walls in which were iron doors that led to the underground ammunition storage areas. At the top of the circling hills, I could see the concrete artillery emplacements. I realized that I'd stood atop these emplacements on my last visit here and had looked down into this courtyard.

Still crouched in the bushes, I peered across the open expanse of cracked concrete, but couldn't see any movement and neither did I see the light again.

Drawing my revolver and moving cautiously into the courtyard, I began working my way in a counter-clockwise direction around the perimeter, keeping the lichen-covered concrete wall to my back.

I came to the first of the big steel double doors in the concrete. They were closed, and I could tell by the hinges that they were outward-swinging doors. I could also see by the rubble and debris in front of them that they hadn't been opened recently.

I continued on around the perimeter of the court-yard, realizing I was a sitting duck, a dead duck, and a cooked duck if anyone was on the parapets overlooking this open space. I came to the second door and found the same thing as the first—old, rusted steel doors that apparently hadn't been opened in decades.

On the third wall of the courtyard, the south wall, one of the double doors was slightly ajar. The debris on the ground had been swept aside when the door had been opened. I peered into the four-inch crack, but couldn't see or hear anything.

I pulled the door toward me a few more inches and the hinges squeaked loudly. *Damn it.* I stood frozen and listened, but all I could hear was the wind and the rain, and the faraway cry of the siren telling everyone that the unimaginable had happened.

I took a deep breath and slipped through the opening.

I stood very still for a full minute, trying to sense what kind of place this was. Again, as in the firehouse, coming in out of the rain was a treat. I was pretty sure that was the end of the treats here.

The place felt damp and smelled damp, like a place where there was no sunlight, ever.

I moved quietly to my left for two long paces and came into contact with a wall. I felt the wall and determined that it was concrete and that it was curved. I took four paces in the opposite direction and again came to a curved concrete wall. I assumed I was in a tunnel such as the one we'd seen on our first trip here—the tunnel that led to the Roswell aliens or the Nazi laboratory.

But I had no time for Nazis and no interest in aliens. I had to decide if this was where Tobin had gone. And if so, was he heading for the treasure? Or had he spotted me and led me into this trap? I didn't really care what he was up to as long as he was here.

I saw no flashlight ahead, just total blackness of the sort you get only underground. No human eyes could adjust to this darkness, so if Tobin were here, he'd have to turn on his flashlight to get me in his gun sights. And if he did that, my shot would go directly along his beam of light. There would be no second shot in this situation.

The rain slicker and rubber boots were making squeaky noises so I removed both along with my life vest. Clad now in a fashionable leather shoulder holster, jeans, sans underwear, and a fleshing knife stuck in my belt, and a dead man's wool socks, I began walking in the pitch darkness, stepping high to avoid rubble or debris, or whatever. I thought about rats, bats, bugs, and snakes, but I pushed those thoughts right out of my head; rats and stuff weren't my problem. The problem was anthrax in the air behind me, and a psycho with a gun in the dark somewhere in front of me.

Hail Mary... I've always been very religious, actually, very devout. It's just that I don't talk or think about it much while things are okay. I mean, when I was lying in the gutter bleeding to death, it wasn't that I called on God just because I was in trouble. It was more like it just seemed a convenient time and place to pray, what with nothing else going on at the moment.... *Mother of God...*

My right foot stepped on something slippery, and I almost lost my balance. I went down into a crouch and felt around near my feet. I touched a cold metal object. I tried to move it, but it wouldn't budge. I passed my hand over it and finally figured out that it was a rail embedded in the concrete floor. I remembered that Stevens had said there had once been a narrow-gauge railroad on the island that delivered munitions from the ships in the cove to the artillery batteries. Obviously, this was a rail tunnel that led to an ammunition storage room.

I continued on, keeping my foot in contact with the rail. After a few minutes, I sensed the rail bending to the right, then felt something rough. I knelt and felt around. There was a switch here, and the rail split and veered right and left. Just when I thought Tobin and I were nearing the end of the line together, there's a damned fork in the road. I remained kneeling and peered into the darkness in both directions, but I couldn't see or hear anything. It occurred to me that if Tobin thought he was alone, he'd have his light on, or at least he'd be treading heavily and noisily. Since I couldn't see or hear him, I made one of my famous deductions, and deduced that he knew he wasn't alone. Or maybe he was just too far ahead of me. Or maybe he wasn't even here.... *pray for us sinners* ...

I heard something to my right, like maybe a piece of concrete or a stone hitting the floor. I listened harder and heard what seemed like water. It occurred to me that this tunnel might have cave-ins with this rain... *now, and at the hour* ...

I stood and walked to the right, guided by the rail. The noise of falling water got louder, and the air got better.

A few minutes later, I had the sense that the tunnel had ended and that I was in a bigger space—the ammunition magazine. In fact, my eyes were drawn upward and I could see a small piece of dark sky overhead. Rain fell through the hole and onto the floor. I could also make out a sort of scaffolding rising up to the hole, and I realized that this was the ammunition elevator where the shells were hoisted to the gun emplacements overhead. This, then, was the end of the line, and I knew that Tobin was here, and that he was waiting for me.... *of our death. Amen.*

CHAPTER THIRTY-SIX

Fredric Tobin didn't seem in a hurry to announce his presence, and I waited, listening to the dripping rain. After a while, I almost thought I was alone, but I could feel another presence in the room. An evil presence. Really.

Very slowly, I moved my left hand to my waist and pulled out the fleshing knife.

He knew, of course, that it was me; and I knew it was him and that he'd led me into this place that he intended to be my tomb.

He also knew that as soon as he made a move, or a sound, or flipped on his flashlight, I'd fire. He understood that his first shot in the dark had better be his best shot because it was going to be his only shot. So we both stood frozen, cat and mouse, if you will, each trying to figure out who was the cat.

The little prick had nerves of steel, I'll give him that. I was prepared to stand there for a week if I had to, and so was he. I listened to the rain and wind outside, but avoided looking up at the opening in the ceiling because that would ruin whatever night sight I'd developed.

I stood there in the damp, cavernous room, the cold working its way through my socks and soaking into my bare arms, chest, and back. I felt a cough coming on, but fought it down.

About five minutes passed, maybe less, but not more. Tobin must now be wondering if I'd backed out quietly. I was positioned between wherever he was and the entrance to the tunnel behind me. I doubted he could get past me if he lost his nerve and wanted out.

Finally, Tobin blinked, figuratively speaking; he tossed something like a piece of concrete against a far wall. It echoed in the huge ammunition room. It startled me, but not enough to draw my fire. *Stupid trick, Freddie.*

And so we both stood in the dark, and I tried to see through the blackness, tried to hear his breathing, smell his fear. I thought I saw the glint of his eyes, or of steel, reflected in the dim light of the opening in the roof. The glint came from my left, but I had no way of judging distance in the dark.

I realized that my knife might also reflect a glint of light so I moved it to my left side, away from the dim light source overhead.

I tried to see the glint again, but it was gone. If I saw it one more time, I decided, I'd rush toward it and do a knife number—lunge, slash, parry, stab, and so forth until I came into contact with flesh and bone. I waited.

The more I stared at what I thought had been the glint, the more my eyes began to play tricks on me. I saw these sort of phosphorescent blotches dancing in front of my eyes, then they took form and turned into gaping skulls. *Wow.* Talk about the power of suggestion.

It was hard to breathe quietly, and if it weren't for the sound of the wind and water overhead, Tobin would have heard me, and I'd have heard him. I felt another cough coming on, but again fought it down.

We waited. I assumed he knew I was alone. I also assumed he knew I had at least one pistol. I was sure he had a pistol, but not the .45 with which he'd killed Tom and Judy. If he was carrying a rifle, he'd have tried to kill me out in the open from a safe distance when he realized John Corey was on his tail. In any case, a rifle was no better in here than a pistol. What I didn't count on was a shotgun.

The roar of the shotgun blast was deafening in the enclosed room, and I nearly jumped out of my skin. But as soon as I realized I wasn't hit, and as soon as my brain registered the direction of the blast—about ten feet to my right—and before Tobin could dive for another firing position, I fired my single round right where I'd seen the muzzle flash.

I dropped my pistol and charged, lunging and slashing blindly to my front, but I didn't come into contact with anything and didn't trip over a body on the floor. Within a few seconds, my knife scraped the wall. I stopped and stood frozen.

A voice, some distance behind me, said, "I guess you had only one shot left."

I surely didn't reply.

The voice said, "Speak to me."

I turned slowly toward the voice of Fredric Tobin.

He said, "I think I heard your pistol hit the floor."

I realized that each time he spoke, he had moved. Clever man.

He said, "I can see you in the light from the overhead opening."

I noticed now that my charge toward the shotgun blast had put me closer to the dim light.

Again, the voice moved, then said, "If you so much as flinch, I'll kill you."

I didn't understand why he hadn't fired again, but I figured he had an agenda of some sort. Taking advantage of this, I moved away from the wall and said, "Fuck you, Freddie."

Suddenly, a light came on behind me, and I realized he'd moved around me, and I was caught in the beam of his flashlight. Tobin said, "Freeze or I'll shoot. Freeze!"

So, I stood there, my back to him, his flashlight on me, and an unseen gun of some caliber pointing at my ass. I kept the knife close to my body so he wouldn't see it, but then he said, "Hands on your head."

I slipped the knife into my waistband and put my hands on my head, my back still to him.

He said, "I want you to answer some questions."

"Then you'll let me live. Right?"

He laughed. "No, Mr. Corey. You're going to die. But you'll answer my questions anyway."

"Fuck you."

"You don't like losing, do you?"

"Not when it's my life."

He laughed again.

I said, "You don't like losing, either. You got wiped out at Foxwoods. You're a really stupid gambler."

"Shut up."

"I'm going to turn around. I want to see your capped teeth and your hairpiece."

As I turned with my hands on my head, I sucked in my gut and did a little jiggle so that the knife's hilt and handle slid down into my tight jeans. That's not where I wanted it, but it was out of sight.

We were facing each other now about ten feet apart. He was holding the flashlight on my midsection, not my face, and I could make out an automatic pistol in his right hand aimed along the beam of light. I didn't see the shotgun.

The flashlight was one of those halogen types with a narrow-focused beam that are used to signal over long distances. The light wasn't diffused at all, and the room was as dark as before, except for the beam hitting me.

Tobin played the flashlight over me from head to toe and commented, "Lost some of your clothes, I see."

"Fuck you."

His beam paused on my shoulder holster and he said, "Where's your gun?"

"I don't know. Let's look for it."

"Shut up."

"Then don't ask me questions."

"Don't annoy me, Mr. Corey, or the next round goes right into your groin."

Well, we didn't want Willie the Conqueror getting shot, though I didn't see how I could avoid annoying Tobin. I asked him, "Where's your shotgun?"

He said, "I cocked the hammer and flung it across the room. Thankfully it fired without hitting me. But you went for the bait. *You're* stupid."

"Hold on—it took you ten minutes standing in

the dark with your finger up your ass to think of that. Who's stupid?"

"I'm getting tired of your sarcasm."

"Then shoot. You had no trouble killing those two firemen in their sleep."

He didn't reply.

"Aren't I close enough? How far were you from Tom and Judy? Close enough to leave powder burns. Or would you prefer to bash my head in like you did to the Murphys and to Emma?"

"I *would* prefer that. Maybe I'll wound you first, then smash your head in with my shotgun."

"Go ahead. Try for a wound. You get one shot, prick. Then I'm on you like a hawk on a chicken. Go for it."

He didn't go for it and he didn't reply. Obviously, he had some issues to resolve. Finally, he asked, "Who else knows about me? About any of this?"

"Everyone."

"I think you're lying. Where's your lady friend?"

"Right behind you."

"If you're going to play games with me, Mr. Corey, then you're going to die a lot sooner and in a lot of pain."

"You're going to fry in the electric chair. Your flesh will burn and your toupee will ignite, and your caps will glow red, and your beard will smoke, and your contact lenses will melt into your eyeballs. And when you're dead, you'll go to hell and fry again."

Mr. Tobin had no reply to this.

We both stood there, me with my hands on my head, him with the flashlight in his left hand and the pistol in his right. Obviously, he had the advantage.

I couldn't see his face, but I imagined it looking very devilish and smug. Finally, Tobin said to me, "You figured out the part about the treasure, didn't you?"

"Why did you kill Emma?"

"Answer my question."

"You answer mine first."

He let a few seconds go by, then said, "She knew too much and she talked too much. But mainly, it was my way of showing you how extremely displeased I was with your sarcasm and your meddling."

"You're a heartless little shit."

"Most people think I'm charming. Emma did. So did the Gordons. Now you answer my question. Do you know about the treasure?"

"Yes. Captain Kidd's treasure. Buried here on Plum Island. To be moved to another location and discovered there. Margaret Wiley, Peconic Historical Society, and so forth. You're not as clever as you think."

"Neither are you. You're mostly lucky." He added, "However, your luck has run out."

"Maybe. But I still have all my hair and my original teeth."

"You're really annoying me."

"And I'm taller than you are, and Emma said my dick is bigger than yours."

Mr. Tobin chose not to respond to my taunts. Obviously he needed to chat before he put a bullet in me.

I said, "Did you have an unhappy childhood? A domineering mother and a distant father? Did the kids call you sissy and make fun of your argyle socks? Tell me about it. I want to share your pain."

Mr. Tobin did not speak for what seemed like a really long time. I could see that the flashlight was trembling in his hand, and so was the pistol. There are two theories when a guy has the drop on you—one is to play meek and be cooperative. The other is to needle the guy with the gun, call him names, and get him riled up so he makes a mistake. The first theory is now standard police procedure. The second theory has been ruled dangerous and crazy. Obviously I prefer the second theory. I said, "Why are you shaking?"

Both his arms came up, the flashlight in his left hand and the automatic in his right, and I realized he was taking aim. *Uh, oh.* Back to Theory One.

We stood looking at each other and I could see him trying to decide if he should pull the trigger. I was trying to decide if I should let out a bloodcurdling scream and go for him before he got the shot off.

Finally, he brought the pistol and the flashlight down. Tobin said, "I will not let you make me angry."

"Good for you."

He asked me again, "Where is Penrose?"

"She drowned."

"No, she didn't. Where is she?"

"Maybe she went to the main lab and called for reinforcements. Maybe you're through, Freddie. Maybe you should give me the gun, pal."

He mulled this over.

While he was mulling, I said, "By the way, I found the chest and bones and stuff in your basement under the wine boxes. I called the cops."

Tobin didn't reply. Any hope he had that his secrets might die with me were now finished. I expected a bullet any second, but Fredric Tobin, ever the deal maker, asked me, "Do you want to go half?"

I almost laughed. "Half? The Gordons thought

they were going halves and look what you did to them."

"They got what they deserved."

"How so?"

"They had an attack of conscience. Unforgivable. They wanted to turn over the treasure to the government."

"Well, that's who it belongs to."

"It doesn't matter who it belongs to. It matters who can find it and keep it."

"The Golden Rule according to Fredric Tobin— whoever has the gold makes the rules."

He chuckled. Sometimes I pissed him off, sometimes I made him laugh. In the absence of another cop, I had to play both good cop and bad cop. It's enough to make a guy schizoid.

Tobin was saying, "The Gordons came to me and asked if I'd consider working out a deal with the government whereby we'd get a fair share of the treasure as a finder's fee, and the rest would go into new state-of-the-art lab equipment with some money left over for a Plum Island recreational facility, a day care center on the mainland for employees' children, some environmental cleanup on the island, and historical restoration and other worthwhile projects on Plum Island. We would be heroes, philanthropists, and legitimate." Tobin paused a second, then said, "I told them I thought it was a wonderful idea. Of course, at that point, they were as good as dead."

Poor Tom, poor Judy. They were completely out of their league when they made their pact with Fredric Tobin. I said, "So, the Fredric Tobin Toddler Town didn't appeal to you?"

"Not one bit."

"Oh, Freddie, you just act tough. I'll bet you have the heart of a young boy." I added, "I'll bet you keep it in a jar on your mantelpiece."

Again, he chuckled. Time to change his mood once more and keep him interested in the conversation. I said, "By the way, the storm destroyed your vineyards and your boathouse. I wrecked your wine cellar and also your apartment in Tobin Tower. I just wanted you to know that."

"Thank you for sharing that. You're not very diplomatic, are you?"

"Diplomacy is the art of saying nice doggy, until you can find a rock."

He laughed. "Well, you're out of rocks, Mr. Corey, and you know it."

"What do you want, Tobin?"

"I want to know where the treasure is."

This sort of surprised me, and I replied, "I thought it was here."

"So did I. It was here in August when the Gordons took me on a private archaeological tour of the island. It was right here in this room, buried under old ammunition crates. But it's not here any longer." He added, "There was a note."

"A note? Like a fuck-you note?"

"Yes. A fuck-you note from the Gordons saying they moved the treasure, and if they had met an untimely end, then the treasure's location would never be rediscovered."

"So, you fucked yourself. Good."

Tobin replied, "I can't believe they didn't share this secret with someone they trusted."

"They may have."

He said to me, "Someone like you. Is that how you knew this had nothing to do with germ warfare? Is that how you knew about Captain Kidd's treasure? Is that how you knew I was involved? Answer me, Corey."

"I figured everything out all by myself."

"Then you have no idea where the treasure is now?"

"Not a clue."

"Too bad."

The automatic came up again into the firing position.

"Well," I said, "I might have a small clue or two."

"I thought you might. Did they send you a posthumous letter?"

No, but I wish they had. I said, "They gave me some hints that didn't make any sense to me, but they might to you."

"Such as?"

"Well . . . hey, how much do you think it's worth?"

"Worth to you? Or worth all together?"

"All together. I just want ten percent if I help you find it."

He shone the flashlight on my chest, just below my chin, and he regarded me awhile. He asked me, "Are you playing games with me, Mr. Corey?"

"Not me."

Tobin stayed silent awhile, torn between his burning desire to plug me right then and there, and his faint hope that I might actually know something about what happened to the treasure. He was grasping at straws, and he knew it on the one hand, but he couldn't come to terms with the fact that the whole scheme had come apart, that he was not only broke and wiped out, but that the treasure was missing, years of work were down the tube, and he stood a very good chance of being tried for murder, convicted, and deep-fried.

Finally, Tobin said, "It was incredible, really. Not only were there gold coins but also jewels...jewels from the Great Mogul of India...rubies and sapphires and pearls set in the most exquisite gold settings...and bags and bags of other precious stones....There must have been ten or twenty million dollars' worth of jewels...maybe more...." He made a small sighing sound and said to me, "I think you know all of this. I think the Gordons either took you into their confidence, or left you a letter."

I really wish they'd done one or the other, preferably the former. However, they'd done neither, though maybe they'd intended to. But as I suspected, the Gordons had apparently given Tobin the impression that John Corey, NYPD, knew a little something; and that was supposed to keep them alive, but it hadn't. It was keeping *me* alive at the moment, but not for many more moments. I said to Tobin, "You knew who I was when I came to see you at the vineyard."

"Of course I did. Did you think you're the only clever man in the world?"

"I know I'm the only clever man in this room."

"Well, if you're so damned clever, Mr. Corey, why are you standing there with your hands on your head and why do I have the gun?"

"Good point."

"You're wasting my time. Do you know where the treasure is?"

"Yes and no."

"Enough. You have five seconds to tell me. One—" He steadied his aim.

"What difference does it make where the treasure is? You'll never get away with the treasure or the murders."

"My boat is equipped to take me as far as South America. Two—"

"Get a grip on reality, Freddie. If you're picturing yourself on a beach with native girls feeding you mangoes, forget it, pal. Give me the gun, and I'll see that you don't fry. I swear to God you won't fry." *I'll kill you myself.*

"If you know anything, you should tell me. Three—"

"I think Stevens figured out some of this. What do you think?"

"It's possible. Do you think he has the treasure? Four—"

"Freddie, forget the fucking treasure. In fact, if you go outside and listen carefully, you'll hear the biohazard warning siren. There's been a leak. We all have to get to a hospital in the next few hours or we'll be dead."

"You're lying."

"No, I'm not. Didn't you hear the siren?"

He stayed quiet for a long time, then said, "I guess it *is* over, one way or the other."

"Right. Let's make a deal."

"What sort of deal?"

"You give me the gun, we get out of here and get to your boat, quick, then to a hospital. We talk to the DA about your voluntary surrender and you get out on bail, then a year from now, we go to trial and everyone has his or her chance to tell lies. Okay?"

Tobin stayed silent.

Of course, the chance of getting out on bail on a charge of multiple murder was zero; also note I didn't use words like arrest or jail or anything negative like that. I said, "I really will go to bat for you if you voluntarily turn yourself over to me." *Right, pal.* "Really. Cross my heart."

He seemed to be contemplating this offer. This was a tricky and sticky moment because he had to choose between fight, flight, or surrender. I kept in mind that Tobin was a lousy long-shot gambler with an ego too big to cash in when he was down.

He said, "It occurs to me that you're not here as a law officer."

I was afraid he'd figure that out.

"It occurs to me that you've taken all of this personally. That you'd like to do to me what I did to Tom, Judy, the Murphys, and Emma...."

Of course, he was dead right, and that made me dead anyway, so I dived left, out of the beam of light, into the dark, and shoulder-rolled across the floor. Tobin swung the flashlight and fired, but I was much farther across the floor than he'd judged. In fact, I did another roll in the opposite direction as the shot echoed and covered the sound of my movement. I got the knife out of my pants before it sliced off my dick.

The narrow beam swung wildly around the room, and now and then he'd fire blindly and the bullet would ricochet off the concrete walls as the blast echoed into the blackness.

Once, the beam passed right over me, but by the time Tobin realized it and swung the light back, I was gone again. Playing tag with a flashlight and bullets is not as much fun as it sounds, but it's a lot easier than you'd think, especially in a big space like this with no obstructions.

I felt around for the shotgun each time I did a roll or a scramble, but I never came into contact with it. Notwithstanding my lack of firepower, the advantage was now mine, and as long as the idiot kept the light on and kept firing, I knew where he was. Clearly, cool Freddie had lost it.

However, before he figured out that he should shut off the light, I charged like a linebacker right toward him. He heard me coming at the last second and swung the flashlight and the pistol simultaneously toward me just as I collided with him.

He made a sound like a popping balloon and went down like a tenpin. No contest. I wrenched the pistol out of his hand easily enough, then pulled the flashlight from him. I knelt with my knees on his chest, one hand holding the flashlight in his face, the other hand holding my fleshing knife to his throat.

Tobin had trouble breathing but managed to say, "All right....All right....You win...."

"Correct." I brought the butt of the knife down on his nose and smashed the bridge. I heard the crack and saw the blood spurting out of his nostrils as he screamed. The screams turned to whimpers and he looked at me wide-eyed, then let out a groan. "No... please...enough...."

"No, no, not enough. Not enough." My second blow with the butt of the knife cracked his capped teeth, then I reversed the knife and sliced at the base of his hair weave, and I ripped the rug off. He let out another groan, but he was in semi-shock and wasn't fully reacting to my nastiness. I heard myself screaming in the darkness, "You bashed her head in! You raped her! You fucking bastard!"

"No...oh, no...."

I knew I was not rational anymore, and I should have just gotten out of there. But those images of the dead were truly lurking in the darkness, and by this time, after the terror of the boat ride, the chase across Plum Island, the biohazard leak, and dodging bullets in the dark, John Corey had reverted to something best kept in the dark. I smashed the butt of the knife down on his forehead twice but couldn't crack his skull.

Tobin let out a long, pathetic wail. "Noooo...."

I truly wanted to stand up and run out of there before I did something that was irretrievably evil, but the black heart that lurks in all of us had awakened in me.

I reached behind me with the fleshing knife and sliced through Tobin's pants into his lower abdomen, a deep, lateral incision that parted the flesh and muscle and caused a rupture of his intestines out of the abdominal cavity.

Tobin screamed, but then went strangely silent and stayed motionless, as though trying to figure out what happened. He must have felt the warmth of the blood, but otherwise his vital signs were fine and he was probably thanking God he was alive. I would soon put an end to that.

I reached back with my right hand and grabbed a nice big handful of warm guts, which I pulled out and dragged along beside me; then I threw the entrails into Tobin's face.

His eyes met mine in the illumination of the flashlight and he looked at me almost quizzically. But since he had no point of reference for the steaming stuff lying across his face, he needed a word or two from me. So I said, "Your guts."

He screamed, and screamed again, his hands flailing at his face.

I stood, wiped my hands on my trousers, and walked away. Tobin's screams and cries echoed in the cold, cold room.

CHAPTER THIRTY-SEVEN

I wasn't looking forward to the long walk back through the dark tunnel. Also, it's good tactics not to go back the way you come; someone may be waiting for you.

I looked at the opening above. A dark, stormy sky never looked so inviting. I moved to the steel structure that rose from the floor to the ceiling of the ammunition magazine. This was, as I said, the elevator by which huge cannon shells and gunpowder were once hoisted to the gun emplacements above, so I figured it was built right. I got up on the first crossbar and it held. I went up another few crossbars and noticed that they were pretty rusty, but they also held.

Rain fell on me from the opening above, and Fredric Tobin's screams assailed me from below. You'd think a guy would run out of screams after a while. I mean, once the initial horror has passed, then a guy should get a grip on and see about stuffing his guts back where they belong and shut up.

Anyway, the air was better the higher I got. At about fifteen feet, I could feel the wind blowing through the hole. At twenty feet, I was at the opening and the rain was driving hard and horizontally; the storm had returned.

I saw now that the opening above was surrounded by a barbed wire fence, obviously put there to keep animals from falling into the hole when the gun emplacements were used as animal pens. "Damn it."

I stood on the last rung of the elevator structure, half my body out of the hole. The wind and the rain drowned out Tobin's screams now.

I contemplated the four-foot-high barbed wire fence that surrounded me. I could climb the fence or go back down and get out through the tunnel. I thought about Tobin down there screaming his life out with his entrails all over the floor. And what if he got himself under control and found his shotgun or his pistol? So, having gotten myself this far, I decided to go the last four feet.

Pain is mostly mind over matter, so I made my brain blank and climbed up the barbed wire fence, got to the top, and leapt down to the pavement below.

I lay there awhile catching my breath, rubbing the cuts on my hands and feet, happy that the hospital docs had given me my tetanus booster in case the three slugs were dirty.

So, ignoring the pain of the cuts, I stood and looked around. I was in a circular artillery emplacement about thirty feet in diameter. The emplacement was cut into the hillside and was surrounded by a shoulder-high concrete wall that had once protected the big gun that sat here. Embedded on the concrete pavement was a steel traversing mechanism once used to swing the gun in a 180-degree arc.

I saw on the far side of the sunken gun emplacement a concrete ramp that led up to what looked like an observation tower. As far as I could determine, I was on the south side of the pork chop bone, and the artillery piece had pointed south, out to sea. In fact, I could hear the waves crashing on the shore nearby.

I could see how these emplacements would make good animal pens, and that in turn reminded me that the air was filled with plague. Not that you can easily forget something like that, but I guess I was suppressing it. Point is, I could make out the whine of the siren if I listened hard. I could also make out the screams of Fredric Tobin—not literally, but in my mind, and I knew I'd hear that for some time.

So, there I was—Tobin in my head, the biohazard siren in my ears, wind and water in my face, cold, shivering, thirsty, hungry, cut up and half naked, and I was feeling on top of the world. In fact, I let out a little whoop and did a sort of jig. I yelled into the wind, "Alive! Alive!"

Then, a little voice in my head said, "Not for long."

I stopped doing my victory dance. "What?"

"Not for long."

It wasn't actually a little voice in my head; it was a voice behind me. I turned.

Up at the top of the five-foot-high wall, looking down on me, was a big figure, clad in dark rain gear with a hood so that the face was barely visible, and the effect was sort of like the Grim Reaper standing there in the storm, probably smiling and all that. *Creepy.* I asked, "Who the hell are you?"

The person—a man by the size and voice—didn't reply.

I guess I felt a little foolish having been caught dancing around in the rain, making whooping sounds. But I had the strong sense that this was the least of my problems at the moment. "Who the hell are you?"

Again, no reply. But now I saw that the person was holding something across his chest. *A standard Grim Reaper scythe?* I hoped so. I could deal with a scythe. But, no such luck. The guy had a rifle. *Shit.*

I considered my options. I was at the bottom of a circular, five-foot-deep hole and someone with a rifle was standing on the wall near the exit ramp. Basically, I was in a deep, round, tight spot. I was profoundly fucked.

The guy just stood there staring down at me from about thirty feet away—an easy shot with the rifle. He was too close to the exit ramp for me to consider that way out. My only chance was the hole I'd just come out of, but that meant a fifteen-foot run toward him, a dive over the barbed wire fence, and a blind plunge into the elevator opening. That would take about four seconds, and the guy with the rifle could aim and fire twice in four seconds. But maybe the fellow meant me no harm. Maybe it was a Red Cross worker with brandy. *Right.* I said, "So, friend, what brings you out on a night like this?"

"You."

"Moi?"

"Yes, you. You and Fredric Tobin."

I recognized the voice now and I said, "Well, Paul, I was just leaving."

"Yes," Mr. Stevens replied, "you *are* leaving."

I didn't like the way he said that. I assumed he was still pissed off about me cold-cocking him on his back lawn, not to mention all the abuse I'd heaped on him. And here he was with a rifle. Life is funny sometimes.

He said again, "You will be gone soon."

"Good. I was just passing through, and—"

"Where's Tobin?"

"Right behind you."

Stevens actually glanced quickly behind him, then faced me again. He said, "Two boats were spotted from the lighthouse—a Chris-Craft and a speedboat. The Chris-Craft turned back in the Gut, the speedboat made it through."

"Yeah, that was me in the speedboat. Just out for a spin." I asked, "How did you know the Chris-Craft was Tobin?"

"I know his boat. I've been expecting him."

"Why?"

"You know why." He added, "My motion sensors and microphones picked up at least two people at Fort Terry, plus a vehicle. I checked it out and here I am." He said, "Someone murdered two firemen. You?"

"Not me." I said, "Hey, Paul, my neck is getting stiff looking up at you and I'm cold. I'm coming up that ramp, and we're going back to the lab for some coffee—"

Paul Stevens raised his rifle and pointed it at me. He said, "If you move one fucking inch, I'll kill you."

"Understood."

He reminded me, "I owe you for what you did to me."

"You have to try to work through your anger in a constructive—"

"Shut the fuck up."

"Right." In some instinctive way, I knew that Paul

Stevens was more dangerous than Fredric Tobin. Tobin was a cowardly killer, and if he sensed danger, he'd run. Stevens, I was sure, was a more natural killer, the kind of man who'd face off with you, mano a mano. I said, "Do you know why Tobin and I are here?"

Still aiming the rifle at me, he said, "Of course, I do. Captain Kidd's treasure."

I said, "I can help you find the treasure."

"No, you can't. I have the treasure."

Oh, my. I said, "How did you—?"

"Do you think I'm stupid? The Gordons thought I was stupid. I knew exactly what was going on with all this idiotic archaeological digging. I followed every move they made. I wasn't sure who their partner was until August when Tobin arrived as a representative of the Peconic Historical Society."

"Good detective work. I'll see to it that you get a government efficiency award—"

"Shut your fucking mouth."

"Yes, sir. By the way, shouldn't you be wearing a mask or something?"

"Why?"

"*Why?* Isn't that the biohazard warning siren?"

"It is. It's a test. I ordered a test. Everyone who has hurricane duty on the island is in the lab wearing biohazard gear, going through the drill of biocontainment."

"In other words, we're not all going to die?"

"No. Only you are going to die."

I was afraid he was going to say that. I informed him, in an official tone, "Whatever you may have done is not as serious as committing murder."

"Actually, I haven't committed a single crime, and killing you is going to be a pleasure."

"Killing a policeman is—"

"You're a trespasser, and for all I know, a saboteur, a terrorist, and a murderer. Sorry I didn't recognize you."

I tensed my body, ready to make the dash for the hole, knowing it was a useless try, but I had to give it a shot.

Stevens continued, "You knocked out two of my teeth and split my lip. Plus you know too damned much." He added, "I'm rich, and you're dead. Bye-bye, bozo."

I said to him, "Fuck you, asshole." I charged toward the hole, looking not at the barbed wire, but at him as I ran. He steadied the rifle and drew a bead on me. He really couldn't miss.

A shot rang out, but there was no muzzle flash from his rifle and no searing pain shooting through my body. As I reached the fence and was about to vault over the barbed wire and plunge headfirst into the hole, I saw Stevens jumping down into the pit to finish me off. At least that's what I thought. But in fact, he was falling forward and he landed facedown on the concrete pavement. I collided with the barbed wire and came to a halt.

I stood there a moment, frozen, watching him. He twitched around awhile, like he'd been hit in the spinal column, so he was basically a goner. I heard that unmistakable pre-lights-out gurgle. Finally, the twitching and gurgling stopped. I looked up at the top of the wall. Beth Penrose was staring down at Paul Stevens, her pistol trained on him.

I said, "How'd you get here?"

"Walked."

"I mean—"

"I came looking for you. I spotted him and followed."

"Lucky for me."

"Not so for him," she replied.

I said, "Say, 'Freeze, police!'"

She replied, "Fuck that."

"I'm with you." I added, "He was about to kill me."

"I know that."

"You could have fired a little sooner."

"I hope you're not critiquing my performance."

"No, ma'am. Good shooting."

She asked me, "Are you okay?"

"Yeah. How about you?"

"I'm just fine. Where's Tobin?"

"He's...not here."

She glanced down at Stevens again and asked me, "What's with him?"

"Just a scavenger."

"Did you find the treasure?"

"No, but Stevens did."

"Do you know where it is?"

"I was about to ask him."

"No, John, he was about to put a bullet in you."

"Thank you for saving my life."

"You owe me a small favor for that."

"Right. So, that's it—case closed," I said.

"Except for the treasure. And Tobin. Where is he?"

"Oh, he's around here somewhere."

"Is he armed? Is he dangerous?"

"No," I replied, "he has no guts."

We sheltered from the storm in a concrete bunker. We huddled for warmth, but we were so cold, neither of us slept. We talked into the night, rubbing each other's arms and legs to ward off hypothermia.

Beth bugged me about Tobin's whereabouts, and I gave her an edited version of the confrontation in the ammunition storage room, saying that I'd stabbed him and he was mortally wounded.

She said, "Shouldn't we get him medical attention?"

I replied, "Of course. First thing in the morning."

She didn't reply for a few seconds, then said, simply, "Good."

Before dawn, we made our way back to the beach.

The storm had passed and before the helicopter or boat patrols came out, we replaced the shear pin and took the Whaler out to the Chris-Craft. I pulled the self-bailing plug in the Whaler and let the small craft swamp. Then we took Tobin's cabin cruiser to Greenport where we called Max. He met us at the dock and drove us to police headquarters where we showered and got into sweatsuits and warm socks. A local doc checked us over and suggested antibiotics and bacon and eggs, which sounded fine.

We had breakfast in Max's conference room and made a report to the chief. Max was amazed, incredulous, pissed-off, happy, envious, relieved, worried, and so forth. He kept saying, "Captain Kidd's treasure? Are you sure?"

During my second breakfast, Max inquired, "So, only Stevens knew the location of this treasure?"

I replied, "I think so."

He stared at me, then at Beth and said, "You wouldn't hold back on me, would you?"

I replied, "Of course I would. If we knew where twenty million bucks in gold and jewels were, you'd be the last to know, Max. But the fact is, the stuff is missing again." I added, "However, we know it exists and we know Stevens had it for a short period of time. So, maybe with some luck, the cops or the Feds can find it."

Beth added, "That treasure has caused so many deaths that I really think it's cursed."

Max shrugged and replied, "Cursed or not, I'd like to find it." He added, "For historical reasons."

"Absolutely."

Max seemed unable to take all of this in and process it, and he kept repeating questions to which he'd already gotten answers.

I said to him, "If this debriefing is becoming an interrogation, then I have to either call my lawyer or beat the shit out of you."

Max forced a smile and said, "Sorry...this is just mind-blowing...."

Beth said, "Thank us for doing a good job."

"Thank you for doing a good job." He said to me, "I'm glad I hired you."

"You fired me."

"Did I? Forget that." He asked me, "Did I understand you to say that Tobin was dead?"

"Well...not the last time I saw him....I mean, I guess I should have stressed that you need to get him some medical attention."

Max looked at me a moment, then inquired, "Where exactly is this underground room?"

I gave him directions as best I could, and Max quickly disappeared to make a phone call.

Beth and I looked at each other across the table in Max's conference room. I said to her, "You're going to make a fine detective."

"I *am* a fine detective."

"Yes, you are. How can I repay you for saving my life?"

"How about a thousand dollars?"

"Is that what my life is worth?"

"Okay, five hundred."

"How about dinner tonight?"

"John...." She looked at me and smiled sort of wistfully, then said, "John...I'm very fond of you, but... It's too...complicated...too...I mean with all these deaths...Emma..."

I nodded. "You're right."

The phone on the table rang, and I picked it up. I listened and said, "Okay...I'll tell her." I put the receiver down and said to Beth, "Your county limousine is here for you, madam."

She stood and went to the door, then turned back to me and said, "Call me in a month. Okay? Will you do that?"

"Yes, I will." But I knew I wouldn't.

Our eyes met, I winked, she winked back, I blew a kiss, she blew it back. Beth Penrose turned and left.

After a few minutes, Max returned and said to me, "I called Plum. Spoke to Kenneth Gibbs. Remember him? Stevens' assistant. The security guys already found their boss. Dead. Mr. Gibbs didn't seem all that upset or even too curious."

"Never look too hard at an unexpected promotion."

"Yeah. Also, I told him to look for Tobin in the underground ammo rooms. Right?"

"Right. Can't remember which one. It was dark."

"Yeah." He thought a moment, then said, "What a mess. What a ton of paperwork this is going to—" He looked around the room and asked, "Where's Beth?"

"County PD came and took her away."

"Oh…okay…." He informed me, "I just got an official-looking fax from the NYPD asking me to locate and watch you until they arrive about noon."

"Well, here I am."

"You gonna give me the slip?"

"No."

"Promise. Or I have to give you a room with bars."

"I promise."

"Okay."

"Get me a ride to my house. I need stuff."

"Okay."

He left, and a uniformed officer, my old bud Bob Johnson, stuck his head in the room and said, "Need a lift?"

"Yup."

I went with him and he drove me back to Uncle Harry's house. I got into nice duds that didn't say "Property of Southold Town PD" on them, and I got a beer and sat on the back porch, watching the sky clearing and the bay calming down.

The sky was that almost incandescent blue you get after a storm has blown out the pollutants and washed the air clean. This is what the sky must have looked like a hundred years ago, before diesel trains and trucks, cars and boats and oil furnaces and lawn mowers and chemicals and pesticides and who knew what the hell else was floating around.

The lawn was a mess because of the storm, but the house was okay, though the electricity was still out and the beer was warm, which was bad, but the good news was that I couldn't play my answering machine.

I suppose I should have waited for the NYPD as I

promised Max I would, but instead I called a taxi and went to the train station in Riverhead and took the train to Manhattan.

Back in my apartment on East Seventy-second Street after all these months, I noticed thirty-six messages on my answering machine, which was the maximum it would hold.

My cleaning lady had stacked the mail on the kitchen table and there was about ten pounds of the crap.

Amongst the bills and junk was my final divorce decree, which I stuck to the refrigerator with a magnet.

I was about to give up on the piles of unwanted mail when a plain white envelope caught my eye. It was hand-addressed, and the return address was that of the Gordons, though the postmark said Indiana.

I opened the envelope and took out three sheets of lined paper, each side of which was filled with neat script, written in blue ink. I read:

Dear John, If you're reading this, it means we're dead—so, greetings from the grave.

I put down the letter, went to the fridge, and got a beer. I said, "Greetings from the land of the living dead."

I continued reading:

Did you know that Captain Kidd's treasure was buried close by? Well, by now, maybe you do know. You're a smart man, and we'll bet you figured out some of this. If not, here's the story.

I took a sip of beer and read the next three pages, which were a detailed chronicle of the events that had to do with Kidd's treasure, Plum Island, and the

Gordons' involvement with Fredric Tobin. There were no surprises in the letter, just a few details that I'd missed. Regarding things about which I'd speculated, such as how the Plum Island location of the treasure was discovered, the Gordons wrote:

Not long after we arrived on Long Island, we received an invitation from Fredric Tobin to attend a wine tasting. We went to Tobin Vineyards for the event and met Fredric Tobin for the first time. Other invitations followed.

So began Fredric Tobin's seduction of the Gordons. At some point, according to the letter, Tobin showed them a rough map drawn on parchment but did not tell them how he'd come by it. The map was of "Pruym Eyland," complete with compass headings, paces, landmarks, and a big X. The remainder of that story was predictable, and before long, Tom, Judy, and Fredric had struck a devil's deal.

The Gordons made it clear they didn't trust Tobin and that he was probably the cause of their deaths, even if it was made to look like an accident or foreign agents or whatever. Tom and Judy had finally come to understand Fredric Tobin, but it took them too long and it was too late. There was no mention in their letter about Paul Stevens, about whom they were totally clueless.

It occurred to me that Tom and Judy were like the animals they worked with—innocent, dumb, and doomed from the first minute they stepped onto Plum Island.

The letter ended with:

We both like you and trust you very much, John, and we know you'll do everything you can to see that justice is done. Love, Tom and Judy.

I put down the letter and stared at nothing for a long time.

If this letter had reached me sooner, the last week of my life would have been far different. Certainly Emma would still be alive, though I'd probably never have met her.

A century ago, people occasionally came to a cross-roads in their lives and had to choose a direction. Today, we live inside of microchips with a million paths opening and closing every nanosecond. What's worse, someone else is pushing the buttons.

After about half an hour of contemplating the meaning of life, the doorbell rang and I answered it. It was the cops, specifically some clowns from Internal Affairs who seemed annoyed with me for some reason. I went down to One Police Plaza with them to explain why I'd failed to return official phone calls and why I'd missed my appointment, not to mention my moonlighting as a Southold Township cop. My boss, Lieutenant Wolfe, was there, which sucked, but Dom Fanelli was there, too, and we had a nice reunion and a few laughs.

Anyway, the bosses went through this crap about all the trouble I was in, so I called my lawyer and my Detective Endowment Association rep, and by evening we were close to a deal.

That's life. The meaning of life has not much to do with good and evil, right and wrong, duty, honor, country, or any of that. It has to do with cutting the right deal.

CHAPTER THIRTY-EIGHT

A light snow fell on Tenth Avenue, and from where I was on the sixth floor, I could see the flakes swirling through the streetlights and the headlights below.

My class was filing into the room, but I didn't turn to look. It was the first class of the new semester, and I expected about thirty students, more or less, though I hadn't looked at the roster. The name of the course was Criminal Justice 709—subtitled, Homicide Investigations. There would be fifteen two-hour sessions, meeting once a week on Wednesdays, plus conferences. The course was worth three credits. We would examine techniques of securing the crime scene, identifying, collecting, and safeguarding evidence, working relationships with other specialists including fingerprint technicians and forensic pathologists, plus interrogation techniques. In the last four sessions, we would examine some notorious homicide cases. We would not examine the multiple homicides on the North Fork of Long Island. I would make that very clear from the beginning.

The students in my course usually ranged from cop wannabes to visiting detectives here in New York on somebody else's nickel, some city and suburban uniformed cops who had their eye on the gold shield, or wanted a leg up on the promotion exams, plus, now and then, a defense lawyer who would learn from me how to get his scumbag clients found not guilty on a technicality.

Once, I had a guy who never missed a session, listened to every word I said, got an A in the course, then went out and murdered his wife's boyfriend. He thought he'd committed the perfect crime, but a random eyewitness helped get him a room down the hall from Old Sparky. Goes to show you. I think he still deserved the A.

I'd written my name on the blackboard, and under my name I wrote the name of the course for the would-be Sherlock Holmeses who needed more than the instructor's name and room number to be certain they were in the right place.

So, part of my deal with the NYPD was their cooperation regarding my three-quarter disability, the dropping of all contemplated charges against me, and the department's help in securing me an adjunct professorship and a two-year contract at John Jay College of Criminal Justice. There is a strong connection between the NYPD and John Jay, so this wasn't too difficult a task for them to accomplish. For my part, all I had to do was retire and make positive public statements about the NYPD and my superiors. I'm living up to my end. Every day when I'm on the subway, I say aloud and publicly, "The New York Police Department is great. I love Lieutenant Wolfe."

The bell rang, and I moved from the window to the rostrum. I said, "Good evening. I'm John Corey, formerly a homicide detective with the NYPD. On your desk, you'll find a general course outline, a list of required and recommended reading, and some suggested topics for papers and projects." I added, "You'll all make in-class presentations of your projects." *And this will cut down considerably on me having to give thirty hours of lecture.*

I babbled on a bit about the course and about grades and attendance, and such. I caught the eyes of some of the students in the first rows, and indeed they ran the gamut from eighteen to eighty, about half male and half female, whites, blacks, Asians, Hispanics, a guy with a turban, two women with saris, and a priest with a Roman collar. Only in New York. What they all had in common, I guess, was an interest in homicide detection. Murder is fascinating and frightening; it is the great taboo, the one crime, perhaps, that every culture in every age has condemned as the Numero Uno offense against society, the tribe, the clan, the individual.

So, I saw a lot of bright eyes and nodding heads as I spoke, and I guess we all wanted to be here, which was not always the case in the classroom.

I said, "We'll also examine some nonscientific approaches to the investigation such as the idea of hunches, instinct, and intuition. We'll try to define these—"

"Excuse me, Detective."

I looked up and saw a hand raised and waving around in the last row. *Jeez.* At least wait until I finish my spiel. The hand was connected to a body, I guess, but the female who owned the hand had positioned herself behind a huge guy and all I could see was the hand waving. I said, "Yes?"

Beth Penrose stood and I almost fell to the floor. She said, "Detective Corey, will you address the issues of lawful search and seizure, and suspects' rights regarding unlawful searches, and also how to get along with your partner without pissing him or her off?"

The class laughed. I was not amused.

I cleared my throat and said, "I...Take a five-minute break in the classroom, and I'll be right back." I left the room and walked down the hall. All the other classes were in session and the corridor was quiet. I stopped at the water fountain and took a needed drink.

Beth Penrose stood a few feet away and watched me. I straightened up and regarded her awhile. She was wearing tight blue jeans, hiking boots, and a plaid flannel shirt, sleeves rolled up and a few top buttons opened. This was more tomboyish than I would have expected. I said, "How's that bullet wound?"

"No problem. Just a graze, but it left a scar."

"Tell your grandchildren about it."

"Right."

We stood looking at each other.

Finally, she said, "You never called me."

"No, I never did."

"Dom Fanelli has been kind enough to keep me up-to-date on you."

"Has he? I'll punch him in the nose when I see him."

"No, you won't. I like him. Too bad he's married."

"That's what *he* says. Are you enrolled in this class?"

"Sure am. Fifteen sessions, two hours each, meet every Wednesday."

"And you come all the way in from...where is it that you live?"

"Huntington. Takes less than two hours by car or by train. Class ends at nine so I'll be home for the eleven o'clock news." She asked me, "How about you?"

"I'll be home for the ten o'clock news."

"I mean, what are you doing besides teaching?"

"That's enough to do. Three day classes, one night class."

"Do you miss the job?" she asked.

"I guess....yeah. I miss the job, the guys I worked with, the...sense of doing something...but I definitely don't miss the bureaucracy or the bullshit. It was time to move on. How about you? Still gung ho?"

"Sure. I'm a hero. They love me. I'm a credit to the force and to my gender."

"I'm a credit to *my* gender."

"Only your gender thinks so." She laughed.

Obviously she was having a better conversation than I was.

She switched subjects and said, "I heard you've been out to speak to the Suffolk DA's office a few times."

"Yeah. They're still trying to sort out what happened." I added, "I'm being as helpful as I can considering my head injury, which has caused selective amnesia."

"I heard. Is that why you forgot to call me?"

"No. I didn't forget."

"Well, then..." She let it go and asked me, "Have you been out to the North Fork since—"

"No. And I'll probably never go out there again. How about you?"

"I sort of fell in love with the place, and I bought a

little weekend cottage in Cutchogue with a few acres, surrounded by a farm. Reminds me of my father's farm when I was a kid."

I started to reply, but decided not to. I wasn't sure where this was going, but I figured that Beth Penrose wasn't making a three- or four-hour commute every Wednesday night just to hear the master's words of wisdom, words that she'd already heard and partly rejected in September. Obviously Ms. Penrose was interested in more than three college credits. I, on the other hand, was just getting used to being unattached.

She said, "The local realtor told me your uncle's place was sold."

"Yeah. It sort of made me sad for some reason."

She nodded. "Well, you can come visit me in Cutchogue any weekend."

I looked at her and said, "But I should call first."

She replied, "I'm alone. How about you?"

"What did my ex-partner tell you?"

"He said you're alone."

"But not lonely."

"He just said you had no one special."

I didn't reply. I glanced at my watch.

She changed the subject and informed me, "My sources at the DA's office said it's going to trial. No plea bargaining. They want a Murder One conviction with the death penalty."

I nodded. I may not have mentioned this, but the eviscerated and scalped Fredric Tobin had survived. I was not too surprised because I knew I hadn't delivered a necessarily mortal wound. I'd avoided his arteries, avoided putting the blade in his heart or cutting his throat, like I probably should have. Subconsciously,

I think, I couldn't commit murder, though if in my efforts to subdue him, he'd died of shock or loss of blood, that would have been okay, too. As it stood now, he was sitting in an isolation cell in the county jail, contemplating either a life behind bars with Bubba, or an electric jolt to his central nervous system. Or maybe a lethal injection. I wish the state would make up its mind. I'm in favor of Old Sparky for Fredric, and I would like to be one of the official witnesses to observe smoke coming out of his ears.

I'm not allowed to visit the little shit, but I made sure he had my home phone number. The little turd calls me every couple of weeks from the slammer. I remind him that his life of wine, women, song, Porsches, powerboats, and trips to France is over, and that someday soon, he will be taken out of his cell before dawn and executed. He, in turn, says he'll beat the rap, and I'd better be careful when he's out. What a monumental ego this prick has.

Beth said, "I visited Emma Whitestone's grave, John."

I didn't reply.

She said, "They buried her in this beautiful old cemetery among all these other Whitestone graves. Some go back three hundred years."

Again, I didn't reply.

Beth continued, "I only met her that one time, in your kitchen, but I liked her, and I felt I wanted to leave some flowers on her grave. You should do the same."

I nodded. I should go to Whitestone Florist and say hello, and I should have gone to the funeral, but I didn't. Couldn't.

"Max asked about you."

"I'm sure he did. He thinks I'm sitting on twenty million dollars in gold and jewels."

"Are you?"

"Sure. That's why I'm here to supplement my disability pay."

"How's the lung?"

"Fine." I noticed that a few of my students had gotten restless and wandered out into the hall, heading for the restrooms or taking a smoke. I said to Beth, "I should get back."

"Okay."

We walked slowly down the hall together. She said, "Do you think they'll ever find Captain Kidd's treasure?"

"No. I think paranoid Paul Stevens hid it so well that it will stay hidden another three hundred years."

"You're probably right. Too bad."

"Maybe not. Maybe it should stay wherever the hell it is."

"Are you superstitious?"

"I wasn't. Now I'm not so sure."

We got to the door of my classroom.

She said, "I discovered there's a swimming pool in this building. Do you ever use it?"

"Sometimes."

"I'll bring my swimsuit next week. Okay?"

"Okay.... Beth?"

"Yes?"

"Well . . . is this going to be awkward?"

"No. But I expect an A in the course."

I smiled.

"I'll do whatever it takes."

"I can't be bribed."

"Wanna bet?"

A few students in the room were looking at us, smiling and whispering.

We went into the classroom, me to the front, Beth to the back.

I said to the class, "We have another homicide detective with us, Detective Beth Penrose from the Suffolk County PD. Detective Penrose's name may be familiar to you from a recent and ongoing murder case on Long Island's North Fork." I added, "I worked with her on that case, and we each learned something from the other's distinctive style and techniques. Also, she saved my life, so to repay her, I'm taking her out for drinks after class."

Everyone applauded.